Nocticadia

Keri Lake

NOCTICADIA
Published by KERI LAKE
www.KeriLake.com

Cover art by Okay Creations
Editing: Julie Belfield
Warning: This book contains explicit sexual content, and violent scenes that some readers may find disturbing.

Playlist

- *You're All I Want* - Cigarettes After Sex
- *Liar* - Paramore
- *Memento Mori* - Nathaniel Drew X Tom Fox
- *Goodnight Baby* - Tarune
- *Achilles Come Down* - Gang of Youths
- *Please* - Omido, Ex Habit
- *You, The Ocean and Me* - Thalles
- *Without You* - Lana Del Rey
- *Glass In The Park* - Alex Turner
- *Sleepwalk* - MOTHICA
- *bad idea!* - girl in red
- *Feel Real* - Deptford Goth
- *The Secret History* - The Chamber Orchestra of London
- *Two Evils* - Bastille
- *Bloodstream* - Stateless
- *The French Library* - Franz Gordon
- *She's Thunderstorms* - Arctic Monkeys
- *Crave You* - Robinson
- *Crush* - Sebastian Paul

- *Misery* - Michigander
- *October* - Broken Bells
- *Sextape* - Deftones
- *I Would* - Coin
- *Romantic Homicide* - d4vd
- *nostalgia* - Teodor Wolgers
- *we fell in love in october* - girl in red
- *Melancholia* - Daniel Paterok, Roman Richter
- *Cinnamon Girl* - Lana Del Rey
- *Make Me Feel* - Elvis Drew
- *Old Letter* - Imaginary Poet
- *Run* - Coin
- *Without You* - Omido, Bibi Silvja
- *Reflections* - Toshifumi Hinata
- *Shakespeare* - Fink
- *Tell Me The Truth* - Two Feet
- *RU Mine* - Arctic Monkeys
- *Fuck Em Only We Know* - Banks
- *Knee Socks* - Arctic Monkeys
- *Not Just A Girl* - She Wants Revenge

Author's Note & Triggers

Welcome Fellow Nocticadian,

Thank you so much for taking a chance on my book 🖤 I hope you enjoy Professor Bramwell and Lilia's story. Before you slip into this world, I just want to mention that a number of elements featured throughout the book are completely fictional, including the organism, Professor Bramwell's medical condition, and the species of moth. In order to remain consistent with the pathology, the medical conditions/symptomatology described are also fictional. I've included a glossary, for quick reference.

In addition, I took liberties with Professor Bramwell's background and profession as well as the laboratory in order to fit the story I wanted to tell. I fully acknowledge his lab would never pass the accreditation process.

This is a dark gothic academia romance. Therefore, you can expect subtle supernatural elements, a dark and atmospheric setting, a slow burn romance, a moody and Byronic/morally gray male lead, and sprinkling of mystery. Like most of my gothic romances, this is a standalone, and since I'm not planning to write additional books for this couple, I decided to hold you captive in this world a little longer.

A word of caution ...

This book contains a number of potentially triggering situations. You can find the full list of trigger warnings-with spoilers-on my website:

https://www.kerilake.com/nocticadia-full-trigger-list

GLOSSARY & TRANSLATIONS

***Casteyon** – An element found in the black rock caves on Dracadia island
***Jestwood Plant** - A plant native to Dracadia which is considered poisonous in high doses
***Nocticadia** – The name given to the Midnight Lab that studies Noctisoma, specifically
***Noctisoma** – Long, black worms that are parasitic in insects, but will infect other species. Their natural host is the Sominyx moth.
***Sominyx Moth** – A nocturnal species of moth found only on Dracadia Island and the natural host for Noctisoma
***Stirlic Acid** - An antiseptic discovered by Dr. Nathaniel Stirling, made from the Jestwood plant that was used in gruesome experiments on patients
Tapetum Lucidem – A light-sensitive biologic reflector system in invertebrates (not typically present in the human eye, but is described as a symptom of Noctisoma in the book)
***Vonyxsis** – The darkening of veins that appears as black lines on moths and humans infected with Noctisoma
***Zigliomyositis / Voneric's Disease** – A rare congenital

neuromuscular disorder named after a famous painter who was diagnosed with it.

*** Fictional element of the book**

Translations

"Voulez-vous boire un verre, mademoiselle?"
Would you like another drink, Miss?

"Si vous comprenez, retrouvez-moi dans le placard dans dix minutes."
If you understand, meet me in the closet in ten minutes.

"Je comprends. Et je décline votre offre."
I do understand. And I decline your offer.

Prologue

Dracadia Island
October 12, 1753

Lord Adderly had seen plenty of death in his lifetime. As commodore for the Royal Navy, its cloying scent had clogged the back of his throat more times than he could recall. He'd felt its cold vaporous breath skim across his flesh, with a longing that would have made most men shiver.

Lord Adderly did not fear death. Some had even dared to accuse him of welcoming it.

Yet, as he stared across the turbulent stretch of wintry sea, toward an ominous black smoke that rose from the surrounding fog, a shiver of dread coiled down his neck. The order to have his men row back from whence they'd come sat heavy on his tongue, when, in the distance, the island's shadowy silhouette split through the mist–an arched rock formation which loomed on the horizon like a sleeping dragon.

Halfway between the coast of Massachusetts and French-settled Acadia, the small Dracadia Island had long been a source of contention–a stretch of land that one could argue had belonged to the British. It hadn't been until most of the Acadians had mysteriously abandoned the island that it'd been annexed as a province of Massachusetts. Lord Adderly had led the charge himself, prepared for battle, in the event the French returned to reclaim the village of Emberwick on the north end.

It had never come to pass.

The British who'd settled there instead had eventually come to suffer a series of misfortunes, and had fled the island, leaving Dracadia abandoned once more.

Of course, rumors had spread. Some had blamed the indigenous Cu'unotchke tribe, who'd sequestered themselves in the southern mountains, for having roused their heathen gods. Whatever the cause, speculations of bad spirits and inexplicable maladies had kept most from the enticement of land ownership on Dracadia. As a result, the island had failed to house any more than the heretics who'd been exiled there. The worst offenders of the holy doctrines.

Lord Adderly did not avert his gaze from the path ahead as the shore broke through the fog and the water grew shallower. Over the devastated landscape, black birds clustered in thick flocks. Murders. The ravens, whose presence had long stirred fears of evil. Lord Adderly had watched their kind follow men to war with the promise of carrion. The circling birds could only be an omen.

A sign of death.

"Dear God," Lieutenant Christ said, where he sat beside the commodore. "Is it the savages, My Lord?"

"No." While the commodore answered assuredly, the truth was he didn't know. He'd fought all sorts of savages, and while they battled with unconventional fervor, they were hardly inherently evil.

"Rumors speak of sharpened black stones for teeth, and eyes like wolves in the darkness," Christ prattled on.

"Perhaps you give equal merit to stories of sea monsters and sirens."

"Of course not, My Lord. But the men who speak of such things are of sound mind. Good Christian men."

The commodore had little doubt of their integrity, but to offer the truth behind their voyage would have sparked panic.

Perhaps even mutiny.

For, unbeknownst to Lieutenant Christ, they had been summoned there by correspondence from the church, after several clergymen had failed to return with three accused witches. Under the care of Dr Jack Stirling, the three women had been ordered to trial in Massachusetts proper. There'd been suspicion that the good doctor had gone mad, possessed by the very demons he had been charged to bleed out of the women months ago. The commodore had heard horrific stories of patients with black veins, who'd been left to hang, bleeding, by their feet. Those whose mouths and eyes had been sewn shut, and tongues removed. The commodore and his men had been sent to investigate the claims, and given the sinister warnings in the distance, he feared what they'd find there.

Closer, the boat tottered across relentless waves, and as shadows lifted to reveal the charred husks of trees, Lord Adderly inhaled deeply, swallowing back the greasy scent of burnt meat on the air. The familiar scent of death.

Six of his men jumped from the boat, dragging the small vessel through the shallows, and once ashore, Lord Adderly set foot on the unhallowed grounds to which he'd sworn never to return. He swept his gaze over the impossible destruction, contemplating what, in God's name, could have accomplished such a feat.

An entire island burned to ash.

The fog around them thickened, and Lord Adderly frowned as it settled between them and the seared forest.

Lieutenant Christ strode up alongside him. "Forgive me

for saying so, My Lord, but I've no inclination to venture beyond the shore."

"Hold your tongue," Lord Adderly spoke low. "Lest you long to invite mutiny."

"My Lord!" one of his men shouted, and the commodore turned to see him pointing toward the trees.

Lord Adderly followed the path of the man's finger toward shadows within the fog. A figure moving toward them. The sharp clank of his men readying their weapons echoed around them, but when the white vapor parted for a young boy, perhaps only twelve years of age, Lord Adderly stepped forward. "Lower your weapons."

Dressed in the robes of a young acolyte, the boy stumbled toward them, his skin covered in black soot and robes stained with what was undoubtedly blood. Before reaching the commodore and his men, the acolyte tumbled to the sand.

As Lord Adderly strode toward him and lowered to one knee alongside the boy, Christ knelt at the boy's feet, where small bleeding wounds on their tops suggested they'd been impaled by something sharp. "Careful, My Lord. We've no idea to *what* he's been exposed."

Cuts, bruises, and patches of glistening flesh where skin had been peeled back marked signs of unspeakable abuse.

The sight of him brought the commodore's own son to mind, and he fought tears as he took in the acolyte's condition. "What happened here?"

"Blackness," the boy whispered on a ragged breath. "The sky ... turned to blackness. All of them burned."

Lord Adderly brushed the sticky, blood-stained hair from the boy's face. "Who did this?"

Through the exhaustion that darkened the boy's eyes lay a flicker of fear. "They commanded the flames. And the flames did their bidding."

"Who commanded the flames? Witches?"

One slow blink, and the boy exhaled. When he breathed in, his chest rattled like coins in a tin cup. "Not witches. Worms. Black worms, spilling from the mouths of madness."

A hush fell over the men, the boy's words raising the hair on the back of the commodore's neck.

Christ moved closer and, leaning in, whispered, "The boy does not seem well, My Lord. He is speaking of evil."

Ignoring his lieutenant, the commodore placed a hand on the boy's bony shoulder. "You are the only one left?"

"All of them burned."

Lifting his gaze to Lieutenant Christ, the commodore kept his voice level in spite of his nerves. "We'll take the boy and return to the ship. Now."

"You cannot leave." A wet, barky cough sent a trickle of blood from the acolyte's mouth. "They will not allow it."

The commodore frowned at the boy and pushed to his feet. He ordered two of his men to carry him back to the ship.

"My Lord!" the coxswain cried out with an edge of panic, and the commodore turned to see him stumbling through the sand toward them. "The boat! The boat is gone! It's gone!"

"Fear not, My Lord." Over the din of panic, as the other men caught on to the bizarre disappearance, the boy's weakened, almost ghostly voice reached the commodore's ears. "Your boat was never there to begin."

"I do not understand your words, boy."

"You and your men ... arrived with the priests ... days ago." Heavy wheezing filled each pause, as the boy seemed to struggle with breath.

"You are sick with delirium. I was summoned here by correspondence from the church itself."

Eyelids hooded, the boy's dry and cracked lips stretched to a slight smile. "You are dreaming now. But soon, you will wake to the sound of crackling fire, and find you and your men tied to stakes. Your flesh will be seared. And your pain and misery will echo for eternity." The boy's eyes fluttered shut, and he let out a hiss of air, before his body turned limp in his officer's arms.

Cold dread clawed at Lord Adderly's belly, the scent of burning fat and skin clogging his throat again. He closed his eyes, finding solace in the pitch blackness, and when the first sounds of agony pierced the air, he dared not open them.

Chapter 1

Lilia

Present day ...

God, that stench.

Too-crisp Spam sizzled in a pan as I held my arm to my nose. The popping sound of fatty meat was loud enough to carry over Jean Valjean's heartfelt plea to Javert from *Les Misérables* playing in the theater below our apartment. I'd accidentally burned the thinner pieces while peeling the potatoes and there was no salvaging it at that point.

Whatever finesse my mother had always had in the kitchen had failed to grace my genetics.

I hated cooking the canned crap, but Mom had developed a weird craving for meat lately, and we'd run out of the thin round steaks she'd come to like eating rare. I couldn't help but wonder if her strange requests might've been her body trying to get better.

I hoped so, anyway.

Watching her devour rare meat with the blood running out of the corners of her mouth had me feeling like a spectator in a gory episode of *Hostile Planet.* An appetite-withering sight. Particularly since my mother had never really been much of a meat eater, anyway. Spam was a far cry from steak, but my stepdad Conner, if I could even call him that, hadn't worked a couple days, which left us short on grocery money.

"Bee!" I called out for my younger half-sister, the nickname short for Beatrix, and tossed the charred spam onto awaiting plates. "D'you check on Mama, like I asked?"

"Oh, shit!" The thud of footfalls followed her curse, and with a smirk, I shook my head. At twelve years old, about four years younger than me, she carried a lot more responsibility than most girls her age.

Both of us did.

Mama's illness had gotten worse. So much worse, and the fact that she refused to see a doctor about it only put more pressure on Bee and me to navigate the progression of her strange symptoms ourselves. While Mama still seemed to have her wits about her, there were moments. Terrifying moments. Like the nights she'd tell me that evil men were coming for me. The nights she'd be covered in sweat, her eyes glowing with unseen horrors.

Monsters, she called those invisible tormentors, but in her mind, they were as real as the deep black circles beneath her eyes. Although, as horrible as it was to say, with her sickly, distorted spine, silvery glowing eyes, and deep protruding bones, she'd begun to look like the very monsters of which she spoke.

Praying had never really been my thing, but I'd done an awful lot of aimless pleading on my knees over the last few weeks, and if God existed, he sure as hell didn't offer much hope.

As I spooned the last glob of mashed potatoes for Bee, a knock at the door halted my plating. Frowning, I quietly placed the pan back onto the stovetop and wiped my hands onto a nearby kitchen towel. With cautious steps, I padded toward the hallway and peered at the entry door. Another hard thud jerked my muscles, and the audacity of whatever was behind that obnoxious racket heated my blood. I tromped toward the door and, through the peephole, spied a man I didn't recognize.

Deep-set, beady eyes, a scar at his left eye, and an oddly crooked nose, like he'd been in one too many fights, made him look like a walking mugshot.

One thing I'd learned from living in a city like Covington–you didn't answer the door to strangers. Particularly ones who looked like criminals.

He pounded against the door again, and I ground my teeth with annoyance.

"Yeah?" I called through the barrier. "What do you want?"

At first, he didn't answer, and I watched him look around toward the hallway. Something about him–those dark eyes I'd only caught a glimpse of and the smirk of his lips–sent a crawling chill beneath my skin.

What a creep.

I glanced at the door's deadbolt, making sure it was engaged. Unfortunately, the apartment didn't have the greatest, or most robust, locks.

"I'm a friend of Conner's," he finally said. "Is he here?"

"No."

"Any idea when he'll be back?"

Studying his face proved challenging, since the guy seemed to refuse to look up. "Look, I don't–"

At the sound of a piercing scream, my spine snapped straight, and I swung my attention toward the back rooms. Abandoning the weirdo at the front door, I dashed across the apartment toward the sliver of light shining beneath the bathroom door.

Light—the first sign that something was wrong. Mama had grown to hate the light. Said it hurt her eyes.

"Mama! No!"

A whisper of fear spiraled down the back of my neck at

what I recognized as Bee screaming at my mother on the other side of the door, and I pushed through into the brightly-lit bathroom.

Mama stood alongside the tub, making a strange growling sound while water splashed onto the floor. Two pink-socked feet kicked out over the edge of the basin.

Oh God.

Bee!

Icy pulses of adrenaline took over as I rushed toward them and knocked my mother aside, into the wall.

The moment she was released, Bee shot up out of the water, her upper half sopping wet, and she let out a barky cough.

"What the hell are you doing!" I shouted at my mother, whose eyes gave off an iridescent flicker in the light.

On a screech, my mother barreled forward again, knocking into me, and pushed Bee back into the water.

Panic exploded through my muscles, my body no longer moving at my will, but on instinct. I grabbed my mother by the hair, throwing her off Bee. A chunk of dull, red locks sat in my palm as my mother slipped from my grasp and fell backward against the toilet. The slippery floor had her scrambling to get to her feet again, and I yanked Bee out of the bathtub, sliding on wet tiles as I pushed her toward the door.

Once out in the hallway, I hauled the door shut after us, tugging the knob to keep it closed.

"Go to your room! Lock the door and do *not* come out until I tell you!" I commanded.

"I was ..." She coughed and sniveled. "I was ... just trying to keep her ... from drinking the water, and she ... attacked me!"

The door thumped and jerked my arm as Mama fought from the other side. "She's one of them! She's one of them!"

Mama screamed through the barrier. "Don't let her get away! She'll tell them I'm here!"

"Go! Now! Lock the door! Don't open it, no matter what you hear!" I braced my feet against the wall and leaned back into the pull of the knob, holding the door closed, as Bee scampered toward her bedroom.

After another minute of fighting to keep her contained, the thumping stopped. Mama's screams silenced.

With heaving breaths, I eased my muscles and straightened, no longer feeling resistance from the other side. "Mama?" I spoke low through the door, hoping she'd give a coherent answer. An explanation for what the hell just happened. She'd spoken of someone coming after her before, but had never projected those paranoid thoughts onto me, or Bee.

Nothing.

But the cloying scent that had been companion to my mother's illness seemed stronger than usual. Thick and sticky, it clogged my throat, and I raised the back of my palm to my face in a poor effort to stifle the odor.

Over the past few months, Mama's sweet floral scent, a comforting smell I'd known my whole life, had somehow faded under the weight of that unfamiliar stink.

Now it was all I breathed.

Ignoring the urge to gag, I turned the knob and entered the bathroom.

Mama lay slung over the edge of the tub, her face submerged in the water.

"Mama!" I sprinted toward her, and on a splash of water, she swung around, screaming again.

I reached for her arm, but she swung out first, plowing the back of her knuckles against my cheek. Pain zapped my bones on a burst of floating stars that wobbled my vision.

I shook off the dizziness when she swung out again, and

ducked. That time, she failed to connect as her hands flailed in a fit of rage. Gathering her arms in a tight grip, I dug my nails into her frail bones, but a sharp sting pierced my hand where she sank her teeth into my flesh.

"Ouch! Shit!" I pushed her off me, and she slipped, arms thrashing around as she fell backward into the tub. When I tried to pull her up, her hands reached out for me and gripped my shirt, wrenching me toward the water.

A rush of fluids shot up into my sinuses on a deep burn, her grip unrelenting as she held me underwater. Panic crystallized my muscles. Water splashed with her frenzied kicking and grappling of my neck.

I reached out for the only thing I could get my hands on in the melee. Palm to her throat, I squeezed just enough to lessen her grip, and I held her there as my face breached the surface of the water on a gasped breath.

She yanked me down again, dunking my face underwater with her.

I squeezed her throat harder, and once again, she loosened her hold.

Each searing lungful of air scorched my throat and shot out of me on a coughing fit.

Frantic, she scratched at the back of my neck, trying to pull me under again.

"Mama! Please!" Breath weak in my lungs, I could hardly push out the words as my muscles locked around my chest. My legs slid across the tiles as I wrangled her arms to keep her from pulling me.

Submerged beneath the water, my mother opened her mouth. Eyes wide in a shocked expression.

As if her fight relented, she stilled while a haunting resolution flashed over her face, one that tickled the back of my neck.

I pushed away and stood over the tub, no longer holding her, but she didn't bother to emerge.

Surely, the air had withered in her lungs by that point. Surely, she needed oxygen.

C'mon! Get up!

I lurched for her arm to pull her up, but halted when, from her mouth, a long, skinny, fibrous creature slithered out past her lips and into the water.

Three more tumbled after it–two from her nose.

A scream shook out of me, and limbs frozen with horror, I watched as the worms wriggled over the tub's porcelain floor and forged a path through the water to gather at the drain holes. At least two dozen more poured free, forcing her mouth and nostrils wide. More still after that. They all wriggled toward the plugged drain.

My breaths arrived in small panting gasps as I watched the horror.

Until blackness consumed me.

Chapter 2

Lilia

Four years later ...

"Lilia?" a voice cut through the void.

I blinked my eyes open and found myself hunched over the drain of a yellowing sink.

"Earth to Lilia," the familiar voice said again.

Confused, I turned to find my coworker, Jayda, standing alongside me, and I pushed up from the sink I'd been cleaning. It was in the haze of confusion that I remembered scrubbing the sink, during which I'd caught wind of a strange, but familiar scent, like rot and dirt. So heavy was the odor that I'd fallen into memories again.

A sheepish grin tugged at my lips and I cleared my throat. "Sorry, I must've spaced out."

It happened sometimes. Something would trigger thoughts, and those thoughts had me slipping into the most horrific memory of my life. One that never failed to pull me under so deep that I lost sight of my own reality.

It'd been four years since my mother's death, yet I remembered every detail. The scents. The sounds. The cold.

"I was just saying, I'm going to work on the office next door." Forearm across her nose, Jayda coughed. "I don't know what the hell the last person in here ate, but that does not smell healthy. So, I'm gonna leave all these latrines to you," she said on a chuckle.

Still spacy, I grabbed the rag I'd dropped on the floor and tossed it into the sudsy bucket beside me. The usual nausea gurgled in my belly, and I tried to hide the shakiness in my arms by busying my hands–wiping them on my scrubs and swiping up the bucket for the next sink. "You're the sweetest."

Snorting, she stepped toward the door, but paused. "You sure you're okay? You look a little pale."

"Fine. Totally fine. I just fell deep into thoughts."

"*Real* deep, from the looks of it. Seriously, you don't mind if I start on the other room? Just figured the two of us could get out early if we hustle."

Half-smiling, I shrugged. "I don't mind."

In truth, I hated cleaning the bathrooms, the patient rooms, the offices, but I suspected it was the closest I'd ever get to working in an actual hospital. The dream of medical research seemed to fade every day, my body growing weary of life. At my age, I should've been finishing up my bachelor's degree and trying to decide whether to take the MCAT or GRE, but with as few classes as I was able to squeeze in at the community college around work, it'd be a decade before I reached that point in my schooling.

"Thanks, girl. Early pregnancy and sewage do not mix."

The bathrooms in the hospital's basement reeked as a general rule, but the stench on the air right then was particularly potent. "I got it," I said, waving her on. "Get out of here. I don't need to be cleaning your puke up next."

Chuckling, she slipped out the door, and alone, I exhaled a long, shaky breath. Hands braced at either side of the sink, I closed my eyes and attempted to clear my mind.

Screams. Black worms. Vacant eyes.

With a shake of my head, I buried those thoughts in the

shadows of my mind, refusing to let them consume me. *No. Not tonight.*

What sounded like the faint plink of water reached my ears, and I opened my eyes to the reflected stalls behind me in the mirror.

At the very last stall, I spotted something I hadn't noticed when I first walked in—the soles of socked feet beneath the door.

I spun around, my heart clenching with the shock of the discovery. Those were definitely feet beneath the door. "Is someone there?" I asked, knowing damn well that someone was, in fact, there. Above the feet, I caught sight of the hem of the familiar hospital gown that every patient wore.

Patients who shouldn't have been using the basement bathroom assigned to staff.

A faint splashing sound reached my ears again. Given the position of the feet, the person likely wasn't indisposed right then, but they could've been vomiting.

"Do you need some help? Because I can run and get someone, if you do ..." I hiked my finger over my shoulder as if they could've seen me.

No answer.

I tiptoed closer. "Are you sick?"

Still no answer.

I finally reached the stall door, peering through the skinny cracks. Long, straggly, red hair lay draped across a patient gown, half-opened enough to revealed a pale mottled back and white underwear. An uneven purplish tone colored the limbs that I could see, particularly the leg and hand.

My first thought was livor mortis, but I pushed that thought aside.

A stinging dryness settled in my throat, and I swallowed a gulp.

Please just be okay.

I gave a slight knock, noting the minute swing of the unlocked door, and hoped the person would volley back an undignified protest to my prying.

They didn't say a word.

I pushed open the door.

The person's head rested just below the seat inside the toilet, those straggled bits of hair hiding the face.

I reached out a trembling hand and gripped a slender shoulder, tugging just enough to totter her to the side. She rolled onto her back, knocking her head on the wall of the stall, and the moment her hair fell away from her face, I stumbled backward.

The familiar milky glow of my mother's eyes stared back at me.

Movement flickered in my periphery, and a rush of air flew out of me when I snapped my attention there and just caught sight of a long, black, slithery object slipping down the toilet bowl.

An icy fear gripped my muscles. I blinked. Triple blinked.

I swung my attention back toward my mother. Another black, slithery form glided past purple lips, down her plum-colored cheek to the tiled floor. It wriggled straight for me.

A scream tore from my chest as I jumped backward, tumbling onto my ass.

The worm came at me, fast and determined.

Before it reached me, though, it slipped down the floor drain, halfway between me and my mother's lifeless body.

The crash of the door sent another shudder through me, and I jolted upright as Jayda came bounding into the restroom.

"Lilia? You all right? I heard you scream."

Nose stinging with the threat of tears, I shook my head, unable to form the words.

Frowning, she stepped cautiously toward me, eyes scanning the room. "What's wrong?"

"We need to call someone," I managed, pointing toward the stall.

"Call someone?" Expression carved in confusion, she turned toward where I pointed. "Lilia? Are you okay?"

I swung my attention back toward the stall to find nothing. Not a single trace that anyone had been there. "I, um ..." Humiliation burned in my cheeks as the shock of reality settled over me. "I ..." My mind scrambled for a reason, something to steal away the possibility that I'd lost my damn mind.

Jayda stepped over my legs and cracked the door of the next stall, jumping back on a scream. "What the hell!"

My pulse hammered.

Had she seen them, too?

Burying her nose in her arm, she gagged and stepped back. "Hang on ... I'm ... I'm gonna call someone down. Just hang on."

Frowning, I pushed up from the floor, as she exited the bathroom, and peered into the stall next to the one where I'd seen my mother. A ball of dark fur with a long naked tail floated on the surface of the toilet water. A rat.

That explained the smell, at least.

Heaving breaths sawed out of me, as I leaned against the wall across from the stall and slid to the floor again.

A heavy weight weakened my legs. A numbing cold pulsed through my limbs and chest. No doubt, I was having a panic attack, because a cold, clammy feeling settled over me, like ice water filling my lungs, and I was pretty sure that if I hadn't sat down, I'd have passed out.

Eyes closed, I breathed through my nose in counts of four. Over the incessant thud of blood pounding in my ear, I could hear Jayda's calm voice, as she made the call to maintenance.

A simmering nausea shot up from my stomach into my

throat, but I swallowed back the urge to throw up. Acids burned in my sinuses, and I clenched my eyes tighter, breathing harder through my nose.

Daring to lift my lids, I stared at the empty stall, hating myself for having slipped into another episode in front of my coworker. On unsteady muscles, I pushed to my feet again, and thankfully, the sickness from before settled from my throat back down to my belly. Breathing through my nose helped.

At my neck, I clutched the small vial of my mother's ashes that I wore, hanging from her old rosary she used to keep in her pocket. It was a silly superstition my mother had told me once. She'd always worn a ring of my grandmother's strung on a necklace. When I'd asked why she wore it all the time, she'd told me that the dead never harmed those who carried something that belonged to them. I didn't even believe in God, but my mother did, and a part of me felt compelled to keep the rosary for that reason.

My muscles flinched when the door flew open again.

Jayda stepped just inside, keeping her distance. "I called maintenance. They're on their way down. You okay?" Her reassuring voice reminded me of my mother's. At twenty-three years old, she was only a few years older than I was, but life seemed to have aged both of us.

"I think so. Just ... a little rattled."

"No, honey. I mean, are you *okay*?"

I knew what she meant. Everything seemed to make me jittery nowadays. Who knew what had triggered the episode that time. Maybe the smell. Maybe I'd seen the rat and processed it as something entirely different. Wasn't the first time that'd happened. Jayda had witnessed a couple incidents when I'd seen something that wasn't there.

"I'll be fine." The three words that'd become my mantra in the last four years.

I'll be fine.

For the most part, I had been fine, except for the times when something had triggered flashbacks.

Or I'd seen the occasional hallucination of my mother.

Was I okay, though?

I guessed that remained to be seen.

Chapter 3

Lilia

Riding the subway after work sucked. Riding the subway after having seen my dead mother at work was downright unnerving. Although Jayda had urged me to leave an hour earlier than usual, I'd stayed a bit longer just so I didn't saddle her with all the work.

I'd never bothered to mention the hallucination to her, even if she was more friend than coworker. And the times I *did* talk about my mother's death, I never bothered to mention the black worms in her mouth, either.

Mostly because I had a bad feeling they weren't real, either.

According to Bee's dad, Conner, my mother had slit her wrists that night. The story went that Bee had eventually come out of her room to find me passed out on the bathroom floor and Mom in the tub with her wrists slashed. She'd run back into her room and called Conner, and by the time he'd arrived, she was hiding under her bed shaking and muttering to herself.

The story had a plot hole, though. A void that'd never filled after years of trying to remember the details of that night. I couldn't recall my mom having cut her wrists. Surely, I'd have mentally clocked such a gruesome sight in the timeline.

When I'd insisted that I'd seen the worms spill from her

mouth, though, Conner had denied their presence and produced the coroner's report. There, plain as day, her cause of death had stood out from every other gory detail: *severe blood loss due to suicide*. That was when I'd first spiraled into a dark place where I couldn't trust myself. A place where reality and nightmares blurred.

I'd followed up with our family doctor a few months later to ask about the worms, and he'd pretty much argued with me, telling me he'd never heard of such a thing. Which made sense, I guessed, if I'd made them up. A number of Google searches had failed to produce anything about the worms, too, and every medical journal I'd read on parasites had lacked the complications and progression of symptoms that I'd noted throughout my mother's illness.

I had no choice other than to accept that I'd imagined them. Trauma could do shitty things to a person's head, after all.

By the time I finally left work, I felt like I'd run a mental marathon. Still didn't entirely have my wits about me, which made the subway feel different tonight. Scarier.

At just after midnight, the only route open was the red line, and aside from smelling like piss, it was sparse. The only folks out and about were the junkies and bar-hoppers, a few of whom sat zoned out, or sleeping. Covington wasn't the worst city in the country, but it certainly wasn't the safest.

The potent stench of urine, stagnant with the July heat, was only a minor distraction, though, to the turbulence still churning in my head.

The problem was, I didn't sleep much. A vicious cycle, really. I suffered horrible nightmares that kept me awake for more hours than the average person. It meant that I sometimes saw things. And sometimes, the things I saw made it hard to determine whether I was awake or asleep.

Eyes closed, I took deep breaths, clutching the rosary.

When I finally opened them again, I caught the leering stare of an older man across the aisle from me. Had to be in his late forties, judging by the speckles of gray in his beard and hair. Pale white skin told me he didn't get much sun. Only one other woman in the car, perhaps sixty, lay passed out in the corner. The other dozen scattered about the car were men.

My social anxiety came courtesy of my mother, who'd always shunned the notion that people were inherently good. In her eyes, everyone was a serial killer until proven otherwise, and somehow, a small bit of that paranoia had manifested in me over the years.

I released the rosary and slipped my hand into my pocket for the knife that I carried everywhere–even to bed. One I'd bought for myself a while back when I'd decided to work the night shift.

As if the older man sensed my unease, he lowered his gaze toward the pendant at my neck. Strung by a black-beaded chain, the ashes inside made up the purest form of my mother–all of the disease that killed her burned away. The urge to clutch it again, to protect my mother from his stares, tugged at me, but instead, I looked away, although I still felt the man's gaze on me.

The voice overhead announced my stop was next. Relieved, I pushed up from my seat, and without looking at the guy, I hustled down the aisle as the train rolled to a stop. The moment the door opened, I dashed out onto the empty platform.

"Hey!" a raspy, gravelly voice called after me. "Hey, girl!"

Stupid drunks. I dealt with them at least three times a week, and I just wasn't in the mood tonight.

I ignored him and kept on toward the staircase ahead, my whole body shaking, knuckles burning with the grip of my blade inside my pocket. A click of the button popped the blade open and offered a small bit of comfort where I could feel it press through the fabric against my thigh.

"Hey! Girl!" The voice was closer than before, but I didn't dare turn to look at him. "Stop!"

Heart thundering in my chest, I ran for the stairs, and the moment I hit the first step, a firm grip of my arm jolted my muscles. Twisting around showed the man from the subway, and I swiped the blade out of my pocket, holding it with a trembling hand between us.

"I suggest you let me go. Now."

He did, at the same time lifting my canvas bag up. "You left this."

Eyes flicking to the bag and back to him, I stood dumbfounded. The tension in my muscles loosened, and I let out a shaky breath. I snatched up the bag, tucking the blade back into my pocket. "Thanks."

The man's bushy brow winged up. "Stay safe."

At that, he hobbled off, back toward the platform.

Once out of sight, I closed my eyes and took a deep breath. *Get it together, Lilia.*

The flashing marquee sign of the Luminet Theater cast a bright light across the sidewalk, as I made my way down Prather Street to the unremarkable door just past the theater's entrance. The apartment complex where I'd basically grown up most of my life, situated above the theater, had been built in the early twenties, when theater was booming in the city. The building itself was something of a landmark in Covington–the place where the first known serial killer in Massachusetts had left his victim, a well-known actress back then, carved up in her dressing room. In spite of its infamy and history, the building hadn't been well-kept over the years. Just wasn't enough money to properly restore it, I guessed.

I climbed the narrow staircase, their tired bones creaking under my boots. Not even the heavy scent of mold and mothballs could erase the odor of piss still clogging my nose. When I finally reached the apartment, the sound of voices sent a pulsing dread through me, particularly when I recognized one of them belonging to Conner's friend, Angelo. He'd shown up about four years ago and stuck around like an ugly mole on my ass–the kind with a cancerous core.

"I don't know, man. Those guys have ties to the cartel," Conner said through the door. "I got my daughter to think about."

My mom had gotten in touch with Conner for Bee, mostly, before she'd passed. For the first two years of Bee's life, he'd lived with us, until Mom had kicked him out and he'd ended up in New York, living with roommates in some crappy neighborhood. A couple years before mom got sick, he'd agreed to move back in with us, to help out and attempt to establish a relationship with his daughter. Considering I wasn't an adult at the time she died, we would've probably gotten thrown into foster care, since my mom didn't have any family that I knew of. Conner was an absolute jerk at times, but at least he'd kept us together, for the most part.

"It's a fucking grand. Look around," Angelo spat back. "You're not exactly living the high life here."

Sometime after Mom had died, the two of them went into some covert business together that Conner claimed was nothing more than selling scrap metal they'd scrounged. I didn't buy that for one second, not since the time I'd watched the two of them beat the shit out of a guy in the back alley of our apartment. Any time I brought it up, though, an argument would ensue, always ending with Conner telling me to mind my own business.

I didn't like it, and I sure as hell didn't like Angelo. The guy was a creep sundae with a rotten, moldy cherry.

Frowning, I entered the small apartment and found Angelo kicked back in one of the kitchen chairs, while Conner chugged a beer beside him.

Conner straightened, likely surprised to see me home a half-hour earlier than usual. "Hey, Lil, what's going on?" Just a few years shy of forty, Conner was a mess, with his grease-stained hands and shirts courtesy of the auto shop where he'd worked the last six years.

His friend, on the other hand, came a bit tidier, but carried an odor that reminded me of freshly churned dirt mixed with a hardware store.

As he sipped his beer, Angelo's beady black eyes tracked me to the opposite corner of the room, where I kept my distance.

"Had a maintenance issue at work." Glancing between Conner and Angelo, I pulled my bag up higher onto my arm. "Found a dead rat in one of the restrooms."

"Nice." Conner snorted and downed another long swill.

"Surprised you didn't bring it home for dinner," Angelo said, his lip only half curved with a smile.

"Had I known you were going to be here, I would have."

His lip twitched. Angelo didn't like to be challenged, particularly if it made him look like a fool. "Think your daddy needs to do something about that smart mouth of yours." The implication in his words had me swallowing back my repulsion.

"Easy." Conner, obtuse as ever, gave a light kick to Angelo's chair just as the brute raised his beer to his mouth. Fluid splashed out onto his lap, and the murderous glance he sent Conner seemed to have my stepdad shifting on his feet. "You don't have to be a dick."

"Manners is a foreign language to assholes," I blurted

before I could stop myself. Unfortunately, Conner didn't have the balls to stand up to his friend if he retaliated, so spouting off at the mouth wasn't exactly wise on my part.

Angelo sailed a scathing glare my way, but didn't bother to say anything more, thankfully.

From the countertop beside him, Conner reached for a paper plate that held a single slice of pizza. "Saved some dinner for you, Lil, if you're hungry." He tossed the plate onto the table, across from Angelo, the impact knocking the cheese off to the side in such a way that the sight of it withered my appetite.

Not that I'd have eaten much, anyway. Not when those worms played on repeat inside my head.

The phone rang, interrupting Angelo's death stare, and Conner answered. After a few clipped *yeps*, he hung up. "Fuck! Those fucking birds! Callahan's bitching about the shit all over the cement again."

My mother's birds. Large cages on the apartment's roof housed about twenty different birds—pigeons and sparrows, mostly. Our neighbor, Winnie, a friend of my mom's who lived down the hall from us, had offered to care for them after Mom passed, but she wasn't always good about cleaning up after them. "I'm sorry. It's been a busy week, I'll clean it."

"Nah, it's all right. She wants me to check her kitchen sink, too, I guess." In addition to working at the auto shop up the street, Conner had been appointed the unofficial fixer for the apartment complex, for which we got a hundred dollar break on rent. "Be right back," he said, and set his beer on the counter before slipping past me.

Seemed like the widow Callahan had been calling him frequently lately, and I'd have had to have been comatose not to see something was going on between them. Not that I cared, except that I hated being left alone with Angelo.

Once gone, Angelo lit up, the scent of cheap cigarettes filling the room.

"There's no smoking in here."

The corner of his lips curved upward in a sickeningly sly grin. "Come put it out. I dare you."

Rolling my eyes, I stepped past him toward the sink for a glass of water, seeing as my throat had suddenly gone bone dry. I would've gone straight to my room, but I was afraid he'd follow me there. It was better to be closer to the kitchen knives. "Why are you here this late?" I glanced back, and catching him looking at my ass, a wave of acid climbed my throat. I tipped back the glass of water, drowning the urge to call him out on it.

"Little Lily cat," he said, ignoring my question. "You're not so little anymore, are you, kitten?"

"Don't call me that."

"Why's it bother you? You got a boyfriend, or something?" The sound of his chuckle when I didn't answer him grated on my nerves. "No. Of course you don't have a boyfriend. Men are dicks, right?"

"Pretty much."

"You ever touched one before? A dick, that is."

Shaking my head, I set the glass on the sink. I'd officially surpassed my patience level. When I turned to leave, though, he was standing behind me, caging me against the counter.

"Pretty girl like you. Seems like you'd have touched a whole lot of dicks by now."

I pushed off the sink to step past him, but he pressed his body against me, sending off alarms in my head. "Let me go, you fucking freak," I gritted past clenched teeth and wriggled my arm from his grasp.

Sharp-nailed fingers gouged my throat, and I froze, grinding my teeth in anger, as he leaned into me, as if he'd dare kiss me.

Eyes riveted on my lips, he smiled, his breath reeking of beer and cigarettes. "Sometimes, I imagine your blood all over my cock, and it makes me hard." Cold, black eyes shifted from my lips to my eyes, the smile on his face fading. "Does it bother you when I say that?"

I bit the inside of my cheek to steady the trembling of my jaw. The guy scared the shit out of me, but I refused to admit that to him. Something told me he got off on fear.

The knife. The knife sat in my pocket, but as badly as I shook, I'd have probably dropped the damn thing before I even got to cut him with it. "If you don't let me go, right now, I'll fucking scream."

"*I'll fucking scream,*" he mocked. "So, scream. You think anyone in this neighborhood gives a shit?" He took a drag of his cigarette and blew it in my face.

Lips sealed, I twisted as much as his grip would allow, refusing to breathe it in.

"If it weren't for me, your old man would be drowning in bills right now. It's me who keeps your sister in that fucking quack school. And who keeps you from having to sell your pretty little kitty ass on the streets to pay for college."

After my mother had died, Bee's mental health deteriorated rapidly. She'd sank into the kind of depression that had me checking on her throughout the night and calling the school during the day. My therapist had suggested a boarding school—Bright Horizons, centered around mental health—and offered to evaluate her for admission. Bee had passed with flying colors and even managed to get a small bit of financial assistance to cover some of the cost of her tuition. Conner and I split the rest–an unwilling contribution on his part, seeing as he thought mental illness was a bunch of bullshit. The asshole actually had the nerve to say that to me once, and I swore it took a stampede of willpower not to haul off and smack him.

I couldn't risk his anger, though. I needed him to cover

part of her tuition, so pissing him off wasn't an option. It was the reason I stayed in the cramped apartment over the theater, working a shit night job and taking the bare minimum classes each semester at community college.

And dealing with Angelo, of course.

"You better not be roping us into the cartel." Bold words on my part, and I regretted them the moment I'd said them.

Teeth bared, he squeezed my throat harder, the pressure amplifying the rapid pulse in my neck. Not enough to completely close off my windpipe, just enough to scare the shit out of me that he could've. "You think you're so fucking smart, don't you? What *promising little scientist* scrubs shit stains in toilets? Huh? Huh?"

I clawed at his fingers, refusing to let the gurgling fear show on my face. One palm still crushed my throat, while his cigarette-toting hand gripped my wrist, and he glanced downward. "*Memento mori*," he read from the tattoo on my forearm. "You're one of those dark bitches who fantasizes about death all the time, is that it?"

That wasn't it, at all. In fact, the tattoo was a reminder of humility, but what did the dumb ass know about that?

"Let. Me. Go."

Angelo chuckled and released my jaw.

Finally free of his grip, I skittered as far away from him as I could, my body still trembling from the encounter.

He stamped his cigarette into my dilapidated slice of pizza. Not that I'd have eaten it anyway, with my stomach roiling and acids burning my throat. Sneering back at me, he strode out of the room. Not a minute later, the door clicked, announcing his exit, and I let out an exhale.

Keep it together.

After tossing the pizza in the trash, I kept on toward my bedroom. Once inside, I slammed the door shut and pressed my forehead to the surface, letting the adrenaline from that fucked-up encounter with Angelo settle as I fought tears.

I hated him. Hated that Conner trusted him around me. Hated how weak I felt in his presence. How vulnerable.

Through deep breaths, I calmed the thrumming of my heart. *He's gone. It's okay.*

On that note, I turned to my room–my sanctuary, brimming with books, candles, small apothecary jars filled with my favorite dried herbs and tissue salts, given to me by Glinda, the woman who owned the homeopathic store just up a block. A place I'd frequented when my mom had gotten sick.

I dropped my bags beside my bed on the way to my closet, where I drew down a small trinket box from the top shelf. Cracking it open revealed a number of unrelated objects–small treasures I'd collected over the past couple of years. Bones of a long-dead sparrow, the bright red feather of a cardinal, which my mother had always told me was a gift from the angels, a squirrel's rib bone, and six of my baby teeth in a tiny, corked bottle. Beneath all that sat a picture of me and my mother from before her sickness had taken hold, one of Bee's barrettes with a yellow- and white-stone bumblebee, odd coins and rocks I'd collected, and a crystal Glinda had given me for protection.

Inside the box, I deposited the rosary, then closed it up and set it back on my top shelf. From there, I kicked off my shoes and plopped down on my bed, exhausted. I needed to get some sleep. After all, I had a meeting with my professor first thing in the morning.

Two weeks ago, I'd written a paper for my microbiology class. A case study. Although meant to be fiction, the assignment was to come up with a *fictional* disease, and I'd taken the opportunity to write about my mother's illness. A purging of guilt, really, seeing as writing the events down helped me realize how screwed up it was that I'd been her main caregiver in those weeks before she'd died. She'd refused to see a doctor and remained adamant that I not take her to any hospital, no matter how bad it'd gotten.

Instead of detailing the suicide at the end, though, I wrote about the worms. Figured it wouldn't hurt, seeing as they didn't exist anyway. I referred to the disease in the paper as Blackworm Syndrome, and, apparently, that delightful little case study had earned me a meeting with my professor first thing in the morning, before class.

I hadn't mentioned my mother's name in the study. Hadn't referred to her as my mother, either. She'd always been what I'd considered ruthlessly protective of her privacy. Still, even if I'd only been sixteen at the time, I couldn't help but feel a small bit of blame for her rapid decline. For not insisting that she'd had it checked out when things had begun to worsen and she'd begun seeing things that weren't there.

Especially if it could've saved her in the end.

Across the room, over my makeshift desk of stacked wooden crates and plywood, hung a picture my mother had painted years before she'd gotten sick. A scenic cliffside seascape, with an ancient-looking oak whose curved branches held a small swing. It'd always brought me a sense of peace–such a faraway place from the shitty apartment in the shitty city. I'd asked her once if she'd ever been there before.

"In a dream," she'd said.

A somber ache bloomed in my chest as I plucked a picture pinned to the wall beside my bed, of my mom, me and Bee, taken about two years before my mom got sick. My mother had always had a radiance about her, but even more so that day, as the sun shone down through the almost burgundy locks of her hair. She'd possessed the beauty of an untamed flame, destructive and wild.

My whole life, I'd been told that I was a spitting image of her.

I'd never had the chance to be wild and untamed, though. Always felt more like the flame in those electric fireplaces—a fake contained by glass, without much potential to do anything. Life had shackled me the moment she'd gotten sick, and somehow, I just couldn't break from those chains.

While Bee had inherited some of her traits, too, she seemed to have gotten a lot more of Conner's features. Where mine and my mother's eyes were bright bluish green, hers were hazel, like her father's. Unlike Bee, I'd never met my father. According to my mother, he was a deadbeat, so I never had much interest.

Also different to me, over Bee's right eye was a bump, a dermoid cyst that she'd been born with–one that had been a source of insecurity for her since she was old enough to attend school, where her asshole classmates had poked fun at it. Unfortunately, my mother had never been able to afford to have it removed, so it still deformed her eye a bit, though she didn't seem quite as troubled about it these days.

As I stared down at my small, but broken family, a snaking dread twisted and writhed inside of me.

Help me!

Mama, no!

Distant screams echoed through my thoughts, and eyes squeezed shut, I shook my head.

No, no. Don't look at it. Don't look.

The blackness seeped back into the corner of my mind, and I exhaled a shaky breath, opening my eyes again. A slight tremble in my hand shook the picture as I slowed my breathing.

Relax. It's gone.

I pinned the photo back to my wall, and from beneath the bed, fetched out one of the black restraints I kept hidden there–a literal BDSM wrist restraint that I'd had to buy at a sex toy shop a while back. After securing one end to the metal frame of my bed, I paused for a moment, making sure Angelo hadn't decided to return for more harassment. Nothing but the quiet sounds of the apartment–the hum of the air conditioning unit in the living room window, the cars down Prather Street, and muffled music from the theater below filled the small room.

Reassured, I tucked my pocketknife beneath my pillow and secured the restraint's other end to my wrist. Just Velcro, so if necessary, I could release myself quickly. It was about the only effective thing to keep me from sleepwalking, even if it might not have been the safest. I'd tried the medication route once, but without insurance, that was no longer an option. And given the number of times I'd found myself standing outside of the apartment, I figured I needed to do something. As strange as it may have been, the restraint worked, and I only had to do one side, as the tugging and clanking against the metal usually woke me up. Good thing, too.

I had a feeling I was in for a restless night.

Chapter 4

Lilia

Professor Wilkins sat across from me, his eyes stern and unreadable, as always. Unlike those of my other professors, his office boasted a rich quality, with burgundy leather chairs, a thick cherry-wood desk with matching credenza, natural light lamps, and bookshelves behind him. The room matched the guy's personality, as he was probably the only professor I knew at Covington Community College who wore a bowtie every day and talked like something out of an old Cary Grant movie.

After a moment of straightening a few scattered papers on his desk, he entwined his fingers and looked up at me. "Miss Vespertine ... about the paper you wrote ..."

A sharp sting across my bottom lip reminded me to stop biting it—a bad habit I'd picked up to avoid biting my nails. "Sir, may I ... am I in trouble for something? I just want to get that out of the way first. Rip the Band-aid off, so to speak."

He leaned back in his chair, eyeing me for a moment. "No. You are most certainly not in trouble."

Exhaling an easier breath, I unclutched the chair handles I'd been clawing at. "That's a relief."

"The paper you wrote, Miss Vespertine, it was quite engaging. Fascinating, with all the detail. You seem to have exceptional insight into the *fictional* organism you wrote about. These worms that you described sound terrifying."

I closed my eyes to a flashback of those worms slipping out of my mother's mouth in the vision I'd had the night before. All night long, I'd suffered horrible nightmares of seeing them crawling over the floors and out of mouths. "I suppose I have quite an imagination."

"I'm curious as to what happened to the individual that you cared for in the paper."

"What do you mean, Sir?"

"You never included their fate in the summary at the end. Only the course of the disease, the progression of it, and your observations." Fingers steepled together, he eased back in his chair, his eyes brimming with concern.

"Well, I ... I suppose, given the fact that I hadn't offered a cure for it, I didn't care to mention her fate."

"And why didn't you craft a cure?"

I shrugged, clearing my throat. "The assignment was simply to write a fictional disease and its impact on human physiology."

"Which you did brilliantly. So brilliantly that I feel compelled to ask how you came about this particular disease?"

Had someone else written the same thing? I didn't understand why he would've called a meeting to ask me these questions. "I beg your pardon, Sir. I made it up. You said that I wasn't in trouble, yet I feel like you're accusing me of something."

The tension in his face softened to a slight chuckle, and he shook his head. "Forgive me, I am not accusing you, Miss Vespertine." With a sigh, he stared back at me again. "The organism that you wrote about isn't fictional. While I understand there are thousands of parasites, the symptoms you described are quite telling of this particular species."

A beat of shock pulsed inside my chest, and my mind spun

backward, replaying his words. "Wh-what did you just say?" I asked with a weak voice.

"I said, the organism described in your paper is not fictional. It *exists.*"

It exists. Real.

Not made up in my head. No. That couldn't be right.

"Are you joking?"

Lips flat, he shook his head. "I would not have called a meeting based on a joke."

Except that it had to be. For years, I'd been told that it was a figment of my imagination. Was led to believe that what I'd seen had been skewed by the trauma of my mother's suicide. It'd taken time, but I came to accept the explanation. The lie my head had told to protect my heart because my mother's suicide made little sense otherwise. She'd loved Bee and me too much to let herself decline that way, to end her life so gruesomely.

Everything unraveled inside of me. Snapping away like fragile branches that'd grounded me to some truth.

The news was somehow both validating and terrifying at the same time.

"You won't find it in any textbooks or online searches." Professor Wilkins interrupted the maelstrom of thoughts in my head. "That's because the research is ongoing and happens to be privately owned."

"Privately owned? It seems to me that something capable of infecting another human being should be made public."

"I'll come back to that in a moment." He lifted a stack of papers from beside him, and I just caught the title of my case study that he'd printed off. "After reading your paper, I submitted it to a colleague of mine for review. Her name is Loretta Gilchrist. She's the entomology professor and Department Chair for the College of Natural Science at Dracadia University. You're familiar with the school?"

The overpriced yuppy university that I'd half-heartedly applied to the summer before my senior year, when I'd hoped to one day become a lawyer, even though I knew damned well I wouldn't be accepted. Yeah, I knew of it. And of course, I'd been rejected. Good thing, too, because it was later that I'd made the decision to switch majors and find the cure for the perplexing disease that'd ravaged my mother. "Yes, I've heard of it. Law school, right?"

"They do have a law school, yes. But they're far more renowned for medical research."

"Well, I mean, they're a little out of my league, so I suppose it makes sense that I didn't know that."

"They're very selective about their applicants. The school, as you know, is quite prestigious. A number of prominent individuals have walked the halls of Dracadia." He rolled his shoulders back, a look of pride coloring his expression. "It happens to be my alma mater."

As much as I wanted to ask why, if that was the case, he was teaching a general microbiology class at community college, I kept my lips zipped.

"As I suspected, Dr. Gilchrist was also quite impressed." He reached into his desk and withdrew a black envelope, which he handed to me. "She apparently shared your paper with the Dean of Admissions, Dr. Langmore, who asked me to pass this along to you."

Frowning, I accepted the unaddressed envelope and turned it over to see it'd been sealed with gold wax, stamped with an Old English 'D'. "What is this?"

"It's for you. Open it." The usual austerity that had given him the reputation of being a jerk twisted into something completely out of character for him. The man wore a giddy smile, and the sparkle of excitement in his eyes had me both curious and concerned.

I broke the wax seal to find another black envelope inside,

that one addressed to me in beautiful gold calligraphy. Opening that envelope revealed thick parchment, folded at perfect thirds. A stamped seal marked the top of the page with the same English D as on the wax.

Dear Miss Vespertine,

On behalf of Dracadia University, I am pleased to offer you admission into the College of Natural Science. Our university prides itself on academic excellence and groundbreaking medical research. We believe your credentials, along with Dr. Wilkins' personal endorsement, makes you a perfect fit for our undergraduate program.

In accordance with the academic scholarship we've awarded for fall semester, all expenses will be covered for travel, textbooks, and housing.

Should you choose to accept this invitation, the midnight train at Covington Park will provide transportation to the port city of Thresher Bay, Maine. You will then take the ferry to Dracadia Island.

Matriculation is contingent on successful completion of your registration. I encourage you to sign in to your student account, which I've taken the liberty of setting up for you, to begin registering for fall classes. As a reminder, classes will begin on the first of September.

Due to the competitive nature of our admissions, we ask that you contact us at your earliest convenience with your decision. I am available at the email address and/or telephone number listed below with any questions or concerns you might have.

I am very much looking forward to hearing from you.

Warm regards,
Gilbert Langmore
Dean of Admissions

LangmoreG@dracadia.edu
Office: 555-721-3699

I stared down at the letter, the confusion probably scribbled across my face as I read bits of it a second time. "I don't .... I don't understand. I was denied admission. And I mean, rightly so, it's way out of my league. This doesn't make any sense."

"You applied for their medical science program before?"

"No. I originally planned to go into law back then. Changed my mind."

"Well, it seems they've reconsidered, also. While I certainly didn't expect my discussion with Dr. Gilchrist to result in admission, I will say, academically, you do possess the aptitude, Miss Vespertine. Make no mistake about your qualifications." A strange enthusiasm carried on his words, which somehow failed to stir me.

"I appreciate that, but ... this letter is offering one semester. There's no way I can afford a school like this. I can barely afford Covington's tuition."

"One semester *with the opportunity to continue*. The school prides itself on retention and academic success. I suspect they'll evaluate at the end of the semester and make a new offer."

Still holding the letter in one hand, I rubbed the tension pulling at the back of my neck. "Forgive me, I don't mean to sound ungrateful, but receiving an acceptance letter this way just feels ... unofficial?"

The excitement in his expression dulled to earnestness. "Given the fact that you, yourself, did not apply, perhaps Dr. Langmore felt that, had he sent it to your home, it may not have been taken seriously."

It was true. Had I received some fancy invitation like that at home, to a school that'd previously rejected my admission, I'd have probably thought it was a scam and tossed it.

"Understand, Miss Vespertine, that between researchers and those wishing to pursue medical careers, in particular, Dracadia receives upward of *thirty thousand* applications every year. Their acceptance rate is two and a half percent. Well below Yale, Harvard, Stanford, Princeton. That's *less than* one thousand students."

I understood the math. If I *had* applied to the school myself for medical science, my chances of getting in without Wilkins' referral were exceptionally slim. Probably impossible. "This university ... it's actually located *on* Dracadia?" A small island off the coast of Maine, if my geography was right.

"It is, yes."

I rubbed harder at my neck. "That's over three hours away."

"I believe your scholarship includes dormitory expenses and travel."

Another scan of the letter confirmed the inclusion of housing and travel. Dracadia was one of those locations that, like Martha's Vineyard, I'd always assumed to be a summer vacation spot for the wealthy. The cost for even one semester at the university must've been ridiculous–a thought that continued to make the invite a little hard to swallow. "How did they acquire my recent transcripts, my test scores?"

"As a private entity, they are under no obligation to review each candidate by the usual standards. They could offer you a scholarship merely because they like your name. And believe me, that happens."

"For a school that prides itself on retention and academic success, that doesn't seem wise."

Giving a slight huff, he nodded. "I understand your apprehension. And perhaps disbelief. Allow me to circle back to your question regarding the organism and research. It's

Dracadia that owns the research, Miss Vespertine. The organism in question is called *Noctisoma*. It's a parasite that exists predominantly on the island and rarely infects humans. We're just not a very reliable host, and not all physicians are aware of the organism as a *human* pathogen. Which is why it's interesting to me that you know so much about this, considering that it's almost never diagnosed outside of Dracadia."

Not a typical human pathogen. "Perhaps it's just coincidence."

"I don't think so. The way you described them expelling from the subject's mouth is fairly indicative, as I understand from Dr. Gilchrist. At the beginning of the year, you told me that you were interested in finding the cure for what took your mother's life. Were those not your exact words during introduction?"

They were. I guessed I hadn't realized he'd made a mental note of them.

"I didn't want to pry into what had ailed her. However, if the patient in your case study is truly your mother, surely you wouldn't pass up the opportunity to attend the only university authorized to study this particular parasite? Even if only for a semester. Aren't the answers to your questions worth it?"

Yes. They were. My whole life, I'd wanted answers. Answers that doctors and specialists I'd made a point to contact on my own hadn't provided. "What makes this organism capable of infecting humans?"

"Evolution, of course. But it requires a vehicle of transmission. Admittedly, I am not well-versed enough on this parasite to know the how of it, but there is a Noctisoma expert at Dracadia. Professor Bramwell. He teaches Neuroparasitology and gross anatomy, and is board certified in anatomical and forensic pathology. He's also the one who performs autopsies for those suspected of Noctisoma."

Bramwell. I made a mental note of that. "It was my paper that decided admission?"

"I'd be willing to bet on it. As I said, it was quite impressive and demonstrates the breadth of your understanding. Of a number of topics, really–parasitology, as well as physiology and research." He pushed up from his chair and grabbed a photo from the bookshelf behind him. He stared at it a moment before placing it on the desk. On it, a much younger version of him stood before an aging stone building, with pointed spires that reminded me of Notre Dame Cathedral. "I can tell you from personal experience, once you attend Dracadia, you will not want to leave."

The worms existed. Not in my head. Real.

And there was a university that specialized in studying them.

The possibility just seemed impossible. A dream that had tapped into the most unsettling memories and thoughts, and conjured something completely outrageous, like an ivy league school extending an invitation to a girl who could barely afford the bus fare to get there. "Can I think about it?"

"Of course. But first semester starts after Labor Day. I wouldn't take too much time. As I said, these positions are few and rare."

A peculiar, inexplicably nostalgic warmth settled over me, as I stared at the picture again. "I understand. And thank you, Professor. I appreciate your confidence."

Chapter 5

Lilia

I should've been studying for my online physics exam. Definitely not *Googling* Dracadia University. Especially since it wasn't a possibility for me. Being at a university that far away, with a full-time schedule, would mean not being able to cover half of Bee's tuition. Not only that, but Conner would definitely freak out if I'd told him I couldn't cover my share of the rent anymore. He'd undoubtedly throw Bee's tuition in my face, and pull her right out of Bright Horizons.

Clicking on the images of the university hurt, though.

Nestled on an island, the school had once been an old monastery for clergymen–a place predominantly built for religious study. While it appeared that a few newer buildings had been added to the campus, it maintained the same overall look of the gothic academic architecture seen at old schools like Harvard and Yale. The enormous building I'd seen in Professor Wilkins' picture sat on a steep cliff, as if the foundation itself had been built into the rock formation. It looked to be centuries old, with its lichen-covered stones and intricately carved masonry rarely seen nowadays.

A stone wall separated the campus from the surrounding woods, and what looked like a small town sat in the foothills of the cliff. The campus reminded me of something out of *Dead Poets Society*. Rich with tradition, opportunity.

A dream.

One too far out of reach for me.

For kicks, though, I entered the admissions address into the search bar and logged in with the temporary credentials provided to me in the letter. There, on the screen, was an account already set up for me, just as Dean Langmore had mentioned–a profile lacking an image, but a number sequence had been assigned, and all of my general information had already been populated. Below my name, a button to register for classes taunted me to click it. I checked the URL again against the one I'd Googled. Everything seemed legit.

Unfortunately, I had too much on my plate.

With a sigh, I clicked out of the search and eased back into my chair, staring up at the painting of the tree and the swing and the vast ocean beyond it. Somehow, it captured my sense of longing right then.

"I wish you were here, Mama," I whispered to myself. "I could really use your advice right now." When I wasn't occasionally spotting ghostly visions of her, I'd sometimes hear her in my head. That soft-spoken voice which cracked any time she'd tried to yell at me and Bee. I smiled at the memory of laughing whenever she'd gotten mad at us and that gentle voice had failed to intimidate.

Leaning forward again, I pulled up the search bar and typed in *Noctisoma*. Now that I finally had a name, perhaps the internet might offer more information.

A few medical studies popped up through Medscape, but when I clicked, it only offered a brief synopsis–nothing in-depth, or accessible to me without the proper login credentials. I pulled up the CDC website and typed the parasite there. Only a data report for a Geneva conference had listed it amongst pages and pages of other parasites.

There was literally *nothing*.

To be thorough, I typed in *black worms* and *Dracadia*

University. The first article to populate the screen was from a *Dracadian Gazette*, dated only a few weeks ago, whose headline read: *Homeless Woman Assaults Provost With Intent To Kill*. It went on to describe a woman believed to be named Andrea Kepling, who'd been living in one of the abandoned houses on the island and had broken into the home of a Dr. Lippincott, the Provost of Dracadia University. Armed with a pickaxe, she'd accused him of putting worms in her belly, according to Lippincott's wife, who'd witnessed the attack.

I paused there. At the peak of my mother's illness, she'd accused me of putting something inside of her, too. Infecting her intentionally. Those had been the times when her eyes had turned spacey, her pupils blown. They'd been the times she'd looked positively feral enough to kill me. I couldn't imagine having someone break into my home in that state. With a pickaxe, no less.

Apparently, the woman had managed to wound Lippincott's leg, but escaped before authorities arrived.

The associated police sketch of Andrea didn't look like a criminal, though. In some ways, she reminded me of my mother, with her long hair and weary eyes.

At a knock on the door, I groaned and closed my laptop. "I'm studying."

"Just need to chat for a second," Conner's muffled voice said from the other side of the door.

"Fine. A second."

He cracked the door open and peeked inside before stepping into the room. "Hey, ah ..." Rubbing his hands together, he cleared his throat. "I know that things have been pretty hard for you lately. And, uh ... you know, you could've left a long time ago. But you hung around here and helped with Bee ... and I know .... I know you didn't have to do that."

I didn't like where this might be going. Conner rarely acknowledged my contributions. If anything, he often criticized me for turning down extra shifts at the hospital–shifts I'd reluctantly turned down to get some studying in.

"I want to make things easier on you."

Definitely didn't like where it might be going. That wasn't Conner. Conner was a blue-collar who'd lectured me at sixteen years old that nothing in life was free. Something was amiss. "Okay."

"We've talked about this before ..." The moment his hand raised to rub the back of his neck and his gaze fell from mine, I knew exactly what he was going to say, and I breathed a sigh.

"I know. You want to rent out Mom's old room." I supposed it was out of respect for me and Bee that he hadn't yet, and I'd appreciated that for a number of years. Struggling for the sake of her memory didn't make sense, though. It'd been long enough. "It's fine."

"You're sure, kid? I mean ... you know, I could wait a little bit longer."

"No," I said, waving my hand dismissively. "We need the money." In the pause that followed, I glanced up to see him picking at his fingers, seemingly anxious. Maybe he'd been nervous to ask me about the room. I was nervous, too. "Can I ask you something?"

"Yeah, shoot."

"Remember after my mom died, I told you about–"

"The worms. Yeah. I remember." Brows furrowed, he lowered his gaze. "I don't .... I don't blame you, kid, that was a pretty rough scene with your mom bleeding out everywhere."

"You're sure you didn't see anything in the tub?" I'd always found it strange how vividly that visual remained in my head for something that hadn't actually happened.

"Why are you asking me this?" An air of suspicion bled through his voice. "You read the coroner's report, Lil. The autopsy. Multiple times. It's all there."

Sighing, I slouched back in my chair. I had, but Professor

Wilkins had also said that not all physicians were aware of the organism as a human pathogen. Perhaps they'd missed it in autopsy. "I know. I just ... thought maybe you'd seen something else."

"Everything I saw is detailed in that report," he said. "You okay?"

"Yeah. I'm fine. I just miss her." There was no point in arguing with him. He supposedly hadn't seen what I'd seen. Maybe the blood had darkened the water too much. Maybe all of the worms had gotten down the drain somehow.

"Yeah." He let out a long exhale and cleared his throat. "So, uh. What would you say if I asked Angelo to come stay here?"

A turbulent dread curled through my stomach as my mood quickly shifted, and I shook my head. "You're not serious, are you?"

"I just figured he's over here all the time. And he's living in that shithole down on Sumler."

"No. No! C'mon, Conner! Seriously?"

"He's my best friend, Lilia." He ran his hands through his hair, the stress etched into his expression more apparent to me in that moment.

Fingers clutching the pillows around me, I stifled the urge to throw something across the room at him. "The guy's a creep, Conner. You know he cornered me the last time he was here, and basically threatened to kill me."

With a dismissive wave, he shook his head. "Nah. He wouldn't do that. He's just a dick, is all."

"That is not a dick. That's a goddamn predator!"

Hands splayed to the side, he shrugged. "'The fuck do you want me to do, Lilia? Huh?"

"Tell him *hell, no*! That's what I want. He's a freak."

"Who could help with the fucking bills! I'm drowning here!"

"I'm not opposed to a roommate, but not Angelo. Please. I still have to live here and work!"

"And I work, too!" The way he thumped his finger into his chest gave off the caveman vibes I loathed. "I work, and this fucking apartment is in my name. So, I get to say who lives here!"

The one thing that I wish my mother would've thought through a bit more before her death. Not that she'd had a lot of choices–I'd only been sixteen at the time, and certainly couldn't have had the apartment in my name. But adding Conner had made for some really tense and frustrating situations.

"It'd be a fuck of a lot easier around here," he said.

"And what happens when Bee comes home for the holidays? You really want her around him? You think that's good for her mental health?"

"Bee is fine! She doesn't need a fucking quack school and therapists. She needs friends! A life!"

The rage exploded inside of me, and I shot to my feet, hands balled to tight fists at my sides. "She has a life. And friends! She's doing better because she's *finally* getting the help she needs! Someone is finally listening to her. And now you want to destroy that by inviting Angelo The Creep over for slumber parties! He's a loser, Conner. You need to ditch him before he gets us wrapped up in something dangerous!"

"He saved my fucking life!"

Not that I'd been present for that, of course, but apparently some guy they'd gone to see a while back had pulled a gun on the two of them. It just so happened that Angelo had been quicker on the draw.

"Goddamn, you bust my balls like your mom!"

"Fuck you, Conner. Fuck. You! You never deserved my mother."

"Yeah? None of you ungrateful shits deserve me. So, fuck

you, Lilia." He slammed the door on exiting, rattling my mom's painting off the wall.

Pissing me off even more.

The rims of my eyes burned with the threat of tears. *Don't break*. Angry heat rose in my cheeks, and I ground my teeth, wishing I could've blinked myself somewhere else. Somewhere far away. Like the tree and the swing and the open sea.

I plopped down on my bed and cradled my face in my palms. *Do not break*.

I couldn't live in the same place as Angelo. I couldn't. What little sanctuary I'd made of the apartment would be torn to shit by his presence. Hopefully, Conner would come to his senses about it. Otherwise, I'd have to make arrangements to have Bee stay at the dorms for the holidays. I'd make a point to visit her on Christmas, still a few months away. It wasn't like we'd had wonderful Christmases at the apartment anyway, since Mom had died. It'd mostly been Bee and I sitting in our bedroom, playing Mom's old Beatles records and drinking too much hot chocolate. Technically, we could've done that anywhere.

As for me? I needed to find a way to pay at least two months of Bee's tuition up front. If I could do that, then maybe, just maybe, leaving this place wouldn't be so impossible.

"Ever consider, like, an OnlyFans, or something?" Jayda peeled off a white sheet that bore an enormous yellow stain.

Still scrubbing at dried piss that'd somehow dribbled over the bed's rails, I shook my head. "Definitely not." Nothing against those who posted there. Hell, if I had the guts, I might've actually considered it. I didn't, though.

"I can tell you, I've thought about it a few times myself. Shit. Be a whole lot better than grabbing up bedsheets, praying not to get stabbed by a dirty needle." She tossed the wadded-up ball of sheets into a soiled linen bag. "A friend of my cousin's did it. Was making a couple grand a month before she found herself a sugar daddy. Now her lazy ass sits by a pool all day long, reading romance novels."

I didn't know why I chuckled in response. Probably just needed something to laugh about, after the conversation with Conner.

"This is your chance, Lilia. The Lord put you on a path that you did not see coming, and you need to walk it."

Sighing, I paused scrubbing the piss and tried to imagine myself walking the halls of an ivy league university. "I know. But ..."

"But nothing. You took care of your mama. Now you're taking care of your sister *and* her daddy. You're done. The Lord is telling you, it's time for *you* now."

Even though I wasn't all that religious, I didn't mind Jayda's Lord talk. I'd have loved to believe that all this turmoil actually meant something. "Why didn't you become a preacher, if you're so up on what the Lord has planned?"

"Because I like fucking too much," she said, rubbing her hand over her rounded belly. "And Lord knows his daddy is good at it. So he didn't put me on that path."

Back to my scrubbing, I huffed. "Can I just come live with you and Quentin?"

"You know you can. You're always welcome. But that's not what you really want. You want to be some *Harry Potter* bitch living it up with all those pretentious, rich, white folk, and don't tell me you don't."

I snorted and shook my head. "Actually, the thought of living with them kind of scares me. I don't know that life. Covington is my home."

"*They* don't matter. What matters is your dream. You deserve to be wearing a lab coat, not some nasty, shit-stained scrubs."

"Well, posting videos of myself on OnlyFans isn't going to be good for my reputation."

"Why not?" She set her hands on her hips. "Why the fuck not? Some girls strip to get themselves through med school. You do what you gotta do, Lilia." Brow raised, she pointed a finger at me like a mother chiding a kid. "Don't let nobody shame you."

"Why do you always have to be so ..."

"Right?"

"Positive, is the word I was going for."

"Because I'll be damned if I'm sitting here scrubbing floors and trash with you next year, when you have a full ride scholarship waiting on you like that. Go. Figure the rest out later."

What if I did? My mother had always been spontaneous like that. Always throwing caution to the wind. She believed, wholeheartedly, that things worked out. Maybe I was just obtuse to all her struggles, but it seemed like we always ended up okay. We'd never starved. We'd never gotten kicked out, or had the heat turned off in the winter. We'd survived.

I wanted more than anything to study the disease that'd ultimately killed my mother, and Dracadia was my chance, as Jayda had said. I needed this. To know that I wasn't crazy, that I had seen those damned worms crawl out of her and that it hadn't just been a figment of my imagination, as I'd been led to believe.

I had to figure something out, anyway–whether I considered Dracadia, or not–because I had a bad feeling about the crap Conner was getting wrapped up in with Angelo lately. For my and Bee's future and the sake of our safety, I needed to find a way out.

Chapter 6

Devryck

"Please don't do this!" The Accused stood before the council, locked inside an enormous, gilded cage. "I'm begging you."

The surrounding chamber was one of three ritual rooms in the catacombs of The Roost–a sprawling cathedral just outside of Dracadia University, owned by The Seven Rook Society. Or The Rooks, as we were more commonly referred. Gray concrete walls and floors added a sense of suffocation, like being buried alive inside a tomb. Fitting, really, given how utterly mind-numbing the ceremonies could be. Not even the multitude of flickering candles could brighten the cold and dreary crypt, at the center of which, etched in gold tiles, was the society's emblem–two crossed medical canes, like those used during the plague, with a number seven. The same emblem that had been branded into my chest.

Outside of the cathedral walls, we were a rumor. A myth. A secret whispered amongst the student body. Fodder for conspiracies.

Never seen. Never heard.

Crossed in front of his body, The Accused's arms shook like fragile branches ready to snap. He was the only one not wearing one of the signature plague doctor masks that concealed the face of every other member in the room, including me.

Deep black circles shadowed the Accused's eyes, telling of little sleep, and the way he kept his gaze lowered, refusing to look at anyone, assured that he understood the severity of his crimes and what level of shit he was trudging.

After all, every member of The Rooks knew not to steal. It was in the fucking handbook given to us as fledgling freshmen and still clueless to the utmost serious manner in which the Society upheld its laws. Laws that were separate from those of the outside world.

Laws that had been in place for centuries and would continue to outlive every member in the room.

The man standing before the council had been a member for nearly a decade. Nearly a decade of privilege and unimaginable power, whittled down to the thread of hope he so desperately clung to right then. The single prayer that The Rooks would forgive his offenses.

"Do you have anything to say for yourself?" Chairman Winthrop's articulate voice remained entirely recognizable even slightly muffled behind his mask. His successor's untimely death had promoted him nearly four years prior, and since then, he'd kept to his vow of *cleaning house* in the organization.

The Accused stepped forward, gripping the golden bars of his cage, and lowered his gaze. "Only that I know I've committed a grievous crime against my brothers. It was a moment of desperation and despair that inspired this unforgivable act. I beg your mercy. Grant me clemency, and I swear I will do whatever necessary to win your trust and your respect."

I snorted a laugh and the sound echoed through the room, earning me the attention of a few masked faces, and a terrified glance from The Accused. Understandable, seeing as I happened to be the one from whom he'd stolen. Years of research that The Accused had nearly sold off to some pharmaceutical mogul. One that would've surely exploited the work I'd tirelessly committed myself to since having won back some modicum of respect after my father's disastrous exit.

Fortunately, The Accused had gotten caught.

They always got caught.

His actual name was Paul Darrows, but that didn't matter anymore. As I understood, Darrows had a wife and kids. Tragic, given the trajectory of his fate at that moment, but the man had witnessed enough executions to be well acquainted with the consequences of his actions. The Rooks were one of three most powerful secret societies in the world, comprised of former CIA, FBI, presidents, inventors, all of whom had once sat in this very room at some point. How he thought he could've outsmarted them was beyond me.

I'd only laughed at his *earning trust and respect* remark because the idiot had been caught with his pants down–literally pegged in the ass by his mistress, who'd probably wished she'd spent the night counting cracks in her ceiling instead of pounding the one that had undoubtedly made for a shitty night.

Darrows had likely been swept up without a wisp of suspicion. No one, aside from the men in this room, would ultimately know his fate. And no one would ever tell, lest they wanted to be in the same position as the poor bastard.

"Let us vote on the matter." From his black, hooded robe, Winthrop removed the object pinned at his chest–what looked like a coin, about the size of a half-dollar, it bore The Seven Rook Society emblem. One side of the coin was gold, representing the brotherhood–safety, and loyalty. The other side was black. A death sentence.

Six other members removed their pins, as well. Conviction required seven votes altogether, and the majority, a simple plus one, determined whether or not Darrows lived or died.

One at a time, they lay their pins on the table before them. From my spot on the balcony, I watched a unanimous decision unravel–every pin, black side up.

The Rooks did not take kindly to thieves among us, after all.

Particularly since my research happened to be important not only to the members in the room, but the university and future of Dracadia.

"Brother Darrows, for the crimes of treachery, larceny, and the intended dispersal of confidential material, you are hereby deemed guilty." Winthrop sat back in his chair and signaled to the right of him, where two other Rook members stood by.

"No!" An outcry reverberated off the walls, and the caged man twisted away from the council, slamming himself into the unforgiving iron bars. He rattled the barrier, screaming and pleading for his life.

There was no escape, though.

His ties with the brotherhood had been severed. He'd broken the sacred vows, the promise branded into his flesh–in all our flesh–the scar that bound all of us.

He was no longer worthy of our mercy.

Darrows made a hoarse plea, as if his executioners had any say over his fate. As if they would've dared to grant him mercy in the face of their superior brethren.

The member known as The Executioner stepped forward. Unlike the black masks worn by every other member but Darrows, his glistened a resplendent gold, the surface of which reflected the many flickering candles set about the room.

I caught a flash of gold in The Executioner's palm–a remote. A click of the button, and a glass wall slid down from the top of the cage to surround the bars, enclosing Darrows inside. Two objects that looked like stage lights emerged from the floor within and snapped into place. A moment later, a sound, like running water, filled the room. The emitted gas was invisible, odorless and colorless. Unlike the masks used during the actual plague, the ones worn by the members effectively blocked out any fumes that might've seeped from the cage–a safety measure, in case the glass bore a crack, or gap.

Darrows covered his face with his hands and dropped to his knees. A futile attempt to stave off the deadly fumes that filled his enclosure. It didn't matter anyway–the gas took hold, invading his lungs and his brain through the cracks in his fingers. It perfused his muscles, and he collapsed to the side, seizing. Moments later, his body went still.

The sound of scraping concrete erupted through the room as the tiled floor lowered, carrying the cage and Darrows' lifeless body within to the lower level, where he'd be incinerated and forgotten. A second, unoccupied, tiled floor bearing the emblem rose up in its place, free of any evidence that Darrows had ever stood before the council. That he had existed, at all.

His name would never again be spoken.

Chapter 7

Lilia

Two weeks had passed since I'd received the invite to Dracadia. Unfortunately, the prospect of going was no closer to my reality than pink unicorns swooping down from the sky. I couldn't figure out a logistical way to make it happen, and no doubt the stress of that and everything else had gotten to me, because I'd begun to see visions of my mom more frequently. Ever since Wilkins had told me those worms were real, my brain went haywire trying to convince me. Consequently, I'd grown overly exhausted, sleeping in class on occasion, only to startle awake, humiliated when I'd call out for her.

I'd avoided my last microbiology lecture for the summer, not only for the embarrassment of having been awakened in class, but because I'd feared Professor Wilkins would ask me about Dracadia. Fall semester was due to begin in a week, and I hadn't done anything to secure my enrollment there. As if my finances weren't enough of a stressor, Conner had begun cleaning out my mother's room for a new roommate. Thankfully, he'd given up on the notion of Angelo moving in, a small sliver of light in the chaos. He must've teased out the stupidity of having a man like that around all the time. I hoped that was the case, anyway.

I'd left for work that evening without a word, while he

stacked boxes of what personal belongings of my mother's I was willing to part with. Having put off going through her stuff long enough, Conner had finally threatened to toss everything, if I didn't separate what I'd wanted to keep. So I'd made a stash for Bee and me–albums, jewelry, paintings, and some of Mom's old clothes.

The sight of her empty room left a hollow ache in my chest, and as much as I knew we needed the cash, I couldn't stand the thought that a stranger would eventually be filling that space.

Exhausted with stress, I entered the staff lounge and crossed to the lockers there, forcing myself to meet Jayda's bright-eyed smile with my own. "Hey," I said, twisting the dial on the lock.

"Hey!" The enthusiasm in her voice seemed a little off, and I glanced back to find she'd moved in closer.

Still smiling.

"Is everything okay?" I turned back toward the dial, pained from having to hold a cordial expression so long, and clicked open my locker where I tossed my bag inside.

"Yes. I got something for you, but ... I want you to know, giving it back isn't an option, okay?"

Head muddled with new curiosity, I pressed my locker door closed and turned to face her, noticing her arms hidden behind her back. "What is it?"

"Just a little congratulations." From behind her back, she drew a purple envelope about the size of a card and handed it to me.

"For what?"

Her face pinched to a frown. "What do you mean, *for what*? Why do you have to act like getting a scholarship to an ivy league school is no big deal?"

I suddenly wished I'd never told her about Dracadia–as if

my guilt hadn't already reached peak levels, as it was. "I can't afford to just up and leave."

"So, you're going to let that opportunity languish?"

"I don't want to, no. But my options are shit at the moment."

"Open the card, Lilia."

At a cautious pace, I pulled open the envelope to find a congratulations card inside. Flipping it open loosed a stack of bills. Hundreds. Fifties. Twenties. Tens. I didn't even have to count to know there was at least a thousand dollars inside.

My heart kicked up.

The sting of tears burned my nose, and I shook my head.

"I told Danica about you getting accepted into school." Danica was our lead manager for the department, with whom I'd always had a decent relationship, so it didn't trouble me that Jayda had told her. "Anyway, she rallied all the docs and nurses to pitch in for some extra cash. About a thousand and some change."

Enough to cover two months of Bee's tuition. My cut, anyway. Plus a little extra. It'd give me a head start, let me find a job and possibly save up a couple more months.

"I can't accept this. It's .... It's too much, Jay."

"Non-negotiable, baby. That money is yours." She threw up her hand in a dismissive way and shook her head. "And you don't have to pay it back, so don't even go there."

"But classes begin Monday. A *week* from today. I don't even know if they'd let me enroll this late. I missed orientation and registration."

"I don't know anything about that school shit. But I will say, you better hustle to see if you're still good to register."

Holding that thick stack of bills in my hand, the impossibilities from before seemed ... well, *possible*. I couldn't imagine a world where the only thing I had to worry about was school.

"I don't know what to say. No one has ever done anything like this for me before."

"What you say is simple. Repeat after me: I, Lilia Vespertine." Brow winged up, she paused, waiting on me.

"I, Lilia Vespertine."

"Am going to fucking Dracadia University."

I released a tearful chuckle. "Am going to fucking Dracadia University."

A beam of pride glinted in Jayda's eyes, as she folded her arms and smiled. "And there you have it. All the thanks we need."

I wrapped my arms around her, desperately holding back a sob, because goddamn it, she didn't have to do what she had. And there was no way I could pay her back. Not until I finished my degree in a decade's time. "Thank you."

"You're welcome."

"Would it be selfish if I asked for one more favor?"

"Depends on the favor," she said in a flat voice that made me smile.

Releasing her, I stepped back. "Can I stay with you this week? Conner's cleaning out my mom's room. Just ... not really interested in sticking around for that."

"You absolutely can. Pack your bags and do what you gotta do tonight." From a shelf beside our lockers, she grabbed a head cap and wound her long braids into it–a practice she'd put into place after having haphazardly dipped her hair into a dirty bucket of water. "I'll bring Quentin along to come pick you up."

"Are you sure?" I pulled my hair back into a loose ponytail at my neck. "I don't want to put you guys out. I can take an Uber to your place."

"I insist. You don't need all that weight on you right now. You got shit to plan for."

Again, I found myself trying to wrap my head around the

possibility that I might soon be walking that mystical-looking campus.

At break, I used one of the staff computers to shoot Dean Langmore a quick email, asking if it was too late to register for classes. At a little after ten, I didn't expect a reply, but when his name popped up in my inbox just before I closed out, my tongue damn near fell out of my mouth.

Absolutely, Ms. Vespertine. I've attached the link for registration, as well as the welcome packet you would have received at orientation last week.

The attached file read: *Welcome to Dracadia University.*

Biting my cheek failed to contain the smile itching to break free. Because I, Lilia Vespertine, was going to fucking Dracadia University.

My shift flew by, and before leaving for home, I'd made a point to both thank and chide Danica. As I sat on the subway, clutching my bag, I stared through the window, desperate to hold back a smile so I didn't look like a weirdo smiling at my own reflection, while I imagined myself as an ivy league student. My campus. My school.

Life felt unreal. A dream.

I'd left for my shift that evening, weighed down by hopelessness and disappointment.

Suddenly, I had a plan.

The moment I entered the apartment, I quieted my footsteps, eyes scanning for Conner in the dim light. No doubt, he'd have given me a hard time about leaving, and I just couldn't afford that when my head still grappled with the decision. I headed straight for my bedroom, the knots tightening even more as I turned the knob and dashed for the closet to grab my suitcase, pausing to nab a few sweatshirts. I hoisted the suitcase onto the bed and twisted for the dresser, sloppily piling in jeans, a couple of skirts that I'd bought for job interviews, dresses I'd taken from Mom's old wardrobe, sweaters, underwear, socks, my trinket box. I tossed in my favorite blanket, a picture of Bee, Mom, and me, and my mom's painting. A charger and toiletries. From my desk, I grabbed the invitation to Dracadia and stuffed it inside my bag. Everything fit perfectly inside the suitcase, and it was only when I grabbed the zipper that I felt an ominous presence at my door.

"Think you forgot something." The distressing sound of Angelo's voice skated down the back of my neck, and I turned to see him clutching a pair of my satin panties to his face.

Lowering my gaze, I reached out a hand. "Give them to me."

"Think I'll keep them as a souvenir."

Hiding my irritation with him, I finished zipping up my suitcase. "Do what you want, Angelo. I'm done with you, this town. All of it."

"Tell me where you're going, and I'll give them back."

"Don't you think you're a little *old* to be playing games?" I hoisted the suitcase off the bed. No way I planned to stay in the apartment with this walking shitstain. Even if I had to wait on the street for an hour until Quentin arrived, at least there'd be witnesses to whatever bullshit he tried to pull. "What the hell are you even doing here, anyway? How'd you get in?"

"Tell me where you're going," he said again, ignoring my questions.

"No." Muscles straining, I carried the suitcase across the room, halting in front of the door he blocked. "Move."

He didn't budge so much as an inch.

A rush of something shot through me–fear, adrenaline, I couldn't tell, but the potency of it vibrated my bones. "Get out of my way, Angelo. I'm not playing games."

He still didn't move.

"Fuck you," I said, ready to plow into him.

He clamped his hand over mine and pushed down on the suitcase that I struggled to lift, weighing it down until it was too heavy to hold. "You're not going anywhere, little girl."

God, the stench that wafted off of him. Who'd have guessed a man could smell like a literal grave? Pretty sure cutting him open would've sent a corpse spilling out.

"Lil! Angelo! Brought some coneys home! Come on an' eat!" The sound of Conner's voice stoked a turbulent mix of relief and alarm. I'd hoped to be gone before he got home.

The note I'd written was a sad and inadequate exit, but I couldn't take a chance he'd try to guilt trip me. Or that we'd fight, and I'd end up pissing him off enough to withdraw Bee's tuition.

"Sounds delicious!" Angelo called back, his lips curving to a smile. "By the looks of things, you weren't planning to tell Conner, either." He pushed off the wall and headed down the hallway toward the kitchen. Much as I had the urge to slip out the window of my bedroom, I owed it to Conner to at least tell him what was going on.

Exhaling a sigh, I left my bag in the bedroom and made my way through to them.

Coney in hand, Conner frowned as I stood in the doorway. "Hey, Angelo says you're heading out. Where to?"

"I'm staying at a friend's. Why the hell was he here before you?"

"We were having a meeting. I ran out to grab dinner. He stayed." Brow winged up, he stared back. "What friend you staying with?"

"Someone from school," I lied. "You don't know her."

With a shrug, Conner bit into his coney, dribbling sauce down his chin.

Angelo tapped his finger against the table, while his uneaten coney sat in its paper tray in front of him. "That's it?"

he asked, not taking those creepy eyes off me. "Aren't you gonna ask who?"

Frowning, Conner wiped his chin across his forearm, taking the bit of sauce with it. "'The fuck do I care? She's twenty years old."

Relief uncoiled some of the knots in my gut, so much so, I didn't want to dare disrupt the mood by telling him about Dracadia. I'd call him. Leave the note in his lunchbox. Send a carrier pigeon. Or owl. Something that didn't involve Angelo.

"Ahh, there's something else, though, isn't there, Lil?" Angelo's face stretched to a wicked smile that I could've slapped with a fly swatter right then.

I shook my head, swallowing back the dryness in my throat.

"Oh, come now. There was something about a ... Dracadia, I believe." The theatrics in his voice grated on me, and I would've happily sacrificed my pinky toe to watch the ceiling cave in on him.

The asshole had clearly opened the envelope on my desk. He had been in our apartment for God knew how long and had rifled through my shit.

"'The hell is that?" Conner asked, shoving another bite into his mouth. "Sounds like something out of one of them vampire movies."

"It's a university. I was accepted there," I offered reluctantly.

Conner's brows winged up, his eyes bright with surprise. "Oh, yeah? That's great, Lil. Congratulations. Is this, uh ... another community college?"

Shifting my attention brought Angelo's smug grin to the fore. "No. It's an ivy league college about three hours north of here."

"Three hours?" Conner buried his frown into a long swill of beer, and when he placed the bottle down, the frown had deepened. "And did you just say ivy league? Is this a joke? You can barely pay for two classes at Covington."

I had to tread carefully, for Bee's sake, in spite of the tensity simmering in my blood. Telling him that I had been gifted money would've been stupid–particularly in front of Angelo. "I received a full paid scholarship."

The cluck of his tongue told me he wasn't happy. "Well, that's not gonna work. You got Bee and half the rent here."

"This is my one and only opportunity, Conner. My one chance. And I'm not going to be made to feel guilty. I stayed when I didn't have to. I helped when I could've left. And I never asked you for anything. Ever. But I'm asking you now to be the decent guy my mom loved all those years ago and help me out. Please."

What I surmised as understanding flashed across Conner's face, and he let out a huff. "Angelo, give us a moment, will ya?"

Angelo's jaw shifted, his stare more intense. "I could use a smoke." With that, he pushed up from his chair and, never taking his eyes off me, strode out of the room.

At the click of the door, I let out a relieved exhale. "Thank you."

Arms crossed, Conner stared down at the floor. "So, this school. Wow. You think you can handle all this?"

Finally, a real conversation without all the show of dominance. "I'm gonna try."

He rubbed his jaw and blew out a resigned breath. "Fine. I'll figure out rent. I got some applicants for the room. Callaghan mentioned some interest in it."

Jesus, I'd take lady Callaghan any day over Angelo, that was for sure.

"So long as you can still help me with Bee?" he asked, and I smiled, glad to know that was still a priority for him.

"I've got ... a little cash saved for it. I'll get a job at school.

Chapter 8

Devryck

Hunting the inebriated was horribly anticlimactic.

A white, vaporous mist danced across wet cobblestones, as I made my way down a shadowy alley in the heart of Emberwick, a moderately-sized, moody village just outside of Dracadia University. Like most of the villages on the island, it had retained its old-century charm, with French gothic architecture and vine-covered shops. A dizzying maze of coffee houses, book shops, museums, and as I understood, the most decadent chocolate on the east coast. Hardly a place for depravity, but that was exactly what I sought there.

The lingering scent of rose perfume clung to my shirt, the nauseating stench of a quick, incurious fuck. It was sickening, the way the mind could eventually grow numb to the parasitic needs of the flesh. I'd made a point to meet twice a week with Loretta Gilchrist, the entomology professor, to burn off the pent-up agony of an insatiable sexual appetite. A mundane, but effective therapy, up until that evening, when I'd been put off by the woman. Not because she was ten years older than me, or that she had a tendency to fall into a coughing fit during her climax. Though our routine had gotten somewhat loathsome, I'd always appreciated the intense release I couldn't seem to find during any other physical activity, and even if she

They have work study, and maybe I can get another evening gig."

Lips thinned to a straight line, he nodded. "You were always a smart kid, Lil. From the time you was little, you know? Smart little shit. Your mom ..." With the back of his thumb, he scratched his nose. "I know she'd be proud."

"Thanks."

"The room will be here for ya. And Bee. I won't rent it out, or anything."

Not that I planned to come back for any great length of time, if I could help it. Even if things didn't work out at Dracadia, I intended to use the move as an opportunity to be on my own. Still, it was decent of Conner. "I appreciate that."

"When do you go?"

"I'm leaving right now. Staying with a friend for a few days, then she's going to take me to the train station."

"All right." He rubbed his jaw again and stepped forward, as if to hug me, but hesitated and stepped back again.

Lips pulling to a half-smile, I held out my hand for a shake, to which he reciprocated. "Take care, Conner."

"Yeah. Take care."

wasn't the most exciting conquest, I appreciated the subtlety of our meetings.

Unfortunately, she'd broken my *no touch* rule.

Ordinarily, I'd have bound her arms to avoid the mistake, but that evening, I'd been hasty and irritated by my body's needs. The incessant intrusion of thought which had rendered me anxious to get it over with. To fuck and be done with it, so I could return to my studies.

To my utter disappointment, she took my oversight as a show of growth. Or worse, *affection*. The very thought of such a thing sent a shiver of horror down my spine.

Even then, more than an hour later, I could still feel the invisible mark of her hand on my skin. I ground my teeth at the ghostly imprint of her cold fingertips across my shoulder, from where it faded down the length of my arm to my entirely insensate fingers. Not even the most excessive scrubbing could rid me of her unwanted touch.

I scratched at my shoulder as I kept on down the alley, until, in the darkest corner of the village, I found the man I'd sought out, one who'd been living in hiding. For that, the island made a perfect cloak.

Admittedly, it hadn't been entirely random that I'd chosen him, and on a prior visit to the village, I'd watched the man scurry out of a corner market toward a quiet place beneath a tree in the nearby park. There, with shaky hands, he'd unbagged a fifth of cheap whiskey and swallowed it straight from the bottle, like water. The alcoholism was obvious. What I hadn't known at the time was that the man had abused his wife and sons–his youngest, to the point of his having fallen comatose. Wanted by police, he was on the run for an entire lifetime of crimes for which he'd never paid the piper.

Perhaps that should've been good cause to turn him over to authorities, to act the hero for once in my godforsaken life.

Heroics were boring.

The man in the alley had been lured to Dracadia Island with the promise of money and refuge, but as it turned out, his ticket to asylum had never materialized. He'd been duped, and with no other resources, had remained on the island. A most unfortunate fate.

As I strode closer, an intense jolt of agony struck my skull, bringing me to a skidding halt. Like a shock to my brain, it radiated out from its pulse points at either side of my head, just above my ears. The pain, like blades dragging over bone, vised my muscles and a sharp ringing in my ears dropped me to my knees. Involuntary clenching of my teeth shot piercing spasms to my temples and eyeballs, locking my jaw. Quiet growls rumbled in my throat, my muscles shaking with the stabbing misery. A cold nausea expanded inside my chest, and I breathed through my nose.

One, two, three, four ...

Until the intensity lessened.

The needling ache dulled.

And dulled.

Eyes closed, I took deep breaths, focusing on the relief. The loosening of tension and slackening of clenched teeth. Seconds later, it diminished, and I fell onto my palms, catching my breath. Cold wet stones dampened my knees through the slacks and the balmy air cooled the sweat across my skin. The headaches had gotten worse in recent months, and often struck without warning. A worrisome evolution.

With the pain finally subsided, I pushed to my feet and kept on down the alley.

The man I'd sought lay slumped against the aging brick wall beside a line of trash cans. Remnants of what I presumed was vomit speckled a dark, shabby beard. I gave a light kick to the man's leg, and he didn't so much as flinch. Crouching to check his pulse, I was relieved to find a weak throbbing below his skin.

An object sticking up from the man's ragged coat drew my attention, and with a gloved hand, I lifted a picture from his pocket. A clean-shaven version of him stood beside a young woman, perhaps no more than thirty, and two little boys, who looked to be about eight and ten. I tucked the picture back into the man's coat, making a mental note to burn it later.

With that, I lifted him to his feet, to the sounds of grumbling and mumbling, and wrapped the stranger's arm around my neck for balance. A repulsive odor singed my nose as I dragged him toward the mouth of the alley, where my car remained parked, waiting for him.

I sat in the shadows on an old wooden chair, waiting for Alley Man to fully wake.

Groans echoed through the dank and dreary corridors of Emeric Tower's catacombs, which had housed prisoners centuries before. The maze of tunnels had been closed off and sealed sometime in the late seventeen hundreds, well before it had been purchased and turned into a university for clergymen. It was only by happenstance, during my junior year at Dracadia when, bored with physics recitation held two floors above, my classmate and I had snuck away for a cigarette and had stumbled upon what looked to be a doorframe's mantle. Weeks of hacking away at the rock-like mud, which had hardened to a stony barricade had opened the entrance and revealed the archaic lab once belonging to Dr. Stirling. The pitch-black tunnels, untouched by light for centuries, had led us to the dark, abandoned cells. Long-forgotten prisons that still held the decayed bones of whomever had been unfortunate enough to dwell there. I'd since installed lighting throughout the tunnels, but even in the thick of summer, the ancient passageway casted an unnerving chill.

The man from the alley raised a trembling hand to his head, his eyes slowly fluttering open. He lay on the floor of his cell for a moment, perhaps trying to discern where in the hell he'd been taken. On a gasped breath, he shot upright and kicked himself back against the wall. Panicked eyes fell on me, as I watched with intrigue.

"W-w-where am I?" A thick rattle in his voice hinted at thirst and likely dehydration. The sound persisted on each ragged breath that followed.

"Dracadia University. Emeric Tower, to be exact."

"Wh-wh-who are you?"

I plucked a piece of lint from my black slacks and offered a small but insincere smile. "Professor Bramwell, which is entirely irrelevant."

The man scrambled toward the bars of his cage, fingers curling around the thick iron posts. "What am I doing in here? I want out! Now!"

"Calm yourself, Mr. Barletta." I reached forward, the movement creaking the old chair as I grabbed a fifth of Macallan from the gritty floor beside me. "Tell me, have you ever had decent whiskey in your life?"

A longing in Barletta's eyes told me his craving for alcohol outweighed his fear right then, and the man licked his lips. "I don't think I have."

I held up the bottle in taunting. "It's delicious. Smooth. Like warm hazelnuts with notes of sherry. Would you like some?"

A spark of desperation lit his otherwise dull, rheumy eyes. "I would."

I reached forward, passing through the bottle that only just fit between the bars of the man's cage.

With haste, the stranger swiped it out of my hands, popped the cap, and chugged a good quarter of the expensive liquor before he lowered it from his lips. On a sigh of relief, he fell back against the wall and held the bottle against his chest, like he was cradling a small child. "You're right, Bramwell, it's good. Real fucking good." He kicked back an even longer swill than the last. Two grand's worth of liquor in his gullet. "Now tell me why I'm here."

Exhaling a resigned breath, I sat forward and rested my elbows on my thighs. "Very well. I am a pathologist here at the university. The primary researcher for a parasitology project that's funded by exceptionally wealthy and powerful individuals."

"That's great. 'The fuck does that have to do with me?"

"I'm glad you asked. It so happens, I am in desperate need of human subjects."

Chuckling, he rolled his head against the wall to face me. "The answer is *no*. I'm not your fucking guinea pig. Now let me go."

Lowering my gaze, I smiled and eased back in my chair again. "Oh. I wasn't asking your permission, Mr. Barletta. You see, the whiskey you just chugged contains thousands of tiny eggs, each of them encased in a wonderful spore-like outer shell that protects it from the ethanol. In two days, those eggs will be embryonated as they settle into your very nutrient-rich liver. The larvae will continue to grow inside of you and, in another six days, will hatch from their eggs. That's when the real fun begins." I watched with pointed amusement as the color drained from his face and his jaw slackened with shock and perhaps a bit of disbelief. "The larvae will then release potent toxins that will breach your blood brain barrier. The toxins will intensify your most basic needs–thirst, hunger, sex. When the parasite finally realizes there is no warm and cozy womb to lay more of their eggs and complete their cycle, the adult worms will then aggressively begin to feed on your liver in an attempt to fatten themselves for survival. You will ultimately go into organ failure and die. And that is when you will finally expel them." Sighing, I shrugged. "But I wouldn't fret. You were well on your way to liver failure, anyway."

Barletta jumped to all fours and shoved a pudgy finger down in his throat. Vomit poured from his mouth and nose onto the floor.

As he retched and gagged, I tugged a small pocket watch from my slacks and polished its surface on my shirt, noting the time was just before midnight before I stuffed it away again. "It's futile. Say, for the sake of arguing, you managed to expel a good few hundred eggs. There are still many more. On their way to your liver now. Which, I'm guessing, is in a grotesque state of cirrhosis at this point."

He shoved a finger into his throat again and let out a hoarse cough. "You sick fuck. You sick and twisted fuck! Let me go!"

"Sick fuck? I gave you shelter. Expensive drink. It's not as if I battered your skull with a liquor bottle and left you comatose. That would've been absolutely unconscionable."

His eyes widened, and he fell back onto his heels, letting out a weary sob.

"What separates monsters from good men is only a matter of perspective. In your eyes, I'm a sick fuck for what I've done to you. But I, on the other hand, see you as a *parasite*."

Swiping up the bottle, he threw it at me. On impact with the iron cage bars, the broken glass crashed to the floor.

"Now that's a shame. I estimate in about an hour, you're going to be going through some fairly intense withdrawals." Lips flattened, I shook my head, and pushed up from the chair. With one hand clasped behind my back, I lifted a piece of the glass, where a small amount of liquor had pooled on its surface. While the eggs were virtually invisible, the fluid seemed to move with the wriggling of the parasite contained inside of its cocoon. Smirking, I tossed it away. "I was the one who offered money and asylum on Dracadia Island. The one who lured you here."

Again, a flare of disbelief shined in his eyes. "You? Why?"

"The why will be revealed later. There is a fragile thread that ties us, Mr. Barletta." A sharp strike of pain hit either side of my head, and eyes screwed shut, I let out a grunt, rubbing the heel of my palm where the agony damn near vibrated my skull. Whatever Barletta said to me after fizzled to an annoying blur of sound, until it came back into sharp focus, and I opened my eyes.

A short episode that time, thankfully.

"Fucking let me out of here!" Nabbing one of the broken pieces of glass, he drove his arm through the space between the cage bars in a pathetic attempt to cut me.

I chuckled and shook my head with a pitying expression that undoubtedly pissed him off. "Consider this penance. Your opportunity to save a life, for once." I shoved my hands into my pockets and turned away. "I can see you're upset. I'll return tomorrow with some breakfast."

Barletta's screams echoed behind me as I strode down the corridor.

Chapter 9

Lilia

"Are you sure this is the place?" Jayda asked beside me, as both of us stared through the windshield of her car toward the train station.

At least, I thought it was a train station.

Heat-withered weeds stuck up through the cracked concrete, and the dilapidated building, where a ticket sign hung half-cocked, didn't even look open. The place looked abandoned, with garbage scattered over the parking lot and colorful words graffitied across one of the stationary train cars.

After another glance down at the invitation sitting in my lap, I nodded. "It's the address on the invitation."

"How 'bout I stay a bit, just in case?"

"You have to be up in four hours to work. I'll be fine."

"Girl, it's *work*. It'll be there tomorrow and the day after that. I can't say the same for you, if I leave."

"I've got my blade and my pepper spray. That should at least get me a head start, right? Besides, it's quarter-to midnight. The train should theoretically be here in fifteen minutes."

"If it's *theoretically* coming, at all." Jayda leaned forward, and I had a pretty good idea that we both saw the same guy in threadbare clothes leaning up against the building, when she shook her head and said, "I'm just gonna stay. That way, if it doesn't come, I'm already here to take you back."

Smiling, I eased back in my seat, secretly relieved that she wasn't going. I'd always taken care of myself, but sometimes it was nice having someone look out for you. "I know you don't like sappy, but–"

She threw up a hand between us. "Don't do it."

"I don't know what I'd do without you in my life."

"Stop it. Okay? Stop it." The same hand she used to blockade came to a rest on my knuckles and gave a gentle squeeze. "You're stronger than you realize, Lilia. You just need to start believing it."

"I will, when you start accepting compliments and gratitude."

She snorted and turned away, retracting her hand as I chuckled.

Ten minutes passed. The anxiety knotted my stomach, while I gnawed on my bottom lip. I'd never been outside of Massachusetts before. Had never traveled by train, or plane. We'd taken camping trips sometimes when my mom was still alive, but never farther than a few counties over. To say that I was nervous was a bit of an understatement.

"Maybe we should just go," I said to Jayda at two minutes past midnight.

No sooner had the words tumbled past my lips than a rattling of my water bottle in its cup holder drew my attention there. I glanced down to see the surface rippling.

Jayda turned toward me, wearing a quizzical expression.

Not a second later, light cut through the misty fog. A loud hum rose from the distance, white noise beneath the screech of metal on metal. A horn sounded, pounding in my chest, and I jolted forward to see the homeless guy startle awake.

The two of us climbed out of the vehicle, and after grabbing my suitcase and backpack from the backseat, I walked cautiously ahead of the car to see an enormous shadowy form slice through the overhang of trees. A monstrous vehicle ground down its pace, and on an angry squeal, it let out one final chug and rolled to a stop.

My mouth hung wide as I took in the magnificence of it. A shiny black surface, over which gold details gave it a luxurious appearance. The side of it read *Dracadian Express* in glittery gold font, with the head of a gold dragon curved over the lettering.

It idled while I marveled the exterior, and through darkened windows, I noticed obscure figures moving about–what I presumed to be other passengers inside.

From the right, a man clad in an black suit and hat, with gold embroidery on his lapel, strode toward me. It was only based on a handful of movies I'd watched that led me to believe he might've been the train conductor.

"Boarding pass?" he asked, and I rifled through the envelope I held. The shiny black ticket matched the train, with its gold dragon and beautiful, metallic gold font, and I handed it off to him.

"The university has its own train?"

"It's owned by the university, but it serves all of Dracadia and Maine." The conductor pointed toward an entrance where a ramp slowly retracted down. "You're in car two. Lounge and observation are toward the front. I've a few more stops, and we should arrive to the port city by five in the morning."

With a nod, I smiled, the excitement buzzing inside of me. "Okay."

"Welcome aboard, Miss Vespertine." He lifted my suitcase, and my muscles lurched to take it back. That single bag held everything I owned. My whole life, essentially.

I had to remind myself it wasn't Covington public transportation. What I owned was probably considered junk in the world I was about to enter.

"Well, this is it," Jayda said beside me.

I turned to see the pride-filled smile on her face, as she stared toward the train. "I'll be back to visit."

"You better." She wrapped her arms around me, squeezing the air out of my lungs. "You take care of yourself, Dr. Lilia."

"Thank you for everything," I whispered, and with that, she released me, stepping back so I could see a shine in her eyes.

"Go on. Your future is waiting."

At the first sting of tears, I double-blinked them away and turned toward the train. Willing myself not to cry, I sucked in a deep breath and strode up the ramp after the conductor, past the luggage rack, and through the automated door that opened to car two.

The seats within flaunted a plush black velvet with gold lettering, arranged in rows of two at either side of the long aisle I traversed toward my seat. The handful of passengers I passed peered down at their cellphones. Clad in designer clothes, blazers and blouses, with bags that probably cost as much as I made in a month, they fit the part of an ivy league student.

I'd taken some of the money Jayda had given me to go thrifting for something decent to wear. I had an appreciation for vintage dresses, thanks to my mother, who'd always told me that dresses and skirts were a woman's rebellion against the world's ruthless nature. Soft and vulnerable and bold at the same time. I'd never been brave enough to wear them on the subway late at night, only to classes during the day. For the train ride, I'd opted for a pale butter, ruffled sundress with my mom's faded leather jacket and my combat boots. While I didn't look homeless, I certainly wasn't as put together as the other passengers–those whose jewelry dangled from their wrists and necks like extravagant tinsel. Sprawled in their seats with their phones, they looked completely at ease, perhaps even bored and unimpressed.

Meanwhile, I sat humming like a bee, with so much pent-up anxiety, it was a wonder they couldn't hear me vibrating in my seat.

My knees bounced incessantly as the train trundled forward. I turned toward the window, and waved as I watched Jayda pass me, like I was watching my old life slip away for the new one. I hadn't even had time to let it sink into my head that I'd be attending an ivy league school. A respected university. Clawing at my own arm failed to break me out of the strange dream.

Things weren't entirely worked out with Conner and Bee, either. I'd sent along two months of my half of payment to Bee's school account, but I'd need to find a job right away to begin saving up and staying ahead, in addition to work-study.

My load would be heavy, but hadn't it always been that way,?

Focus on the now, Lilia. The words of my mother who'd always managed to calm my anxiety when I was a kid.

I closed my eyes, resting my head against the cushiony seat —a far cry from the hard plastic I was accustomed to on the subway. I needed some sleep. Even just a few hours, so I wouldn't look like a zombie when I arrived on campus.

As I stole the moment to take a quick snooze, my thoughts grew distant.

Chapter 10

Devryck

Dragging the scalpel down from the acromian, to the center of the chest, and then toward the abdomen, I made a Y-incision on the decedent's body. I'd already performed an external exam and confirmed that she was, in fact, Andrea Kepling, sent from Calypso County Medical Examiner's office for confirmation on the cause of death.

The faded black map of veins, or vonyxsis, I'd noted on external examination served as the first clue. However, a few different parasitic toxins were known to cause the discoloration, so it didn't necessarily confirm a case.

The second clue was the putrid, dark colored fluids seeping from the incision. With how long she'd been stored, I'd have expected some fluid ejection, but not the profuse liquids that dripped into the catch basin under the examination table.

And, fuck, that *stench.* Not even retained shit in the bowels smelled as horrible.

A tickle at my ankle drew my attention to the floor, where a black ball of fur circled my legs like he had any right to be there. A Bombay cat I'd inherited after he'd somehow gotten into my lab, and I couldn't, for the life of me, get rid of the damned thing. He kept the mice and rats away, though, so I'd decided to let the nosy little bastard stick around. "I see you decided to show up," I said behind the mask and shield covering my face. "Almost started without you." The cat, whom I'd named Bane, sauntered his way across the room and settled in the corner opposite me, where he licked his paws.

Forceps in hand, I carefully peeled back the decedent's skin like a butterfly, exposing her ribcage beneath. Nothing exceptionally notable about the skin or the bones still covered in remnants of flesh. Aside from the darkened veins, the state of her body at that point seemed rather unremarkable for one supposedly having been ravaged by disease. It was what I'd hoped to find within that would tell a sinister and grim story for how she might've died.

Next, I grabbed the rib shears and snapped each of the connecting bones. With a postmortem knife, I sliced away the muscles holding it in place, and lifted away the rib shield, exposing the organs beneath. Using the broad end of the knife, I shaved a small bit of the muscle from the bone, noting another defining characteristic of the parasite–bone striations. If I were to remove all of the muscle and flesh, her skeleton would undoubtedly be covered in faint black lines, like tiny fissures in the bones. Why, or how, the parasite managed such a thing remained a mystery.

I collected a small sliver of the flesh onto an awaiting agar plate for later examination and set it aside, then made a quick dictation on visual exam of the heart, lungs, and fluids collected in the spaces. Not water, though. Aside from excessive inflammation, I didn't find evidence of aspiration into the lungs. Only the thicker, serum-like fluid, which I believed had seeped from the GI tract during patient transportation. I ladled about a liter of the moldered fluid from her abdomen and chest cavity into a sterile jar. As I held it up to the light, I couldn't help but wonder how many eggs it might've contained.

Tying a string to the bowel, I cut the fat away from her body, and once free, I dumped the entrails into the awaiting bucket beneath the table.

As I meticulously removed each of the organs and weighed them, I finally reached the one I'd been interested in from the beginning–the liver. In her case, it was about a quarter of the size it should've been, black, nubbly, and oozing the fluids I'd collected earlier. In the absence of the parasite itself, it confirmed *Noctisoma*. I'd never seen another parasite ravage the liver quite the same. Enzymes released by the worm liquified the organ for faster consumption and made for one hell of a slimy mess.

Movement caught my eye.

I peered through the irritating face shield barrier that reflected the light to find something wriggling in a pool of liquid in the interstitium. With the forceps, I poked around and lifted out a long, black, skinny worm, about a foot long.

"Fucking hell," I muttered. The head of the worm latched onto my glove, and though I felt nothing, the sight of it chomping onto my finger startled me, and I dropped it back into the decedent's abdominal cavity. "Damn it!"

The worm slid over the flap of skin, and down the edge of the examination table. I lurched for the floor drain just a few feet away, but before I could cover it with my shoe, the parasite slipped through the drain holes, and just like that, it was gone. Not even Bane, my cat, could get to it fast enough, as he sat pawing at the drain, clearly depressed for the missed opportunity. He somehow had the intuition not to eat the worms, thankfully. At most, he'd have only slowed it down.

"Fuck. Fuck!" I peeled off the glove to find a tiny bubble of blood beading at the surface of my skin.

Since when had they grown fucking teeth?

As I stared down at the carved decedent, my thoughts

rewound to the quick briefing Lippincott had given me before I'd agreed to perform the autopsy.

"She's a special case."

What made her special?

After washing the wound with soap, I covered it with a Band-aid, before donning a new pair of gloves, and set back to seeing if her body would tell me.

By the time I reached her brain, I already had the scenario of her death clear in my head. Having witnessed the progression a few times, I knew what the worms inside of her had ultimately wanted–escape. I sawed the last bit of her skull and, with a skull key, pried off the top crown of bone to expose her brain beneath. Black lines proved the presence of the toxin in high concentration, and the presence of blood lent some insight into how she'd died, confirmed by the attached radiological reports stating she'd suffered a stroke. After cutting away all the nerve connections, I removed the gelatinous organ and set it aside. In cutting away slices, I found what I was looking for in the prefrontal cortex–a pocket contained within a clear membranous sac wherein the purest toxin, aside from what could've been harvested from the liver about a week prior, remained perfectly encased. With a needle tip, I pipetted the fluid from inside and deposited it into a prepared test tube. I held up the bright purple fluid with its black marbled threads to the light. Might've been entirely too late to utilize anything, as she'd been dead for quite some time. Although I'd have gotten the best results within minutes of death, it was still worth hanging onto the sample. Perhaps whatever hell the woman had suffered in life, with her illness, might one day offer a sliver of promise in her death.

Back at my office in the administrative corridor, I stared at my bandaged finger, my head trying to wrap itself around what I'd seen during the autopsy. Clearly, the worm had evolved and I suspected it might've been due to repeated inoculation in humans—a hearty human liver certainly could've been reason enough to grow teeth.

A knock at the door interrupted my thoughts.

I cleared my throat. "Come in."

The door creaked open to Dr. Lippincott, Provost of Dracadia, a longtime friend of my father's. Hands tucked into his pockets, he strode across the room, the sight of him souring my already cantankerous mood. "I don't suppose you have any liquor hiding in here somewhere?" he asked, brows winged up with a sickening hope.

Of course I did. After all, one didn't take a job working for high class assholes without something to numb the misery of it all. I reached down into the bottom drawer of my desk and grabbed a bottle of bourbon, along with two glasses.

"Brace yourself, Devryck." Lippincott was the only one who didn't bother to address me by doctor, or professor. I hadn't decided whether it was a friendly gesture or meant to be condescending.

After pouring him a glass, I passed the liquor to him, watching as he polished it in one gulp then signaled me to pour another.

"I just met with Langmore for an hour. Apparently, he received a call from Albert Wilkins. Do you remember Albert, at all?"

"Yes. Dracadia's finest alcoholic," I answered, watching Lippincott toss back another shot.

"Well, he's done his time, gotten sober, and seems to be working for some community college in Massachusetts. Anyway, Langmore claims he called to tell him of a student of his who was tasked with writing some *mind-blowing* case study involving a parasite."

"Adorable." I kicked my feet up onto my desk, not-so-patiently waiting for the point of his story. "So, what about that, exactly, warranted an hour-long meeting?"

"Langmore requested funds to cover her first semester entirely. I understand she happens to be quite brilliant. Unanimously approved by the admissions committee." He flicked his fingers, seeking more liquor.

"And?" I poured another round into his glass.

"He placed her in your Neuroparasitology rotation."

"That better have been one fuck of a research paper she wrote."

"I didn't actually read it." He snorted and waved his hands dismissively. "Do you have any idea how many student essays cross my desk? It's a literary slush pile of the poor and helpless requesting financial assistance. Who the hell has time for that? My bigger concern is that Langmore might be trying to fast track these students behind my back, and if that's the case, I intend to catch the weaselly bastard red-handed. Therefore, I'd like her to stay in your class. If you detect any monkey business with the asshole, report to me. I've got my reappointment coming up, and I don't need any surprises."

"You're asking me to babysit an undergrad." The tone of my voice couldn't have been more unenthusiastic. "Who is she?"

"Lilia Vespertine. Perhaps you can take her on as an assistant–"

"Absolutely not." I took another sip of my whiskey, relishing the burn in my throat as I swallowed back the urge to punch him.

Lippincott buried a chuckle in his glass. "At the very least, I want to monitor her while she's here. If he attempts to place her in any other advanced class without prior authorization, his ass will be canned." Upper lip curled into his teeth, he shook his head. "I have been *waiting* for the opportunity to get rid of him. And that nosy bitch, Gilchrist," he said through clenched teeth.

"And what of the girl, in that case?"

"We deny her financial assistance for the second semester. She was awarded a Meritus Scholarship for financial hardship. There isn't a chance in hell that she could attend the school, otherwise." He ran his finger over the perimeter of his glass, eyes unfocused. "On a separate note, I understand you've completed the autopsy report for Andrea Kepling. May I ask the findings?"

"Bone striations. Near complete putrefaction of the liver. Vonyxsis. Bilateral tapetum lucidum. Significant levels of toxin isolated from the brain and liver. Nothing surprising." I didn't bother to mention the worm with fucking teeth.

"So we're calling it Noctisomiasis."

"The presence of the toxin is fairly indicative, I think."

He let out a hearty huff and shifted in his seat like the guy had a bad case of hemorrhoids. "I have to tell you, I was not entirely on board with this autopsy being performed here."

"Why?" I had to tread carefully with Lippincott–he was like a politician, in that the more questions you asked, the more diversion he inserted into his responses. "What makes her so *special*?"

Another resigned exhale, and he tapped his finger against the rim of his glass. "She's been identified as one of the patients who went AWOL in your father's study."

Of course she was. Nearly two decades had passed since the scandalous disaster that had loomed over my career like a fucking curse. Six women had died. Two had gone missing. And, somehow, I'd inherited the shitshow job of cleaning up my father's reputation. "Well, it seems she can no longer speak about it. So, what's the problem?"

"The problem is, she broke into my house and tried to kill me. How incredibly fucked would that look, if you then submit an autopsy report on a patient who went missing from a study twenty years ago, which demonstrates a rare parasite that I happen to have contributed a large sum of funds to research. She did accuse me of putting fucking *worms* in her belly!"

"Last I checked, all evidence of those women having participated in the study was eliminated." It was sickening the way someone's entire life could be turned into a lie. How easily one's existence could be wiped out without question, or explanation. Every detail of the two who'd participated in the study and subsequently left had been thoroughly erased without a shred of consequence. While I'd been given all of my father's formulations, I knew nothing of the women involved in the study.

Was probably better that way.

"Reports were still submitted to the board prior to that. I don't need the media catching wind of this and conjuring stories that I had any part in this woman's death. She was deemed psychologically unfit, and therefore, uncredible, but as you are well aware, *corpses* never lie."

My thoughts returned to the moment, during Andrea's autopsy, when I'd pulled a foot long worm from her abdomen. "I do find it surprising that she only recently became ill. It's been twenty years. This is not an organism that longs to inhabit the body for any great amount of time."

"Police said she was homeless on the island. Maybe she got herself infected. I have no explanation. I played no part in your father's sadistic studies, nor have I gone out of my way to contact this woman, after what she did to me."

"Yet, you're here for something. What is it?"

"I want you to alter the report."

I snorted at that and poured myself another drink, uncertain if the crazy son of a bitch was serious, or joking. "You're asking me to falsify my findings?"

"Don't you dare get technical and legal with me. Remember who saved *your* ass last year with that Harrick girl." Yet another scandal with absolutely no merit. "Your family name has cost me excessive damage control. I'm simply asking you to remove the toxin detail."

"And the bone striations? How the hell do I explain that in the absence of any genetic abnormalities or dysplasia?"

"Strike that finding, as well."

Groaning, I rubbed a hand down my face, listening to him turn a simple report into a complex web of lies that even a novice pathologist worth his salt could untangle. "She has an entire medical profile based on the damage this organism has caused. What happens when someone questions my findings and she's exhumed?"

"She's due to be cremated afterward. Neither the hospital, medical examiner, nor this university is interested in absorbing the cost of a burial. As I understand they've tracked an uncle who can sign for cremation. Therefore, your report is the gospel. Quietly remove those findings, and no one will be the wiser."

Falsifying a report was nothing new–I'd done it before, with reasonable and logical explanation. Trying to conjure a reason for every physiological assault this woman had endured, however, was a puzzle I didn't need thrown into my lap.

"You think I'm a bastard for requesting such a thing."

I twirled the last bit of liquor in my glass, convincing myself it'd be a bad idea to bash his face with it. "I'm more impressed that you could so easily ask me for a favor that would cost me my license."

"What is it you want in exchange, Devryck?"

Now we were talking. I could justify the work for a bargain. "I want the cameras removed from my laboratory."

"Those cameras are a requirement of funding. They're in place as a result of—"

"I know why they're in place." I tipped my head just enough to stretch the scar that spanned from my neck to elbow. An acid attack, courtesy of the ever-vigilant student body, who'd felt compelled to villainize me for the disappearance of a girl–without proper evidence, of course. I'd spent two months on hiatus, recovering from it, which had put me further behind in my work. "I do not work with student assistants, as I've explained a number of times to the board."

"Why do you insist they be removed, then?"

"I don't appreciate feeling as if I'm being watched while I work. It upsets my focus. Quietly have them removed, and no one will be the wiser." I echoed his words from just moments ago.

"Fine. Consider it done." Legs crossed, he looked around my office and took a sip of his liquor.

I couldn't help fantasize how incredibly gratifying it would be to slip a few larvae into his drink. Of course, that was just laziness talking. I loathed the idea of having to edit my report.

"I'm surprised I managed to catch you in office hours, at all. It's a wonder you sleep." Lippincott pushed his empty glass onto the desk. "How is the research coming along?"

My mind wouldn't let it go, this fantasy, so vivid and entertaining. Thinking about those wriggling things making their way down his esophagus and into his belly. *Snap out of it, Devryck.* I cleared my throat, rolling my shoulders back. "Steady and tedious, as always."

"Any headway on the latest variant?"

"Yes. I now have a moth with a fully extended proboscis that'd prefer a nice, rare steak over sliced oranges."

"I find that utterly fascinating."

"If it didn't equate to failure, I might, as well."

"I don't mean to add further pressure, but with the quarterly evaluations coming up, there will be unwanted interest in the program." His hands curled around the arm of the chair, and the muscles in his face tensed.

It was no mystery, what had his panties twisted. Having to face members of The Rooks–those practically born into excessive power–with a stagnant report wouldn't be an easy task. Fortunately, I enjoyed a somewhat insulated status, in that my lineage with the group went so far as my great-great grandfather–one of the founders. It was the only reason The Rooks hadn't thrown my father into one of their pretty cages, after the humiliation he'd caused. Humiliation that I'd since been tasked with sopping up.

While ambitious and brazen enough to climb the ladder of power, Lippincott was only a first-generation Rook. *Nouveau riche* who only married into money, and his not being born into it made him practically expendable. Easily knocked from his rung, if he were to fuck up.

"I've commandeered the midnight lab to assist in moth propagation and inoculation, in hopes of testing multiple variants at once," I offered as a stale consolation. It didn't matter how long I took to complete my work. Unless I suddenly became a threat to the society, I'd suffer nothing more than a slap on the wrist.

Lippincott, on the other hand, carried the weight of failure.

Fortunately for him, I had other reasons riding my ass to stay motivated. Most notably, the fact that, at any moment, every muscle in my body could lock up and seize, including my heart, and throw me into cardiac arrest. So, yeah, I felt the pressure.

"But we are still far from *human* clinical trials." Lippincott slumped in his chair like a child who wasn't getting what he wanted for Christmas.

"Inoculating a human at this stage would be disastrous. Deadly. *Irresponsible.*" An image of the alley drunk I had locked in a cell right then flickered through my mind.

"As will failure to produce results. Bear in mind the difficulty in getting this study approved, particularly with a Bramwell at the helm." He rubbed his hands together, clearly anxious. "My opportunity to become president of this institution depends on the success of this, Devryck. I'm counting on you to come through with results. Your study could change the entire landscape of medicine and pharmaceuticals." As if I needed him to remind me. The man hadn't set foot in a lab in twenty years. At one time, he was brilliant, but he'd chosen politics and administrative drama instead–a path I avoided with the fervor of an unwanted syphilis infection. "I look forward to your next IBS report."

"I need more time. The toxins produced by this parasite are ever changing and evolving." Practically turning into monsters, with their teeth and scorpion tails.

"If it's more time you need, I'll make that happen. But know that there will be enormous pressure placed on the university in the upcoming months. The board, the sponsors, they want success. They want results. The promise of this study was the only redeeming point for the sponsors."

"I'll have results."

"Of course you will. That's where you and your father differ." His gaze fell toward my hand, where I'd placed a Band-Aid on my little parasitic love bite. "What happened there?"

"Papercut. Nothing serious."

He snorted. "Until it becomes infected, grows some resistant form of bacteria, and turns into septicemia."

"I washed it, Edward. Thoroughly."

With a chuckle, he tapped his knuckles on my desktop as he pushed to his feet. "I'll let you get back to it, then.

Chapter 11

Lilia

The blare of a horn startled me, and I awoke on a gasp pressed against the cool pane of a window. Drool wet my cheek, and I dragged my arm across my face in as subtle a movement as I could, glancing around to see other passengers also rousing out of sleep. In the moon's light, a thick fog hovered over the water, as I peered through the window toward the ocean in the distance.

The ocean.

I'd only seen it once as a teenager. As much as my sister and I always dreamed of going to the beach, my mother had always refused, opting instead for camping trips in the woods. As if my mother had feared the water.

I found it mesmerizing.

"Attention, passengers, we've arrived at Thresher Bay, Maine, where the time is five-oh-six in the morning. Weather is a balmy sixty-four degrees with patches of thick fog. The ferry will depart at approximately five-thirty to transport you to Dracadia Island. Please gather your luggage, and be sure to watch your step on the exit ramp. If this is your first year at Dracadia, congratulations and welcome!" The train entered an enormous glass dome and slowed to a stop between two other stationed trains, each separated by a narrow platform on which a clock stood upright above a sign with the next departures.

Across from me sat a guy, about my age. He removed his earbuds, his bright blue eyes, a stunning contrast to his dark skin, staring past me, presumably toward the window at my other side.

I felt a small bit of relief on seeing someone else not clad in designer clothes.

Having unbuckled myself, I pushed to my feet and waited as a line of passengers made their way to the luggage rack. An inexplicable tension wound through me as I eyed my suitcase too far away to grab.

Relax, nobody wants your damn suitcase.

At the end of the lineup, the kid across from me gestured to let me go first, and with an appreciative nod, I stepped out into the aisle behind everyone else.

"First year?" he asked, falling in line behind me.

Lips tight, I smiled. "Is it obvious?" I hoped so, considering I was about two years older than I should've been for a first year.

"You just look a little nervous."

"I'm actually a sophomore, but it's my first year at the university. What about you?" The line moved forward, and I slid my suitcase off the rack, stumbling forward as I hefted it into the narrow aisleway.

"Sophomore." He pulled a much fancier suitcase off the rack and, in the brief moment before the line moved forward, stuck out a hand. "Name's Briceson Williams."

I returned the handshake. "Lilia. Nice to meet you."

"You, too. Where are you from?"

I glanced over my shoulder, at a blonde passenger who was busy scrolling through Instagram, and turned back around, lowering my voice. "Covington."

"Ahh, home of the Luminet." Lips stretched to a smile, he

shrugged. "I'm a few towns over, in Lansmot. And I'm kind of a theater nerd."

Last I checked, Lansmot was the second most wealthy city in Massachusetts. Yet, I didn't feel like a pauper around him, in fact, I found him to be relatable.

"I actually live above the theater," I said.

"Seriously? No way! I'm so jealous!" He chuckled and gave a jerk of his head, alerting me that the line had moved forward.

"Yeah," I said over my shoulder, making my way for the exit. "I know just about every word to *Les Misérables* at this point."

"I do, too. But for different reasons, I suppose." All of us made our way down the platform toward the main part of the station. "What are you studying?" With the wider space, he strolled up alongside me, the two of us walking side by side.

"Medical microbiology. You?"

"Chemistry."

"Wow. Redox balancing. Hated that with every fiber of my being."

"Simple computation."

"Ahh, that was a subtle insult." I chuckled, my arm straining as my suitcase bounced over the cracks in the concrete behind me.

The station opened out onto a road, where everyone crossed to the ferry boat launch across the street. Pale rays of sunlight had begun to crest over the clouds, though it would probably be another half-hour, or so, before sunrise. Eyeing a statue out in front of the launch, I studied the stony profile of man in a colonial style uniform. The placard at his feet read, *Lord Commodore Adderly,* and below that, *In memory of those who perished enroute to Dracadia*.

As I followed everyone onto the small boarding bridge, I caught sight of the murky ocean water below. I'd never been on a boat before, and I really hoped I didn't get seasick. Especially in front of a load of people I'd only just met for the first time.

Just as on the train, we all stored our luggage in a small rack. Briceson gave a slight jerk of his head. "If you tend to get a little nauseous like I do, the cabin is probably best," he said, as if reading my mind.

A nervous smile lifted the corner of my mouth, and I nodded. "Yeah. Okay."

He led the two of us inside an enormous passenger cabin with tables and benches, and gestured toward a seat by a small window. Being enclosed by walls had me feeling less vulnerable, and I slid onto the bench across from him. "How long is the ride to Dracadia?"

"About ninety minutes, or so. Not too long."

"So, the university ... what's it like?"

"It's a great school. Beautiful campus. If you can get past the ghosts and creepy history."

"A chem major who believes in ghosts?"

He snorted a laugh. "I didn't believe in a lot of things before I attended this school. But it comes with the territory. You kinda just have to roll with it."

After a short announcement from the captain, the ferry idled away from the dock, and I peered out of the window to see the ocean water splashing up as we picked up speed. I'd studied the map of Dracadia, had seen its position miles out into the Gulf of Maine, where I'd read that the water reached depths of over a thousand feet in some spots. The thought sent a shiver across the back of my neck. *Please don't send any tidal waves to tip the boat over.* Getting stranded in the middle of the ocean happened to be a recurring nightmare for me, for some reason. My therapist had told me that it might've been my mind feeling trapped in my circumstances. Google had suggested that I might soon be facing a dangerous time in my life.

I hoped it was just a stupid nightmare that didn't mean much of anything, at all.

"Have you actually seen a ghost, or something?" I asked Briceson, searching for distraction from the gurgling in my stomach. As much as I wanted to stare out at the ocean, seeing it dip and swell with the waves sent a cold tickle to my chest, and I decided *against* the possibility of painting the table between us in puke.

"All I'm gonna say is, you might see some weird stuff. But as far as I know, no one was ever *killed* by a ghost there."

"Well, that's good to know."

He hiked his arm up over the top of the bench and eased back into his seat. "So, what does a medical microbiologist do?"

"I want to study diseases. Find cures. You know, save the world. You?"

"Would you believe me if I said I don't know? I'll probably become a professor and mold the minds of those who have their shit together better than I do."

"Well, at least you have a plan."

Somehow, an hour and a half passed with light conversation, and only a minor case of nausea that I was able to keep in check by breathing hard through my nose. Watching the sun rise over the horizon, its salmon-colored rays stretching across the water's surface, also provided some distraction. Fleeting, as those golden rays disappeared too quickly behind the gloom of overcast.

When, finally, the dark silhouette of the island could be seen through the fog, I marveled at the arched curve that did, in fact, look like a sleeping dragon. Gray clouds, swollen with rain, loomed like puffs of black smoke billowing upward.

"Hello, Dracadia," Briceson said, peering through the window.

"Wow. It's beautiful."

"Even more beautiful up close."

The boat ferried through the crack in the rock, beneath the arch, toward the other side of the island. Stony spires speared the sullen sky over the dark, wispy crowns of the pine trees, which cloaked the university grounds. The ferry's engine slowed as the boat tottered across the choppy waves toward a stone, castle-like structure at the foot of the cliff, whose center looked like it had been carved into an archway. Flickering torches lit the way through the small tunnel, which opened up into a domed interior, where a number of small boats had been docked. Attendants inside the rocky boathouse scurried around the ferry, tying it up as we made our way toward the ramp.

Standing on deck beside all the stacked luggage, a middle-aged man smiled at me, and as I reached for my suitcase, he set a gentle hand on my arm. "I got it, Miss. Your luggage will be delivered to your dorm room."

That same uneasy feeling as before nagged at me. I suspected every other student on the ferry could've probably afforded to replace a wardrobe, or missing gadgets, but that wasn't the case for me. If he lost it, or worse, it got stolen, I'd have nothing.

"Trust me," he added, and I realized that I was still clutching the handle of my bag. "You're not going to want to drag this thing up the hill."

At that, I bowed to the side, noticing through the brick tunnel where the path disappeared up the mountainside.

"Don't worry, they're really good about delivering everything with care," Briceson said behind me. "I was a little uncomfortable at first, too."

From his coat pocket, the attendant pulled a pen and

flipped through the first few pages of the clipboard clutched in his other hand. "Name?"

"Lilia Vespertine."

"Lilia ... Lilia ... ah, yes. Crixson House. Room three-ten." He peeled away a sticker from the page and secured it to my luggage.

"Okay. Thanks." I threw one more glance toward my suitcase, before exiting the boat.

A stone platform led toward the tunnel, and I stepped in that direction, assuming it was the way to my dorm, when a grip of my arm brought me to a stop.

Briceson released me, pulling a messenger bag up onto his shoulder. "Hey, can I get your phone number?"

"Oh. Um. I'm not–"

"It's not like that. I, um .... I have a boyfriend?" A lopsided smile slanted his lips as he scratched the back of his head.

Idiot, I silently chided myself. I somehow had to pry myself from the mindset that every guy who asked for my number was looking for a hookup.

"Right. Sorry, um, yes." As we made our way toward the tunnel, I rattled my cellphone off to him, and he sent me a text with a smiley face emoji that said, *hello.*

"Now you have mine. I just thought it'd be cool to exchange theater lines sometime."

Smiling, I nodded. "I'd like that."

"Lilia? Is there a Lilia Vespertine?" At the sound of my name, I turned toward a bright-eyed blonde, who, like the attendant, also carried a clipboard.

Briceson gave me a light shoulder tap. "I'll catch you later. Good luck!"

"Thanks. You, too." On those parting words, I headed toward the blonde who'd called me. "I'm Lilia," I said, strolling up to her.

After an appraising once-over, she flashed a too-wide smile

that creased her eyes. "I'm Kendall. I work with the dean's office. Dr. Langmore asked that I fetch you for a quick introduction."

"Of course." I trailed after her, away from the tunnel and up a winding stone staircase, to what looked like a gondola ski lift.

Some students, including Briceson, took the walking path that led upward toward the castle-like building ahead, and as I stared down, dozens of feet below me, I could see them making the steep climb.

Once we'd settled onto our seats, the gondola lurched into motion, exiting from its tower, and at that height, I could finally take in the breathtaking school grounds set against the ocean backdrop. Sunrise fought to break through the overcast, offering a soft glow over the bustling campus, as students arrived for the new semester.

The university buildings were arranged in a square, enclosed by an ancient stone wall that lined the perimeter of the surrounding woods. Like a small village made up of weathered buildings, with their pointed arches and ribbed vaults, some covered in sprawling vines, with lush gardens and courtyards interspersed between them.

Wealth flowed through the veins of the university, that much was clear. Yet, deep within its bones hid the slumbering tragedies of its past, ones that had bled through in the irreparable decay that had aged the exterior like a smoldering infection.

"Dracadia was once a monastery," Kendall said, staring out through the gondola window.

"And an asylum, right?"

"Yes. It has a rather dark history. But I'm sure that wouldn't impress someone like you."

At that, I frowned, not quite catching her meaning. While a snarky comeback sat perched on the tip of my tongue, I didn't want that on my first day, so instead, I turned back toward the window, and for the rest of the ride, I remained quiet as she prattled on about student life on campus.

When the gondola finally slowed to a stop on the grounds of the monastery, I stepped out onto a narrow platform and down a flight of stairs, which led out to the manicured lawn of an expansive courtyard. From there, I followed after her, cutting through the center of campus, toward what must've been the main admin building. Situated directly across from an enormous clock tower at the opposite end of the courtyard, the building rivaled the height of every other on campus.

My eyes wandered in awe of the place, before we entered the building and headed up to the second floor, to a hallway of offices. Something tingled the back of my neck, as we slowed to a stop at a door where a gold plaque engraved with *Dr. Gilbert Langmore* hung beside it.

"Wait here one moment." Kendall knocked on the door before slipping inside.

The sound of a voice carried down the corridor, and I turned toward a slightly ajar door, catching sight of a man who slouched in his chair with a bored expression, as another man, unseen from my angle, spoke without taking a breath. When the bored man turned toward me, that tickle in the back of my neck flared again.

Copper colored eyes, set beneath long, black lashes and a naturally stern brow, stared back at me. The shift of his jaw dragged my attention toward the perfection of his profile, sharp and angular and shadowed in a light stubble. A shivering warmth scattered beneath my skin and fluttered in my chest, as he gave an aloof blink of his bedroom eyes before turning back toward the voice.

"Lilia?" Kendall's voice snapped me out of my staring. "Dr. Langmore is ready to see you now."

Nodding, I cleared my throat, stealing one more glance of the man, who didn't bother to look my way again.

"Ah, Ms. Vespertine. Come in." Behind the desk sat an older man with graying hair and spectacles. He pushed up from his chair, gesturing to the one across from him, where I took my seat. "I trust you had a long morning, so I will keep this meeting brief so that you can get settled. I'm Dr. Langmore, and I would like to personally welcome you to Dracadia University." He settled back into his chair. "I was thoroughly impressed by the paper you wrote for Professor Wilkins."

"Thank you, Sir," I said, gaze trailing over the walls, where inspirational quotes hung beside framed degrees that highlighted each step of his credentials. Displayed on his desk sat a picture of him in a deep burgundy tuxedo, his arms wrapped tightly around a slightly taller, slimmer man in a pale pink tuxedo.

"Your analysis was exceptionally detailed. May I ask how you *designed* this particular organism?"

I didn't know why I still harbored a sense of duty in upholding my mother's privacy. She was dead, after all, and I had little doubt the organism responsible was something I'd since learned rarely infected humans. I wanted to tell Dr. Langmore that I knew firsthand how the disease affected a human being, because I'd watched it every day for weeks. Instead, I smiled and shrugged. "Just a basic understanding of parasites, paired with a wild imagination."

"Interesting." Wearing a pensive expression, he adjusted his spectacles and nodded. "I look forward to seeing that knowledge blossom during your time here. As stated in my letter to you, all expenses are paid while you're here. I want you to feel comfortable in this environment. If you need anything, I want you to reach out to me personally."

Wow. I'd never been personally greeted by the dean of any

college, let alone invited to contact him. "I appreciate your hospitality." Hospitality? Was that even the right word?

"You've received your dorm assignment, correct?"

"Yessir."

"Good, good. Any questions regarding your classes?"

"One, yes. There is a parasitology class and accompanying lab that was already on my schedule. I looked at the requirements, and it seems I've not taken the prereq for that class."

"Yes, I enrolled you in that rotation. That's Professor Bramwell's midnight lab. No worries. I'm certain you'll do well there."

Bramwell. The expert Professor Wilkins had mentioned the day he'd given me the invitation. "I'm sorry, I didn't realize he taught it. The course guide listed–"

"His associate professor and teaching assistant. Dr. Bramwell oversees the course and gives the lectures for the accompanying class, but his associate and teaching assistant run the Midnight Lab and recitations. Dr. Bramwell is the lead in charge."

"I see. There's another class I didn't sign up for, as well. Entomology. I'm assuming you put me in that class, too?"

"No. That was likely Dr. Gilchrist. She's the Department Chair for the College of Natural Science. The one who petitioned your enrollment."

"Yes, Dr. Wilkins informed me."

"I'm imagining she hoped to have you in her class, but you're welcome to remove it, if you'd like."

"No, that's okay. I'll leave it."

"Very good. Now, Ms. Vespertine, I imagine you're quite tired. Get settled, get some rest, and allow me to welcome you to Dracadia. I'll have Kendall show you to your dorm."

Chapter 12

Lilia

Shit.

Like an idiot, I'd decided to look for my assigned dorm alone while exploring the campus a bit along the way. I stared down at the map I'd gotten from the dean's secretary, twisting it around in a poor effort to figure out where the hell I was. *Leave it to me to get lost in a perfect square.*

I glanced up toward the building where I'd stopped, an ominous tower whose lichen-covered surface, laced in lush green vines, gave it a much older appearance than the other buildings on campus. Etched into the stone was a plaque indicating it was Emeric Tower.

The campus boasted six different houses, each with its own crest. Beautiful dormitories with their flags waving proudly out front, none of which appeared to be Crixson Hall. At least, not on the map I was looking at.

Growling in frustration, I spun around and straight into an unyielding wall of man. A burning humiliation thoroughly heated my face, as I stepped back. "I'm sorry!"

I trailed my gaze up a black button-down shirt, to a perfectly chiseled face with copper eyes blazing in irritation. The handsome man I'd seen back at the dean's office. Without a word, he stepped around me.

"Excuse me," I called after him, but he didn't so much as acknowledge me.

The warmth in my face intensified with my growing irritation, and I twisted the map around, trying to figure out where the hell I was. I scanned my surroundings, watching students bustle to and fro, all of them well-composed and dressed like they belonged in an academia editorial spread.

I zeroed my attention on a woman, about my age, hoofing it toward me. Long, black hair cascaded over her shoulders, and her berry red lipstick emphasized the pallor of her skin. She wore a crop top with a skull on the front, and black and white striped pants paired with red boots. A bit eclectic, from what I'd seen so far. Maybe she was an art major, or something.

"Excuse me." My voice hardly carried over the hum of voices, but she ground to a halt and twisted toward me, one pierced brow raised. "I'm looking for Crixson House. It's not on the map."

"'Cause it's not called Crixson."

"Wait, what? The guy at the dock told me."

"*We* call it Crixson, but its actual name is Corbeau House."

As soon as she said the name, I snapped my attention back to the map, finding it directly across campus from where we stood. "Ah."

She gave a jerk of her head. "C'mon. I'm headed that way."

Falling into step behind her, I stuffed the map into my bag. "I'm Lilia, by the way."

"I'm Melisandre," she said over her shoulder. "Mel for short. You're new at Dracadia?"

"Yes. It's my first day. I feel a little like a fish out of water." Finally caught up to her, I glanced around at all the other students, who seemed to know exactly where they were going as they buzzed past with determined strides. "So, Crixson, why do you call it that?"

"Are you familiar with the Crixson Study?" At the shake of my head, she nodded. "Figured as much. There's a whole conspiracy theory about how they tried to suppress all the information about it."

"They?"

"The Rooks. They're Dracadia's *super* secret society," she said on a dramatic whisper, while I chewed on the news that secret societies actually existed outside of books and movies. "Anyway, rumor has it they were somehow involved in this clinical trial that happened about twenty years ago. A bunch of women were invited to participate in some study for a new medication that supposedly reversed diabetes. They all stayed in Corbeau Hall, which as you saw on the map, is somewhat separate from the campus." It did seem hidden in the illustration of trees that surrounded it. "So yeah, one night, six out of the eight women drowned themselves in Squelette Lake. And voila! Six skeletons were swept under the rug."

"All six? Like ... at the same time?"

"Yep." As we passed another dark-haired girl, who flipped her off, Mel smiled and blew her a kiss. "Some kind of weird mass suicide."

"What happened to the other two?"

"No one knows. They just disappeared. Some say they live in the tunnels beneath the dorm. Others say they were murdered and their souls haunt Crixson Hall. It's mostly just staff who refer to the dorm as Corbeau."

Confused, I shook my head. "*The Rooks* conducted this study?"

"Well, they played some role. Doctor Death's father was the project's primary investigator."

"Doctor Death?" My gaze wandered the lush greenery of the campus courtyard, with its benches and aged statues. The stone walkways that weaved through well-kempt gardens and hedges.

"Professor Bramwell. He's the–"

"Pathology professor. Why do you call him *Doctor Death*?"

"Well, aside from the fact that he plays with corpses all day, he was allegedly involved in a totally separate disappearance two years ago. A student by the name of Jenny Harrick. Was a total scandal. Rumor has it that he got jealous of her boyfriend and killed her. One of those, *if I can't have her, no one can* deals."

"Really?" That didn't add up to a man who was considered brilliant in his field. I knew brilliant men. I'd worked alongside them. They rarely noticed anything outside of their own bubble.

"Yeah. He's got scars across his neck and shoulder. Her boyfriend snapped. Stole some sulfuric acid from the chem lab and attacked him." She snorted a laugh at that, as if it wasn't an absolutely horrific visual she'd just planted in my head. "Boyfriend was permanently expelled, and Doctor Death got off with nothing more than a slap on the wrist."

"But you said disappearance. So, not a confirmed murder, or anything?"

She rolled her eyes. "Okay fine. Disclaimer: all accusations of murder are based on speculation and rumor. Except that she never turned up, and he was the last to see her alive. Happy?"

Jeez. Touchy. I was just clarifying that there wasn't actual proof that he'd murdered her.

The shady overhang of trees swallowed the open space, as the path continued on through a shallow forest, beyond which

I could see a stone building ahead–one that looked significantly aged compared to the rest of the dorms we'd passed. "It sounds like you believe the rumors?"

She shrugged. "I believe in the underdog, and I can assure you, Professor Bramwell is no underdog at this university. He's old money, and old money at this school equates to power."

"Going back to the Crixson study, you said not much is known about it. How do *you* know so much about it?"

"Research. I wanted to know why everyone on campus avoided the dorm. You dig in a cemetery, you eventually find a bone." We crossed the yard and arrived at the entrance of the building, where dark, weathered stones, covered in moss and vines, made for an eerie exterior. "Anyway, here it is. Crixson House." The flag sticking out from the pediment of the building's entrance bore a purple and black shield with a raven, or crow, it was hard to tell which. "One of the original buildings when the place was still a monastery. Before some of the buildings burned down."

"Was that recent?"

"Nah. Centuries ago. It's what the whole Adderly monument is about back at Thresher Bay. That we commemorate a British soldier who drove off the natives on the island and participated in the burning of accused witches is precisely what's wrong with this country."

I recalled having seen the monument just before boarding the ferry. "Why *would* they commemorate him?"

"Because no one gives a shit about the actual history. You have to scrape past all the lies to get to the truth. In their minds, he's some kind of savior for having killed off a bunch of *deranged patients and savages*," she said in air quotes. "What we would call those with mental illness nowadays, but back then, they were *possessed by demons*." Sighing, she shook her head. "Anyway, I'll spare you. What floor are you on?"

"Third."

"I'm the RA for the third floor. If you smoke, crack a window, or light some incense. All rooms in Crixson have ensuite bathrooms, so if you drink? Hide the evidence in the shower during rounds. We never check the showers. And if you decide to have company over, I suggest the basement, if you're a moaner."

"I'm actually pretty quiet. I'm just here to study."

She snorted and rolled her eyes. "That's what every student here says on their first day. Anyway, check in at the front desk for your room's key card. Don't lose it. And if you haven't yet gotten your ID card, go do that right away. You need it for the dining room. Dracadia Bookstore is at the opposite side of the clock tower, in the Plaza." She waved her hands in a dismissive way, as if trying to flap away all the information flying out of her mouth at once. "It's like its own small village, with lots of cool little shops, there."

"Thanks. I appreciate the help."

"No problem. Oh, and one other thing. Unless you have a class at Emeric Tower, I'd stay away from there, if I were you, particularly at night."

A glance at my schedule earlier indicated that I did have classes there. At least three of them. One at night. "Why?"

"It's just creepy. It's where Doctor Death *actually* works. There's a morgue for the cadavers and whatever autopsies he performs. And an incinerator room."

"He performs autopsies here on campus?"

"Only special cases. The university hospital is about two miles outside of campus. Just past downtown Emberwick." The small village I'd only acquainted myself with on a Google search before I'd arrived. "You don't actually see the bodies, thank goodness, unless you're in the med school program. They bring them in through the tunnels outside of the gate."

"Interesting." The more I learned about Professor Bramwell, the less I seemed to be able to visualize the man who'd garnered such a dark and macabre moniker. "He performs these autopsies by himself?"

"Yeah. He's not the friendliest guy. Like I said, unless you have to be on that side of campus, maybe just steer clear."

I couldn't tell if she was trying to scare me, knowing it was my first year there, or being genuine in her warning. "Got it."

Nothing she'd said had scared me, though. I'd already seen my fair share of ghosts and dangerous men. At least the ones at Dracadia wouldn't smell like a grave digger.

After checking in with the front desk for my key card, I was directed down the hallway to an office, where they took an unflattering photo of me for an ID card, attached to a black and gold Dracadia lanyard. From there, I finally made my way to my room.

The keycard clicked green as I stuffed it into the card reader and turned the knob, before swinging the door open to a small but cozy room, with shiny hardwood floors and a simple bed. The dorms, while rich with antiquity, seemed to offer a few modern features. To my left was a small walk-in closet made of thick wood in the same shade as the rest of the room, with a heavy-looking dresser pressed against the wall. A lot of storage space that I likely wouldn't fill.

The window on the south facing wall showed the ocean in the distance, and at the opposite wall sat an actual desk and chair, which looked out onto Dracadia's courtyard. Why the room hadn't been snatched up right away, with such a beautiful, almost panoramic, view was an absolute mystery.

My suitcase had been placed beside my bed, and on the mattress sat a stack of folded white sheets next to a folded black sweatshirt and T-shirt with the gold Dracadia logo. Beside those was a small black satchel that I opened to find a pin, a journal, pad of paper, pen and water bottle, all with the same school colors and logo. A small card tucked inside read: *Welcome to Corbeau House, Fellow Dracadian!*

As I smiled down at it, a strange and foreign sensation swept over me.

For the first time since my mother had died, I felt a sense of belonging.

Chapter 13

Devryck

"I feel … fucking great," Barletta said. "Aside from sleeping most of the day. Turning into a bit of a night owl lately. But other than that, I feel better than I ever have before. Why is that?" He shoveled in a mouthful of eggs, his appetite as hearty as that of the tiny intruders which had undoubtedly begun to settle in to his gut. The yellow pallor of his skin had already warmed to a healthy shade and even in his disheveled state, he appeared in better condition than when I'd first captured him.

"The organism growing inside of you doesn't like a filthy home. It happens to be very particular about where it lays roots."

"Can you not say that? It's gross. Don't like thinkin' about that." After only a few hours of agonizing detox, he'd become more compliant, even pleasant. It was amazing how manipulative feeling good could be. Barletta had probably lived a good chunk of his life in chronic pain, due to his vices, and now they were gone. He likely didn't have so much as a headache right then. "How? How does it *clean*?"

"It produces a toxin, a very powerful toxin, that eliminates competing organisms and incites the mechanisms to repair cells. Lucky for you, the liver is the only organ capable of regenerating, so the toxin enhances the growth factors that increase cell division, resulting in rapid repair."

Eyes wide, he shook his head and snorted a laugh. "No idea what the fuck you're talking about, but whatever it is, is working. I ain't had one craving for drink. I don't feel all the pain. No shakes, or the urge to puke. Nothin'." He shoveled in another bite of his breakfast. "Can taste again," he said around a mouthful of food. "Smell. I ain't felt this good since I was a teenager. I don't even care to drink."

"Of course you don't." Elbow kicked up over the top of my chair, I casually watched him devour his breakfast, feeding the parasites that would soon emerge from their tiny cocoons and wreak havoc on his body. "The toxin itself produces chemicals that essentially control the part of your brain that craves alcohol. Alcohol would be detrimental to all the work it's doing inside of you. It tells you that you no longer need it, and your body responds."

"What, like ... mind control?"

I smiled. "Exactly."

Halfway to his mouth, he paused in eating, staring off with a thoughtful expression. "Then, how are these worms so bad, if they do so much good?"

The urge to stifle a laugh tugged at my throat. "Because they are parasites. It repairs your liver to feed. It cleanses your blood to feed. It uses your body to feed, and when it's finished, it will discard you as a used-up corpse."

His thoughtful expression sobered into something more serious. "Ain't there some kind of medication for it?"

"Not yet."

"But that's what this is about, right? You're working on one?"

"More, or less."

"So, I'm gonna die?" he asked, as if just catching on.

"Eventually." I shrugged. "You were dying, anyway. Little

by little. Every day. I'd have probably given you a year at the rate you were going. If that."

Frowning, he chewed slowly, as if tasting the bitter truth in my words. "You don't, uh ... you don't strike me as a killer. So, why are you doing this?"

I leaned forward and rested my elbows across my thighs. "Because, like the parasite inside of you, I am only interested for my own selfish gain."

Brow flickering, the man looked like he was about to break into tears right then. "I got kids, man. A family."

"You don't give a shit about your family," I said without a speck of empathy. "If you did, you wouldn't have hurt them."

"I didn't mean to hurt my son." His words shook out of him on a defensive snarl, and his eyes shone in the light of the naked bulb overhead. "It was an accident."

"I don't mean to kill you, either. It's just a consequence."

"Then, why don't you just let me go?"

A stab of pain struck my skull, the ringing in my ear sharp and intense, and I stumbled backward, teeth clenched while I waited for the agony to subside. Blackness crawled into my vision like shadows swallowing up the light. Sound faded for distant laughter.

"Let me go!"

"The crooked army is coming! C'mon!" My brother, Caedmon, drags me by the arm down the long hallway of the cellar. Perhaps the scariest place in the old mansion that once belonged to my grandfather, and his father before him. According to stories I've heard the nannies and maids tell, my great-grandmother's bones lie somewhere in this house, and I'm certain it's down in this cellar.

The sticks we gathered from outside to use as swords scratch across the cement floor behind us. We pretend an entire horde of the infected is after us. The ones we call the crooked men, who walk with a twitch in their step and enjoy the taste of human flesh.

I follow Caedmon through the halls, laughing as I try to keep up with him and keep from getting eaten by the invisible monsters with glowing eyes.

The laughter dies away to a creepy quiet when we turn the corner to another hallway and come to a screeching halt before a cracked door. One that's usually locked.

My father's office and laboratory.

It is forbidden to enter, but maybe one peek won't hurt.

"Father will be angry if we go inside," Caedmon says beside me. He's only three minutes older than I am, but he acts like he's the boss all the time.

"Father is always angry." I step toward the door, using my stick to push it open. "Have you ever seen him smile? I certainly haven't."

A grip of my shoulder stops me in place.

"Devryck, don't. Let's go."

I wrench my arm from his hand. "Don't be such a chicken," I say, twisting back toward the door, but the darkness there brings me to a stop, and I'm a little ashamed to admit, it scares the bejesus out of me.

"What is it that you want from inside? I'll get it."

"I want to see her." The only picture of our mother lies in Father's desk drawer. I've seen it a mere handful of times in my life, as my father sometimes enjoys tormenting Caedmon and I by showing us how beautiful she was. She died giving birth to the two of us, and therefore, my father has crowned us—specifically me, as I was the latter to be born—as her murderers.

"What's the point, Devryck? We never knew her. And we never will."

The irritation of my brother's words scratch at the back of my neck, and on a whim, I dash into the dark space.

The temperature feels as if it's dropped ten degrees, the air brushing across my skin like a ghostly whisper. From what little light streams in through the cracked door, I catch the shimmer of glass jars lined on shelves. Ones that hold strange-looking creatures suspended in fluids. Skulls and books fill the space between the jars. More books sit in neat piles on counters and the floor. Silver tables gleam with cleanliness. My father is a stickler for neatness.

The room is hundreds of years old, with a morbid history. My great-great-grandfather was a renowned doctor in the early 1900's, known as the Beast of Bramwell Estate. He was arrested for the very gruesome experiments he performed on prostitutes looking for abortions. The stories terrified me growing up, and I often had nightmares about him, which kept me out of the west wing of the mansion where his portrait hangs beside the other Bramwell men. His crimes plagued two generations of our family, up until my grandfather helped to develop a vaccine against a virus, saving thousands of lives. My father says that was when we finally crawled out from under the Bramwell curse and were once again respectable.

I want to be like him someday, my grandfather. I want to do something incredible and save lives.

Father's office lies past the laboratory, and as I venture closer, I turn to find the closed door of the refrigerator. The body fridge, where the dead are stored.

Sometimes, men bring big bags that they carry down to this laboratory. Sometimes, I spy and catch them pushing carts of bags into the fridge.

"Bah!"

At a rough shake of my arms, I let out a scream.

Caedmon belts out a hearty laugh.

I hammer a punch into his shoulder, earning nothing more than a grunt from him. "Asshole!"

While rubbing his shoulder, he laughs again. "Should've seen your face!"

Attention returning to the fridge, I nod. "Do you think there are bodies in there now?"

"Probably."

I stare at the gleaming, silver surface, on the other side of which could very well be a dead body. "Have you ever been curious what they look like?"

"No."

"Not even a little?"

Caedmon groans with irritation, and at a nudge to my arm, I stumble a step to the side. "You came to see a picture. Look at the picture, and let's get out of here."

"Why are you so scared?"

Eyes trailing over the room, he snarls his lips. "I hate this laboratory. This office. I hate everything about it."

"Father says his work is going to save lives." I want to believe that. Truly. But I know my father's true nature.

"Only good men save lives, Devryck. Father isn't a good man."

With another nudge from my brother, I keep on in my intended task and round the perfectly tidy desk to the other side of it. Clicking on the desk lamp sends a reflective shine across the spotless desktop. After running my hands across it, I open the drawer beside me. A picture frame lies tucked within, and I lift it out to an image of the most beautiful woman I've ever seen. Eyes a fiery amber, hair as black as ink, there is no doubt where Caedmon and I inherited our most notable features.

In the photo, she's looking over her shoulder, a bright smile on her face, her eyes sparkling in the light. It made sense why my father loved her so much. Why he obsessed over her.

She was an incomprehensible light in his darkness.

"What are you doing in here!"

At the sound of the furious voice, my muscles jerk in fear, and I drop the photo.

Clattering against the wooden desk, it sends tiny shards of glass scattering over the shiny surface. My mother's photo dislodges from the frame on impact.

Panic rises up into my throat, as I lift my gaze toward the man standing in the doorway. Perhaps there was a time when he was handsome, worthy of my mother even, but right now, he embodies the very essence of a monster.

Brows pinched to fury, eyes blazing with madness, he stares toward the mess I've made. "What have you done?" he growls through clenched teeth, just like a monster.

"He didn't mean it, Father!" Caedmon pleads on my behalf, but I know it's no use. "You startled him!"

In what feels like no more than a blink, he storms across the room toward me.

I should run, particularly when I feel Caedmon tugging on my arm, but my muscles are frozen in place, eyes fixed on my mother.

Caedmon lets out a cry as, in my periphery, the monster pushes him out of the way, sending him backward into the wall.

Something flashes at the corner of my eye, but before I can make out what it is, an intense pain strikes the side of my head. Jagged light flickers behind my eyelids. The room tilts. An unyielding force strikes the other side of my head.

Caedmon screams.

Everything turns black. Quiet.

So quiet, I can hear the thud of blood pulsing in my ears.

I blink my eyes open.

My father is standing over me, holding Caedmon by the arm, as my brother claws at his grip. "If it's the dead that fascinates you, then you will sleep with them tonight."

The darkness slinks back into its shadowy corners, the view opening to my surroundings. I glance around at all the jars. Ears and fingers, and other bits of meat I can't identify, all suspended in fluid. The specimen closet, situated beside the corpse fridge.

"No! No, please!" Intense ringing blasts inside my ear, as pain strikes my skull again. Eyes clamped shut, I grind my teeth, clutching either side of my head.

The light shutters with the slamming of the door, and as I lurch for it, I hear the lock click from the other side.

"No! Please! Don't leave me here!" Warmth trickles down my leg, the smell of piss burning my nose. A cold sensation, like ice crystals crawling beneath my skin, slithers from my neck down to my fingertips, a thick numb throbbing in my hands, and when I lift my arm to wipe away tears, I can't feel anything. Not my skin, nor the closet's rough floor beneath me. Only an agonizing tingle lingers with the pressure. "Father! Please! Help me!"

Caedmon's screams echo through the door, growing distant. Distant.

Until all is quiet.

"Hey. Hey! What the hell's going on? You okay?" A familiar, but unfitting voice for my memory invaded my thoughts, yanking me back into the present.

I blinked out of the void and found myself on the gritty concrete floor where I must've collapsed. "Do you give a shit?" I asked, pushing to my feet. Dizziness hooked my brain, jostling my field of view for a moment, and I stumbled to the side. Fuck. I hated coming out of these dreams.

"Yeah, I give a shit. You're my meal ticket. I'm guessing the only person that knows I'm down in this shithole." He leaned back against the wall of his cell, watching me compose myself. "So ... your father, he made you sleep with them corpses?"

"What?" Had I verbalized the memory? I'd only ever had them alone, so I wouldn't have had any awareness.

"You were talking kind of spacey. Said your brother and you were playing where you shouldn't've been. Your father hit you."

Hit me was putting it mildly. It so happened, he'd struck a very specific part of my brain, consequently dislodging and activating a latent congenital prion disease. Zigliomyositis was the technical term for it, or Voneric's Disease, as it was more commonly known–a rare condition only seen in an exceptionally small fraction of the population. Incurable and unstoppable in its destruction.

Rubbing my temples, I breathed through my nose, banishing the mist of confusion still clouding my head. "He was like you, Mr. Barletta. Terrified of anything that might challenge him. He was weak. Impatient. Utterly detestable."

"Ain't there a small part of you that cares about your old man, though? Even if he knocked you around, you still give a shit about him, right?"

I snapped my eyes open, the acerbic response sitting on the tip of my tongue and begging to be said. Instead, I swallowed it back, mostly for the sake of my blood pressure. "To answer your question, yes, he did make me sleep with the corpses. I spent the night hearing things. Whispers through the walls. Whether it was my father trying to scare the ever-loving fuck out of a twelve-year-old boy, or something else, I suppose I'll never know."

Barletta stared off toward the center of his cell. "My old man was a hothead, too. Always flying off with his fist." He tapped a finger against the side of his head. "Used to say my brain was made of stone, as many times as I got hit and got back up."

"You and I have nothing in common."

A pathetic shame darkened his eyes as he glanced at me and to the floor. "Yeah. I guess not." He fidgeted for a moment, seemingly deep in thought. "My death ... it'll help someone?"

I shrugged. "Perhaps. If nothing else, it will give me a better understanding of the toxin, so I can save lives."

His brows came together, and he didn't bother to look at me when he asked, "Is it painful?"

"Yes," I answered in a flat tone. "But no more painful than what you've inflicted upon others."

He flinched and covered his face with his palms. Without the alcohol shielding him, I imagined his guilt was eating him alive faster than the worms hatching in his belly. "This is fucked, you know? The way I am ... the way I feel. I could really turn shit around. Do better with my life."

"Yes, I suppose in some alternate universe you could've. Unfortunately for you, I found you first."

Chapter 14

Lilia

Wind howled at the window, as I lay in bed, staring out at a dark sky. Classes would begin first thing the next morning, and no surprise, I couldn't sleep. The heavy ache of exhaustion burned in my eyes, but every time I closed them, my head spun with thoughts. Probably didn't help that my stomach growled incessantly. Seeing as I wasn't yet ready to head down to the dining room myself, I'd eaten nothing more than a granola bar from the vending machine on our floor. One that hadn't filled me up much.

Earlier, I'd ventured to the Dracadian bookstore, an absolute monstrous building packed with students buying supplies and books and even some of the Dracadian merch they sold there. Most of my classes had opted for online texts, meaning I only needed the few books that I'd neatly stacked on the shelf above my desk.

Noting the time on the clock was just after midnight, I climbed from the bed and crossed the room to the south window, beyond which the moon's light glistened off the ocean's dark surface. Staring out at the expanse of black water, I imagined myself out on that sea, alone. Adrift. Terrified of what lurked below the water.

For weeks after my mother passed, I'd had dreams about the sea, even though it seemed as foreign to me as outer space. I'd felt hands pulling at me. The water reaching for my mouth. The icy cold embrace crushing my ribs. Voices I hadn't recognized telling me to let go.

Below the surface, I'd see my mother, so calm and still, as if she'd fallen asleep.

At the first sight of black worms slithering past her blue lips, I'd shake awake, panting and trembling.

As time went on, I'd slept less and less. Ten hours to seven, then six. Nowadays, I'd been lucky to get four in a night. Sleeping pills weren't an option, after the insurance had run out, so I'd suffered through lack of sleep, nodding off in class and throughout the day. My only saving grace was that I had knack for acing tests. Otherwise, I'd have probably failed out of every class.

With a long and tired sigh, I stood staring. In all my twisted thoughts and nightmares, I'd never once anticipated how mesmerizing the sea would be. How utterly magical, even in what little I could make of it from my window. How calming. Vast. I liked that it made me feel small and insignificant. That it could be dark and domineering, yet beautiful at the same time.

A flickering movement caught the corner of my eye, and I looked down to see an insect hopping across the sill. A black moth, from what I could make out. I'd never personally seen a black moth before. Bent at an odd angle, its wing looked injured and left behind a fine black dust on the white sill. Moths had always scared my mother, for some reason. Whenever one had managed to fly into our house, she'd chased it with a broom, smashing it to bits of guts and dust.

I stuck out my hand, letting the creature hobble onto my palm, and studied its wounded wing, noting tiny gouges that looked oddly like bite marks. It fluttered its good wing, tickling my palm, and with a smile, I placed it back on the sill to resume my vigil.

As my muscles loosened and my focus waned for an oncoming trance, the sound of rattling carried across the room. Frowning, I turned toward the exit door, catching the slight movement of the knob.

What the hell?

At home, when the door rattled in the middle of the night, I didn't answer it, because it was either Conner stumbling home drunk after a night with friends, or a street junkie looking for a place to crash. I was no longer at home, though.

I tiptoed toward the door, watching the light from the hallway flicker beneath it. Someone was there, for sure. Scarcely breathing, I pressed my ear to the door for a listen.

Silence on the other side.

A chill brushed the back of my neck, ice-cold fingers over my nape.

Unintelligible whispers tickled my ear, and I swatted there, twisting to find no one present but me. Shivers spiraled down my spine, as I threw the door open. The corridor stood empty. Swinging my gaze left then right showed no one.

An object caught my attention, though. At the threshold of the door lay a crudely formed metal button with an iron cross etched into its flat surface. I stepped back and closed the door over the button, but it wouldn't budge beyond the small bit of metal. Frowning harder, I opened the door again and bent to pick it up.

The voice arrived louder that time, as if someone were bent forward alongside me, and I jumped backward, slamming the door shut. The unintelligible sound echoed in my ear, not with the smooth cadence of a foreign language, but something strange and abrupt. Unsettling. Clutching the button, I backed away from the door and climbed into my bed, throwing the covers over top of me. Too rattled, I didn't bother to secure my arm in the cuff, as I peeked out of the blankets toward the door, watching the light from the hallway flicker with the shadows.

Chapter 15

Lilia

"Damn it, c'mon!" I swiped my card through the reader, only to be greeted by the sixth red beeping light in a row. "C'mon!" Twisting slightly to the left showed that the line of seven other students had already doubled in the last two minutes, all of them wearing irritated and impatient expressions. Humiliation gnawed at me as I swiped the card a seventh time.

Another red beep.

"Here." An arm reached around me from the other direction, and I turned to see a tall blond guy with bright blue eyes offer a half-smile, as he swiped his card and punched number two on the pad below the card swiper.

A green light followed.

"Thanks," I said, stuffing my card away, the pressure in my throat settling again.

"Underclassman?"

"Sophomore."

"Only juniors and seniors are allowed to dine at Darrigan Hall." The two of us strolled at an easy pace toward the front of the dining hall. "Freshmen and sophomores are restricted to Cavick. Unless we invite a guest."

Another blast of embarrassment warmed my cheeks. "I

didn't realize. I'm sorry. It was close to my next class, and I thought I could grab a quick lunch and go."

"I'm Spencer." A well-groomed hand prodded my arm as he held it out to me, and I gave it a weak shake. The guy reminded me of Paul Walker, with his boyish charm and the way his eyes naturally held a smile.

"Lilia."

"Any chance you want to have lunch with me?"

The way my chest instantly tightened when he asked that, one would've thought I was allergic to lunch dates. "Oh ... um. I was just ... I was going to eat in the–"

"Spence!" Kendall, the tour guide from Langmore's office, sashayed up to him, both of them looking like Ken and Barbie, standing side by side. When her eyes fell on me, smile falling away, I wondered if she thought I was wearing the same outfit as yesterday. I'd chosen another sundress–one with blue flowers—but it was the same jacket and boots. "I see you've invited a guest."

Clearing my throat, I hiked a thumb over my shoulder, which actually had me pointing at the bathrooms behind me. "I'm going to eat in the courtyard."

Primped brows winged up as she offered a fake smile. "How very boho of you."

"Mind if I join you?" Spencer tipped his head toward me, and a knot tightened in my stomach. Nothing against the guy–he seemed decent enough. I refused to invite distractions, though. My goal was to remain focused on studies and nothing more.

Besides, what the hell would we even talk about?

"Um ..."

"It's okay if you'd rather not. No pressure." He shot me a wink, and when I offered a silent nod in response, he strode off with Kendall toward the long table of chafing dishes.

I opted for the cold bag lunches at the opposite side of the room, and it was only when I headed toward the exit, with no cashier in sight, that I realized he'd swiped his card and essentially paid for my lunch.

Ugh. Did you have to be such an asshole?

As I passed one of the tables, I snagged a glimpse of the guy with copper eyes again, the one I'd bumped into the day before, sitting alone and staring down at a book. When those eyes found mine and he caught me staring, I snapped my attention away, and consequently rammed my thigh into the corner of one of the tables. With a quiet grunt, I brushed off what would undoubtedly become a bruise in the next twenty-four hours.

Once out of the building, I took a deep breath, and on spying an empty bench beneath an impressive red oak, I hustled across the lawn toward it. After settling, I tucked into a chicken salad croissant with grape halves and celery, Cape Cod potato chips, and organic apple juice. Even cold lunch at Dracadia was more impressive than anything I'd have scrounged back home—and mine had been only one of about ten different cold bag options.

Lichen-covered statues, chipped and aged with time, stood about the courtyard in front of me–angels, and children with motherly figures who cradled them. I glanced back at the ominous gargoyles perched outside of the engineering building to my rear. How creepily they'd been angled, as if watching the innocent statues play. Across the yard from me, black birds pecked about. The infamous ravens, I guessed. I'd read in the history of the school that because there were so many that had flocked to the island, it was long believed to have been cursed.

They made for pretty peaceful lunchmates, though.

After eating, I headed toward Emeric Hall for my first class of the day. Like every other building on campus, the gorgeous interior had been well-preserved. Thick hardwood gleamed, as I made my way to a set of wooden doors ahead. I opened one of them into a dimly-lit auditorium, where a handful of students had already claimed seats and sat scrolling on their phones. Every one of them had the sleek, black, to-go coffee cups with the purple and gold dragon logo of the local coffee shop, Dragon's Lair. A pretty popular gathering place, as I understood. They had a few pop up stands in some of the academic buildings, too. Unfortunately, eight bucks for a latte was out of budget for me.

Finding a seat at the opposite side of the room, I sat in the very corner of the second row. Although I'd have ordinarily opted for a rear seat, with this being an advanced class I wanted to make sure I didn't miss anything. Hoping to blend in, I pulled out my phone and spotted a text from Jayda:

How's anglican life?

Snorting a laugh, I texted back:

Surprisingly uneventful so far. I met a Paul Walker clone.

Met? As in talked to?

He spared me the humiliation of my card being declined. Guess he paid for my lunch, too.

Tell me you didn't eat alone, Lilia.

I ate alone.

Jesus on a pogo stick, the hell is wrong with you, woman?

I'm not here for men. I'm here for knowledge. I can't screw this up, you know that.

"Is this seat taken?"

A shock of surprise jerked my muscles, and I looked up to see Spencer standing over me, his brows winged up. Black to-go cup in hand, just like everyone else.

A quick glance around showed a number of open seats he could've chosen.

"Sure. I mean, no. It's not taken."

"Cool." It was when he slumped into his chair that I noticed how uncomfortably close we were situated. Enough that if I hadn't turned my knees the other way, one would've surely touched his. "Thought you said you were a sophomore."

"I am. I was placed in this class." I pulled my laptop from my bag–an off-brand loaner from the tech department, and a far less fancy machine compared to the MacBook that every other student had out on their desks. From the side of the chair, I tugged the small desktop to unfold it, frowning when it refused to flip up.

"Ah. You're a smarty pants, then." Spencer pressed a button I hadn't noticed, and the desk lifted with ease. Smiling, he tugged out his own laptop from his bag–a Mac, of course.

While I appreciated his playful nature, I felt like every response fumbled inside my mouth. Though undoubtedly attractive, the guy wasn't my type, so it didn't make sense that I'd have been so tongue tied. "I do okay, I guess."

"You missed out on a riveting conversation at lunch. Country clubs and fall fashion and everything I don't give a shit about." He chuckled, and I smiled, wondering if he'd said that for my benefit. Perhaps he'd hoped to make me feel more at ease around him, but unfortunately, his comments only left me feeling more like an outcast.

Just as I was on the verge of unzipping my skin and crawling away, a figure strode into the room.

My heart stalled in my chest.

In his black, button-down shirt, black slacks, and black, finger-raked hair, he looked like an ominous shadow moving through the lecture hall with the kind of lethal grace that had undoubtedly obliterated a few hearts. His outfit matched the infamous black, to-go cup clutched in his hand. A tingle at the back of my neck had me scratching there, and when he headed toward the desk and lectern at the front of the hall, instead of one of the audience chairs, I wondered if he might've been one of the assistants Dean Langmore had mentioned.

Bright copper eyes scanned the room, and when they fell on me, my heart slammed into motion again.

The girl in the row in front of me lifted her camera, not-so-subtly snapping a picture of him. I stared down to see her posting a caption with a weary face emoji over it:

Why does Doctor Death have to be so fuckable, tho?

Doctor Death.

I nearly choked on my own spit right then.

Bramwell.

Dracadia's brilliant expert pathologist.

Given his reputation, and the respect he'd gleaned from Professor Wilkins back in Covington, I'd expected him to be sixty years old. The guy couldn't have been much past thirty.

He certainly dressed the part of death with all that black.

A few more students filed in, as Professor Bramwell stood at his lectern and cracked open a book.

Look away, my head told me, but he was one of those men that effortlessly commanded attention. The kind who went about his business looking utterly *fuckable*, as the crude brunette in front of me had pointed out. It irritated me how much of a distraction he posed in a class that was apparently one of the more difficult on my schedule.

Once all of the students seemed to be present, Professor Bramwell snapped his book shut on a thunderous crack, and a unison of gasps echoed through the room.

"Let's get started. I'm Professor Bramwell, and this is my teaching assistant, Ross." He pointed toward the front row, where a slightly younger guy sat wearing glasses beneath a mop of ungroomed hair that told me he must've been a grad student. "The class is Neuroparasitology, and will pick up from the parasitology prereq you should've taken last year."

The deep timber of his voice vibrated in my chest, as I practically swallowed every word out of his mouth. The authority in his tone demanded to be obeyed, and as I glanced around the class, not one student had their face buried in a phone screen.

I placed my phone onto the small folding table, opening up my audio app, and clicked *record*.

"This is your first Bramwell class?" Spencer whispered beside me.

I gave a sharp nod.

"He doesn't like to be recorded. Kinda weird, I know, but if he catches you recording, he'll take your phone. All the notes are available on DracNoti. You can edit as you go."

"Oh. Shit." In swiping up my phone, I knocked it off my small desk, sending it to the floor on a clatter.

After retrieving it, I sat up to find those fiery eyes staring at me with such intimidating annoyance, I had to look away, and clearing my throat, I held the phone in my lap.

His eye twitched. "It's imperative that you keep up and pay attention to the material. There's a lot to cover, and I'll be moving at a fast pace."

Gaze lowered, I prayed hard that the seat would fall out from under me and I'd get sucked into a black hole.

"Is there anyone here who has not taken the Parasitology prereq?"

Oh, God. Just kill me already.

I was the only one in the class who raised a mildly shaky hand.

Again, those eyes fell on me. Hard.

"Name?"

"Lilia. Vespertine. Sir."

"See me after class, Miss Vespertine."

My first *see-me-after-class* since freshman year of high school.

"This class covers topics rooted in ongoing and privately-owned research at this university, meaning you are not permitted to discuss whatever is covered outside of this institution. If anyone feels a sense of opposition?" He pointed to the left of him. "Don't let the door hit you in the ass."

Jesus, I'd had some abrasive professors before, but this guy took the cake.

"You should've all signed the non-disclosure agreement online during orientation. Is there anyone who didn't?" he asked, once more raising my blood pressure.

Freaking hell, fate must've been out to get me, because again, I raised a shaky hand, and his gaze left me feeling like I'd been raked over hot coals. On an obviously frustrated huff, he twisted toward his bag on the desk and pulled out a paper, which he handed off to Ross, who handed it to the brunette in front of me. Wearing a smirk, she handed it over.

At the top of the page, in bold print beneath the Dracadian logo, were the words NON-DISCLOSURE. An entire page of smaller print followed, but I didn't even bother to read it before I signed it, not with the entire class silent while Bramwell waited with arms crossed.

I handed the paper back to the brunette, who handed it to Ross, who handed it off to Bramwell. I could've just signed my soul away to the guy and I didn't care, so long as the class stopped looking at me like the fly who shat on their birthday cake.

After a look of disapproval, followed by a brief glance at the paper, he placed it on his desk and finally resumed his lecture. "The most important function of a parasite is to secure its transmission to the next host." The way he paced back and forth across the room, his voice carrying an intense inflection, kept me riveted, as I jotted as many words as I could into a simple Word doc. "Is anyone familiar with mind-hijacking?"

"I thought this was parasitology, not MK-Ultra conspiracies class," some joker from the back of the room answered, earning a few clipped chuckles.

Bramwell didn't so much as crack a smile, only offering that deadly gaze for an uncomfortable minute, before he resumed his pacing again. "*Paragordius varius*, otherwise known as the horsehair worm, is an aquatic parasite that has, to its misfortune, chosen the common cricket as a host. As you may or may not know, crickets, as a general rule, avoid water. However, this clever worm releases a chemical that confuses the cricket, causing it to commit suicide by drowning. Once submerged, the worm makes its escape. If the cricket is lucky enough, it won't drown before the worm emerges, but often, that is not the case."

"Jesus," Spencer muttered beside me. "Doctor Death kicking things off on a morbid note."

"Another example. The female jewel wasp makes a practical nursery for her young out of a cockroach, by first attacking the roach's front legs with a toxin. It then attacks the head, leading the senseless roach to its burrow like a lost puppy. There, it lays its eggs and entombs the two of them together. The larvae consume the cockroach from the inside and eventually emerge as adults." He paused his pacing, hands still clasped behind his back, the stance opening the unbuttoned top of his shirt even wider and allowing just enough of a peek of the deep grooves there. "Parasitic mind control is an emerging science, not yet well understood. It is a complex and fascinating field of study. For the next sixteen weeks, you will be submerged, much like our unwitting cricket, in a wealth of little-known information about various species of parasites. I recommend you pay close attention to the syllabus and keep up with the reading."

Something in the way he spoke, the passion I could literally feel infused into every word, sent a shudder of excitement through me. The man lived and breathed science–that much I could tell. When the class ended, I found myself looking at the clock in disbelief. An entire hour had slipped by in what felt like minutes, as I'd sat completely enthralled by the man and the ease with which he relayed information, as if he were talking of something so benign as the weather. As the class packed up and exited, my stomach knotted in tight bows of anxiety at the thought of having to talk to him one on one. I'd wanted the opportunity to pick his brain sometime, but something told me he wasn't happy about my presence in his class.

"Professor Bramwell, you wanted to see me?"

His assistant, Ross, shot me a quick glance as he passed behind him toward the exit, but Bramwell didn't bother to take those cognac eyes off of me.

And just like that, I was completely alone with the one they called Doctor Death.

"Miss Vespertine, I understand you're new to Dracadia."

"Yes, I'm technically a sophomore, but–"

"Allow me to acquaint you with my teaching style, since you managed to skip the prerequisite." From the top of his collar, a small bit of his skin appeared to be contracted and discolored. A gruesome scar that I guessed must've marked the acid attack Mel had told me about. Unless that was just a story she'd made up. "I don't like interruptions. This isn't a fuck around class. Know that I've failed more students than I've passed."

"With all due respect, I believe that's the failure of the one teaching."

His jaw twitched as if he were gnashing my words between his teeth to spit back in my face. "I also don't appreciate underclassmen with smart mouths."

"My apologies. Sir."

"Your being here is a mistake. Let's not make it an egregious one. Keep up with the reading. Attend the recitations."

"I will."

He made a grumbly *humph* in his throat, like he doubted me, and breaking his staring, he shoved his book and notes into his bag, along with my signed NDA, unavoidably drawing my attention to the map of veins in his forearm where he'd rolled his sleeves up.

And the fact that he didn't have a wedding band.

Stop, damn it.

I wanted to ask him more about the parasites. Perhaps get on his good side with what small bit of knowledge I had on the one for which he'd been named an expert, but my throat clogged, my tongue heavy in my mouth.

Instead, I exited the auditorium to find Spencer waiting outside. Oddly enough, I felt relieved to see him after such an intense encounter. My lips burned from having bitten the shit out of them the whole time.

"All good?"

I pulled my bag up onto my shoulder. "Were you expecting otherwise?"

"Alone time with Doctor Death? I don't know."

I headed in the direction of my next class, seemingly in the same direction Spencer was headed, from the way he kept in step. "You call him that because he was supposedly involved in some other student's disappearance?"

"Yeah. She dated a buddy of mine. He's expelled now."

"Ah. The one who splashed sulfuric acid on him."

Spencer lips flattened. "You heard the story already."

"Yeah. I think I found that bit less impressive than the rumor."

"He wasn't the sharpest tool in the shed. But Jenny's disappearance fucked with his head."

I slowed to a stop, just outside of the building of my writing exposition class. "What evidence led everyone to believe Bramwell had anything to do with it?"

Spencer stuffed his hands into his pockets and shrugged. "Cameras caught her leaving out some back door of his lab, the night she went missing."

"And you don't think that makes the boyfriend a suspect?"

"He was pissed, for sure. He always thought there was something going on between them, for some reason. But I talked him down that night."

I playfully rolled my eyes at that. "So, you're the campus knight in shining armor."

Rubbing the back of his neck, he smiled in a way that seemed flirtatious. "Something like that."

I'd been the yolk of nasty rumors my entire high school career. I hated gossip–loathed the way something could spread like a wildfire with no merit, or evidence. No doubt, Professor Bramwell was a bona fide asshole with a cherry on top, but I decided to reserve judgment before flat out calling him a murderer. "Well, look. I appreciate your concern. But I like to give people the benefit of doubt before grabbing the nearest pitchfork."

"No disrespect. I just felt compelled to give you a heads up, is all."

"I appreciate it. If you'll excuse me, I need to head back to my next class."

With a nod, he stepped aside and headed off in the opposite direction.

Chapter 16

Lilia

An impressive building, with multiple pillars that reminded me of something out of Washington D.C., identified the campus library where I'd been assigned work-study duties. Once past security and the metal detector, a soaring vaulted ceiling, adorned in gorgeous frescos of angels in battle, seized my attention as I entered the open space. Balconies stood at either side, converging into a winding staircase at the center of the main floor. I'd heard there were multiple levels, with an impressive gallery of baroque paintings and artifacts in the library's attic. I'd also heard of other things known to go down in the attic—a hotspot for campus hookups, so I'd have to be careful venturing up there. Fancy chandeliers loomed over long hardwood tables, which made up plenty of study spots, each with multiple desk lamps, outlets, and pencil cups.

I'd always had to carve out times in the day when no one was around to get any quiet study. Yet, there, I could've heard a pin drop.

I followed the signs to the second level, passing private little study nooks–tables amid walls of bookshelves. The upward path led me to the beautiful rotunda room, where white marble floors and banisters gave a bright contrast to the dark wood of the other rooms. Impressively carved stone heads on pillars stood about the room in small alcoves, giving it a Romanesque look. Through the windows of the Adderly memorial room, I took in the gorgeous view of the yard, with its magnificent oaks I imagined would soon be snow-covered, making for a cozy scene. The room itself held the history of Dracadia, from what I could gather of old photographs and glass cases that held artifacts. I looked forward to perusing more of the school's history when I got the chance.

I couldn't even begin to imagine how many secret places this magical school held. I could've probably attended for years, and I'd never explore the many wonders of it all. The more I saw, the more I wanted to see and know.

As I entered the Stirling room, dedicated to science texts, I found an older man, with dark skin and graying hair, reaching to place a book onto the shelf over his head.

"Excuse me," I said on approaching. "I'm looking for Kelvin Reed?"

The man spun around, his spectacles halfway down his nose as he regarded me with a tip of his chin. "I'm Kelvin Reed." The articulate nature of his voice matched his appearance of sweater vest over a gray shirt, looking like a lifelong academic.

Smiling, I gave a respectful nod. "Lilia. I was assigned work study here."

"Ah, yes. Miss Vespertine. Very good to meet you. I'm the Master Librarian for the Adderly Memorial and Stirling Science wing." Truly, I could've listened to the man talk for hours, his voice was so pleasant to the ear. "I'm assuming you've acquainted yourself with the Adderly Memorial room already?"

"Yes. Is that the same Adderly as the statue in Thresher Bay?"

"It is. Lord Commodore Adderly was a widely respected pillar of Dracadian history." His comment brought to mind

Mel's irritation over the memorial. Maybe I'd learn what had brought her to those opinions.

"I'm looking forward to learning more about the history of the school."

"Well, you're in luck. It so happens to be a requirement for working in this department. It's our duty to preserve the precious texts we managed to recover from Adderly's ship. So, your job for the next week is to familiarize yourself with our history so that you might be a resource to others."

"Would I have access to these texts, as well?"

Brows knitted, he sighed. "For the most part. Some texts are restricted and require certain *permissions* to access."

Those were suddenly the ones that piqued my curiosity most.

With a nod, I followed Kelvin back to the Memorial room, which was decorated to look like something out of an old ship, with all the nautical details–ropes with thick knots, a porthole, and oars. Perhaps items they'd recovered from Adderly's ship.

"We'll start here," Kelvin said, gesturing to the many books in the room. "Leave any books that you read on the table. I'll take care of them. It's important they return to their proper places."

"Got it. I just ... spend the couple hours I'm here reading?"

"Yes, exactly."

I couldn't have picked a more perfect job. Except maybe one that required sleeping.

Kelvin left, and I perused the room, looking for an interesting place to start. I came to a halt before a painting of a woman with fiery auburn hair. She wore a plain white dress and held white lilies in her hand. The name below read Sister Mary Elizabeth, though she didn't wear any religious garb in the painting. Beneath the painting a thick book sat cracked open on a table lectern, a bible given the looks of it. *Romans 12:17* had been underlined: *Do not repay anyone evil for evil.*

Another glance at the woman drew me into staring at her. How much she reminded me of my mother. I nabbed one of the books from the shelf beside her painting and sat down at the table near the window.

According to the text, she'd come to Dracadia as a young nun to care and watch over those deemed mentally unsound and exiled to the monastery. The book described her as a kind and benevolent woman, particularly admired by Dr. Nathaniel Stirling.

The book included a picture of the doctor, known for wearing the infamous plague doctor uniform while caring for his patients, whom he believed were infected by bad spirits. An unsettling shiver coiled down my spine as I stared at his image on the page, in his beaked mask and long black cape. The sight of him must have given his patients nightmares. It seemed the science wing had been named after him, based on him having unwittingly discovered Stirlic acid, an antiseptic made from the Jestwood plant. It had apparently changed the outcome of surgeries he'd performed, and he'd been hailed the godfather of sterilization.

Except, he'd employed his discovery in a much more sinister way when banishing evil from his patients.

I found myself immersed in the history of the monastery as something of an early mental institution, where patients had been subjected to a number of experiments to exorcise the so-called bad spirits from their bodies.

By the time I finally broke my concentration, I noticed it was already dark outside. A glance at my watch showed that I'd stayed over an hour past my work study time.

"Shit," I muttered, placing the books in a neat stack on the table, as Kelvin had requested. I gathered up my book bag and twisted around, knocking into the person behind me on an explosion of papers that flew up into the air before scattering over the marble floors.

"Oh, my!" Dr. Langmore stepped back, adjusting his spectacles. "I didn't mean to startle you, Miss Vespertine."

Cheeks red with humiliation, I dropped to the floor and gathered his fallen papers into a somewhat messy pile. "It's my fault, Sir. I wasn't watching where I was going." I pushed to my feet and handed off the stack, which he received on a smile.

"Please, I insist on sharing half the blame."

"I was just leaving. My work study shift ended an hour ago."

"Ah! Ambitious. We like that." His gaze skated toward the window and back. "It's fairly dark outside. Will you be walking alone?"

"Um. Yeah. My dorm isn't far."

His eyes squinted with unease. "Still, I would advise caution."

"Of course." Movement beyond him caught my attention, and I looked past Langmore to find a shadowy man striding toward us, his eyes scrutinizing as he entered the memorial room.

Clearing his throat, Langmore seemed to follow the path of my gaze, twisting around toward Professor Bramwell. Seemed the man's intimidation radius was fairly broad, as even the dean appeared somewhat uncomfortable in his presence. "Yes, well. Take care, Miss. I've a staff meeting."

"Sure," I said, still caught up in my staring. When Bramwell's gaze flicked to mine, I finally broke my ogling and lifted my bag up onto my shoulder.

Bramwell didn't say a word to me as he passed, in spite of my polite nod and smile, which quickly faded when I turned away.

What an asshole. It was a wonder he saw anything past his own nose.

With that, I made my way toward the exit.

The moon shone high in the sky as I hoofed my way across the courtyard. For the most part, the campus seemed to have settled in for the night, though a few students still bustled about. I'd survived the first day, and even in spite of the crappy moments, I'd enjoyed it. For all its faults, the school had a dark magic about it. The history, the architecture, the mystery of the campus and its people–it spoke to me and inspired a longing to drink it all in.

Such a sense of belonging was foreign to me. Even though I hadn't been born into wealth, like most of the students, there was so much to Dracadia that went beyond old money. It existed in its own little pocket of intrigue, like stories of Pan and worlds far beyond.

To imagine that I'd become part of its fabric had yet to sink in.

Vigilantly scanning my surroundings, I skittered toward the shallow stretch of woods that separated my dorm from the others in the square.

"*Lilia*," a voice whispered from behind, and I startled.

Turning around showed nothing more than tree branches swaying in the breeze. I scanned over the courtyard, eyeing two students off in the distance. Another hustling toward a dorm.

As I turned back to my path, something caught my eye on the other side of an oak tree. A dark figure that I had to squint to see in the dim light given off by the streetlamp halfway between me and the tree. A long, black cloak. A long, beaked nose. Two black holes for eyes.

The plague doctor mask I'd seen.

On a gasp, I spun back around, straight into the wall of a human being standing behind me.

"Whoa!" Spencer chuckled, grabbing my arms as I crashed into him. "Someone's in a hurry."

"I saw some–" I twisted back toward the tree, finding nothing there. A longer scan showed not even the students from before. "There was someone by the tree. I ... I swear I saw ..."

"You really shouldn't be out walking alone. I know you said you're all about giving people the benefit of the doubt, but some people are just assholes."

Muscles sagging on a sigh of relief, I turned back to him. "Are you?"

"An asshole? I thought we already established that I was." On a snort, he knocked my arm. "C'mon. I'll walk with you. Where are we going?"

"Crixson."

"Ahh. Crixson. Get used to seeing things that aren't there."

I hated to admit, I was a small bit relieved to have company on my walk. Dracadia wasn't Covington, not by a long stretch, but that didn't mean it wasn't crimeless, either. "So, what makes you think *you're* so safe to walk around by yourself?" I craned my neck, searching for the figure behind us.

"This is where you see if I insert something sexist, right? Tell you it's because I'm a guy?"

"I don't know. Is it?"

"The truth is, I stayed late training. Otherwise, I'd be stuck back at my room watching *Big Bang Theory* reruns with my roommate."

I chuckled at the visual of that. "That sounds exciting."

"Riveting. Where are you coming from?"

School flags rippled in a light breeze that scattered my hair around my face. Every sound seemed to catch my attention, as I kept stealing glances over my shoulder, the unsettling feeling still vibrating my bones.

"Work study," I said, trying to tame the wild strands ticking my cheek.

"Cool. Where'd you get assigned?"

"Library." Damn the strand that slipped into my mouth, heightening my irritation. My hair had always been wild and unruly, but add a bit of wind? It had a mind of its own.

"I was assigned there last semester. I got kitchen duty this semester."

Slapped with surprise, I frowned. "You .... You're in work study?" I'd always had the impression that only kids who couldn't afford school got placed there.

The shallow forest just before my dorm seemed darker tonight, the trees even creepier for some reason, and again, I was reluctant to admit that I appreciated Spencer's company.

"Yeah. Oh, wait ... is this where you insert something about rich kids being brats?" He chuckled, loosening the accusatory tone in his voice.

"I guess I'm a little guilty of passing judgment."

"I guess," he said, as we finally reached the front of my dorm.

"Thanks for walking me."

"Anytime." He brushed his finger over my hand, and on reflex I jerked back, clearing my throat to cover up the slight gasp that escaped me.

Stuffing his hands into his pockets, he flattened his lips and took a step back, either offended or embarrassed by my reaction. "I'll see you tomorrow."

"Yeah. I'm ... sorry. 'Night."

I didn't have much experience with friendships. Male friends, in particular. I'd had too much going on at home to pay attention to guys my age, and the few times I had gotten involved with them, it certainly wasn't friendly. Every exchange with Spencer just felt awkward and forced on my part. I'd barely been cordial with the poor guy.

So, why the hell did he bother?

As I entered the dorm, I passed the lounge and caught

sight of the TV, where a news report brought me to a skidding halt.

Namely, the face that popped up on the screen

Angelo.

Frowning, I darted toward the lounge, just catching the news anchor talking about some billionaire CEO who'd been found brutally slain a few days ago. For a moment, I slipped into an alternate reality, thinking it might've been Angelo who'd killed him, but the report went on to say that he was wanted for questioning.

"*Authorities believe Angelo DeLuca may have had dealings with a cult and is considered armed and dangerous.*"

"Jesus," I muttered. With shaky hands, I tucked myself into a quiet corner and dialed Conner, biting my nail while waiting for him to answer.

"Hey, what's up?"

"Did you see the news? They're saying Angelo was involved in that rich guy's murder!" I whisper yelled, the panic in my throat squeezing the words.

"Nah, wasn't him. He's been here the whole time. Poor asshole's freaking the fuck out over it. One of his cop buddies said Angelo's name was written in blood on the wall. He thinks he's marked by someone, but he won't say who."

"And what's this cult they're talking about?"

The sound of Conner's long exhale crackled through the phone. "Some sadist group. They call themselves Schadenfreude—but don't go repeating that. They're dangerous, according to Angelo. Asshole didn't even want to tell me about them, at first."

"Sadist?" I lowered my voice even more. "Like ... *torturing* people?"

The moment he said, "I guess," my stomach curled into itself.

"Maybe you should stay away from him, then?"

"He just needs to lay low until the police find out who did it."

"Conner, what if the killer comes after you? Jesus, are you drunk right now?"

The guy had absolutely no concept of the danger he might've been in. A sadist group affiliated with Angelo? It didn't get any more messed up than that.

"A little, but no one is coming for me, Lil. We're fine. No one's gonna connect the two of us. He hasn't used the DeLuca name in five years."

"Except that his face is plastered to the TV. Someone might recognize him."

"The guy's so fucking paranoid, he won't even leave his place. Been making me run his damn errands for him."

"I just think you should inform the police, is all. Maybe they can protect you." At the very least, the shady ones Angelo seemed to be associated with. While grateful not to be in the thick of all that, I wasn't stupid enough to think criminals stopped at the men they'd sought. Sometimes, they went after friends and families, too, in an effort to make a spectacle out of their revenge.

"Police ain't gonna protect shit. Relax. Bee's at school. You're away at school. I'm the only one who might be caught up in this shit, and I'm telling you, I'm fine."

I rubbed a hand down my face, groaning at Conner's misplaced disregard when it came to things that mattered. Things that could turn really bad, real quick. "Just ... don't do anything stupid. Okay?"

"Yeah, yeah. How's school?" Such a benign question for the topic at hand.

"Great. It's great, Conner."

"Good to hear. I meant what I said, kid. I'm proud of you."

"Thanks. Keep me updated, okay?"

"Will do."

With that he hung up, and I exhaled a shaky sigh.

"Hey." At the sound of a new voice, I looked up to find Mel standing over me. "All good?"

"Yeah. I just needed to make a private call." I stuffed my phone away, hoping she hadn't heard any of the conversation. "I'm heading up to my room now."

"I saw you walking with Spencer," she said flatly.

"Oh. Yeah, he walked me to my dorm. We're just friends."

"Can I give you some unsolicited advice?"

With my head still spinning, I honestly wasn't in the mood, but I responded with, "Sure?"

"I'd be careful around him."

What the hell? Had she crowned herself the resident messenger of shady men, or something? First Bramwell, then Spencer.

"Why?"

"Because he's a lying piece of shit. A manipulator."

I shrugged, mildly frustrated at the way she'd nosed herself into my business. We'd had a neighbor like her back in Covington. An older woman who'd constantly inquired about my mother's state of health and whether, or not, her illness could pass through the apartment vents. As my mother had progressed, we'd decided to keep her confined to her room, so as not to rouse all the gossip in the building. "He's been pretty cool to me."

"Of course he has. That's what manipulators do."

Perhaps her warning was warranted, but I had a shitshow on my hands with Conner hanging out with what seemed to be a wanted criminal, and I just didn't have the headspace for her right then. "I appreciate the heads up."

"I'm serious, Lilia. You don't want anything to do with that."

"Noted," I said, heading back to my room.

Chapter 17

Lilia

Cavick Hall had to be the most intimidating lunch commons I'd ever seen. A high vaulted ceiling, tall enough to have accommodated a freaking space shuttle, loomed over thick wooden trusses that buttressed the walls. Elegant candelabras and stained-glass windows, set above white bust sculptures, gave a gothic feel to the expansive space. Like the lunch spread at Darrigan Hall, rows of chafing dishes sat out on long tables, but Cavick had twice the number —almost overwhelming, how many options the place offered.

Given the opulent spread, I opted for a somewhat pathetic breakfast of avocado toast and coffee. I'd lost a bit of my appetite since that conversation with Conner and, after a mostly sleepless night, still hadn't gained it back. I'd debated making an anonymous call to police and turning Angelo over, but who knew what that would've meant for Conner, if they started nosing around in Angelo's shady affairs. I couldn't risk that they'd find him guilty of something, too.

I decided to let it go. After all, ruminating about it wouldn't make it go away.

As I nibbled on my toast, I glanced around the room at the other students who'd flown in for a quick bite. Unlike high school, where I'd been ousted as a loser for sitting alone, Dracadia seemed to embrace its loners sprinkled about the room, unbothered by their solitude. Some studied as they ate. Others scrolled through phones. A handful lunched in groups, but their clusters were few by comparison. Strange, the way I felt less lonely in my being alone.

After breakfast, I scampered across campus and, once again, found myself in Emeric Hall for another class I hadn't signed up for–entomology with Loretta Gilchrist. Seeing as she was the one who'd had some influence in my acceptance, I was in no position to complain, though, and I hoped to make a good impression, in case she had anything to do with my tuition for the second semester.

"Miss Vespertine?"

At the sound of the feminine voice, I leaned back from hunching over myself to grab the laptop from my bookbag. A fairly attractive, dark-haired woman with speckles of gray roots, perhaps in her late forties, stood before me, holding the signature black and gold coffee cup, her eyes scrunched with a smile.

"Yes?"

"Dr. Gilchrist." She held out a slender hand, which I promptly shook. "I see you accepted the invitation. Wonderful."

"Yes, of course. Thank you for whatever magic you pulled to get me in. I am both grateful and thoroughly impressed. The campus is incredible."

"It is. As was your paper on Noctisoma." With both hands, she lifted the cup and slurped some of the fluids in an unbecoming way for a woman who seemed well put together. "I found the clinical details absolutely engrossing. Tell me, have you had the chance to meet our provost, Dr. Lippincott yet?"

"The provost? No." I couldn't imagine a reason I'd have needed to–I couldn't even have said who the provost was at

Covington Community. Maybe they hadn't had one, but I found it strange she'd have asked that.

"I recommend you make an appointment. He'll be very pleased to make your acquaintance, I'm sure."

"Okay. I didn't realize the provost took appointments with students."

"It isn't common, he's a very busy man, but for you, I'm sure he'll make the exception." Her eyes scrunched again, and she gave a small chuckle and lifted her cup for another slurp of coffee.

"Well, look who it is." As Spencer strode up to me, Gilchrist lowered her cup and turned toward him.

"You two have met?" she asked.

"Yeah. We have another class together." He dropped his bag into the chair next to mine, indicating he had every intention of sitting beside me in this class, as well. "Bramwell's parasitology class."

Gilchrist frowned, her gaze shifting from mine to Spencer's. "Dr. Bramwell's neuroparasitology class? That's a junior level advanced class. He doesn't *allow* underclassmen." The argumentative tone in her voice struck me as odd, as if I'd *chosen* to be in grumpy's class.

"Smarty pants here seemed to get in."

"Dr. Bramwell is quite particular about his students. I can't imagine how you managed to charm him." Again with that smile that I'd begun to think was as feigned as Kendall's.

"I actually didn't sign up for his class. I was placed there."

One would've thought I'd smacked her, the way she flinched in response. "Placed there. By whom?"

"Not sure, to be honest. I logged in to register, and both of your classes were already on my schedule."

"Yes, well, my class is an appropriate level class for *you*. The other is not."

I shrugged, increasingly uneasy with the conversation. "Professor Bramwell seemed okay with it."

"Of course he did. But he is not the Department Chair for the college of natural science. I am. If you'll excuse me ..."

It must've been a bigger deal than I thought. Hopefully, she wouldn't have me removed, though, because even if he was something of an asshole, I still intended to needle some answers out of him.

"We must've been on the same wavelength with class scheduling, huh?" Spencer's question snapped me out of my thoughts as he leaned in closer. "I'm actually the TA for this class. Just so you know, she can be a little strange. Woman studies insects all day long."

I snorted at his comment, watching Gilchrist dial her phone before she turned to face the wall, speaking low enough that I couldn't hear the conversation.

Very strange.

When she turned back around, tucking her phone away, her eyes were on me again. Gone was the tepid welcome there, replaced by a cold expression that had me shifting in my seat.

"I'll definitely keep that in mind," I whispered back to Spencer. "Didn't realize I'd broken the rules."

"If Bramwell's okay with you being there, there really isn't much she can do. He's pretty tight with the provost and deans."

"I'm not trying to make waves. I just find his class fascinating."

"Fascinating?" Spencer snorted that time and leaned back into his chair. "Give it some time. A couple campus parties, and you'll be right in the head again."

I frowned at him, a snippy comeback parked at the back of my throat, but as Gilchrist took her place at the lectern to begin, the insult died on my tongue.

Gilchrist's lecture was, by no means, anywhere near as

riveting as Dr. Bramwell's. Not by a long shot. Her delivery was bland enough that I could hardly stay focused without my mind wandering into other thoughts, and the tug of my eyelids from little sleep the night before had me wishing I'd brought a cup of coffee to class. The struggle to stay awake and focused overrode my ability to absorb anything she'd said, and by the time class had ended, I felt like I had taken an unrestful nap.

"I'm impressed," Spencer said, catching up to me as I headed toward my next class. "Pretty sure I fell asleep on the first day of her class."

"She's a smart woman, no doubt, but robots have more personality when they speak."

Spencer let out a chuckle and waved to a small group of guys walking by. "I heard her say something about Provost Lippincott."

"Yeah. She thinks I should make an appointment with him. I'm going to go out on a limb and guess that he's pretty busy."

"I can get you an appointment."

This guy. If I didn't find him to be genuinely nice, I'd wonder what the hell his motives were. "You've got pull like that?"

"He's my father."

Oh. Shit. My mind suddenly found itself rewinding back to all of our conversations, and I tried not to let myself cringe too much at the memory of the first day when he'd bought my lunch. "Wow. That's crazy."

"Don't be too impressed. My father is a strict believer in following the rules. Believe me, there are no special privileges."

"That's why you're kitchen duty?"

"The man insists that I show some *responsible effort* in contributing to my education." He let out a long sigh and shook his head. "Anyway, I'm happy to put in a word with his secretary."

"If I can get her number, I'll just contact her myself." I reached into my bag for my phone, noticing it was gone. "Oh shit. I think I left my phone back at class. Look, I'll catch up to you later."

"Tonight, right? Midnight lab?"

"Right!" I called out over my shoulder and darted back toward the lecture hall, scrambling through the empty seats until I spotted my phone on the floor. As I bent to pick it up, voices neared, and it was only by some weird instinct that I ducked down behind the row of seats in front of me. Chiding the decision, I shook my head, but just before I could push to my feet, the click of a door echoed through the room, shutting me inside with whomever just entered.

"My time is limited. I'll ask that you make this quick." At the sound of the bone-penetrating baritone voice, I peered through the gaps in the seats to spot Professor Bramwell standing at the front of the lecture hall with Professor Gilchrist, who sauntered toward him from the door that I could clearly see had been shut.

Shit.

"I don't understand why you placed her in a class that requires a prerequisite. As Department Chair for this college, I should be informed of any exceptions made as they relate to students. It's very strange, and on the heels of you not returning my phone calls, even more so."

"I'll ask that you not confuse the two circumstances. It has nothing to do with you and me."

"Of course not. And I know you despise any accusation of you and a student. Please accept my apologies, Devryck." Her shoulders sagged as she stepped closer, keeping a small distance between the two of them. "I meant no disrespect, and I know that you would *never* consort with a student that way."

My suspicions about him must've been true, then. The guy seemed more apt to make out with a textbook before hitting on any of his students.

"I'm just ... was it touching you that pushed you away?" Hands clasped together, she dared another step toward him, and the desperation in her tone had me shaking my head. "I promise it won't happen again. Please give me another chance."

Another chance? Why she pined over the asshole was baffling and, as a fellow woman, painful to watch. I wanted to leap out from behind the seat and shake some sense into her.

He stepped away, seemingly uncomfortable. "Do not question my decisions as they relate to my class. Miss Vespertine is there because I allowed it, and because I think she'll excel."

"Really?" Realizing I'd spoken aloud, I slapped a hand over my face, the panic shooting through my muscles like jolts of electricity. Peering through the gap showed no indication that either had heard me, though. They didn't offer so much as a glance in my direction, thank God.

"Excel? That's a stretch. She's smart, I'll give her that. But she isn't *that* smart, Devryck."

Lowering my hand from my lips, I frowned. What a bitch thing to say.

"Are we finished here?" he asked with an air of boredom.

"You tell me."

"I'll call you if I have a change of heart."

Ouch. The way he spoke with such detachment left me feeling a little sorry for her. As hot as he was, particularly for a professor, he sure as hell had a moody side to him.

She scoffed and shook her head. "You are, without a doubt, the most confusing man I've ever met."

"That's the problem, Loretta. You seem to be easily confused."

My phone lit up with a text notification, and I damned near dropped it trying to shut it off. Eyes clenched shut, lips tight, I waited for one of them to approach. Surely, they'd seen the flash of light in the dim room.

Surely, I'd be picked up by the scruff of my neck and tossed out, accused of being a snoop.

The door clicked shut. I looked through the gap to find neither of them standing there. Exhaling a shaky breath, I glanced down to a message from Jayda, asking about Angelo. No doubt, she'd seen the news report.

I finally pushed to my feet to find Professor Bramwell hadn't, in fact, left. He stood before the row of seats in front of me, hands in his pockets, eyes pissed off, as usual.

Shit.

"The next time you decide to eavesdrop, perhaps you might opt to be more subtle."

"I, um ... I didn't mean to eavesdrop. I forgot my phone." On a nervous chirp of a laugh, I held up my phone, as if that proved anything.

He didn't bother to respond, only stared at me like he was silently conjuring the door to hell so he could toss me into the flaming pits and call it a day. Instead, he turned to leave.

"Professor!" I lurched, nearly dropping my phone. "I was wondering if I could ask a few questions? Regarding Noctisoma."

"I've no time. I hold limited office hours, Miss Vespertine. You're welcome to make an appointment."

"Right. Sure. I'll do that."

Without so much as another glance, he exited, and I exhaled a shaky breath. Man, the guy was intense.

My thoughts drifted back to his conversation with Gilchrist–namely the subtle compliment he'd handed off. "Excel," I whispered to myself, emphasizing the word. "Ex-*cel*." Had he known I was there when he'd said it? That I'd heard him? What was it about a man known to be brilliant but grouchy handing out a random compliment like a decadent piece of chocolate that I wanted to savor before it melted?

He's an asshole, the voice inside my head argued back. *Don't put too much into it.*

Yeah, he was. An exceptionally good-looking and smart asshole.

Sighing, I headed to my next class.

Chapter 18

Lilia

According to the syllabus for Professor Bramwell's class, I was to wait outside of my dorm for the campus bus to pick me up. At ten-to midnight, I got a little antsy, because damn it, I did not want to be late to that man's class. On the verge of abandoning the bus idea and walking across campus, I caught the flash of headlights coming toward me. A small shuttle bus with purple, interior lights rolled to a stop. Painted along the side of the bus in black letters was *Nocticadia*, and below it, *Midnight Lab.*

Nocticadia?

The whole thing seemed a bit too theatrical for Professor Bramwell, so I guessed it must've been something arranged by the students, or the college itself. I climbed inside, finding about two dozen students, and Spencer who waved to me from the back.

Swallowing an internal groan, I made my way to the seat across from him. "I was getting nervous for a minute there," I said plopping into the cushy seat.

"Griggs is never late." He canted his head toward the driver. "Not even when it snows. The guy always gets us there on time."

"You've taken this class before?"

"Pretty much. I took Bramwell's pre-req last semester. Lab was the same."

"What's *Nocticadia*?" I asked, glancing out the window, as the bus rolled to a stop for two more students outside of Hemlock Hall.

"It's what we call the Midnight Lab. A play on Noctisoma."

"Ah. Right. So why midnight?"

"That's when the parasites are most active."

Somehow, that made sense. I remembered in my mother's illness that she'd always seemed to be most active at night. Wandering for food, or staying up watching TV. I once awoke to her eating raw hamburger and just about lost my mind. She'd always seemed to get weird cravings like that after we'd all gone to bed.

Two stops later, the bus arrived at Emeric Hall, where everyone piled out. I followed the group that obviously knew where they were going down a flight of stairs. We descended three levels before we finally arrived at a set of double doors and filed into a room with a high-domed ceiling and wooden benches where candles had been lit. I'd never been in a lab lit by candles before. Bunsen burners, sure, but never candles.

Books and specimen jars, flasks and beakers lined the walls of the room that carried a soft purple glow, given off by large tanks situated around the room. Scattered over the benches sat domed mesh cages that housed bright purple butterflies fluttering about. While it held modern amenities, the place didn't look like any lab I'd ever worked in before. It reminded me of something out of a sci-fi movie.

"Welcome to Nocticadia." Spencer said from beside me, as I took in the strangeness of it all. "This is where we study the Sominyx moth and propagate Noctisoma."

"Sominyx moth?" I swung my gaze back toward the cage domes. "Those are *moths*?"

"Yeah. Weird, huh? They used to be black. But when they're infected with Noctisoma, they turn purple. They're nocturnal, so they sleep during the day."

"That's why the lab is so late at night."

"That, and like I mentioned earlier, the parasite likes to party when the sun goes down."

Fascinated, I veered toward one of the domes on a bench, staring in on the moths inside. Yes, I could see it up closer, the thicker, fuzzier traits that differentiated moths from butterflies. Purple wings practically glowed against the thin, black vein-looking lines. In the dimness, I could hardly see the detail, and I turned on the flashlight of my phone for a better look.

A quick hand covered it, and I turned to see Spencer standing beside me. "They're sensitive to light."

As soon as he'd said the words, I looked back to see the glowing reflective eyes of a moth staring back at me, while it jabbed a long slender appendage that I guessed to be a proboscis through the mesh holes. It reminded me of the way my mother's eyes had changed toward the latter stages of her illness, and the way she'd almost hiss when I'd turned the lights on in her room.

"I'm sorry. I didn't realize."

"It's why we have candles. Natural candlelight and bioluminescent light is okay, but anything fluorescent, or ultraviolet, phone lights, that's a no-no. They tend to get aggressive, making it hard to handle them."

In the corner of the dome sat a dish containing what looked like a small piece of steak.

"Is that … meat?"

"Yeah. They're not much for sweets. These guys like their steak rare and bloody."

Like my mother's cravings. Strange.

I stared down at the proboscis, wondering if it was strong

enough to break through gloves and skin. "I've never heard of such a thing in a moth."

"Happens with infection. Otherwise, they tend to be pretty docile in nature."

"They're infected with Noctisoma worms?"

"Yeah. Bramwell will go over that in lecture, but they're the primary host, like his morbid little crickets. Don't worry, though. We only handle them with gloves. It's the larval stage we're interested in, anyway."

"Have you seen them? The worms?"

"Yeah. C'mon." With a jerk of his head, he led me to a tank along the wall, which glowed a bright purple. "There's bioluminescent bacteria in the water. Doesn't harm the worms, at all."

About a dozen long, black, skinny worms squirmed over the floor of the tank, and my jaw hung open as I leaned in to get a better look.

The worms. The exact worms I'd seen expelled from my mother.

Real.

Strange, how differently they looked at home in the tank. Less like the monsters I'd made them out to be in my head.

Help me!

Mama!

At a flash of memory, I flinched and looked away to find Spencer pointing at something.

I followed the path of his finger to a moth sitting at the bottom of the tank. The occasional flutter of its wings told me it was still alive. "Doesn't it drown?"

"Only the males do. Females submerge themselves in water to lay eggs, as a general rule. If the eggs are deposited quickly, they actually live to see another day."

Frowning, I stepped closer and watched as tiny clusters of

eggs emerged from the moth to be deposited on the glass surface.

"Once they hatch, they'll make their way to the noxberries on the surface."

I glanced up to see what looked like little water lilies on the water's surface, where tiny berries stuck out from the petals. "That's how the larvae disperse, isn't it? The moths eat the berries."

"Yep. Unless Bramwell sweeps through and grabs all the infected berries."

"For what?"

"All right, class, find a seat so we can begin!" Ross, the guy I remembered from Professor Bramwell's lecture stood toward the front of the room unloading a stack of notebooks from his messenger bag onto one of the empty benches, before he passed them out to everyone.

I opted for the bench at the back of the room, from where I could easily see the glowing tank and the moth that fluttered her way to the water's surface.

Ross tossed one of the journals onto the benchtop, and I flipped through the pages to find empty boxes for dates and descriptions and notes.

"You will record everything in detail." The sound of Professor Bramwell's voice dragged my attention back to the front of the room, where he stood with an air of authority that tickled my stomach.

I rested my hand over the irritating sensation, annoyed with my reaction.

"Failure to update your journals will result in automatic dismissal. Ross will lead the lab, so any questions are to be directed to him. Not me." His eyes found me, lingering for a moment, before he stepped around the desk. "I have separate office hours for general inquiries. I encourage you to make your appointment in advance, or you will be turned away."

Without another word, he breezed through, his gaze locked on mine as he passed. A delicious mixture of coffee and spicy cologne trailed after him.

As Ross began with his lecture, I turned to see Professor Bramwell exiting through a door at the back of the room.

"Where does that door go?" I whispered to Spencer, who sat at the bench in front of me.

"Basement level. That's where his research lab is. The morgue is down there, too. Off limits."

"You mean to tell me no one's ever snuck down there before?" I couldn't have been the only one curious enough to even consider such a thing.

"Can't. There's a steel door that he keeps locked at all times."

"Why so secret?"

Spencer threw a smile over his shoulder. "Depends on who you ask. Theories span the gamut. Some think he's got a Frankenstein shop down there. Reanimating his corpse friends."

Snorting a laugh, I lowered my gaze, when Ross flicked his attention my way.

"Others say he's working on some secret government project. No one really knows."

"You said he takes the larvae down there, though?"

"Yeah. Every so often, he grabs a few berries and disappears with them."

"Interesting." So, it wasn't just him cutting up corpses in the basement. He was studying the parasite, as well, leaving me to wonder if he was working on a cure for it.

If so, I needed to be part of that. Since my mother's death, my entire reason for studying science and medicine centered on finding out what had ailed her in those weeks before her death.

As the hour passed, I kept stealing glances at that door,

wondering if Bramwell would return. He didn't, only prodding my curiosity and distracting my thoughts. It turned out, watching the moths took only a small fraction of lab time. We spent most of the hour prepping stains, viewing Noctisoma fragments through a microscope, and filling agar plates. Not the most thrilling time of my life.

But it did inspire one objective for the semester:

To find out what Bramwell did in that lab.

Chapter 19

Devryck

What had started out as an inquiry into how much of a pain in the ass my new student was going to be had left me intrigued. A cursory search proved Lilia to be both smart and athletic, seen in a school announcement for Covington High that listed her as Valedictorian for her class and an All-State Champ for track and field. I was curious to know more, though.

I hadn't yet bothered to read the paper she'd written on the fictional parasite that'd apparently landed her a spot in my class, but in an effort to learn more about the girl, I'd had Lippincott's secretary send me her file. I casually scanned over her case study, and as I read the progression of symptoms, I sat forward in my chair, frowning at what I read.

Aversion to light. Intense thirst. Glow to the eyes. Episodes of paranoia.

She noted a butterfly tattoo just below the patient's navel that they'd claimed a small hand would poke through. Strange delusional visions that were common with the infected.

Even the timeline of events was spot on for Noctisoma.

While her knowledge of the organism seemed to be lacking, rightly so as not much had been published about it, I found her observations of the physiology interesting. In my reading, I hadn't noticed any mention of a rather significant symptom in her paper–vonyxsis. The darkening of red blood cells in the latter stages was due to extreme depletion of oxygen, caused by a protein the worms produced. In the patient she detailed, she had noticed fever and muscle fatigue, and had consequently administered a tissue salt known as ferrum phos–an oxygen carrier cell salt that would have destroyed the protein's byproduct. In doing so, she had completely averted vonyxsis and possibly prolonged her patient's lifespan by another couple of weeks.

Impressive.

The occasional patient infected with the parasite had been known to pop up from time to time, but were often isolated cases, and only on the island. Physicians on the mainland, unaware of the parasite as a human pathogen, never made the connection. How the girl had come across such a case was the mystery of it all. Suspicion from Wilkins, her former professor, suggested that the patient in the study had been her mother, since she hadn't bothered to identify them.

I pulled up my computer and typed her name in the search bar.

An obituary for a woman named Francesca Vespertine popped up, where Lilia had been listed as a living relative, along with her half-sister, Beatrix. No picture. No other information.

With her mother's name, I logged into my PathNet account, which gave me unlimited access to coroner and autopsy reports, so long as they were properly filed. A quick search brought up Francesca's file, and a skim of the coroner's report revealed that she'd committed suicide in the bathtub. Slit her wrists, apparently, a finding that *wasn't* consistent with Noctisoma patients. In my experience, the infected had a strong sense of self-preservation up until the parasite was ready to eject, resulting in drowning more often than not. However, the autopsy also didn't list any of the other telling pathology, either.

I'd have thought the coroner's report and Lilia's case study were two separate people, based on that, except that I scanned down, noting that same butterfly tattoo covered in small lacerations, where she'd undoubtedly clawed at it. I didn't recognize the coroner's name, but if the patient had suffered all the symptoms that Lilia had detailed, then he'd omitted obvious signs that would've been present in autopsy. Most notably, the bone striations and liver decomposition.

The finding left me wondering if he'd altered the report.

If that was the case, he must have done so to cover something up.

A thought that left me puzzling over who Francesca Vespertine was and how she'd become infected.

Hopefully, Lippincott would remain lazy about reading the case study, or investigating Lilia's mother. I certainly had no intentions of sharing my findings with him. The girl had just earned a spot on my list of curiosities, making her secret safe. For a while, anyway.

My cellphone buzzed beside me, and I turned to see Langmore's number flashing across the screen. Frowning, I answered it.

"Dr. Bramwell, excuse the interruption, but I just received a call from Dr. Gilchrist, requesting that I have Miss Vespertine promptly removed from your class and accompanying lab."

"On what basis?"

"She claims that she's not equipped to handle your curriculum, and that she hasn't taken the required pre-req. I personally felt she had a good handle on the subject matter, but I apologize for overstepping. Before I move forward, I just wanted to get your thoughts."

Get my thoughts. I wanted to laugh at that. The man was

probably holding back a torrent of piss in his pants right now.

"Yes, of course," I responded cordially, biting back the anger that tautened my muscles. "Allow me to impart my thoughts. Dr. Gilchrist needs to keep her fucking nose out of my business. I approved Miss Vespertine's enrollment. End of story. If Gilchrist has a problem, she can take it up with me. Directly."

The woman wouldn't have dared. It was a wonder she'd grown the balls to approach Langmore in the first place, unless she honestly thought I'd have not given a shit. Had it been any other student, that might've been the case. But something about this one had me intrigued enough to challenge the department Chair.

"Very well. I will uphold her enrollment and inform Dr. Gilchrist of your decision. I appreciate your time."

"Yeah. Thanks." At that, I hung up the phone, rattled that the woman would dare to go behind my back that way. Clearly, she still harbored animosity over what'd happened between the two of us. It was a snake move trying to have Lilia quietly removed from my class. The fucking audacity of it nettled me, and good on Langmore for having contacted me. Of course, I suspected he'd probably calculated the consequences of not doing so first. No one touched what belonged to me without repercussions.

My class.

My requirements.

My student.

Without a doubt, Lilia Vespertine was going to be a massive headache. But she was *my* headache.

Chapter 20

Lilia

How was it, the more I watched him, the less I knew of the man?

Four days had passed, and on a campus that housed thousands of students and staff, between classes, I'd somehow become hyperaware of Doctor Death's whereabouts. In addition to neuroparasitology, he taught fourth year and graduate level anatomical pathology, which seemed to take up most of his afternoons, besides the occasional visits to the admin building, where I suspected he attended staff meetings. Every morning, at precisely seven, he could be seen jogging past the clock tower in his usual campus circuit, four times around, equating to about ten miles. Not that I could possibly track every moment of his day, of course, I did have quite a bit on my plate, but he rarely passed by without my noticing.

Today was the exception.

Some students had left for the long Labor Day weekend, but I'd stayed. The last thing I intended to do was return to the shitshow with Angelo, though that seemed to have settled over the past week.

I'd gone all morning, to the dining halls, the library, and one of the coffee shops across campus, without having seen Professor Bramwell hustle to and from Emeric Tower, leaving me to wonder if he'd left the island for the holiday weekend, as well.

Since the weather was a balmy sixty-eight degrees, I decided to take one of the campus bikes for a spin. A swipe of my ID card allowed me to rent a bike for six hours at a time, and with the island being about eighteen miles long, I suspected I'd need the time to do some exploring.

Following a five-minute interview from the gatekeeper, who insisted on knowing where I was going, when I was coming back, and if I planned to meet up with anyone, I headed through the campus gates. The bike accelerated down a slightly terrifying narrow road, steep enough that I nervously kept my hand off the brake for fear of flipping forward. The path that split the forest wound down the cliff, and as I passed thick stretches of trees, I wondered how the hell I'd get back without destroying my thigh muscles.

Swells of a sprawling forest opened around the occasional cottage-style home–adorable, old-century structures, with asymmetrical, rounded roofs and steeply pitched gables that had me feeling like I'd fallen into a small European country. Properties in Covington tended to be the usual bungalows and Cape Cods, whereas those on the island were adorable storybook cottages, drowning in overgrown ivy, and beautiful wooden arches brimming with colorful blooms.

The entire island had a magical appeal about it, unlike any place I'd ever been. Like the school itself, it quickly grew on me, luring me into its charm, just as Professor Wilkins had predicted.

The first week of school seemed to have flown by. I liked my classes—even the dreaded calculus and quantitative physiology lectures—and I finally felt like I was falling into a routine. A strange, but welcomed, change of life. Days of trying to squeeze in class and study around full-time work had shifted to long study sessions around lectures and exploration.

Unnerving subway rides at night, surrounded by complete strangers, had given way to shuttle buses with familiar faces–all of them there for the same thing. While I knew I still had to work out extra cash for Bee's tuition, I no longer felt the tremendous weight of it pressing down on me.

A few miles up the road, I passed a sign that read Emberwick, and entered what appeared to be a small seaside village–a charming town that ran parallel to a boardwalk and the endless blue beyond it. To my right, seagulls soared above the pier that stretched hundreds of feet out toward the few fishing boats anchored offshore. The tires of my bike bounced over aged cobblestones, as I admired ivy-covered brick shops lining either side of the road. While a few cars buzzed through town, mostly those two-seater smart cars, the bike racks outside of the shops stood packed–-undoubtedly the main source of transportation for most of the island.

When I caught sight of the apothecary shop, I slowed my bike, spying an open spot on one of the racks in front. Once parked, I peered through the window of the shop next door to the apothecary, called Glaucus, a place which appeared to sell good luck charms to fishermen and sea travelers. Small trinkets lay displayed in front of the window, a variety of engraved medallions, stones, hooks, and what looked like strings of tiny bones. A wooden brochure rack beside the door held booklets of Dracadian Folklore, and I nabbed one when I noticed *Free to take* scribbled on a paper stapled to the wooden post.

Flipping through showed a brief description of different stories–*Sirens of Bone Bay, The Cazanute, Mangurdame of Devil's Perch, Nereides of Squelette Lake*–all of them tales of different locations on the island. The place had so much history and lore, I could've probably spent hours studying it.

Tucking the booklet into my bag for later, I pushed through the old wooden door of Salty Sea Apothecary, to be greeted by the ring of a bell and a delicious ginger scent.

Candles burned throughout the shop, and a wall of jars stood off to the right of me, filled with all sorts of colorful fluids. Matcha ginseng elixir. Lion's mane. Maca. Moringa. I lifted one of the jars, examining the clarity of the liquid inside, which almost appeared crystal-like.

"Can I help you find something?" a voice said behind me, and I turned to see a striking older woman, with deep, almond eyes and graying hair, whose skin glowed with ageless perfection. Her brows came together as she stared back at me. "Oh, my, you look like someone I once knew."

"I do?"

"Yes. Did you by chance happen to know a Vanessa Corbin?"

"No, I'm afraid not."

A flash of surprise lit her eyes, and she shook her head. "You are a spitting image of her."

Smiling, I shrugged. "They say everyone has a twin."

"Well, I knew her about twenty years ago, so I suspect she isn't much of a twin these days." She twisted toward a small collection of jars on a table behind her and stowed them away on one of the nearby shelves. "Do you live on Dracadia?"

"Sort of, I guess. Going to school here." I lifted one of the bars of soap and, placing it back on the table, caught a whiff of that delicious scent again. "What is the ginger I'm smelling?"

"Oh, it's just some black rock tea I made earlier."

"Black rock tea?" I'd frequented a few holistic shops back in Covington, but had never come across that before.

"Yes, it's a local tea that we brew here. Takes a bit of time to prepare, but it'll cure whatever ails ya."

"Do you have it for purchase?" Not that I had tons of money to spend, but I always kept an eye out for anything that might keep the seasonal bugs away. And with winter right around the corner, it was better to start building up my immunity now.

"Oh, no. It's too much work to sell it. But how 'bout this, I can give you a couple tea bags of it."

"Really? I can pay you."

"No, no. It's all right." She waved her hand in the air and made her way toward the cash register. "Don't get too many young ones in here," she said, rummaging through something below the countertop, only the top of her head visible.

"My mom was always into herbal remedies. Never took so much as an aspirin her whole life."

Frowning, she shot back up, holding a small white satchel of what looked like black crystals inside. "Are you sure you don't know a Vanessa Corbin?"

"Positive."

"So strange. She and her mama were long time customers of mine. Vanessa loved the herbal teas and honey gums. Here, I'll throw in a couple to try." From a bowl on the counter, she plucked two golden-colored pieces of candy wrapped in wax paper and deposited them into a small bag. "Anyway, here's the tea." After holding it up for a moment, she slipped the satchel in with the candy. "Just add hot water, a bit of ginger and some honey, and you will be in heaven. You can even drop the honey gum into it. It's just raw hardened honey with a hint of elderberry." She pretended to shiver and smiled. "So good for cold winter nights."

"Thank you for this," I said, accepting the bag from her. "Why is it called black rock?"

"Sourced from the rocks at Bone Bay. Which is why we don't sell it. It's dangerous trying to get to it."

"Dangerous? Is it guarded by dragons, or something?"

"Sharks, mostly. You have to dive into Devil's Perch. My grandson knew those underwater caves like the back of his hand. But it's a nursery for some of the bigger sharks. *Legendary* sharks."

I couldn't even imagine diving into something named

Devil's Perch, let alone knowing a nursery of sharks awaited me there. "Is he a shark whisperer, or something?"

Smile fading, she lowered her gaze. "He passed a few years back."

"Oh, I'm sorry to hear that."

With a sigh, she stared off for a moment, then smiled again. "Yes, so his brother brings me some black rock on occasion."

I stared down at the supply in the bag, no more than a small satchel, but considering the danger in retrieving it, I no longer felt right taking it. "Are you sure about giving this to me? I don't want to take your supply."

"I insist."

"Well, in that case, I'll take some of the matcha ginseng, as well."

"Very good." With a quick wink, she nabbed a small box of the matcha from the shelf behind her and rang up the goods for me. When she'd finished, she handed me a slightly bigger bag containing everything I'd bought. "Don't be a stranger around here, eh?"

"Oh, I'll definitely be back." As I exited the shop, I sighted a few maps of Dracadia and, when I stopped to snag one, noticed a poster beside the rack. It showed a man, apparently wanted by police for the brutal abuse of his son, who was believed to have been hiding away on the island. *Wanted* and *Missing* posters decorated just about every pegboard back in Covington, so seeing one wasn't anything special. It just seemed out of character for the island.

Salt and pepper hair put the man about mid-forties, and his sunken brown eyes gave me the creeps. He *looked* like a child abuser. I glanced down at his name. Barletta. Not one I recognized, but what stood out to me was how much he reminded me of Angelo, for some reason. Just that disheveled look of a criminal.

Which took my mind right back to home. I hadn't heard anything more from Conner since our phone call, and nothing more had been reported on the news. Hopefully, things had died down.

Beside Barletta hung a *Missing Persons* poster whose corners were curled a bit, as if it'd been there a while. A blonde with bright blue eyes stared back at me–Jennifer Harrick–the girl who'd gone missing. The one Mel had told me about on my first day.

On a somber note, I left the shop and hopped back on my bike. After stowing my goods in the little wicker basket, I opened the map. The main street looped all around the island and came back around on the other side of the university, where I hoped the incline would be less steep. Ten miles up the road, the complete opposite side of the island, stood Bone Bay. I pushed off, pedaling an easy pace toward my next stop.

Wind sifted through my hair, the salty sea air thick on my tongue as I inhaled it. A blissful warmth scattered over my skin where rays of sunlight touched me, the first full sunny day we'd had in a week on the island. Again, I found myself thinking how much my life had changed in just a few days. How I'd transitioned from carrying around a pocketknife and scurrying home in the dark, to a quiet, seaside bike ride.

The sense of freedom scared me a little, like I'd become naive and soft. After all, the place hadn't entirely earned my trust yet, so it didn't make sense, the way I felt so at ease there. I hadn't even bothered to bring my pocketknife on my excursion, which was still tucked in my desk back at the dorm. Conner would've called me stupid for the oversight.

After my mother's death, I'd gained certain freedoms that I hadn't had growing up, mostly out of necessity. Conner had moved in and needed help with the rent, so I'd had to get a job, and going to school meant working late at night. Because Conner couldn't drive, thanks to too many DUI's, I'd had to rely on public transportation. It was a scarier brand of freedom. One I didn't care to exert, but again, necessary.

I'd been thrown out into a world that would've eaten me alive, had I not learned how to navigate it quickly and so young. I supposed I could've thanked Conner for that, since he'd been the one to give me a good shove into adulthood, but honestly, having had the mother I'd had, living the life I'd lived, maybe I'd been preparing for it my whole life.

It didn't take long before the winding road curved alongside a stretch of cliffs, and I came upon a weathered and cockeyed sign that read Bone Bay, with a crude blackbird carved into the wood. About a hundred yards away, an archway of spindly branched trees created a tunnel over a long, descending staircase. I tugged my phone from my pocket and snapped a quick shot, thinking how absolutely enchanting it would look if it were decorated in lights.

The stairs creaked and groaned as I made my way down to where the tree tunnel opened onto lush green pines and white sandy dunes that tapered into the rocky shore of the cove.

Black birds, whether crows or ravens, I couldn't tell, had settled in trees and along the shoreline. So many of them. At the end of the staircase stood a sign that urged me not to feed the birds, and to avoid the south end of the cove during late winter, as that was where they might be most aggressive.

I stepped off onto the rocky shore, and two birds scattered toward the sky. Before me stood the vastness of the ocean. Beautiful, yet utterly frightening. Docile waves reached for my feet, but I backed away, not allowing the water to touch me. Maybe someday I'd be bold enough to dip my toes in, but certainly not today. Not when it could've easily pulled me out and no one would've even cared, or have thought to look for me.

With the cliffs surrounding me, trees at my back, the stretch of beach held a peaceful tranquility. I followed the curve of the cove toward a mass of rock, and there, a hard *thunk*ing sound echoed above me. For a brief moment, I thought back to the *Wanted* poster I'd seen in town.

What if it was the child abuser? What if he was hiding out in the wood there?

The city girl inside of me begged me to walk away, while chiding me for not having grabbed my knife.

A flicker of movement overhead drew my eyes to the rock's flat peak, where a muscled figure in a black Tee swiped up a bottled water and looked out over the sea.

Curious, I climbed up the stretch of jagged boulders, careful of my footing. The moment I breached the top of it, the view sharpened, and I caught sight of Professor Bramwell about twenty five yards off.

Slapping a hand to my mouth, I ducked alongside the rock on a gasp. Not that I was shocked to see someone at a *public* beach. It was the *someone* I'd seen. At the sound of retreating footsteps, I peeked over the rock to find him locked in a stance, holding something in his hand. Sunlight glinted off its steel surface.

A blade.

He drew it back and hurled it toward one of the trees.

From the ground, he swiped up another blade and chucked that one, as well. I followed the path of his throw to see the first had landed smack in the middle of the tree trunk. The second, directly beside it. I watched him toss a third, which landed beside the first two.

It wasn't the blades that held me captivated, though. Beneath those unassuming dress shirts he wore to class, the man apparently sported a carved physique that stretched the fabric of his T-shirt. Paired with the careless mess of his usually perfect hair and the casual jeans hanging low on his hips, he held me enthralled.

Staring at my professor.

Stop, Lilia.

I felt like a predator watching him.

The way he easily manipulated the weapon left me convinced he practiced frequently. A hobby? Probably fitting for a man who cut bodies up for a living.

A chill wound down my spine as that thought rooted itself in my head. In a normal human being, it might've triggered an urge to get the heck out of there, because what the hell kind of person would've been caught on a rocky cliff, in the woods, with a man who carved corpses at night? One who seemed exceptionally proficient with his weapons.

Me, apparently, as I kept on staring, watching him throw a few more tosses, lunging and pivoting, without a single blade bouncing off that trunk. For reasons I couldn't explain, I was mesmerized by his skill.

Confused, but fascinated.

Chest heaving, a shine of sweat coating his neck and arms, he tossed off his blade and turned toward the edge of the cliff, opposite me, where the ledge of rock stuck out over the sea. The moment his fingers hooked the hem of his shirt, like he was about to strip, I ducked.

Oh, God.

My brain urged me to leave and give the man some peace, but when I pushed off the rock to make sure he wouldn't see me exit, he wasn't standing there. Only his discarded clothes lay in a heap.

I jolted forward, down the jagged slope, until I just caught the tail end of his body splashing into the waves. Eyes darting back toward the top of the cliff, I estimated about a fifty, or more, foot drop.

"Oh, shit!" I scrambled down the rock, back onto the stony shoreline to search for him. Seconds ticked away, and the horrific realization that I may have just watched the man leap to his death pummeled my conscience.

C'mon. Don't be dead. Don't be dead.

Off a little way, his head breached the water. The distance from the shore sent a chill down my spine, when I imagined the depth there and what creatures might've lurked below him.

I screwed my eyes shut on a shuddered breath, and when he began his swim back toward the rock, I decided I'd had enough excitement.

Once again, I'd found myself more perplexed, the more I observed.

Who was this man?

As I made my way back up the staircase toward my bike, I decided the questions would never be answered by watching him from afar. I needed to get closer.

Which meant I needed to make a dreaded office hours appointment.

Chapter 21

Lilia

It took a damn week to get a meeting with Dr. Bramwell. The guy never answered his email, nor the phone number he'd listed on the syllabus. In lamenting to Jayda, she told me to *be audacious* in my dealings with men in power positions. So, five minutes into his lecture, I'd boldly asked him if I could make an appointment, and in return, he'd pinned me with a dagger-hurling glare.

Then agreed to meet with me after class.

Palms sweating, I trailed after him from the lecture auditorium, all the way to his office. Knots wound impossibly tight in my stomach, and as delicious as his cologne smelled, it only heightened my nausea.

Eyes focused on the surrounding rooms kept me from staring at the way his ass moved in his black slacks. Undoubtedly firm, given what little I'd seen of those ass-hugging jeans he'd worn back at the cliff.

Stop it, Lilia!

Wincing, I mentally insisted that my eyeballs not veer back for another look, but that was the problem with my brain. Once I'd thought it, I couldn't unthink it, and it became a dangerous game of trying to ignore the issue.

Thankfully, we reached his office, where he stuffed a skeleton-looking key into a black iron lock and swung the door open on a creak. The interior was relatively small but brimming with medical texts and journals that lay in neat stacks on his desk and floor.

The man liked tidiness.

I took a seat in one of the chairs across from him, as he fell into his seat on the other side of the desk.

"Miss Vespertine, I'm allotting fifteen minutes for this meeting. Make them count."

I didn't waste any time. "I understand Noctisoma is rare in humans. How was it introduced?"

Easing back in his chair, he steepled his fingers, staring at me, and I realized right then that I hadn't quite calculated just how intense his undivided attention would feel. How utterly consuming and threatening at the same time. "I will be covering the history of Noctisoma in an upcoming lecture."

"I understand, and I am looking forward to that section, but according to your syllabus, you don't cover it until December."

He quirked a brow. "And?"

"Well, it's for personal reasons that I ask." Mostly, that the class was a full two semesters back-to-back, and I might not get the information I needed, if for some reason my tuition didn't cover a second semester.

Annoyance colored his expression, and he sighed. "In the colonial era, the disease was believed to have been spread by the natives, who shot the larvae using blow darts into those they deemed a threat. It's hard to say how many cases emerged after the fall of the tribe, seeing as the island remained abandoned for a number of years. It re-emerged about thirty years ago, when a wanderer camping in the woods stumbled upon the noxberries and consumed them."

"You're working on a cure for it, aren't you? In your lab? Is that why you remove the larvae?"

He stared at me silently for a moment, and as much as I

wanted to look away, because goddamn the man was intimidating, I didn't. "Your questions have begun to traipse a delicate line, as they relate to *my* activities."

"Sorry. I'm just curious, is all."

"Curiosity often leads us down a precarious path."

"You say that as if you've walked it yourself."

The corner of his lips twitched, and he leaned forward, resting his elbows against his shiny desk. "To answer, I am studying the organism to gain a better understanding of how it affects the human body."

Instead of blurting off the first question that popped in my head—namely, *how the hell had my mother become infected?*—I considered my words carefully. "Do you get many cases from the mainland?"

"No."

"If one were to contract it, though, is it spread person to person?"

"Rarely."

I frowned at that–how the hell else would my mother have gotten it? I'd never seen a noxberry in my life until I came to Dracadia. "Well, it must be."

"Are you asking questions, or trying to convince me, Miss Vespertine?"

"My mother died of Noctisoma." I dared him to argue that.

"Our facility would have been the one to confirm such a diagnosis, if it had been properly diagnosed. What's her name?"

"It doesn't matter. She refused to see a doctor."

"And the autopsy?" he asked in an almost bored tone. "Surely, it would've shown evidence of Noctisomal pathology.

If it had, it'd been encrypted in coroner language that I didn't speak. "What kind of pathology?"

"Bone striations and liver decomposition, most notably."

I couldn't recall seeing any of that. The most notable issue, aside from blood loss, was fluid in her lungs. "Perhaps they missed that."

Jaw shifting, he narrowed his eyes. "Is your mother from the island?" he countered.

"No."

"Did she attend Dracadia? Visit here? Live here for any length of time?"

I didn't like the way he was ruling it out before my very eyes, but I answered honestly. "No."

He gave an insouciant shrug that made me want to reach across the desk and smack him. "Then, chances are, it wasn't Noctisoma."

"I know what I saw, Professor. Black worms. Like the ones in the Midnight Lab. I saw them crawl out of her body." I gestured toward my mouth. "Like they were trying to escape."

"Death can be difficult to process, Miss Vespertine."

Frustration curled in my stomach with the way the guy was trying to refute everything, like I had imagined it all? I'd gone too many years believing that lie. To hell with that. And to hell with him. I hadn't imagined any of it–I knew that now. "It was not shock, or hallucination. It was real."

Maybe I looked to be on the verge of crying, because he eased back in his chair and let out a long, exasperated exhale. "Very well. It was real. Unfortunately, I did not examine your mother, so I can't say for certain how she may, or may not, have become infected. I'm only sharing what decades of study have taught me."

Releasing a sigh, I nodded. I'd gotten worked up again, and he was right. Maybe I had gotten caught up in trying to convince him. "My apologies for getting upset."

"If I've answered all your questions, perhaps you might let me return to my work."

"May I ask one more question?"

"Of course."

My mouth suddenly turned dry, as the strong possibility of rejection needled me. "I wondered if you might have any lab assistant positions open?"

"Ross can direct you to available positions, but they fill quickly."

"I don't mean general lab. I mean ..." *Be audacious*. "I mean working with you."

He didn't even give the question enough time to linger before he batted it away with a swift, "No. I'm afraid not."

"It wouldn't have to be the whole semester." I scooted forward in my chair, the desperation goading me to sound like a whiny beggar. "I'm happy to be a dishwasher, or prep reagents. Maybe just–"

"*No*, Miss Vespertine. I do not take student assistants in my lab, in any capacity. Now, if you'll excuse me, I'd like to return to my wor–" He let out a grunt, and his hands flew to either side of his skull. Eyes screwed shut, he clenched his teeth, and a hiss of a moan was the only sound he made before tumbling from his seat to the floor.

"Professor!" Dropping my bag, I rounded his desk to find him curled into himself, his hands covering his ears.

"Fuck!" He pressed the heel of his palm to his temple.

My whole body shook with adrenaline, my heart racing in my chest. The scenario took me back to the nights when my mother would suffer horrible headaches. Not knowing what else to do, I dropped to the floor beside him. A look of agony claimed his face, his body shaking uncontrollably.

Seizure. It was a seizure.

I mentally ran through the checklist of what I remembered reading about seizures in one of my medical textbooks. Remove anything dangerous.

I pushed his chair out of the way, and as I glanced around the room, tip number two came to mind. Nabbing his suitcoat draped over the arm of a leather couch, I crumpled it into a ball and gently pushed it under his head. After that, I loosened his tie and unlatched the top two buttons of his shirt. While part of me felt strange, another part didn't feel or think, at all. I ran on pure adrenaline in that moment.

He trembled and shook, as I gingerly pushed at his shoulder to turn him on his side.

Biting my nail, I looked up at the clock to see that it had already lasted about four minutes. I slipped my hand in his, just to let him know I was there, as I'd always done with my mother.

He whispered something, and I leaned forward, trying to make out what he'd said. "Impervious," he whispered again.

Impervious? Had I heard him right?

The trembles slowed. His breathing slowed. Beads of sweat had gathered on his forehead, and his face had turned ghostly white, but it seemed the seizure had subsided.

"Professor?" I gave his hand a light squeeze, and his eyes shot open.

He jerked back, nearly cracking his head on the desk. "Don't touch me! Don't fucking touch me!" The command arrived as a growled warning, and I tumbled backward, kicking myself away from him.

"I'm sorry. I ... I just wanted to make sure you were okay."

Wearing a mask of confusion, he pushed to a sitting position and looked around. As his gaze landed on his balled-up coat, his jaw hardened. "That's a five-hundred-dollar coat crumpled on the floor," he said, tossing the jacket onto his chair. "Next time you decide to crumple something, consider using your own."

Any sympathy I may have had drained out of me right then. "Seriously? You just had a seizure in front of me, and you're worried about a little dust on your coat?"

"Welcome to my Tuesday. This is nothing new." He pushed to his feet until standing over me.

I didn't like the dynamic of him looking down on me right then, so I jumped to my feet, as well. "I guess I shouldn't have bothered to stick around, then."

"I guess you shouldn't have."

Assholeprickbastard! "Forgive me for being a decent human being."

"A decent human being would've given a man some dignity by leaving when she was *excused*." He ground the last word through his teeth.

It occurred to me then, he wasn't angry at me, per se, but perhaps a bit embarrassed. In spite of the urge to verbally duke it out with him and not back down, I softened my voice. "My apologies. I sprang into action without much thought."

"You certainly–" His jaw hardened again, the muscle ticced, as he clearly fought to restrain his words. On a sharp breath, he buttoned his shirt and adjusted his tie back into place. "A bit overboard."

With a shrug, I clasped my hands so that he wouldn't see how badly I was shaking right then. "I was just trying to make you comfortable, is all. Sir."

His eyes skated to me on the last word, his jaw shifting. "You may leave now, Miss Vespertine."

With a quiet nod, I gathered my bag. I didn't know why I felt disappointed leaving his office, aside from the fact that my plan to assist in his lab had been savagely turned down. It wasn't like I was expecting him to wrap me in a hug for sticking around through all of that.

A thank you would've been nice, though.

Chapter 22

Devryck

"Ah! Damn it!" Barletta held up his hand, shielding himself from the flashlight I shined through the bars at him. A silvery glow reflected from his eyes, giving him an unsettling appearance, one common in those infected with Noctisoma.

"Tapetum lucidum."

"What?"

"It's what makes certain animals appear to have glowing eyes." I lowered the flashlight and took a seat in the chair just outside of his cell. "Humans, of course, don't have this. But the organism is nocturnal and requires it."

With the heel of his palm, he rubbed his eyes, groaning. "I can't stand the light. It hurts."

"You no longer need it."

Lowering his hands, he stared off, a troubled look twisting up his expression. "I don't want to see the things I've been seeing lately."

"What kinds of things?" I hiked my arm over the back of the chair, already knowing what he was going to tell me.

"My son." Blinking hard, he seemed to choke back tears and cleared his throat. "The blood from his skull," he said, gesturing to his own. "He came to me last night. It was like a dream. A fucking nightmare."

"Hallucinations are common. The organism sometimes uses these images to manipulate you."

The sadness in his eyes from moments ago darkened to dread. "You mean I'm gonna be seein' my son like this again?"

"Yes. Guilt is a wonderful manipulator."

He stared off, the slow furrowing of his brow indicating the news troubled him. "You said a while back that you'd reveal the why of all this. Why me?"

"I did say that, didn't I?" I sat forward and rested my elbows on the tops of my thighs. "Perhaps it's best to revisit the story of my childhood. After all, what good is a reveal, a twist, if it has absolutely no impact."

Crossing his arms, he shook his head. "Did I wrong you, somehow?"

I let out a mirthless laugh. "Yes, Mr. Barletta. You absolutely wronged me, but we'll get to that soon enough."

"That night with corpses. Is that what messed you up? Why you took me off the streets to watch me go through this shit? You got some kind of trauma that you need to take it out someone else?"

Messed me up. Abusers had such a warped view of reality. Unamused with his accusation, I didn't bother to answer the last question. In fact, every muscle in my body fought not to reach in through the bars and strangle the life out of him right then. It was only the consolation of knowing what was coming to him that settled my thoughts. "That night would be one of many. My father had effectively found a means to scare the shit out of me, and he used that power every chance he got. Until I eventually became as dead inside as those corpses."

"Didn't you have a mother lookin' out for ya?"

"My mother died giving birth." My brother and I only had Hannah, the maid. And because she was older, and my father had no interest in fucking her, she was the only one who stayed.

A vision of Hannah gently rubbing my back during one of my episodes somehow brought to mind Lilia in my office. Her gentle movements and caring eyes. Her delicate hand in mine. There was something about her–so genuine and real.

I'd hated that she'd seen me like that, on the floor. Helpless, as the pain wracked every muscle in my body like a jolt of white-hot flames. It was as I came out of it, when her blurred out face had sharpened into view, and those blue-green eyes watched me with worry and panic, that something had shifted inside of me, rousing an inexplicable ache in my chest. Yet, all that had come to mind in that moment were the words of my father whenever I'd had an episode as a boy.

"You were always the weaker one."

"Pathetic."

"So, how did I wrong you?" Barletta's voice snapped me out of my musings.

The answer slipped on the fringes of my mind, but I refused to dip my thoughts into those dark and murky waters. Not yet. A swelling ache throbbed at my temples. Inky blackness slithered into my consciousness, and once again, I fell prey to the memories.

"Tell me who laughed at you." Caedmon sits on the edge of the bed, staring at me, as I stare out the window.

I was sent home earlier that day when a headache struck. My whole body froze with it, and I ended up pissing myself in front of my classmates. "All of them."

"Then, I'll punish them all."

I don't respond, just keep staring out the window.

"What did the voices say to you?" he prods.

I sometimes hear them when I'm locked away in that closet. Strange voices that whisper secrets. Promises of death. "I don't remember now."

In my periphery, Caedmon reaches for my hand. "You're cold."

It's only the realization that he touched my skin that breaks my staring. Not that I could feel it. I feel nothing in my hands or arms, not since the night my father struck me in the head.

I yank my arm away, repulsed by the lack of sensation. It's an unnerving thing to watch someone touch you, yet feel nothing. "I have to leave this place, Caedmon. We have to go far away from here."

"Where?"

"I don't know. Far away, where he can't hurt us anymore."

"Or perhaps you should stop inciting his anger. Every day, you test his patience, Devryck." He quickly looks away, knowing damn well that my punishments have never once fit the crime. Father has always been harsh with me. Doesn't matter what I do, how hard I try to stay on his good side. He hates me. He always has, and Caed knows it.

"I had two headaches today. Doctor Meinsh says they'll get worse."

Caed snaps his attention back toward me, that pathetic and all too familiar look of worry in his eyes. "And the spasms?"

"I couldn't move. Couldn't breathe. I thought I was dying."

His lips peel back to an angry snarl. "And, so, what's he doing about it?"

I'm the one who turns away this time. I stare out on the yard below my window, watching a hawk swoop down on a smaller bird. "There's nothing he can do. Someday, they'll get so bad my heart will stop. I don't want to die in this place. In this house." Panic washes over me, and I curl into myself, trembling as the fear grips me. "He's going to put me back in that room with the corpses again. He's going to make me sleep in there! I need to get out of here. I need out!" I rub the top of my head raw. "Death is coming for me, Caed! He's going to get me!"

"Hey." Caed wraps his arms around me, but I push out at

him, thumping the heel of my palm against his chest to break his embrace. "Shhhh. It's okay, Dev," he whispers, trying to settle me. "The next time he throws you in there, I want you to say a word. A powerful word, okay?"

I still in his embrace and breathe hard through my nose. "What word?"

"Impervious."

"Impervious?"

"Yes. It means nothing bad can hurt you. Ever. When you feel like Death is coming for you, you say that word. Death can't touch you, then."

"You're sick." Once again, the sound of Barletta's voice broke me from my memories. "That's why you're doing this. Something made you sick."

"Not something. Some*one*." I paused for a moment, wondering how much I should divulge to a complete stranger. Didn't matter, really. The man would soon succumb to infection, and all our conversations would slip into the void along with him. "I have a rare genetic disorder. It's called Voneric's Disease. It remains dormant until late in life. Unless triggered by trauma."

"The whack to your head. Your old man triggered it."

"Yes. Every day I live with the risk that it will seize up my heart and I'll go into cardiac arrest."

"If it's genetic, does that mean your brother has it, too?"

"*Had*," I corrected.

His brows flickered, and he shifted where he sat on the cot. "He's no longer alive."

"No, he isn't." As many years ago as it was, the anger still clawed inside of me, begging to be cut loose. "And no, not every child is affected by the disease. But as I said, we'll get to that soon enough. I suspect you're probably starving right now."

"I am." He eyed the dish I'd placed beside the chair when I first arrived. "I've been craving weird shit. Like ... rare meat."

"Noctisoma utilizes iron to produce the proteins that create physiological changes. Your reflective eyes, for example. It depletes the iron in your blood, and you will crave it." I removed the silver platter lid from a plate of rare steak, potatoes, and green beans that I'd had the chef at Darrigan Hall prepare for me. At the bottom of the cell bars was a small door, through which I slipped the food to him.

With a frenzied excitement, he yanked the plate toward him and lifted the thick slab of meat with both hands, consuming it like an animal. Blood dripped down his arms, the meat rare enough that it probably bordered on carrying a potential foodborne illness. Not that it mattered. Any bacterial infection he might've otherwise suffered would've been swiftly destroyed by the Noctisoma, who didn't much care for competition.

As he plowed through his dinner, I shoved a small cup of water into his cell, which he quickly swiped up and swigged to the point of an obnoxious slurp.

"Why so little to drink? I'm thirsty," he said, handing it back to me as if I had any intentions of giving him more.

"Your brain is telling you that you're thirsty."

"My fucking lips are dry as a bone." He shoveled in a forkful of potatoes, and I grimaced, watching it slide down the corners of his mouth onto his plate, from where he scooped it up again.

"Yes, I suppose they are. The parasite wants you to move toward a source of water so it can eventually kill you. In fact, if it didn't require your healthy organs to grow, it'd be perfectly content living inside of you underwater."

He paused his abhorrent eating and stared off for a moment. "Fucking hell, every time you tell me about this thing, I get more freaked out. Is this gonna be like one of those *Alien* scenes, where it pops out of my chest?"

"It won't be pretty, or pleasant, but nothing quite so theatrical as that, no."

Gaze lowered, he shook his head as he scooped up some of the green beans. "It's fucked up," he said around a mouthful of veggies. "I feel like I'm in the best shape of my life right now. Like I could run a goddamn marathon."

I shrugged. "You probably could."

"But that won't happen right?" He speared another round of green beans onto his fork, not bothering to look at me. "You don't plan to let me go after all this."

"No. I don't." Why lie to the guy, or sugarcoat the inevitable? "I need the organism growing inside of you, and I intend to harvest them when you die."

"What for?"

I rubbed my fingers together, but only the uncomfortable tingle of pressure there prickled my skin like tiny jolts of electricity. Again, I found myself thinking back to Lilia's hand in mine. How the prickling sensation had marked her gentle caress. "So that I can feel again."

"What, like you can't feel anything? At all?"

"No. It's like being trapped inside a corpse."

He snorted a laugh and shook his head, diving into his mashed potatoes again. "Must drive you nuts."

I ground my teeth while watching him, something dark twisting my guts. "It drives me."

He must've picked up on the ire in my voice, as he glanced up and rolled his shoulders back. "These worms are the cure?"

"No." I pushed up from the chair and stuffed my hands into my pockets. "Their toxins are the cure. Unfortunately, they're not easy to manufacture in a lab. It takes a fresh human body."

"Am I the first you've ... you know, infected like this?"

Gaze lowered, I paced. "No. There was another before you."

He ran his tongue over his teeth and tapped his fork against his plate. A plastic plate, after the little mishap with the bottle he'd thrown at me. "How long you think you can get away with it?"

"I suspect until I do something foolish and get caught."

"I can see you're no fool," he said with an air of disappointment. "Can I ask you a favor?"

I stopped pacing. "No."

"It's nothing big. Just some pencil and paper. I'd ... I'd like to write a letter to my sons."

Of course I wouldn't allow it, not even if I read the damn thing before mailing it off. He didn't deserve forgiveness. He didn't even deserve to ask. Yet, it might've served as a bargaining chip later. "I suppose I can accommodate this one request."

"I'd appreciate it. You know, my son has seizures. Since he was little."

"Yes. I'm aware."

He let out a shaky breath and dropped his gaze to the plate again. "You think I caused 'em?"

"I'm not his physician. I wouldn't know. However, you've certainly not made things better for him."

The silvery glint of his eyes wavered with what I imagined were tears. "You won't hurt them, too, will ya? My wife and my sons?"

"I have no reason to harm your family. I don't hurt children, like you."

He flinched and swiped at his nose. "You know, this sobriety thing? Really fucking sucks."

I waited a few more minutes, watching him shovel in the last bites of his meal.

"You gonna finish your story?" he asked, pushing the plate

back through the bars of his cell. "Still curious to know what all this has to do with me."

"Next visit," I promised, and I swiped up his plate before heading back to my office.

Chapter 23
Lilia

As I approached Emeric Hall for my entomology class, my book bag buzzed. I lifted my phone out, and seeing the academic advisor from Bee's school calling sent my brain into panic.

"Hello?"

"Miss Vespertine?"

"Yes."

"It's Janet Kemphell. Everything is okay with Bee." A flash of relief shot through me, quickly snuffed when she added, "I'm calling in regard to Bee's tuition. Do you have a moment?"

With only four minutes before class, I rounded the corner to something of a narrow alley between Emeric and Descartes Halls for privacy. "Yes."

"I'm just wondering when you might be able to send payment? The account is sixty days behind, and ... well, I don't want to have to do this, but we may need to disenroll your sister."

"Wait. What? What do you mean, sixty days? I sent a thousand dollars just a few weeks ago. Conner's payment should've put us two months ahead."

"Miss Vespertine, we've not received a payment from Mr. Doyle since June. We've tried numerous times to contact him, but he never seems to return our calls. The payment you sent covered July's tuition, but now August and September are due."

Pangs of nausea needled my gut. Bending over, I clutched my stomach, which had begun to fold into gnarled knots of shock.

"I truly hate to make this phone call, Miss Vespertine. I know how much your sister loves the school, and–"

"Please. I'm begging you, Miss Kemphell. I will get you the money." I clenched my eyes shut and breathed through my nose to keep from throwing up. "Can you give me some time?"

"I know you're doing what you can. And you've always been very timely with your half of payment. There is a low-income grant that might offer a thirty-day extension. I can certainly speak to our provost and look into that for you. Beyond that, though, you would need to make payment for the thirty days you're still behind."

"I understand. I promise I'll get you the money."

"Again, my apologies for having to make this call, Lilia. Your sister is one of our best students, and she has made great progress here."

"I appreciate your investment in her, and I will do everything I can to keep her enrolled."

"I appreciate it. We'll talk soon."

"Thank you." On those parting words, I clicked out of the call and scrolled through my contacts for Conner's number. The phone rang and rang before going straight to his voicemail. Teeth grinding, I ended the call and dialed again. And again. After the fourth try, I texted him a simple message:

Call me immediately.

Enraged, I ground my teeth as I stuffed the phone into my

pocket. Voices from the other end of the alley caught my attention, and I backed myself to the wall, alongside an arborvitae shrub. Peering around it showed Gilchrist and Spencer walking toward the alley. Once inside the shady passage between buildings, she shoved Spencer against the wall and ran her palm over the crotch of his jeans as she slammed her lips against his.

Frowning, I only just caught her leaning in to kiss him, before I flattened myself to the wall, feeling like I'd seen something forbidden. A buzz of discomfort hummed through me as I scurried back toward the front of Emeric Hall, my head trying to process whether, or not, I'd just seen some kind of messed-up hallucination. The sight of it wouldn't have shocked me near as much, if I hadn't witnessed Gilchrist pining after Professor Bramwell just a week ago.

When I glanced up, the devil himself strode up, a black, leather bag slung over his shoulder, and his gaze buried in whatever book he was reading. As the two of us converged toward the entrance, he finally peeled his attention from his reading, eyes on me as he breezed past while folding his book closed.

"Miss Vespertine," he said, the acknowledgement nearly kicking me backward onto my ass.

"Professor Bramwell," I responded, offering a respectful nod.

He disappeared inside, and I trailed after him, scurrying toward my usual seat in Gilchrist's class.

The moment I took my seat, my phone buzzed with a text from Conner.

What's up?

I choked back the urge to throw my phone against the wall as I texted back.

What the hell is going on with Bee's tuition?! Kemphell said you haven't made a payment in months!

Something came up. I planned to catch up this month, but then this shit with Angelo went down and now I'm drowning in bills.

In other words, the shady deals he had going with Angelo to make extra cash had gone awry.

You promised me! They're going to kick her out.

I told you, she doesn't need that school. She just needs more friends.

Don't do this. I am hanging on by a thread here. Can you at least make one payment?

I need a few weeks.

I need you to swear you'll make this payment. Please.

"Hey, how goes it?"

Irritated by the intrusion, I tucked my phone away and looked up to see Spencer looming over me. A flashing image of Gilchrist fondling his crotch flickered through my brain, and I shook my head, mentally batting it away.

"Good. Thanks."

"Everything okay? You looked *stressed*."

"Family issues."

With a snort, he slid into the seat beside me. "You, too?"

The frustrated bitch half of me wanted to tell him rich people problems weren't the same, but instead, I mustered as much of a smile as I could, despite the absolute chaos inside my head right then.

"Hey, wanna meet for lunch later?"

Schooling my face so as not to look entirely confused, I glanced toward Gilchrist, who stood at the lectern unpacking her computer, her eyes locked on Spencer.

How the hell was I supposed to respond without looking like the creep who'd spied on them?

"Don't you have a girlfriend?"

"Nah." He sank further in his seat and hiked his elbow up on the back of it. "But what does it matter? It's just lunch. Gotta eat, right?"

"Right."

Another glance toward Gilchrist showed her still staring up at him. It was then that Mel's words from before echoed inside my mind. *He's a manipulator.*

Not that I'd entirely take her word on who, or what, someone was, but his persistence in being around me did strike me as odd. Even if I gave him the benefit of being a nice guy, I found it a little strange.

"I think I'm going to pass this time. I've got a lot going on." Not that I wanted to be a jerk, I just wasn't in the right headspace for casual lunch conversation when my world had flipped on its ass.

While his smile wilted to a downcast expression, he nodded. "Were you able to get a meeting with my father?" he asked.

"No, I didn't bother, to be honest." Aside from thanking him for allowing me to attend the school, I really had no other reason to take up his time. I wasn't sure why Professor Gilchrist had insisted I seek him out.

Still feeling slightly bad about turning Spencer down for lunch, I sighed. The guy had consistently been decent to me, and I suspected it was my own insecurities and thoughts about guy friends in general that had me skeptical of his intentions. I hadn't planned to *avoid* making friends here, after all. "Would you consider meeting up *tomorrow* for lunch?"

His eyes lit up. "Yeah, sure. Cool."

That would at least let some of the chaos settle in my head. Because at that moment? I had no freaking clue how I was going to make up those missed payments.

"I'm just starting to get settled here, and Conner has already shit on things. Like, it doesn't matter how far away I get, the guy shits on everything." Lying in my bed back at the dorm, I stared up at the ceiling while listening to Jayda yell at her two other kids, who were apparently getting rowdy in the background.

She returned with a groan. "How desperate are you feeling right now?"

"Not enough to consider sex for money. Yet." I rolled onto my stomach and traced the yellow stitching in my quilt.

"It's not exactly *sex* for money." Her voice was lower that time, and the lack of noise in the background told me she'd cornered herself in a quiet place.

I frowned. "What are you talking about?"

"There's a website I heard about."

I fell onto my back again, slapping a hand over my forehead. "Jayda, I'm not–"

"Now, wait a second. Hear me out. It's all anonymous. You don't show your face, or anything."

Pinching the bridge of my nose, I shook my head, already knowing I had no intentions of agreeing, but I was admittedly curious. "What is it?"

"Just be open-minded, okay? Because I happen to know someone who got paid to do this."

"Your cousin?"

"No. It wasn't my cousin."

The tone of her voice told me she was hesitant to say, and I shot up in bed. "It was you! *Was* it you?"

"Look, I wouldn't suggest this, but you're in a tight spot, and I can speak from experience. The payout is worth it." The excitement in her voice had me a little more than curious, all of a sudden.

"What did you do?"

"So … just keep an open mind, okay?"

"You already said that."

"Right." She blew out a breath that rattled through the phone. "So, I softened the peach in public."

"What?"

"I paddled the pink canoe in the parking lot at Daly's Market."

"Paddled the *what*?" I shook my head, trying to decipher what the hell she was talking about. "What are you saying?"

"Damn it all, I finger-banged myself, okay?"

"You masturbated in public?"

"Yeah. And I'm not gonna lie, it was the hottest fucking thing I've ever done." She let out a nervous chuckle, as I sat daring myself to imagine her pregnant self doing something like that at Daly's Market, of all places. "You get paid by tokens, and the site includes a small fee in those tokens, so it all basically goes to you. I made *two hundred* off that video, plus tips. And I didn't even need to show my face."

Damn. Two hundred? Jayda wouldn't have lied about that. "You get paid right away?"

"Yep. The more risqué, the more you get paid. I guess some men are into pregnant women. You could totally play the schoolgirl, with your short skirt and knee-high socks."

"Jayda, I'm not showing up to class looking like Britney

Spears circa nineteen ninety-eight. This is college, for fucks sake. No one wears knee-high socks."

"Suit yourself. But I'm telling you, a young thing like you, with your toned little thighs and short skirts, would make a lot of bank."

I shook my head in a desperate bid not to seriously consider what she was suggesting. "Don't you have to verify your age, or something? I'd be outing myself with an ID."

"Not on this site. Don't know how they get away with it, but they do. Look, it's not like you're making a career out of it, Lilia. A few videos, and you could be back on track with tuition. Shit, they might like the schoolgirl thing and you could make tuition with a *single* video."

God, I hated the way she made it sound so damn easy and enticing. That all my problems could potentially be solved in a single conversation with her. "Do I have to make any sounds?"

"They just like the wet sounds."

"Well, this just keeps getting worse." I groaned, and she shushed me.

"You don't have to moan, or anything. But maybe do it where other people are talking, so they know it's in public."

Covering my eyes with a palm, I huffed. "This is just … wrong."

"Look, Conner is an asshole. He's never gonna be there for you and Bee, okay? And now that he's hooked up with Angelo? Any hope of decency is gone. You gotta figure shit out yourself, Lilia. Remember when I said *be audacious*? Don't let a man take away this dream. Do whatever the fuck you gotta do to keep it."

She was right, damn it. Relying on Conner was like praying for snow in Hell. As decent as the guy might've been, he just wasn't cut out for dad shit. Uprooting Bee and throwing her into the same space as Angelo, and whatever criminal shit he had going on, would've been detrimental. I needed to take the reins on things. To figure things out myself. When she graduated, it'd be on her, but until then, I needed to step up. "How is it possible for me to hate and love you at the same time?"

Jayda chuckled. "You love me more than you hate me."

"True." I blew out a resigned breath and glanced around my room, wishing I could've just done the video there. But as Jayda had said–the more risqué, the more money, and I couldn't think of anything more risqué than in class. "Okay, I got my midnight lab coming up, so I need to let you go."

"Take care of yourself. And let me know if you decide to do it."

"I will." The moment I hung up the phone, I thumped my palm to my forehead and shot Jayda a quick text.

I forgot to ask the name of the site?

VoyeurBait.

Even the name has to be creepy right?

Ignore the name

I slipped out of bed, and on an exasperated sigh, I stared out the window at the courtyard below. Students bustled about, looking as carefree as birds hopping to and fro. I couldn't help but wonder if any of them were trying to wrap their heads around some massive roadblock in life right then, or were actual classes their only source of stress?

Why the hell does my life have to be such a mess all the time?

As I scanned over the grounds, I caught sight of something off in the distance. Squinting, I leaned forward, peering through the window toward the oak between Shanlot Hall and the clock tower.

A figure cloaked in a long cape and what looked very much like a plague doctor's mask.

A sharp breath flew out of me, as I stumbled backward, tripping over my desk chair, and landed with a hard thud on my ass. Hot needles of pain shot up my spine, and I flinched, pushing to my feet. When I stared out the window again, I saw nothing there. Only students walking about.

Great. Not only is my life a shit show, but I'm still seeing things that don't exist.

With a huff, I fell onto my bed and rested my head against my palms.

My phone screen lit up with a text from Bee.

Hey, is everything okay? I tried to buy snacks with my food pass earlier and it says it was reduced.

I wanted to cry right then.

Everything is fine. Just a little confusion with your account, is all. The reduction is temporary.

It's fine, Lil. I don't need to be eating snacks between meals anyway. Just wanted make sure all was okay.

I wanted to tell her it wasn't. That I was on the verge of tears trying to figure out what to do. Instead, I texted back:

No worries, all is great!

If you and Conner are having a hard time right now, I can get a job. I'm going to be seventeen, you know?

Her offer would've been wonderful, but I didn't have the

heart to remind her of the last job she'd taken a few months back, which had swiftly come to an end when she'd had one of her episodes and screamed at one of the patrons. She'd thrown a milkshake in the woman's face, ultimately ending her very short stint at the ice cream shop.

Not that I was free from having suffered episodes myself, but mine, so far, hadn't resulted in attacking anyone.

No need. Just a temporary issue.

Okay! How's Dracadia?

It's beautiful. Like Hogwarts without the wands.

Ah cool. Can't wait to see you at Christmas.

Same. Love you.

Love you too.

Fuck. I was going to do it, wasn't I? I was really going to film myself in class.

But when?

Lab would be perfect. The TA usually lectured for the first twenty minutes of class, and we all had our own benches with cupboards at either side. Mine was the back bench, which meant no one would see me. Not unless Spencer got snoopy, all of a sudden.

The thought made my stomach curl.

Two hundred dollars, Lilia. Two hundred that could reduce the two thousand still owed.

The decision slowly cemented itself in my head. I was really going to do it.

Chapter 24
Devryck

With gloved hands, I lifted Barletta's tongue. "Superior and inferior lip, as well as sublingual papilla, demonstrates vonyxsis," I dictated into my phone. "Dentition is otherwise normal. Bilateral scleral icterus. Bilateral tapetum lucidum. Dry mucous membranes." I placed my stethoscope against his back, listening for a moment, then moved it higher and across his spine to the other side. "Upper airway sounds are heard diffusely across all lung fields. Slight rattling, but non-productive cough. End dictation."

"Dictation ended," the robotic feminine voice answered back.

A horrific, yet distinct odor clung to the air–one reminiscent of death—which was typical in the infected. I didn't have much explanation for it, seeing as humans weren't the parasite's natural host. Perhaps it served a purpose in its other victims.

"What's vonyxsis?" Barletta asked, sitting calmly on his cot.

I turned his arm over, to a skinny, black map of veins in his wrist.

"That can't be good. Fuck, what's happenin?" He quickly

turned his head away and coughed, shooting bright red spittle onto the concrete. "I'm so thirsty. I need water."

"The amount of water I give you throughout the day is enough. I told you what's happening, Mr. Barletta. These are all normal progressions of infection."

"It's not enough water. I'm getting cramps at night. Hallucinating. Shit's worse than detox."

It had only just begun.

I didn't turn my back on him as I packed up my equipment and made my way toward the cell door.

While he didn't seem to have much motivation for escape right then, that would inevitably change. Physical exams would become wrestling matches soon enough. Thankfully, guilt kept him in check for the most part, and it was a weakness I intended to play off for as long as his conscience mattered to him.

But it'd soon be a fleeting emotion.

"You're not leavin', are ya?" He ran his hand through his hair and frowned when he lowered his arm to see a clump of strands in his palm. Throat bobbing with a gulp, he tossed it away. "It's so fuckin' ... quiet down here. I can't stand the quiet."

"I've some papers to grade."

"Wait." He lurched forward. "You were supposed to tell me some more of your story. Your childhood. Remember?"

I actually needed to get back to the lab, but I responded, "Very well."

"You said, if the seizures reach your heart, you'll have a heart attack. That ever happened?"

"Not quite cardiac arrest, no. But I did have quite a scare once." I closed my eyes on the memory of that fateful day–the one that forever changed the course of my life.

"Her tits are sheer perfection," Caedmon says with an air of awe in his voice, from where he sits crouched inside a small linen

closet. "I cannot believe she hides them beneath those ugly fucking sweaters she wears."

The closet adjacent to the women's staff locker room holds a small carving–an eyeball hole that peers in at the perfect angle on of one of the staff showers. Story goes, some screwball maintenance guy put the hole there two years ago and got caught jacking off. He apparently never told anyone about the hole, though. Not that I'd ever personally peered through it. Still can't stand closets. Not since that night.

Von Naerick Academy is a small prep school affiliated with our father's alma mater, Dracadia University. Our family name affords us the kind of pardon few other students are offered, and the two of us exploit it to the utmost degree. At seventeen, we've gone through five other prep schools, each one offering a quiet exit to keep from marring our record. One more, and my father will probably have us sent off to some drug cartel farm in the heart of Mexico.

The hole, as everyone calls it, is one act of insubordination we can't pass up, though. Caedmon and I are like tour guides for the depraved, leading small groups of underclassmen to our secret peep show. My brother has seen damn near every female teacher's tits and ass, and is something of a self-professed expert on the topic.

One of the kids pushes at Caedmon for a peek, and with a smirk, I shake my head.

Not a beat later, my brother wails him in the face with his fist. The poor kid flies backward onto the concrete floor, groaning. Blood trickles from what will probably be a split lip.

"Next one who pushes, gets knocked out. Asshole." With a nod toward the group, he asks, "Who's next?"

Three boys cluster around him, but Caedmon chooses one. I stay in the hallway of the tunnel to keep a lookout and light up a smoke, waiting for each member of the group to get their peek. Fifteen minutes later, the boys file out, some dragging their feet with disappointment. Probably didn't get much of a look, seeing as the teachers only shower for so long.

Once the boys have cleared out and begun their trek back to our dorms, Caedmon exits the closet, counting cash.

"Fifty bucks." He hands off twenty five of it to me, and taking another drag of my smoke, I stuff the cash into my pocket. It's not like either of us needs the cash, just gives us something to do. "Aren't you even the least bit curious, Devryck?" He snags the cigarette from my fingers and takes a long drag.

"Of course I am. Not even a nice pair of tits is worth it, though." Besides, I don't need to watch them through a peephole. I'd already gotten intimate with Miss Chandler's tits in the boathouse after row practice. The same day she confessed to wanting a threesome with my brother.

"He really fucked you up."

"Anyway, we better head back. Caesar said, if I'm late to first hour again, he's going to sever my hand and send the bones home to Father."

Caesar is the guard Father hired to keep an eye on the two of us. Not a bodyguard, of course. The asshole is a former mafia soldier who only cares about his own ass. His only job is to make sure Caedmon and I stay out of trouble. Or, rather, out of Father's hair.

"A man after our own father's heart." Caedmon grabs the knob of the closet to close the door, when a clacking sound, like shoes on concrete, echoes down the hall.

The two of us dart toward the curve in the hallway, toward the sound, and flatten ourselves against the wall, peering around the corner of it into another corridor.

Naked lightbulbs in rusty cages illuminate the long passage down which two figures stride toward us. Men we've never seen before, but both of them wear black suits, and in each of their hands is a gun.

"C'mon!" I whisper-yell to Caedmon, and yank him back.

The door at the end of the hall is locked as always, a dead end, so we run in the other direction, back toward the closet.

The sound of footfalls grows louder. Any moment, the men will turn the corner and find us. Who knows who the hell they are, or what they want, but them finding us down here isn't a good idea, either way.

At a hard yank of my arm, I turn to see Caedmon pulling me toward the closet.

I shake my head. I can't. I won't. "No! No!"

"We have nowhere to go, Devryck. C'mon!"

The footsteps close in on the corner.

Caedmon slaps his hand over my mouth and drags me into the closet with him. Panic stirs in my gut, winding upward like a tornado to my chest. I wheeze behind his hand for a breath, the small bit of air through my nose not nearly enough. Light thins as he closes the door, still holding me against him.

Until we're bathed in darkness.

"I'm right here, Devryck," he whispers in my ear. "Focus on my voice."

Through shaky breaths, I close my eyes, my whole body trembling and stiff. The vague grip of his hand breaches the numbness that has my arms feeling ice cold and thick.

"You're going to be okay. Nothing is going to happen. Focus on my voice, Dev."

A stabbing pain strikes my skull, and I throw my hands up, knocking his arm away. I collapse to my knees. Warmth trickles down my thighs and pools onto the floor, leaking beneath the crack in the door. My muscles harden, a thousand tiny knots pulling beneath my skin.

Light blasts into the closet, and through a blur in my eyes, I stare up at both men. A blackness slinks in from the fringes, threatening to pull me under. Something jostles my body.

"Leave him alone!" Caedmon cries out.

A dark nightmare swallows me whole.

"He pissed himself!" an unfamiliar voice growls. "Take the other!"

An intense pain strikes my muscles, and I collapse to the floor into a wet puddle. Through a haze, I watch one of the men drag Caedmon away.

Hauled off by an arm to his throat, my brother stares back at me, eyes wide with fear. "You can't leave him! He's going to die! He'll die!"

Impervious.

I open my mouth to scream the word. Nothing comes out.

"Impervious!" I finally cry out. "Impervious."

Shoes step into view, and its then I realize the second man is standing over me. For a moment, I think he's gonna drag me off with my brother. Instead, he draws back his fist and hammers it into my cheek, setting off an explosion of light that flares at the back of my eyes, the impact rattling my teeth.

My brother disappears behind a pitch black shield.

"What's that mean? *Impervious*?" Barletta's question ripped me out of the memory, dragging me back into the present.

"Impenetrable, essentially."

"Who were they? Who took your brother?"

"At the time, I didn't know." I'd later learned they were ordered to take one of us. And because I'd pissed myself, they'd opted to take my brother.

"What happened to your brother?"

"We'll save that bit for next time."

Chapter 25

Lilia

My pulse throbbed in my ear, as I climbed off the Nocticadia bus to Emeric Tower. While Spencer prattled on beside me, talking about some campus event coming up, I ignored him, my mind glued to the visual of me touching myself in public.

What the hell was I about to do?

I'd touched myself before, but only a couple times, and never outside of piles of blankets and pillows. I'd always been too nervous of Conner walking in on me, so the sessions had always been quick, and rarely ever satisfying.

Earlier, I'd stumbled upon some blog offering tips for how to create one of the videos without drawing a lot of attention. Tips for masturbating in public–that was what my life had become.

The blog had advised not wearing underwear beneath a skirt, to avoid the awkward task of having to pull them down or push them aside while filming. So, I chose a skirt that reached my knees and spent an hour walking around my room while trying to banish the absolutely unnatural vulnerability of having my nether region uncovered. I hated the feeling of being naked. Even after showers, I felt the need to dress quickly, so the cool air breezing up my skirt as I walked to class sent a chill up the back of my neck.

The bad kind of chill.

We made our way into the lab, and I scurried to my desk, donning my lab coat, as usual. My mind wound over how to logistically carry out the task, and I frowned, trying to imagine holding the camera between my legs with one hand.

Two hundred dollars. Two hundred dollars. The easiest two hundred dollars you'll ever make.

My whole body trembled as I settled onto my stool and spread my knees apart in the little alcove cut into the desk. Thankfully, drawers boxed in either side of me, and in as subtle a movement as I could muster, I removed my camera, while the other students took their seats, and glanced down to press the camera app. After shifting it to video, I snagged a glimpse of Spencer quickly turning away.

Please don't let him watch me the whole time.

It was bad enough thinking about doing the unthinkable in the middle of class. But to have Spencer's eyes on me the whole time would make it absolutely miserable. In an effort to keep with the school girl theme Jayda had mentioned, I'd worn my gray plaid skirt that fanned out at the hem.

When Ross finally arrived, and all of the students had settled in, my pulse hammered harder. The worst part was over–showing up to class without underwear. According to the website, all I had to do was record for two minutes.

Two minutes, one hundred twenty seconds, two hundred dollars, I reminded myself.

Exhaling a shaky breath, I pressed play and positioned the camera between my thighs, holding it there. As Ross launched into his lecture, I swallowed a gulp, breathing hard through my nose.

C'mon, Lilia. Two minutes.

Camera lodged between my knees, I assured it was positioned correctly, and pushed it closer, up my thighs. From the bottle clipped to my bag beside me, I took a quick squirt of hand sanitizer and cleaned my hands as thoroughly as possible. Then, resting one arm against the tabletop, I slid my other hand up my skirt, wincing when my fingers met my bare flesh.

Oh, God. I can't believe I'm doing this.

One deep breath, and I moved my finger up and down my seam, my thigh muscles clenching on contact. Swallowing a gulp, I kept my eyes on Ross, who went on, giving a recap of last week's lab, and as he talked, I kept on with the gentle strokes. Up and down. Up and down. Acclimating myself to the task.

Thirty seconds down.

My mind scrambled to process what the hell I was doing, and when it finally caught up to reality, something shifted inside of me. A slippery wetness slid across my fingertips. In the dull black benchtop, a face came to mind. Copper eyes. Deep voice. Stern brows.

"My apologies for interrupting."

My gaze snapped toward the front of the room, where Professor Bramwell strode in like a dark knight, in his black shirt and slacks beneath a stark, white lab coat.

A tickle low in my stomach had me shifting in my seat, as he took his place at the front of the room. I pulled my hand away from my sensitive flesh, resting my soaked finger against my inner thigh, where I attempted to wipe the fluid away.

"I'm seeing a slight reduction in larvae, and I believe the issue is that you're squeezing the forceps too hard when you transport the adult worms to the tank."

As he went on to describe how to delicately handle the parasite, I watched his hand movements, focusing on his fingers and tuning out the topic. They were the perfect length. Not too thin, but not too thick, either. Perfect enough to imagine them buried inside of me.

Oh, God, stop.

Without much thought, I found myself mindlessly

brushing my finger over my seam again. Unlike earlier, when Ross had lectured, I couldn't look away from Professor Bramwell. His deep voice caressed my ear, sending a shiver across the back of my neck. I kept my eyes locked on those hands as he spoke and imagined rough palms over my skin.

Before I could stop myself, the fantasy took root in my mind, and I plunged my finger in and out of me. A tenacious need curled in my belly. Muscles stiffened.

My thighs shook, as he continued to address the class, and I lost myself in the vivid fantasy of him fingerfucking me. A glance around the room showed no one, not even nosy Spencer, looking at me.

Once I could get past the reality of what I was doing, and accepted it? Contrary to my initial thoughts, it was thrilling, the game of quietly bringing myself to climax in a room full of people.

I panted as I focused on Bramwell with enough intensity I noticed the slight scar at his neck, peeking up from his collar. My fingers plundered with greed, so wet that the fluids leaked down my thighs.

My muscles tightened. Tighter.

Bramwell's eyes landed on me then.

I sucked in my bottom lip, panting hard through my nose, trying to keep a poker face while my body shook in chaos. A cramping ache seized my hand where it was bent at an odd angle, and I fought to keep the upper part of my arm from moving while my fingers went to town.

An insatiable need to climax coiled low in my stomach.

I needed it.

The tension inside of me wound so tight, the phone slipped.

En route to the floor, it smacked one of the drawer handles with a clattering *thwack* that echoed through the room, before it bounced out of reach.

A zap of horror shot through me, and I scrambled from my seat to pick it up.

In my panic, I didn't notice the lecture had quieted, and Ross had taken over again, until shiny, black shoes stepped into my periphery and I followed the length of the black slacks upward to find Professor Bramwell's disapproving stare. My eyes shot to the phone, still recording, and I prayed he wouldn't look down.

I recalled Spencer's words on the first day, how he didn't like to be recorded and would confiscate the phone, if he found evidence of it. As a distraction, I held that scornful gaze far longer than I wanted to.

Please don't look.

My heart caught in my throat when he glanced down at it.

I bent further to swipe it up, but not before he snatched it first.

The blood drained from my face. *No, no, no. Please!*

While Ross continued to speak to the class, who didn't seem to notice the chaotic scene going on at the back corner, Professor Bramwell leaned into me.

The feel of him being so close, his delicious cologne snaking its way down my throat, and his warm cinnamon breath against my cheek, shot my pulse into a frenzy. "Tell me you aren't recording my classes, Miss Vespertine." He spoke low, but the depth of his voice tickled my senses.

Swallowing past the dryness in my throat, I shook my head. "I'm not," I whispered.

"The NDA you signed gives me permission to confiscate your phone, if I suspect that you are."

Alarms blared inside my head as the scene played out like a terrifying nightmare. "Please don't."

"Then, you will delete whatever you were recording in front of me. Right now."

A quick glance at Spencer showed him staring over his shoulder at the two of us, a quizzical frown wrinkling his face.

"And if you confiscate it? What will you do? Delete it yourself?"

"I'm not legally allowed to look through your phone, Miss Vespertine." He leaned in even closer, and God help me, it took the willpower of a freaking nun not to turn and confirm how close his lips were to mine. "That would be an invasion of privacy. Grounds for consequences."

Gaze glued to the black benchtop, I breathed through my nose to stifle the shaky panting breaths clogging my throat. "But you would still ask me to delete the recording after?"

"I would be more inclined to trust you to do it yourself, if you were willing to turn over your phone. You're either guilty, or you're not."

I didn't have much choice. If I deleted it in front of him, he'd surely see the video of my pussy, right in his face. No doubt, I'd get kicked out of his class, and possibly the university. If I allowed him to take the phone, there was a chance he'd see it, anyway, but then he'd have to admit to having watched it. It boiled down to confessing what I'd done, or playing into the lie.

"Take it. I wasn't recording intentionally. I dropped my phone and the record button accidentally went off. But if you don't believe me, you're welcome to take my phone." Damn near sweating, I waited for the guy to call my bluff and ask, if it was so innocent, why not just show him?

Straightening, he stood over me in that authoritative stance of his, jaw flexing as if he were grinding his teeth right then. "Very well. I'll return it at the end of the lab."

The moment he walked away, I let out a shaky breath and returned to my seat.

Stupid. Stupid. Stupid!

As if life couldn't get any shittier, I faced the possibility that my phone wouldn't have locked right away and he'd watch the mortifying video, and of course, not say a word about it. Humiliation flared in my cheeks, and I wanted to collapse with the exhaustion of having to stress about that on top of everything else. Would he search for a reason to fail me? Or say to hell with invasion of privacy and view it, anyway, then turn me in for indecency?

Either way, my chances of finding out more about his research had just slipped through my hands.

Literally.

Another glance toward Spencer showed him flicking his brow, as if to ask what had happened. With a subtle shake of my head, I turned away from him, my eyes burning with tears while anger rose up into my throat. He wouldn't have understood. None of them understood the desperation. Especially not Bramwell. I hated their perfect, little, privileged lives, where all they had to think about was what designer purse to pair with their outfit the next day.

Stop it, Lilia, my head chided. *Just stop it.*

I reluctantly dragged my attention back to Ross, desperate for distraction, but the monotony of his lecture only threw me back into the visuals of Bramwell watching what I'd done. All he'd have had to do was tap the screen to keep it from locking within that first two minutes. Would he have bothered? The questions battering my skull were endless.

My only saving grace might've been the man's reputation. If the rumor behind the scars I saw on his neck were true, then surely he would never risk the accusation of another scandal with a student.

Chapter 26

Devryck

I carried the phone down into the lower level lab, staring at the brightly-lit screen. The moment it dimmed, I touched the space between icons to keep it from locking. Fuck invasion of privacy. I'd already trusted people attempting to steal my research twice, and I'd be damned if I'd let some newly-minted adolescent attempt the same. The fact she had such in-depth knowledge of the organism already put her on my radar, but to have detailed its clinical manifestation in such depth sent up a red flag where her intentions were concerned.

I reached my office in the lower lab, where Lippincott had so kindly removed all of the cameras. Once there, I clicked on the photo icon, and the image in the small preview window had me frowning. In the tiny corner square, the background of which was mostly dark, I could just make out what looked like her hand beneath the hem of her skirt.

Fuck.

I tossed the phone onto the bench and stepped back, staring down at it.

I was wrong. So very wrong.

Don't do it.

I wanted to say it was the bullshit story of needing to know if she'd recorded my class, but that was a lie. The infuriating truth was, I needed to see if she'd had the balls to do something so bold and outrageous right in front of me.

Rubbing the back of my neck, I paced beside the desk.

Why? Why look, when I had a perfectly good idea of what was on that video?

The screen dimmed, and I lurched to keep it from locking me out. The moment I tapped the screen, it sent the video into motion.

In the background, I could only just pick up the mumbled voice of Ross. The camera seemed to be positioned between her knees, given the short length of her thighs and the hem of her skirt at the top of the viewing screen.

An unrelenting ache twisted in my stomach, and I wanted to say it was disgust churning there, but I knew better. A long-slumbering and vile greed throbbed in my groin.

The camera slid closer toward the dark depths beneath her skirt, and the moment she peeled back the hem, allowing some light, my knees damned near buckled. Her pussy arrived in perfect view, shaved clean of every hair, and when she pressed two fingers against her folds, opening herself up, I bit my knuckles while staring down at that beautiful, pink shell.

Fuck me.

Fuck. Me.

At first, she only toyed with her seam, tickling the tiny pearl of flesh that had the tips of my fingers tingling.

"My apologies for interrupting," I heard myself say in the background, and her thigh twitched, making the view jump.

All at once, she stopped, her finger resting on her thigh, where I watched her wipe away the glisten on her skin.

Stop. Stop it now, you crazy fuck.

After all, I'd been embroiled in enough scandals throughout my life. The last, involving a student, hadn't even warranted the reputation I'd earned. I'd never touched her, never felt the slightest inclination, and yet, I'd been made out as some kind of predator. Thankfully, a complete lack of evidence and a fairly solid alibi had cleared my name, but I swore I'd never get tangled in a mess like that again. Not when my research was on the verge of greatness. Not when this dreary stretch of failures I'd been living was about to take flight into a whole other stratosphere of success.

Just as I reached to turn off the video, she moved her hand again. I froze, watching her finger tease that mouthwatering bit of flesh.

Eyes screwed shut, I shook my head. *Don't do this.* The girl had to be at least twelve, maybe thirteen years younger than me. A woman, but young.

And a student, for fucks sake.

A lewd, wet sound, like ASMR porn had me opening my eyes, to see two of her fingers disappearing up inside of her, my voice still prattling on in the background. In and out, she pumped those wet digits, while I unwittingly gave my lecture.

Again, I bit my knuckles, damn near gnawing them to keep from taking hold of the painful erection blooming behind my zipper. I couldn't take it anymore.

I paused the video and swiped out of the app altogether.

A ravenous hunger shook my muscles. In all the years I'd taught–as a TA in grad school, a resident in medical school, and as a professor—I'd never felt such sexual temptation. Ever. I'd been boldly propositioned by students, and endured their flirtations, but I'd always been very adept at ignoring it all. I'd never had any interest in my students, not even the ones who'd shown up to class wearing makeup and tight, revealing clothes, making eyes at me and leaving gifts. One even left a scrap of paper with a note to meet her in the library at a certain time.

Beautiful girls with money and bright futures, and yet, I'd never once taken the bait.

I wasn't stupid enough to destroy my reputation over some silly schoolgirl fascination. Not even when that fascination had bordered on a strange obsession, as was the case with Jenny Harrick.

But it was the audacity of this girl that crawled beneath my skin. The way she sat in my class with her wild hair that reminded me of autumn leaves, her mouthy comebacks, and those eyes. Bold, aquamarine eyes that constantly challenged me. Eyes I imagined were staring straight at me while she fingered herself in my class.

I should've been furious with her, but it was the most exciting fucking thing I'd ever seen. Perhaps an effect of the last injection I'd taken.

I'd thought the sexual urges had declined over time, seeing as I'd lost interest with Loretta so quickly. Yet, clearly they hadn't.

In fact, I dared say it'd gotten worse.

The light on her screen dimmed again, and I swiped it up, keeping it from locking. On a whim of absolute adrenaline, I sent the video to my phone, then clicked on her texts and deleted it permanently. While there, I saw a couple of text threads–one to someone named Conner.

I clicked on the thread, reading through her most recent conversation. All I could gather was that Conner owed some money for someone named Bee's tuition. Whether he was her boyfriend, or husband, I couldn't tell. There were no other texts prior to that, as if she'd erased them.

The second thread was to someone named Jayda, regarding a website named VoyeurBait. Frowning, I punched the address into my phone in incognito mode, and was greeted by a video of a woman masturbating at a library. The header on the page read: *Easy Money! Submit your videos and get paid!*

It occurred to me right then that she'd made the video for cash. I clicked back to her texts with Conner, and suddenly, the story came together in my head. It seemed whoever he was had screwed her out of much-needed money.

She wasn't into public gratification by nature, from the looks of it, as I perused boring campus shots on her camera, but only out of desperation.

A flash of her wet fingers plunging into her pussy slid into my thoughts like a poisonous vapor that quickly evaporated, leaving me sick and drunk. The fact she'd seemed to enjoy her little assignment sent a shiver down my spine.

A wiser man would've kicked her out of his class and avoided the inevitable headache that was sure to follow.

I'd certainly never professed to be the wisest.

Before the end of the hour, I returned to the lab where I found Ms. Vespertine sitting at her bench, well-composed, looking completely innocent with her bright doe eyes and cupid bow lips. As I approached, my gaze caught on her legs, and I winced at the visual of them flexed around the phone camera. Fucking hell, how could I ever look at the girl again after that video.

I was grateful it hadn't shown her face in the throes of all that, or I'd have lost all composure.

I handed off the phone, which had long since locked.

Gaze lowered, she didn't bother to look at me as she accepted the device. It should've made me feel sympathetic toward her, but the bastard in me found her humiliation utterly enthralling.

"I trust you'll delete whatever you recorded in my class."

For a moment, she stared down at her phone, then lifted her gaze to mine. The way her eyes studied me, as if she knew I'd watched it, only hardened my cold expression. I'd learned from an early age to uphold the face of a liar in front of those far more powerful than a crafty young girl. I waited to see if she had the balls to challenge me.

Instead, she tucked her phone away, gaze never wavering. "Of course, Professor."

Damn her.

Damn that innocent face and those cherry blossom lips she sat nibbling on that probably *tasted* like cherries.

Without another word, she gathered up her books and left.

Chapter 27

Lilia

My finger hovered over the *submit* button. *No going back after this.*

Damn it.

Damn it!

I hated that this was the easiest solution for me. That I had backed myself into a corner, by being so naive as to think Conner gave a shit about my sister. Or me, for that matter. Jayda was right, though. It was time to stop living under the shadow of men. Even if I had to resort to sex work, it was better than being chained.

Be audacious, Lilia.

Ugh. I wasn't, though. I was shy and quiet, and entirely uncomfortable when it came to sex.

But I was desperate, too.

A text from Bee popped up, startling me enough, the phone slipped from my fingers, but I caught it before it hit the floor.

And in doing so, I unintentionally clicked the *submit* button.

My heart thudded in my chest.

In that split second, I changed my mind, and I scrambled to close out of the app before it was too late.

But it *was* too late.

No. *No!*

I fell onto the edge of my bed and doubled over, my stomach twisting with needling pangs of nausea.

Shit. *Shit!* I'd never done anything like that in my whole life. Had never sent so much as a nude to a boyfriend, not that I'd had many of those in my life.

"No, no, no."

A ding drew my attention to my dropped phone, which lit up my dark dorm room. *Your video has been successfully uploaded! Get ready to get paid!*

"No. God, please. No!" I damn near dove for it and clicked onto the website, searching for a delete button. There was nothing.

No way to undo what I'd done.

Another notification popped up. One view. Ten views. Thirty views. Fifty views.

No!

Why was there no way to delete!

I scrolled down to the bottom of the page, where I found an email address for a removal request. With shaking hands, I typed out a plea to have my video promptly removed from the site and clicked send. Tears welled in my eyes as I watched the views climb higher and higher with every passing minute. I clicked on the video in my photos, and with teeth grinding in anger, I deleted it.

The pangs of sickness in my gut twisted again, and closing out of the image app, I checked the text that Bee had sent:

> I just wanted to tell you how much I appreciate you and all you do for me. That's all. Love you.

Not even her sweet words could erase the agony burning a hole in my chest right then, though. I placed the phone on my desk and curled up into myself on my bed. I closed my eyes over tears.

A quick check of my email showed no one had responded yet. Ten minutes later, I checked again. Nothing.

By morning, those views would be at a sickening level. It was entirely possible that my professor had been one of the many to watch it, though he didn't offer a shred of insight when he'd handed me back the phone. His face had remained as stoic as ever, completely unreadable. And now? Who knew how many were watching it?

Through a black void, an incessant beep rattled inside my head. I opened my eyes to weak rays of sunlight streaming in through my window, and the first thought to pop in my head was that video. I scrambled for my phone, my stomach instantly twisted in knots all over again. Overnight, it'd reached five thousand views. My account showed eight-hundred and sixty-seven dollars in tokens.

Not that I cared about the money.

I checked my email to find a new message from VoyeurBait:

Dear CollegeChick20,

Unfortunately, because you've already begun to earn tokens on this video, we cannot delete it.

Thanks for getting in touch,

Tony B.

A sharp cold filled my chest as I stared down at the email. The screen lit up with a text from Jayda.

So did you do it?

I left her unread and dashed toward the bathroom, just making it in time to expel last night's dinner into the toilet. Acids burned my throat as I wiped away the last bits of vomit, and I undressed for a quick shower, eyes burning with new tears. Why I cried about it didn't make a whole lot of sense, seeing as I'd done it to myself. I just hated feeling helpless, was all. Not even the prospect of earning all that money was worth knowing strangers had watched me touch myself. I didn't shame those who did it, like Jayda. I was glad she'd found a way to make extra cash for her family, and I didn't think any less of her for it. But it wasn't for me. I'd never been extroverted like that, so why I thought I could've posted something so personal and intimate without beating myself up for it was a mystery I'd never untangle.

In the warmth of the shower, I tried to think about Bee, and how the money would allow her to stay in school. She could go back to her regular lunch pass, instead of the reduced one. But the only visual I could summon was a cluster of faceless voyeurs watching it. Doing God knew what as they did.

Once finished showering, I dressed quickly. I didn't bother to look at the views before setting out for my next class.

Chapter 28

Devryck

Curiosity gnawed at me.

I should've been reviewing student journals, and studying their observations of the larval stages. Instead, I found myself scrolling through the new videos posted on the Voyeur site. Page after page of men and women masturbating in public. It wasn't until I reached the bottom of the third page that I stumbled upon the familiar thumbnail image, posted by a CollegeChick20.

I clicked on the free preview.

Just like the few times I'd watched it on my phone the night before, my body hardened at the sight of her slender thighs. I scrolled down to find six thousand viewers had already watched the same video. Teeth grinding, I searched the site for a takedown link, only finding some lame fucking email address that likely wouldn't result in a damn thing.

I swiped out of the app and pulled up the number to my lawyer. Not only was he the best in the country, he happened to be a fellow Rook, so anything I asked of him, he would carry out immediately.

And I wanted that video taken down, like, yesterday.

It wasn't just about the fact that she'd posted a video of my class online, as much as I wanted to believe such a pathetic excuse, though that certainly pissed me off, as well.

No, there was a whole fucked-up psychology going on inside my head right then that I had no intentions of trying to untangle.

Griffin answered on the third ring. "Devryck! So good to hear from you. What's going on?"

"I need a favor." Bane jumped up onto my desk and strutted in front of me for a pet. In spite of the irritation tensing my muscles, I carefully stroked a hand down his back, willing myself not to grab a fistful of fur.

"Anything."

At the risk of losing my temper and taking it out on the cat, I scooped Bane up and set him down on the floor, giving a light pat to his flank. "There's a website called VoyeurBait. A video was posted under the name CollegeChick20. I need it taken down. Immediately."

"Is this a student of yours?"

"Does it matter?"

"No. Of course not. I'll track down the owner and send a notice right away."

Only some of the knots in my gut unraveled. Whatever the hell was wrong with me right then, I'd work it out after the video had been taken down. I just needed it off that fucking site. "I appreciate it. And if I can return the favor, please let me know."

"I will. Keep an eye out for a follow-up call."

"Of course." I hung up, finger tapping against my desk as I watched the views climb. Imagining every *ding* to be some asshole, sitting slack-jawed and stroking his dick while watching her, had my muscles bunched with rage. I threw my glass across the room, and it crashed on impact against my bookshelf. That lying little shit had posted the video anyway, and I'd be damned if I'd let a bunch of perverted fucks watch her like that.

Ungrateful little pricks who only saw her as a set of toned

legs and pussy. They had no idea the girl was brilliant and witty. Too damn smart for her age.

Too damn beautiful to be seen as something so simple and entertaining.

Not even fifteen minutes later, Griffin called me back.

"Spoke to a guy named Tony. Says he'll take it down in the next ten minutes. I told him if it's not gone in ten minutes, his whole fucking operation would be taken down by the end of the day." It wasn't a bluff. Griffin was powerful enough, had the right connections to make things like that happen. He'd once taken down a darknet site on behalf of a client in a matter of minutes–a task the FBI had failed to accomplish for months. Honestly, it wouldn't have surprised me if the guy had ties to Anonymous, the way he so swiftly got shit done.

"I appreciate your diligence. And again, let me know if there's anything I can do in return."

"You've always been a wonderful ally." I'd assisted him with a few cases where bodies had to be exhumed, resulting in his favor in court. "It's my pleasure to help."

At precisely ten minutes later, I refreshed the site.

The video was no longer there.

Smiling, I eased back in my seat. If she was that desperate for money, she'd have to find another way of getting it. I refused to let a whole population of swinging dicks ogle her. I'd fuck over every person who ever posted there and burn the site down before I'd let that happen.

My head couldn't leave it alone.

The visuals of men getting off to her spun through my unsettled brain like a wicked web, and my hands balled into tight fists at my sides. So caught up in the thought, I didn't catch Barletta's question at first.

"Professor? Is this fuckin' normal?"

I snapped my attention to where he hunched over himself, pants pooled at his ankles. A moment ago he'd been sitting on his cot, but instead he faced the wall, his arm jerking with abrupt movement. The telling sound of slapping skin, coupled with his hearty grunts, confirmed what I already knew.

Clearing my throat, I turned away. "Yes. Sexual urges heighten during infection." Damn the stench on the air that'd gotten worse, invading my nose as I tried to clear my throat of it.

Seconds later, his moans reverberated off his cell wall, and he cried out. "Fuck! Fuck!" When he pulled his pants back up and fell onto the cot, I noted the wet spots on the wall where he'd shot his release. "This is fucking humiliating," he said, wincing as he shifted position, drawing my eyes toward the odd curve of his back. Spine distortion was a normal progression, as the parasite began to attack and deplete parts of the body. "It's like ... it hits out of nowhere, and if I don't take care of it? Worst case of blue balls I ever had. My apologies for doing that in front of you."

"No need to apologize."

"I was thinking about the story you told me. With your brother gettin' hauled off like that." He coughed, sending a spray of red to the concrete, and his eyes winced when he swallowed. "Don't know why I haven't stopped thinkin' about it. What happened to Caesar? Didn't he try to help you?"

I pried my thoughts from Lilia and the video, to the memory of Caesar that night. "He had no loyalties to us."

"You think he had somethin' to do with your brother gettin' taken?"

Staring back at the man, I studied his expression for any sign of reaction to asking that question. A flinch. A muscle tic. A shift of his gaze. Nothing.

Stabbing pain struck my temple, and I clenched my eyes and jaw, rubbing at the spot. *Ten, nine, eight, seven, six.*

"You all right?" Barletta asked, as jagged lights flashed behind my lids.

"Fine." Took a good couple of minutes to subside that time, and I rolled my shoulders back on a long exhale, as the last of the pain withered. "My father punished him. Interrogated him in an effort to find out who'd had the balls to take Warren Bramwell's son. But it was all in vain."

I peer through the crack of the door in one of the rooms adjacent to my father's lab. Caesar sits tied to a chair, his face bruised and battered, with bright red plums that marked every merciless punch to his face. Eye puffy and distorted, lips swollen and bleeding, he hardly looks human. My father stands before him, two men flanking him, both wearing suits and black gloves, and weird masks that remind me of a creepy bird. Ones I've seen in books about the plague. Doctors' masks designed to keep germs out. Why the men are wearing them right now is a mystery.

"Where's my fucking son?" my father asks for the dozenth time.

Caesar doesn't answer. His head sways like a watermelon balanced on a toothpick, the sight of which sickens me.

I want to knock the melon clean off and watch it splat against the concrete. Seeing a man beaten within an inch of his life isn't easy, but I want my brother back, and I can't fault my father for being violent about it. In fact, I want more violence. More blood.

One of the masked men beside my father rails his face again, the impact of his fist sending blood and a dislodged tooth to the floor.

Still, the guard refuses to talk.

Hands balled into fists, I grind my teeth, wishing I could throw some punches.

My father groans and turns away from him, running a hand down his face. "Get him out of my sight."

No. No!

He hasn't revealed anything, and six days have passed with no sign of Caedmon.

I give my father some credit for his efforts. I've always been under the impression that he hates the two of us and would happily write us off. He even negotiated a reward with the police–a pretty enticing amount of money for a man who acts like he doesn't give a shit.

The two men drag Caesar toward the door where I'm hiding, and I scramble to my feet. In a small, shadowy alcove, I press my back to the wall, watching them carry his limp body past. A phone rings from the room where my father still stands, and after peeking to make sure the guards are out of sight, I tiptoe back to my spot and peer in.

My father answers. "Yes."

I can't hear what the other person is saying, but my father's expression shifts from exasperation to a tight-knitted frown.

"What do they want?" A pause follows, and he lodges his fingers through his hair, pacing. "I have money. I can pay them whatever they want."

Another pause.

"No! It's not possible! No! Tell them, no!" A beep ends the call, and he slams his phone down on a roar of anger. "Fuck! Fuck! Fuck!"

With both hands lodged in his hair, he paces again.

On a bold breath, I push closer until standing just inside the room.

He doesn't notice me at first as his paces lead him toward the wall. When he pivots around, angry eyes lock on mine. "What are you doing in here?"

"Who called you just now?"

"None of your fucking business!"

"It's about my brother! Tell me!"

Eyes ablaze with fury, he snarls back at me. "I told you. It's none of your fucking business. If you hadn't been so busy pissing your goddamn pants, he might be here now!" His words strike me like a hard blow to the chest, and I choke beneath the impact.

"Fuck you! They had guns! There were two of them!"

"And the shame of it all is they let you live."

Tears form in my eyes, but I won't give him the satisfaction of knowing just how much his words stab my heart. Instead, I grit my teeth and let the anger swallow me. "You know who took him, don't you?"

"No."

"They want something from you, though. What is it! Tell me!" The rage snaps inside of me, and I lurch toward him, my hands tingling with a longing to throttle him.

No more than two steps forward, and he draws a gun from his back, pointing it at me.

I skid to a halt, my head trying to process the scene.

"Get out of my sight. Or, so help me God, I will put a bullet in your skull."

"Tell me where he is. I'll go after him. I'll go after all of them."

He snorts a laugh. "You'll piss your pants and fall into a seizure," he says, curling one of his arms into his chest and jerking, mocking me.

It's a wonder I don't taste dust in my mouth, as hard as I grind my teeth. "I fucking hate you. He hated you."

"You've ruined my life. The day you took your first breath, and she died. Now Caedmon. You're no son of mine."

The tears cut loose, and staring at him through a watery shield, I mentally search for one single reason I shouldn't coax him into shooting a bullet in my skull. The answer arrives in a haze of red. Revenge. "You may have rued watching me take my first breath, Father. But know that I will rejoice in watching you take your last."

"Jesus. Your old man sounds like a real prick. D'you ever find out what that phone call was about?" Barletta rested his elbows on his bent knees, where he sat tucked against the wall.

"I did, yes."

"But I'm gonna have to wait to find out, right?"

"Yes. I'm certain you'll be riveted."

His jaw shifted, fingers rubbing together. Fidgeting. "Is this when I find out why you took me?"

"Yes."

"How much longer do I have?"

"I don't think you'll make it another week." My toneless voice lacked any shred of empathy.

Bottom lip quivering, he turned his head to the side just enough that I caught a glisten across his cheek. Unfortunately for him, there was nothing left in me to appeal to, only a bottomless hollow in which to cast his useless tears.

My heart was a graveyard. A cold and starving apathy entombed within slumbering bones. Nothing could make me feel sorry for him.

He slipped two sealed envelopes through the bars. "Can you make sure my sons get these?"

"Of course," I lied.

Chapter 29

Lilia

I endured an hour of lecture and absorbed nothing. The phone lay beside me the whole time, taunting me to click on the site and look at how many nauseating views had accumulated in that amount of time.

As I walked out of class, I finally dared myself to click on it, and finding a quiet spot beneath a tree, I logged onto the website and scrolled through three pages of videos in search of the one I'd posted.

Nothing.

I clicked on my profile, and under the My Uploads tab, there was nothing.

Wait. What? Had it *actually* been removed?

The tokens I'd accumulated sat at about nine-hundred thirty-five dollars, but I hesitated to hit the transfer button. What if that made the video populate again?

No. Leave it alone.

It wasn't worth the anxiety of the video showing up again. I had no idea what the hell had given Tony, or whatever his name was, a change of heart, but I was grateful enough not to press my luck. A potent relief swept through me as I made my way to Darrigan Hall for lunch.

Spencer met me at the entrance, and after swiping me in, we both made our way to the buffet. I'd only had warm breakfast meals since I'd been there. For lunch, I typically ate in the courtyard, and dinner was often nothing more than soup that I smuggled back into my room.

I grabbed my plate, eyeing all the many choices–fresh fish with lemon and capers, red spiced chicken, Korean BBQ beef, ravioli, vegan options, endless sides and desserts, all prepared by on-site chefs.

"Is everything okay?" Spencer asked behind me, piling potatoes on his plate.

"The food is overwhelming."

"Yeah, it's nutty how much they prepare every day."

I spooned roasted veggies onto my plate, along with some rice and salad, and the two of us found a table toward the front. I glanced around as I took a seat on the long bench, and my eyes locked with Professor Bramwell's, where he sat watching me from a table beside what I presumed was another professor.

It was then the other professor seemed to catch sight of me, too, his eyes scrutinizing, the way they narrowed on me. He set his fork down on the plate in front of him and immediately leaned into Professor Bramwell, who never broke his stare.

Frowning, I turned around, wondering if I was the subject of their whispering, and caught sight of Spencer staring beyond me, presumably toward the professors.

"It seems my father does make time for a select few."

"Your father?"

He nodded and I followed the path of his gaze toward the professor who had stared at me a moment ago–who gathered up his bag and plate of half-eaten food.

"That's Provost Lippincott?"

"Yeah."

Lippincott Senior paused to stare back at me again, his brows pulled to a frown, and in my periphery, Spencer waved at him. The older man didn't wave back. Instead, he shook Bramwell's hand and headed toward the exit.

As he passed us, Spencer leaned to the side, presumably to get his attention. "Dad, I want to introduce you–"

The elder Lippincott hobbled past without so much as a nod in acknowledgement, and out of the dining hall.

"He ignores you?"

"On the good days. On the bad? Well, let's just say I prefer the good ones. Not sure what has his panties in a bunch today, though."

The slight limp I'd noticed in his gait brought to mind the article I'd read a while back about the homeless woman, Andrea Kepling, who'd attacked Lippincott in his home. "Hey, are you familiar with a woman named Andrea Kepling?"

"Who?"

A furtive look around confirmed there were no other students within earshot of my whispering, and I leaned forward. "She's the woman who attacked your father."

"The psycho who claimed my dad put worms in her? Never met her, but yeah. He has a gnarly-looking scar on his leg because of her."

I'd forgotten that bit of information–her claims that he'd somehow infected her. "Like ... Noctisoma worms?"

"Who the hell knows? Lady was a fruitcake."

"Was?"

"Yeah." A quick glance around, and he leaned in closer. "Overheard my dad telling someone she died a few weeks back. Someone found her slung over the bathtub in some house she was staying in." His tongue swept over his lips, and he glanced past me and back. "Guess Bramwell did the autopsy on her." He spoke low, as if the guy might hear him over the din that echoed through the dining hall.

Worms in her belly. Bramwell performing the autopsy. As

I poked at my lunch, I silently absorbed the picture he was painting inside my head, one that had me questioning how she might've died.

"Any chance your dad might actually have known her at one time?"

"Nah. He said he'd never met her in his life."

"Lippincottttt!"

At the startling shout of a voice from behind, I turned to see four guys stroll up, all dressed in polo shirts and khaki shorts, one carrying what I guessed to be a rugby ball, like something straight out of an Abercrombie catalog.

Blood thudding in my ears, I prayed they wouldn't sit down at our table.

Please don't sit down.

Every one of them piled in around us, though, two on either side of me. In my periphery, one of the guys stared so hard, I almost expected laser beams to come shooting out of his eyeballs. Tension wound in my muscles, the urge to crawl out of my skin scratching at my bones.

"Who's your new friend?" the one staring beside me asked.

"None of your business." Though Spencer's words were honed, his tone carried an air of amusement.

"Well, *none of your business* looks pretty bored sitting here with you. You're new here, eh?" He finally addressed me directly, and I gave a sharp nod. "Where are you from?"

"Not around here."

The guy chuckled and straddled the bench, fully turning toward me. "No one is from around here."

I hated that he was well within my personal space enough that I could feel his breath on my shoulder.

"Thank fuck for that," one of his friends added. "All the ghosts and stories about this place would probably drive a person mad. Like *Doctor Death*," he whispered and snorted a laugh.

"So, tell us, Red. Where are you from?"

Lifting my gaze to Spencer, eating his lunch as if oblivious to my growing irritation, told me he had no plans of sparing me from his friends. "Why do you care?" I asked, the edge of annoyance punctuating the question.

"Just curious. Why are you so reluctant to say?" The slight smirk pulling at the corner of his lips left me pondering the possibility that he already knew.

"C'mon, Jared, just leave her alone," Spencer finally chimed in.

"I don't get why it's a big secret. Now I *need* to know."

"Well, this just got weird. Thanks for lunch, Spencer. I'll catch you later." I pushed up from my seat, and feeling a grip on my arm, I glared down with clenched teeth at the asshole who held onto me. "Let go of me. Now."

"Miss Vespertine. May I have a word with you?"

At the sound of the much more mature voice, I turned to find Professor Bramwell standing behind me, his pissed-off looking eyes locked onto Rugby boy. The mood shifted, as if his very presence cast a cold stab of ice across the table.

My pulse hastened, and the grip of my arm fell away.

Swallowing a gulp, I nodded. "Sure."

With a slight jerk of his head, he urged me after him, toward the exit, slowing his pace as I caught up. "My apologies if you had hoped to finish your lunch. You looked like you needed an exit."

"You're very observant. So, I'm not in trouble, then?"

"I don't know. You tell me." He came to a stop just outside of the dining hall and turned to face me, glancing over his shoulder when a group of students passed by. "Have you deleted the video?"

"Yes. Of course."

"So, if I asked for proof, you'd willingly hand over your phone to me."

Eyes locked on his, I pulled the phone from my bag, holding it out between us."

He merely glanced down to the phone and back to me, not bothering to take it from me. "Good." An awkward silence lingered for a moment, before his gaze shifted to the dining room and back. "I see you and Mr. Lippincott have become well acquainted."

I shoved the phone back into my bag, catching his eyes tracking the movement. The man had the mannerisms of a panther, the way nothing seemed to escape him. "He's a nice person. Genuine."

"I've found *nice* and *genuine* rarely go hand in hand."

"That seems not to be the case with Spencer."

"Of course not." His hand flexed, and in the brief interlude of conversation, I found myself staring at the way the strap of his bag crossed over his chest, somehow emphasizing his broad shoulders. "I've graded the quizzes from last week. In a class of sixty-eight students, ten of whom failed it altogether, you're the only one with a perfect score." A slight curve of his lips told me that pleased him.

For reasons I couldn't explain, the thought of that tickled me.

"For one who seems to have a good handle on neuroparasitology, perhaps you find the class a bore," he suggested.

"Absolutely not. I find your lectures riveting."

Again, his lips curved, higher that time. Without warning, he tossed me an apple that I hadn't noticed him carrying. "In case you get hungry later. Good afternoon, Miss Vespertine." With that, he strode off into the courtyard.

"Hey," Spencer said as he ambled up to me. "I'm really sorry. Those guys are dicks. Everything good with Doctor Death?"

"Yeah." I watched him cross the yard, like a thunderstorm passing over the sky. That was the perfect way to describe him–ominous and foreboding, yet mesmerizing at the same time. "He just wanted to ask me about one of my journal entries." It was strange, the way I couldn't look away, the way I couldn't stop thinking of that seemingly innocuous smile. One that still had my stomach in a fluttery mess.

"Huh. Hey, I actually asked you to lunch because I wanted to know if you're doing anything next Saturday?"

I finally dragged my attention from Bramwell. "Studying, most likely."

"Any chance I can convince you to take a night off and attend a charity event with me?" A complete look of disinterest must've been plastered on my face, because he kept on, with "It's a gala with a candlelight concert. But I promise, it's not a date. I just ... would rather go with someone who doesn't drive me nuts."

"I don't think so. I'm sorry. Besides, I don't really have anything to wear to something like that."

"You wouldn't have to worry about that. The dress would be my treat. My thanks for saving me from having to go with Kendall."

Having to go with Kendall? Not like she wasn't beautiful, and she definitely fawned over the guy. Not exactly a chore to ask her. "There's a whole campus, Spencer. And candlelight sounds a little too ... *intimate*."

"I promise it won't be. Please. I'm willing to beg, if that's what it'll take."

I exhaled a sigh, my head refusing to give in. I hated social engagements as a general rule, but one for the wealthy would undoubtedly give me hives. "Surely, there's someone else you can ask."

"There isn't, I can assure you."

Arms crossed, I huffed, hating myself for being so damn

empathetic that I was actually considering his request. "What time?"

"It starts at eight. Ends at midnight."

"I'm not staying out until midnight."

"No problem. I'll get you home whenever you need to be back. Scout's honor."

Damn, the guy did not give up easily. "You're sure there's not someone else you'd rather take?"

"Positive."

Don't do it, Lilia. Don't give in.

"Fine, I'll go."

Chapter 30

Lilia

Bored during work study, I found myself reading through texts in the Adderly Memorial again, and as it had before, the story of Mary Elizabeth sucked me into the history of the school. While a number of Adderly's journals were off limits, I was able to get my hands on one that detailed some of the experiments performed on the patients. He described a young woman, only a year younger than me, who'd had an affair with a married man. Due to his respectable background, the clergymen of her town had decided that she must've been a witch to seduce someone so pious.

I scoffed at that.

As a result, the woman had been sent to the island to await trial. Dr. Stirling, who I'd read about last time–the creepy doctor who wore the plague uniform to ward off his patients' bad spirits–had apparently convinced the clergymen that he had methods of saving her soul, and thus, had averted a public trial and burning.

I read on to find her fate was no safer in the hands of Dr. Stirling, though. While in his care, she'd had one of her eyeballs removed, her tongue removed, and her mouth sewn shut. The notes detailed that she'd been fed Stirlic acid to purify her body, however her manner of death was excessive blood loss, after she was forced to bleed out for black blood.

I paused there, frowning.

Black blood?

Her mental health had declined significantly while at the monastery, and she had expressed terror over hallucinations and the feeling of snakes in her belly.

Again, I found myself staring off. *Was it possible ...*

The note prompted me to scan for any other symptoms. And I found one more–glowing eyes, deemed to be a demonic trait. A few more pages in, I paused on a crude sketch of a human skull with sharpened black teeth. The accompanying note described it as having belonged to the Cu'unotchke tribe, who'd inhabited the island around the same time the first colonists arrived. They were deemed savages, monsters, by early Acadians, with black stone teeth supposedly used for tearing flesh, and eyes that glowed like an animal's. I snapped a quick picture of the skull sketch, focusing specifically on the strange markings in the bone–thin and black, they almost looked carved into it, like tiny fissures.

My mind swirled with thoughts. Professor Bramwell had said there was a long-standing history of the organism. Was it possible that it went back as far as the 1700's? He'd also mentioned bone striations as an autopsy finding, in my meeting with him, and that it had surfaced thirty years ago. Had his father been working on Noctisoma? Was that the basis of the Crixson study?

My thoughts quickly switched to earlier, in the lunchroom with Spencer, and the discussion of *his* father and Andrea Kepling, who had also mentioned worms in her belly. Bramwell had performed the autopsy on her. If what Professor Bramwell said was true, that he rarely stumbled upon cases outside of the island, and that it didn't spread person to person, was it possible that Andrea Kepling had been from Dracadia?

Was it possible she had been one of the patients to escape the study?

I scooted myself over to the computer with its sketchy internet connection, and typed *Andrea Kepling* into the search bar, just as before. The article I'd already read was one of three results–two of which were newspapers that boasted the same headline about her attack on Lippincott. The third one, though, had been written by a blogger who went by the name of Anon Amos, and I clicked on it. While it gave much of the same details as the other two articles, there was one difference–it questioned Andrea's participation in the Crixson Project, just as I had.

I immediately searched The Crixson Project, only to find an article about the six unexplained deaths.

All deemed to be suicides, somehow.

All of them drownings, with no mention of the other two patients.

Intrigued, I dug deeper and pulled up another article that offered a very brief synopsis of the experiment, led by Dr. Warren Bramwell, a long-time professor at Dracadia.

Professor Bramwell's father.

The project aimed to test an inoculation said to reverse the effects of insulin-dependent diabetes. Apparently, whatever was given to the women targeted the body's immunity, blocking the lymphocytes that attacked insulin-secreting pancreatic beta cells. A possible cure for diabetes.

Except for the tragic outcome that quickly shut down the project. Unfortunately, not much was available on the alleged suicides.

After gathering up the journal, I quickly ran back to the check-out desk, where Kelvin checked in books on the computer. "Do we have any information on the Crixson Project?"

"We do, but I'm afraid those references are locked and inaccessible, due to the tragedy associated with the project."

"Is there anything I can get my hands on? Maybe even just a synopsis of the project?"

"'Fraid not, Miss Vespertine. Are you finished with Adderly's journal? I need to get it back to the vault before I clock out for the evening."

"Yes. Thank you."

There had to be information about it. How else would Mel know so much?

Perhaps she had other resources that I could tap into.

On a sigh, I turned around, and across the science wing, I spied Professor Bramwell reading through some texts at one of the tables. The air in my lungs deflated like a balloon at the sight of the man hunched over a book, intensely studying with his fingers lodged in his hair.

"Can I trouble you for a moment?" Kelvin asked behind me, breaking me from my spell.

With a shake of my head, I spun around. "Absolutely. What do you need?"

He handed me a stack of physics texts. "Please return these to their shelves."

"Of course." I glanced down at the call number, realizing it was the same aisle where Professor Bramwell sat. Keeping my eyes on him, I carried the binders over, trying not to ogle the man while he studied–particularly when my head urged me to interrogate him about Andrea Kepling.

Don't be a nuisance.

Why the hell did my pulse hasten when the man was in the room?

His gaze never lifted from the book flattened on the table below him, and when he rubbed the back of his neck, my fingers tingled for reasons I couldn't explain.

Closer.

Closer.

I reached the aisle, my head spinning with how I could broach the topic of Andrea Kepling. *Do you have to be so investigative all the time?* my head chided. *Just ask the weather. Or sports.*

I hated sports.

Ask if he needs a goddamn water, but for the love of Christmas, do not ask about Andrea Kepling.

I neared the table, my nerves turning bolder by the second. *Be audacious.* Breath gathered in my lungs, and on a fruitless exhale, I kept on toward the shelf.

He turned his head just a little, as if he sensed someone passing.

I paused alongside him for a brief moment, lips parted for whichever of the millions of questions floating around in my head might've broken loose.

"Devryck!" a familiar voice called out, and I turned to see professor Gilchrist sauntering over, her eyes lit and focused on Professor Bramwell.

It was when I twisted back around that his eyes were locked on mine. A strange sensation fluttered in my belly, and I clutched the texts tighter, moving past him toward the shelves. In my periphery, I watched Gilchrist slide into one of the chairs at his table adjacent to his workspace.

"I've good news! I was able to secure dozens more uninfected specimens. The Preservation Society wasn't thrilled, but they understood the importance of this research."

Eavesdropping was such an unbecoming trait, but I couldn't help myself.

"Wonderful. Thank you."

A beat of silence hung between them, and I rounded the other end of the aisle to the next row over, pretending to shelve a book there.

"Why are you ignoring my calls?" She spoke in a lower

voice than before, but I could just make out the words. “I’m … confused. I keep rehashing the last time we met up, trying to imagine what I could’ve done to upset you.”

“I’m not having this conversation again.”

“Devryck … I am …. I think I’m in love with you. I can’t stop thinking about you.”

Through the books, I watched his fingers tap impatiently on the table, his shoulders bunch with irritation. The more the woman talked, the more this bomb ticked.

“One more time,” she said in a flirtatious voice. “In my office. I promise I won’t call you again.”

“No.”

“No?” Brows winged up, she gave a look like she’d just been slapped. “Is it someone else?”

I paused, not so much as uttering a single breath, as I waited for him to answer. For some reason, I needed to know, too. Peering through the books, I caught the clench of his fist.

“Why won’t you answer me?” she prodded, clearly not picking up on the guy’s cues.

Stay out of it. It’s none of your business.

What had happened in the dining hall earlier wasn’t his, either, yet he hadn’t hesitated to step in. And I was grateful for it, too.

With a deep breath, I rounded the aisles again, and clearing my throat, I came to a stop at his back. “Professor Bramwell?” Heart pounding in my chest, I couldn’t believe I’d worked up the balls to insert myself into the situation.

He kicked his head to the side without saying anything in return, and I clasped my damp palms together to keep them from shaking.

“I tracked down the eukaryotic pathogenesis text that you requested.” A total lie, and I truly couldn’t believe the words were tumbling out of my mouth with such ease.

Frowning, he twisted in his seat and seemed to study me for a moment.

Please don't make me look like an idiot. "If you want to follow me, I can show you where."

Another agonizing beat of silence, and he rolled those broad shoulders back. "Yes. Of course." He glanced back at Gilchrist, and I didn't dare look at her right then. The woman was probably carving me up with a murderous glare. As he pushed to his feet, I finally chanced a glance, and the look on Gilchrist's face blazed with something that sent a chill down the back of my neck.

"Professor Gilchrist," I said in acknowledgement with a nod.

Her lips curved into a feigned smile.

With a jerk of my head, I urged him to follow me four aisles down, and once sufficiently out of earshot, I turned around to see he had, in fact, followed me.

Hands sliding into his pockets, he strode closer. "You're either incredibly astute, or exceptionally nosey."

Clearing my throat again, I lowered my gaze. "My apologies. You looked like you needed an exit," I said, echoing his words from earlier in the dining hall.

Through narrowed eyes, he stared back at me in that unsettling, studious way of his. "You work in the science wing?"

"Yes."

"How frequently?"

"Four nights a week, Sir."

He stared a minute longer, the weight of his gaze bearing down on me. "Thank you, Miss Vespertine."

As he stepped past me, I spun around. "Professor Bramwell, wait."

When he paused, I instantly regretted my impulsive nature.

"May I ask a question?"

"Depends on the question."

It was then or never. Snagging his full attention like that probably wouldn't happen again. "I know you won't tell me anything specific, but I wondered if you might answer one question regarding Andrea Kepling."

He turned to fully face me again, but didn't say anything. The question was etched in the tight knit of his brow, though. *How do you know about her?*

"I know she was sent here for autopsy."

"And just how did you come by that information?"

"I'm not at liberty to say." Having seen me with Spencer, though, I suspected he was smart enough to figure it out. While I didn't want to rat Spencer out, my desperate search for answers pushed those concerns to the back of my priorities.

With an exasperated huff, he crossed his arms, drawing my attention to the bulge of muscle at his biceps. "What is your question? Bear in mind, I am not permitted to disclose any information regarding her medical record."

Which meant I had to be clever in my inquiry. "Any thoughts on how she might've acquired Noctisoma?"

Cheek twitching with a smirk, he stepped closer. Closer. Until I picked up on a hint of his delicious cologne. "I never confirmed such a diagnosis."

Yet, the fact that he didn't outright dispute it told me he might've been lying.

I pinned him with a hard stare. "She claimed Lippincott put worms in her belly. She was sent to you for autopsy. I find that highly coincidental."

"Allow me to caution you, Miss Vespertine. You are a confused moth dancing about a wild flame. Blind to the incomprehensible danger of your curiosities."

"I want to know the truth."

"The truth is an intangible luxury of the powerful."

I didn't doubt that, especially in a place like Dracadia, but I refused to accept it. "I came here to find answers, Professor. I'm not afraid to ask questions."

"At what cost? Your scholarship? Your future? Your *life*?"

"Is that a threat?"

"Yes." One step forward backed me against the shelf behind me, and he threw out his hand, creating something of a cage. "You have no idea who you're fucking with."

I'd been cornered by men before, terrified of them, but that wasn't the case with Professor Bramwell. This almost felt like an invitation. A dare. Heart pounding in my chest, I gave a defiant tip of my chin. "Who am I fucking with?"

His gaze fell to my lips in a way that felt too intimate. Too riveted to mistake the thoughts that must've been churning in his head right then. "It's fascinating how you can be so meek and bold at the same time." His tongue swept over his lips, and I prayed he'd do something fucking bold, like press them to mine. "You are inarguably brilliant, so quit acting foolish. Leave this alone."

He stepped past me, and once he rounded the corner, I blew out a shaky breath. Holy hell, the man was intense.

But not even Doctor Death could intimidate me at that point. My curiosity had been piqued. The walls of this place held dark secrets, past skeletons, that I intended to exhume with a sledgehammer.

Chapter 31

Devryck

"We have a fucking problem." Lippincott paced in front of me, as I leaned back in my office chair, watching the man unravel over something. He kept muttering to himself about someone having lied to him, his hair a mess atop his head from where he'd damned near rubbed his skull raw. "The girl. The girl is a problem."

"What girl?" I asked, casually sipping my drink. Although, I had a pretty good idea who he was talking about.

He shook his head, not bothering to slow his pacing. "Don't fuck with me. You know what girl. *The* girl. The one I told you to watch."

"And I have. So, what's the problem?" Ordinarily, I'd have found his anxiety somewhat amusing. In light of the fact that I had something much more exciting, in the form of a newly-prepped injection of the toxin, waiting on me back at my lab, I was bored.

"The problem? Have you seen her?"

Damned near every night when I closed my eyes, but I didn't bother to say that aloud.

"She's a spitting image of her mother!"

"A number of children are."

"Quit fucking mocking me, Devryck!" He slammed his

fist against my desk, though he failed to intimidate me with his anger. Shoulders squared, he stared at me with unflinching bravery, seeing as my patience had begun to wear thin already. "Her mother is the other *missing* woman. The runaway in your father's fucked-up study."

Fuck. I frowned at that. Was hoping he'd have remained obtuse enough not to make the connection—one I'd had my own suspicions about since having read that faulty coroner's report. "You're certain of this," I said, playing dumb.

"Do you imagine I'd forget a face like that?"

Given the questions that Lilia had asked, I didn't get the impression she was aware that her mother had participated in the study. Otherwise, I suspected she'd have been much more specific in her many inquiries.

"I told you I'd keep an eye on her, and I will." I reached for the decanter of bourbon to fill his glass, because goddamn, with his face beet red, he looked like he was two breaths away from a stroke. "So far, she hasn't stirred any trouble," I added, as I filled my own glass. Since he'd confirmed my suspicions about her mother's participation in Crixson, I couldn't wrap my head around the odds of it. Fate must've hit the crack pipe again, the way it kept reminding me how much of an absolute prick my father had been in life.

"She's here for a reason, Devryck. She's undoubtedly trying to dig up information. And when she does, I'll once again find myself in front of the firing squad. Your fucking father *ruined* my life with this." He pushed off my desk, pacing again. "Ruined it!" He punched the air like a madman, as if my old man were standing in front of him right then. Not that I blamed him. I'd have had a few punches to throw myself.

"Relax. She's merely curious about the organism."

Ignoring me, he swiped up his drink from the desk,

spilling drops of liquor onto the shiny surface–an observation that annoyed the hell out of me. "Gilchrist fucking assigned her *Crixson Hall*. Do you think that was an accident?" He tipped back his drink, nearly choking when he didn't wait long enough to answer his own question. "No. The woman has it in for me. She's trying to sabotage my fucking life for not having promoted her!" He shook his head, then returned to pacing and sipping his drink. Growling, he loosened his tie, furthering the lunatic look. "That lying piece of shit. Slimy motherfucker lied right to my face!" It was hard to tell if he was talking about Langmore, the girl's mother, or someone else. "I was wrong. Granting her a semester here was a fucked idea. Fucked!"

"You're only just now coming to this conclusion?"

"I had no idea who the hell she was. Her last name isn't the same. Wasn't like her transcripts arrived with a fucking family album!" It was a wonder he hadn't rubbed all of the hair clean off his skull, the way he kept running his hands over it. "She has to go."

"Wouldn't it be wiser to contain the problem? She signed a nondisclosure, meaning she can't speak a word of anything related to Noctisoma. Not without legal repercussions."

He scratched at his jaw, obviously considering my words as he stared off. "Does she have any other family?"

I didn't like the idea of telling him Lilia's personal information, but not telling him might've only stoked his curiosity, had him watching her closer, instead of trusting me to keep an eye on her. "A half-sister and the mother's ex-boyfriend."

Another sip, and he flicked his fingers, asking for another refill. "And the mother passed? We know she passed away?"

I pushed the decanter in front of him, refusing to oblige the man every time he sucked down his drink, but God help the bastard if he spilled it again. "Four years ago, from what I've gathered."

He poured his drink, and I watched as it splashed around the rim, but lucky for him, it remained in the glass. "She hasn't come to you with any questions?"

That was laughable. "Yes. A fucking barrage of them. None of them concerning." The chair creaked as I leaned back and kicked my feet up on the desk. "She's just a girl dreaming of finding a cure for the disease that took her mother's life."

"She hasn't inquired about Crixson, at *all*?"

"No. And what does it matter? Those files are locked away. The information on her mother and Kepling no longer exists. You're being paranoid." Aside from sheer fascination, I had no connection, no loyalty to the girl. The fact that I was protecting her made zero sense to me.

Exhaling a long breath, he slid into the opposite chair. "Perhaps you're right. What the fuck can she do? Nothing." He blew through the entire glass of liquor in one swill and slammed the glass down on my desk. "Fine. She stays. For now."

It was then it occurred to me that I had just negotiated Lilia's ability to remain enrolled.

Hell if I knew why.

I stared down at my phone, where Lilia's video sat paused. I'd dreamed about her the night before. Those long, slender fingers tracing over my arms and up the back of my neck. A torment I'd carried with me all afternoon and into the evening, when she interrupted my concentration at the library. Gilchrist was a nuisance, but Lilia, she was a distraction. An irritatingly welcomed one.

I thought back to the look in her eyes when I'd had her cornered against those bookshelves. The defiant glint that made me want to seize those pouty fucking lips of hers and end whatever the hell it was that held me hostage to the girl's poisonous spell. That infuriating scent of hers that messed with my brain chemistry. The delicious enchantment that undoubtedly lured men to their doom.

One touch. One touch would end this agonizing curiosity, but might just send me spiraling into madness.

Damn her for being so inquisitive. The questions she'd begun to ask had dipped into dangerous waters, particularly since Lippincott had suspected who her mother was, and if the wrong person happened to overhear her, who knew what that'd mean for her.

I loathed this secret obsession I'd begun to develop with her.

It was wrong.

While she might've been of age, a woman essentially, she was still forbidden, and the fact that I had any sense of yearning at all served as a testament to the effectiveness of my last inoculation.

I lifted the syringe from its case, where the pale purple substance had my veins tingling for a sip. The toxin had begun to metabolize at a much slower pace for me, after all the weeks I'd taken it, but it was nowhere near stable enough for clinical trials. In the absence of the parasite, it had no true mechanism of replenishing itself, and therefore, its effects were short-lived. Subsequent generations of the parasite had proven to be more specific toward human genetics, but there remained a flaw. Sustainability.

And the matter of requiring human sacrifice to breed the parasite and teach it our pathophysiology.

The other issue was a side effect that triggered my own need to breed.

Even in the absence of the parasite itself, as the inoculation I gave myself consisted of nothing more than purified toxin, it still compelled my brain to fuck something. An urge I'd managed to control for the most part, even in the presence of the many young, fertile women on campus. A chemical mechanism carried out by the very toxin that I willingly injected into myself.

Because it was also this toxin that compelled my immune system and helped to create protective proteins that effectively repaired the damage of my medical condition. Reversed it, if only temporarily. Every new episode, where my muscles locked up and my head pounded in agony, was fresh destruction that had to be reconstructed by the toxin's potent army of proteins.

And I still ran the risk of it reaching my heart.

I longed for the day when I could better control the toxin in a way that might allow a complete reversal of the faulty genetics that caused the disease. The same disease that'd ultimately killed my father.

It wasn't the exaltation for what my research had the potential to achieve that I sought. I just wanted to fucking feel something again.

After cleaning the site with alcohol, I lined the needle to my vein and pushed it into my flesh. No sting. No burn of the liquid. Only a small bit of blood gathered around the wound, which I covered with cotton, then removed the syringe.

In any other lab, I'd have been disgraced for having used myself as a test subject. Lost my license and been blacklisted from academia.

Fortunately, Dracadia wasn't any other university.

Had they been privy, I suspected they'd have turned a blind eye, so long as I continued to report progress. And didn't die. While I maintained a sense of legitimacy in the labs upstairs, here, in my private lab, I could get away with anything–even murder.

It hadn't been without coaxing that I'd agreed to take on my father's research. Upon his deathbed, I'd vowed that his lifelong studies would die with him. It was Lippincott who'd encouraged me to consider it. To investigate the potential for curing my own affliction. He'd agreed to fund the research, and worked to reinvigorate interest in it, after my father had turned the entire academic community away from himself.

I needed it to be a success.

I was desperate to untangle myself from my father's humiliating legacy.

The room tilted and shifted as the toxin pulsed through my veins. A euphoric high swept over me with the intense surge of dopamine. Grunting and moaning, I tensed and flexed as the toxin worked its way into my bloodstream. While it failed to return my sense of touch, each dose lessened the seizing episodes with which I suffered. And, of course, stoked my libido.

I reached for my phone, and Lilia's paused video.

Stop this, my head urged. *Not her*.

What was it about the girl that had me breaking my own rules?

Perhaps it was knowing that Lippincott was watching her. That she unwittingly swam in a placid sea where sharks lurked beneath the surface, and the vulnerability spoke to me.

Maybe it was the way she challenged me and defied all of my prejudices against her, that unbreakable resilience that I found so utterly alluring. A shot of fire in my veins that stoked my blood.

I was drawn to her, for reasons I could neither justify nor understand. A realization that annoyed the shit out of me. She was an itch on my brain that I couldn't scratch. The maddening shimmer in the corner of my eye during lecture that distracted my thoughts. The kind of girl who seduced with nothing more than a single glance. A bite of the lip.

And she'd captured my attention with steel hooks.

I wanted to know more about her, who she was, where she came from, how that brilliant mind of hers worked.

It wasn't right, though.

I pushed the phone out of reach, because fuck, I'd have easily gotten off like every other pervert who'd watched that video. Instead I eased back in my chair, and sprang my cock free. In the past, I'd have called Gilchrist to ease the ache and transport me to the kind of bliss that escaped me most times during sex. I closed my eyes, imagining the last session with Gilchrist, when I'd had her on her knees, her lips wrapped around my shaft. An edge of disappointment rode every stroke of my hand. Her rhythm was always off, and for some reason, she mistakenly believed I enjoyed the feel of her teeth against my cock.

I could feel myself frowning as I pumped my hand up and down my shaft, the flesh growing soft, as the fantasy didn't quite do it for me.

A new image flashed through my head.

Fiery auburn hair.

Arctic green eyes.

Soft, pouty lips exploring my flesh.

My body hardened as every drop of blood shot straight to my cock. Before I could stop myself, I was fucking my own hand to the visuals of Lilia—her short skirt hiked up and no panties, teasing me. While my stomach lurched and flexed with an unsettling discomfort, my cock reveled in it. Fist pounding out a beat of intoxicating depravity, I imagined it tangled in her hair, using her mouth in the most exquisitely filthy ways.

I kicked my head back on a blast of light that hit the back of my skull. Hot jets exploded onto my fist, slickening the final strokes. Body shuddering, I let out a groan, a fucking groan. I never made a sound when I came, but the agony was bittersweet. I rested my head against my arm, banging out the final spurts, and shuddered again.

Breathing hard through my nose, I tried to catch my breath, and it was when my conscience finally caught up to me that I groaned again, but that time in frustration. "Fuck."

Just like that, Lilia Vespertine had become more than a student.

She was a serious problem.

"I can feel them. Inside my guts. You put them there! You son of a bitch!" Barletta paced inside his cell, hobbling from one end to the other. "Th-th-they crawl in and out, and in and out."

"Relax, Mr. Barletta." I scanned the walls, noting more wet stains–multiple spots where he'd likely relieved his sexual cravings. The urge to stifle a gag had me wishing I'd brought a dab of Vicks for my nose, or NeutrOlene to spray. I'd gotten used to the smell of dead bodies, but this was something else entirely.

"No! I will not relax!" He slammed himself against the bars of his cage. "They're eating me from the inside out! You don't think I can feel it!"

I let out a sigh, my head still wound around an annoying redhead with a smart mouth. "They only begin to consume at death. What you're feeling is a surge of growth. And perhaps hallucination."

"I want them out. Get them out of me!" He pounded against the bars with what had to have been a painful crack against his knuckles. "Please!"

"In time. I promise. Have a seat." I gestured toward the chair he'd knocked over earlier with his little tantrum. "I'll finish my story, and give you some water."

Wary eyes stared back at me, brimming with distrust. “Not some small piddly ass Dixie cup of water. I want a full glass! With ice.”

“Consider it done.”

Hands trembling, he pulled the chair closer to the bars and took a seat, seemingly calmer than before. With the progression of the disease, his outbursts would eventually become increasingly violent in his desperation to escape.

“Aside from the crawling sensation, how are you feeling?” I asked.

“My muscles ache. Sometimes, I feel like something’s crawling on my skin.” He scratched at his arm, grimacing, as if he could feel it then. “And I’m seeing my fucking son. Constantly. Only, he isn’t my son. He’s some … warped version that carries a hammer and tells me he’s gonna break my skull open.”

Oh, the justice of guilt. It was almost too entertaining at times. “He isn’t real, I can assure you.”

“He feels real.” Eyes wavering with a shine, he looked away. “So fucking real.”

“It’s your guilt toying with you.”

He lowered his gaze to his fidgeting hands. “You ever see hallucinations of your brother?”

“Yes,” I answered honestly. “Frequently.”

“So … that call your old man received. The one you told me about in your last story. What was that about?”

It was sickening, the way his question sucked the joy, the rapture, right out of me. The toxin’s euphoric effects sobered into something dark and twisted that pulled at my stomach. “I actually didn’t find out until much later. Not until I learned of my brother’s fate.”

Liquor in one hand, I stare down at the deadly jagged rocks, where the ocean’s waves crash in a chaotic spray of water. The world billows around me in the same rhythmic pattern, setting me swaying back and forth. The words of my father echo inside my head in a vacuum of toxic thoughts.

"Don't do it." *At the sound of Caedmon's voice, I turn to see him standing beside me. Not him, though, but the intangible version of my brother who visits me nearly every night.*

The sight of him fills me with shame, and I turn back toward the rocks below. "I failed. I'mma failure."

"You're not. This is Father's doing."

"It shoulda bee'me."

"Stop it," *he chides in his usual impatient tone.* "Stop being a whining cunt and get off this ledge. You're too fucking smart to waste it on guilt."

"I have nothing, Caed. Nothing." Without my brother, whatever callous part of me that remains has been sliced in half with his disappearance, leaving nothing more than a husk. "I feel empty and carved out. So hollow, it's cold."

"Listen to me." *His voice is pleading, and even in my drunken haze, I can sense the desperation in it.* "Father has something they want. Find out what it is and set me free."

"It's pointless. He'll never tell me." I throw back another swill from the bottle of liquor and sway again.

"Of course he won't. You have to find it yourself, Devryck. Damn it, think!"

Caedmon's voice holds a sobering anger that pierces through my drunken haze. "He keeps all his secrets in his lab."

"Yes. Very good."

"It's his life's work. They want it."

"Yes. Precisely." *His tone, brimming with hope, anchors my focus.*

"How?"

"You know how. You've seen it, tucked away. Locked in that closet."

"The safe?" I can visualize it in his office. In the back corner

of that closet. The small safe, where he stored mother's picture after I broke it.

"Yes. What's inside the safe?"

"Aside from her picture? I've no idea. I could never open it." Who the hell would've wanted his failed experiments? The study that disgraced our family name.

"Find a way. And for fucks sake, man, get away from the edge. You're making me nervous."

An erratic gust of wind kicks me off balance and I stumble backward. My footing falters. I slip on the rock.

The ground slips from beneath my feet, and I slide against the slippery stones, the searing jagged surface slicing at my stomach as my fingers catch on the ledge. "Fuck!" I dare a glance below, where the ocean beckons me to let go. It taunts me to release my hold and slip into the void.

"Get back up, Devryck. Climb!"

I tighten my muscles and pull myself, arms trembling with the effort.

"Pull yourself up!" *His words are a painful screech that jabs my skull.*

"Ahhhh!" The agony hammers against my bones, while my muscles lock themselves into a deadly rigidity. "I can't! I'm going to fucking die!"

"You are not going to die. Pull yourself back onto this ledge, you fucking sap!"

"No." I loosen my muscles and hang from my treacherous grip. "No, Caedmon. I don't want to."

"I need you, Brother. I'm begging you. Try."

I imagine my brother, wherever he is, holding on. Clinging to hope.

At that, I breathe through the cramping ache, fingers digging into the rock. Gripping tight and sure, I pull myself up, and before I can slip, I quickly adjust my arms so they're anchoring me to the ledge. I kick my leg up, using my muscles in my thigh to propel me upward. In a concerted effort of all limbs, I manage to pull myself back onto the ledge and away from its precarious rim. Lying flat on my back, I breathe through my nose, desperate to catch breath in lungs that feel as if they've been crushed by an iron palm.

Caedmon stands staring down at me. "Set me free."

I stumble back home, thoughts of my brother sobering me along the way. Through the front entrance, I plow past Dmitry, our butler, who calls after me, but his words are lost to the mire of thoughts racing through my head. He tries to stop me when I reach the door to the cellar, but I push him off in a rage. The air cools as I make my way down the long, winding staircase, towards my father's laboratory. Shouts from behind grow wilder, the words a blur in my drunken state.

Down a lengthy corridor, I reach the lab, where the door stands cracked.

From inside, I hear my brother's screams.

Caedmon!

I push through the door to find my father standing over a box on one of the examination tables. His hand is curled around a small camcorder, his face a mask of rage and tears.

"Father?" I lurch toward him, confused. "Caedmon?"

He drops the camcorder and stumbles backward, as if he almost passed out.

Before he can swipe it up again, I scramble for the machine and lift it, eyes instantly finding the small screen, on which my brother sits tied to a chair. From the cameraman's view, I watch as flames spray out from a blowtorch, licking my brother's raw and blistered legs.

Panic rises into my throat. I fall forward, my palms slapping the concrete. A torrent of vomit pours past my lips, splashing onto the floor. Another round hits the pooling fluids, splashing up into my face.

On shaky legs, I push to my feet and peer down into the

box. My father rushes toward me, but I turn in time to give one hard shove that knocks him backward onto his ass. From inside the box, I remove a small black box with a note attached:

As requested, we've returned your son.

Hands trembling, I open the lid to find a pile of ashes inside.

My breaths come too fast. The room spins out of control.

I slip into the blackness.

"They killed him." Barletta's grim tone pulled me back into the present.

My muscles tensed at the question. "I find it amusing that you listen to this story as if it's the first time you've heard it."

His brows flickered, his reflective eyes shifting in his dark cell. "I don't .... I don't know what you mean."

"You're the one who transported my brother to his killer." There it was. The reason I'd taken a man off the streets and infected him with the deadly worms that had begun to ravage his body. Revenge. Revenge for my twin who'd been brutally slain for greed. For the very research to which I'd dedicated my life.

Barletta's gaze shifted away and back to me. "Me?" he asked on a nervous laugh. "Nah, you got the wrong guy. I don't know what you're talking about."

"Don't insult me. On the night of October twenty-third, you drove two associates and my brother to an abandoned building outside of the city. You were the last to see him alive."

Silence hung on the air, as he rolled his shoulders back and fidgeted, perhaps realizing there was no way I planned to let him live. "I only did that gig for about a year."

"Gig. Is that what you call handing over humans for slaughter?"

He shook his head, the sickening denial painted on his face making me wish I could cut it away with a sharp blade. "I didn't know anything about him, or you, or your old man. I was told that I'd be taking some kid to a place on the east side. I didn't know who for, or why."

"Yet, you did it, anyway." My voice held no inflection. No empathy. As lifeless as a corpse. "You never questioned, nor followed up to make sure said kid was still alive." I shrugged, easing back into my chair. "Why would you, when you beat the shit out of your own son?"

Expression screwed up with fear, he rocked back and forth in his chair. "That's why I'm here, then, huh? That's why you brought me here. Some sick fucking revenge plot?"

"You're too brilliant."

"I never meant to hurt any kid. Had I known that they were gonna torture him ..."

"You'd have what?" I tipped my head, watching the man spew lies as easily as if they were truth. "Saved him? Called the police? Done what any decent human being would've done?" I let out a mirthless chuckle. "No. I don't think so, Mr. Barletta. You're shit. Food for the worms."

"What do you want? You gotta want something."

"It so happens I do. And now is the time to request it, before your brain begins to deteriorate."

"What?" He fell out of the chair onto his knees and gripped the bars of his cell. "Anything! I'll do anything!"

Unimpressed with his plea, I watched with an air of disgust as the man shed his worthless tears. "The reason I brought you here is simple. I need a name. A name only you can give me."

"Who? Who!"

"It seems I was too late getting to Victor Rossi, one of the two associates who transported my brother. He unfortunately passed of a heart attack. The other succumbed rather quickly to the worms. But not before he offered up your name. So, it's up to you, Mr. Barletta, to tell me the name of the man you handed my brother off to."

"You're talkin', what? Almost twenty years ago?" He released the cell bars, slouching in defeat. "How the fuck would I remember that?"

"I don't know." From the inside pocket of my coat, I pulled a capped syringe and held it up for him to see. "This is the antidote that will keep you from dying. I suggest you remember. And if you lie to me? You can kiss it goodbye."

"Ahhh, Jesus. Jesus, Mary and Joseph, what the fuck?" He rubbed a hand down his face. "Victor Rossi … yeah … I know the name. So … the guy … he was …" Frowning, he seemed to think hard on the name, desperate to remember. "From New York … It was … Angelo. Angelo! It was Angelo! Angelo DeLuca!"

"You're certain of this?"

"Yeah. The guy was a prick. I can see his face clear as day." His eyes lit with a sickening hope that I was all too eager to snuff. "His nose was crooked, like he'd been punched too many times. And he had a nasty scar at his eye." Amazing what a person could remember under the right circumstances.

I made a mental note of the name–my next test subject. "So, you're going to sit tight while I do some research on Mr. DeLuca."

"What about these worms, man? I can't take them moving around inside of me. It's freaking me the fuck out!"

I shrugged with a smile. "Hopefully, I'll find him fairly easily. But before I begin this goose chase, you're absolutely certain this is the guy?"

"Yes. I swear on … on my own fuckin' grave. It's him. Please. Get these goddamn things out of me!"

I pushed up from the chair and straightened my slacks, unaffected by his desperation. I had no intentions of helping him. The syringe I lifted held nothing more than sterile saline. "I'll let you know how the research goes."

"Please hurry, man. I can't take this shit anymore."

Rubbing his skull, he rocked back and forth on the floor. "I can't. It's fuckin' with my head."

"Yes. It does fuck with your head. That is the nature of it. We'll speak soon, Mr. Barletta. Enjoy your evening."

"Enjoy .... Enjoy my fuckin' evening? In a prison? Where's my water? I want my water!"

"Ah. Yes, I almost forgot." I strode down the hallway, where a plastic cup sat beside a hose that I'd fed down into the lower levels. I twisted it on and filled the cup half full–about twice the amount I'd given him every other time.

His eyes lit up when I returned with it, his hands outstretched through the bars of his cell. "Please," he said in a shaky voice, carefully accepting the drink, and he took a hearty sip. His brows pinched to a frown, and he opened his mouth, as if to gag. A long black worm slithered past his lips into the cup, and he slowly lowered it with trembling hands, eyes wide and panicked. "Oh, fuck," he whispered in a shaky voice. "Oh, fuckin' hell."

I reached through the bars, urging him to pass it to me.

As if in a trance, he didn't take his eyes off the cup as he handed it over. "This ..." He swallowed a gulp and stifled another gag. "This is what's inside me?"

Holding up the scant bit of water left to the naked bulb, I studied the worm coiled at the bottom of it, noting the teeth that attempted to latch at the surface. "Yes. It seems they've evolved."

He slapped a hand over his mouth, breathing hard through his nose. "I don't want to throw up. I'm afraid more of those fuckers will fly out!"

"Yes, it's better to keep them contained, otherwise they'll try to get away." I lowered the cup and turned back to Barletta, who crouched in the corner of his cell, shaking.

"You're not right in the head, are you? Ain't no way you're right in the head."

The sound of my chuckle echoed down the corridor. "Says the man who beat his son with a bottle?"

"I was drunk. I would never intentionally hurt someone. But this? This is sick!"

Sighing, I stared down into the cup at the fully grown worm. One who'd spent the last few weeks feeding on the man's liver. "I suppose you're right. Must've been all those knocks to the skull." I tapped a finger to my temple. "Have a look at what happens when you beat your children."

"You're not letting me go."

Head tipped in disbelief of the man's ignorance, I snorted a laugh. "Is that what you thought? That our time together would end with me setting you free? I'm afraid not."

Whimpering, he rocked back and forth, his hands running across his skull. "I was in a bad place when I was working for those assholes who took your brother. I'm not there anymore."

"That's great. Truly. I suspect the next time we chat, you'll be a bit preoccupied."

He stilled and looked up at me, the desperation in his eyes almost laughable. "With what?"

"Trying not to vomit your own bowels." I strode back down the corridor, and at the sound of Barletta's outcry, I smirked, glancing over my shoulder. Something caught my eye.

A shadowy figure at the opposite corridor, past Barletta's cell.

Frowning, I turned around, examining the shape, and walked back in that direction, until I was standing in front of Barletta once again.

The figure didn't move. He only stood staring, mostly hidden by the shadows.

"Who's there?" I called out.

"Someone's there? You see someone?" Barletta slammed

himself into the bars of the cage and reached out for my coat. "Get me out of here, doc! I want out!"

Scowling, I looked down to see his fingers curled into my coat, and I pried him loose. When I lifted my gaze again, the shadowy figure was gone. To be sure, I strode closer, the cup holding the worm still clutched in my hand.

Nothing but the empty corridor stood ahead of me, brimming with the sound of Barletta's screams.

Chapter 32

Lilia

After two hours of gathering snippets from various articles and studies on *symbiosis as an evolutionary perspective* for Gilchrist's upcoming essay exam, I was sick of it.

Freaking sick of it.

Who knew beneficial relationships between insects could be so boring?

At least Bramwell's class offered a bit of horror and action with his mind-controlling parasites.

As I eased back in my chair, I caught sight of Mel hustling past my opened dorm room door. Strange thing, university. At home, I'd always kept my door closed, hating the lack of privacy. At Dracadia, I welcomed the occasional hello as one of my floormates breezed past. They were often respectful enough not to enter, and never came off as particularly nosey, or caring of what I kept in my room. Maybe that was why I didn't mind.

"Mel!" I called out, knocking over the coffee cup I'd left on the floor beside my chair ... so that I wouldn't knock it off my desk. "Shit." Nabbing some Kleenex from the box beside my laptop, I knelt down and daubed it, not immediately noticing she'd stopped at my door.

"What's up?" she asked, leaning against the doorframe.

Abandoning the sopping tissues, I wiped my wet hands on the skirt of my dress and pushed to my feet. "Hey, can I ask you a few questions?" With a frantic wave of my hand, I corralled her inside my room and closed the door behind her.

"Sure?"

"It's about the Crixson Project. See, I work in the library, and ... well, I can't find anything on it. The librarian I work with says there are some texts, but they're off limits."

"Those texts are useless and meaningless."

Useless and meaningless. Meaning what? She had better information? "So ... how .... How do you know so much?"

"Why do you want to know?"

Telling her that I had suspicions about Andrea Kepling and the nature of the experiment led by Professor Bramwell's father would've been laying too many of my own cards down at once. I wanted to see what she had on it first. "I find myself questioning Professor Bramwell's current research." I lowered my voice. "I don't trust him."

"You and everyone else."

Okay, seemed I needed a bigger bargaining chip. "I know what happened to one of the participants who escaped."

"How?"

Instead of answering, I shook my head. Had she known it was Spencer who'd informed me, I doubted she'd have given it much merit.

She stared at me for a moment, her jaw shifting. Contemplating. "Come to my dorm tonight, and I'll show you."

Just like that. I thought I'd have had to do something crazy, like sacrifice a goat to get her to tell me the information, but there she was, offering it up like free booze at communion. "Okay. What time?"

"After ten."

A knock on the door interrupted us, and frowning, I opened the door to find a strange blonde wearing fancy threads that, to my untrained eye, looked designer. The harder lines in her face put her at about forty, or so, but her hair and dress gave her a sense of youth. I caught the twitch of her lip, as she gave a quick once-over, clearly examining my less impressive outfit.

"Miss Vespertine?" she asked, like the name left a bitter taste on her tongue.

"Yes?"

"I'm Missy Finch. I own the boutique in Emberwick. Mr. Spencer Lippincott sent me to measure you for a dress."

The air deflated out of me at the reminder that I'd committed myself to that charity event with him. "Oh, God."

"Spencer?" The air of disgust in Mel's voice had me flinching. Not that I cared that she had something against him, but the timing was a bit off. I didn't need her clamming up when I was on the brink of getting somewhere in my nosey inquiries. "Are you seriously hanging out with that guy? He's a creep!"

The blonde's gaze snapped to Mel's, and judging by the repulsed expression on her face, it seemed that Lippincott was more than some rando who'd sent her over to measure me. "I beg your pardon."

"Look, it's a misunderstanding," I intercepted before an all-out brawl could break out in my dorm room. "Miss Finch, I appreciate you dropping by, but I don't need you to measure me."

Her bright blue eyes flared with indignity. "I came all the way over here, leaving my boutique unattended, battling the tyrant at the gate, and now suffering insult to a family friend."

On a huff of irritation, Mel stormed out of my room, and I turned my attention back to the blonde.

"My apologies. Can you just give me a minute?"

She crossed her arms and gave a haughty tip of her chin. "Only a minute."

I chased after Mel, who'd only gotten about three doors

down from me. "Wait. Can you please tell me what the hell is up with Spencer that you hate him so much?"

"I get it. You don't give a shit what the freak has to say. Go off and enjoy your little romance with the provost's privileged son."

Emo Jesus in a black dress, I didn't have the patience for her right then. "I give everyone the benefit of doubt. Including you. Just as I wouldn't give a shit what someone had to say about you without finding out myself, I'd like to be my own judge where he's concerned."

"Then, find out by yourself. But don't say I didn't warn you."

"And what about meeting up? Are we still on for that?"

A furtive glance around and she leaned closer to me. "You're asking for sensitive information. Why the hell should I trust you when you so *openly* trust others?"

"Because you still want to know what I know. And I never said I fully trusted Spencer. Where I come from, spilling secrets gets you killed."

"As is the case here." She ran her tongue over her teeth, and arms crossed, studied me again like she needed to internally ask her other moods for permission first "I don't know why I bother with you, Vespertine. Maybe because you're not a pretentious little trust fund bitch. But you still annoy the shit out of me."

"Is that a yes, then?"

She rolled her eyes and huffed. "Yeah. I guess."

Thank goodness. Breathing a sigh of relief, I returned to my room to find Missy rummaging through the dresses hung in my closet.

"Hey!"

"It's not that you're entirely tasteless, mind you. It's just, well, you have no sense of balance."

"I have balance."

She studied me for what felt like minutes, her eye squinting on occasion as if in disapproval of whatever thoughts ran through her head. "You remind me of someone. Are you related to the Corbins, at all?"

"No. But you're the second person who's asked."

"It's uncanny. The hair." She motioned to her own, wearing a frown as if there was something wrong with mine. "The face. The eyes. It's like I'm staring right at her again."

"Who?"

"An old classmate of mine. Vanessa Corbin. She lived here on the island for a number of years."

"But she looks like me?"

"A spitting image." Waving her hand in dismissal, she shook her head. "Let's get this over with, shall we? I'll take measurements back to my shop and see what dress would best compliment your figure."

"Wait, wait, wait." I threw up my hands at that. "I don't get to pick the dress?"

She glanced toward my outfit and back. "I don't think that's a good idea."

"Well, I happen to be very particular about what I wear. And I'm not really in the position to spend–"

She threw up a hand, refusing to hear what I had to say. "The cost is inconsequential. As I said, the Lippincotts are *friends*."

"Okay. Fine. But I'd like to try it on first before the event. I refuse to wear anything that makes me uncomfortable."

"No can do, darling. Depending on the dress, adjustments could take me right up until the night of."

"Fine." If it happened that I hated the dress, I'd wear one of my own, or fake being sick. Either way, the woman was not about to dictate what I wore.

As she took hold of my shoulders and urged me upright, her gaze landed somewhere on my neck, and she frowned, lifting up the small vial of my mother's ashes dangling from its beaded chain there. "What's this?"

"It belonged to my mother," I answered lamely.

"It'll have to go, the night of the gala. It certainly won't pair well with any dress I provide."

I groaned and shook my head. "Okay. Can we just get to measuring?"

For the next twenty minutes, she must've taken about a hundred different measurements, as if she was about to clone a three-dimensional version of myself back at her shop. With impatience, I let her do her thing, mildly irritated by the slow-mo pace in which she moved.

When she finally finished and left my room, I was actually eager to jump back into the symbiosis of insects.

And I would've dove head-first back into those studies, if I hadn't caught sight of Professor Bramwell reading beneath the tree in the courtyard. Unusual, seeing as he rarely spent a moment outside of his office, or lab, from what I'd observed over the last couple of weeks.

That the guy had to be utterly delectable with a book in his hands made me want to scratch my eyeballs out. I snacked on an apple as I sat on my windowsill, staring down at him, hating that my determination to focus had been completely derailed by the man again.

Yes, a man. Not a boy. Not a classmate.

My professor, whom I found myself thinking about far more than I should've.

What started as a curiosity over what he was reading quickly turned to thoughts of what it must've felt like to be the sole object of his focus, like that book. I imagined him to be intense. Passionately reading every page, desperate to soak up as many of the words as he could.

Staring intently, I ran my thumb over my bottom lip, imagining it caught between his teeth.

All at once, he lifted his gaze, eyes locked on mine.

On a squawk of humiliation, I startled and fell off the windowsill, crashing onto the floor below me. A zap of pain shot up from my ass into my spine, and I grimaced, rubbing the cheek that'd taken the brunt of the fall.

"Classy. Real classy."

Chapter 33
Lilia

Tick. Tick. Tick.

I hawked the clock, until at precisely ten-oh-eight, I headed out for Mel's dorm room. The hallways were never quiet, always bustling with late night study sessions. The commons room at the end of the hallway buzzed with the same physics students cramming for another exam, just as they had the week before. Each of them made obvious because they plastered the chalkboard with their equations and often yelled '*bazinga!*' from *The Big Bang Theory* whenever they solved it correctly. It was the only time the entire corridor smelled like weed, too.

When I reached Mel's room, I only had to knock once before the door swung open, and she peered out into the hallway, looking left and right. A hard yank of my arm had me tumbling forward into the room.

"Hey, a simple *come in* would've worked." I scowled, rubbing the raw spot where her nails had dug into my skin, and glanced around her room, significantly bigger than mine, with a small living room and a hallway that I presumed led to a bedroom.

Ignoring my complaint, she jerked her head for me to follow, and led me down the small hallway to a door she swung open on a bedroom, as I'd suspected.

What I hadn't expected was for her to lead me to another door, a closet, where at its rear stood yet another small door.

"What in the wannabe Narnia is this?" I asked, staring at the frame which appeared to be half the size of a normal door.

"Decades ago, when the dorm was first built, it housed children, like an orphanage. The settlers were terrified of the *savage monsters*," she said in air quotes, "coming and taking the children in the middle of the night. So they built these little doorways leading to the cellars to hide them in the event of a raid."

"I'm guessing the raids never happened."

"You guessed right." Hinges groaned as she opened the door on a creepy stone stairwell, and from the shelf of her closet, she nabbed an LED lamp. "C'mon. Gang's waiting to meet you."

"Gang?" Hopefully that wasn't crazy talk for a pile of dead bodies. I followed her down the staircase, where the air grew thicker and colder. Rubbing my shoulders failed to keep the chill off my skin, and when we finally reached the bottom of the stairs, shivers wracked my bones. "Jesus, you should've given me a heads up to wear a sweatshirt."

"Don't be a wimp." Tiny bells on her bohemian skirt clinked as she led me down a narrow corridor off the staircase that curved to the left.

I couldn't help but think how freaking creepy it would've been to stumble upon something while wandering the passage alone. "What made you want to explore down here? I feel like this is the perfect place to hide dead bodies."

An impish curve of her lips told me Mel definitely had a dark side as she glanced over her shoulder, leaving me to wonder if I was stupid for having followed after her. "The dead have stories," she said. "Have you had any encounters yet?"

"What? Like, ghosts?" Of course I had–a man in a bird

mask, though I hadn't yet worked out if he was the result of too-little sleep, or real. Either way, I had no intentions of mentioning him.

"Yes. The whole campus is plagued with hauntings, but this building? It's the worst."

"Why is that? The Crixson Study?"

"In part, yes." She kept on down the dark hallway, while my gaze wandered the ancient stone walls that seemed to close in on us, the deeper we ventured. Again, I couldn't imagine her exploring down there by herself. "In addition to the experiments, it's also where exorcisms were conducted on kids, back when the place was a monastery. Apparently, some of the builders who worked on the university were superstitious about all that, so about a third of the crew left, and others refused to venture into these little passages, so they were never properly investigated and got sealed."

"The exorcisms .... Is that during the time of Dr. Stirling?"

"You've read about him?"

"Yes." The memory of my readings and the tortures he inflicted certainly didn't put me at ease, as we walked through the tunnels.

"So, in the mid-to-late seventeen-hundreds, the place was sort of a dumping ground for heretics and those accused of witchcraft. They sent anyone with mental illness here, as well, thinking they were possessed. In the early eighteen-hundreds, an asylum opened. That's when things got really disturbing."

"How so?"

"They began torturing the patients, and discarded them in mass graves on what is now Bone Bay. These hideout tunnels became solitary confinement for a number of patients. Where they were starved and left to die."

"Jesus. That's messed up. How do you know all of this?"

She shrugged, running her hands over a stretch of wall that, when I looked closer, appeared to bear scratch marks in the stone. "I spend way too much time reading. But also, there was an investigator back in the eighteen-hundreds, who disguised himself as a patient. Before he mysteriously disappeared, he apparently sent one of his friends encrypted journal entries that detailed the tortures he'd witnessed. They're part of the no access journals in the library."

"So, how did you get access? I work in that department and can't get my hands on them."

"My father is a massive donor for the library and chairman of the Board of Overseers. Administration and board members have access to just about anything. And Kelvin, but there's no bargaining with him. He's too much of a straight shooter."

The corridor finally opened up on a moderately-sized circular room with no windows or doors. A shiver spiraled down my spine as I imagined being trapped there, like the patients she'd mentioned. Candles lit the space where three others sat on large, multi-colored cushions–an Asian guy with pink hair, a young woman with short black pixie hair and tawny skin, and a collection of piercings in her ears, nose, lip and eyebrow. And Briceson, who tipped back a fifth of what I recognized as Jack Daniels.

"Lilia!" he said in a more spirited tone than the last time I'd seen him.

With a slight smile, I waved. "Hey."

The pink-haired guy crossed his arms, eyeing me up and down. "So, you brought fresh blood, Mel?"

"This is Lilia. Lilia? This is Ken."

Pink Hair waved a hand over himself, then lit up what I guessed to be a joint, given the way he held it between thumb and forefinger and took a puff.

"Seems you already know Briceson. And this is Catalina, who we call Cat, for short." In response to her unenthusiastic wave, I gave a curt nod, and the dark-haired girl went back to reading the book in her hands. Squinting, I could just make out *The Anti-Christ* by Nietzsche on its cover.

A bottle of Patron sat in the middle of the circle, which Mel swiped up and poured into a shot glass.

She kicked back the mouthful, filled the glass again, and handed it off to me.

With a shake of my head, I declined, and she shrugged, tipping back a second shot.

Scattered about the room sat beaten up boxes filled with manila folders, and two laptops. Other equipment lay about that I didn't recognize–electronics of some sort that Briceson tinkered with, between stealing sips of whiskey.

"What is this?" I asked, gaze wandering their secret little gathering space.

"Welcome to Anon Amos." Mel slumped onto one of the open cushions and flicked her fingers toward Ken, who passed the joint to her.

"Wait. What? That's you?"

"Yeah, we're kind of the underground version of *Snopes,* here at the university." Voice hoarse, she blew off the smoke and passed the joint to me. Again, I declined, and she shrugged, handing it to Cat instead. "If it's true, we dig up facts. If it's false, we find proof to back that."

"So, when I asked you about the Crixson Project?"

Never taking her eyes of mine, Mel stretched toward Briceson that time and flicked her fingers. From one of the banker's boxes, he grabbed a stack of folders and handed them over. "These files were stolen by two computer science majors back in two-thousand-five. They hid the files down here, never speaking of them. Both were expelled the following year, but since then, this has become a dumping ground for inaccessible information."

"Hasn't the school caught on to that?"

"Not yet." Pushing up from the cushions, she crossed the

room, flipping through the files. "So, I suggest whatever facts you're looking for, now's the time to dig. And when you're done, you'll tell me what you supposedly know about one of the participants." She shoved the folders against my chest and sat back down beside Cat, who still didn't bother to put her book down.

Strange that she didn't require me to offer up my end of the deal first.

I took a seat on the floor beside one of the candles at the opposite end of the room, and laid the folders out in front of me. No idea why the hell I was so nervous, like opening a vault of dead bodies. Oddly enough, it was when I cracked open the first folder that a cold dread brush the back of my neck. Rubbing my hand over it failed to settle the disturbing feeling, especially when I flipped the first enclosed paper over to reveal a slightly familiar face.

"Warren Bramwell," Briceson said from beside me, alerting me that he'd moved from across the room. "Doctor Death's–"

"Father. Yes, I can tell." The eyes may have been a different color, his hair lighter and peppered in gray that hadn't yet touched his son's, but their relation was undeniable. His eyes held the same striking intensity, as if he were peering into the soul. Handsome was an understatement, but perhaps that made up his sinister charm.

"The university's very own Dr. Stirling."

As Briceson spoke, I skimmed through the incident report which must've been taken by a representative of the university, the way it praised his credentials and work. "His background was endocrinology?"

"Yes. As I understand, his wife had battled diabetes since childhood. He hoped to cure it for her."

I flipped the page to a picture of a young, dark-skinned woman clipped to what I recognized as a medical chart.

Yolanda Murdock, age twenty nine, with a history of insulin-dependent diabetes.

Another flip of the page, another woman clipped to a medical report. The next one was a blonde, thirty years of age, who also suffered from diabetes. Same with the next, and the next, and the next. After skimming the medical record of all six women, I kept on through the file to where I found a synopsis of the experiment.

OBJECTIVE: To evaluate the efficacy and safety of NuBram1 Toxin on Type 1 diabetes management in routine clinical practice.

SECONDARY OBJECTIVE: Demographic and biometric data, treatment compliance, adverse drug reactions

METHODOLOGY: Serial injections of NuBram1 purified Toxin over a period of six months. Efficacy measured by increased beta cell mass and insulin levels.

At a glance, the summary painted a picture of legitimacy. Included were detailed graphs that displayed the incremental dosages given to the participants and the symptoms they reported. Digestive changes. Hallucinations. Sensitivity to light.

I frowned, reading through the report. What the hell had the NuBram1 Toxin been purified from? The answer revealed itself on the next page:

Purified toxin derived from Noctisoma larvae.

I knew it. I knew Bramwell Senior had had some dealing with Noctisoma.

An adverse event table detailed more symptoms. Horrific symptoms of suicidal ideation. Night terrors. One of the women stabbed herself in the stomach, claiming she had felt something moving around inside her. Another suffered hallucinations of her dead daughter after she'd refused to eat, telling her that she had to *feed the babies inside of her*.

I flipped quickly for the outcome of the experiment, and found it in a police report, for which an autopsy had been performed on the women after their bodies had been pulled from the lake. All of them had died by mass suicide. The coroner had come to that conclusion based on ongoing mental disturbances documented in the study and no evidence of foul play. The women had apparently submerged themselves into freezing waters, willingly. Two of them showed signs of stroke. All of them had likely suffered hypothermia due to winter temperatures.

I folded the file shut to grab another, when something fell from inside.

A picture.

In it stood three men dressed in lab coats–one I recognized as Dr. Warren Bramwell. The other was Dr. Lippincott. I had never seen the third man before. They flanked eight women, whose faces I scanned over.

My gaze landed on one of the women. A familiar face.

Too familiar.

The picture slipped from my fingers. My heart hammered like a drum against my ribs. Ribbons of panic wrapped themselves around my lungs and squeezed. I took hold of the vial at my collarbone and ran my thumb over the surface of it.

"What is it?" Briceson asked beside me, breaking me from my shocked spell. He lifted the picture from the floor, bringing her to my attention once more.

Hand trembling, I pointed to the woman, third from the right. "That's my mother."

"Wait. You know her?" Mel strode from across the room, plopping down beside me.

"I have a picture back in my room. Yes, that's my mom."

"Holy shit." She snatched the picture from Briceson, staring down at what I couldn't bring myself to look at again. "I was aware of Andrea, thanks to her little tantrum with

Lippincott a few weeks back. Not sure if they ever found her after that. We've not been able to track down any information on the last one though, aside from her intake sheet. It's believed she and Andrea are the two that left the study, but there's nothing on them."

"What name have you searched?" The toneless cadence of my voice mirrored the shock still pulsing through me. I felt like I was caught up in some suspended state of reality. Like I'd slipped underwater and taken a breath.

"Vanessa Corbin. Andrea is actually June Galloway. The locals tell me both of them lived on this island."

Lived on the island? My mother?

"I knew her as Francesca Vespertine. My mom."

Mel tipped her head, as if just then catching on that I wasn't processing the news well. "You okay? You look pale."

I didn't know how to answer that. Was I okay? Not particularly. My brain didn't know where to begin piecing things together. So many flitting strings clamoring inside my head, all of them in need of tying before my brain would settle. And I couldn't. I couldn't tie the pieces together because they didn't make any sense to me. "Fine," I lied.

"Where's your mom now?"

Where's your mom now? The question echoed inside my head, and my thoughts latched onto it like a lifeline. Dread clawed at my stomach and an itch across my forearms had me scratching there. Furiously scratching.

"She died four years ago. Both women are dead, actually." A hollow chill twisted in my gut, churning and gnashing with the stress of feeling like I'd been broken into. Vandalized and robbed of what I'd come to know as truth. I felt numb. Like a dream. It had to have been a dream. No way my mother would've done this to me. To us. Every memory ended on a question mark. Every story she'd told left me wondering how many had been fairytales.

"You're certain that June is dead, as well?" Mel's questions remained a welcomed intrusion to the blackness pulling me in. The impossible void of not really knowing who I was in that moment.

June. Andrea. The names tangled inside my head. "As I understand."

"How do you know this?"

I didn't answer because it was none of her business.

"Okay, can I ask how your mom died?" Mel looked away, the expression on her face a delicate balance of empathy and intrigue. "If you don't want to share the details, that's okay. I understand."

"Suicide. In the bathtub," I said coldly, and squeezed my eyes shut on the images flashing inside my head.

Mama! Please stop!

I cleared my throat and shook my head in an attempt to bat the echo of voices away.

"Don't you find that a little fucked up?"

From her perspective, it probably seemed that way. From mine? It made absolute sense, given what I knew about the *organism* and the way it hijacked the mind. It wanted a water source to mate and breed more eggs.

What made absolute zero sense to me was how my mother had ended up infected, if these women were supposedly only injected with a purified toxin. And why, after twenty years, would she have suffered symptoms? According to what I'd learned in Bramwell's class, they began fairly soon after infection. Was the toxin capable of mind control like that, in the absence of the organism? Could it have delayed her infection somehow?

Unfortunately, nobody in that cramped and suffocating room could likely answer that question. But one man undoubtedly knew.

A heavy weight of exhaustion fell over me, pressing down

on my shoulders. The burden of having to unravel a mystery that made no sense. "What is your conclusion?" I asked.

"That Bramwell Senior killed all those women and had some connection to the pathologist who *conveniently* reported them as suicides for him. How would that look, after all, if Dracadia–the top medical research facility in the world–was plagued by a scandal where six women died and two went missing?" It was plausible. Plausible and shady.

I held out my hand for the picture again, and turned it over to the date on the other side: January 9th, 2003. I was born November thirteenth of the same year.

Was I the reason my mother had left the study? Had someone tried to keep her from leaving?

"Do you know if Bramwell Senior is still alive?"

"He's not. There was a big obituary in the Dracadian Gazette. He died maybe eight years ago? Before my time here. You can probably pull the obituary in the library records."

"Then, I need to talk to his son about this."

A rough shake of my arm dragged me from the trance I'd slipped into again. "No! Are you fucking kidding me? Did you miss the part where I said these were *stolen* files?"

"If my mother was a participant, if she died based on these experiments, then I have a right to get the answers."

Cat groaned, snapping her book shut and setting it aside. "I knew it was a bad idea inviting an outsider. For fucks sake, she probably reads vampire smut."

"Shut up, Cat," Mel spat and turned her attention back to me. "Look, I get it, okay? If it were my mom, I'd be all over that shit, too. But you can't just waltz up to the son of the psychopath who orchestrated all of this. If he's smart, he won't tell you a damn thing, and we all know Doctor Death isn't dumb. Or he wouldn't have gotten away with Jenny's disappearance, the way he did."

"You honestly think he had something to do with that?"

"I was her roommate, okay? And I can tell you there's no way she'd have just up and ran off. He knows what happened to her. Just like he undoubtedly knows what happened to those women. But he's not going to tell you shit. These men are powerful. That power is the reason there isn't any information on these murders. They wipe it all out of existence."

I had a feeling she might've been right about that. Meaning all those flitting strings in my head would forever wriggle and taunt me for answers I'd likely never find. "I'm not stupid. I wouldn't outright ask him."

"Ask him what, anyway? You have your proof. She participated in the study."

"But she didn't die when they did. She died four years ago. What happened in that time?"

As if she could finally see my dilemma, Mel huffed and slouched against the wall. "Well, what do you expect from him? Even if he knows the details of the study, do you think he'd come out and tell you? How the hell do you plan to ask that question?"

"I don't know yet. I'd wanted to work as an assistant in his lab."

She rolled her eyes at that. "Yeah good luck. He doesn't take assistants, and he sure as hell wouldn't want anything to do with a first year. Trust me, I know. I was so desperate to gain access to the missing files that I asked Ross out for coffee." She made a puking gesture, which I would've made a point to tell her was a bit dramatic, seeing as the guy wasn't ugly, except that my head still spun and I kind of felt sick myself. "He's Bramwell's beloved TA, after all. He doesn't do dates, in case you decide to go that route."

"What files?" I asked, ignoring her comment.

"The ones that describe the results of the toxin before these women *committed suicide*?" she said in air quotes. "There's a whole section of notes missing. Daily inoculations that weren't recorded. And what happened to this guy?" She pointed to the one researcher in the photo that I couldn't identify. "There's nothing on him, either. As if he never existed. He's not even in the reports. Neither is Lippincott. No surprise there."

It made sense why Lippincott would've distanced himself from the botched project, if he'd had aspirations to become provost one day. What didn't make sense, and what continued to plague my head through all of this speculation, was why my mother had expelled worms from her mouth. As if she'd somehow gotten infected. How? And why had her and Andrea just recently succumbed to the illness?

"Well, I guess it doesn't matter," I said. "You're right. He doesn't take assistants. I already asked."

"Probably covering his ass. Jenny was dying to work on the Noctisoma project with him. It was all she talked about. *He* was all she talked about." Mel rolled her eyes again, as if it troubled her that her roommate had been so taken with him.

"He refused her, as well?"

"I'm guessing so. She went to meet with him after the midnight lab. She was never seen again."

"And you're convinced it was Bramwell who had anything to do with that."

"CCTV cameras caught her leaving his secret little lab. That was the last anyone saw her."

If that was the extent that they had on the guy, it certainly wasn't enough to convince me that he'd murdered her. He barely gave me, or any other girl in class, the time of day, and I'd never seen him so much as react to those in class who very obviously flirted with him. Surely, the university wouldn't have kept an accused murderer as a tenured professor. "Was he ever arrested?"

"Of course not. Are you kidding me?"

I had to figure out a way to get closer to him. Perhaps

asking him for tutoring lessons, but he'd probably just direct me to Ross for that. There had to be another way. Somehow, Jenny Harrick had found her way to his lab, so it wasn't impossible. I just needed a hook. Something to draw him in, but considering the guy showed absolutely zero interest in any of the students, I'd probably have an easier time capturing the attention of aliens in space.

Mel's finger prodded my arm, once again dragging me from thoughts. "I swear on my dog's grave, if you tell anyone about this place, or these files, you will regret it. Are we clear?"

"Crystal."

"Good. And steer clear of Bramwell. They call him Doctor Death for a reason."

While the mystery of Jenny Harrick's disappearance was certainly a draw, as it related to Professor Bramwell, the bigger curiosity for me was Bramwell Senior. I needed to know more about those experiments and what had happened to my mother. If he'd played some role in her death.

The file I'd read made me question everything. It couldn't have been mere coincidence that the the woman in that picture looked exactly like my mother.

The more horrifying thought plaguing my brain was that everything I'd come to know about my mother appeared to be a lie. Where she'd come from. Who she'd been.

Had she lied about her parents, as well? Was it possible I had family on the island?

The questions seemed endless, but proved to be a motivator for my investigations. Because I intended to get to the bottom of who my mother really was and what had really happened to her.

And not even Doctor Death would stand in the way of that.

Chapter 34

Lilia

Having finished a list of tasks that Kelvin had requested during my work study shift, I hustled to the Adderly Memorial room for some peace and quiet. There, I pulled my laptop from my bag and Googled: *Corbin Dracadia Island*. An obituary popped up for Arabella Corbin, who'd apparently passed just four years ago. Preceded in death by her husband, Richard Corbin. Survived by her only daughter, Vanessa Corbin, who'd gone missing in 2003. The attached picture offered an eerie glimpse of what my mother would've looked like, had she aged to seventy-four years old.

My grandmother.

I tried to wrap my head around that, but it refused to go there. It refused to believe that my mother, a woman I'd adored, respected, trusted, for so many years had lied to me. She'd told me to my face that her mother had passed at an early age of a stroke, and that she'd never known much about her father, either.

For years, I'd believed that.

Even if I assumed that I *had* been the reason my mother had left the study, why lie about her family? In what little I'd gleaned about the Corbins, I hadn't gotten the impression they were terrible people.

Tears formed in my eyes as I Googled more pictures of Arabella. She appeared to have been an active woman, a potter, who'd often attended various craft shows on the island. She seemed to be well liked and respected by her community, who'd spoken highly of her in the comments below the obituary. The younger photos showed her long, auburn hair, like mine, and bright blue eyes—beautiful and vibrant, just like my mother.

Another article on her told of an estate sale held two years before her death. I peered at the address, jotting it down in a notebook. When I Googled the address, it appeared that the house had been in foreclosure at some point.

As soon as work study ended, I headed for the bike rental shed with the address clutched in my palm. After the usual interrogation from the guard at the gate, I biked toward town. Past the strip of shops, I rounded the corner onto a dirt road that ended at a white picket fence. Beyond it stood a small, yellow cottage with a white door, and a bow window half-blocked by a bush with bright pink flowers. The courtyard in front surrounded a sturdy oak tree and a small, white bench beneath it. Stone paths weaved through a wild mess of flowers, and birds flocked around a small stone fountain in their center. While it had a slightly unkempt and unlived in appearance, it was no less adorable with the vast blue of the ocean behind it.

After rubbing away some of the salty residue on the window, I peered through into an empty and quiet space that hadn't looked lived in for years. Keeping on with my nosing around, I unlatched the fence and padded through the small courtyard toward the back of the house. As soon as I rounded the corner, I skidded to a halt. The air caught in my lungs.

A vibrant American elm with bent branches stood off to the side, a single swing hanging from a bough, and behind that, a cliff tapered down to a gorgeous ocean backdrop.

My mother's painting.

The sight of it stabbed my heart. A place I'd thought to be nothing but fictional in her head, one that had always brought me such peace and serenity, turned out to be the home where she'd grown up.

How sad that it now stood alone and abandoned. Unwanted. I wished right then that I had the money to snatch it up and bring it back to life, to own a small piece of my past–a place where Bee and I could come and try to reconcile the mess our mother had left.

I had to assume my mother had had her reasons, though. Maybe those reasons had something to do with Professor Bramwell's father and that study.

Staring out over the ocean, taking in the serenity of the view, I recalled something from my reading. My grandmother had passed four years ago. Frowning, I tugged my phone from my pocket and opened the notes app where I'd jotted the few dates I'd gathered in my research.

July fifteenth.

Around that time, my mother had gone out of town to look into a specialist and financial assistance for the small benign tumor on Bee's eye.

I'd been left in charge of Bee for those two days, so my mother could go alone, which I'd thought strange at the time–she'd never gone anywhere without the two of us. Although not life-threatening for my sister, the cyst had always been part of her insecurity, and perhaps even contributed to the anxiety she'd always felt around others. It'd troubled my mother that we couldn't afford to have it removed, with us not having insurance or any means of paying for it. A little over a week later was about the time when my mother had first started showing signs of illness that we'd thought might've been something she'd picked up in her travels. From there, it had progressed over a period of weeks, up until her death.

Was it possible that my mother had returned home for the funeral? Maybe Bramwell and Crixson had had nothing to do with it. Had she somehow exposed herself to Noctisoma then?

If so, how?

Chapter 35

Lilia

Three days had passed since the night I'd met with Mel. Three days of obsessing over every smidge of information I could squeeze out of Google on my mother and grandparents. Three days of questioning every moment of life. Of trying to construct who Professor Bramwell's father was in my head.

My whole world had turned upside down, thanks to that file. The mental snapshots of my life, up until that point, seemed like an alternate ending to a story that had already been written.

Who the hell was my mother, and why had she lied to me and Bee?

How had she ended up at Dracadia University and connected to Warren Bramwell?

Aside from the few articles covering the suicides, wherein the media was careful not to frame an accusation against Warren Bramwell—for legal reasons, I presumed—I'd found absolutely nothing useful on the man. Some published journals, and his obituary, of course, but nothing significant. Not even those creepy websites that claimed to have access to addresses and public records. Not one photo on Google images, which was weird, given that he had been a professor a number of years. As if he'd been wiped out of existence.

Standing at the front of the class, Professor Bramwell delivered his lecture on Cordyceps–a parasitic fungus that infected ants. It released a chemical that compelled the ant to climb a tree, where the fungus would emerge from its body to release spores that would fall to the ground and infect more ants.

I couldn't help but stare at him, studying his body movements as he lectured. As riveting as the topic may have been, the only thought running through my head was: did the guy's father kill my mother?

Of course, thoughts of Jenny Harrick then came to mind. Were both father *and son* killers?

The accusations I'd heard had seemed nothing but speculation and rumor, hardly enough to pin a murder on the man, unless evidence had been intentionally overlooked.

Even the Crixson Study and my mother's involvement in that left little for me to connect Warren Bramwell to *her* death. It seemed my mother had gotten pregnant and left the study well before the other women had committed suicide.

What if Mel was right, though? What if there was more information that I hadn't seen yet? What if they were powerful enough to get away with murder? To wipe all evidence clean? Was that what they'd done to my mother?

I'd Googled Bramwell Junior, as well, and the results were much the same. Published research journals galore, and some doctoral dissertation award he'd won a few years back, but nothing too in-depth, or personal.

I couldn't leave it alone, though. Fate had brought me to Dracadia, placed me in the path of Professor Bramwell, for a reason. For my mother's sake, I needed to move past the discomfort I felt around the man, or I'd never find out what had truly happened.

At one point during the lecture, his eyes caught mine, and something strange stirred in my stomach. His stare lingered with intensity, forcing me to look away, and when I did, I noticed Spencer's glancing between Bramwell and me. As if he'd caught on, as well.

I wondered how many other students noticed, and the thought heated my cheeks and stomach.

"Miss Vespertine," a deep voice called out, and I turned to see Professor Bramwell with his arms crossed at the front of the room, staring up at me. "What reason would the fungus have for urging the ant to climb the tree instead of remaining on the ground?"

A look around the room showed all eyes on me, and my heart pounded a chaotic beat inside my chest. I'd never been called on in a college class before. Not unless I volunteered information on my own. Most professors only knew me as a number, not a face, and certainly not by name, aside from Dr. Wilkins when I'd attended Covington. He'd never called on me in class, though. "To expand dispersal and the chance of infecting another ant."

"Precisely. And why is that important, Mr. Lippincott?"

"Uhhhh. Because the ant population is too high?"

"Do you agree, Miss Vespertine?"

"While it may be true that parasites do help control insect populations, I think they tend to be far more selfish. What's important to Cordyceps, in particular, is the need to fulfill its lifecycle. And of course, as you said at the beginning of the class, the most important function of any parasite is to secure its transmission to the next host."

His lips curved into the kind of smile that made my stomach flutter and stoked some deep-seated guilt lingering there. "Very good, Miss Vespertine."

Assuming I did suspect that Crixson had had anything to do with my mother, and I wasn't sure it had, given the facts that didn't line up, it didn't make sense that I would harbor any reservations around my professor, when the experiments took place twenty years ago. He couldn't have been more than thirteen, or fourteen, years old at the time.

As he kept on with his lecture, I caught another glance toward me, and the slightest curve of his lips that quickly faded when he turned his attention away.

Perhaps something simmered there. A small flicker of interest on his part, unless I was looking too deeply. Did I have it in me to flirt with my professor as a means to get closer to him?

To *seduce* him?

Absolutely not. The very thought had my guts in acrobatics. But the man was a closed vault, sealed with hot molten steel that I'd never otherwise penetrate. The few interactions I'd seen between him and Gilchrist told me that not even sex managed to crack him. I'd have to appeal to that brain of his, somehow, and in a way that didn't seem annoying. Doing well in his class wasn't enough. I needed him to see me as an exceptional student. As passionate about the organism as he was.

Harmless flirting. Nothing that would've gotten either of us kicked out. I just needed to gain his trust.

At the end of class, I packed up my notebook and headed for the exit.

"Miss Vespertine, a word, if you will," Professor Bramwell said, as I reached the door.

"Of course."

The class cleared out, and once again, Spencer shot me a glance full of disapproval.

As Professor Bramwell gathered up his notes, I forced myself to ignore the way his muscles bulged at his biceps whenever he bent his arm, or the way he'd rolled up his sleeves to expose the map of veins in his forearms. And those hands. Hands that looked both delicate and barbaric, like they could gently wring the very life out of you. They were handsome hands, with trim nails and strong but slender fingers that I could imagine wielding a scalpel with utmost precision. An artist, no doubt.

To flirt with him, even intellectually, I'd have to allow myself to appreciate these things about him. Allow myself to be attracted to a man who was otherwise off-limits. A man that I imagined was powerful enough to have me kicked out of the school faster than I could say *elitist privilege*. And what then? If that happened, I'd never discover the truth about my mother.

"I want to apologize for the other night in the library," he said. "I didn't mean to speak so crass."

"It's fine. Crass is polite where I'm from."

"And where is that again?" The flexing of his left hand invited a momentary distraction.

"Covington."

"Interesting."

"How so?"

"You don't strike me as particularly hostile." His eyes reminded me of pennies in a flame, a searing metallic gaze that warmed my blood.

"I have a feisty side."

"I don't doubt that." And just like that, an invitation to flirt. Whether intentional, or not, I couldn't tell, but it didn't matter. It was an opportunity to begin chipping at his armor.

Flirt, Lilia. Say something back. Something witty, not stupid, or awkward. "It's rather presumptuous of you, though. Assuming that, because I'm from a bad area I should be automatically hostile."

"The fight response is an ancient part of our defense mechanism that has allowed us to adapt, defend. Survive. I'm certain it's served you well."

"You're speaking science again."

His lip twitched as if he might smile, but didn't. "Always." He leaned in, and I could smell the warm cinnamon on his breath over the delicious spice of his cologne. "I didn't say it was a bad thing." His brow winged up as he straightened himself and shoved another notebook into his bag. "That will be all."

I willed the calming of my heart as I gave a sharp nod. Had he flirted back? I wasn't the wittiest or most in tune when it came to men, but the man was close enough to my face to have breached the invisible barrier between professor and student. "Wait … um. Can I ask you a question without you getting mad?"

"Probably not. But go on with your question."

"A while back, when I told you that I believed my mother to be infected with Noctisoma, you asked if she was from here. Do you find it's prevalent in the locals?"

"Prevalent? Not as a general rule, no. They have their own folklore surrounding the berries. They believe they're the poison of bad spirits and tend to stay away from them. It's only ignorant tourists who occasionally consume the berries."

"I'm pretty sure Andrea Kepling wasn't a tourist." I'd have mentioned my mother wasn't either, but no point wasting all of my new-found facts in the single encounter with him.

"And I'm pretty sure we've already had this discussion. You're skirting the flame again, Miss Vespertine."

"Behavioral fevering. I'm merely trying to rid myself of the endless questions plaguing my head." It was almost criminal how at ease I felt flirting over science, and worse, I didn't even feel like I was pretending.

His jaw shifted, eyes narrowed with an amused appraisal. He crossed his arms, and stared down at me, his muscles really working the fabric of the poor shirt that clung to him for dear life. "While I'm intrigued, I'm not at liberty to speak on this matter. And I'd appreciate no more inquiries."

He was intrigued?

By what? The fact that Andrea wasn't a tourist? Or had I actually chipped a small divot in that steely exterior?

"Then, just a general question about the organism itself. I swear it'll be my last."

"What's your question?"

"Are there any cases of delayed symptoms? As in, over the course of years?"

"*Years*? No. The parasite settles in quickly."

Just as I recalled from lecture, but I wanted to confirm. "So they don't go into a latency phase, or something?"

He shook his head, stuffing a stack of papers into his bag. "Not that I've observed. The eggs do have a tough outer coating, like spores that allow them to resist hostile environments, such as extremely cold temperatures, for example." The fact that the small bit of skin peeking between the top two unclasped buttons of his shirt could distract me even a little bit was a testament to the man's allure. The tone of his voice, his extensive knowledge, it was easy to get lost in his words. "But they eventually infect when conditions are favorable–and they are quite favorable in a human."

Which really didn't make sense where my mother was concerned. There was never a time throughout my childhood that I recalled my mother having had so much as a bad head cold, up until she'd gotten extremely ill four years ago. What had triggered her infection? Did it have anything to do with the Crixson Project?

There just didn't seem to be enough evidence pointing me there.

"Have I answered your endless stream of questions?"

Not really, but I didn't want to annoy him with the barrage still kicking around inside my head. After all, the objective was to flirt, not piss him off. "Yes. Thank you."

When he hoisted his leather bag over his head, crossing it over his chest, I caught a glimpse of the scar on his neck, reminding me the man had little reason to trust any of the students at the school, particularly a first year like me. He'd been branded, both physically and by rumor, thickening his armor. Making him harder to crack. That he bothered to entertain my questions at all was surprising. "Stay out of trouble, Curious Moth," he said, as he strode for the door.

Curious Moth.

A nickname.

A fitting one, too, given the fact that I had no intentions of avoiding the flame.

"Hey, smarty pants. Way to make me look bad," Spencer said, as he hustled to catch up to me after class.

"I can't make you look bad. Only you hold the power." I chuckled, pushing my bag up onto my shoulder.

"So, what's the deal with you and Bramwell?"

"What?"

"Like ... the way he looks at you in class. It's weird."

"He probably just noticed that I was kind of drifting off."

"Nah. It's something else. Like, guy body language. I can pick up on that shit."

I snorted at that, trying to imagine how those heated and heavy glances might've looked to Spencer. "Is that the same as mansplaining?"

"I'd just be care–"

"Careful. Yes. I'm very careful. What is it with the warnings?"

"Has someone warned you against me?"

"As a matter of fact, yes."

"Who? Mel?"

I ground to a halt. While I didn't really need another round of drama thrown in my lap, particularly when it neither involved me, nor had happened during my time at the university, perhaps I could clear some of the questions in my head. "What about Mel?" I asked, playing dumb.

Cheeks puffed, he blew out a breath and stuffed his hands into his pockets. "I got drunk. I kissed her. She got squirrely when I didn't want anything to do with her, so she made up some story that I *assaulted* her. I get it, the kiss went too far, but nothing else happened."

"Why would she make that up? Why would any woman?"

"I've known Mel for a couple years now. All I can tell you is, she's not running on all cylinders."

I groaned and started toward my next class. "Right. She must be psycho."

A grip of my arm brought me to a stop, before Spencer released me. "That's not what I'm saying. Stories are her thing. She likes to stir up conspiracy theories and dirt on everyone. I guarantee, if you piss her off? She'll go digging up shit on you, too."

"Yet, you both agree that Dr. Bramwell had something to do with Jenny Harrick. If that's true, why take his class?"

"Because I need the credit for my degree. No other reason. And believe me, it isn't easy to sit in a class when you suspect someone of something like that. I try to see him as innocent, because I know that my friend was wrong for what he did in retaliation. But the way he interacts with you?" Frowning, he shook his head. "It makes me question things all over again."

"His interactions haven't been at all inappropriate." Not obviously so, anyway. Except when he'd cursed in the library. "But I don't need you hawking me, either. I can take care of myself."

"I'm not trying to be disrespectful here. On the contrary. I think of you as a friend, Lilia. That's all."

“Is that all?” As he opened his mouth, I interrupted, “Because I’m not interested in a relationship beyond that.”

His mouth clamped shut and he cleared his throat. “I understand. Are we still on for tomorrow night?”

Swallowing hard, I forced myself to not look surprised that I’d been caught off guard. “Tomorrow night?”

“The Charity Ball?”

“Oh. Right.” I couldn’t back out when he’d likely already paid for the dress. “Sure. As friends, right?”

“Definitely.”

Damn it.

Chapter 36

Lilia

Billie Holiday droned on in the background of my dorm room, as I jotted notes from my expository writing class. I had a meeting with my preceptor to discuss one of the topics that would make up a shit ton of essays I'd be expected to write before the big final at the end of the semester. I'd selected *The Evolution of Biomedicine*, thinking it'd be relevant to my degree, but I hadn't preempted that the class would be boring as hell and taught by a man who didn't know the meaning of inflection.

The Very Thought of You came on, and I paused, the song taking me back to when I was younger and my mother would play an entire record of Billie Holiday while she cooked. With a glass of wine in her hands, she'd dance around the kitchen, making an absolute mess that my sister and I would have to clean up.

It'd made me happy to see her so happy, though. Even at the prospect of having to scrub spaghetti sauce off the cupboards, I'd loved when she cooked.

Beside me sat a steaming mug of the black rock tea I'd gotten from the apothecary in town. I'd added the honey gums to it, which sweetened the bitter flavor, making it a delicious complement to my studies.

A knock at the door interrupted my thoughts, and frowning, I shuffled across the room and swung the door open. Missy Finch stood in the hallway holding a long garment bag.

Damn it. I'd hoped that maybe she'd forget me. Or maybe the dress would accidentally fall into a shredder.

"It's time!" she squealed enthusiastically, and she pushed past me, into my room. "Let's try it on!"

"Oh, this is actually a really bad time for me. I'm trying to write–"

"It's imperative that I make sure it fits. I'm not dealing with the gate tyrant again. We're doing this now."

Shoulders slumped in defeat, I watched her unzip the garment bag, and when she pulled the dress from inside, the air wheezed out of me. *The Dress* was a long, deep burgundy satin skirt with delicate black tulle. Its off-the-shoulder bodice, adorned with black and burgundy star flowers and accented with gleaming diamonds, had my jaw cocked open.

"I thought the burgundy would complement your hair. Come, come. Let's get undressed." That snapped me out of my trance.

"Wait, what? Here? I'll go into the bathroom and change."

Her face pinched to a frown. "Drag the train across a bathroom floor? I think not." With that, she draped the dress over my desk chair and turned around, crossing her arms with a huff. "Ridiculous. Had we been in a proper boutique ..." She shook her head and huffed again. "Never mind."

Eyes on her, I quickly slid out of the ratty sweats I'd worn, which would undoubtedly had her nose turning up, had she not been so excited about that damned dress. With nervous hands, I slid my legs into the unlatched dress and carefully pushed my arms through the sheer sleeves that also held the gorgeous starflower detail. Once dressed, I turned to face her, catching my reflection in the mirror.

On a gasp, I stared at myself.

Me, but so … elegant. A far cry from the poor Covington girl who wore her mother's hand-me-downs.

"It's lovely, isn't it?" Missy's voice, so close, snapped me out of my staring. "Fits like a glove," she said, fidgeting with the buttons at my back. From the foot of the garment bag, she grabbed a black leather case, which she opened. Inside, lay a beautiful diamond starflower choker, with diamond leaves between each flower, and a set of diamond earrings to match. She removed my vial necklace, dropping it gently into my palm, and fastened the choker in its place. So beautiful and delicate against my skin tone.

"Perfect," Missy added.

I couldn't stop staring. The dress held such a darkly alluring appeal that, when paired with the diamonds, made it almost seductive in itself. Way too much for a friendly date with Spencer. Way too much. "I can't wear this."

"Excuse me?"

"It's gorgeous. Absolutely stunning. But Spencer is going to get the wrong idea."

She loosed what sounded like a cross between a laugh and a scoff. "That is the tragedy of women, isn't it? We deny ourselves beauty for the sake of *misleading* men."

Ugh. When she put it that way, it did sound ridiculous. Still, I didn't want to draw attention. From anyone. "I get that, but I feel like an oyster without a pearl." Missy's lips curved to a smile, and she brushed a strand of hair behind my ear. "And what of the other oysters once their pearls are plucked?"

I'd have hated getting into an argument with her, because the woman probably had some plucky comebacks, judging by the last two she'd thrown at me.

"I can't get over how much you look like her. Vanessa, the woman I–"

"I know who she is. Were you friends?"

"Hardly. She was my competition in everything. Sports,

academics, *men*. Things that don't really matter anymore." She twisted around and cracked open my Caboodle, which held small things like the mascara I almost never wore, chapstick, some hair ties, and a lipstick the same shade that my mother would never leave the house without wearing.

Missy popped its cap and twisted it up, revealing a deep berry color, and with a glint of intrigue, she plastered it onto my lips.

"She was my mother," I finally confessed before rubbing my lips together. "Do you know if she has any family on the island?"

I only wore lipstick on rare occasions, but as I stared at myself in the mirror, I couldn't help but appreciate how perfectly it matched and added a much needed pop of color to my face.

Lips pressed to a hard line, she shook her head. "Her mother passed about four years ago. Her father about a year before that. Good honest people. Fashion-challenged, of course. But good people."

"That was all the family she had?"

"As far as I know. The Corbins were a pretty tightly-knit family. I personally found it a little unbelievable that Vanessa would up and leave. Just ... completely out of character."

"Did you know a June Galloway?"

She snorted and rolled her eyes. "*Everyone* knew June. A bit strange, that one. She hung out with the burnouts, mostly."

"Was she friends with my mother?"

"Not that I know of. Your mother was a bit more *goody-two-shoes* than June."

"Do you know if either of them attended Dracadia?"

She made a face like I'd said something outrageous and let out a snooty chuckle. "No. I don't think so. The school was a little out of budget for their families. Particularly

June's. Only the elite and wealthy attend this school. And ... you."

"Thanks," I said in a flat tone.

"It wasn't an insult." She circled me, fussing with the dress. "I love money, but wealth is exhausting. The look on your face when you first saw yourself in this dress is something I rarely see. I found it ... gratifying."

"I do love the dress."

"Good." Brow winged up, she sauntered in front of me. "Wear it. Feel beautiful. And for god's sake, Lilia, enjoy yourself."

Chapter 37

Devryck

"Stay away from me! Stay the fuck away!" Wild, silvery eyes glowed in the dark from where Barletta crouched in the corner of his cell. "Don't touch me!" A sob ripped from his chest, and he clawed at the wall, his back hunched further than the last time I'd fed him. Dried blood coated his nails, the tips of which had broken off with his scratching. His body held long, red marks–slices he must've somehow made in his skin.

Frowning, I scanned over the room, finding nothing but the mattress, the Bible he'd requested on my last visit, and a small, plastic comb filled with hair that'd fallen out. "How did you get those marks?"

A whimper echoed in his cell, as he shook his head and scratched at the walls harder than before. "Please," he whispered in a shaky voice. "Please don't hurt me."

At that point in the infection, I'd have expected more hostility out of him. More desperation for escape. The cowering in the corner was something new. "Would you like some water?"

He breathed hard, clearly scared shitless for some reason, as he clung tighter to the wall, his eyes shifting.

Impatient, I strode toward the hose and filled a cup halfway, just like last time. When I returned to his cell, he didn't bother to come closer when I held the paper cup through the bars, so I set it down on the floor and stepped back.

He took an uncertain lurch forward, then halted, eyes flitting from me to the cage, as though gauging the distance. His behavior reminded me of a small animal, like a rodent.

"I'm not going to touch you. I've no idea why you're so skittish, all of a sudden."

Scrambling on all fours, he drove forward, swiped up the cup, and gulped back the proffered fluids. A long scratch ran the length of his wrist, from the bottom of his palm to his elbow, as if he'd toyed with the idea of cutting deeper.

Again, I scanned over his cell in search of whatever he might've used to cut himself, but still only found the comb as the sharpest object.

Just as before, he lowered the glass on a gag, and palms flat against the concrete, he retched. Blood-tinged fluids expelled from his mouth, splashing onto the concrete. The movement in the puddle directed my attention to about four worms wriggling there.

Moaning, Barletta backed himself to the wall again. "Fuck! Fuck!"

"Tell me how you got those cuts on your skin."

"Are you crazy?" A cross between a sob and laughter reverberated off the walls. "You put them there! You crazy son of a bitch!" He dug his fingers into his forearm, scratching and scraping, until the first red drops appeared. "Just like you put the worms in me. It was you!"

Self harm wasn't unusual in the infected, though only to a certain degree, and as I examined his flank, I supposed it was possible that, with some impressive twisting, he could've done it to himself. With the hallucinations he suffered, it wouldn't have surprised me if he'd gotten caught up in a scene inside his head, of something attacking him that way.

As much as I would have loved to end his suffering and get

on with harvesting the toxin, though, it was important to let nature take its course.

And it seemed nature had already decided the man's fate.

Staring down at the papers strewn across my desk, I tried to make sense of Barletta's behavior. He'd begun to enter the stage of aggression in his illness. The effects of the organism tended to make its victims combative and violent, but his earlier reaction baffled me.

My cellphone rang and, recognizing the number as one of my contacts, James, a fellow Rook I'd gotten in touch with a while back, I answered it. "Yes?"

"I have to admit, Devryck, this task of finding Angelo DeLuca was probably the most challenging yet."

"How so?"

"There's really nothing on this guy. Spent some time in prison. Seems his family cast him out for being something of a loose cannon. Had a few jobs–odds and ends. But his last known location was New York about four years ago."

Four years ago. Great. The asshole could've been anywhere. Easing back into my chair, I pinched the bridge of my nose and let out a groan.

"Not sure if you saw the news a couple weeks back?" James asked, but as of late, the barrage of political bullshit, along with my own preoccupations, had kept me away from television. "He was apparently involved in the murder of some bigwig investor out of Massachusetts. Guess his name was smeared in blood on the walls."

"You got a picture of this guy?"

"I got an older mugshot of him. Looks like he was imprisoned for some drug charges a while back. He was also charged with human trafficking, but prosecutors apparently dropped that because the victim was unwilling to cooperate."

I blew out an exasperated breath. "So, you have nothing recent?"

"Aside from that murder a couple weeks ago, no. Sounds like he fucked with the wrong person, and my guess is he got himself killed."

My feelings were mixed on that. Partly relieved that I wouldn't have to track him down and deal with dragging him back here, but also disappointed that I wouldn't have the opportunity to kill him myself. "If you could send over the mugshot, that would be great."

"Yeah, no problem. Sorry I couldn't scrounge up more than that, but it sounds like the FBI can't even track the asshole down. I'm thinking he's dead."

"What a shame that would be."

"Yeah. One less scumbag in the world." He had no idea the level of scumbag the guy was. That I suspected he'd been the one to ultimately murder my brother. The one who'd tormented Caed with a blowtorch.

How miserably I could've made him suffer for it.

"I appreciate your efforts. If you manage to come up with anything else, don't hesitate to contact me."

"Always. Take care."

On those parting words, I hung up the phone. *Fuck*. Was probably for the best that I hadn't found him. Getting involved in FBI matters would throw a bullseye on my back, and I certainly didn't need that right then. Not when I already held a man skating the edge of death. It would only be a matter of time before Barletta succumbed. Besides, I'd done enough to exact my brother's revenge, hadn't I?

The motive for Caedmon's kidnapping had been clear to me all those years ago, when I'd first learned of how important my father's discovery was, and to what lengths he'd gone to protect it. The ability to cure the incurable amounted to millions of dollars. Even in the incapable hands of criminals, the science could've been sold. Replicated. If not for the protection of The Rooks and the university, I'd have probably been just as much at risk as my brother had been. It was a shame my father had never acknowledged the ruthlessness, the depraved lengths others would go in order to claim his discovery. Perhaps if he'd extended the protection offered to him, my brother would've still been around.

For the sake of not drawing any attention to myself, I decided to pause my pursuit of Angelo DeLuca. I'd soon have a dead body to deal with, anyway.

Barletta was enough. For now.

My phone buzzed again, and I looked down to see a text from Lippincott:

I hope to see you at this evening's gala.

Groaning, I sent nothing more than a thumbs up in response. I hated the fucking dog and pony show of academic funding. Why the rich couldn't quietly hand over their money without the need for caviar and banal conversation was beyond me.

Before packing up and heading back to my campus quarters to get ready for the evening's crap crusade, I decided to check on Barletta one more time.

The quiet, as I made my way down the dark corridor, marked the first sign that something was wrong. The sound of my footsteps against the concrete should've surely triggered his moaning and pleas. It was the blood pooling out of the cell into the corridor that had me slowing my steps. I finally reached his cell, where he lay slumped to the side, his back pressed against the bars of the cage. Frowning, I withdrew the key and unlocked the door, rounding his body to find an absolute macabre scene. One mangled eyeball lay popped from its socket against his cheek. The other had been gouged, completely mutilated, oozing blood down his face. Clutched in his hand lay a crude looking tool–a sharpened piece of stone in the same aged shade as the surrounding walls. I flicked on the light of my phone and trailed it over the cell, not finding any divots or broken stone. How he'd gotten his hands on it left me puzzled. At the same time, it made sense how he'd managed the scratches on his body, even if finding him this way didn't add up. Suicide of this manner was extremely uncommon. The worm sought water to mate and reproduce. To live.

I thought back on the coroner's report for Lilia's mother, and how she'd slit her wrists. Was this evolution? Or was something sinister at play?

As I crouched beside him, the stone in his hand snagged my attention again. Earlier, when I'd offered him the drink, I'd noticed a long scratch on his inside wrist. From the angle he faced, he would've tipped the cup back with his right hand. I'd also seen him write with his right hand. Double checking, I twisted his wrist to confirm the scratch there. Yet, the stone to gouge his eyes rested in his left hand. Just a theory, on my part, but it seemed his right hand was dominant and would've been the one to gouge his eye, had he done it to himself.

"Fuck." I had to cast my inspections aside and hustle, as the parasites would only stay contained within the body for so long before escaping for a water source.

Grabbing a stretcher parked at the opposite end of the corridor, I hustled back to the room and awkwardly hoisted Barletta's body onto it. A glance at my watch showed it was just after seven. Enough time to deal with Barletta and head to the dreaded gala.

I wheeled Barletta to a separate room down the hallway–one that housed a large, silver hydrotherapy tank I'd purchased. A hose sat just inside of it, and I cranked on the water, allowing it to fill. I flipped on the naked bulb overhead, then slid Barletta's body from the stretcher and into the tank, where he slumped to the bottom. The water rose quickly, swallowing his legs, arms, and, finally, his face. Angling my cellphone's flashlight over the water, I watched as, without fail, small black objects wriggled out of his mouth and nose. A few down by his legs had undoubtedly emerged from his anus, somehow finding their way out of his clothes. Over a dozen parasites emerged from the corpse, darting around the water in frantic search of a mate. His belly shifted with more of them.

As I stared down at the horrific scene, I couldn't help but think of how far I'd come from the boy who'd cowered in the supply closet, hearing voices of the dead. The frightened teenager who couldn't stand to be in the same room as a corpse. It was my brother's demise that had pulled me from those fears and into the macabre fascination I'd developed with death. My curiosities had led me into that cold refrigerator, where my father kept bodies he'd been asked to examine. And it was there, staring into the eyes of one of the decedents, that I imagined my brother laid out. The visual had somehow humanized the monsters inside my head, and I no longer feared them. The more I learned about the human body, the less I heard those terrifying voices, until at some point, they faded entirely.

Only a blissful silence.

After a good couple of hours, most of the worms will have escaped into the water, which I would collect and allow them to mate with the other worms I'd harvested. I'd then take him to the autopsy room and open him up, to collect brain and liver samples, where the toxin would be most potent for isolation and purification.

Each time the worms infected, their toxins became more

specific for human genetics, and the elixirs became more effective. The effects lasted longer.

Unfortunately, I was running out of test subjects. I'd been able to justify tracking down the men who'd taken my brother, but with news of Angelo missing, I could only pray that the latest elixir was successful. Otherwise, I'd have to seek another victim.

Chapter 38
Lilia

Just breathe. Just. Breathe.

I sat at the back of the campus bus, hoping to avoid any and all attention. Spencer had offered to pick me up at my dorm, but that felt a little too *date-like*. In retrospect, given the number of eyeballs glued to me right then, I regretted the decision.

My leg shook incessantly beneath the puffy tulle as the bus jostled about, and I prayed one of my boobs wouldn't pop loose, because wouldn't that have been the icing on the shit-cake?

The bus slowed to a stop at Carmady Hall. One more stop, and I'd finally break free of the ogling from the other students returning to their dorms after the evening classes. They weren't even discrete about it, for crying out loud, and I had to keep my attention toward the window just to prevent any confrontational remarks flying out of my mouth.

The bus jolted into motion again, my breasts jiggling and testing the integrity of every stitch in the bodice. Kudos to Missy for whatever magical thread she'd used to keep it all together.

The next stop was Jaxstone Hall, but because the campus bus didn't travel as far as Wattscrick Hall, where the gala was to be held, I'd have to cut through Canterbury Gardens. It was a ten minute walk, past the old mausoleum.

A little creepy.

Of course, I wasn't entirely stupid. I had pepper spray tucked inside the ribbon at my waist, the one Jayda had given me just before I left for Dracadia.

When the bus finally stopped again, I damned near leapt to my feet. Mercifully, Missy had let me get away with black, embellished flats, when I told her how accident prone I was in heels. Not entirely enthused, but she'd conceded without much more than a quiet grumble.

"Can I get your number?" one of the passengers asked, as I breezed past. Probably a freshman.

I didn't bother to turn and look at him as I hustled off the bus before the anxiety rattling through me could shake me off balance and send me tumbling to my face. Once on solid ground, I closed my eyes and took a breath, but at the sound of the door closing, I spun around and knocked on the glass.

Face scrunched with obvious irritation, the bus driver opened the door again.

"When is the last pickup?" I asked, fidgeting with the tulle of the my skirt.

"You're looking at it."

"Wait. You don't come through here again?"

"Nope. You need a ride back? You'll have to call a DracUber."

"DracUber?" Of all the cheesy names ... "Is it ... like Uber?"

"Something like that." She slammed the door shut on a waft of air that ruffled my hair, and took off down the street.

I hadn't brought any cash with me to call for a ride. Shit.

Temperatures had dipped slightly, but the humiliation of the bus ride kept me nice and toasty as I stepped onto the path of the gardens. My dress rustled over the concrete, and I was grateful Missy couldn't see me right then, or she'd have probably thrown a fit about the hem getting sawed. Overhead, the moon shone high, thank goodness, or it would've been a pitch-black trek around what had once served as a burial site.

Walking alone in the dark was nothing new for me, I'd done it so many times back at home, it didn't even feel abnormal, or unusual. While I'd definitely run into my share of weirdos, I'd never actually been harmed.

However, I'd never worn a gorgeous ballgown with my breasts half sticking out of it before.

What few stray hairs hung from the loose French twist I'd clipped up stood on end, my muscles poised and ready to draw the pepper spray if necessary.

The gardens were peaceful, though.

Serene.

It felt a little like walking through a pristine, old English courtyard in a dream, with all the perfectly trimmed hedges, vibrant mums and colorful late summer blooms. I couldn't wait to see the university in the thick of autumn. How beautiful it could look with all of the fiery oranges and reds.

The sound of crunching leaves sent me skidding to a halt, and I spun around, eyes scanning the surrounding shrubs and trees. I watched for any sign of movement, but found nothing. Not wanting to stick around, I kept on through the garden, ears piqued for any other sound.

Light up ahead caught my eye, and I could make out what looked like a glass-enclosed solarium. My heart caught in my throat, and I stopped. From where I stood, I sighted a crowd of people in their fancy dresses and tuxedos, the crisp white tablecloths below the soft glow of candles. The place oozed wealth.

Oh, God. What am I doing?

It was too fancy. Way too fancy for me.

I turned to leave, but paused when my gaze snagged on

someone standing just outside of the solarium. Cigarette in hand, he stared up at the stars, but the sight of him in a perfectly-tailored black coat and slacks made my heart catch in my throat.

Bramwell.

Mascara'd eyes clenched, I sucked in three deep breaths, and swayed when a wave of dizziness swept over me. Shaking it off, I kept my eyes glued to Professor Bramwell's back, and I stepped out of the garden onto the Solarium's patio, only a few feet from where he stood. As if sensing my presence, he kicked his head to the side, not yet having turned to look at me, and panic wound in my stomach as I took in his perfect profile and that model-worthy jawline.

Hide, my brain urged. Don't let him see you like this.

The moment he turned around, though, it was too late. Our eyes locked. A chill wound down my spine as I took in the expression on his face. Not an exchange between student and professor, but like two strangers. Intentional and intense. I wanted to crawl inside myself and become invisible, for the way his gaze devoured me.

His broad shoulders tapered to a fit waist, and he stood with a drink in one hand, a cigarette in the other. I'd never seen him look so casual, yet imposing at the same time. The man filled his suit with a sharp, lethal grace and an air of authority.

An utterly thigh-clenching sight.

The world around me turned silent, a dark galaxy spinning with a gravitational force that drew me closer. Every nerve kindled to life under his stare, and my skin prickled.

"Lilia?" The voice from behind hit me like a cold bucket of water, and I turned to find Spencer, also decked out in a tuxedo. His eyes scanned me up and down, wide with fascination. "Jesus. You look ... wow."

A glance over my shoulder showed Professor Bramwell

turning back toward the stars, undoubtedly disinterested in our meeting.

"Did you walk here?" Spencer asked, looking past me toward the garden.

Snapping out of my daze, I shook my head. "No. Campus bus."

"You took the campus bus?" His brows winged up, and he shook his head. "Okay, it's settled. I'm driving you home."

"You have a car? I thought students weren't permitted to have cars on the island."

Wearing a smug grin, he shrugged. "Most aren't. My family actually lives on the island, though. If you have residence here, or you're staff, you can get a pass."

"Must be nice." Not that I had a car—or could afford one, for that matter.

"C'mon. You gotta be freezing." He offered a bent arm, into which I reluctantly slipped mine.

"Just to clarify–we're friends."

Spencer chuckled, shaking his head. "Who hurt you?"

"What does that mean?"

"I've never met someone so adamant about avoiding a date."

"You're not calling this a date, are you?" Frowning, I pulled my arm back, and he gripped it, holding it in his.

"Relax. We are two friends attending a charity gala."

"Good." Having established that, the tension in my muscles eased a bit. "What's the charity for, anyway?"

"A pissing match for the wealthy, mostly. Pardon my French."

"I prefer your French. It makes me feel less ... posh."

"The gala ultimately funds Professor Bramwell's research, under the guise of conservation breeding." Another glance over my shoulder showed Professor Bramwell was no longer there, as Spencer led me through one of the glass doors. "If I recall from the invitation, it's to help maintain genetic diversity for the moths that are indigenous to the island. Guess it was a requirement for using the Sominyx moths in research."

The air warmed to a very toasty temperature, as we stepped inside the solarium.

"Ah. So replace the moths in the environment that are killed in the lab."

"Precisely," Spencer said, leading me farther into the elegantly decorated room.

Black candelabras flickered about the space, giving a soft luminescence. A sea of elaborate gowns and tuxedos had my stomach in knots, despite fitting in for the style of dress–in that respect, Missy did well. Aside from a few younger faces–Kendall being one of them, as she sent me a death stare from where she stood beside one of the rugby guys that I recognized from the other day in the dining hall–the crowd seemed to be mostly older folks, which I supposed made sense at a charity event.

The stiff elegance was somewhat softened by the piano music that filled the pause between all the many conversations going on around me.

At the center of the room stood a glass enclosure that reached up to the high arched glass ceiling. Like an enormous version of the glass domes from our midnight lab, and inside, hundreds of the black Sominyx moths fluttered about.

"I'll grab us a drink," Spencer said, but his words hardly registered, as I released his arm and made my way over to the moths, fascinated by them. Their black wings indicated no sign of infection, as I'd learned in midnight lab. One moth had perched itself against the glass, and when I pressed a finger there, its wings flitted. More moths flocked to my side of the glass, as if drawn there. I glanced down to see the light reflecting off the little starflowers on my dress.

"Drawn to light." At the sound of the deep voice, I turned

to see Professor Bramwell staring through the glass only a couple feet away from me. The sight of him stirred my pulse, just as before.

"There are so many of them. Where did they come from?"

"Purchased from a breeder here on Dracadia. The university's penance for using them to study Noctisoma. Dracadia is the only place these moths call home, so their numbers could deplete, if we're not careful."

"They're the organism's natural host, though, aren't they?"

"Yes. But not every moth is doomed to be infected. Only the curious ones." With a glass of champagne in hand, he stepped closer, toward me, yet careful to keep distance between us, it seemed, as he came to a stop at some invisible line. "Do you see the latch on the ceiling up there?"

Peering upward showed a glass door, of sorts, at the roof of the solarium, a gap between the panes where it didn't fuse as tightly as the others. "Yes."

"They'll open at the end of dinner and release the moths into the wild."

"I'm sure the bats are looking forward to it."

His lips curved upward, and the dark chuckle that followed had my stomach as much aflutter as the moths. "Fortunately, the uninfected ones are a bit savvier at survival. Although, that would be a much more merciful end, don't you think?"

"I suppose it would. I couldn't imagine being an insect. Pursued by so many dangerous things." I dared a glance, and found him looking at my lips, where I'd reapplied the lipstick before leaving my dorm.

"You need to pay closer attention, Miss Vespertine." He twisted around, as if scanning the room, which compelled me to do the same.

Spencer, staring at me from across the room, wore a curious expression.

"I see you and Spencer are hitting it off." Professor Bramwell kicked back his drink and, as one of the uniformed women passed with a tray of champagne flutes, signaled for another. I couldn't help but notice the flirtatious smile on her face, as he took the drink without even bothering so much as a glance at her.

She turned toward me, her brows winged up over striking gray eyes. *"Voulez-vous boire un verre, mademoiselle?"*

While I recognized the sultry words as French, one of the native languages spoken by locals on the island, I had no idea what she'd asked. "I'm sorry, I don't entirely understand. Are you asking if I'd like a drink?"

A smile slanted her lips and when she nodded, I answered with a polite, "No, thank you."

Her smile lingered another moment, before she slid her attention back toward Professor Bramwell whose eyes were on me then. *"Si vous comprenez, retrouvez-moi dans le placard dans dix minutes."*

A muscle in his jaw twitched and he dragged his attention from me to the server. *"Je comprends. Et je décline votre offre."* The smooth cadence of his voice held an alluring fluency that left me both intrigued and wanting more. Whatever he said to her, though, seemed to knock her composure off kilter, as the server rolled her shoulders back, offered a clipped nod, and sauntered off.

I stared after her, puzzling their interaction.

"You never responded to my inquiry," Professor Bramwell said, interrupting my thoughts and sipped his new glass of champagne.

My mind wound back to his last comment about hitting it off with Spencer. "We're just friends."

"Friends," he echoed, as his eyes cruised south, down the length of my gown and back.

I'd been ogled by men since I'd first sprouted breasts, but Bramwell's gaze held something different. Something I wanted to study and unravel, without all the other people in the room. An unspoken command, and the unsettling tension that had my bones vibrating.

An intricate maze I wanted to get lost inside.

Warmth rushed beneath my skin, undoubtedly leaving me flushed.

It was strange seeing him that way–without a book in his hand, or antsy to stride off somewhere. It almost seemed as if he didn't know what to do with himself in the setting.

Not unlike me.

"To be honest, I feel a little out of place here." I glanced around, catching the stares of a few guests–men and women. "It feels like everyone knows I'm dirt poor."

"You think they're staring at you because you're poor?" He buried a smirk in his drink and tipped back a long swill that emptied the glass. His jaw flexed with the clenching of his teeth as he swallowed. "The wealthy possess an insatiable appetite for the rare and priceless. They stare because you're the only thing *worth* staring at."

The air turned heady, tickling my chest with each intoxicating inhale. Cheeks flushed, I turned away and caught sight of Spencer waving me over to where he stood among a few men, including his father.

I didn't want to go to Spencer, though. I wanted to stay there, with my professor, fighting to catch my breath. Beside me, the moths fluttered about, their movements mirroring the sensation in my stomach every time the man opened his mouth.

"Go, Miss Vespertine," Professor Bramwell whispered, his proximity setting my nerves aflame. "You're far too young to live a life without mistakes." On those parting words, he strode off with an air of arrogance that made my knees weak.

My head urged me to follow him. I wanted to.

Instead, I made my way over to Spencer, who handed off a dark, purple-colored drink.

Studying it, I frowned at the deep color, through which I couldn't see the bottom of the glass. "What is this?" I gave it a sniff, noting nothing more than a sweet berry scent.

"Just punch," he said and took a sip. "If you think the good provost would let me get away with spiking it, think again."

Mouth dry after the encounter with Professor Bramwell, I took a sip, and the sweet flavor hit my tongue with an unexpected delight. "It's really good." I took another sip, trying to place the taste of it. "What's it made out of?"

"No idea. But I guarantee a shot of rum would've made it even better."

"I've never tried rum."

"Oh, we have to remedy that. Not tonight, obviously." With a slight nudge to my arm, he urged me back toward the group of men with whom he was standing a moment ago. "I want to introduce you to my father."

The thought of coming face to face with a man who had participated in the research study that may, or may not, have resulted in my mother's death felt a bit heavy for the evening. While I'd have loved to have needled his brain for some answers, the dress had me feeling off-guard. "I don't know."

"It's fine. He's had a few drinks. It's probably the best time to meet him."

Perhaps if he got drunk enough, he'd forget ever seeing me there. With reluctance, I followed after Spencer, stealing another sip of my drink.

"Father, I would like to introduce you to someone. This is my friend, Lilia."

A flicker of consternation flashed over the provost's face, before he smiled and reached out a hand toward me. "Lilia. It's a pleasure to meet you. Spencer tells me you're a pre-med major, as well."

"Well, I haven't exactly decided on med school yet. I'm wavering a bit."

"I, um ... I'm sorry for my strange behavior that day in the dining hall. I didn't mean to be rude. You simply took me by surprise."

"How so?"

"You remind me of someone I knew."

"Oh? Who?" I played, knowing damn well who. While the question tickled the tip of my tongue, begging me to ask him what he knew about the deaths of those six women, I bit it back.

Waving his hand in dismissal, he chuckled. "I see so many faces pass through this university, it's hard to pinpoint where, or who, exactly. Strange how our brains work that way, isn't it?"

"Very strange. You seem familiar to me, as well," I lied.

Another one of the servers, a young, bright-eyed blonde, stepped toward us and placed a hand on the provost's arm in a way that struck me as a bit intimate. She leaned in to whisper something in his ear, and I caught his gentle squeeze of her hand.

He nodded and released her. "Dinner is to be served soon. Lilia, will you join us at our table?"

"Sure." Even if I'd have preferred to sit with the moths.

The provost led our small group toward a round table that sat eight, and everyone settled into a chair, Spencer beside me.

An older man I didn't recognize offered a wink, as he slid into the seat to my left, instantly kicking up my discomfort. An equally-aged woman, dressed in embellished jewels, claimed the seat on the other side of him.

Across from us, the provost took his seat, stealing the occasional glance toward me and only breaking the maddening habit when a man passed behind him, patting him on the shoulder.

"May I ask how old you are, young lady?" The man beside me leaned toward me just enough that my defenses reared up again.

I cleared my throat and took another sip of my drink, before setting it down on the table. "Twenty."

"Such a wonderful age. I remember being twenty years old. Attending this very university. Rugby captain."

"Wow. That's great."

"Charles Dandridge," he said, holding out a pudgy hand toward me.

"Lilia," I answered, returning his handshake.

"It is a pleasure to make your acquaintance, Lilia." His gaze dipped low, and there was no doubt in my mind where it had landed. "I was quite the ladies' man back then."

"I'm sure." I cleared my throat again and turned away from him. In doing so, I caught sight of Professor Gilchrist making her way toward our table.

Don't sit here. Please don't sit here. Please don't sit here.

To my utter dismay, she took the seat beside the provost, and the smile on her face faded the moment her gaze landed on me.

With a sheepish, tight-lipped smile, I gave a small wisp of a wave.

Of course, she didn't wave back.

A forced smile creased her eyes as she slid into the chair. In as subtle a move as I could muster, I turned toward Spencer. "I didn't know Gilchrist would be here," I whispered. My mind flashed back to the day in the alley when I'd seen the two of them together.

"Yeah, she kind of arranged the gala. She's the one who

negotiated all of these moths. Stupid really, they're just going to go back into circulation, and we'll be plucking their carcasses out of cages in no time."

"That's horrible. Speaking of horrible, the guy next to me is kind of creepy," I whispered in an even lower tone.

"Ahh, he's harmless. Stinking rich, but harmless. An old friend of my dad's."

Beyond Spencer, a figure strode toward the table, and my heart caught in my throat for the second time that evening, when Professor Bramwell eased into the seat two down from Spencer. When his eyes found me again, a rush of warmth shot through my veins.

The chair between him and Spencer remained empty, and it was only then I took notice that everyone at the table had a companion. Except him.

My eyes darted toward the provost, who quickly looked away from me. I leaned into Spencer again. "Are your dad ... I mean ... is your mom–"

"She's home. Sick. Which just means she took too many sleeping pills again."

"Oh. I see."

"Yeah. Happens a lot."

"I wasn't sure if Gilchrist was ..." Hesitating to say, I shook my head. "Never mind."

In a subtle gesture, he covered his mouth with his hand and leaned in closer. "They actually can't stand each other. Kinda makes this really awkward."

At a flash of her cupping Spencer's crotch, I nodded. "I can imagine."

In the quiet that followed, I stared down at the elaborate table setting–three forks on the left, two knives and a spoon on the right, a smaller fork and spoon above my plate, and some odd-looking pronged utensil I'd never seen before.

Our waiter brought out a variety of appetizers that had my

eyes popping–tuna tartare, halibut ceviche, seared octopus, salmon latke. I had no freaking clue what any of them were, but sampled one of the salmon latkes only because they were bite-sized.

Next course consisted of a shellfish bisque, and as I reached for my silverware, I caught Professor Bramwell staring at me.

I tried not to notice the seat beside him, still absent of a date.

"Doctor Bramwell," the man to my left grumbled around his food. "While in Vegas last month, I visited a restaurant where you can order caterpillar fungus soup for a mere seven hundred dollars a bowl. Supposed to have amazing healing properties. A natural cancer treatment. *And* an aphrodisiac." He elbowed me under the table, and I frowned. "What are your thoughts?" For a man who supposedly had an obscene amount of money, he certainly lacked table etiquette in the way he slurped his soup.

I turned my attention toward Professor Bramwell, who stared back at the man with undisguised disinterest. It made me wonder if they knew each other outside of the gala, because I could almost feel the hostile chemistry between them.

"*Ophiocordyceps sinensis*. A cousin of the cordyceps species that turns ants into zombies. Harmless to humans, but if you're foolish enough to pay seven hundred dollars for what you think is the next panacea, then I'd wonder if it did, indeed, infect your brain."

Biting my lip failed to contain the quiet chuckle in my throat.

Undoubtedly rattled, the man beside me bristled and *hmphed* and sat back in his chair. "Isn't that the basis of your research, Professor?"

"My research focuses on a single toxin and its effect on

autoimmune response. No, I do not believe it is the cure-all that has the power to improve your sex life. I suspect not even Viagra has that much ambition."

Eyes wide, I snapped my gaze to the plate in front of me. They had to have known each other. Professor Bramwell certainly had a coarse edge to his social skills, but I'd never heard him outwardly insult someone.

Mrs. Dandridge coughed into her napkin, and I couldn't tell if she ended her fit on a snicker or a choke.

Provost Lippincott let out a nervous chuckle. "Devryck has a ... quite a sense of humor." An air of discomfort clung to his words, but the tension remained thick.

I stole another glance at Professor Bramwell, who downed another glass of champagne, those copper eyes landing on me, the moment he set the glass on the table.

A strange pull tugged at my chest. I couldn't explain it. Even as abrasive as he was, I found him utterly captivating. Magnetic.

When the main lobster course arrived, I kept light conversation with Spencer about the food and interesting spots on Dracadia where I'd yet to venture. Still, I couldn't help stealing more glances at Professor Bramwell, every one of them met by his unabashed stare. My dress scratched at my skin where it felt too tight, caging me in, as my skin flushed and my stomach fluttered.

The blonde server from before made a second appearance and, with a gentle touch of his shoulder, whispered something in Lippincott's ear. When she glanced back at me, I realized I'd been staring a bit too intently, and clearing my throat, I snapped my gaze toward my hands in my lap, catching Dandridge gripping his crotch under the table beside me, in a crass adjustment.

"Excuse me for a moment," Provost Lippincott said, sliding his chair back and depositing his napkin on the table.

The moment he strode out of the dining room after the server, the cramping tension in my stomach loosened a bit, reminding me how uneasy I felt around him.

The reprieve was short lived, though, as only a few minutes later, the provost returned to his seat, and my anxiety cranked a notch tighter than before.

Dessert arrived. Mine was a tiny square of a cheesecake with some kind of berry topping, each person at the table served something different.

"They know how to skimp out, don't they?" Spencer snorted and popped what looked like a cheesecake filled strawberry into his mouth.

Toying with my dessert fork, I willed myself not to look at Bramwell again. It was ridiculous and perhaps even inappropriate.

But part of me didn't care.

Professor Bramwell had taken notice of me, and as much as I'd originally loathed the idea of going to the gala, I was glad that I had.

I took a bite of the delicious berry cheesecake, the flavor reminding of the drink I'd had earlier. As I licked the sauce from my lips, I caught Professor Bramwell turning away. My attention swung toward Gilchrist, who glared at me from across the table, her lips snarled in disapproval.

"Where are you from?" Mr. Dandridge asked, and I inwardly cringed at the question.

Perhaps telling him the truth would inspire him to leave me alone, though. "Covington," I said as unflinching as I could muster, and forced myself not to fidget too much when his face pinched to a frown.

"Covington? That horrible city in Massachusetts?"

"Yeah."

"Good God. How did you, um .... How did you end up here, at Dracadia?"

"Decent test scores and grades."

"Everyone at Dracadia has decent test scores and grades." He leaned into me, close enough that I could feel his hot breath against my cheek. "Or was it extracurricular activities that gave you an edge over your fellow classmates, hmmm?" Beneath the tablecloth, his hand landed on my thigh. "I have a number of connections here, as well."

My muscles lurched with the urge to slap him, my cheeks so red with anger and humiliation, I could hardly spit out a word. It had to be written all over my face.

A cold paralysis settled in my bones, though. *Do something!* my head urged me, but my body felt stiff and heavy with shock. As his hand moved higher, I finally reached under the table and gripped his wrist, eyes stinging with the threat of tears.

He took hold of my hand and drew it to his thigh, and my muscles trembled to pull myself from his grasp. The entire silent struggle seemingly oblivious to the others, who went about eating their dessert without a single word. Not even Spencer seemed to be privy, as he smiled at me, before popping another strawberry into his mouth.

"I wonder what your wife would think, if she knew you were groping the young girl beside you, Charles?" Everyone at the table gasped in unison, as Professor Bramwell casually took a sip of a new glass of champagne. "Or do the two of you partake in extramarital activities, which gives you a pass, hmmm?" Professor Bramwell's tone carried an edge of mocking that echoed Mr. Dandridge's from moments ago, and I didn't know what was more shocking–what he'd said or that he'd heard Dandridge's words to begin with.

The grip of my thigh quickly fell away, and while I was relieved, my face burned with the shame of not having stood up for myself.

"Devryck!" Provost Lippincott shot to his feet and threw

his napkin onto the table. "Is it your intent to insult my guests at a very important gala which happens to fund your research?"

"Is it your intent to ignore the fact that another of your guests is clearly uncomfortable? Or is it only the wealthy donors whose comfort matters most, *Edward*?"

"Enough of this. Please," the provost said.

"Yes. I've had *quite* enough." Bramwell turned his attention to Spencer. "Be a gentleman and switch seats with her." His gaze flicked my way, and hardened into something almost murderous when it shifted beyond me. "And if you value your anatomy, I'd strongly advise you keep your hands to yourself, Mr. Dandridge." With that, Professor Bramwell tossed his napkin onto the table and pushed to his feet.

My heart sank to my stomach watching him stride toward the exit.

"Is that a threat? Did he just threaten me, Edward?" Dandridge shifted in his seat, knocking me in the arm.

"No … he …. No, it wasn't a threat." Provost Lippincott let out that nervous chuckle again.

"He absolutely did! I heard it. Everyone at the table heard it."

"Can it, Charles," his wife finally said beside him. "You are an embarrassment."

I'd heard it, though. Professor Bramwell *had* threatened him. For me. In all of my twenty years, no one had ever stood up for me. No one had ever intervened on my behalf.

Compelled to go after him, I stood up from my chair, and the moment I did, a surge of dizziness had me wavering backward.

"Lilia?" Spencer grabbed my arm, steadying me. "Are you okay?"

"No. I feel. Strange."

"Do you need some fresh air?"

Mouth pinched tight to avoid throwing up, I nodded.

Lowering my gaze to avoid all the prying eyes, I allowed Spencer to lead me out of the Solarium and back onto the patio.

“Sorry. I didn’t mean to–”

“Stop. You made my father uncomfortable. I’m thrilled.” Spencer snorted.

Another wave hit me, and I swayed on my feet. “Whoa. I’m really .... Are you sure there wasn’t alcohol in that drink?”

“I’m pretty sure there wasn’t. Of course, my tolerance has grown a bit in the last few years. Do you need some water?”

Running a hand over my forehead, I nodded.

“Stay right here. I’ll be back in a sec.”

A blur had settled into the edges of my view. Looking around showed Professor Bramwell nowhere in sight.

Another bout of vertigo hit, and I stumbled to the side, catching my hand on one of the heavy iron chairs sitting out on the patio.

The sound of rustling off in the garden snapped my attention that way.

I scanned over what I could see through the shrubs, but found nothing there. The blur in my vision intensified, and as the view shifted, I stumbled again.

“Whoa!” Spencer said, swiping up my arm before I could tumble to my ass. He handed me the glass of water, and in spite of not really wanting to drink anything, with my stomach gurgling the way it did, I took a couple sips. “Better?”

“Not really.”

“Let’s walk and see if the air and muscle movement helps.”

Hooking his arm in mine, he led me onto the garden path, and I kept an eye out for Bramwell, or whatever had made that noise. The path wobbled, but the movement did help a small bit.

"I'm sorry, I should've switched seats with you back there. Did Dandridge really touch you?"

The question had me grimacing at the memory of him gripping my thigh under the table. "Yes. He really was creepy."

"Forgive me. I can honestly say he's never groped me under the table, so I didn't know how creepy he could be."

"I just want to forget it all."

"Everything?"

A look of hurt in his eyes sent another round of nausea to my stomach. I turned away, and caught sight of a figure standing in front of the mausoleum off in the distance. Long, black cape. The plague mask. My imagination? Or was it real? A sharp breath shot out of me, and I jerked back into Spencer. A quick look back at him, and I stepped to the side, clearing my throat.

"What is it?" he asked.

"By the mausoleum." I pointed in that direction and had to shake my head to dislodge the double-vision corrupting my view. When the scene settled back into a single blurry form, there was nothing there. "I saw ... there was ... someone in a mask."

"A mask?"

"I keep seeing him." Confusion clouded my head. "Someone following me in a mask. Like ... the kind the doctors wore during the plague."

"Plague mask?" Brows pinched, he recoiled. "That's weird. You saw him near the mausoleum?"

"Yes. He was just ..." Another zap of dizziness. "Standing there a moment ago. Staring."

He unhooked his arm from mine, and when he stepped in that direction, I reached out for his arm.

"What're you doin'?" My voice carried a slight slur.

"Just stay here. I'm going to check it out."

"No ... you don' ... never just go check it out." Tension

pulsed inside my skull, and I winced, rubbing the heel of my palm over the ache.

Ignoring me, he stepped in that direction again, and I clutched his arm harder.

"Spencer ... what if ... it's dangerous?"

"If someone is harassing you, it needs to stop. Stay put."

"No. Thassa *bad* idea."

He frowned, staring back at me, as if just now catching on that this thing with me was getting worse. "Fine. C'mon."

We stepped off the path into the gardens, toward the mausoleum.

The figure appeared again, and I pointed, skidding to a halt. "There!"

Spencer yanked his hand free of my grip and strode that way. "Hey! Asshole! You got a fucking problem?"

"Spencer!" I wanted to follow, but damn it, I wasn't even sure I could manage ten steps, let alone defend myself. Instead, I backed toward the path, watching Spencer through a fog, as he disappeared around the mausoleum.

Seconds passed.

The air turned colder.

A minute.

Two minutes.

"Spencer!" I whisper-yelled, feeling completely vulnerable. Alone. I awkwardly tugged the pepper spray from my waist-band, teetering again with the movement. Why I didn't think to give it to him, I didn't know, but right then, I was glad I had it.

Get help. Go get help.

I turned back toward the path, but the world continued to spin, the dizziness thick as I careened and staggered around shrubs. The surroundings had somehow shifted. I'd lost my sense of direction, and worse, my view was waning.

Blackness crawled into my periphery, creating a narrow field of view, as I scrambled for the familiar path.

One slow blink.

I opened my eyes to the dark sky above me, the stars twinkling high and bright. Had I fallen? I couldn't remember.

Slow blink.

When I opened my eyes again, a terrifying figure stood over me. The plague mask. I wanted to scream, but nothing came out. The figure tipped its head, studying me.

Take the mask off!

I willed myself to reach up, but my arm felt like lead weights.

"Le'mee 'lone."

The figure snapped its attention away, as if it heard something.

Slow blink.

My body jostled as something slid beneath my back. "Hel'me." Nothing more than a weak mewling that mirrored the softness in my bones. I opened my eyes to see the world moving too fast, the sight twisting my stomach.

I closed my eyes again.

Warmth engulfed me. Wonderful, relaxing warmth, and the scent of leather and cologne. I roused to find a gloved hand on a gearshift. The monotonous purr of an engine. Lifting my head to see who'd taken me captive, I was greeted by a light far too bright through the window behind them. I groaned and screwed my eyes shut, seeing only jagged flashes behind my eyelids.

Perhaps I was dying.

Perhaps I would die by the end of the night.

Death felt like a warm blanket.

Chapter 39

Lilia

I awoke with a start and jolted upright. At the restriction of my arm, I looked down through the dim light to see it tethered by a handcuff to the steel frame of a bed.

My gaze shifted to the dress I wore, which carried small flecks of … food?

Confusion settled over me, my head throbbing with the task of trying to catch up to my eyeballs.

Piano music. Moths. Dinner. Spencer. Bramwell. The masked man.

A gurgling nausea churned in my gut as I slowly trailed my gaze over the surrounding room. My vision wobbled with the ache in my brain.

The darkness. The stone walls chipped with age and covered in moss. A gravelly floor. The air, so cold, it felt like I'd been cast into a tomb. The heavy, damp scent of earth and decay invading my sinuses. And the bars. Not a room. It was a cell. A prison.

No. No!

He'd captured me. The man in the mask.

My pulse raced as I thought about all those sick, serial killer movies, where the victim ended up chained in a basement. The horror of that goaded my escape, and I tugged at the cuffs, trying to slip my hand through it. Skin raw and burning, I shook with the effort, folding my hand to make it as small as I could.

The ache in my skull intensified with my stress, and I abandoned my escape to rub my throbbing temples.

"You could just ask for a key."

At the sound of the deep voice, I sucked in a sharp breath, and the shadows to my right shifted as a form came into view. A strange current snaked over my skin, devouring my fear, as I took in the sight of him.

Black slacks. White, button-down shirt. Devastatingly handsome face. The pressure in the room seemed to change, as his presence pervaded the space like a dark storm.

Professor Bramwell?

My head spun with a million possibilities, nothing springing forth a familiar memory of what had happened the night before. My professor kidnapping me?

I thought back on the way he'd defended me at dinner. No way.

Still, tension wound in my stomach, as he strode toward me, my fight or flight buzzing with the urge to do one, or the other. Light glinted off a metal key as he held it up for me to see. The sleek, black, leather gloves he wore had me questioning things. Perhaps I'd watched too many crime shows, but there was only one reason that came to mind for why someone would wear black gloves. He knelt down beside me, and at the click of the handcuff, I yanked my hand free and backed myself to the headboard, away from him.

"You cuffed me?"

"You apparently sleepwalk." He pushed up from the floor and, hands tucked in his pockets, made his way toward the cell door, which he pushed open as if to let me know I was free to leave.

"And the prison?"

"I couldn't exactly take you to my office. Or your dorm.

These cells are connected to my lab. The midnight lab is two floors above us."

"You don't store corpses in here, do you?"

"No. I don't store corpses in here."

My stomach settled only slightly, seeing as nothing made any sense still. "What happened?"

"You were drugged."

I rubbed at the red mark that'd been left on my wrist from the cuff. "How? With what?"

"Noxberries."

Air whooshed out of me. Noxberries? Shit. Shit! "How do you know?"

He crossed his arms and leaned against the iron bars of the cell. "You had a few bouts of vomiting in the night. I performed a litmus test on it. One specific for the enzymatic reaction found only in the berries."

Oh, God, not only was the thought of that humiliating, but the tickle in my stomach and chest told me he might've been looking at round two any second. "So, I'm ... I'm infected with Noctisoma?"

"Just as every moth isn't doomed for infection, neither is every noxberry."

"How do you *know*, though?" The moment I said the words, the answer came to me. "You studied my puke?"

"There would've been trace larvae. Eggs. I saw neither under the scope."

Again, the thought of Professor Bramwell studying my puke somehow seemed worse than him handcuffing me to a bed inside what must've been a prison at one time. Crazy, but that was my state of mind right then. "Oh, God. I don't remember anything. Throwing up. Being brought here."

"Noxberries are a very strong hallucinogenic. More powerful than any natural drug in existence. It's only their association with Noctisoma that keeps them from being abused more frequently. Otherwise, I suspect they'd be making the rounds at frat parties across campus."

I rubbed a hand across my forehead, trying to imagine at what point in the evening I might've been drugged. The cheesecake. It had berries. And the drink. It'd tasted like the cheesecake. "Why would anyone drug me?"

Brow furrowed, he drew in a deep breath, and—*God, strike me down*—I glimpsed the deep grooves of muscle in his chest where he'd unbuttoned his shirt. It brought to mind the day I'd spied on him throwing knives in the woods. The muscles in his arms. The sweat. But he was damned good with those knives. Would he throw knives at me?

Unfortunately, a thick fog still muddled my head, making it impossible to stay a step ahead of the man if he did have something sinister up his sleeve.

"*Why* is inconsequential at the moment. The question you should be asking right now is *who*?"

Was this where he confessed that it was him?

"I don't suppose you'd have any idea?"

Again, he stuffed his hands into his pockets and paced toward the wall across from me. "Spencer Lippincott was accused of giving another student noxberries. After which, she claimed he assaulted her."

"Mel."

"Yes." He turned and paced toward the cell bars again, back and forth, as he had a tendency to do whenever he lectured.

"She never mentioned the berries. Neither did he."

Pausing his pacing, he shot me a look as if to say, *Come on, Lilia, you're smarter than that.* Ordinarily, I was, but in addition to feeling woozy, I was freaking starving, for some reason. "He wouldn't have, for obvious reasons. And I suspect she didn't know."

"How do *you* know?"

His jaw shifted, his eyes unreadable as he stared at me. He wasn't going to tell me.

Arms crossed with stubborn resistance, I shook my head. "Spencer wouldn't do that."

"I told you, nice and genuine don't mix when it comes to Spencer. And now, we're right back into a scandal."

"How?"

"Cameras caught me carrying you away."

The torment of that visual sliced through my concentration. Me, passed out in his arms, as he carried me through the gardens. The gardens. Yes, I remembered that much. Walking through the gardens with Spencer. And a man. A man in a mask. "Canterbury garden has cameras?"

He rubbed his jaw as if frustrated with my lack of brain power, as if it was my fault. Whatever I'd been given may not have infected me, but it'd surely killed a few brain cells. "The lot where my car was parked has cameras."

"No, I'm asking because I saw someone. In the garden. A man wearing a bird mask."

"A bird mask?"

"Not a bird mask, one of those plague masks that docs used to wear."

Frowning again, he stared back at me. "You saw someone in a plague mask?"

"Yes. He was standing by the mausoleum." An irritating, slow drip of memories trickled in, feeding me one scene at a time. "Then Spencer ran off. Toward him. I got dizzy and fell. The man in the mask was standing over me."

"Did Spencer see this masked attacker?"

Had he? Or was he only going after him for my benefit? "I can't say for sure."

"Did he take his mask off at any point?"

"No. I kept blacking out. Did you see him when you found me?"

"Unfortunately, no. I heard a scream. When I found you, you were lying passed out. There was no one else. Did he touch you, at all?" The question carried a hard edge, like the thought of such a thing angered him.

Touch me? Not that I recalled. I couldn't summon so much as the memory of fingertips on my skin. I shook my head, flexing way too many brain cells trying to remember a single detail past that mask. "I swear I saw him."

"The noxberries are fairly strong. Perhaps you were–"

"I've seen him before. All over campus. Watching me."

He stared off, as if deep in thought. "You sleepwalk."

It wasn't a question, yet I answered anyway. "Yes."

"Do you take any medication?"

"No."

"Do you find yourself tired during the day?"

I knew where he was going with that, and with a roll of my eyes, I answered, "Sometimes. Look, I'm not hallucinating the guy, okay?"

"I'm merely teasing out a possibility, Miss Vespertine. Have you come across anything plague-related recently? Perhaps a reading? A picture of the mask?"

I had read about Dr. Stirling when I'd first arrived on campus. Admittedly, that was about the time I first began seeing the man in the mask. "I have, yes," I answered honestly. "You think I *am* hallucinating him?"

"I'm only suggesting that exhaustion can fuck with your head. I know this from experience."

Maybe I *had* dreamed it up. The sickening possibility that it might've been nothing more than another hallucination smothered the argument cocked at the back of my throat.

"If that's the case, then I feel silly. About all of this."

"Hallucinations don't drug individuals. There's still the mystery of who accomplished that, and I suspect that I will find myself on the chopping block once again."

"But they didn't catch you bringing me *here*."

"I brought you through the cadaver entrance. So, no."

God, the thought of that twisted my stomach inside out. But I was alive and untouched. Although, as disturbing as it may have been, the visual of him touching me while I lay passed out didn't quite sicken me as much as it probably should have.

"So, it's only my word that would get you in trouble." It wasn't a question, and just like that, my horribly manipulative mind shifted back into gear, because it was in that moment, I realized that I had something on Professor Bramwell. A bargaining chip.

Eyes narrowed, he did that annoying studying thing, where I couldn't read what the hell was going on in his head. Maybe he wanted to throttle me for saying that aloud. Or throw knives at my skull.

"Make me your assistant, and I won't speak a word," I quickly added.

"No. I told you before, I don't take assistants." Arms crossed again, he ran his thumb over his bottom lip in a way I found mesmerizing, unintentionally seductive. "I can offer you money. A significant amount."

"No." The answer came out faster than I'd have expected at the prospect of money, especially when I desperately needed to catch up on Bee's tuition. But I desperately needed to know more about the worms, too—and faster than I was learning in Nocticadia. "I'll leave. I'll take off for a few days, and you won't have me here to clear your name." I didn't even know who was talking at that point. Maybe I had been infected and the parasite was steering the ship, because no way in hell was Lilia Vespertine *that* bold.

His dark chuckle tickled the back of my neck, and his eyes held a ruthless glint that slid through my bones. "My, you are a wicked little moth."

I hated the way my stomach fluttered when he said that. "I want to work in your lab. Not the midnight lab, not some lame duck lab, where I'm assigned to washing dishes and making agar. I want to work on the toxin with you. And I want to be paid in cash for my time." I swallowed a gulp. While, on the outside, I might've looked cool and calm, my insides were screaming right then.

He tipped his head, and I caught a flicker of intrigue in that coppery gaze. "Look at you. Such a bold moth. Far bolder than I gave you credit for."

"Make me your assistant, and I'll make you the hero this time."

"Or I can lock you in this cell and toss the key. No one would find you. And after a while, no one would care."

I'd forgotten the part where I hadn't yet confirmed whether, or not, he was a psycho killer. Damn the fog still thick on my brain.

My gaze flicked to the cracked cell door and back to him. In a pathetic effort to beat him to it, I scrambled over annoying tulle and satin, getting caught up in the skirt of my dress for a moment, and dashed toward my only exit. The moment I reached the barred door, the world tilted on its axis, and the iron spindles crashed into my spine. His gloved hand pressed into my throat, sealing off the oxygen.

A rush of adrenaline pounded through me, colliding with an inexplicable titillation that had my nerves flaring like livewires.

"You will take the money that I'm offering. And you will not say a word about this. Do you understand?" Eyes trained on my lips, he leaned into his grip, his tongue sweeping over the edge of his teeth.

Mouth gaped for air, I stared back at him, studying the flicker of fascination that slipped over his otherwise stern expression.

Chaos exploded inside my head, as I tried to make sense of the fact that my professor had his hand to my throat, had just threatened to lock me in a cell and toss the key, and that I still had no intentions of accepting his offer. Perhaps *I* was the psycho. After all, I could've negotiated the answers I was looking for about my mother and maybe he would've told me.

But maybe he'd have lied, too.

Or subjected me to some *three questions only* rule.

I only just managed to shake my head. "Imprisoning me ... doesn't ... cover your ... ass."

His hand squeezed harder with his frustration. "Fucking hell, why do you have to be stubborn!" Jaw flexing with his rage, he released me on a growl.

I threw my hands to my neck, rubbing the spot where he'd choked me, and bent forward as a cough sputtered out of me. "It's a curse. But I promise not to annoy you, and to be helpful. And I won't say a word to anyone about it. No one has to know that I'm working for you."

Another frustrated growl told me I was whittling him down. "I knew the moment you arrived at this school that you were going to be a major fucking headache for me."

I straightened, ignoring the annoying blossom of hope that warmed my chest. "That's a yes, then?"

He ran his hands through his hair, ruffling the ordinarily thick and smoothed strands into a disheveled mess that I found painfully attractive. "Fine. You'll work as my assistant. You'll do as I say. You will not touch anything, or venture where you're not wanted. You use the cadaver entrance only. And should you decide to break any of my rules or speak of this arrangement to anyone, I will make you regret the moment you tried to blackmail me."

"Did you just threaten me? Like, with death that time?"

He didn't flinch beneath the accusation. "Don't fuck with

me, Miss Vespertine. You want to play hardball? Know that mine are made of steel."

"That sounds painful."

His lips twitched as if he were trying to hold back a smile. "Leave through the back entrance. And don't return until tomorrow at eight in the evening."

"Can I ask one more question before I go?"

He let out an almost pained groan. "What?"

"Are there any buildings on this campus that *don't* have cameras?"

Chapter 40

Devryck

The girl was a problem. An incredibly beautiful, but annoying, problem.

That she could stand there, making bold demands, while staring me straight in the eye had me wishing I could either throttle, or kiss, her. I couldn't tell which compelled me more than the other.

It'd been shitty of me to manipulate her into thinking that what she'd seen was nothing but a hallucination, but I'd had to. Lying to her was for her own safety. She had no idea what world of corruption and mayhem she'd be inviting in by getting herself tangled up with The Rooks.

I'd find out who the hell was harassing her and deal with it.

My guess was Spencer. As a new member, he had yet to learn that ceremonial garb wasn't some fucking Halloween scare. Wearing those masks outside of The Roost brought heavy consequences, and I would see to it that the offender was adequately punished.

Especially since I didn't like the idea of someone fucking with her. And I was pretty sure that was exactly what Spencer had in mind, having drugged her. The kid had done it before, and with as delectable as Lilia looked in that dress, I suspected the asshole hadn't been able to help himself.

A realization that irritated the shit out of me.

Since having found that video on her phone, I'd made a point of ignoring the girl–an impossibility, as a general rule, particularly when she wore those short skirts that danced around what I imagined to be a pert ass. When she'd arrived to the gala the night before, though, looking like a walking aphrodisiac topped with whipped cream, and catching the eye of every swinging dick she passed, something had snapped inside of me.

I'd never wanted anything so badly in my life.

Calling her beautiful was like calling the sun lukewarm. She'd blazed like the hottest part of a flame in that dress. And fuck me, I'd felt the heat.

I knocked on Lippincott's door and, at a sound of acknowledgement from the other side, stepped into his office. Papers lay scattered about his desk, along with empty water bottles and discarded granola bar wrappers. I took a seat in the chair across from him, swallowing back the urge to tell him how much I wanted to beat the shit out of his son.

"Devryck, what a nice surprise." The flat tone of his voice told me the little incident with Dandridge at the gala still rankled him.

I'd always loathed the pervy bastard, a former dean at the university, who'd never even attempted to rein in his affinity for younger women. The man was approaching seventy-two years old, and I'd watched his hand grope more thighs than a starving man at an *all-you-can-eat* chicken buffet.

It just so happened, he'd groped the wrong thigh that night.

"What brings you out of your crypt?"

"I thought you might want to know that someone was seen wearing ceremonial garb outside of The Roost. I suspect it might've been your son."

He reached for a bottle of Tums on the other side of his computer and popped two of them. "When was this?"

"Just after I left the gala. He was roaming about the gardens."

"Ah. Yes. The night you gave Spencer a black eye?"

I frowned. "I didn't lay a hand on your son."

"He insists that you were the one wearing the ceremonial garb and that he caught you without the mask. He said you punched him in the face and knocked him out cold. He has a lovely black eye to mark the occasion."

While I had seen Spencer run off toward the mausoleum, I never pursued him, nor laid so much as a finger on him. "As I said, I never touched your son."

"But cameras did pick up on you carrying Miss Vespertine to your vehicle."

"She'd passed out. I was merely trying to get her somewhere safe."

Leaning back in his chair, he ran his fingers through his hair and blew out a sharp breath. "Dean Langmore is getting her side of the story, and for your sake, Devryck, you better pray the girl doesn't throw you under the bus. One accusation is fairly easy to contain. Two is a bit more challenging. And it would entirely fuck up the opportunity to move toward clinical trials, if you were to be investigated for inappropriate conduct with a student. So, my advice? Stay the fuck away from this girl, in particular."

Unrattled by his comments, I tipped my head. "What exactly are you accusing me of?"

"Everyone at that table could damn near feel what was going on between the two of you."

I highly doubted that. If the unscrupulous prick sitting next to her had felt even a fraction of what I was feeling right then, he'd have made a better effort to keep his hands from getting severed. Dandridge was nothing more than a waste of human body parts and precious oxygen.

"Fucking hell, are you crazy?" he prattled on, his voice growing annoyingly hostile. "And then you have the audacity to insult our most generous donor! In front of his wife!"

"He was fondling Miss Vespertine's thigh while you were nibbling on your goddamn cheesecake."

"I don't care if he threw her on the table and ate her pussy for dessert! The man has damn near carried this project with his funding! He can do whatever the hell he wants!"

I clenched my teeth to hold back the rage, until a spasm of pain shot to my skull. The visual he'd planted in my head had my control completely unraveled, and for the sake of dignity and reputation, I kept my hands gripping the chair, calming the urge to grab Lippincott by the throat and tear out his windpipe.

Whatever the hell was going on with me had shifted into something unrecognizable. Something dark and violent, and at the center of it was a troublesome girl, with her ridiculous berry lips that I wanted to bite, who'd somehow corrupted me. A crafty little shit who'd bulldozed right through my defenses.

"You are brilliant, Devryck. Perhaps the most brilliant man I know. Do not let some lowly Covington girl fuck up years of research and innovation. I'm tempted to have her removed from your class and placed somewhere else just to eliminate the *temptation*."

Exhaling a rage-filled breath, I rolled my shoulders back. "That won't be necessary."

"Good. I'll consider Spencer's black eye a *misunderstanding*. And I will inquire about who the fuck decided it was a good idea to wear ceremonial garb as a costume. In the meantime, go back to your work."

Only the small modicum of respect I had for the man kept

me from telling him to shove his misunderstanding and opinions up his ass and fuck himself. Years ago, after my father had finally given up on Caedmon, Lippincott organized something of a task force, comprised of a few tight connections of his, to track down one of the men who'd kidnapped my brother. He'd always been kind to Caedmon throughout our childhood, treating him like something of a son before Spencer had come along. I'd always felt bad for him after the night Caedmon and I had stumbled upon our father fucking his wife, during one of the Lippincott's dinner parties. Hadn't been much the poor bastard could've done, seeing as it was her money and status that'd given him any clout at all at the university. He was horribly pathetic when it came to his wife, but the man had undoubtedly climbed the ranks and amassed enough power to avoid his shitlist.

I didn't need the headache of pissing him off. Not when my research had begun to make major strides.

And he *had* been right about one thing. I didn't need Lilia fucking things up for me. Not because she was some *lowly Covington girl*, as he'd said, but because she was the only thing in the last ten years that'd managed to distract me from my research.

Which meant agreeing to let her work in my lab might've been the dumbest decision I'd ever made.

Chapter 41

Lilia

It was clear Dean Langmore didn't believe me, as he stared back at me with skepticism shimmering in his eyes. Not that I could blame him, really. Playing ignorant wasn't something I enjoyed, but for the sake of securing my place in Bramwell's lab, I was willing to risk scrutiny.

"So ... let me get this straight," he said, flattening his hands against his paper-cluttered desk. "You were attacked in Canterbury gardens by some masked man. A bird mask, is that correct?"

"Yessir. Like a plague mask." If it was true that I'd only hallucinated the mask, I didn't see any harm in mentioning it, if for no other reason than to derail whatever theories they'd constructed around Bramwell.

"Right. And Spencer was where?"

I honestly couldn't recall exactly what had happened to Spencer. The last thing I remembered was that he'd jogged off toward the mausoleum. "He took off."

"He left you there to be attacked by this man in a bird mask?"

"Yes. I don't know where Spencer ran off to, but he wasn't there to help."

"But you claim Professor Bramwell heard you scream and came to your aid."

"Yes. He fought the bird man." Even if I hadn't actually seen that happen, I had to admit, I enjoyed the fantasy of it.

"Right. And in the meantime, you escaped back to your dorm?"

As much as I'd have loved to end the story there, I couldn't tell him that. There were cameras posted outside of every dorm. He'd have surely called me out on the lie right then and there. "No. I wasn't feeling well when I left the party. I ended up passing out. Professor Bramwell carried me to his car, *intending* to drive me back to my dorm."

"But ..."

"I threw up. In his car. And I was humiliated. I asked him to pull over and that's when I jumped out and ran."

"To where?"

"The chapel." After speaking to Professor Bramwell, I knew the chapel had no cameras posted outside. Apparently, Jesus didn't like spies, and that was fine with me. It also happened to be the only building left unlocked that late at night. "After what happened, I was horribly shaken and scared. I hid in the pews of the chapel all night and prayed."

"Uh-huh." The disbelieving tone of his voice matched the look he gave me right then. "But you did not report this to campus police?"

"No. I know it was wrong, and I should have." Gaze lowered to my lap, I fidgeted with my hands, wondering if any of my lies sounded remotely believable. Were victims allowed to be disputed, or was that just an unspoken rule? "But I'm reporting it to you now."

"I've spoken with Spencer. He did say you weren't feeling well when you left, and that you did, in fact, see a figure in the gardens. Where your stories differ is the part when he ran away. He says something, or someone, attacked *him*." Of course he did. It was almost artistic, the way Spencer manipulated stories. If I'd had even the slightest doubt about what'd happened between him and Mel, my situation surely cemented it in my head that the guy was shady.

"As I said, I can't recall where Spencer ran off to."

"He claims it was Professor Bramwell who attacked and knocked him out."

The urge to choke out a laugh wobbled in my throat. All that came to mind were the few times throughout the night when I'd talked to Professor Bramwell and noticed Spencer's disapproving scowl. "That's absurd. I specifically saw Professor Bramwell fight off the man in the mask. Spencer ran off."

"Spencer does have injuries that support his claim. A rather unpleasant-looking black eye."

"And, what? Because I don't, my claims are dismissed?"

"I didn't say that." Langmore threw up his hands and shook his head, clearly uncomfortable with my rebuttal. "Those words did not come out of my mouth, Miss Vespertine."

"I have reason to believe I was drugged, Sir." The moment I said the words, his mouth clamped shut.

"Perhaps you should consider testing–"

"I was given noxberries. A known hallucinogenic. I suspect that Spencer gave me the drug." I'd avoided the accusation up until that point, because accusing Spencer would've undoubtedly made my life all the more complicated. He was Lippincott's son, and Lippincott happened to be the keeper of my scholarship. As the provost, he held the ultimate decision whether, or not, I'd be permitted to continue my education at Dracadia, and considering that I'd finally gained an opportunity to find out what'd really happened to my mother, I didn't want to screw that up by pissing him off. Yes, the right thing to do would've been reporting Spencer, but I kinda lacked evidence at that point, and getting myself kicked out of Dracadia over speculation would've pissed *me* off. "I accepted a drink from him earlier in the night–I'm sure there are a number of witnesses from the gala I attended who can attest. Unfortunately, urine tests won't pick up on noxberries."

"You're certain that you were given noxberries."

"Of course not. The only one who could confirm that is Professor Bramwell, but at this point, you might deem that a conflict of interest, based on Spencer's accusations. So, why don't we do this, since I am the victim in this situation ..." Having to admit that, to actually say the V-word, burned like acid on my tongue. In my own quiet space, I'd deal with the anger of having been drugged, and since my suspicions led me to believe it was Spencer, I'd make a point to keep my distance from him. "In the interest of not rousing a bunch of scandal, I won't press charges against Spencer. I will avoid him, as I should have from the beginning. You have my report on the man in the mask. Perhaps you might put your efforts into him, since I'm telling you he is the one who attacked me." Unfortunately, he'd be chasing thin air with the lead, and while I felt slightly bad for leading him on that goose chase, I didn't need Spencer throwing Bramwell under the bus–particularly after I'd negotiated a pretty sweet deal with the professor. Not to mention, Spencer knew damned well that Bramwell hadn't attacked him. The whole situation felt a little vindictive, if anything, especially considering Spencer still harbored animosity about his friend getting kicked out. It wouldn't have surprised me if the guy had given himself that black eye, like something straight out of *Fight Club*.

"Are you certain of this, Miss Vespertine? We do not take these attacks lightly. I want you to feel supported in your account of what happened."

"I'm certain. We'll consider this a wash. I'll be much more careful not to venture out at night." *Ugh.* That went entirely against my femininity, but I held onto the fact that it was for a good cause. I had the opportunity I'd been waiting for, to learn more about my mother's illness, and I had no intentions of getting wrapped up in Spencer's vengeful little web as a distraction.

"Very well. We will pursue this masked man in the meantime, for the sake of campus safety. And I would ask that you report any additional concerns directly to me."

"Of course."

Chapter 42

Lilia

The cadaver entrance was an old, brick tunnel with two points of entry. The door outside the university gate, which would've left me dealing with the tyrannical gatekeeper and made the whole point of remaining unseen pointless. Or the door leading to the incinerator room that was connected to the cadaver tunnel. Neither entrance had cameras. Both were creepy as hell, particularly at night.

A chill wracked my body, as I walked through the open space, carrying nothing more than the flashlight on my phone. To the left stood six steel doors, like old ovens, and beneath them, smaller sliding doors, which I guessed held the flames used to burn the bodies. A charred ash scent on the air told me one had been used recently.

Casting that thought to the back of my mind, I hustled through the room to a full-sized door, which spat me into the halfway mark of the cadaver tunnel--an arched brick tunnel, the ends of which were shrouded in darkness, like something out of a horror movie. The temperature inside the tunnel had to have been ten degrees cooler, the crisp bite of cold gnawing on my bones. A few more feet ahead, and the tunnel opened onto the autopsy room, with its stainless-steel beds, sinks, scales and white tiled floors, and a steel door to the left that led to the refrigerator, where med school cadavers were stored. If possible, the room was even colder than the tunnel with a sterile bleach scent that burned my sinuses and overpowered the faint whiff of formalin.

I only vaguely remembered the path based on the quick introduction I'd gotten when Professor Bramwell had whisked me out of there earlier that morning. The cells where I'd awakened were down some other obscure tunnel that I probably couldn't have found again, if I'd tried.

I kept on through the autopsy room, to the lab door, where I punched in a code he'd given me on the keypad beside it. A red light on the keypad flicked to green, and the door clicked, allowing me to push through into a wide-open space, with wooden benches and microscopes, stacked books, and walls of bookshelves. Candles flickered in lanterns and large hurricanes throughout the room, and like in the Midnight Lab, tanks around the room gave off a soft purple glow. I passed one that housed dozens of worms squirming across the tank floor—far more than those in the lab upstairs. Rows of shelves housed specimen jars in which unidentifiable objects sat suspended in what I presumed to be formalin. Amidst the old, outdated echoes of a lab from the 1800's were a few modern amenities sprinkled in–two large steel refrigerators, a centrifuge, incubators, scales and fume hoods. A strange clash of old and new that left me scratching my head. Surely, the university could've afforded to outfit such an important project, particularly given the extravagant gala I'd just attended.

Professor Bramwell breezed through the door at the other end of the lab, which led to his office, wearing a long, white lab coat, and a pair of goggles cocked up on his head. On seeing me, he skidded to a stop. The frown on his face gave me the impression that he hadn't *actually* expected me to show up.

I cleared my throat, wearing a sheepish smile, and waved.

Grumbling to himself, he kept on toward one of the

benches, and as I stepped in that direction to follow him, he pointed toward the door from where he'd just come. "My office."

Nerves humming with intimidation, I obeyed his command and made my way toward his office. Through the door, I came upon another small corridor, with three closed doors and one ajar. At the end of the hallway flashed an exit sign, which I guessed led to the staircase that opened up on the midnight lab above us–a much more sophisticated laboratory.

With curious steps, I entered the moderately-sized office, where the scent of leather, polished wood, and old books mingled on the air along with the mouthwatering echoes of his cologne. If the lab was the heartbeat of his research, this room was the brain, given all of the medical and parasitology references that lined the bookshelves on each wall. Sketches of human anatomy lay scattered on the coffee table as I sauntered past it. My gaze fawned over the exquisitely carved, cherry-wood desk gleaming in the dim light. Behind it, a vintage-looking record player in a wooden cabinet sat with the lid cocked open. And above that, on the wall hung a plaque with the Latin phrase: *Mortui vivos docent*. I recognized it from a forensics class I'd taken two semesters ago.

The dead teach the living.

Unlike his office in the admin wing, this one held more amenities, which gave the impression he spent more time here–a small refrigerator, a leather couch and ottoman with a blanket draped over the arm, a small fireplace radiating a cozy warmth, and a standing coat rack where an umbrella had been hooked. Like the lab, his office held skulls of various sizes, jars of strange objects–dissected organs and bones, from what I could make out. A full-sized human skeleton stood propped on a stand. Books claimed space everywhere I looked in perfect stacks. Two microscopes. Candles flickering in large hurricanes.

Something brushed across my ankles, and on a panicked jolt, I leapt onto Professor Bramwell's desk. Twisting around showed a black little furball staring up at me with golden eyes. I blew out a relieved breath and chuckled, climbing off the desk. "Hello there," I said, kneeling down to give the cat a pet. "What the heck are you doing in a lab?" I frowned the moment the words escaped me. "He better not be experimenting on you." The cat leaned into the scratching, and I smiled, indulging the attention-loving rascal. "Strange, he doesn't strike me as a cat person."

Footsteps alerted me to his approach, and I abandoned the cat and scurried toward one of the chairs at his desk, plopping down just before he entered the room.

Crossing toward his desk, Professor Bramwell removed his lab coat and goggles, hung them neatly on the coat rack, and slid into his chair. The tight fit of his dress shirt certainly didn't go unnoticed, as he sat forward, resting his elbow on the desktop. With an unreadable expression, he stared at me for a moment. "I understand you spoke with Dean Langmore."

"I did."

"What did you tell him?"

I shifted in my seat, because the man's gaze felt like hot laser beams across my skin. "That you tried to help me, but I ran off. Humiliated for having thrown up in your car."

"To the church, I presume."

"Yes."

"Good." Leaning back in his chair, he steepled his fingers, not bothering to direct his laser beams somewhere else. "You'll don a lab coat every time you enter the lab. I'll be sure to have them available to you in the autopsy room. Gloves and goggles are also required."

"Okay. Can I ask you a question?"

Though he didn't make a sound, his unamused expression told me he was inwardly groaning.

"Why does this lab look like something out of the dark ages?"

"The specimens you've worked with in the midnight lab are newly infected. Those in this lab are in the tertiary phase and happen to have a rather intense sensitivity to light. We'll also be working with adult Noctisoma, which also possesses a very intense aversion to anything that isn't natural light."

"They can survive in sunlight, then?"

"They *can*, although they're nocturnal and *prefer* night." His comment brought an observation to mind.

"My mother, she hardly slept at night. Do you think the worms affected that?"

"I have no idea what may have caused your mother's insomnia, seeing as you claim she wasn't from the island, or had never been here, but yes, they can affect circadian rhythms. As for the outdated state of the lab, I've plenty of equipment in the three other labs throughout this building. I'd much prefer to concentrate funds into the actual study versus giving this particular lab a makeover. It suits its purpose."

Definitely touchy about the lab. "Of course. I meant no disrespect." The labs upstairs were certainly well-equipped, I just hadn't expected to be working in a crypt. Probably fitting, though, for a moniker like Doctor Death.

"Have you ever worked in a lab outside of your degree requirements?" he asked.

"Um. Briefly. A mycology lab when I first graduated high school. It was basically just counting spores through a microscope."

"Then, perhaps you have a very *basic* understanding of lab etiquette and safety."

Except for the times my colleague and I would spray down

the bench tops with alcohol that we ultimately lit on fire. "Sure."

"No food or drink. Practice good hygiene. Do not sniff, or taste. And, for God's sake, don't use your mouth as a pipette."

"No one actually does that. Do they?"

Brow cocked, he let out a sound of exasperation and reached for a to-go cup on his desk, with the infamous gold dragon label of the *Dragon's Lair* coffee shop. "I'll also have you assist in the occasional autopsy. Do you have any experience with cadavers, Miss Vespertine?" He kept his eyes on mine as he sipped his drink.

"No."

"Then, you will follow my every direction without a fuck-ton of questions. I like quiet when I work. Observe, and you will learn."

"Yessir."

"I will give you two hours each night. You will be compensated in cash, as requested."

I scratched the curious itch at back of my neck. "May I ask what the compensation will be?"

"Two hundred dollars a week. You will clean dishes and keep the lab tidy. You will not nose around."

Jesus. Two hundred a week? I'd expected a meager fifty, at most. While I certainly appreciated the paycheck, the bigger benefit would be learning about the organism itself. I needed to understand its mechanisms better, the details that weren't expected to be covered until next semester, according to his syllabus. By gaining knowledge on the worm, perhaps the progression of my mother's sickness would make more sense. "I understand."

"There are three other rooms in this corridor. They are off limits."

Which, of course, only piqued my curiosity.

Even so, I answered, "I understand."

"Good. Let's begin."

For the first hour, I followed closely behind him, as he acquainted me with all of the different machinery throughout the lab. Some, I was already familiar with, like the microtome, centrifuge, and flow cytometer. Others, like the organ bath, were new to me. He also introduced me to a moderately-sized steel structure–the autoclave, where I'd be expected to sterilize instruments and agar.

As he led me toward the host of different microscopes out on a table, I paused at the shelf where I'd first noticed the strange specimens in formalin.

Chunks of unidentifiable dissections of meat and bone lined four shelves, each with tiny labels. Gaucher disease, staghorn calculus, fibrous dysplasia. Conditions that I made a mental note to look up once back at my dorm.

"Medical oddities I've stumbled upon," Professor Bramwell said from behind. "The human body is a magnificent puzzle."

"It must be fascinating to open the body and look inside." It was strange, the way he collected from the dead in much the same way I did with trinkets. It made me wonder if he did so for the same reasons as my own. If harvesting a piece of them in jars as he did kept the nightmares away.

"You don't find this grotesque?" he asked, staring off at his wall of trophies.

"Yes, of course, but that's what makes it fascinating. I want to learn based on that curiosity."

"You are a curiosity in yourself, Miss Vespertine."

After a brief introduction to the histological exams I'd be studying, he set me to work on chores. Small petri dishes lined the bench as I poured agar into them while silently grumbling to myself. Although I appreciated an easy start, I'd hoped to get my hands dirty with the nitty gritty.

Across from me, Professor Bramwell sat with his back to me, peering into a microscope.

"May I ask a question?"

"That is a phrase that will echo in death," he said, not bothering to look up, and I smiled.

"Why moths? Aside from them being the natural host, why use them to study a toxin in humans?"

"Because they're cheaper than human beings, and it's not considered murder when they die."

I let out a snorty chuckle, spilling some of the agar onto the plastic mat beneath it.

"They also happen to have a similar immune response."

"Really? What is it about the toxin and human response?"

"You're delving into toddlerhood with all of these questions." It was the flat tone of his voice that struck me as amusing. Not that I wanted to annoy him, by any means— it somehow seemed to come natural between the two of us.

"I'm just trying to understand the nature of the research I'll be assisting with."

"While you may be aware of the negative aspects of infection, Noctisoma happens to have a number of benefits."

"Such as ..."

He let out a huff, and I lowered my gaze to hide the smile cracking at the seams. "You claim your mother was infected. Tell me, prior to the week of her death, did she ever complain of illness, pain, or something as benign as indigestion?"

"Not that I recall, no. In fact, she'd suffered with arthritis in her hands for years. But I don't recall her complaining much about it then."

Lifting his face from the eyepiece, he swapped samples from those out on the bench and peered through the microscope again. "If that's true, it's interesting, particularly in the case of her arthritis."

"Why?"

"The organism cleanses the body. It removes all other pathogens." His voice carried the drawl of his trying to focus the lens as he talked. "And in the case of arthritis, it redirects the immune system and keeps it from attacking the joints."

"So, it's a possible cure for autoimmune diseases?"

"The possibility is there. The methodology is an endless maze. For now, my focus is more narrowly concentrated."

I shook my head, imagining all of the diseases that would've fallen under that umbrella. "This project is huge."

"An understatement."

"Then, why do it yourself? It seems you'd require a team to carry that out."

"As I'm sure you've discovered, I don't get along well with others. *And* I first have to establish and prove that the toxin holds potential."

I nibbled my lip, debating whether, or not, to ask the next question. "I understand your father was a professor and researcher, as well. Did he study Noctisoma?"

He twisted around in his chair, away from the scope. "Are you finished pouring the agar?" he asked, ignoring my question.

"Yes."

"Good. You may leave."

"I … I still have twenty minutes. Is there something else you'd like me to do?"

"No. That will be all. Careful walking back to your dorm." With that, he turned back toward his microscope.

Disappointed, I let out a huff and I slinked past him, toward the autopsy room.

"Miss Vespertine. Wait."

Midstride, I turned back around.

"I'll walk you to the campus bus stop. It's a fairly dark path at night." He pushed up from his seat, and I had to turn back around so he wouldn't see the alarm flashing across my eyeballs.

"I can handle it. I've walked worse."

"I'm certain you have. But as you are now a liability for me, *I insist*."

A liability. What the hell did that even mean?

Even if I refused to admit it, I was a bit relieved to not have to walk solo through that creepy incinerator room. As he removed his coat, it seemed to catch on his shirt, pulling the collar down just enough that I managed a peek of the grisly scars across his collarbone and shoulder. The ones that still held the raw, pink coloring of a recent wound. I tried to wrap my head around what had given his attacker the balls to throw acid, of all things?

The abrupt pause of his movements caught my attention, and I glanced up to see him staring back at me. Clearing my throat, I removed my own coat, and after hanging it with his own on the hook outside the lab, he strode ahead of me, like he was leading me out instead of accompanying me.

I jogged to catch up, walking alongside him through the dark tunnels. "How are you not creeped out when you leave at night?"

"I've a reputation as *Doctor Death*. Seems most would be frightened of *me*."

"I suppose. Though, I don't find you all that frightening. Grouchy, but not frightening."

He slid me an unamused glance. "My grouchy nature serves a purpose, Miss Vespertine. Unfortunately, you seem to have some inexplicable resistance."

I smiled, ignoring the crematory ovens as we passed by them en route to the exit. "I like to arrive at my own conclusions about people."

"Admirable, though not entirely wise when the warnings are legitimate."

Legitimate? Like, murder legitimate, or just a play on the fact that he hung out with corpses? "Are you confessing something, Professor?"

He skidded to a halt, the exit just up ahead of us. "Ask me."

"What?"

"You're dying to ask me. You were staring at my scars just a moment ago. If I wanted to kill one of my students, I certainly have all the tools at my disposal." He glanced over his shoulder toward where the ovens stood as an ominous reminder of how quickly he could eliminate the evidence.

"Am I foolish for thinking you didn't kill her?"

"I don't know. Are you?"

"What I've learned doesn't point to you killing her. But you did invite her to your lab."

"I did not *invite* her. She apparently came in through the incinerator room, while I was in the upper lab gathering some samples. I suspect she realized there was no getting past the code to the lab and abandoned her quest, whatever it may have been." Arms crossed, he let out an exasperated breath. "It wasn't until the next morning that I learned of her disappearance, and by then, I'd already been labeled a murderer."

I didn't know Jenny Harrick, but based on the interactions I'd had with Professor Bramwell, that story sounded like the most plausible of any I'd heard so far. It was sickening to think how quickly everyone had arrived at the conclusion of murder. Particularly without any evidence that she'd been killed, at all. "I don't believe you're a murderer."

His brow winged up, and he strode off in the direction of the exit. "And so the moth befriended the flame."

"Huh," I said, falling into step after him. "I didn't think the flame was capable of being friendly."

"You assume I'm the danger to *you*."

Smiling, I lifted my bag up onto my shoulder. "Well, I

suppose you would've locked me in that cell, if that were true."

"I suppose I still can. But it'd be a shame to cage a specimen so ..."

"Intriguing?"

"Annoying. Truly, you'd make the worst captive in the history of kidnappings. A pack of howler monkeys would cause less headache." He pushed the door open, allowing me to exit first. The heavy door slammed behind us as we made our way over the small hill toward the open yard where the road stood about a hundred yards away.

"Is it wrong that I'm insulted by that?" I let out a laugh and turned to see a smile stretch his lips. A true and genuine smile, and holy shit, it was the most beautiful smile I'd ever seen. Straight, white teeth, and a dimple in his cheek. I wished I could've captured it, but it faded as quickly as it arrived, and I watched as his brows tightened and a look of panic claimed his face.

He bent forward, his hands balled into tight fists, and he let out a grunt.

When he collapsed to the ground, adrenaline exploded through my veins, and I dropped my phone, collapsing next to him. "Professor!"

Teeth clenched, he trembled and shook, but it wasn't like the seizure he'd had a while back. His eyes locked on mine, pleading in a way that clawed at my heart.

I didn't know what to do!

"I'll call for help." I said, scrambling for my fallen phone.

"No!" He reached out and grabbed my arm, his warm palm crushing my forearm as he held onto me. Eyes screwed shut, he kept hold, as his body shook and trembled and he grunted and gasped. His lips moved as he whispered something I couldn't hear at first, until his face twisted up and his body bowed as if he'd been struck by a jolt of electricity. "Impervious!"

That word again. I'd heard it the last time he'd suffered one of these seizures.

I didn't move, or try to wriggle from him. There'd surely be a bruise there tomorrow, but I didn't care, as I watched him suffer through whatever had hooked itself into him.

Call someone, my head urged, his refusal for help echoing the times my mother had refused. *Call now!*

As I lifted my phone to dial campus emergency, the grip of my arm loosened. I looked back to see the tension in his face softening. His body trembled less as he exhaled through his nose. Eyes still closed, he seemed to calm, and the brush of something on my forearm was his thumb stroking me. Back and forth, back and forth. When he opened his eyes, there appeared an almost intoxicated serenity, before it morphed before my eyes. The laxity in his face hardened again, and he released me, kicking back as he jolted upright.

Gaze diverted from mine, he scowled, patting his chest and slacks, and fished out a silver case that housed cigarettes.

"Are you okay?"

Shoving the cigarette between his lips, he patted again and pulled out a lighter, igniting the end of his smoke. One long drag, and he rested his elbow on his bent knee, pinching the bridge of his nose. "I suspect you're good to walk the rest of the way to your stop."

"I'm not leaving until I know you're all right."

"I'm fine." He waved me off. "Now, please. Go."

"No."

The look he shot me was one I'd have expected if I slapped him.

"I'll wait a few minutes. For my own peace of mind." Dropping my bag beside him, I plopped down on the grass that'd gotten significantly colder in the last few hours. "You have a condition."

"No shit," he said, and took another drag of his smoke.

"What is it?"

"Voneric's Disease. A rare congenital disorder. Happy?"

"An autoimmune disease."

"Yes."

Just like that, it became clear to me why the man was so dedicated, so single-mindedly passionate about a bunch of freaking worms. "That's why you're working on the toxin. But I thought you said your work focused on diabetes. Is this a diabetic complication?"

"No. It so happens the mechanism is similar. Unfortunately, no one gives a fuck about a disease that only affects one in five-hundred-thousand people."

I wanted to ask him if his father had set out to study the same thing, but didn't want him shutting me out again. "Is it ..." I clamped my mouth shut, not wanting to say it.

"Deadly? Yes. If it reaches my heart, it's game over for me."

God, the sound of that had such a swiftness to it. The thought that I'd almost witnessed his death, twice, had my stomach flipping on itself. "What is *impervious*?"

His brow flickered. "It's nothing." Cigarette dangling from his fingertips, he rubbed his face against his outstretched bicep. "My apologies for putting my hand on you."

"No need to apologize. I'm happy my arm was here." Flinching, I shook my head. "God. Scratch that comment all together." What a stupid thing to say. "So, this toxin ... how do you know it affects autoimmunity like that?"

"It's been demonstrated in mice."

"You said earlier that you have to prove the toxin holds potential. Doesn't its effect in mice prove it?"

"It does." Another drag of his cigarette, and he smashed it into the grass. "Unfortunately, death is a major fucking potential side effect. Until I can isolate a stable toxin variant, I'm stuck studying moths."

"Here, I thought you liked studying moths, the way you carry on in your lectures."

"Depends on the moth I'm studying." Eyes on me, he pushed to his feet, stumbling back a step.

Head winding through whether or not he'd just flirted again, I absent-mindedly reached out for him. When he jerked his arm away, I recoiled. Right. He didn't like to be touched.

"I'm sorry," I said.

"It's not my intent to be–"

"You're not. Not at all. Please don't feel the need to explain. I shouldn't be touching you. God, I didn't mean that to sound weird. Or creepy." Ugh. *Just stop already*. Shaking my head, I gathered up my bag. "I'm gonna go. I think the last bus is in about ten minutes."

"Miss Vespertine." At his call, I swung back around. "I'll see you tomorrow."

With a smile, I nodded.

Chapter 43

Lilia

A mild ache throbbed in my arm where a bruise marked Professor Bramwell's grip. As I lay in bed, I studied the pale purple outline of his fingers, tracing their edges with my fingertip.

After securing my non-bruised arm into my restraint, I flicked off the lamp beside my bed and settled into the covers. The moment I closed my eyes, I could almost feel his hand still gripping me. Holding me. The curl of those strong fingers digging into my bones.

The cool sheets dragged across my bare legs as I turned over to my stomach, the chain of my restraint clanking against the metal frame of the bed as it slid across the steel rail to the other side. I imagined his hand guiding mine down my body, slipping beneath the hem of my panties. Through parted lips, I let out a heavy sigh as I skated my fingers down an already wet seam.

So fucking wet, I imagined Professor Bramwell whispering in my ear. In my mind's eye, he was bent over me, the muscles of his bare chest pressed against my back, while he ran his fingers over that excited bundle of nerves that practically purred against his fingertips. I turned my face into the pillow, and darker thoughts emerged. Ones where he held me by the back of my neck, warning me to come, or suffocate.

My finger stroked faster, my breaths panting into the unforgiving cotton. I shoved one of my pillows between my legs, letting the firm surface press against the sensitive cleft. The bed let out a quiet squeak as I moved my hips. With my hand freed up, I pulled down my nightgown, springing my breast free. I could almost feel his palm gripping my flesh, fingers tickling my nipple, and his warm breath on my neck.

Be a good little moth, and I'll fuck you hard. As I rubbed myself against the pillow, I imagined him pounding into me, my smaller body jostling beneath his much bigger form. The feel of his cock pushing deep inside, filling me.

Hot and desperate, I pushed to my knees, propping my ass up slightly, and plunged two fingers up inside of me, shocked to discover how wet they were when I pulled them back out and plunged again. *Please fuck me*, my mind begged, still caught up in the fantasy of being bent over his desk. *Please, Professor Bramwell. Fuck me hard.* My belly tightened into hot coils of need, every muscle shaking as the orgasm crashed over me, and I moaned into my pillow. Loud, throaty moans that carried the lust-drunk pleasure of a hard climax.

I ground out the last of it into the pillow still wedged between my legs. With my ass still propped up, I turned my face to the side, drinking in the first sip of cool air, and breathed heavy and fast.

From the nightstand, I nabbed a half-consumed bottle of water, and gulped it back until the sting of thirst faded with my high. Once the lingering swells of euphoria died down, I pulled the pillow from between my legs and arranged it beneath the one I'd nearly smothered myself with. The restraint clanked again as I turned back over, and when I fell back onto my bed, I stared up at the dark ceiling, still trying to catch my breath.

Holy shit. I'd masturbated a few times in my life, but it'd never felt quite so good as *that*.

Groaning, I turned to my side, letting the small bit of shame settle over me. I'd just fingered myself to thoughts of my professor. Who also happened to be my boss. He had to be at least thirty-something, and while I wished that would have been a deterrent, unfortunately, it only stoked the flames. Something about the man crawled beneath my skin, unraveling dark fantasies like a spool of silk ribbon.

I liked that he was older. More mature. I'd always been attracted to older men.

I remembered having a conversation with my mother when I was about fourteen. Well before she had gotten sick. She'd told me that boys my age were immature and that I needed to wait until they grew up a bit. I'd carried that thought to the end of my freshman year at high school, when I'd met my first real boyfriend, if I could've even called him that. I'd mostly referred to him as Ghostboy. He was a senior, about to graduate. I'd been assigned to help him with physics, so that he might actually pass twelfth grade. He'd spent our tutoring sessions trying to get me to jerk him off, and when he turned eighteen, the dynamic of our interactions changed. I'd thought it would've turned him off, knowing he could've gotten in trouble, since he'd been considered an adult and I was still a minor. On the contrary, it seemed to make him much more interested. Somehow, I'd found it a turn on, too.

He'd told me that I was more mature. Smarter. More beautiful. I'd been so certain that I had fallen in love with him, up until I'd caught him fucking another girl in the alley behind the movie theater, where she'd worked at the time. A sophomore. That had marked the end of my little explorations with Ghostboy, but the experience had unlocked something else. Something much more depraved.

The visual of being dominated and ravished by an older man had somehow entrenched itself into my fantasies.

Until Angelo had started taking notice of me. That'd been

about the time my fantasies had fizzled into the recesses of my head.

I'd thought they were banished for good—until Professor Bramwell had gripped me earlier in the night. I hated to admit that I'd enjoyed his bruising grasp a bit too much.

A sound roused me out of sleep, and I opened my eyes to the darkness of my bedroom. The creak of old wood echoed through the room, and I turned to see the closet door across from me cracked open. A breath caught in my chest, as something shifted in the darkness there. The willowy shape of a woman stepped forward, wearing a white gown.

Fiery red hair danced around her shoulders as she glided across the floor, and when she came into view, my heart caught in my throat. "Mama?"

Eyes black as coal gave her a terrifying, demonic appearance. Pale, wrinkled hands reached out as she hobbled across the room toward me. She came to a stop alongside my bed, staring down at me with those doll's eyes, and her mouth opened wide, wider, too wide. The abnormal unhinging of her jaw had my skin pebbling with goosebumps.

A tingling paralysis seized my muscles. I couldn't move!

Black worms spilled from her mouth, falling onto me.

A scream ripped from my throat, and I shot up in bed with a loud clank. Confused, I turned to see my arm stretched.

Tethered. Restrained.

The restraint was connected to the headboard. Yes, I did that. I restrained myself. I snapped my attention to the closet, where the door stood closed.

I'd dreamed it. Not real. Only a dream.

Exhaling a shaky breath, I lay back on my pillow, staring

up at the ceiling again, clutching the vial of my mother's ashes that lay against my throat. Tears wobbled in my eyes. I hated these visions of her as a monster. She wasn't a monster. Not before she'd gotten sick, anyway.

A dark and shadowy memory sat on the fringes of my thoughts. Echoes of screams. Nails digging into arms.

Mama! Please! No!

I can't breathe!

Eyes screwed shut, I shook my head and buried my face into the pillow.

No, no, no. Don't look at it. Push it away. Push it away!

The screams faded at the same time the ache at my arm flared again. The bruise from Bramwell.

My thoughts shifted to his pleading eyes and trembling muscles. The laxity on his face as he'd gripped my arm and stroked my skin.

The ache withered.

I unlatched my tethered arm and pressed my thumb into the bruise, desperate for the pain to keep that nightmare from earlier away.

And it did.

Chapter 44

Lilia

The lab coat I'd worn the last time I'd worked in the lab hung from its hook just outside of the door. I donned it, as Professor Bramwell had asked of me, and entered the code for the keypad. The door clicked open to the laboratory, where I found him typing on a laptop at one of the benches. Candles flickered about the lab, giving off an eerie feel, like something out of a *Jekyll and Hyde* novel.

I licked my lips, where I'd applied the same lipstick I wore on the night of the gala. The shade that'd seemed to snag his attention.

Beside him stood a stereo microscope, and on the opposite side, a large glass dome held two, small, purple Sominyx moths, which didn't cling to the walls as they should have, but lay on the floor of their cage.

"New pets?" I asked, noticing the small holes in the top of the dome and the bowl of berries provided to them, and of course, a chunk of bloody meat that had me grimacing.

"Test Group Ten," he grumbled, keeping on with his typing.

"These are the moths you're using to study the toxin?"

"Yes."

"Do you have names for them?" A quick examination of the moths showed enough distinctions in coloring to distinguish them. One had a white spot, and the other, a crooked probiscis.

"No. I don't have names for them." He still hadn't peeled his gaze from the eyepiece.

"What a shame. I mean, seems like it would be bad luck not to name them individually."

Brow cocked, he shot me a glance that turned into a double take, as his gaze seemed to catch on my lips. Clearing his throat, he turned away again, brow furrowed, and I bit the inside of my lip, feeling victorious that he'd noticed. "Feel free, if you're so inclined."

"Me? Wow. The *pressure*. They have to be good names, if we want the experiment to be successful, right?"

"I'm afraid the name is inconsequential."

Smiling, I turned my attention back to the moths. "By the way, what's the cat's name?"

"Bane."

"What are you, a DC fan, or something?"

"No. I'm simply *not* a fan of curious cats that like to invade my workspace."

Without a doubt, he'd inherited the cat. Still kind of cute that he'd allowed it to stay. And had named him. Turning my attention back to the moths, I studied the unnatural kink to their wings, which brought to mind the way my mother's spine had begun to bow in the latter stages of her illness. How helpless and sad it'd always made me feel, watching her hobble around in pain. A somber ache throbbed in my chest, and I cleared my throat. "So, names. I think the one in the back with the white spot on its wing should be Achilles, and the one in the front, with the goofy proboscis, should be Patroclus."

From his profile, I caught the lowering of his brows, and I chuckled, thinking about how many muscles the man must flex in a day with all those frowns.

"Is this an obsession with Greek mythology?"

"In your canonical world, I suppose it would seem that way."

"Dare I ask what it represents in *your* world?" he asked, making a quick sketch in the notebook beside his microscope that appeared to be the melanization of larva, given the dark pigmentation.

As I peered down at his artwork, a small white scar just below his knuckle caught my eye and had me wondering how it'd gotten there. At his abrupt pause, I glanced up to see his brow cocked in expectation and realized I hadn't answered his question. "A romance novel I read a while back."

He let out a disapproving sigh. "I'm sure it was enriching."

"You shouldn't knock romance, Professor. It so happens that love is *biologically* important to human beings. It reduces blood pressure and depression, and improves sleep."

The contemplative expression on his face twisted to a smirk. "And just how does that benefit you as a *reader*? A voyeur, essentially. You have no intimate connection with these fictional characters."

"Says who? I happen to get very attached to my fictional boyfriends."

Yet another frown. "*Boyfriends*?"

"I read a lot."

With a shake of his head, he huffed. "Fine. Achilles and Patroclus," he conceded.

"Has a nicer ring than Test Group Ten." I drew my finger over the glass, curious that the moths didn't bother to flutter off, or startle, at my presence. "What's wrong with them? Why are they hanging out on the floor of the cage?"

"They suffer with a condition that affects their ability to fly. The muscles used to contract their wings are faulty."

"And so, you intend to inject them with the toxin in hopes it'll reverse it?"

"Precisely."

"Have you had success before?"

"No. The moth metabolizes the toxin before it can repair the muscles."

"Then, the puzzle is slowing the speed it metabolizes. How?"

"If I knew that, I'd be on a yacht sipping champagne, instead of fielding all of your millions of questions. Again."

I smiled as the moth hobbled, trailing after my nail that I dragged across the glass. "The ferry ride here was my first time on a boat. First time on the sea. I've never actually touched the water, at all."

In my periphery, he lifted his head from the microscope and turned to me. "You've never touched the sea?"

"I was always scared of it. The vastness. The power. The way it could sweep a person off their feet and carry them miles away from shore. Then you're alone and adrift in the middle of nowhere. With God knows what swimming beneath you." I stared off, imagining the visual I'd had on the ferry ride. "Deep waters terrify me."

"Or perhaps it's the sea who fears the depths of you, Miss Vespertine." The amusement in his voice and dimple in his cheek told me the comment wasn't serious, but it left me wondering if there was an element of truth in his humor. If the man buried his compliments that way, or softened his insults behind handsome smiles and poetic words.

"That's ridiculous," I played along. "The sea doesn't fear anything." Turning back toward the moths, I fought the urge to smile. "Well, these moths are named, therefore this experiment cannot fail."

"If you say so." Eyes still peering through the microscope, he reached for the notebook beside him and handed it to me. "I've detailed a list of chores for you." A small Post-It flag stuck out from the side, labeled 'Vespertine', and I opened the book up to a list of illegible scribbles.

"Jesus. Did you have to take a class to write this bad?"

He let out a disapproving grumble. "Keep in mind, it's *you* who wants this job. Not the other way around."

I chuckled to myself, trying to decipher the first chore on the list, and got to work on the menial tasks I'd specifically requested not to do.

The hours passed quickly, and once again, it was time to go. Just as he had the night before, he walked me to the bus stop. A sharp tension rattled my nerves, recalling the last we'd walked together and he'd collapsed in front of me, without warning.

"No millions of questions tonight?" he asked, staring up at the stars, as we strolled across the yard.

Smiling, I lowered my gaze. "Okay, fine. Remember, though, you asked for it.

"I take full responsibility."

"You seem kind of young for a tenured professor with a medical degree. What's up with that?"

"I was fast-tracked. It pays to have the right connections. Remember that."

I bit the inside of my cheek, debating whether, or not, to ask the next question. One that'd toyed with my mind for days, and I wouldn't have been ballsy enough to ask out of the blue, but since he was actually entertaining questions, why not. "Why did you carry me to your car that night? You could've left me in the gardens. Someone might've found me."

When he glanced back at me, his brow did that painfully attractive kicking-up thing. "Had I known you were going to blackmail me, I might've."

I chuckled. "You don't strike me as a man who's easily blackmailed."

"And you don't strike me as a young woman who longs to sequester herself in an antiquated lab with cadavers and parasites, either. Yet, here we are."

The smile on my face faded as I contemplated why I was still so drawn to this after my mother's death. Why my curiosities had so much of a chokehold over me. "I feel compelled to do something meaningful with my life. I owe it to my family."

"You owe nothing to your family," he said abrasively, as if I'd insulted him. "Passions are useless, if we pursue them for others. They become obligations. Undesirable."

"This project is your passion."

"I suppose. In spite of all the political bullshit." He glanced over at me. "What's yours?"

It was a question I'd answered so many times, on applications and in interviews, and my benign response of wanting to help people was always the same. But that wasn't true, either, and in light of his last comment, I got the sense he'd see right through it, so I answered honestly. "I don't know. I guess I'm still searching for it. I love science. I love learning. And I want to cure Noctisoma someday. Put you out of business."

"Good luck." It was clear from the way his lips twitched that he was holding back a smile. "To answer your question about why I didn't leave you in the gardens that night, I find you to be an intriguing annoyance."

"I guess that's appropriate, coming from a man I find to be brilliantly antisocial," I quipped.

The crease at the corner of his eye hinted at the slightest smile. Man, the guy was stingy when it came to them. "I suppose that's fair. I have a gift for repelling."

I snorted and shook my head. "Not the brunette who sits in front of me in class," I blurted.

"What about her?"

I instantly regretted having brought her up. "She seems to be very ..." An image came to mind, of two days before when she'd snapped a photo of him rolling up his sleeves before lecture, with the caption: *Professor Hand Necklace [tongue emoji].* "Observant during your lectures." I dared a glance and found him staring at the ground, frowning, his hands tucked into his pockets, sleeves rolled up over those exquisite forearms she'd captured in her photo. "She's pretty," I added, gauging his reaction. "Seems your type."

A short distance away, the headlights of the bus flickered as it approached my stop.

"Hardly. I don't have a defined type, particularly when it comes to my students."

"She'll be thoroughly disappointed, I'm sure." At that point, I didn't even know if I was talking about the girl anymore. "Under different circumstances, she might've been the perfect match."

"Under different circumstances ..." The pause in his words carried a laborious heartbeat that smothered my own, as I watched the slightest smile play on his lips. A beat of hesitation. "I might've pursued you."

A nervous rush of breath escaped me. I gripped the strap of my bookbag in some faulty attempt to hold my composure, and swallowed past the dryness in my throat. "And I might've let you." The bus rolled to a stop, absolutely killing the moment. If it counted as a moment. "Goodnight, Professor."

"Good night, Miss Vespertine."

Chapter 45

Lilia

What?

I stared down at my first entomology exam, trying to make sense of the grade that'd been populated into the computer.

Forty-five points out of eighty, which equated to a fifty-six percent. I hadn't received a fifty-six percent on an exam since middle school.

Scrolling through the document that I'd submitted showed pages and pages of red notes alongside my essays, and at first, the grade almost seemed legit for all the red ... until I scanned over them. The notes marked ridiculous technical errors, like a comma that should've been a semicolon, a paragraph that Gilchrist felt should've been new, except that the information had related to the previous paragraph, and I had apparently not tabbed over enough on my bullet points, to her liking.

Cheeks red hot, I held back the urge to cry as I waited for the class to end. I'd have loved to compare grades with another student, but the only other person I knew was Spencer, who hadn't bothered to show up, and I had no interest in interacting with him after the events at the gala. Although he'd attempted to call me since then, I'd ignored him.

Once class ended, a small line formed, as other students

waited to speak with Professor Gilchrist, and I patiently waited my turn, in spite of wanting to crawl out of my skin right then. When I finally reached the front, I stepped forward, my hand shaking with the anger that had blossomed over the last hour.

"How can I help you, Miss Vespertine?" Her voice held an air of boredom that only goaded my frustration.

"My grade ... it seems content-wise. All of my essays and multiple-choice responses were correct?"

"Mmm-hmm. And?"

"I received a fifty-six on grammatical and *formatting* errors? You never specified the importance of these issues and how much they weighed on the grade."

The unbothered expression on her face didn't waver with my complaint. If anything, it grew smugger. "It's a college course. You should be well-versed in how to format a proper essay."

"I understand, but ... *fifty-six*? I mean, I got every answer correct. I understood the material, and you had no comments on the composition and content of my essays."

Shoulders rolled back, she rested her elbows on the desk, entwining her fingers. "Tell me, do you intend to conduct research someday?"

"Yes."

"Yes." Her brows winged up with a smile that was both pitiful and condescending at the same time. "And so, grant writing is a huge part of funding for those research projects. If you can't format properly, well, you'll look inept." She threw her hands up dismissively. Dismissively doling out a grade that weighed heavily on my cumulative score.

"That would make sense ... if this was a grant writing class."

"Please tell me you're not one of those students who feels a sense of entitlement based on your circumstances."

"Excuse me?" I cleared my throat, the shock of her words rendering me stupefied.

The haughty tip of her chin told me I hadn't misheard her, nor misunderstood the meaning.

"I'm not trying to be difficult," I added. "I'm just concerned what this will do to my overall average."

"It'll certainly bring it down, which is a shame. It seems the underprivileged aren't meant for a proud and dignified institution like Dracadia. I was wrong about you."

"How so?"

Her finger tapped on the lid of her black coffee cup. "I saw you glancing over at Spencer twice during this exam. You're lucky I didn't fail you for *cheating*."

Cheating? *Cheating!*

The accusation struck me like a punch to the throat. I'd spent hours studying for that exam.

"I do not cheat, and if I ever thought of cheating, it certainly wouldn't be off Spencer."

On a mirthless laugh, she shook her head. "You are an arrogant little thing, aren't you? So smug and full of yourself."

"What? I'm not .... I don't understand. I swear to you, I never cheated. I *wouldn't* cheat." I hated that my voice wobbled with the threat of tears. "I want to do well while I'm here."

"I'm sure you do. And I'm sure your manipulative behaviors work on some professors here at Dracadia, Miss Vespertine. But I'm not one of them." The arrogant smile that followed sank into my gut like a rusty fork. "Now, if you'll excuse me, I have an important meeting. The grade stands."

A cold despair stirred in my chest, as I exited her class. I'd planned to get lunch at Cavick, but decided the best thing for me to do was head back to my dorm to sleep it off. Exhaustion and anger weighed heavy on me, and I still had two more afternoon classes to get through.

As I rounded the building, past the small alley, something grabbed my arm, and a hard yank had me stumbling backward into a solid surface. I opened my mouth to scream, but a hand smothered it, and my body was dragged backward, toward the alley. Once there, the hard stones of the building smashed into my spine.

Spencer stood before me, one eye swollen and purple, both eyes red with deep, black circles beneath. His body shook, his lip downturned as if he would cry.

I let out a scream, and he pressed his hand harder, his jaw clenching with frustration.

"Please! Listen to me! Just for a moment. I'm begging you."

My heart hammered in my chest as I stared back, wondering what he would do. Was he crazy enough to strangle me? Angry enough to punch me?

"I know you think that I tried to ... hurt you ... that night. And I swear to you, Lilia. I didn't. I wouldn't hurt you. Ever." His voice was shaky, as if he were on the brink of cracking. "There are things you don't know about ... people who ... are very bad here. And Professor Bramwell is one of them. Do you understand?"

I didn't bother to shake my head, or nod at his comment.

"He beat the shit out of me that night. He did this to my fucking eye." At that, I did try to shake my head, and he pressed into me, lip snarled up in rage. "Yes, he did! I fucking saw him. He took off that fucking mask, and he beat the ever-loving shit out of me. And no one believes me. Not Langmore. Not my fucking father. Not even you." He lowered his gaze, eyes shining with tears. "Did I have intentions that night? No." Eyes screwed shut, he shook his head. "Yeah. How could I not, with how you looked in that dress? But I did not drug you. I wouldn't do that. Not to you."

I kicked my head to the side, and he lowered his hand from my mouth. "Did you drug Mel?"

His brows came together, and he let out a huff. "Yes. But it's not what you think. I was just trying to find out what she knew about Jenny and Bramwell. I just needed her to relax a little."

"Did you try to have sex with her?"

"I flirted. Tried to kiss her, is all. Again, it was just trying to get her to talk to me."

"She was telling the truth, then. You really are a scumbag."

Fingers curling into my arms, he held me tighter. "I didn't do this shit because I wanted to. I did it because I had to."

"What the hell does that even mean? Your dad put you up to drugging her?"

The expression on his face blackened, and a cold brush of alarm palmed the back of my neck. "I told you. There are bad people at this school. Some worse than others."

"I saw you with Gilchrist. I saw her ... touch you."

A look of shame crumpled his brow, and he lowered his gaze from mine.

"You kissed her."

"She threatened to fail me, if I didn't–" He grimaced and exhaled a shaky breath, the repulsion crimping his lips.

"If you didn't what?"

Tears shone in his eyes as he shook his head.

"Spencer, if you didn't *what*? Was it Gilchrist who put you up to all of this?"

He looked toward the mouth of the alley and back to me, his hand frantically stroking my hair. "I like you, Lilia. A lot. Too much. I can't stop thinking about you, and it kills me to know that you hate me right now."

"I don't hate you. I just really need you to tell me the truth."

"If you care for me ... even the slightest bit ... even as a friend, you'll stay away from Bramwell."

"What are you talking about? He's my professor."

"I see him watching you sometimes. You don't even realize how much he watches you. He's followed you to class. He's probably watching you now, for fucks sake. The guy is nuts."

Undoubtedly wearing the confusion that clouded my brain, I shook my head.

"Yes. He does. Watch yourself, Lilia. In fact, fucking leave this school. You're better off." Placing a palm at my throat, he didn't squeeze, only stroked the column of my neck with his thumb. His face pinched, as if he might cry right there. Instead, he darted off back down the alley.

A strange vulnerability settled over me, as I walked down the cadaver tunnel toward Professor Bramwell's lab. Even though I'd spent the afternoon convincing myself that Spencer was wrong, that I had watched Bramwell enough to know that he hadn't been watching me like that, his arguments still left me confused. Spencer clearly had it in for Bramwell, and while his friend being kicked out seemed reason enough to suspect he might harbor some animosity toward him, to what extent would that animosity go? That he would frame Bramwell as an attacker? Make him out to be a total creep who followed me around?

As if my problems weren't already stacked like a Jenga tower ready to tumble, Bee's school had called me earlier, letting me know they could only get half of the back tuition approved with the grant, and that I'd have to get them five hundred as soon as possible.

Five hundred I didn't happen to have right then.

Feeling pummeled by the day's events, I entered the lab,

and found Professor Bramwell hunched over, studying something on the bench he stood before. A candle flickered near him, as he poked a set of forceps toward the benchtop. It was enough distraction to banish the thoughts of Spencer and Bee and Gilchrist, and every other woe that'd reared its ugly head.

At the brush of my ankles, I knelt down to give Bane a quick pet, grateful for his sweet little greeting on such a shitty day, and I approached Professor Bramwell to see it was a moth he had spread out on the extra wide stage plate of the microscope, its thorax sliced open to reveal the organs beneath. He lifted a long, skinny black worm up into the air, where it wriggled and thrashed around. Professor tipped his head and grabbed another set of forceps, which he used to hold one end of it still while he examined the parasite. "Son of a bitch."

"What is it?" I asked, intrigued by the awe in his voice.

"Another one with teeth."

"Teeth?"

He laid it beside the moth, restraining the end of it, and when he shifted it beneath the lens, I peered up at the small square viewing screen to see tiny fang-like structures snapping at the forceps. "It seems they've evolved."

"You're telling me those things ..." The thought of it curled my guts. Probably didn't help that I'd skipped both lunch and dinner after what had happened earlier.

"Yes. They can apparently latch now." He lifted the worm and plopped it into a jar of clear fluid and placed a cap over it. From beside him, he lifted the burning candle, holding it over the moth as if looking for more of the worms.

At the angle he held it, the flame flickered over his knuckles, and I frowned as it seemed to have no effect on him. He didn't move. Didn't even flinch, as if he couldn't feel it.

"Professor!" I lurched toward him, and he startled, knocking the jar with the worm onto the floor, where the glass shattered. The worm wriggled across the tiles toward a drain.

"No! Shit!" He jogged toward it, sliding over the slick tiles, but caught himself and planted his shoe over the drain. The worm slid up onto his shoe, lifting its upper half, which it tapped against the leather's surface. "Hand me the forceps!"

I sprang toward the bench and swiped up the forceps, slipping on the small bit of water like he had moments ago.

He leapt back toward me, catching my arm before I fell and pulled me upright.

Momentarily stunned, I stole a moment to catch my breath, and at the same time, both of us snapped our heads in the direction of the worm, only catching its tail end as it slipped down the drain.

He let out a sigh. "Fuck."

"I'm so sorry. I didn't mean ..." Perhaps it was exhaustion coupled with hunger, and add in the fact that I'd just disappointed him, but my voice shook and I blinked away tears.

As if realizing he still held my arm, he frowned and stepped back, stuffing his hands into his lab coat. "What's wrong with you?"

I shook my head, not wanting to tell him, because telling him would've definitely made me cry, and I was *not* crying in front of the man. "I'll clean up this mess." As I stepped in the direction of the utility closet, he sidestepped and blocked me.

"Lilia, tell me what's wrong."

A strange feeling stirred in my chest on hearing him say my name, and when I lifted my gaze to his, saw the concern brimming in his eyes, I couldn't hold back the tears.

"I can't."

"Tell me. Now."

Why did I protect Gilchrist? Had she given me even a fraction of consideration when she'd said those things earlier? No. In fact, it probably tickled her black heart to know how much her words had crushed me. The way she'd somehow seen right through me and reached down into the deepest pits of my self-doubt. "Gilchrist accused me of cheating on an exam. She gave me a fifty-six on it."

His eye twitched, jaw hardened. "Did she now?"

"I don't know if she plans to pursue the cheating accusation, but if she does, then that will ruin everything. I'll be kicked out, and I won't be approved for next semester."

"Relax. She would need proof." While the confidence in his tone cut through my worry like a jagged blade, it didn't settle it entirely.

"She accused me of cheating off Spencer. She's threatened to fail Spencer before. He's not going to tell the truth for my sake."

He snorted. "As if Spencer held a candle ..." He trailed off in a grouchy grumble.

I didn't know why that half comment filled me with satisfaction and withered some of the mire in my head. Maybe because the man rarely threw out compliments. Or perhaps it was because I felt like he was on my side.

"It takes tremendous effort to prove a student has cheated, and I don't think even she has the energy, or motivation, for that."

The relief I felt in telling him just that small piece of my day left me wanting to offload everything, every miserable detail, until I'd purged and emptied myself of it, but I wouldn't. He didn't need to know my financial woes on top of everything else.

The man probably had more money than he knew what to do with. The fact that I owed thousands for Bee's tuition, with a mere ten bucks left in my account, would've probably seemed absurd to him. To all the students who attended this university, too. I'd yet to meet one weighed down by their finances, the way I was. "Sometimes, I think coming here was a mistake. I just feel like everything is stacked against me all the time. There's no winning."

"And so, what? You go back to Covington?"

"I don't know. I don't want to, but ..." Even if I paid Bee's school the two hundred Bramwell had agreed to give me every week, it'd still take over two months to pay everything back. And that was assuming Conner kept up his half to bring the account current. "Everything just feels so heavy sometimes."

"So, your solution is to quit school. Forego your scholarship."

"As I said, I don't want to do that, but–"

"But nothing. You may be smart, but you sure as fuck say foolish things."

I could've given him some benefit of doubt, not knowing what was going through my head right then, that Gilchrist was only one of many worries, but his response still pissed me off. People with money somehow always pissed me off, and I hated myself for that, but goddamn it, sometimes they acted like their problems were on par with everyone else's. What would he have thought, had he known that I'd uploaded a fucking porn video to a website just to pay for my sister's tuition? Would he have judged me for that? Lectured me on virtue and human decency?

"Since when do you care? I'm sure you'll appreciate going back to your quiet lab, where no one breaks jars and lets specimens escape down the drain. I don't belong at this school, with students who drop hundreds on dresses for one night. Who can afford their fancy latte coffees in cute little cups with the gold dragon logo," I said, giving a snobby flip of my wrist. "Who don't have to think about anything but their grades and studying. I'm tired of stressing about things that never cross their minds."

"So, going back to Covington is going to relieve you of all these struggles?"

"Of course not. But everyone in Covington struggles. At least I'm not some freak outcast there."

"Yes. Brilliant. You'll be thrown into some shit job that you'll hate and resent for the rest of your life."

"What does it matter to you if I stay, or not?" I searched those usually apathetic eyes for some explanation for why he suddenly seemed bothered.

"It matters."

"Why?"

"Has anyone treated you like scum here? Has anyone thrown your lack of money in your face?"

Gilchrist came to mind, her comment from earlier that'd apparently sunk its claws into me, given the way I was feeling right then, but I didn't bother to mention it. Instead, I kept my lips shut, which he apparently took as a response to his question.

"Stop feeling sorry for yourself. You sound ridiculous."

"I sound ridiculous? Why? Because I don't share the same problems as the rich elite?"

"No. That you bother to compare yourself to them at all is ridiculous."

"Ah, yes. I almost forgot they were in a different league. Thank you for yanking me back down to reality." Tears formed in my eyes as I dared to confess what had ground at me all afternoon. "Perhaps Gilchrist was right when she said the *underprivileged aren't meant for a proud and dignified institution like Dracadia*."

Scorn darkened his eyes. "She said that to you?"

As much as I regretted having said it aloud, it felt good to have told someone. To offload some of the humiliation still chipping at my pride. "Yes. After she accused me of being entitled, based on my circumstances. So, tell me again why *I* sound ridiculous. Why I have no right to compare myself to my fellow students. Why I shouldn't go back to where I *belong*."

His jaw shifted, lip curled in disgust. "Because you're better than them. Stronger. And unfortunately, you'll have to fight harder for what you want. But you have an understanding of things beyond their comprehension. You're exceptional, Lilia. And by God, if you waste that intellect on the ignorant words of an envious shrew like Loretta Gilchrist, it will be the most egregious offense you've ever committed."

Heat burned my face red-hot. My arms shook with the urge to throw them around him and kiss him. Instead, I stared, focusing on the unsteady breaths that sawed in and out of me.

The suffocating tension between us threatened to ignite on one bold move, a single strike of a match. His hand curled around the bench where he leaned, and it was then I noticed the glossy red mark and inflamed skin where he'd burned himself with the candle.

"Oh, my God." I reached out for his hand, and he jerked it away, holding his fist at his chest. "You're burned pretty badly. You need to clean and wrap that."

"I know what I need."

"Right," I said, taking a step back. Of course, he'd probably done clinical rotations in the ER and burn units at some point in his life. "Can you not feel, at all?"

"No. Not at all."

"I can't imagine how awful that must be. How terrifying not to feel."

He lowered his hand, flexing his fingers. "It's grown on me."

"You've suffered with that your whole life?"

"Yes."

"I'm sorry."

"I don't need your pity, Miss Vespertine." His voice hardened, the space between us colder, all of a sudden. "If you'd be so kind as to clean up the broken glass, I'd appreciate it. Be careful not to cut yourself."

"Of course."

For the next two hours, I busied myself with menial lab tasks–autoclaving, sterilizing new agar solution, and catching the occasional glance from Professor Bramwell, like the night at the gala–stolen glances amounting to nothing, really. Nothing but curiosity. I thought back to the evening before, when he'd told me that, under different circumstances, he'd have pursued me. Whatever had compelled him to confess that must've slinked back into its shell and covered itself up with a blanket.

As I wiped down the fume hood, I noticed a tray of tubes carrying a strange purple and black solution. Frowning, I turned my head to the side, reading the vertical label on the test tubes–NyxVar2.10, NyxVar2.12, NyxVar2.15. Beneath that was Noctisoma toxin and the date. Pretending as if I was scrubbing hard at something, I studied the strange fluid inside, the almost marbled mixture of purple and black that must've been what he planned to inject into the moths.

At the end of my shift, Doctor Bramwell walked me to the bus stop, wordless. Shoulders bunched, gazed glued to the ground, he seemed preoccupied. And I supposed I was too tired to bombard him with questions, so the two of us walked in silence. Just like the last time, he watched me from a distance, until I caught the flicker of bus lights coming up over the hill, and I waved him on. Hands stuffed in his pockets, he turned around and headed back toward his lab.

Drops of rain hit my arm, and when I tipped my head back, cold sprinkles dotted my face. Perfect. Fortunately, the bus was close, because the longer I stood there, the faster the drops fell. Faster. Faster.

When the bus finally reached me, the rain had picked up intensity, pattering hard against the sidewalk. It was then I realized I'd left my purse and my ID back at the lab.

Shit! Shit!

I'd need it to get into my dorm.

Shit, shit!

Groaning, I waved the bus driver on, and as the downpour assaulted me along the way, striking my skin like dissolving bullets, I jogged my ass back toward the laboratory until I reached the incinerator room, where I shook off the freezing water still clinging to my skin. Shivering, I made my way down the frigid cadaver tunnel, clenching my teeth to keep them from chattering. I'd worn a skirt that day, thinking I'd beat the forecasted rain for the evening. It was my luck to have to walk in it, anyway.

There was no sign of Professor Bramwell when I entered the autopsy room and strode toward the hooks holding the lab coats. As I approached, I noticed something sticking up from the pocket of my lab coat. A note.

I opened it to find a small plastic card with the Dragon's Lair coffee shop logo on it. The attached paper simply said: *Now you can buy coffee whenever you like. –B*

It was a yearly pass, one he must've purchased for himself, and at the echoes of my self-wallowing earlier, I winced. It wasn't like me, at all, to be so pathetically self-deprecating, but I was tired. Stressed. Confused. Angry. A whole host of emotions that made the perfect storm. Even then, I felt kind of stupid for dumping all of that on him.

I unhooked my coat to find my purse hidden beneath it, and I nabbed it, just then remembering the dreaded walk I'd have to make back to my dorm, seeing as the last pick up of the night had already come and gone. I'd be a sopping mess and, with my luck, would end up with a horrible pneumonia, proving my mother right all those years.

A sound reached my ears–loud, pained, brimming with suffering. A chill skated up my spine, the hairs on the back of my neck standing on end.

It arrived again, that time carrying a distinct masculine pitch that I recognized. Bramwell?

He could've been having another attack.

Without too much contemplation, I punched the keypad code and dashed through the door, into the lab. I yanked my phone, ready to make a call in the event that his heart had suffered the attack that time. Eyes scanning the candlelit space, I caught sight of the glass dome, where Patroclus and Achilles fluttered around inside. Flying? Though my head begged to tease out the possibility of such a thing, it was only a brief distraction in my otherwise cursory search, and I kept on through the other set of doors, toward Bramwell's office. I slowed my steps on hearing the sounds of quiet moaning and peeked into his office.

He sat at the desk, turned toward his bookshelves, shirtless, his muscles glistening with sweat, a tourniquet wrapped just below his bulging bicep.

I trailed my gaze to the tray of test tubes in front of him, the purple marbly tubes that I'd seen earlier under the hood. Beside them lay a syringe.

Unless I was mistaken, those were the test tubes labeled NyxVar. The Noctisoma toxin. Had he injected them into *himself*?

Jarred with disbelief, I stood paralyzed, watching him writhe in his chair, grunting and moaning, as I presumed the toxin worked its way through his body. My phone slipped out of my hands, clattering to the floor.

Shit. Shit!

Slapping a hand to my mouth, I swiped it up and backed myself away. As I heard him moving about, undoubtedly getting up out of his chair, I turned to the nearest door beside me and ducked inside. Footsteps approached, and in a panic, I stumbled through the dark room, until I felt a cold metal surface beneath my fingertips and slid my hand over a latch. With a yank, I swung it open and shut myself inside. Through the barrier, I heard the other door creak open. Footsteps.

I bit my lip, praying he wouldn't find me there. Given how staunchly he protected his privacy, who knew how he'd react if he suspected I'd seen him?

The footsteps retreated, and I exhaled a jittery breath.

When I reached for the latch to open the door, though, it wouldn't budge. *Oh, no. No, no, no.*

I wriggled the latch, yanking on it, but to no avail. A putrid stench assaulted my senses, so repulsive, it sprang tears to my eyes, and I covered my nose with the back of my hand, swallowing back a gag. Blindly patting the wall, I found a light switch and flipped it on. A fluorescent tube flickered overhead, and I turned around to find that I had locked myself in what looked to be a smaller autopsy room with only one examination table. A white sheet covered what I had little doubt was a body beneath.

Muscles quaking, I tiptoed toward it, my heart my heart rioting inside my chest with every step closer, and I peeled back the sheet.

There on the table lay a man with the telling post-autopsy Y-incision stitches, and whose eyeballs had been removed, leaving empty sockets. Another gag punched the back of my throat, the acids burning as I breathed hard through my nose. The sight of him sent an icy trickle of fear down my spine, and with a sharp exhale, I threw the sheet back over him to quickly cover him up. Even without his eyes, something about him looked vaguely familiar, but I couldn't quite place why. And I didn't care, because the realization that I was stuck in there with him hit me right then.

I ran for the door. No fucking way I was staying all night with a corpse who had no eyeballs. No fucking way! When the door wouldn't budge again, I pounded. The panic rose up into my throat, and I let out a scream.

Cold tentacles of fear slithered over the back of my neck.

A glance over my shoulder revealed a ghostly figure of the

man standing alongside the examination table. Forehead pressed to the door, I squeezed my eyes shut. *No, no, no.* Hysterics commandeered me, and I slammed the heel of my hand against the door. A sob broke from my chest. "Help me! Somebody, help me!"

The door swung open, and I dove headfirst into the body standing in the doorway. I wrapped my arms around it, fingers clawing into flesh to keep me rooted there, away from that room and the death it held. Every muscle in my body convulsed in terror, and I let out a shaky breath, the tears spilling down my cheeks.

At first, he didn't move, but then strong arms engulfed me, pulling me closer. "Oh, fuck, Lilia. I'm sorry. I'm so sorry."

I clung to him, letting the fear work its way through me. The realization that I could've been stuck all night in there gnawed at my bones every time I dared to imagine the visual. It was when I felt the gentle stroke down my damp hair that I glanced up to see Professor Bramwell embracing me, his eyes brimming with remorse.

Remorse that shifted to confusion, as he stroked my hair slower.

Curiosity and trepidation clashed his eyes, and he skated his palm down my cheek, pausing to rub his fingers together. His thumb caressed my bottom lip, and his hand moved to my hair again, where he let a strand slip through his fingers, eyes alight with fascination. "I feel you."

I stared up at him, the fear inside of me dissolving, and I raised my hand.

He placed his much bigger hand against mine, palm to palm, and curled his fingers around mine, swallowing them. "I feel everything." He let out a choke of a laugh. "I fucking feel everything!" He whisked me into his arms and spun me around.

My stomach flipped, and a giggle slipped free, in spite of my earlier tears.

The room settled as he placed me back onto my feet and held me against him. Tightly. I didn't move. Like the night before, I let him hang onto me, breathing. "You're so cold," he said, the heat practically radiating from him, as I sagged into his embrace.

"It was raining hard, and ..." My words drifted off the moment his fingers feathered across my back and to my arms where they drew a light caress.

He let out a shaky exhale, as he ran them up my shoulders and to my throat, where he held my face in his palms. The delicious spice and musk of his cologne mingled with the cinnamon on his breath, the intoxicating mix watering my mouth. His gaze fell to my lips, and I wondered if he'd kiss me.

The restive beat of my heart marked each passing second, as I waited for it.

With a shake of his head, he stepped back. "Forgive me. You're the first thing I've felt in a long time."

As he drew his hands back, I reached out to clutch his forearms, holding them there. "What was the last thing you remember feeling?"

Pain flashed over his face. "My brother's hand, just before he was taken away and killed."

"Oh, God. I'm so sorry."

Brows tight, he ran his fingertips across my clavicle and licked his lips. "You feel good."

My nerves caught in my throat as I said, "You do, too."

Curious eyes seemed riveted on my lips, and he ran his thumb over their surface. Before I could gauge his next move, he leaned forward and pressed his lips to mine.

All sound faded. The world around us disappeared. The kiss began slow, a mere sampling, as he brushed his lips over mine. He grabbed either side of my face, pulling me closer, fully committing to the kiss, and a tingling deluge of excitement scattered across my skin.

Some kisses were said to feel like fireworks. His felt like a slow-drip anesthetic, silently siphoning my senses, until all I could smell, taste, and feel was him.

I held his biceps, as he ate the breath from my mouth and ran his palms over my exposed skin. He pulled me closer still, kissing me with such passionate fervor that my knees weakened. I'd never been kissed by a man. Boys, yes. But never a man. Not even Ghostboy, who was technically an adult, held a candle to Professor Bramwell's skill and mastery. The way he teased with his tongue, and held me as if I were fragile porcelain. It was right then that I realized, I'd never truly been kissed before, at all.

As his grip hardened, the need for oxygen burned in my lungs, punching at my ribs. I tugged my head back, but he held fast, threading his fingers through my hair, jaw flexing as he dipped his tongue to deepen the kiss. Dizziness settled over me, the need to breathe setting off alarms inside my head. I whimpered against his lips and pressed my palms to his chest.

When he pulled away on a sharp inhale, a coldness filled the space between us, and the dizziness heightened, claiming my balance. I teetered to the side, and he caught me, holding me upright.

Forehead pressed to mine, he breathed hard. "I'm sorry. I don't know what the fuck I was thinking."

"It's okay."

"No. No, it's not okay." He released me and stepped back. "I can't fuck this up. Not now."

Don't take that personally, my head warned.

Running a hand over his brow, he turned away from me. "Forgive me. I'm just overwhelmed right now. I didn't mean–"

"It's okay. I understand. It was a pretty tense moment for both of us."

His gaze flicked toward the autopsy room behind me and back. "You'll not speak a word of what you saw in there."

"Of course not. But ... you injected yourself with the toxin," I countered. When he didn't respond, only stared at me with that chilling, sobering look in his eyes, I kept on. "I remembered seeing the vials under the hood. You're performing clinical trials on yourself, aren't you?"

He slowly turned back around to face me. "You're in a very precarious situation, Miss Vespertine."

Spencer's words echoed inside my head. Those warning me that Professor Bramwell was a bad man.

"Are you ... infected with the worms?"

"No. Of course not. The toxin is purified."

"So, you can't become sick from it?"

"Not at all."

Swallowing hard, I lowered my gaze. "I won't tell anyone."

"How can I trust you? How do I know you won't use it against me?"

I reached for his hand and linked my fingers in his, keeping my eyes on him. "I give you my word."

With a gruffness, he shook off the connection. "C'mon," he said in a surly voice. "I'll walk you back to your dorm."

"My dorm? Won't someone see us?"

"There's a path through the woods."

"It's pouring rain," I argued back, because I didn't want to be alone, and I didn't want to leave him alone. What if he fell into a seizure again and there was no one there? "Maybe I should stay a bit. What if you have a bad reaction?"

Not a single cell in my body imagined that he'd actually consider such a thing, and the argument to stay sat perched on the tip of my tongue, ready to fire off, when he gave a short nod. "Fine."

———

As Bramwell furiously scribbled notes into a journal, I sat sprawled on the couch in my long socks, reading a chapter from my textbook on my phone for the next day's lecture. Soft piano music drifted from the record player, the cozy ambience colliding with the feverish thrill still humming through my bones. My lips tingled where he'd kissed me earlier, and as subtle as I could muster, I ran my thumb over them, wishing I could capture the feel of his mouth on mine again.

Focus, Lilia.

I turned my mind back to my reading, then yawned and stretched, settling further into the cushions, willing my eyes to stay open. Between the laboriously detailed text and the lingering echoes of that kiss, the maelstrom of thoughts in my head exhausted me.

"If you're tired, the couch folds out to a bed. You can sleep there."

Sleep there? I'd only expected to stay a couple hours to observe him. I never imagined he'd invite me to stay overnight, and I didn't dare question it aloud. "What about you?"

"I'll sleep here in my chair." He planned to stay, too. The two of us, sleeping in the same room. "It's raining pretty hard." He'd gone to lock up the incinerator entrance about fifteen minutes earlier and must've noticed it then.

We were rained in together. Alone. In the dungeon of the building.

I was going to be sleeping over with Professor Bramwell. *Doctor Death.*

Perhaps that should've terrified me, especially since there was an eyeless corpse laid out in the room across the hall. Unfortunately, it didn't. As naive as it might've made me, I felt something with Bramwell that no other man in my life, including Conner, had ever made me feel–safe. I let that thought wrap itself around me like a blanket, as I stared back at him, then snapped my focus back to the issue at hand. "No need to be a martyr. You can sleep on the bed. I'll just make a bed out of the couch cushions."

"I'll use the cushions."

"Don't be ridiculous, you're twice my size."

"Have you always been so damn stubborn?"

"Since the womb, I'm afraid. I was born nine days after my due date."

He grumbled and scribbled more notes. The man looked absolutely delicious in his half-buttoned black shirt that he'd since donned and the thin-rimmed glasses he wore as he read through books. In the thick of his note-taking, he paused and ran his fingers over the shiny desk surface, then held his hand over the candle and quickly withdrew, rubbing his skin where it must've burned.

I smiled, watching him explore all the different sensations around him. How exquisitely rich his world must've seemed now that he could feel again. "So, what happens next? Now that you've had a successful variant?"

"I wait and see how it affects the moths. If they continue to respond favorably, we move to the next step."

"I thought moths didn't have a nervous system like us. How do you measure success in them?"

"So long as Patroclus and Achilles continue to fly, the toxin is working."

"You're going to be famous, Professor Bramwell." Burying a smile into my phone, I mindlessly read the same line in my book that I'd read ten times already. "In all the textbooks for having cured Voneric's Disease. Arthritis. Diabetes."

"Let's not get ahead of ourselves."

"It's called manifestation. And it actually works."

"Yeah? What have you manifested?"

I quirked a brow. "Working in your lab."

He groaned again, in disapproval. "Blackmail is hardly manifestation."

"The mechanisms for achieving your goals are inconsequential, so long as they're successful." I sucked my bottom lip between my teeth, marveling at the man's unbreakable focus on his work. "Perhaps I manifested that kiss."

He froze, staring down at his notes, then slowly removed his glasses. "Now, why would you do that?"

I lowered my gaze to my fidgeting hands and shrugged. "Are you angry?"

"I'm angry at myself. Not you."

"Why?"

"Because you're my student. I'm your professor. I also happen to be a decade older than you. You've got a lot to lose, if someone found out. We both do."

"Who would find out? There's no one here."

He ran his tongue over his lips, his eyes lost to whatever thoughts churned inside his overthinking mind. With a shake of his head, he snapped out of it. "I can't do that, Lilia. This lab is still subject to the occasional visitor. The school provost, in particular."

"I like when you say my name." Not something I would've ordinarily confessed so boldly, but the kiss reminded me that I wasn't alone in my attraction. A heavy silence filled the space between us as we stared back at one another, the intensity only broken when I cleared my throat and stood up from the couch. "So, I can start pulling these cushions off, then, to make my bed?"

"Yes." He pushed up from his chair and helped me remove the stiff leather cushions, arranging them in a row to form a bed. "You're not sleeping here. You can sleep on the mattress," he said, folding out the bed.

"Be serious. Look." I pointed to the row of cushions, which must've only measured about four feet in length.

"You've got to be over six feet tall. It'll be like sleeping on a dollhouse bed for you."

"Six-foot-two. And I'll be fine." From the closet, he pulled down a stack of sheets and unfolded them onto the mattress. He returned to the closet for four pillows, handing off two to me.

Before he could stop me, I plopped down onto the cushions. "Look, you see? It suits me better."

"Up on the bed."

"Don't be ridiculous. I'll be fine."

"On the bed. Now."

The deadly authority in his voice prodded something deep inside of me. Something that begged to be cracked open and cut loose. A flash of fantasy slipped through my mind, of him holding my throat, spouting off commands in that voice.

"You'll have to haul my dead rotting corpse there."

"I'm quite familiar with the task." Lips tight, he bent forward and to my utter shock, slid his hands beneath me, lifting me up into his arms.

I let out an unattractive squawk as he threw me into the air, my skirt flying up around the spandex shorts I'd worn underneath, and the soft, cushy mattress caught my fall. "Talk about stubborn."

He strode over to the fireplace and lit a small flame, stoking it enough that it caught quickly and let off a blaze of radiant heat. As if mesmerized, he stared back at it and raised his hands, twisting them in front of him. "I never thought I'd feel warmth again. Not like this." In his profile, I caught the slightest curve of his lips. "My brother used to tease that I was half-dead, for how cold my hands were all the time."

"You said your brother was taken away and killed?"

The look he cast over his shoulder held an expression of *Oh, yeah. About that.* He turned back to face the fire, and I pulled the blanket he'd set out up over myself. "He was kidnapped when we were about seventeen years old. Boarding school. They sent what we believed were his ashes. For years I questioned whether, or not, they were his. But even if they weren't, the message was clear. He was gone."

A cold dread stirred in my stomach, as an image of Bee's terrified face flashed through my mind. I quickly blinked it away. "I'm so sorry."

"I blamed myself for what happened to him."

"Why?" I stared off, wondering if his guilt weighed as heavily as mine. If it ever pressed down on him, drowning him, as it often did for me.

His brows knitted together, and he lowered his hands. "The day he was taken, I fell into one of my episodes. I couldn't fight back."

"You were a kid. It wasn't your fault."

He shook his head, as if refusing to believe me, then pushed to his feet and strode over to his desk. From one of the drawers there, he withdrew a picture that he handed to me.

I stared down at two adorable boys with dark hair and copper eyes, one with a more prominent dimple on the left, the other more prominent on the right. "You're identical," I said, running my finger over the one I knew was Professor Bramwell, based only on his dimple.

"He was three minutes older."

After examining the two of them side by side, I handed it back. "I couldn't imagine losing my sister. She's going to be seventeen this year. I worry what that'll mean for her."

"What do you mean?"

"She's in a sort of boarding school herself now. A special school designed to help her. She kind of had it rough when my mom died, and ... well, she's just been lost. Has some mental turmoil to work through. She, um ... found my mother in the bathtub." My nerves hummed, as they usually did, with the creeping visual of what I'd actually seen that night. Except, that time, I felt sliced open, like he could see the ugliness of it all. The dysfunction that'd felt like a shadow for so many years. "Anyway, the school has been great for her, but it's so expensive to keep her there."

He looked thoughtful for a moment. "Your mother's trust pays for her tuition?"

"Trust?" I wanted to laugh at that, but it occurred to me right then how disconnected the two of us were. How inconceivable it must've been for a man like him to imagine a woman living so irresponsibly as to not leave a trust behind for her child. My world must've been as foreign to him as his was to me. "My mom didn't have anything when she died. Her boyfriend, Conner, is Bee's father. The two of us split tuition."

"You pay for your sister's tuition while going to school?"

"Yeah." I didn't want to admit that I was a couple of months behind. "It's why I was so hardball about getting paid in cash. I don't want to be that way, but sometimes, you do things out of desperation, you know?" I tried not to wince at the thought of the video I'd filmed in his class weeks ago. "Or maybe you don't."

"Don't ever feel ashamed of being ruthless in the pursuit of what you want, Lilia. The path to success is rarely a virtuous one." After returning the picture to its drawer, he fell back into his chair. "And how is this Conner?"

I shrugged. "He's okay. He sticks around, so I guess I can't complain. Has some pretty shitty friends, though."

"They give you a hard time?"

I bit my cheek to keep the repulsion from showing on my face, as Angelo came to mind. "One. He's the only one who really scares me."

"What's his name?" An edge of hostility hardened his voice, and I looked up to see rigid lines of malice darkening his expression. As though it angered him to know the man scared me?

"It doesn't matter." Shameful as it might've been to say, I liked his defensive reaction. I'd never relied on a man to protect me. Ever. But something primal played on the back of my thoughts that went hand in hand with the visual of him choking me, and I found myself oddly turned on by it. "Anyway, I know what you mean about feeling the guilt, though. I was sixteen when my mom died. I knew things were going downhill with her, and I tried to get her to go to the hospital, but she refused. She was so paranoid of everything and everyone, and ..."

"It wasn't your fault."

Those words hooked themselves in my belly and pulled a blackness from my guts that twisted and writhed. My head begged to ignore it. To cast him off as a liar. I turned away, forcing a smile. "You're throwing my words back at me."

"They're fairly wise words." He reached down into his desk and brought up a decanter of amber-colored liquid.

I watched him pour a dose into a glass and take a sip, mesmerized by the sheen that I wanted to lick off his lips. Every small gesture, from the lazy swirl of his drink, the way he inhaled the scent, to the gentle press of the glass against his lips, held a provocative undertone. "Can I have some?"

"How far away is twenty-one for you?"

"Only a few weeks."

He cocked a brow and reached down into the desk for another glass, pouring half as much. "Seeing as I don't know how you hold your liquor, we'll start with this." He handed it off to me, his finger brushing mine when I accepted the drink.

I swirled it just as he had, taking in the woodsy, fruity scent with a subtle hint of what reminded me of caramel. One small sip, and I closed my eyes, letting the liquor sit on my tongue a moment, where it burned, before I swallowed it back.

"Mmm. That's good." I liked the feel of it sliding down my throat into my belly, warm and tingly. When I opened my eyes, he was staring at me over the rim of his glass. "I've never had this before."

He tipped back his drink, polishing off about half the amount I had left in one sip. "It's good shit."

"Can I ask you a question?" The moment he winced, I chuckled and cleared my throat. "Who's the guy in the autopsy room? He looks familiar."

"You recognized him without eyeballs?" Not looking my way, he snorted. "Just someone I was asked to examine."

"I thought I was going to be stuck in there all night with him. I was terrified. And then you came in, and ..." I buried the visual of his kiss in another sip of my drink, remembering the taste of his lips on mine. "I was so relieved to see you."

His lips twitched as if to smile, and his gaze fell as he seemed to slip into thought. "The dead themselves are harmless. It's what they leave behind that inspires fear." He blinked out of his staring and poured himself another glass of liquor. "I need to finish my notes. You might consider going to bed, Miss Vespertine. It's going on midnight."

"I wish I would've packed a toothbrush. Whiskey will kill any bacteria in my mouth, though, won't it?"

"I wouldn't rely on that as a regimen, but I suspect you'll survive tonight."

I placed my glass down on a coaster atop the side table next to the couch, where I'd set my phone earlier. Beneath the blankets, I unlatched my skirt and shimmied out of it, leaving me in the shirt I'd paired with it and my spandex shorts. As I discarded it on the floor beside me, I noticed him staring at the garment, perhaps thinking that I wore nothing beneath. I wondered if I should've said something about the shorts, that I shifted around a lot when I slept which made my clothes shift so they tended to drive me nuts. I figured I'd better just leave it alone, particularly when his attention veered back to his notes.

Except, there was the one issue. "I don't suppose you have anything to secure one of my arms? I don't want to wander off into the corpse room half-asleep. I'd probably have a heart attack."

From another drawer of his desk, he pulled out a set of cuffs, presumably the ones he'd used to secure me in that cell. He strode over to the bed and snapped one to the metal frame, the other to my wrist. When he failed to release my arm, I looked up to see him staring down at it.

"*Memento mori*," he read aloud, running his thumb over my tattoo, his soft caress stirring an irrepressible fire beneath my skin. "Remember you must die."

"It's just something I did after my mother passed."

"A reminder to appreciate life as a gift."

Smiling, I lowered my gaze. "Some days are easier than others."

"Having purpose helps. Keeps you from doing foolish things, like dropping out of school."

I winced at that. "Earlier, when I said that stuff ... I was just angry. I didn't mean to badmouth Professor Gilchrist. You won't tell her I said those things, will you?"

"No. I won't say a word about it. So long as you promise not to leave Dracadia."

I gave a playful smile. "And abandon the opportunity to annoy the hell out of you? Never."

"Good." He held up the key to the cuffs and placed it on the side table next to my glass.

If I thought about it, perhaps it was strange asking my professor to cuff me, but it spoke to the level of trust I felt around him. I probably could've slept naked and he wouldn't have laid so much as a finger on me. The man was rigid to a fault, in that respect.

No other male in my life had ever instilled such confidence in them—not even Conner, though I'd have never tested the theory.

I settled into the bed, covers up to my neck, and watched him ease back into his chair. After giving one more glance toward my skirt on the floor, he returned to scribbling his notes, stopping every now and then to glance over at me, and the moment our eyes met, he went back to his writing.

Much as I wanted to keep talking to him, to learn more about this enigmatic man, I didn't want to bother him while he worked.

In the quiet, sleep weighed heavy on me.

Heavier.

Until at last, I could no longer keep my eyes open.

Chapter 46

Lilia

A sound startled me upright. I looked around the dark space, with a vague awareness that a fire crackled in my periphery. The door ahead stood cracked open. An unseen force compelled me to go to it. I didn't know what, or why, but as I pushed up from the bed, a tug at my arm sent me backward. I trailed my gaze down the length of my arm to find something silver flashing at my wrist, but my mind didn't register was it was.

Instead, I tugged. And tugged.

"Lilia," I heard a voice whisper, and I turned toward the door once again. Stared. Waiting.

The darkness shifted for a form that stepped into the light. A man with a grotesque curve of his spine. The one I'd seen earlier, on the examination table. The eyeless man, whose deep dark sockets held a world of terror. "Come sleep with us," he whispered. "At the bottom of the lake."

He hobbled closer.

I tugged at my wrist. "No."

"It's time, Lilia. Your mother is waiting for you at the bottom of the lake."

"No!" I pulled harder, and a sharp pain struck my wrist, but I didn't care. I needed to get loose! Now!

He inched closer and closer, until he was standing over

me. “Lilia!” He gripped my shoulders, and I let out a blood curdling scream.

“Lilia!”

A light flicked on. Something shook me. Hard. I opened my eyes to find Professor Bramwell standing over me, his hands gripping my shoulders.

I snapped my attention toward the door and, finding it closed, choked on the air that arrived too fast.

Just a nightmare. It was only a nightmare.

My whole body trembled, though, the deep vibration rattling my bones.

I didn’t realize he’d asked me a question, until he said, “Lilia,” tipping his head to the side.

“What?”

“Are you all right?”

I cleared my throat, shifting my attention back toward the door to make sure it remained closed and that the corpse was gone. “Yes. I .... I had a bad dream.”

“You damn near woke the dead with that scream.” From the side table, he swiped up the key for the handcuffs and unlocked them, setting my hand free.

I released a nervous breath, still shaken. I’d had visions of the dead before, but something about that guy I’d seen earlier in the autopsy room freaked me out. Probably his lack of eyes. The sight of empty eye sockets made my skin crawl. “Yeah.”

As Bramwell turned away, a restless fear spiraled through me again, and I reached out, grabbing his arm. “Wait. Can you stay with me? Here? Just ... just for a couple minutes, until I fall asleep again?”

He lowered his gaze to where I’d grabbed him, staring down at it for a moment. It was then I noticed he had on nothing but a pair of boxer briefs that contained an exceptionally well-endowed package beneath. “Yes,” he said, and I couldn’t help taking in the whole of his physique.

It wasn't even necessarily ogling the man, but appreciating the utter perfection of his form—his broad, muscled shoulders that tapered down to a slim waist, and that chiseled V disappearing into his briefs. Not overly bulky, he had just enough muscle to make a girl stare without wondering how many hours he spent at the gym.

Gaze trailing over his body brought me staring at the mutilation scattered over his arm and shoulder and a strange black marking just below his collarbone. Not a tattoo. Something deeper that seared the skin and created a horrific groove in his flesh. A branding of what looked to be two crossed medical staffs and a seven, contained in a circle. I nodded toward it. "What is that?"

His lips flattened. "A mistake I made early on in my college career."

"Like a fraternity thing?"

"Something like that."

I scooted over to make room, and he rounded the bed to the other side and sank onto the mattress beside me, careful to keep some distance between us. Once settled, he threw the sheet over his lower half, relieving me of that hard-to-miss bulge and those muscled legs of his.

Did he always sleep in his briefs? Or nude? Perhaps he was just being decent around me. Or maybe he slept in more clothes. The fireplace had warmed the room with a sticky heat, and he had slept closest to it, so perhaps it was a matter of comfort for him.

"I would think it's dangerous to cuff yourself to the bed every night," he said, interrupting my thoughts.

"I don't typically use handcuffs. And, usually, I can snap myself out of it quickly. I don't know why I couldn't this time."

"You suffer night terrors?"

At a flash of the eyeless man hobbling toward me, I winced. "Yes. They're horrible."

"Paralysis?"

"Sometimes, yes."

"I did, too, as a boy. Of course, it didn't take closing my eyes to throw me into nightmares, with the father I had."

And just like that, the first chip into his past and the mystery of his father. "He was abusive?"

"Forgive me, I shouldn't have brought that up. I don't care to talk about him right now."

Dammit.

With a huff, he eased down onto the bed, jostling the mattress, and faced away.

Disappointed, I turned over and flicked off the light.

Chapter 47

Lilia

"Lilia."

The sound of my name drove me out of the black void of sleep, and my muscles jerked. On instinct, I prodded the pillow in search of my knife, and opened my eyes in a haze of confusion when I didn't immediately recognize my surroundings.

The sound of moaning and movement had me turning over to see that Professor Bramwell had fallen asleep next to me. Writhing on the bed, he seemed caught up in a dream, and when he lifted his arms over his head, tucking them beneath his pillow, the sight of him sent a throbbing ache between my thighs. Jesus, the man looked hot even when he slept. Meanwhile, I probably looked like a drooling Saint Bernard.

Had he been the one to say my name, or was it an echo of my own dream?

"Yeah," he whispered, still shifting on the bed. "Tha's it." The slight slur of his words told me he was still deep in sleep. "T'ch'me, Lilia."

I froze. Heated tingles scattered over the back of my neck.

He was dreaming of *me*?

He turned his head away, and his stomach twitched, his hips grinding out a sensuous wave of unconscious pleasure. "J'slike that."

My thighs clenched at the visual of stripping off my panties and climbing on top of him. With his arms tucked away, muscles flexing with his restlessness, he looked tethered and completely at my mercy. Like having a dangerous animal chained to the bed.

I trailed my gaze lower, over the dips and grooves of his carved abs, to the massive erection tenting his briefs, and God, my palms itched to touch him. I sucked my bottom lip between my teeth imagining my hands on him, the ridges and veins slipping beneath my fingertips. *Don't do it*, my head urged. So badly, though, I wanted to pull it out and feel the weight of his cock in my palm.

A deep, masculine groan vibrated out of him, the sound slipping across my skin like rough hands, springing goosebumps.

Before I could stop myself, I slowly reached out, ghosting my fingers over one of his thighs—those powerful beasts he toned with his daily runs. Long cords of muscle contracted beneath my fingertips as I dragged them upward.

On a sharp breath, his hand shot out and grabbed my wrist. I turned to see his eyes open, but heavy with sleep, as he stared down at me. Furious.

"What're you doing?" he growled. "Get your hand off of me."

Humiliation seared through me as I retracted my hand and scrambled for an explanation. I hadn't expected him to be *angry*. Surprised, perhaps, but not this. "You .... You said my name. You asked me to touch you. I'm sorry." I turned over, wishing I could crawl into a hole and lock myself away, the mortification springing tears to my eyes.

I'm so stupid.

Minutes passed in silence, and I eyed the door, wondering if I should leave and go back to my own dorm. The decision took hold, and I sat up in bed, not daring so much as a glance at him. As I reached down for my skirt, I felt a grip of my arm.

"What do you think you're doing?"

"Going back to my dorm. I shouldn't have put my hands on you like that."

"You're not going anywhere at this hour."

Wrenching my arm free was futile against the unrelenting grip he had on me. "Please. This is embarrassing enough."

A hard yank sent me crashing back to my pillow, and I stared up at him, frowning at the abrupt movement.

That predatory gaze devoured me like a hearty meal, the sharp anger from before devolving to an untamable carnality. "Do you have any idea how fucking hard it is to lie next to you? It's killing me." Another hungry sweep of his eyes and he licked his lips. "I've been numb for as long as I can remember. You're the first thing I've felt in *years,* Lilia. All I want to do is touch you."

"Then, touch me." I turned to face him and reached out for his hand.

Brows pinched to a frown, he gripped my wrist instead, his jaw clenching. "Don't," he warned.

"Touch me."

"No."

I twisted my arm to get loose, a heated mix of embarrassment and frustration blazing across my face. "Then, let me go."

His grip tightened, his nostrils flaring in obvious anger, and when I brought my other arm up to push him off, he swiped up that wrist, too. Something inside of me snapped, and I wriggled to break free from his grip. The strength in his arms proved true, as he held me with little effort or exertion, while I thrashed for freedom. He gathered my arms together and, with ease, turned me to my side and dragged me against him, putting my back to his chest. Heaving breaths sawed out of me, as I lay trapped in his inflexible embrace with no chance for escape. Not a word spoken between us.

As I stared at the bookcase across from me, I took in the rigidity of his arms around me, the way they held me firmly. Tenaciously. And yet, how at home I felt in his embrace. Safe.

Another minute passed and his grip slackened.

His forehead rested against my shoulder, palm skimming down the length of my arm to my hip. The slow, aching grind of his erection pressed against my ass left me fighting to breathe, as I squirmed against him in a silent battle of wills. "This thing with you. It's fucking me up." His voice shook as badly as the muscles in his arms that held me against him like a steel cage. "You're a sickness inside of me that begs never to be cured. Infecting me with this unshakable craving for things I shouldn't want."

"Then, let me *go*."

"No," he said in an uncompromising tone, his fingers digging into my hips. "I can't."

Without a word, I slipped my shorts off, leaving my panties as the only barrier.

As toxic as it was, I relished this game between us, the push and pull, the stolen touches and delicious tension. I knew it was wrong. I knew what hell this would bring.

If anyone found out about us, I'd lose everything and would be forced to return to Conner and Angelo and the life I fucking hated. I'd be forced to abandon however close I'd gotten to finding out the truth about my mother. Bee would undoubtedly get kicked out of her school, and God, if she'd ever caught wind of why, she'd hate me.

I'd hate me, too.

And the consequences didn't end there. Bramwell could lose his position, and what then? Would the project go on? Would they continue to fund it, or move on and leave millions to suffer the loss of his discovery?

I knew all these things.

But I couldn't help myself.

I both hated and craved the addicting way he'd hooked himself into my veins and fed me with this unbridled and reckless desire. It went against everything I was. Everything I believed. And yet, it was everything.

For so long, I'd been forced to bury that side of me. I'd grown up too fast and had left the wild and carefree teenager in the dust. When my friends had talked about boys and going on dates, and getting drunk in basement parties, I was stressing over bills and how I'd take care of my sister, while clinging to a distant dream of getting out of that apartment. On the outside was a smart and responsible young woman with a shit ton of potential, and yet, I yearned for the stupid girl who just needed a break. A moment of recklessness.

Bramwell was my moment. Even if he wanted nothing to do with me tomorrow and would cast me aside like leftovers, he was my greatest risk, and I needed to grab it by the balls and not let go.

Literally.

I slid my hand between my ass and his bulge, feeling his hard length behind his briefs, and his body turned rigid, hard like iron against me.

Hand covering mine, he silently halted my movements, and I waited to see if he'd throw my hand away and tell me to stop. Instead, he squeezed his hand over mine and shifted his hips, feeding his cock into my eager palm. A shuddering breath hit the back of my neck, and his teeth grazed my shoulder.

Victory surged on the wings of butterflies in my stomach. I bit my lip, smiling to myself as he relented some of his control.

With careful strokes, I massaged the erection sticking up out of his briefs, eyes widened as I took in the length and girth of the man, the way it strained behind that measly layer of fabric like it'd tear through any moment. Jesus. No wonder Gilchrist pined after him like a lost puppy.

"We need to stop. Fuck, I can't do this." His voice held a raspy tension, and I would have released him right then, but his hand betrayed his words when it slid up the hem of my shirt. A slow, taunting trail of his fingertips to the lace bra beneath, which he peeled back, springing my breast free. "Tell me to stop, Lilia. I'm fucking begging you."

Opposite to what he asked, I wedged my hand down inside his briefs and stroked the stiff flesh that clearly begged for attention.

He hissed and rolled his hips in the motion of thrusting into my palm. "You're going to destroy me. And I won't stop you. It feels too fucking good to stop." On a growl of frustration, he squeezed my breast as if punishing me for his lack of control, and I let out a moan, but the dominating grip of his palm felt so fucking good.

The heavy ache melted away with his kneading and stroking, and I arched into him with the relief of his touch.

His rough grip lightened as he ran the pad of his thumb over my nipple. "Every inch of you is something new to explore. A new texture. A new curve. Sensations I've been robbed of for so long." In tiny circles, he painted an inescapable pleasure that left me in a dizzy lust. "Goddamn it, your skin is like fine silk. I could spend hours touching you and never tire of it." With a nudge, he urged me onto my back and lifted my shirt up to my neck. He peeled back the cup of my bra and bent forward, sucking my nipple into his mouth.

I gripped the frame of the bed above me and slid my bottom lip between my teeth, biting down as the delicious pull of his mouth tugged the ache that throbbed at my pussy. My fingers curled tight around the metal bar above me, knees pressed together while the soft trickle of my arousal spilled into my cotton panties. I squirmed as he moved to the other breast, sucking that nipple to a hardened peak and flicking his tongue against the sensitive tip.

Seeming to notice the torment, he skated his hand lower, his palm flat against me, until he reached the apex of my thighs and rubbed his finger over my panties.

"Of course you're wet." His voice held a sharp bite of anger at the discovery.

My body slid closer to his chest, one of his arms wedged beneath me and across my chest, holding me to him as if I'd try to get away. Like I would've attempted such a thing right then.

Determined fingers breached the hem of my panties and I bowed in exquisite agony, as he painted gentle lines over my undoubtedly drenched seam.

"Fuck me." That deep baritone voice in my ear innervated this frantic need for him that pulled like a taut string, ready to snap. Whether intentional, or a mindless act, his other hand gripped my throat as he ran his finger up and down my slippery seam, gathering the slick dew he'd worked up. In my periphery, he brought his hand to his mouth, and a deep throaty sound of satisfaction rolled through his chest. "Why do you have to taste like a sweet forbidden fruit? Goddamn, you're killing me, Lilia. I can't do this. I can't."

"Don't stop. Please, I'm begging you. So many nights I've–" I cut myself off, embarrassed to admit that I'd fucked my own pillow to thoughts of him.

"You've what? Tell me everything. Every detail. I want to hear what you do when you're alone." It seemed to keep him interested, and though I risked the most humiliating confession of my life, I was too intoxicated to care right then.

"I dream that you come into my room. And ..."

He flicked a wet finger over my clit, and I arched into him on a moan. "And what?"

"And you ... climb into bed beside me, just like this."

"Are you sleeping?"

"Yes."

Teeth grazed the shell of my ear, his shaky breaths telling me the story turned him on, so I kept going.

"You shove your hand down my panties ... just like this."

He spread me wider and pressed into my clit, giving just enough pressure that I clenched my teeth as he rolled the sensitive flesh between his fingers.

"Do I fuck you with my fingers?"

"Yes, definitely."

At that, he plunged two fingers up inside of me, his thumb still pressed to my clit. The man knew exactly what he was doing, as if he'd earned a goddamn degree in fingering. Wet sounds reverberated in my head as I relayed the fantasy. "You... choke me a little. Not hard. Just enough to make me gasp."

"I like this dream." His palm pressed into my throat, the pressure parting my lips, and fucking hell, it was perfect. The lack of breath. The disheveled state of my clothes that made me look ravished, the feel of his fingers plunging and stroking while he held me captive against him. Every detail culminated into the flawless visual inside my head.

"Tell me, Little Moth. Have I ever eaten your pussy in these fantasies?"

"Not yet. But ... mostly because I've ..." I hesitated to admit the truth that played on the tip of my tongue. It was stupid. Every other girl I knew had had a boy go down on them before. I'd had fingers prod and poke me there, but never a mouth. "I've never done that before."

To my utter disappointment, he stilled against me. "Tell me you're joking."

My cheeks heated with humiliation.

"Are you a virgin?"

The question brought to mind the incredibly awkward and dissatisfying attempts at fifteen years old with Ghostboy.

No, technically I wasn't a virgin, but that didn't mean I'd actually *experienced* sex. At least, not the kind of sex Professor Bramwell undoubtedly excelled at. The rest of my sexual experiences had boiled down to blow jobs and hand jerking–two skills I'd honed during my tutoring sessions. "I'm not a virgin, but I haven't done much at all in the last couple of years. I just ... never had time for boys, so I never really dated after my mother died."

"Fuck." He released me and rolled onto his back, rubbing a hand down his face.

The humiliation squeezed me harder, and I settled on my back beside him. "I want to do this with you."

"No. I'm not going to be your first anything."

"Right. So, it's better for me to experience that with some asshole in the back of his car who'll ghost me the next day."

He made a gruff sound of disapproval, and I turned to see his jaw grinding, as if I'd pissed him off.

"Please, Devryck. I want this." Flares of mortification arrived in rapid fire, when I realized I'd just called him by his first name.

Clearly, he'd caught it, too, as he slowly lowered his hands and turned toward me. "Say that again."

"I want th–"

"Not that."

"Please ... Devryck."

Another agonizing moment of contemplation followed, and I was certain he was about to roll away again. Instead, he pushed up from the bed and rolled over top of me. A carnal darkness shadowed his eyes as he stared down at me, stroking his long, hard cock. He tore away the sheet, exposing my lifted shirt and soaked panties. "I'm not fucking you tonight. But I am going to dine on this obnoxiously wet pussy, and I'm going to enjoy every moment of knowing I'm the only man who's ever tasted you." Eyes locked on mine, he slid my panties down my thighs slowly, until they reached my knees, and only then did he break contact. "And because I'm a selfish prick who has to live with the fact that I cannot have you to myself, I'm going to ruin you so that any *boy* who comes after me will leave you deeply unsatisfied, and you'll be left fucking your own fingers, desperate to remember the time you had your professor's face between your legs."

The crass edge to his words titillated my nerves and sent a tremble of excitement fluttering in my core.

His tongue swept across his lips as he slid the panties over my ankles and tossed them away. "Panties are for the modest," he said with an air of disgust. As if I was the one who'd brought him to this place of desperation. As if I alone shouldered the blame for what was to come of this night.

Once that little layer of cotton was out of his way, he pushed my knees apart, and the disgust carved in his furrowed brow withered to a shimmer of gratitude as he stared down at me. Chest rising and falling, he kept his gaze fixed between my thighs and bit his knuckle, falling back onto his heels. "Damn you, Lilia. Goddamn you." He reverently ran his hand down my inner thigh and dropped forward, propping himself up on muscled arms. He kissed the inside of my thigh, the softness of his lips sending a tickle to my stomach. Lower and lower, he trailed his kisses, and when he finally reached the apex of my thighs, I held my breath, my heart so wound up, it was a wonder he couldn't hear it rattle across my ribs. He rested his nose against my folds, and I twitched on contact.

A deep inhale sent my pulse rate soaring. He was smelling me. *There.* Oh, God. All I wanted to do was slam my legs closed right then, but his head would've gotten crushed.

A whimper slipped past my lips, and I reached down to grab the top of his head. I wanted to tell him to stop, but the humiliation exhilarated me. What the hell was wrong with me? It was so primal. Hot. So hot, I felt the shameless urge to grind against the ticklish stubble of his face.

He took hold of my wrist and pried it from where I'd clutched the top of his skull.

"Devryck, I'm nervous."

"You should be. Your professor is about to eat your pussy, Lilia. There's a whole host of reasons why that's fucked up, but I'm too far gone to stop myself. At this point, there is nothing I want more than to feel that obscenely pink clit of yours against my tongue. And we will never do this again after tonight. Do you understand? This cannot happen again."

"I understand," I rasped.

Wearing that same stern, unyielding expression that he wore in lecture, when he refused to entertain further questions, he lowered his head.

Legs spread wide, I turned away, closing my eyes. In the silence of my mind, I prayed that I smelled okay, that I hadn't missed a spot when I'd shaved earlier that morning. *Oh, God, what was taking so long?* I felt completely open and on display. The anticipation curled in my belly, and when he finally made contact, every nerve ending flared inside of me. My muscles violently twitched, and I dug my fingers into the bedsheets. It occurred to me how much I'd ached for the man, as I bit down hard on my lip and pressed the crown of my head into the pillow, desperate, needy, hungry.

At a long, delirious drag of his tongue, I arched upward, my fingers clawing the sheets while the shock of his invasion seared my insides.

Prickles of stubble grazed my thighs, his warm, wet tongue dancing against my clit, while his fingers held me open for his assault.

I wanted to bite, scratch, scream, but instead, I dragged the pillow over my face, pressed it there, and focused on every sensation he'd commandeered. The sounds he made in his throat. The way his fingers plunged in and out of me, working in tandem with that relentless mouth. It was a level of mastery I couldn't even fully appreciate, because I'd never had someone so boldly dive between my legs before. In my limited experience, boys took. They took without much thought, and they rarely ever reciprocated.

Bramwell was right. He'd ruined me. Destroyed me from the inside out, and there wasn't a chance in hell that I'd ever feel something so raw and thrilling and forbidden again. I threw the pillow to the side and dared to lift my head, watching him devour me like a death row meal. The slurping sounds and moans and growls he made were lewd and filthy, and spoke of a man who fervently enjoyed the task.

He lifted his head for a moment, his ordinarily stern eyes heavy with intoxication, while the shine of my arousal glistened across his face in a way that reminded me of an animal feasting on prey. When he dove back in, I felt him latch onto the sensitive bud, sucking on the bit of flesh with such intensity, my hips jerked toward his face. Strong hands held me down, as his mouth ravaged my clit with unfaltering determination.

A shocked breath missiled past my lips, and I arched back, rolling my head against the mattress, my hands mindlessly fisting the sheets, desperate to claw into something. I'd learned how to stimulate my clit on my own, but it'd never felt like *this*. An intense and delicious pull that had my belly curling, my thighs shaking. A tearless sob broke in my throat as the tension wound tighter and tighter. More powerful than when I'd masturbated with my pillow or caressed myself.

The pressure throbbed and pulsed, like a gluttonous beast fattening itself on my pleasure. I was about to come. Oh, God. I'd never come with anyone before. I'd only ever done it alone, and it'd only ever lasted a second, or two.

My breaths hastened. My muscles trembled and turned rigid. So tight.

Yeah. Yeah. Yeah.

I ground my hips into his face. My *professor's* face. The very thought of that had such a filthy, immoral ring to it, but I'd worry about the utter depravity of it later. Right then, I was too close to stop. So close!

He lifted his face from between my legs, holding my knees apart as he stared down at me.

"Wha … what are you doing?" I sounded drunk, intoxicated. I ground my ass into the bed, desperate for his lips and fingers and that fiendish sucking that had turned my world on its ass only seconds ago. "Please. I need–"

"You need what?" A hard, stinging smack smarted my pussy, and I twitched, moaning at the sensitivity of my flesh, a delicious mix of pleasure and pain.

"I need to come. I need to come so bad!" I circled my hips as the desperation vibrated in my muscles, intensifying the ache. I thirsted for his touch like a withering flower.

The need he'd stirred with his fingers coursed through my body with a punishing violence.

"You're a salacious little nymph, aren't you? Turn over." His command was terse and pitiless, and as I turned over onto my belly, he roughly yanked me up onto my knees.

"Ass in the air. Hands flat on the mattress."

Frustrated and painfully aroused, I did exactly that, letting him position my knees apart however he wanted. I needed this. I needed him to finish me, or I'd die of agony. Was that even possible? Could someone die of the desperate need to come?

His big palms cuffed my ankles to the mattress, holding me spread open. I waited for him to do something. To stick his fingers in me again, or drag his tongue over my throbbing clit. My thighs trembled with a ravenous gluttony I'd never felt before. Instead, he bent over me, those muscled arms caging me beneath him. "I'll bet your pussy is aching to be filled right now." It wasn't a question. The sadist knew what he was doing.

The tension in the air bore teeth and claws, whose jagged edges razed my skin. I'd never wanted to be destroyed so much in my life. "Yes. Please. It hurts. Oh, God, it hurts."

A sharp pain struck my skull as he yanked my hair, lifting my head from the bed. "Did you think I'd feel sorry for you? That I'd be gentle? I feel this torture every fucking time you walk into a room." He pressed a thumb into the crease of my ass, and I sucked in a breath as he threatened to breach the tight ring of muscles there, pushing and massaging. "So, I don't feel sorry for you, Lilia. In fact, it warms my dirty bastard soul to know you ache this way." Holding his thumb there, he alternated between licking my pussy and fingering it. Each time I neared climax, he stopped, dragging me back from the edge, and I was left soaking wet and twice as needy. He toyed with me like that for what felt like an eternity, never seeming to tire of this vicious little game.

I, on the other hand, clawed and scratched and pleaded, damned near sobbing.

Once again lying on my back, I wrapped my arms around my knees, holding myself open for him when he commanded I do so. Wearing the same cold expression as before, he stared down at me while stroking his cock. Teasing me with it. The level of control the man demonstrated only heightened my arousal, as he stared down at me with those mercurial eyes that seared my insides.

"I cannot properly express how much I'd love to shove my cock inside you right now." The mere suggestion had his tip shining with more precum.

I wanted to tell him to do it, but the size of it scared me. Would probably split me in two. Instead, I licked my lips, wishing I could taste the fluid gathered at the head of it.

"Are you ready to come, Lilia?"

"Please don't tease me. I can't stand it anymore."

"Don't tease *you*? The way you tease me every goddamn day, with these short skirts and those pouty, fuckable lips? That obnoxious lipstick that I imagine smeared all over my cock."

"You don't exactly dress like a priest yourself. You don't think every girl in class dreams of fucking you?"

"I don't give a damn about every other girl. There's only one who crosses my mind a fuck-ton more than she should. So, I'm going to finish you, Lilia. I'm going to give you the release you've been craving, and I won't touch you again. But this pussy belongs to *me*. You let any other undeserving prick near it, and I will cut out his tongue and send it to you in a specimen jar."

I must've been sick, considering the rush of arousal that leaked down my ass as I took in his dirty and psychotic words. As well-mannered and refined as he was, the man had a darkness about him that was absolute catnip to my libido. He stirred an ungodly ache that sang to the deep-seated fantasies I kept in a box tied with black ribbons somewhere inside my head.

Red and swollen from his relentless sucking, I imagined myself sitting in lecture the next day, watching him in his button-down shirt and dark jeans, listening to that voice that made every girl in class wish he taught erotic literature. I tried to imagine the terrifying feeling of knowing I'd only had him once but it'd been enough to mess me up for the rest of my life.

I couldn't stay in those visuals, though. Because every speck of thought came spiraling back into the present when he put his mouth on me again. Gentler, that time, as if he knew it was coming to an end and wanted to savor the last bits.

With featherlight tickles, he teased and taunted me toward

the pinnacle again. My body tensed and loosened, hesitant to let him lead me up such a treacherous path, untrusting of his tricks, but he was persistent. He didn't move, didn't jar my senses with some maddening switch of position. He tickled my appetite with the same consistent flick of his tongue, until my muscles trembled again, breaths panted out of me, and my hands balled into tight fists.

Please, please, please, my head begged. The storm inside my belly thrashed and twisted and rolled, like a tide gathering momentum. Faster. Faster. That euphoric crest loomed over me like a wicked threat, one that would pull me under and drown me in a black squall of ecstasy. I wanted to spit the same venom back in his face for refusing to let me come, by making him wait for the finale he so clearly sought from me with that relentless tongue of his.

I couldn't, though. Goddamn it, the man had my muscles cramped and shaking with desperation.

He fluttered his tongue one more time, and the wave crashed down mercilessly, exploding at the back of my head. Body bowed, I screamed his name, writhing under his unforgiving mouth, as he shook his face and gave one long agonizing suck of my clit to finish me off.

He released me on a pop, and I rode out the subsequent shocks that rocked through me like tiny bolts of electricity. It was everything. Everything I ever dreamed it would be with him, and when he moaned, lapping up the fluids spilling out of me, I lifted my head from the bed to commit the scene to memory. Every sensation, every scent, every sound. I wanted him in my blood, pulsing through me, heating my skin on the nights when I'd be alone in my bed, thinking of this moment. Right here. Right now. Forever.

He pushed up from my thighs, staring down at me with a look of awe that made my belly flutter again–one that begged me to look away, to avoid seeing the prideful victory creep across his face like it had with every other boy who'd felt he somehow conquered me after hooking up. "I knew you'd be fucking beautiful when you came, but I didn't imagine you'd look like this."

"Like what?"

He didn't answer, but the carnal and possessive glint in his eyes, as his fingers dug into my skin, said everything. *Mine*. With a firm grip of my ankles, he slid me down to the edge of the bed and fell forward, catching himself on outstretched arms. One hand stroked down my hair as his lips latched to my neck. "You can shower first, if you'd like," he said against my throat.

It seemed almost silly showering separately, after what he'd done to me, but I didn't bother to offer suggestions. "You go first." I didn't want to wash him off me yet. A part of me hoped his essence would seep beneath my skin. That, maybe, he'd feel the same shiver of need as I did, if I kept a part of him inside of me. What a sickening thought.

It wasn't until he pushed away that I caught a glimpse of what must've been a painfully-stiff erection sticking up from his boxer briefs. How badly I wanted to run my tongue over it. The mere suggestion watered my mouth, and I could practically feel my gag reflexes kicking in. When he turned away from me, my focus switched to his broad, muscled back that tapered down into the most deliciously-toned ass I'd ever seen, and long, powerful thighs that I imagined could hold a woman in place with little effort.

He disappeared through a door to the right of the fireplace, closing it behind him. Light radiated through the crack at the bottom, followed by the sound of a shower flicking on.

I turned toward the computer on his desk. The cabinets undoubtedly brimming with old files.

The younger me, the girl who'd grown up on the unforgiving streets, where etiquette and decorum were nothing but the fancy words of the rich, begged to unscrupulously plow through his personal space without care.

The other part of me loathed the thought of betraying his trust.

I pushed up from the bed, fixing my bra and shirt, and swiped up my tangled panties, the crotch of them still damp as I slid them up my thighs. When I stepped in the direction of his desk, I paused, though.

Would a man like him leave information like that lying around for anyone? He probably had a password on his computer. His desk was undoubtedly locked, along with any file cabinets. Was I foolish enough to think he'd make it easy to drag out what must've been a humiliating piece of his past? The experiments that'd marred his family name.

I brushed my finger over the mousepad of his laptop, where I was prompted to enter a password. A tug of the drawers to the right of me confirmed that he'd locked them.

It would be futile to attempt rummaging through his things. Especially when I already had an advantage that, to my knowledge, most didn't. How many could've said they'd gotten that close to the man?

I lifted my gaze toward the bathroom door, where the light flickered beneath, and licked my lips, before I darted for my bag and rummaged for the tube of lipstick. I applied it thickly across my lips and, without much prompting, padded toward the door, carefully turning the knob to find it wasn't locked. A light push cracked it open, and the monotonous sound of running water sharpened as I peeked into the steamy space. It was obvious, based on the simple but modern decor of white tiles, white porcelain pedestal sink and toilet, that it'd been added on at some point, as it didn't fit the aged look of its surroundings. The shower was a simple box with glass doors thick with steam, through which I could just make out his shape, bent slightly over himself, his arm moving quickly, the merciless strokes of his fist echoing through the stall. Turned slightly away, he didn't seem to notice me watching him, and my tongue prickled as I imagined that long cock sliding against his palm.

I yanked the hem of my shirt over my head and snapped off my bra, then slid out of my panties. With careful steps, I tiptoed closer, and when I slid the glass door aside, I was greeted by the full scope of his erection. Jesus. The man was huge.

From where I stood, I could see the entirety of his shoulder and bicep that'd been ruined by the acid attack. The raw shine of newly healed skin. The scars. So many of them scattered over his flesh. The sight of him had my fingers itching with the urge to touch them, to feel the cruelty that had been inflicted on him. I'd noticed it before, but beneath the harsh lights, it was almost glaring.

He twisted around, and his gaze immediately skated down my body, the appreciation in his expression tickling my confidence, and when it trailed back upward, he seemed riveted on my lips.

I stepped into the stall and slid the door closed, shutting me in with him. Eyes locked on his, I lowered to my knees, squinting against the errant drops of water that sprayed in my face.

Cock still in hand, he watched me warily, his chest rising and falling.

I didn't bother to break my stare, as I leaned forward and licked the weeping tip, watching his eyes screw shut.

"Lilia ..." The strain in his voice told me a battle waged in his head. "I can't do this."

I ran my fingertip over the ridges of his shaft, the deep map of blood feeding his engorged cock.

A sharp sting struck my skull as he gripped my hair. "Please. For fucks sake."

It didn't stop me, though. I pushed forward and ran my tongue over his heavy balls, drawing them into my mouth.

He let out a hiss, his grip of my hair tightening. "Stop," he rasped, but when I did, he unraveled his fingers from my hair and pressed his palm to my crown. "Don't stop. Fuck."

I wrapped my lips over the head of his cock, letting my tongue explore the textures along his shaft. A faint smear of lipstick marked the path of my mouth, and I couldn't even imagine what my face must've looked like right then. Flexing my jaw to accommodate his girth, I gave one long, passionate suck.

Brows tight, he bit his bottom lip on a growling moan. "Fuck, Lilia. You feel so fucking good." His praise stoked my senses, while he fed me his cock at a languorously slow pace. About a quarter of the way down, my gag reflex kicked in, and I pushed up higher onto my knees, angling myself to take more of him. "That's it. Take as much as you can. I need to fuck those pouty lips."

Careful not to scrape my teeth over him, I sucked the water from his skin, savoring the flavor as he glided in and out of my mouth with ease.

"You'll swallow my cum, yeah?" A delirious edge clung to his voice, and I released him on a pop of suction and nodded. I drew him back in, sucking harder than before.

His hands shot out to either side, and a look of pained ecstasy claimed his face as he rammed his length into my mouth with unrestrained fervor. A growl slipped past his clenched teeth, his head thrown back, stretching the wires of tension in his throat. Faster and faster, he pumped his thighs, his grunts echoing all around me. "Good fucking girl," he said in a ragged and strained voice.

My whole body jostled with every fevered drive, as he plundered with greed. I slid my hands up the back of his muscled thighs to his tight ass and dug my nails into him, feeling him clench with every retreating suck.

He moaned and panted, and his thighs shook as I held him to my face. "Show me those beautiful eyes," he rasped, and when I dragged my gaze to his, he held the back of my head, fucking my mouth with brutal decadence. Over and over, his thighs flexing with every thrust.

Drool leaked out of the corners of my lips.

His grunts heightened to a mixed sound of pain and pleasure.

Not a second later, he swayed, and warm fluids shot to the back of my throat.

I coughed and gagged, but never once broke contact with his shaft. I gripped his cock tight, holding it steady as the sound of relief that broke from his chest bounced off the tiles and hot jets filled my mouth, dribbling down my chin. I swallowed it back and licked the head of him again, sucking away the water-drenched cum.

The floor scraped across my shins, as he yanked me to my feet and slammed me against the tiles. Vexation and intoxication and exhaustion swirled in his eyes like a turbulent storm, as he pinned me there, heat rolling off him.

"What are you doing to me?" He rested his forehead against my shoulder, his body trembling, chest heaving. "What the fuck are you doing to me, Lilia?"

I threaded my fingers through his hair, and he gripped my bottom, lifting me up, as I wrapped my legs around his waist.

My fingertips ghosted down his neck, where the puckered flesh of his acid scars slipped past.

He pushed away, but I clutched him tighter, wrapping my arms around his neck.

"Don't. Please. I'm sorry."

For a moment, he stilled, and then his lips were on mine,

his body pressing me into the shower wall. "Why did you come in here? Why do you insist on making it worse?"

"Making it worse? Or making you want me as much as I want you?"

"We already agreed. This was only one night." He wiped away the remnants of lipstick smeared across his mouth. "That's all."

"Is it? Do you honestly think everything will just magically go back to the way it was before?"

"It has to. My work is too important."

I didn't want his words to sting as much as they did. I didn't want to feel like he'd punched me in the chest and I couldn't breathe, but that was exactly how I felt right then. I hated myself for letting him crawl beneath my skin. For allowing my guard to fall, to crumble into a pile of miserable rubble, knowing he would kick the pieces around.

Holding back tears, I wriggled to get loose, but his grip tightened. "Let me go."

"No. Not until I know that you won't say a word of this."

"Of course not, *Professor*. Your reputation is safe with me."

"It isn't about that, Lilia. Stop being foolish and emotional. They'll tear you apart to keep me here. Do you understand that? That is what I mean when I say my work is too important. They will make you look like an impoverished whore, to spare my good name."

"So, what? They think that, anyway, don't they? Don't *you*?"

He didn't answer, only stood there, silently snarling at whatever thoughts ran through his head.

I refused to let myself regret this. No matter what he said, what he did, how it all played out in the end, the fact was, he made me feel something extraordinary. Something no one had ever made me feel. Even at the risk of pain and longing. "I don't care what this was to you. It was still worth it."

His eyes softened, and he exhaled a breath, lowering me back to the floor. A gentle hand ran over the top of my head, and he planted a kiss to my forehead. "I don't regret tonight." He stepped past me and exited the shower. Through the glass, I watched him nab a towel from one of the hooks on the wall and dry off. He wrapped the towel around his waist, and with one more glance back at me, he exited the bathroom, closing the door on a quiet click.

Don't cry. Don't you dare cry.

It wasn't as if I'd pined after the man, as if I'd sought him out for any reason other than the opportunity to find out more about the organism and, possibly, my mother. I'd planned to use him, too. Didn't that make me just as shitty?

I'd survived getting ghosted by the small handful of boys I'd given blowjobs to under school bleachers and in the backseats of rusted-out cars. So, this was nothing new for me, right?

Except, it was. Everything was entirely new. The way he made me feel. The way he gave without asking for anything in return. The way his arms felt around me, and the dirty, titillating words he whispered in my ear. It was all new. It was all beautiful. And even if it was fleeting, it was perfect.

When I finally exited the shower, he sat leaning against the edge of the foldout bed, the towel still wrapped around his lower half, cigarette dangling from his fingertips. Seemingly mesmerized by the flames.

He took a drag of his smoke and tipped his head back, blowing it upward, and spared me nothing more than a glance.

Towel wrapped around myself, I scampered toward the other side of the bed and sat down on the edge of it. "Cracking open chest cavities hasn't turned you off to smoking?" I asked, trying to lighten the mood and lessen the awkward silence.

"I don't do it frequently. Only when I'm fucking tense, or reeling from an intense fuck, and right now, I'm both."

"I made you tense."

"Yes. But it's not your fault. It's mine."

"Why is it anyone's fault?"

He snorted and leaned forward to flick his cigarette into the flame. "No more questions tonight." Hiking his arm over the edge of the bed, he went back to staring off at the flame, and I settled into the sheets at the opposite side.

"You should probably hate me right now," he said, his voice stained with remorse.

"I probably should. But I don't."

With a mirthless chuckle, he shook his head. "Here, I thought it was the moth who would succumb to the fire."

Chapter 48

Lilia

I folded the sheet I'd used, draping it over the couch. Due to the dungeon-like office being lit only by the desk lamp, only the chime of the clock alerted me that morning had arrived. Professor Bramwell typed away at his computer. His eyes had been glued to there for most of the morning, aside from the occasional glance my way. He'd helped me fold the couch back and replace all of the cushions, but not a single word was exchanged between us.

Fully dressed, I cleared my throat and turned to face him. "Well, I guess I'll see you in class."

"I'll see you in class, Miss Vespertine," he echoed, going back to his typing.

The cold, detached tone in his voice stabbed me in the heart, and I blinked back tears as I turned for the door. *Stop it*, I chided myself. I'd always been harder than this. Stronger. I'd had boys from school feeding me their false promises, while they stuffed my face with their cocks, but walking away from them had always been easy. Because they'd taken without giving. They took selfishly and made sport of their conquests. I'd never climaxed with one of *them*, never felt their skin against mine, or watched them fall to their knees to pleasure me first.

As much as I tried to convince myself otherwise, Bramwell was different. Exceptional.

And that made it hurt worse.

"Lilia, wait."

I refused to turn around and let him see the torment on my face, the way his actions affected me so profoundly. I wished I could tear all of the emotion out of me, the way he so easily had.

At the sound of footsteps, my head urged me to bolt for the door. *Don't be childish.*

"Turn around." The command in his voice told me he'd gladly spin me around himself, if I failed to comply, so I turned to find him standing there, hands casually tucked in his pockets. "I won't soon forget last night. Tell me you understand how much it meant that you were here for my first success."

His words slashed across my heart like a poison-tipped blade.

His first success. Was he so clueless that he couldn't understand that last night was more than that for me? That he'd turned my entire world upside down in just a matter of hours? That what we'd done had seared itself into my memory forever, and no matter how many boys I'd been with before, or men I ended up with after today, he would always be my true first?

"I understand."

His jaw shifted, and he turned as if he might go back to his desk, but paused mid-stride. Without warning, he prowled toward me, grabbed me by the back of my neck, and dragged me to his lips. His kiss was cruel and blistering, his hands like barbed wire across my skin, and I wanted to push him away and tell him how much I fucking hated his stupid games. That I hated the push and pull and cat and mouse.

Tell him, Lilia! Make him hurt, too!

But I couldn't. Because the unsettling truth of it was, it set me alight. I really was a dumb fucking moth.

I melted into the commotion, and when he pulled me in tighter and clamped onto my neck, I let go, floated on big, fluffy clouds of ignorant and unrequited bliss. It was easier that way, to slip into stupidity and pretend his kiss meant anything to me. The masochist reared her ugly head, swallowing his attention like a love-sick fool. Because even if I knew better, even if I knew it was all a lie, it felt fucking good.

He pulled away, and for the first time since the night before, I saw a flicker of pain in his eyes. Good. I wanted to frame it, study it, just to know that I'd left something inside of him, too. That he could still feel me crawling over his skin.

Eyes locked on his, I reached up the hem of my skirt and pulled down my panties, slipping them over my ankles. I balled them in my palm and stuffed them into the pocket of his slacks, next to the hard length that brushed the edge of my thumb. "Panties are for the modest," I said, and turned for the door.

Chapter 49
Devryck

F*uck!*

I paced my office, running my hands through my hair. Hours had passed since Lilia left. Hours I'd sat at my desk, trying to focus on something that wasn't my tongue in her pussy. It was futile. She'd crawled beneath me, inside of me, infecting me with the kind of drunken lust that had me pausing to fuck my own hand every hour.

My rejection toward her hadn't been personal. I was affiliated with too many corrupt and dangerous individuals. Those who would love to know that I'd all but fucked my student--not just for the scandal, but to have something weighty to hold over me. As it was, they had nothing. I had nothing. I was a rogue, completely detached from anything meaningful enough to reel me in.

And that was exactly how I wanted it to stay.

Unfortunately, Lilia was fucking up my head in that respect.

Palms pressed to the desktop, I stared at the half-written report on my computer screen. The same sentence I'd written a dozen times over in a failed attempt to concentrate. An unbridled flame blazed through me, burning with the urge to pull her out of whatever class she was in right then and fuck her brains out.

Part of it was the toxin that invariably affected my sex drive. The other part was the fact that she'd done something to me no other woman before her had accomplished: she'd actually made me feel. Not just mentally, but physically. Every nerve in my body hummed with the memory of her soft skin. The curves and edges and textures and flaws that made me crave an entire night of touching and exploring. Those defiant eyes that matched the fire of her hair, and that smart mouth that had not only mastered the words to get my blood boiling but also the sheer incontestable art of sucking cock.

She was a sorceress. She had to be. What else could possibly explain the toxic poison running through me right then? The inability to go ten minutes without thinking about her–either sexually, or longingly. My body mourned her. Had spent the last few hours punishing me for letting her walk out of my office like that. Without panties.

I imagined a breeze catching the hem of her skirt, lifting it from the pretty little ass beneath.

Focus. Please. Fucking focus!

The sooner I handed the report over to Lippincott, the more time I could buy. After all, the toxin wasn't perfect. I'd still had a few jitters and the inability to control my body temperature. It also gave the feeling of crawling skin, which I'd noticed more profoundly when Lilia had left.

And the sex drive.

The endless appetite to stick my dick in something was probably the worst of it.

Not something. Some*one*. *Her*.

The fact that she was entirely forbidden only made me want her more, and the hell of it all was, I held the power to either ruin, or change, her life. She was precisely the kind of woman for whom, I'd easily cast aside whatever pathetic morals still smoldered inside my conscience—one whose drive and passion wasn't tainted by power and money. So hungry to learn, and I longed to be the one to feed her every spoonful of depravity she craved.

I pulled the panties out of my pocket for the dozenth time and breathed in that sweet, infuriating scent that left me intoxicated. Like every other time, a rush of blood shot straight to my dick at the same time that pain struck my groin.

Furious, I fell into my seat, unlatching my belt as I had done so many times before, rubbing myself raw to feed that insatiable monster that clawed at my insides, desperate and hungry. *Is this what you want? Will you let me fucking work, if I do this?*

I had class in an hour, would have to see her there, knowing I couldn't touch her, or smell her, or feel her. The misery of that gnawed at my bones.

I'd faced Gilchrist a number of times after having actually fucked her and felt nothing. Not a single twitch of my dick, or desire to have her again. Lilia was different. She made me physically feel things I hadn't felt in a long time—a feat I didn't think was possible, even with my senses having returned. Beyond the superficial caresses of every other woman I'd known, Lilia's touch had branded itself into my flesh and blood, and now it was all I craved.

She was the warmth of the sun on a cold and rotting corpse. The first breath after a lifetime of death.

How could I share an entire campus with her, knowing she could fall in love at any moment with some inexperienced cad who wouldn't have a clue what to do with a girl like her. The very thought sprouted cruel and vile schemes, like keeping her in one of the cells below. Caging her like one of my little moths.

Another swell of pain throbbed deep in my groin, as the visual of her tied and bound danced through my head like dangerous little pixies. I stroked myself fast and hard, punishing my flesh as I beat out those obsessive urges. But like the monster inside of me, they took root and bloomed into a full-on fantasy I couldn't shake from my mind. My sweet, decadent Lilia laid out before me like a delicious meal.

I held her panties to my face, breathing her into me as I imagined burying my dick inside her. Those beautiful, suck-able tits bouncing in my face, a look of pain and pleasure written in her expression, and the disarming sound of her silky moans that echoed in my head like mind grenades.

Lilia.

Her name was a dirty scalpel plunged deep inside my chest, past crumbling bones and decayed flesh. It pierced the only organ I vowed could never be touched again and infected me with insufferable greed.

I wanted the pain of it. The impossibility. The absolute rapture of claiming her for myself. And therein hid the tragic reality of just how tempting she'd become—if fucking her meant an eternity in hell, I'd welcome damnation with a goddamn smile.

My body hardened as climax hooked itself deep inside me, and I called out her name as ribbons of cum sprang from the head of my dick, onto my hand.

Spent and weak, I reached for the same towel that had captured every other ejaculation, wiping my slick hand on wet spots from before. I couldn't deny–every one of them had left me shuddering with satisfaction, but I was in desperate need of accomplishing something other than soaking a fucking towel with cum. Rubbing my clean hand down my face, I let out a relieved breath and took in the flaccid state of my cock. As I leaned forward to pick up where I'd left off in my report, a memory of Lilia knelt before me slipped through my head.

No, no, no!

Blood surged to my cock, my muscles hardening with new arousal, and I looked down in horror, to see the insatiable beast standing at attention again.

What the fuck!

I couldn't tell if it was the toxin, or a fiery redhead who'd managed to mindfuck me before she left. Fumbling to stuff it back into my pants, I shot up from my desk.

No more.

Still battling a massive hard on, I knocked on the door to Gilchrist's office. At her acknowledgement, I entered the office, one hand in my pocket, where I subtly pushed the record button on my phone.

"Devryck, what a pleasant surprise. Have a seat." She gestured toward one of the chairs, and her gaze lingered at my groin. The hell of it was, she probably thought it was for her.

"I understand you accused one of my students of cheating, and gave her a shit grade with some petty bullshit notes."

Peeling her gaze from my dick, she scoffed. "I beg your pardon. Is that what you came in here for? To defend your student?" When I didn't bother to answer that, she rolled her shoulders back. "She happens to be my student, as well, and she failed to produce coherent responses to the essay questions."

"I read her responses, and they were not only coherent, but accurate. As for the cheating accusation, you and I both know Miss Vespertine would have more success cheating off a dead opossum than Spencer Lippincott."

"Spencer happens to be a very good–"

"I've little time," I said, cutting her off, my dick growing more flaccid by the second. "So, let's just get to the root of what this is. I rejected you. You're angry."

Incredulity flickered in her eyes, as she shifted with obvious discomfort. "How dare you inject yourself into this matter."

"You're not angry at me?"

Her gaze flicked to mine, and she opened her mouth as if to speak, shifting again. "Well, of course I am. I'm hurt."

"And you're taking it out on a student who doesn't deserve your wrath."

"I see the two of you. It's a strange relationship."

"You see through jealous eyes," I said, flatly. "There is no relationship between Miss Vespertine and me." Even I was impressed at how easily the lie tumbled free. There *was* something between us, I just didn't know what the fuck it was. "Stop using her as an emotional punching bag."

She tapped an unmanicured finger against the desktop, staring back at what must've been a look of absolute apathy written all over my face. "Fine. Although I stand by my original assessment and observations, for your sake, I will revisit Miss Vespertine's test score and drop the accusation, on one condition."

I waited with not-so-bated breath for her to say it.

"Have dinner with me."

Bingo. Exactly what I was looking for. "No."

"No?" She scoffed a laugh. "Then, do yourself a favor, Devryck, and stay out of matters that don't concern you. Or I'll have other accusations, besides cheating, to report." Brow raised, she crossed her arms. "Like your strange interactions with Miss Vespertine."

"I would invite administration to reach out to Miss Vespertine and inquire of any inappropriate behavior. My interactions with her have been nothing less than honorable and professional." My soul damned near withered with that one.

"Perhaps. But who would believe the man previously accused of such behavior."

"Likewise, who would believe that a respected professor would choose to dole out shitty grades based on jealousy?" I lifted my phone from my pocket to show that it continued to record, and pressed stop, holding back a laugh when her eyes damn near bulged out of their sockets. "Don't fuck with me, Loretta. And stay out of my business, or I'll see to it that every member of administration, *and my lawyer*, receive a copy of this."

Chapter 50

Lilia

He refused to look at me.

Clad in dark jeans and a white button-down, Professor Bramwell stood at the front of the lecture hall, describing chemotactic behavior in Leishmania–a topic I suddenly didn't care about–not sparing me a single glance. I would've been frustrated by that, if he hadn't rubbed the back of his neck a few times, rubbed his jaw, and even loosened a button on his shirt at some point, which didn't go unnoticed by the girl sitting in front of me. She snapped a picture of him with the caption, *Yes Daddy Death*, and had zoomed in on the front of his pants, to the obvious outline of a bulging hard-on.

I shifted in my seat, the impudent brat in me wanting to kick the back of hers. *Hard*. Not like it was her fault, though, when the man oozed sex and raw masculinity out of every pore of his body. The mere sight of him spurred visuals of sweat and muscle, moving like a well-honed machine. I flinched at that, turning away to relieve myself of the gnawing thought that had me crossing my legs.

Damn him.

As I left the lecture hall, rolling my eyes at the lineup of girls waiting to ask a million questions just to get a few moments of his attention, I caught the focused trail of his gaze that followed after me. That was how it was going to be from then on. Stolen glances and awkward silences. I hated it, this dynamic between us. It'd only been mere hours, and my skin already missed the feel of his rough hands, the soft caress of his lips.

For the rest of my day, I went through mindless motions. Muscle memory. Unpacking my laptop, taking my notes, packing it back up, heading to the next class, eating. All the while, my head was wound around Professor Bramwell and what we'd done the night before.

In a long hot shower, I pressed my forehead to the tiles and desperately tried to recreate those sensations with my own fingers. Not even the tickle of the water, the heat, or the slickness of my body could replicate the belly-curling thrill he'd stirred with his mouth. Like a hungry, starving beast that would never be full. Everything after him would be mediocre.

He was right. He had absolutely ruined me. Torn me open to my darkest secrets, which he shifted and molded to fit himself there, and sewn me back together as something else entirely.

I didn't even recognize the pining fool I'd become. As I stared at myself in the foggy bathroom mirror, I shook my head. "What the hell are you doing?" I whispered.

I had to get over it. Over him. It was one night. A night I'd never forget.

And nothing more.

Chapter 51

Lilia

I needed to clear my head.

Running had always been a source of stress relief for me, and since I couldn't sleep, I decided a jog around campus might unkink the tangle of thoughts in my head.

Clad in my Dracadia sweatshirt and a pair of black shorts, I grabbed my pepper spray and headed out into the dimly-lit early morning. Dawn wasn't for another forty five minutes, and a peaceful calm blanketed the campus. It'd been a few weeks since I'd last gone for a run, and it felt good to work those muscles that'd gone soft with my insanely busy schedule.

At the beginning of the semester, I'd acquainted myself with Devryck's running schedule. According to what I'd observed, he wouldn't be setting out for another hour, which meant I was probably safe not to run into him, and earbuds in, I took the path along the dorms, where a few other joggers waved as I passed. Athletes, most of them, given the Dracadia warmup garb I'd seen them wear on the field while practicing. My playlist was a wild mix of rap and alternative, with the occasional pop song thrown in.

Unbidden memories of my night with Professor Bramwell arrived in erratic flashes, though.

The intense stare. His hands on me. His face between my legs.

Running shoes pounding the concrete, I kicked up my pace, my ponytail whipping around my face. I dashed around the Rawlings academic wing and up the small hill toward the Sigma Phi House, as if those thoughts chased after me.

More images poured in.

His lips on mine. Fist threaded in my hair. His palm cuffing my throat.

Mist blew from my mouth as my pulse ramped up, and I pushed more speed from my legs.

Fingers inside of me. Dirty, whispered words. Filthy thoughts. Teeth grazing my jaw.

I ran even harder, my breaths becoming erratic, my heart hammering in my chest. I was no longer jogging, but sprinting across the campus, my muscles growing weak with the exertion. The cool air thickened in my lungs, and I ground down my pace to a brisk walk, heaving for breath. Eyes clenched, I willed myself to banish the visuals of him, because, for fucks sake, I knew it couldn't work. He was my professor. He had the power to affect my grade and maybe even my scholarship. I couldn't afford to lose that. I couldn't afford to leave Dracadia.

Tugging one of my earbuds out, I paused, resting my palms on the tops of my thighs, and breathed. Once sufficiently oxygenated, I stood up, preparing for another circuit around campus, when in the distance, I saw Professor Bramwell round the corner of Pryther Hall, wearing his gray sweatpants and the black muscle shirt that emphasized his brawny arms.

Oh, shit.

A glance down at my watch showed I still had another thirty minutes before he typically headed out for his run. *What the hell!*

Spinning on my heel, I darted ahead of him.

To my utter horror, he caught up to me, coming alongside

me. He pulled one of the black earbuds from his ear. "What are you doing, Miss Vespertine?"

"What does it look like?" I sprinted ahead of him, my face burning with humiliation. Jesus, the guy probably thought I was trying to stalk him, or something. Once again, he caught up to me and grabbed my arm, bringing both of us to a slow halt.

"It's fucking dark out," he said, his furious voice only mildly affected by the run. "You shouldn't be running by yourself."

"I was trying to *avoid* running into you, *Mister Jogs-At-Precisely-The-Same-Time-Every-Morning-Except-Today.*"

"I have an important board meeting later and had to bump my run. So, you put yourself at risk to avoid running into me?"

"You won't even look at me. Now, you suddenly care?" Shaking my head, I turned in the direction of my dorm, but felt a tight grip of my arm.

"What do you want, Lilia? Want me to proclaim my attraction and fuck you in front of the student body and administration? To let everyone know that I'm so bitterly obsessed with you, I've rubbed my dick raw since you left? Maybe I should apologize to the board this afternoon for a half-assed report, because my student's pussy was all I could think about when I was writing it." He ran his hands through his hair, pacing in front of me. "No, I can't look at you right now because I'm crawling out of my skin wanting to touch you." A look of disgust claimed his face as he gestured toward my legs. "And if you think, for one second, I'm letting you jog around here in the dark in those tiny fucking shorts, looking like a midnight snack, you've grossly underestimated just how much of a prick I can be."

I didn't know what to say to that. I was literally speechless standing there, watching him pace with anger and frustration. Because of me. Because of what we did.

"I'm sorry. I haven't stopped thinking about you, either."

Two joggers approached, and he cleared his throat, turning away as if to put some distance between us, as they passed through.

Once they disappeared over the hill, he turned back to face me and dragged a hand down his face. "Let's just call it what it was–one amazing night. One I hope you remember with the same relentless longing and anger and ache that I feel every time I look at you. It fucking hurts to know that I can't have you, Lilia. I lose in that respect. But that is the tragic reality in all of this. What we did that night cannot be repeated. Understand?"

"Yes. I understand." As much as it troubled me, I understood.

He gave a quick nod, ushered me back onto the path, and trailed after me. Watching me, as he jogged at a distance behind me. Instead of taking another circuit around campus, I headed straight for my dorm.

A text popped up from Jayda.

Say hello to Henry Michael Fuller.

A picture followed, of a small little bundle held in the crook of an arm.

As much as it hurt to smile right then, I texted back:

OMG. He's perfect. How are you feeling?

Exhausted. This baby eats every hour. Got my boobs feeling like two boulders hanging off a toothpick.

Sounds painful.

You have no idea. But I don't want to talk about motherhood right now. Whisk me away to academia. What's going on with you?

I bit my lip, debating whether, or not, to tell her about Bramwell. It wasn't like she knew him, or would ever meet him.

I think I screwed up.

How?

My mind spun with how to frame the answer.

Did you fuck your professor?

Leave it to Jayda ...

Define fuck. On second thought, don't. I hooked up with him. But we didn't get that far.

Hang on, this isn't a conversation for text.

Not a minute later, my phone rang, and I answered it.

"Oooh, Lilia." She spoke low, obviously not wanting to wake the baby.

"I know. It's bad."

"Was it, though? Or was it fucking *good*?"

Screwing my eyes shut, I let out a pained sigh, and at a flash of his head between my thighs, I willed the thought away.

"Is he hot? Does he have a big dick?" she whispered through the phone. "C'mon, I need details."

"Really?"

"I have five more goddamn weeks before I can get dicked again. I'm living vicariously through you right now. Please."

I groaned, trying to hold back a smile. "Yes, and yes."

She made a noise of excitement, quickly followed by a broken, "*Sh-shhh*," like she was bouncing the baby. A moment of quiet, and she whispered, "Where did all this nastiness go down? His office?"

"Yes."

"Mmmmm. Are you guys a secret forbidden thing now?"

"We're not anything." I hated the bitter taste of disappointment on my tongue from saying that aloud. It was only weeks ago that I'd sworn off all men, determined to focus on my studies, and there I was pining after my moody professor.

"Does he have a history of hooking up?"

"No. I've never seen him so much as look at another student."

The insensitive chuckle that followed left me frowning.

"What's funny about that?"

"He is not over you, Lilia. Trust me." The baby cried in the background. "Shit. I gotta go. Hungry again. Make sure you send me a pic."

"I don't have a pic."

"Get one." She didn't even wait for me to argue before the phone clicked.

I arrived at his lab that evening dressed in something a bit more conservative, after the conversation with him earlier that morning. A sweater and jeans that scratched at my legs. Every brush of our hands, and he flinched. Every stare, and he looked away, scowling. It was as if he'd grown angrier at me since our last encounter.

While on the way to sterilize agar in the autoclave, I paused alongside the glass dome, noticing Achilles and Patroclus vigorously flapping their wings, their ends attached to one another. Mating. Achilles broke loose and almost looked like he stumbled away, before Patroclus returned again, wings flapping so fast and frantically, I could hear a soft hum through the glass. "Jesus," I muttered. "Somebody's horny."

As I hung up my lab coat in the autopsy room, Professor Bramwell pushed through the door, a look of sheer misery screwing up his face.

"Lilia..." He exhaled hard through his nose, like even the sound of my name brought him grief. "This arrangement is no longer workable."

My heart withered like a deflating balloon. "What? What do you mean?"

"I mean, I'm going to have to let you go. I'll put in a word with Doctor Friedman to have you work in his micro lab, if you'd like the ex–"

"I don't want to work with Doctor Friedman. I want to work here! With you! On this project. It's important to me." I searched his eyes for humor, or even the slightest bit of doubt, but found nothing but a steely resolve burning there.

"It's not going to work."

"Why? Because of what happened between us?"

He winced, as if the mere mention of it wounded him.

"I need this job. I need the cash. Please, I'm begging you." God, I sounded like Gilchrist.

"This is my fault. I should've stayed away. It was on me to stay away, and I didn't. And now ..." A muscle in his jaw twitched with the clenching of his teeth. "It's just not going to work."

"My sister ... she's going to be kicked out of school. I'm

begging you, Devryck. Nothing has to happen between us. I get it. It was irresponsible of me, too. Reckless. I shouldn't have pushed. Please. Please let me stay. I don't know what I'll do."

He handed me an envelope, presumably a check for the wages I'd earned for the measly few days I'd worked. "Go, Lilia. And do not come back tomorrow."

"Please, Devryck." The pathetic tone in my voice sickened me, how quickly I'd shifted from feeling in control to feeling completely helpless, and I hated that this man held the reins. That, no matter what, he would always be in control, because that was the dynamic of professor and student. He didn't have to have a good reason to kick me out of his lab. He'd let me in on a bribe, and now he was trying to dissolve the arrangement like a bad case of heartburn. "Please don't do this."

As he turned to leave, I fought tears.

The options for making up the extra cash had just slipped from my fingers like water. Jobs on campus paid half of what I'd have earned working for him.

My cheeks heated with the shame I swore I wouldn't allow myself to feel. The realization that my sister would be kicked out of the one place she felt safe, and thrown into whatever hell awaited her back at Conner's, because I'd had a reckless moment with my professor.

It was my fault.

All of it.

The bus pulled up to my dorm, and I climbed out, my body weak and exhausted with stress. I made my way through the commons area, where students laughed and watched TV, up to the third floor. Once inside, I pressed my back into the door to close it and slid to the floor.

Tears finally broke free.

On the ride home, I'd contemplated logging back into the porn site, just to claim the money I'd been too scared to collect, fearing that my video would've shown back up on the site. Did dignity matter at that point? I had ten bucks in my account. The coins I'd earned would've given me another few hundred, almost a thousand, if memory served me right. I unsealed the envelope from Devryck and pulled out the check from inside.

Five thousand dollars.

A personal check made out to *cash*.

My throat constricted, the air trapped in my lungs, and I was glad to be sitting on the floor right then because I probably would've passed out.

Five thousand.

I double-blinked, wondering if my eyes were playing tricks. The amount was written out in mostly illegible writing, but I could definitely make out *thousand*. Not hundred. Five thousand dollars. I'd never had so much at once in my entire life. It'd cover all of her tuition until Christmas, including Conner's share, so even if I had to get a job paying a hundred bucks a week, I'd have enough to be two months ahead by then.

Stop, I chided. *Stop right now.*

As much as I wanted to slip into the excitement of it all, the weight of reality pressed down on me. I couldn't accept this from him. While it was a noble gesture, it'd be wrong for me to take the money. I hadn't earned it. Which brought to mind another thought–was this his way of paying me off to keep my silence?

That would've hurt even worse. Part of me wanted to storm back to the lab, to his office, and throw the check in his face like a strong, independent woman with scruples would've done. The other part of me decided to sleep on it.

Perhaps I could come up with an arrangement to pay him back.

Who was I kidding?

It'd take a decade, or more, for that amount. Perhaps in sleep I'd formulate some kind of plan to make it work, because I sure as hell didn't want to do something rash and emotional like throwing it back in his face when I really needed it.

Chapter 52

Lilia

Two days passed.

My knee bounced incessantly as I sat in Midnight Lab, waiting to see if Professor Bramwell would show. He hadn't been in lecture that morning, or the last scheduled lecture, leaving Ross to lead in his absence. I nibbled on my lips, my anxiety blossoming, as students filed in and took their seats.

The check remained tucked away in my trinket box, hidden beneath my bed. I refused to cash it until I at least talked to Bramwell. Unfortunately, I hadn't come up with much of a plan to pay him back that wouldn't continue to put me behind with Bee. The nagging possibility that the money might've been a payoff chewed at my thoughts, and again, the stubborn fool in me wanted to throw it in his face and tell him to fuck off.

That was the shitty thing about being broke, though. Pride was an ever-fading ideal.

Spencer hustled to his bench, his eyes rimmed in dark circles as if he hadn't slept in days. It was the first time I'd seen him since that day in the alley after class. The guy looked like he'd gone on a bender, or something.

Ross stood at the front of the class, unpacking his notes, and the sliver of hope I'd had for seeing Devryck shriveled. For two days, I'd convinced myself it was wrong. That I didn't deserve the cash. That the right thing to do was return the check politely and thank him for his kindness.

And then I'd imagined his response–him calling me a fool and throwing out insults to anger me into cashing it.

Where was he?

I needed to talk to him.

Just as I prepared to settle in for another disappointing lecture, the devil himself strode through the door, and damn my heart for galloping in my chest at the sight of him. Decked out in jeans and a black shirt, he swept through the lab, looking better than he had any right to look. His skin glowed, eyes lacking the dark circles he always wore. He looked good. Too freaking good.

He stopped at the tank beside my bench, where all of the larvae germinated on their beloved noxberries, and with his trusty forceps, he plucked berries and deposited them into a specimen jar.

Say something!

My lips dried at the thought of grabbing his attention in a full class. "Professor?" The meek tone of my voice hardly carried, and my cheeks reddened with the possibility that I'd have to call out to him again.

"Yes, Miss Vespertine?" He didn't bother to turn around, but kept to the task of gathering the larvae.

Of course the class had quieted then. Of course they had.

"May I speak with you for a moment?"

"Regarding?"

Are you kidding me? I should've been bold and told him I wanted to speak with him about the check he'd written me.

That would've pissed him off, though.

"It's about my grade," I lied.

"I have office hours available to discuss such matters, Miss

Vespertine. I would invite you to schedule a time that works best for you."

I hated this. I hated that we'd reversed time into this weird dynamic that was worse than before.

"It's urgent, though. I'd really like just a few minutes of your time."

"I'm afraid that's not possible right now. I'm very busy."

Had we not been in a classroom full of other students, I'd have called him by his name. Snapped him out of the cold, aloof front he was putting on.

Ross finally began his lecture, a lively topic on mind control that garnered some engagement from other students.

"Would you happen to have any openings tomorrow?" My voice hardly carried over the rumble of voices, as students held quiet discussions.

"I'm afraid I'm booked all week." Purple light streamed through the glass jar, as he held it up, examining the cluster of berries inside. "You might find an available slot next week."

Booked? With what? His fangirls who showed up with lists of questions just to flirt with him?

"Fine." I wanted to scream. "It's fine. I'm sure I can get a private appointment with Ross."

At that, he finally turned around with an absolutely murderous look carved into his expression. "Tomorrow, Miss Vespertine. After lecture." The snippy edge of anger in his tone told me what the man would never admit to my face.

He was jealous.

And damn it, the thought of that made my twisted little heart sing.

———

As I left the midnight lab, I caught sight of a light in one of the other labs across the hall, where Briceson sat at a bench, furiously typing away at his computer. Curious, I abandoned the group heading toward the bus and entered the room, which was empty for all but him.

"Hey."

He glanced up from his computer and smiled. "Hey, what's up?"

"Burning the midnight oil in here, or what?"

"Yeah. I have a research project due tomorrow."

"Oh. I probably shouldn't bother you, then."

"No, it's okay. I could use a break." He gestured to one of the stools across from him.

I'd have to walk back to my dorm, but it wouldn't have been the first time I'd done that. Now that I knew the man in the bird mask had been nothing more than a hallucination, I hadn't seen him as much. That, or I'd just stopped looking for him.

"So, what's the topic?" I asked, peeking at his notes on the bench.

"I'm actually really excited about this. So, you're familiar with black rock, right?"

"Like the stuff they sell at the apothecary stores in town? Yeah."

"Well, the chemistry department is actually working on cataloging a newly-discovered metal found in the rock, called casteyon."

"Wow. I thought this rock was pretty difficult to find. One of the locals told me it's dangerous to harvest."

"It's definitely not as abundant as it once was. Centuries ago, the basin became unstable, forming a huge rift, and part of the island sank into the ocean," he said with a gesture of his hands, the excitement for his project pouring into his explanation, and it made me think of Bramwell. "It's how we ended up with Bone Bay," Briceson prattled. "The rock split away and now makes up one of the deepest drop-offs around Dracadia. It's pretty creepy, actually. The shallows are about five feet deep, and then *boom*, a quarter mile vertical drop. That's where you'll find the most concentrated black rock, inside the underwater caves, but it's all over Bone Bay, in the gravel onshore. That's how we found it, actually. In the gizzards of seagulls and ravens that eat the small stones."

I knew from taking care of my mother's birds that they didn't have teeth and used the small stones, gastroliths as they were called, to mill the food during digestion. It brought to mind a sketch I'd seen in one of the books I'd read on the history of the island. The skull with the black stone teeth, belonging to a member of the Cu'unotchke tribe. Could it have been the same stone? "That's fascinating. A whole new metal? Isn't that going to change the whole periodic table?"

"Well, yeah. We have to confirm that it is, in fact, new and meets the criteria for discovery, then submit to the International Union of Pure and Applied Chemistry. It's pretty cool, though. I just need to get my shit together on this paper. But ... think I'm gonna call it quits for the night. Can I walk you back to your dorm?"

"You don't have to do that."

"I insist. It's not Covington here, but you still have to be careful. Better to walk in twos."

"And what happens when *you* have to walk back alone?"

He snorted a laugh and shrugged. "My dorm isn't far from yours. There's one camera and an emergency station. All lights."

"Then, how about we walk each other to that point and split off there."

"I don't think so. I offered to walk you, so I'm walking you."

"Well, if you insist." I waited for him to pack up his laptop and scattered notes, and the two of us headed out of Emeric Hall together. "Can I ask you something that's been bothering me?"

"Sure."

"What was the relationship between Jenny Harrick and Mel? I mean, as far as I know, Jenny dated Spencer's best friend, right?" The drop in temperatures had my skin pebbling as we cut across the courtyard.

"Admittedly, I don't know a whole lot outside of Mel's perspective, but yes. I guess Mel agreed to a couple dates with Spencer. Up until he, you know ..."

Strange that he didn't want to say it aloud. "Do you think it was Spencer's father who let him off the hook? Seems drugging a student would be cause for expulsion."

"Could've been, if we assume Mel is telling the truth."

I already knew she'd told the truth after my conversation with Spencer, but it was interesting that he questioned it.

"It was actually Professor Gilchrist who backed his story."

"What?" The visual of her cupping his groin flashed through my head. Again.

"Yeah. She claimed that she had been tutoring him at about the time Mel would've been drugged. She claimed the same thing when Jenny went missing."

I knew the first was a lie, based on Spencer's confession. Was it possible she'd lied for him again? "Was Spencer suspected, at all?"

"Maybe briefly. But everyone was pretty certain that Bramwell had something to do with her disappearance. Story is, he killed her and threw her into one of the incinerators."

What a horrible rumor. Even if I was pretty sure it wasn't true, it still sent a chill up my spine. "Were there cameras?"

"Yeah. Guess some of the footage is missing from after Jenny left Bramwell's lab. They *claim* there was some interruption when the footage was stored to the cloud. The sequence of video somehow went missing, and the timestamps were off."

"But someone likely tampered with it, you think?" I sure didn't know enough about surveillance cameras and cloud storage, but it seemed unusual that such a critical sequence had simply disappeared.

"I think so. But what do I know? I'm just a chem major."

"Do you think Bramwell had anything to do with her disappearance?"

He let out a huff and shrugged. "I don't know. I'd like to think not, but his family has such a morbid history. Murder is definitely in his genetics. He had a brother that went missing, too. It's like their whole family is a string of conspiracy theories."

I knew the story behind his brother, and I'd seen the pain in Devryk's eyes when he'd told me about him. It was only out of curiosity that I asked Briceson, to see what the student body had conjured about that piece of his past, as well. "Then, you think Bramwell Senior was also behind the mass suicide."

"It's documented in the study that he injected those women with something. Something that messed with their heads. Do I think he drowned them himself? Maybe not. But I do believe he's the reason they're dead."

We finally arrived at the dreaded stretch of woods. A chilling prickle palmed the back of my neck, as the two of us walked in the darkness. Different than the feeling I got walking from the subway at night back at home. There, I was one of hundreds walking the street at night. A random. Here, an attack seemed more intimate. Personal.

The brief copse opened to the lawn of my dorm. "Well, I

guess this is where we part ways, huh?" I asked, pulling the wallet that held my ID card from my bag.

"Yeah. Hey, don't mention to Mel that I told you that stuff about Jenny."

"Okay. Can I ask why?"

He glanced around, as if she were anywhere within earshot, and stepping toward me, he lowered his voice. "She's really sensitive about speculation. She and Jenny were close. In her mind, Bramwell did it."

"She really has it in for the guy, huh?"

"I guess. Wasn't always that way, though. There was a time she went on and on about him, like every other student who's smitten with the guy. But then Jenny went missing, and she all of a sudden pulled out the pitchforks. Like I said, it's not as if he doesn't have a history to suspect him, though."

"Yeah." Funny how I felt the opposite–that there wasn't enough for me to condemn him. "Anyway, I'll let you get to your dorm. Goodnight."

"'Night."

I jogged up the staircase and threw back the door to the residential staff checking ID's. I exhaled a sigh as Mel flicked her fingers, impatient for my ID card.

"C'mon, Vespertine. I've got fifteen minutes before I can hit the sack."

From my wallet, I tugged my card, holding it out for her to scan me in.

"Midnight Lab, huh?" she asked, handing it back to me.

"Yeah. Just getting back."

"You walked?"

I glanced toward the other staff member scrolling through his phone, seemingly uninterested in our conversation. "Briceson walked me home."

"Surprised it wasn't Spencer," she said bitterly.

"I've distanced myself from him a bit. You were right."

She rolled her eyes. "When am I wrong, though?"

Perhaps I should've been as bold and outspoken about Spencer drugging me, too. My situation was a bit more complicated, though. Inquiries would've led into deep examinations that would've pointed to Professor Bramwell's involvement that night. Having Gilchrist on my back was bad enough. She hadn't said anything more about my test score, or cheating off Spencer, so perhaps she'd decided to drop the accusation. Maybe it was as Bramwell had said–not enough evidence to prove it. However, I couldn't help but wonder, if I had come forward with the accusation against Spencer, made it public, as Mel had, would she have lied for him again? Made me look bad to prove her point that I didn't belong?

As I stepped past Mel, she gave a quick tap to the other staff member's shoulder. "Hey, I'm going up now. You got the last few minutes?"

"Yep."

I stepped inside the elevator, and she followed after. The moment the doors closed, she turned to me.

"What's going on with you and Bramwell?"

As the elevator lurched into motion, she pressed the stop button, halting our ascent. A surge of panic locked my muscles. Elevators had always freaked me out, just the thought of getting stuck in one, but old elevators, in particular, terrified me. I kept my eyes on that button, while she stared at me expectantly.

"There's nothing going on."

"Please. I'm not stupid. I've seen you leave his lab at night." Considering the back entrance to the lab was tucked behind Emeric Hall, she'd have had to be spying on me.

"Are you following me around, or something?"

"Does the thought of that worry you?"

The bottom line was: she had no proof of anything.

Bramwell's lab was like a fortress, so what the hell was I doing cowering to her like a frightened schoolgirl, anyway?

I had grown up with worse than Mel. I'd been approached by those far more dangerous.

I reached for the elevator button, and when she grabbed my arm, I threw her off me and shot her a look of warning that must've been pure death, with the way she backed away. Once the elevator lurched into motion, the clamp of anxiety over my lungs loosed itself. "What I do is none of your business."

"I'm only warning you to be careful. It started out as obsession with Jenny, and–"

"You. Were you not attracted to him once?"

The elevator dinged, and the door opened to the empty corridor of my floor. When she didn't answer, I stepped out of the carriage and turned to face her.

"Yes. I found him attractive once. Then I learned that the good professor is actually a monster. Watch yourself, Lilia."

The doors closed.

I pulled up the picture I'd snapped on my phone of the Cu'unotchke skull and zoomed in on the sharpened teeth again. Curious, I logged into my Dracadia Library account on the laptop, and clicked on the Adderly Memorial texts. Scrolling through pages of history on the Cu'unotchke tribe brought me to a picture of a young girl with long black hair and dark eyes. It had been taken in the early nineteen-hundreds–about the time when the tribe had been mostly wiped out. Two of her teeth had been replaced with black stones, which was interesting in itself, but when I zoomed in, something else caught my eye. The buttons of the doll clutched in her arm.

Frowning, I zoomed closer, noting one of the buttons

appeared to be a small, misshapen metal button with an iron cross etched into it.

Scrambling out of the chair, I dashed toward the closet and removed the small wooden box that held all of my found trinkets and lifted the small button I'd noticed wedged in the door my first night here. I returned to my desk and studied it against the one I'd zoomed in on.

The same button.

Chapter 53

Lilia

The conversation with Briceson consumed my head as I exited the Dragon's Lair, having eaten nothing more than a piece of avocado toast and a latte that I'd charged to Bramwell's card. I spent half the night thinking about the black stones Briceson had mentioned in the birds, and the skull I'd seen in the photograph, trying to establish a connection between them.

Black to-go cup in hand, I made my way to Bramwell's lecture, if he bothered to lecture today, and felt the pressure of an oncoming storm tickling the back of my neck. Vibrant red, oranges, and yellows colored the trees, as the full breadth of autumn had settled over the campus, and gray clouds hung heavy and thick in a sky that promised rain. The euphony of early morning birds lent a peaceful song to my walk, while an errant breeze stoked the scent of wet leaves. Although the temps remained in the mid-fifties, warm for those of us who suffered brutal winters as a general rule, the air cast a chill over my bare legs. The temps were expected to climb up to sixty at some point during the day, so I wasn't too concerned about the outfit I'd chosen, but it sure as hell made for a chilly walk.

I sipped my overpriced latte to keep warm, looking like every other student hustling to class, the lid of my cup marked with the lipstick I'd made a point to wear.

Because I wasn't every other student. I was the one who'd given her professor a blow job and carried his check for five grand in her bag.

He wasn't like any professor I'd ever known, either.

He was moody, like rainy days and bitter coffee. Sensual whispers in dark corners and the slow burn of fine whiskey.

A torment I both hated and welcomed at the same time.

Aside from a couple of early birds, the auditorium was mostly empty, and I hustled to my seat. A completely foreign face strode up to the lectern, where he unpacked books and papers, and my heart sank as he introduced himself as the assistant professor.

In other words, Professor Bramwell had either forgotten about our meeting, or had blown it off.

Deflated and bored, I took notes, while Professor Humdrum gave a bland account of Noctisoma's lifecycle–a topic we'd already witnessed first-hand in the lab. It was only when he mentioned that some seagulls and ravens managed to avoid infection, despite their fondness for consuming noxberries and Sominyx moths, that I perked up.

I raised my hand, and when he acknowledged me, I asked, "What about bats?"

"Bats, unfortunately, are *not* immune. When they feed on an infected Sominyx moth, they succumb rather quickly to infection, and are often found floating in bodies of water."

"They don't have gastroliths, correct?"

He looked thoughtful for a moment. "To my knowledge, no."

"Why do only some seagulls and ravens avoid infection?"

"That would be a question for Dr. Bramwell, I'm afraid."

Of course it would.

With a nod, I settled back into my chair. My head puzzled the pieces I'd been given, as the professor kept on with his lecture. Bats succumbed. Some seagulls and ravens did not.

The latter used gastroliths to digest food. The question was–of the birds who became infected, how many had black stone gastroliths?

I wished Professor Bramwell was there to answer and tame the curiosity swirling in my head.

Spencer sat two rows behind me, and each time I felt a burning gaze at the back of my head, I'd turn to see him staring at me. Trying to ignore him, I slogged through the rest of the lecture, grateful when it was finally time to pack up. It was then that Professor Bramwell entered the class with that arrogant and dominant gait that made a girl's ovaries ache. The sight of him stirred a flurry in my chest, like dried fallen leaves in a wind tunnel. He took a moment to shake the assistant professor's hand, and when his gaze landed on me, I nearly stopped breathing. Why the hell did he have to look so good in his dark jeans and white button-down standing next to Mr. Khaki-Pants-and-Pullover? As if he was trying to torment me?

One of the other girls in class sauntered up to him, as if to ask a question. I watched as he gave her no more than a minute of his attention before directing her to the assistant beside him. I could almost feel the disappointment radiating from her.

As I slung my bag over my shoulder and made my way down to the front of the auditorium, his gaze caught mine, and he jerked his head for me to follow.

Not waiting for me to catch up, he strode from the room.

I hustled after him, and when I exited the class, I sighted him striding toward the corner at the opposite end of the hallway.

"Hey," Spencer said from behind. "Can I talk to you for a sec?"

"Hey, sorry. I gotta run."

He reached out and gripped my wrist. "Please."

It was only the look of pleading in his eyes that made me pause, at all. "What?" An air of annoyance thickened my tone. When he didn't answer, I jerked in his grasp. "Spencer, I don't have time for this," I said, my impatience blossoming to full-on irritation.

Instead of answering, he dragged me to a small alcove in the hallway, and I twisted my arm to get loose.

"Spencer!"

Once out of the main corridor, he pushed me into the wall behind me. "My mother told me ... something," he whispered, his throat bobbing with a swallow, voice shaky. "Lippincott isn't my father."

I froze, frowning as I peered up at him. "What?"

"He's not my real father."

Words failed to come to mind. I didn't know what to say to him. How to respond without sounding like an idiot, and the seconds ticked before Bramwell would become impatient and forego our meeting.

"I'm so sorry, Spencer. I don't know what to say."

"I'm not sorry. I'm elated. Fucking elated." Through tears, he chuckled, the contrast of his emotions unsettling, as if he might snap at any moment.

"Then ... I guess I'm happy for you?"

His face softened. "I knew you'd be." Before I knew what hit me, he took my face in his palms and pressed his lips to mine.

My spine snapped to attention, muscles stiff with the shock that sputtered up my throat, clamping off the air. As I let out a muffled protest, he broke the kiss, his chest heaving, tears breaking over his cheek. "Please, I'm begging you. Meet me tonight. The courtyard outside of the commons."

At the shake of my head, he leaned in, as if to kiss me again and I pressed a hand to his chest to stop him. "Don't."

The aggrieved expression on his face might've earned a

small bit of sympathy from me, if he hadn't so boldly trampled my boundaries.

"I'm sorry," he said. "I shouldn't have done that." What might've been a genuine apology hardly carried over the warring thoughts in my head, as I tried to wrap my mind around what the hell had just happened.

Stepping to the side offered just enough distance to regain some of my lost composure. "Spencer, I told you from the beginning, it's not like that. I'm not ... I can't–"

"Lilia ..."

"I have to go." Head pounding in calamity, I jogged down the hallway toward where I'd seen Bramwell go. Rounding the corner brought me to another hallway, but he was nowhere in sight.

"Shit," I muttered, peering into a packed lecture hall. The next was a small auditorium, but equally packed. The next two rooms at the opposite side of the hall were the same. It wasn't until I reached the last room, which opened on an empty auditorium, that I found him leaning against the wall at the front of the room with his arms crossed.

Mouth suddenly dried, I swallowed a gulp as I approached, my head still swimming with what had happened with Spencer. "Wouldn't it have been easier to meet down in your lab?"

"Easier for you? Perhaps." His gaze cruised over me, lingering on my legs for a moment before he lifted it to mine. "For me? No."

Still reeling from the unwelcomed kiss, I reached into my bag and pulled out the uncashed check, slightly humiliated when it shook like a leaf from my outstretched hand. "I can't accept this."

Nothing more than a quick glance at it. "You want to so badly, you're probably tearing yourself apart right now."

Unable to look him in the eye, I shook my head. "It's too much, Devryck."

He pushed off the wall, not bothering to uncross his arms. "Cash the fucking check." The sharp tone in his voice swung my attention to the equally annoyed expression on his face.

"Why? So you can look at me with pity? Call me pathetic?"

"Why do you have to be so goddamn stubborn? You need the money. I'll be just fine without it."

I silently tried to wrap my head around the thought that what would save me right then was nothing for him. A pittance. Lowering my arm, I stared down at it, telling myself that I shouldn't take it. "Working for you wasn't about the money, you know." Clearing my throat, I blinked away the mist in my eyes, a cataclysm of emotions hammering my brain. "I'll pay you back."

"You won't. You can't."

"Then, tell me how I *can* repay you?" I folded the check in half, wondering what he'd do right then if I tore it to pieces in front of him. "I can't just accept this. It isn't right."

"Neither is intentionally letting yourself sink in quicksand. Focus on yourself for once. And eliminate the roadblocks that stand in your way."

I sighed at that. "You were never a roadblock."

"Only because we weren't caught."

I hated that he could hold himself so composed, while I felt like my insides were being crushed by a wrecking ball. The utter chaos of wanting to wrap my arms around him for having single-handedly eliminated months of stress and worry, while at the same time wanting to tear at him, the way his indifference tore at me. "Why are you doing this to me?"

"What am I doing?"

Was it not written across my face? Had I hidden the ache that well?

I tucked the check into my bag, because if nothing else, it just felt too heavy in my hands right then. "You push and you pull, and I feel like I'm being torn apart."

His dark chuckle echoed through the room, and I looked up, scowling at the audacity of him laughing at me while I felt at my most vulnerable. "You think you're the only one?" His jaw hardened, lip curled in disgust. "There isn't a sharp enough blade to carve you out of my head, Lilia. I'd have to tear out my own goddamn eyeballs to keep from noticing your every move. Who you talk to. Who you fucking *kiss*."

The breath shot out of me at the realization that he'd seen what had happened with Spencer. Oh, God, how that must've looked. I opened my mouth to offer an explanation, but the resentment sketched in his expression told me it didn't matter. At the same time, a twisted part of me enjoyed that I could hurt him that way. That something poked at his emotions, when it seemed like he'd been trying to forget what had happened between us.

"We're just professor and student. Just like before." I forced the same aloof tone that he'd fed me. "Isn't that what you wanted?"

"We're more than that, and you know it." The tight clench of his teeth almost made me think he was insulted by what I'd said.

"I don't, actually."

Rubbing the back of his neck, he looked away. "For the love of Christ, stop biting your lip."

It was only then I realized I'd been gnawing the hell out of my bottom lip as I swept my tongue over a slight sting there.

"These little things you do that mess with my head." Hand raking through his hair, he paced. "There's a violence in my blood. This rage that twists in my gut, and it makes me sick. I'm fucking sick when it comes to you. That I could even fathom breaking his neck ..." He paused his pacing, eyes lost to whatever images spun through his head, like he could vividly see himself in them. "I can't control it," he said, curling his hands to tight fists. "I can't reel it in because I still feel you. I still smell that nauseating sweet scent on your skin that drives me fucking crazy. That sickening shade of lipstick that takes me back to that night. I'm losing my mind!" His voice thundered around me, shaking every nerve in my body to life, as I watched him unravel.

There was a beauty in it. The vulnerability I longed to see in him. The visible distress creeping over him was unfitting for a man so otherwise collected and detached. He was coming apart at the seams. Finally, a dent in the armor he wore like a second skin. What I'd mistaken as indifference wasn't that, at all. He ached and burned as much as I did.

I wanted to watch him come completely undone, to turn reckless, just like me. To grab me by the throat and tear away this resistance between us. "Why are you fighting it?"

"You know damn well." He stepped closer, backing me against the wall. "I'm not one of your goddamn classmates, Lilia. I'm your professor. Your future would be destroyed. You'd be kicked out and sent home to whatever life you were living, and I'd be here, hating the fact that I fucked you up. That I took *everything* from you."

"That's only if we get caught," I whispered.

Every emotion seemed to flash across his face, like a battle waged inside his head. He lifted his hand, brushing only his finger across my cheek as his tongue swept across his lips. "The things I want to do to you ..." Wincing, he looked away, and as he recoiled, I snatched up his hand. A look of torment claimed his expression as I dragged his palm across my cheek.

Eyes closed, I focused on the texture of his skin, the sensation taking me back to that night. I kissed his palm, drawing it across my lips, and latched onto his finger. Gaze locked on his, I sucked it into my mouth, moving up and down the length of it, just as I had done to his cock in the shower, a trail of lipstick marking the path.

Jaw slack, he watched me with heavily hooded eyes. "Lilia …" His grip hardened around my face, the veins in his neck popping as he snarled back at me. "You want to know how you can repay me?" The grit in his voice sharpened his tone. "Stop making me think of fucking you every hour of the day, so I can get back to my work!"

Exasperated, I gnashed my teeth. "If that's what you want, then okay. I'll stop." I didn't even wait for his reaction as I stepped past him for the door.

A hard grip of my nape was the only warning, before my body spun back around and he slammed his lips to mine in a kiss that was neither gentle, nor calm. One hand fisted my hair, the other took hold of my jaw. He kissed me ruthlessly. Plundered angrily. And he groaned and bit my lip, digging his fingers into my flesh with unflinching possession. And jealousy. God, the jealousy beat through me in punishing fury, as he held me to his face and ate the breath from mouth.

At the sound of approaching footsteps, he broke away, chest heaving, and crossed the room back toward the lectern. In a subtle gesture, he thumbed away the lipstick from his mouth, wiping it onto his pants.

Trying to catch my breath, I somehow snapped into motion after that kiss, and after wiping my lips as he had, I hid my hands behind my back as I scampered in the opposite direction, putting distance between us.

An older woman I didn't recognize popped her head into the room and smiled. "Oh, I'm sorry, Professor Bramwell, I didn't realize you were holding a meeting."

"We're just wrapping up."

I winced at the breathlessness in his voice, something the woman didn't seem to catch onto when she answered, "No problem."

She quickly exited, her heels clacking against the hardwood floor as she made her way back down the hallway.

Exhaling a long breath, he rubbed the back of his neck. "Not getting caught is far more difficult than you might imagine. Even my lab is subject to the occasional visitor."

"We'll have to be creative. Assuming you're interested."

"You know damn well I am," he growled, as if it angered him to admit it.

"Then, I know of a place. Library rotunda. There's a room at the top that's used mostly for storage."

"And how would one go about finding *you* there?"

"I have work study tonight. My shift ends at eight o'clock. The library doesn't close until after midnight. I need to show you something, anyway. Something I think you might find fascinating."

Wearing his usual frown, he swiped up his bag on the way to the door, and came to a stop alongside me. "If you're smart, you won't show."

With a defiant tip of my chin, I stared back at him. "And if you want me as much as you claim, you will."

Chapter 54

Lilia

From the cart, I lifted two physics texts and placed them on the shelf where they belonged. A glance at my watch showed only five more minutes before my shift ended, and I couldn't stand it any longer. My stomach twisted with the uncertainty of whether, or not, he'd even show.

Once the clock struck, I alerted Kelvin, as I normally did, and grabbed my bag, stopping in the restroom along the way to make sure I didn't have any food from dinner lodged in my teeth. I removed my underwear, feeling much more confident about that since the night I'd shown up for class without them, and stuffed them into my bag before hustling to the rotunda room.

The ceiling of the circular structure was a glass dome that loomed over the marble floor two stories below it. An upper level of rooms rounded its perimeter, enclosed by a bannister. Through a skinny door, I climbed a narrow staircase to the second floor, and peered into the rooms in search of Devryck. Shelves of books lined the walls of each separate room, and though there were desks with lamps for studying, the entire floor was often completely empty. I walked through the tall archways, finding Bramwell with his back to me, in a darkened corner of a small study area, hidden behind a wall of books. A small nook beside a window that overlooked the courtyard.

I closed the door to the room, and with a twist of a lock, we were completely alone.

"All the years I've been at this school, I've never been up here," he said, not yet having turned to look at me.

"I've only come up here a few times. This is where all the historical texts for Dracadia are kept." I sauntered up beside him, looking out at where campus life buzzed. "It's so beautiful."

"You showed." His tone carried a bitter snip of anger.

"So did you."

"I didn't have a choice. You're all I've thought about since this afternoon." Quick hands yanked my arm, and my spine hit the wall behind me, knocking my bag to the floor beside us. His lips crashed into mine, fevered and impatient. Tongues and teeth. Frantic.

He lifted my sweater vest over my head, revealing a white button-down beneath, and tossed it aside. His breaths hastened, and his throaty groan vibrated against my lips. After a moment of fumbling with my shirt buttons, he gave one hard yank, jerking my body and tearing it open. Buttons flew off, clattering to the floor. "I'll buy you another," he said against my lips. Cool air hit my breast as he peeled back the lace bra.

Across the room hung an elaborate gold mirror that filled one of the square wooden panels of the wall. In the reflection, I saw the two of us together–me, a disheveled mess with my breast hanging out and a look of euphoria painted in my expression, and him in his black shirt and slacks, a dark specter, whispering dirty words in my ear.

"Have you thought about that night? When I tongued and sucked on that little clit of yours?" He rolled my nipple between his fingers, and my lids grew heavy as an intoxicating need pulled at my belly.

"Yes."

"Do you touch yourself thinking about it?" When I didn't answer immediately, lost to his ministrations, he pinched both nipples, inciting a small shock of pain. "Tell me."

Mouth bone dry, I nodded.

Rough palms slid up both my arms as he guided them over my head and manacled my wrists with his hands above me. "I've been starving for you ever since." Hungry lips hunted my throat, while his free hand palmed my exposed breast. He paused his kissing just long enough to suck one of my nipples into his mouth, the teasing little tug between his teeth coaxing a moan past my lips. Still holding me captive with one hand, his other palm slid up the hem of my skirt, and he froze.

I smiled and bit my lip at his discovery. "I figured it was more convenient without them."

"Fuck me." The moment his finger made contact with my sensitive flesh, I arched into him, leaking a quiet whimper, careful to keep any sound that would echo through the rotunda. "If you ever show up to class like this, I'll take you aside and spank your bare ass."

"Is that a threat, or a promise?"

Groaning, he gave a slap to my ass, as if to prove his point. The pain smarted my cheek, and I jerked against him with a quiet grunt. He returned to his soft caresses over the needy bit of flesh that ached and throbbed for his fingertips.

Another glance at the mirror, and I took in the slackened jaw and drunken lust on my face as he teased me. How utterly intoxicated the man made me.

As though catching on to what had captured my attention, he turned toward the mirror.

"You like to watch?"

Licking my lips, I nodded.

Two fingers pushed up into me on a wet glide, and I felt him shudder around me. “Look how beautifully your body surrenders to me when my fingers are inside you.”

I let out a shaky breath, as he hiked my leg up to his hip. Cheek pressed to mine, he forced my head to stay watching, as he bunched my skirt to my hip, my cocked leg offering a clear view of my bare flesh. “You’re pink and perfect now, but you’ll be a red and swollen mess by the time I’m finished with you.” His words rooted themselves in my head while I clenched around his fingers.

I dug crescent moons into his biceps, and fought to keep upright, as my knees weakened.

Bottom lip caught between my teeth, I rested my crown against the wall as he pumped in and out of me, curling his finger inside of me with each thrust. Wet sounds echoed around me, inside my head, filling my brain with lewd visuals of the two of us. Faster, he pumped while rubbing his thumb over the electric ball of nerves that had me choking on a moan. Eyes clamped, I focused on the pull of his fingers and the wet squelch of fluids that leaked out of me, dripping down my thighs.

“Do you hear that, Lilia? How your greedy little pussy weeps for me. Look at the mess you’ve made on my fingers.”

I turned toward the mirror, in which he held my skirt up, giving a clear view of his skin that glistened with my slick arousal. “You make me this way,” I whispered.

A deep, sneering sound of amusement sent a shiver beneath my skin. “You don’t want to know what you do to me, Little Moth.” He stirred his fingers, so deep inside of me, I pushed up onto my toes, releasing a whimper as his thumb pressed against my sensitive clit. Teeth grazed my jaw. “This is what I see at night when I’m drenched in sweat, stroking my cock to thoughts of you." A kiss behind my ear. "You make me come so hard I can't fucking breathe after."

His dirty words wrapped around my head like dancing devils, pulling at the strings. Tight. So tight that every cell in my body shook, as I ground myself into his fingers, desperate and hot and needy.

"That's it. Come for me."

The deep, burgeoning ache he'd summoned escaped me on a tearless sob, as my muscles relented and an overwhelming pleasure bulleted through my veins. I tipped my head back, mouth gaping around a scream that he captured behind his palm. On a blinding explosion, I succumbed to bursts of ecstasy winding through my muscles in fevered pulses. My knees buckled, but he held me up as he circled his fingers, drawing out the last drops of my orgasm.

"Good girl," he whispered, his palm still pressed to my mouth. He guided my face toward the mirror again, where my heavy-lidded eyes and weak posture made me look drunk. A kiss behind my ear, and he slowly withdrew his fingers that glistened with my release. "I'm going to fuck you delirious."

In the mirror's reflection, I watched him shove his fingers into his mouth, and a rough sound of satisfaction rumbled in my ear as he rested his head in the crook of my neck. He breathed against me for a moment, his fist in my hair, body trembling like he was fighting for control. "You taste like innocence, Lilia. A good man would walk away from you right now."

"Are you a good man?"

Instead of answering me, he lifted me into his arms and carried me to one of the study desks, where he laid me onto my back. After planting my heels on the desktop, my legs fully open for him, he stared down at me with the same reverent gleam in his eyes as the night in his office.

I'd never done something sexual in a public place, where

people scurried back and forth only one floor below. My belly tightened at the thrill spiraling through me. Although the door was locked, I fantasized someone walking in and seeing us, me spread before him like a sacrifice.

His tongue swept across his lips, and he bent forward. One long lick up my tender seam, and I arched, mouth gaping for a scream I couldn't cut loose.

He moaned and grunted as he sucked on my clit, but I wanted more. Not so much the physical, but emotional connection. To have him inside of me and on top of me, and feeling me as much as I felt him.

"Devryck," I whispered. "I need more. Please."

Sighing, he shook his head. "I can't do that, Lilia. Especially if you've not had much experience."

A flare of embarrassment warmed my cheeks. "I told you, I'm not a virgin, or anything. My first just ... wasn't anything spectacular. It stung. I bled. And it probably only lasted about a minute and a half. We did it a few times, and he ghosted me after."

"He ghosted you?"

"I caught him screwing another girl behind the theater."

At that, he stilled, before breathing hard and rubbing a hand down his face. As if contemplating. Overthinking. Battling himself.

"Whether you're a virgin, or not—the fact is, I'm not a gentle lover. I don't want to hurt you." His heated gaze trailed down my body and back, and a pained expression flashed across his face. "But just looking at you stirs my compulsions. This rapacious need to take what I want."

I swallowed past the lump in my throat, unsure about my next words. All I knew was, I didn't want him to stop. In spite of his warning, I still wanted it. *Him*. I was desperate to sate this curiosity burning inside of me. This cliff dive into unknown waters. "Then take what you want."

Brows furrowed, he stared down at me. "You're certain of this."

"Yes. I'm certain."

Lowering his gaze, he rolled his shoulders back, seeming to mull it over. Undoubtedly calculating risk and consequences, as his analytical mind would.

A hard thunk beside me was the heel of his palm hitting the desktop, and on a growl of frustration, he straightened himself, the clink of his belt a small victory. He unfastened his pants, and it was then I realized this was really happening. I was about to fuck my professor.

He pushed down his pants and sprung that monstrous cock free.

I swallowed a gulp as I stared at it, standing tall and erect, heavy and ready to plow into me. Physics told me he'd never get that thing inside of me without some serious damage. The way he casually held it in his palm like a lethal weapon, taunting me with it, left me both desperate and terrified to know what it would feel like moving inside of me.

"I can assure you, this isn't going to last a minute and a half. I'm not some adolescent boy who comes the moment his dick gets wet. I'm a man who fucks hard and thoroughly enjoys the torment of delayed gratification. You're going to be sore. And I really fucking hope you want this, Lilia, because you're going to hate me when it's over."

"Why? Are you going to ghost me, too?"

"I don't think I'll be able to stay away from you after this. But let me be very clear," he gritted through clenched teeth as his hand gripped my throat. "I don't share. If anyone else so much as *looks* at this pussy, I'll take pleasure in dissecting him, starting with his eyeballs."

It seemed the jealousy of Spencer's uninvited kiss hadn't entirely faded just yet, and like before, his psychotic comments shouldn't have sent a flutter to my stomach. The possession in his tone should've had me running in the opposite direction. But I'd known bad guys my whole life. The skeevy, slimy types who took from girls and ultimately didn't give a damn about them. I knew boys who hurt girls for their own selfish pleasure. Who cast them aside afterward, as if they were useless, used-up rags.

Devryck was a different breed altogether. As he'd said—a man, not a boy. The kind who broke the rules in fucking his student, but was courteous about it–giving pleasure before taking. Bad, though? I supposed that was yet to be determined, but I was willing to take the risk. I was willing to lay my pride down just to feel the kind of passion I'd only ever read about in books. I wanted his rough hands and teeth, and to feel his sweat against my skin.

When I reached for him, he gently batted my arm away and stood stroking himself in front of me, drawing his hand up and down his cock in a way that had my thighs trembling in anticipation. "Show me what I shouldn't want. Make it hurt."

Swallowing hard, I slid my fingers over the throbbing ache between my thighs. Eyes on his, I plunged two fingers inside of me and watched the veins in his neck pulse to the surface.

Still pumping his stiff cock, he licked his lips with a ravenous glint in his eyes. "What do you think about at night, when your fingers are knuckle deep inside this pussy? Tell me what you want."

A voracious need curled inside my belly like hot coils. "I want ..."

"Your thighs are trembling. Say it."

"I want your cock."

"That's exactly why you wore this skirt, isn't it? Why you tease your professor to the point of madness. You *need* to be fucked, don't you?"

"Yes."

From his pants pocket, he tore a condom out of a package, and I watched with fascination as he smoothed it down the length of his swollen and hungry cock. It was when he lined himself at my entrance that he paused and lowered his head. The conflict clear in the tensing of his muscles.

"Do it. Please." I wanted him so badly, it physically hurt.

"Goddamn it, Lilia. Goddamn you." He notched himself inside, and a mewling whimper escaped me. He trapped the sounds behind his big palm, and I breathed hard through my nose. "Shhh. Take it a little at a time."

Hands balled into fists at my sides, I nodded.

"I'm gonna go slow. I promise I won't push all the way until you're nice and stretched."

I panted through my nose as he kept his hand held over my mouth. Little thrusts at a time, he tunneled himself deeper. Deeper. My muscles keening with his rigid intrusion.

"Goddamn, you're so tight," he said on a ragged breath. "Take a little more." Inch by inch, he filled and stretched me, the pressure inside of me swelling, reluctantly welcoming him, until at last, on a painful sting, he was fully seated.

Hands balled to tight fists at my sides, I continued to breathe hard through my nose as I took in the dizzying fullness of his cock inside me. My body had tensed so much, I felt light-headed by the time my muscles eased up. *God, don't pass out.*

Bent over me, he stilled, resting his head against my shoulder, his muscles rigid and vibrating with what I imagined to be pent-up energy and frustration ready to tear through me. "Are you okay?"

At my whispered, "Yes", he lifted his head and drew his hips back, then drove forward again.

"I needed this," he rasped, his jaw tense and flexing, as he ground his hips into me so deeply, it stole my breath. "I can't tell you how badly I needed to fuck you, Lilia."

A tortured sound ripped from my throat, captured by his palm, and he rocked in and out of me again with rough and powerful strokes. Plundering, as he'd promised, but each glide arrived smoother. I clawed at his arms, holding onto him, and something inside of me shifted.

I took in the feel of his body against me, the vigor in his tight muscles, the way his skin moved across mine, rousing a humming in my nerves. The quiet stuttering breaths. The frantic digging of fingers and trembling of arms and legs. He was everywhere. Across my skin and inside of me, winding himself into my bones and muscle. Moving like the violent waves of the ocean, that deep, vacillating sea, which pulled me like the tides.

A force of terrifying strength.

I tilted my head back toward the window beside us, through which the stars twinkled with constancy in a world that felt like it was spinning out of control. Time liquefied between us, rippling in slow currents that bent and swayed with our sweat-slickened bodies. I was slipping, falling, tumbling into feelings that I'd never felt with anyone.

The tightness in my chest promised implacable pain, but I didn't care. I wanted this. Needed it. Even at the risk that he'd cast me aside too.

And I hated myself for that. Hated that I was so hungry for passion, starving for the need to feel so much at once, that I could even fathom letting him slice me open that way like one of his dead corpses, somehow brought back to life by his skilled hands.

It was too much and not enough.

The commotion of everything I felt right then sprang forth a mist of tears. What were these strange, foreign feelings taking hold of me?

"Lilia," he whispered, the hand that had quieted me

stroked the top of my head, and I lowered my gaze to find his eyes brimming with concern. "Am I hurting you?"

"No. I didn't ... I feel ... so much." A tearful chuckle slipped out as I tried to reel in my emotions. "I'm sorry, I just don't know what to do with it all."

"Sex should always make you feel something. Just let go."

A tear slid down my temple, and I gave a nod.

He thumbed away the moisture and resumed his thrusts, holding my head in place. "Keep your eyes on me, Lilia."

More tears spilled across my temples, as I watched him staring down at me–our gazes locked, our bodies tightly woven together. Could it have been more perfect? Could I have known another soul so intimately as in that moment, with the two of us wound so tightly together? Entombed by rapture and the shame of knowing we'd breached the forbidden boundary and there was no going back.

The sound of voices and approaching footsteps brought him to a halt. The doorknob rattled, and I slapped a hand to my mouth, not daring so much as a breath.

He hoisted me up into his arms and carried me to the shadows of the room, pressing my back into the wall there.

"I thought you said no one comes up here," he whispered.

"I've never seen anyone up here," I whispered back.

The intruding voices grew louder, telling me they were just on the other side of the wall now.

Devryck slid his hand over my mouth, holding me propped against the wooden surface that pressed into my spine, his tip prodding my soaked entrance.

"There's an entire collection on Dracadian history up here," one of the voices said. "I could spend hours reading through these books."

"Ugh. You're such a nerd." Another voice chuckled. "What are you looking for, anyway?"

As the two prattled on, I could feel Devryck's cock impaling me, pulsing with impatience. He rested his forehead against my shoulder, shaky, warm breath scattering over my skin.

Slowly, I slipped lower. Lower. Until his cock slid back up inside of me, and when I arched, his grip over my mouth grew tighter.

"Shhhh," he whispered, giving small thrusts in and out of, me, his eyes aflame with a burning voracity that refused to be smothered. A feverish craving simmered in my veins, as I dug my nails into his muscled shoulders.

While the two strangers on the other side of the wall spoke of history and their class schedules, and other benign conversation, he fucked me.

I turned just enough to see the two of us in the mirror.

The indent in the cheek of his ass every time he drove forward. The tension in his muscles and neck, and power in his thighs with every controlled thrust and sinuous roll of his hips.

The raw beauty of our reckless fucking reflected back at me like a dark image I wanted to frame inside my mind.

My breaths turned to a sharp staccato, as my muscles wound tight, taking in the swell of his cock filling me.

His teeth clenched, jaw wired and straining. Sweat gleamed over his body while his muscles flexed around me. Destroying me from the inside out.

As the footsteps finally retreated, he let out a shaky breath and slammed into me harder. Faster. Thumping against the wall marked the fervor in his body.

The tension rippled inside of me. Twisted and curled, as I rode the edge of something wonderful. A deep, cramping ache bloomed in my taut muscles, and I arched into him, surrendering to this rapturous destruction. He groaned and grunted while holding me tighter, rutting against me like a feral beast. Faster and faster.

"Fuck. Fuck!" Jaw cocked open, he squeezed his eyes shut and let out a shuddering breath of relief. Long cords in his neck pulsed with each unsteady jerk of his hips. His body shook so hard, I thought he'd drop me. A look of pain and ecstasy claimed his face as he stared up at me, filling me with his release.

I stroked a hand down his damp hair, watching the euphoria wash over him, the focus and intensity as he succumbed to his climax. The most beautiful thing I'd ever seen.

Something shifted, electrifying the space between us. Shadows of a young and naive girl slipped from every sharp breath that quivered out of me. I was different now. Changed to something I didn't recognize–something far more vulnerable. Exposed. I wondered if he could see it in my eyes, the pathetic infatuation that had to be glowing there. Still drunk off what we'd done, I turned away, but felt the grip of my face as he guided me back to him and pressed his lips to mine. My body slid down the wall, as he lowered me to the floor.

"You are sublime," he whispered against my lips and slipped off the spent condom.

I watched in rapt fascination as he tied off the end of it, eyes wide at the amount of fluid captured inside.

"Jesus. That looks like enough cum to impregnate a village."

With a smirk, he tossed the condom into a small trash can. "Let's hope the forensics team isn't the one who empties the trash."

I smiled at that. "Housekeeping arrives at about ten. Maybe we should tie up the bag. Spare them the visual."

"I will. When I'm finished with you."

Reaching out for my arm, he took both of us to the floor, drew me into him, and holding me between his legs, my back to his chest, he wrapped his arms around me. "Tell me you're okay. Tell me I didn't hurt you."

"You didn't hurt me."

"You're not sore, at all?"

An ache pulsed between my thighs, raw and stinging, as if he'd torn me. "I didn't say that. I just said you didn't hurt me."

On a relieved sigh, he buried his face in the back of my neck. "I won't fuck you again tonight. But I will fuck you again." Perhaps it was mindless on his part, when he slid his hand down between my thighs and palmed my pussy. Not probing or caressing, just holding it there with the heel of his hand resting against my pubic bone. It felt wildly possessive yet somehow sexy at the same time. Something of a balm to the lingering sting of his intrusion. He breathed into the back of my neck and kissed the shell of my ear. "I've never felt something so intense before. Every moment with you is something new for me."

"This is all new for me, too."

Together, we breathed in the darkening corner, our quiet little oasis, and I drank in the aftermath of what we'd done.

"What is it you wanted to show me?"

It almost seemed too morbid for the mood right then, but I reached for my bag, anyway, yanking my phone from inside. A quick scroll through the pictures landed me on the one I'd taken of the skull with the black stone teeth. "I'm curious about this."

He shifted around me, taking the phone from my hand, and held it up to his face. "Unless my Dracadian history is off, this looks like the skull of a young Cu'unotchke child."

"The natives who inhabited the island centuries ago?"

"Yes. You see these black stones here?" He reached around me, pointing at them on the screen. "They sharpened them for teeth. Early dental care."

"Were they cannibals?"

"Some believed they were. They were said to have silver, glowing eyes and beastly fangs."

"Noctisoma?"

"I suspect so."

Pieces pulled together, forming a picture that left me questioning the link between the stone and Noctisoma. "Do you think the stones served another purpose, though?"

"Like what?"

"Briceson told me that they isolated a new chemical from black stones called casteyon. They found it in the gizzards of seagulls and ravens. Earlier, the assistant professor told us that some birds tend not to become infected with Noctisoma."

He handed the phone back and pulled me against him, as before. "It's an interesting theory. Perhaps one you might consider pursuing while you're here."

"But not you? What if it's a cure for Noctisoma?"

He kissed my temple. "I'm not looking to cure Noctisoma. The organism has so much potential as an antineoplastic, antimetabolite, antioxidant. And of course, autoimmune therapies."

"Yes, of course. But for those who don't *want* to be infected with the worm itself, it might prove effective."

"It might. And I encourage you to establish a hypothesis. Perhaps something you might consider for a thesis someday. I can direct you to some resources, if you'd like."

Thesis *someday*? It sounded like an unkept promise that a parent would make. Why did that have such a condescending ring to it? "Yes. I would like, as a matter of fact." I didn't mean to have such a snippy edge to my words, but my mother had passed away from infection. Had someone investigated even the smallest possibility of an antitoxin, I'd have surely been willing to administer it to her.

His arms tightened around me. "You're angry."

"I'm not angry. I'm just ... frustrated."

"I don't blame you, but my condition doesn't afford me much time to venture off into other avenues, as noble as they might be."

I sighed, reminded of the cause behind his research. "I know. Perhaps I can study gastroliths and black stones, and you can study the toxin, and we'll compare our studies every night in bed."

"*After* sex, I assume?"

I tenderly ran my nails over his arm. "Of course. No one wants to talk about worms *during* sex. That's gross."

"It is. And besides, I have a one-track mind, the moment your panties come off." He slid his hand down my thigh, giving a slight squeeze.

"Someday, maybe we can have a proper date."

"You're inquiring about activities beyond sex?"

"It'd be nice to eat an actual meal and maybe take a romantic stroll after."

"I've eaten quite heartily whenever we're together." His teeth grazed the shell of my ear, and I tipped my head, smiling at the tickling of my skin. "But if it's a date you'd like, I'll see what I can do."

"See what you can do?" Tonguing my back teeth, I kicked my head to the side. "That sounds like a copout, if I've ever heard one. If you're not careful, Professor Bramwell, the freshman in my exposition class might beat you to it," I teased.

"Freshman," he grumbled. "I doubt his balls have even dropped yet."

Chuckling, I twisted around, resting my legs over top of his. "Are you jealous?"

The dark smile on his face sobered to something serious, and he pushed a stray hair behind my ear. "Jealousy is a callow schoolboy's emotion that ends in hard feelings and bloody noses. What I feel for you, Miss Vespertine, would *destroy* lives." Palm to my jaw, he kissed me hard and bit my lip to emphasize his point.

As we lay hidden in our quiet, little nook, he explored my body with his hands and lips and tongue, until I was spent and boneless. Just before ten, we gathered up our clothes and exited the rotunda separately, so as to avoid any suspicion. He walked me to the bus stop, and I returned to my dorm with a smile on my face.

Chapter 55

Lilia

Somehow another week passed.

Stealing away with Devryck had become my favorite dangerous game. The leering glances in class, the brush of hands as we passed in the courtyard. Stolen kisses behind buildings, and in empty classrooms. In the darkest corners, hidden from prying eyes, we were more than professor and student. We were forbidden. Scandalous passion and the ache of longing, wrapped in a blazing fire too powerful to smother.

At night, we held trysts in the most obscure places. Sometimes, his lab, his office, the top of the clock tower, anywhere that was warm, hidden away from others, and lacked cameras. After sex, he'd pull out his books, and we'd lay naked in quiet study until it was time to return to our sleeping quarters. Three days before, we'd met in our secret little room in the rotunda, where he'd helped me study for my parasitology exam, quizzing me while I rode his cock.

Sex had become easier, more thrilling, and I found myself far more in tune to my body than I'd ever been before. He taught me things I never knew about myself, unlocking the dark fantasies tucked deep inside my head that I'd always feared were some strange anomaly. I felt safe voicing them to him–the desire to have him bind my hands and grab my throat–and I enjoyed the nights when he'd indulge them while whispering dirty secrets in my ear. At times, he was rough and abrasive and used my body to burn off the frustrations of the day, but then afterward, he would lie beside me and trace the contours of my bones with his gentle fingers, telling me how beautiful I was. I knew that what I felt for him had evolved into something completely foreign.

A beautiful complexity that was as pure and thrilling as it was forbidden.

And in the wake of everything, the stresses that'd plagued me only weeks ago withered to calm. It seemed Spencer had finally come to terms with some things, as he hadn't bothered to approach me since that day in the hallway. I'd caught him hanging around Kendall more frequently, and made a point to wave when I passed him on campus, which he awkwardly reciprocated.

I paid off all of Bee's tuition, which in turn eased some of the pressure on my relationship with Conner, and with that off my shoulders, I was able to focus on my studies, acing my exams. The measly four hours of sleep I'd always mustered had somehow blossomed to six, and I'd had to start setting my alarm just to ensure I woke up on time each morning.

I forgot the world outside the gates of Dracadia.

If Heaven existed, I'd found it in those ancient, dark hallways, under cold misty skies with autumn's wet leaves sticking to the soles of my boots, in the scent of coffee and old books. And him. My moody and devilishly handsome professor.

Camped out at my desk, I flipped through one of the texts on the Cu'unotchke tribe I'd borrowed from the Adderly library. While most students weren't allowed to remove the texts, Kelvin had let me check it out on the promise that I would promptly return it afterwards. I'd hoped to learn more about the black stone teeth, but most of what I'd read up until that point had been folklorish tales about the tribe–how they'd supposedly hunted the godfearing and put evil serpents in the bellies of good Christians.

At a knock on my door, I frowned, closing the book. A shock of surprise jolted me when I opened the door to Professor Gilchrist.

"Miss Vespertine, may I come in?"

I didn't know why I suddenly felt like I was in one of those vampire movies, debating whether I *should* invite the demon of the night inside. Was it even normal for a professor to visit someone's dorm? I'd never seen anyone else visited by a professor.

"Sure." Stepping aside allowed her access into my room, and I scanned the space for anything personal I may have forgotten to put away.

Once inside, she closed the door behind her and crossed her arms behind her back. "Miss Vespertine, I've been struggling with something for a while now. And I've come to the conclusion that it's best to confess."

"Okay." I bit the inside of my lip to hide my trepidation.

"I know the woman in the study that you wrote was your mother." She crossed the room, staring at the picture of me, Bee, and my mother. "The moment I saw you, it was as if I was looking right at her again."

"You knew my mother?"

"I was an undergrad when I first heard of the Crixson Project. At the time, I didn't really have much direction in mind. I just knew I wanted to get into some fast-paced science, and the Crixson Project held so much potential. I signed on as a lab assistant and secretary for Dr. Warren Bramwell." She turned to face me, gaze cruising over my room as if looking for something else to examine. "For the participants involved, it paid handsomely. A life-changing sum, in many cases. Your mother was part of the control group. Seeing as she was a native Dracadian who'd lived here all her life, Dr. Bramwell hypothesized that she might have had some natural resistance to the toxin. In hindsight, he was correct, but that isn't what was most compelling about her time in the study. It was the pregnancy."

I'd pieced together that much on my own, and had figured that was the reason she'd left the study. What wasn't clear to me was whether, or not, it had been voluntary.

"One night, I was asked by Dr. Bramwell to stay after and input some data. It was as I was mindlessly typing away that I overheard your mother speaking with a certain doctor about his *indiscretions* leading to her dilemma."

Dilemma. In other words, *me*.

A thick churning nausea roiled in my stomach, as I imagined the possibility that she might've been talking about Dr. Bramwell. Such a thing would've made Professor Bramwell my half-brother.

"He urged her to get an abortion."

As she went on, my pulse revved with impatience, waiting on the damn punch line to this joke.

"She told him she needed to think about it. Consequently, she left the study and never returned."

"Which doctor? Who got her pregnant?" I finally asked.

She smiled and shook her head. "Come now. You don't think I'd hand over such sensitive information without something in exchange."

Of course not, but I couldn't begin to imagine what exchange she'd be looking to make. "What do you want?"

"I want you to finish out the semester and leave quietly."

In one single gasp of breath, I felt spiritless. Soulless. As if she'd reached inside my chest and ripped out my heart. Leave Dracadia? The place that had become my solace, my sanctuary? I couldn't do that. "You're the one who invited me here."

"I made a mistake."

"This is about Professor Bramwell. Isn't it?"

Her lips twitched as if to smile, and she crossed the room toward the window, opposite my desk, that overlooked the sea. "He's exceptional as a professor, you know. He's never once shown the slightest interest in any student on campus. Which is why I certainly didn't believe the crap story about the Harrick girl. It was as if he didn't even notice them." When she twisted around, the humor on her face had withered. "That is, until you came along."

"Nothing is going on–"

She held up her hand, cutting me off. "Don't insult me. While the rest of the campus might be obtuse to your trysts, I can assure you, they've not gone unnoticed."

A person would've had to have made the effort to watch us, as careful as we were. We hadn't even exchanged texts, because Bramwell didn't want a trace of evidence that someone could use against us.

"Why are you doing this? He's made it clear that he's not interested in a relationship with you."

Hands behind her back, she chuckled. "If that were true, he wouldn't have paid me a rather *special* visit yesterday." The implication in her voice had me frowning.

"When?"

"Last night." The woman must've been off her rocker, because the two of us had spent the entire night together in his lab.

Calling her out on the lie wasn't going to get me anywhere, though. "Professor, going back isn't an option. There's nothing for me in Covington. And my home life has become unstable since my mother's death. You can't do this."

"I can. A meeting with Langmore, and it's done."

I didn't know what that meant. What politics might've made that a real possibility. I only knew that leaving was not an option. Not now. "You wouldn't be here, wasting both our time, if it was that easy. You're lying."

For one split second, I thought she'd plow through that door again, out of my dorm room and straight to Langmore's office to prove me wrong. I expected a smug grin and the pathetic explanation that she was giving me an option.

None of that happened.

Which proved I was right. I'd called her bluff.

She reached into the pocket of her skirt and held up a computer chip. "This? It could end my career. Or worse. So, I need more than your crap promise to stay away from Devryck."

"What do you want?"

"I want to know who the members of Anon Amos are."

That was certainly not the significant bit of information I'd imagined she'd be looking for. While tempting, given my distaste for Mel as of late, I didn't have it in me to rat her out. "I wouldn't know."

"Well, I'm asking you to find out. When you do? I'll tell you who daddy dearest is."

"Why? What do they have to do with you?"

After a good few minutes of staring, perhaps debating whether, or not, to tell me, she huffed. "I received a threat recently. That they would expose something scandalous. I need to know."

If I had to guess, it was probably the strange relationship she had with Spencer. What could've been more scandalous than her sexual relations with the provost's son? "Can you at least tell me if Warren Bramwell was the doctor who got my mother pregnant?"

As if my concerns had suddenly dawned on her, she shot back a fiendish smile. "Tell you what. You give me a name? I'll tell you if you're fucking your own brother."

I needed to know. I couldn't stand not knowing. "Fine. Cat. Dark-haired girl. Piercings. She's one of them."

"Cat," she echoed. It wouldn't have surprised me if she

told me Bramwell was my father anyway, just to traumatize me, but a wild surge of relief shot through me when she responded with, "It's not Professor Bramwell's father."

Thank God.

"This is a fun game, isn't it? Let's keep going, Miss Vespertine."

I shook my head. "I don't care. I don't care about my father. I never did. Why does it matter now?"

"This file contains more than your sperm donor, I can assure you. But if that's not enough for you, perhaps you might like to know how your mother became infected with the worms."

"How would you even know that? It was four years ago."

"I'm a scientist. I document everything."

"I thought the files were ..." I hesitated to say, not wanting to risk telling her more than necessary.

"Those files were what? Stuffed in some Bankers Box in the bowels of this school? Some of them were, yes. I was tasked with destroying them. A few of the boxes were stolen from me before I could shred them, but not before I'd scanned my own copies." She twisted the chip around, taunting me with it. "This holds everything those files don't."

"I only have to give you a name? *One* name?"

"Oh, honey. For this? I'm going to need your ass on the next train out of here. It's just too much risk." She tucked it back into her pocket, my gaze trailing her every move. "But I'll tell you what. You give me a significant name this time, and I'll give *you* a significant name. Deal?"

It was true what I'd said. I didn't care to know who my father was, but perhaps knowing would help me begin to piece together the puzzle that still baffled my brain. Namely, how the hell my mother had ended up infected only four years ago. I'd only postulated that she'd come home for her mother's funeral and had somehow gotten sick. Perhaps something more sinister had been at play, though. "You won't tell them that I told you?"

"Of course not. I give you my word."

"Melisandre. She's the group's leader."

Her face blanched. "You're certain of this."

"Positive. They meet in some little dungeon in her dorm room."

Staring off for a moment, she scratched at her face in thought, then quickly snapped out of it. "Very well. Since you've been so *helpful*, I'll extend you the same courtesy. Your father is–"

My phone buzzed at my hip, but I didn't bother to look at it.

Gilchrist glanced down and back. "Do you need to answer that?"

"No. My father is who?" The ringing died down, only to start up again. I inwardly growled at the obnoxious intrusion, not offering so much as a peek at who it might've been. "Just tell me."

"Dr. Lippincott."

The moment she said the name, the world skidded to a halt. I shook my head, trying to process it. Trying to imagine the possibility of truth in it, but I couldn't. It was absurd. "You're lying."

"Why would I lie? He fucked your mother, got her pregnant, and Bramwell kicked him out of the project. So terrified that his wife was going to leave him destitute, he urged your mother to get an abortion. She disappeared soon after."

I couldn't deny that her version of the story made sense, but there were a million possibilities. Less traumatizing versions, for certain. "That's why you invited me here. Why you kept telling me to meet with him. It had nothing to do with my paper. My academics."

She smirked and shook her head. "You're smart, I'll give

you that. While I was intrigued by your knowledge on Noctisoma, I found it lacking. Do I think anything you've done in your life warrants a full ride scholarship to this institution? No. You're a dime a dozen, Lilia."

"How did you even know who I was?"

"All I had to do was Google your name. As I said, you are a spitting image of her. Wasn't rocket science putting everything together."

Still reeling from the shock, I shook my head. "You're a horrible person."

Brows winged up, she sighed. "I wasn't. Truly. Not until you came along and fucked everything up." She held up the chip again. "Before you leave, come see me. I'll give this to you on your way out." Wearing a smack-worthy grin, she exited my room, closing the door behind her.

Whether the information she'd given me about my father was true, or not, I had no intentions of acknowledging, or confirming, it. My mother had always described him as a conniving man, and based on what I'd learned from Spencer, it might've been the only truth she'd fed me.

No. I wasn't leaving. I had no intentions of going down without a fight.

Or staying away from Professor Bramwell, for that matter.

Not now.

Chapter 56

Devryck

I rubbed my thumb across my index finger and flinched at the lack of sensation there. Fuck. I'd just taken a dose of the toxin two days ago, and based on the last dose, it should've lasted a week, or more. Long enough for me to synthesize more of it.

In the glass dome, the moth Lilia had named Patroclus barely fluttered across the floor of the cage, not only no longer able to fly, but in a state of constant paralysis. The toxin was metabolizing too quickly. The effects were wearing off as the body learned how to respond to it. I should've had another test subject lined up, but I'd gotten too overconfident.

Too fucking cocky.

And I didn't have time to go hunt down Angelo DeLuca, to infect him, and harvest more of the toxin, as I had with Barletta. All that remained was a single sample and what I'd harvested from Angela Kepling weeks ago, which might not even have been viable.

If I wanted to save this study, to keep it from slipping into failure, I needed to find another victim. The reality weighed heavily on me, and yet, at the same time, the only reason I'd made progress so swiftly was because I *had* sought out test subjects. Without them, I'd have been in a stagnant state of growing toxin in moths.

At the click of the door, I frowned, turning to see Lilia enter the lab. An unexpected intrusion, seeing as it was early afternoon and she didn't typically come visit the lab until evening, but her presence was certainly welcomed.

Every muscle in my body goaded me to sweep her up, but as I clenched my hands over the numbness that persisted there, I didn't move.

The expression on her face as she approached told me something was troubling her, as well.

"What is it?" I asked, wishing I could reach out and caress her face, but not being able to feel her skin would only stab me in the fucking chest.

She stared off for a moment, frowning. "Can you take me somewhere?"

"Where?"

"Away. I just need to get away for a couple of hours."

"I know of a place." I pushed to my feet and gave a jerk of my head, stuffing my hands into my pockets. For a moment, she looked confused. Rightfully so. I hadn't kissed her. Held her. Offered her any of the affection I'd given her over the past week.

Wearing a downcast expression, she followed after me, and after we'd deposited our lab coats on the hooks in the autopsy room, I led her through the cadaver entrance to the door leading out into the woods behind the school, where I'd parked my car in a small lot. I opened the door for her, allowing her to slide into the seat.

"Jesus, a Maserati?" she asked, the amusement in her voice an improvement from the somber tone moments ago. "And black. How did I know Doctor Death would drive a black car with black leather interior?" She ran her hand over the seat as she settled in.

"It suits me." The Ghibli was a sportier car, but practical, too, as it had a backseat, where I tossed my sport coat, and a trunk big enough to stuff a body. After rounding the vehicle, I slid into the driver's seat and fired up the engine.

Locked in her preoccupations, she remained silent, just staring through the window, stirring my concern.

"What's troubling you?" I asked again, driving down the small dirt road that ran along the perimeter of the school and down the mountainside.

"I learned who my father is today."

When she didn't say more, I cocked a brow and tipped my head to get her attention. "And?"

"I'm not sure I should say. I don't really want to put it out in the universe. He doesn't matter. He never did."

"Then, don't say his name." I shifted the gears on the car, allowing it to pick up speed as we hauled down the mountainside at about seventy miles-per-hour. As though sensing my venturous intentions, she opened the sunroof and tilted her head back, closing her eyes beneath the few scant rays of sunlight pushing through the overcast.

With my own head wrapped up in a mire of shit, I didn't prod her for a response. Instead, I let her enjoy the silence between us, with the cool sea air blowing her hair in disarray, and Chopin's Nocturne in E-flat Major blaring through the speakers. In spite of the mildly cool temps, a strange warmth settled over me, making me wish I'd opted for a T-shirt instead of the dress shirt. An ache throbbed in my muscles, though not necessarily unusual, given the dosage had begun to taper.

As we approached a familiar road, I slowed the car, and Lilia sat up in her seat. I dared to turn down the long, tree-lined drive, even though it sent a pulse of dread through my veins, as memories emerged from the dark corners of my mind like corpses rising up from the grave.

Beside me, Lilia looked around at the dark and dilapidated trees that hid the long stretch of dirt road. "What is this place?"

I rolled the car to a stop just outside of a black, wrought iron gate with *Bramwell Estate* etched into its metal. "It's where I grew up." Beyond the gate stood the dark and dreary gothic mansion with its stained-glass windows, steep gabled roof and turret.

The place had always physically looked to be in a state of mourning, with its weathered, vine-covered stones, chipped and decayed, and the unkempt gardens my father had refused to keep maintained after my mother had passed.

She peered through the window, giving a quick glance to me and back. "You lived here?"

"Generations of Bramwells have lived here. Caed and I were away at school most of the time, so we rarely spent much time here. But, yes. This was my home."

"Is this where you stay while on campus?"

"No. I haven't set foot in the house in a decade. Not since my father passed." I hadn't seen my father in five years, when our family lawyer had contacted me, urging me to pay him a visit. He'd been on his deathbed for some time, afflicted with the same condition with which I suffered. It was the day I'd refused to carry on his work. The day I told him I'd happily watch him die knowing everything would die with him. "The house is mine, though. The bastard cursed me with it."

"Your father wasn't a good man?"

"No. He wasn't."

"So, the rumors of what he did ..." A hesitation carried on her voice, as if she didn't want to risk letting me know she'd heard of it. "The Crixson study. Do you believe them?"

"Are you asking me if my father murdered six women?"

"I'm asking if he murdered my mother."

I couldn't look at her. My feelings for Lilia had grown to be complicated. The lies to protect her no longer came to me as easily as before. "I don't know," I answered honestly. Perhaps the most honest I'd been with her. While the details of her mother's death and the timeline of her illness didn't scientifically add up, I knew my father. I knew his sadistic tendencies, his greed and desires. "It's quite possible. Though, I've never heard of anyone harboring the parasite for so long. I can't even investigate the circumstances. There were files that went missing. A number of them were destroyed."

"I think Gilchrist has those files."

Frowning, I turned toward her. "How do you know?"

"Because she offered to hand them over if I stopped seeing you and left Dracadia."

"These files have information about your mother?"

"Supposedly."

"And you didn't leave? You didn't accept this offer?"

She lowered her gaze to where her hands wrung in her lap, and a smile played on her lips. "After I lost my mother, and Bee went off to school, I kind of spiraled into myself and learned how to find solace in loneliness. It became my home. The only place I felt safe. Then I came here. And I met you. And I learned that loneliness was a choice for me. This place is more than just a school to me." The turmoil bubbled to the surface as she sat fidgeting. "I suppose I could've kept to myself, as I always have, and remained another forgettable face in the crowd. And maybe Gilchrist wouldn't have bothered. Or maybe she would've and I'd have just gone back to my old, lonely life, and had all the answers I've yearned for." She shrugged and looked away. "Answers that don't really matter anymore." From her profile, I watched a hint of a smile play on her lips. "The decision was made the moment I met you, though. To stay here. I choose you."

Damn her. Damn *this*. What the hell was I doing to this girl? What the hell was she doing *to me*?

I pushed past the revolting lack of feeling and hooked my finger beneath her chin, turning her to face me. "I choose you," I said, and pulled her in for a kiss, feeling the smile against my lips. "And believe me when I say, you're hard to forget, Miss Vespertine."

Reversing the car back down the drive, I pulled out onto the main road and kept toward the north end of the island.

"I meant to ask. Why women? Why did your father choose strictly women for the study?"

For years, I'd suffered through the rumors that my father had been no different than my great-great-grandfather, who'd chosen prostitutes as victims. It wasn't until I studied the parasite that I learned the truth of why. "The toxin responds more favorably in women."

"Why?"

"Haven't gotten that far. Genetics? Evolution? There's so much left to learn about it."

"I feel like I should hate this parasite more than I do. Everything about it fascinates me, though."

I sighed. "Welcome to my world."

We finally reached Amorisse Cove, and I parked my car off onto the shoulder. After opening the door for her, I led her down a rickety staircase, to the beautiful cove surrounded by the tall, stone walls of the cliffs. In the distance, about a half mile offshore, stood the arch known to the locals as Lover's Leap. An archway that made up the tail of the dragon-shaped island.

Lilia followed behind me toward the water, the urge to grab her hand smothered by the numb tingling in my fingertips. We finally reached the shore that opened onto white sand and the soft, gray waves of the ocean. I came to a stop on a short stretch the tide hadn't yet reached, and she sauntered up beside me, wind sifting through her hair as if it longed to touch her the way I did.

"It's so beautiful."

As she stared at the arch, I stared at her. "Lover's Leap."

"I remember seeing this one in a booklet I grabbed from town. Haven't read it yet. What's the story behind it?"

"A local native girl, the daughter of a chieftain who fell in love with a simple Dracadian fisherman. She asked the gods for permission to marry him, and the gods refused, banishing him from the island." As I relayed the story, I toed the sand with the tip of my shoe, unearthing a shell that I picked up and rubbed the sand away from with my thumb. "She climbed atop the arch to watch his boat depart, and out of nowhere a white squall struck his vessel, crashing it into the rocks beneath where she sat. Devastated, she leapt to her death." I handed the perfectly intact shell to her, watching her marvel it as if I'd given her a rare jewel. "From that day forward, the gods gentled the waters around the arch, made it shallow there, so no one would ever perish by those rocks again. The indigenous believed the arch to be a gateway to the afterlife."

Her lips curved to a smile, and the wind blew a stray hair loose that I wanted to capture between my fingers and tuck behind her ear, but I didn't dare.

I didn't dare because it would've only infuriated me to confirm I couldn't feel its silky texture.

"Everything about this island is a story. The sirens of Bone Bay. The nymphs in Squelette Lake. And now Lover's Leap. Every corner seems to hold something magical and terrifying."

The waves drew closer. Closer. She backed herself up, nearly tripping, and I reached out a hand to catch her. Biting back the repulsive lack of sensation, I forced a smile, as she chuckled.

"Well, what are you waiting for?" I asked, releasing her. "The sea awaits."

She shot me a look, as if thinking she shouldn't dare to. Her bottom lip slipped between her teeth on a smile, and she yanked off her boots and socks, tossing them to the dry sand behind us. With her feet together, she took in a deep breath and closed her eyes. The waves reached for her again with the kind of longing that I could feel pulsing in my own chest.

On a squeal, she jumped back, then cautiously stepped forward. Another wave followed the first, and I watched her legs jerk, as she lifted her dress and let the water pool around her. Over her shoulder, she shot me a smile–one so fucking beautiful, I wanted to frame it. Capture it. Study the alchemy of it. How wonderfully intoxicating one simple expression could be.

Emboldened, she skittered forward, letting the next wave pool above her ankles. A little more, and the next one pooled at her calves. I watched in awe as she let the sea seduce her, tickle her into a giggling young girl, dancing, hopping, and tumbling in the waves. It was there that my failures and her worries were swept away, cleansed by the salt and air and the sounds of calm that reverberated off the surrounding rock walls.

It was there that I began to wonder if what I felt for Lilia was something more than I cared to admit.

I dared not slip into those thoughts, though, because I knew fate and the world didn't give so freely. It lured us on a siren's call and pulled us to the inevitable depths of pain that followed.

Lilia was a liability. A weakness. The one crack in my armor that threatened to crumble my defenses. I couldn't afford that. Not when The Rooks were watching so closely, waiting for the news of my latest variant.

Yet, the radiance she gave off was fucking addicting. A warmth that reminded me how cold death could be sometimes.

She jumped and stumbled in the waves, trying to lift her foot from the water. After an unsuccessful examination, she hobbled back across the sand with her toes stuck upward, red trailing after her foot. "Think I cut myself on a shell," she said, grimacing. “Damn it.” When she finally plopped down beside her discarded socks and shoes, I took hold of her foot and examined the small cut just below her toe.

“I’ve got something to clean it up. Hang tight.” I strode back up the staircase to my car, and from the glovebox, I pulled a small emergency kit I kept stored there.

An intense pain struck my skull at both sides.

Fuck!

Hands clutched at either side of my head, I screwed my eyes shut on the intense ringing that sliced across my eardrums like hot blades, and fell to the pavement. The agony radiated outward, down my neck, into my arms, where it electrified my bones. As a searing heat struck my spine, I arched and grunted, feeling the attack crawl down into my legs, like my whole body was crystalizing inside. There was nothing I could do. Every muscle had locked itself into paralysis. Inside my coat pocket in the backseat hid the last dose of toxin, but hell if I could get to it. A stabbing pain pierced my chest, and I rolled onto my back, staring up at the birds–ravens–circling overhead.

An omen of death.

This is it.

Impervious. Impervious!

An invisible fist clamped over my lungs, banishing the air on an excruciating gasp.

Fucking figured that just as I’d begin to feel something through this numb existence, fate would tear it away from me like a jealous lover.

I closed my eyes and let the blackness take me under.

Chapter 57

Lilia

Another glance back at the staircase, and I frowned. No way it should've taken that long. The guy was too much of a neat freak to have to rummage through a car for ten minutes. Or maybe it just felt like ten. Either way, I wasn't sitting around any longer.

I tied my boots, after having stuffed my bloody foot into my white sock, and hobbled my way back up the staircase. It mostly just stung, anyway. Not like I needed surgery on the thing.

When I reached the top of the stairs, I nearly fell backward on seeing Devryck next to his car.

His body twitched and convulsed, and ignoring my foot, I darted toward him. A sharp sting streaked through my knees as I skidded across to him.

"Devryck! Devryck!" Like last time, I turned him on his side and looked around for something to place under his head.

Jumping to my feet, I noticed his coat lying in the back-seat, and I snatched it up. As I attempted to crumple it, I felt a hard object inside, and rummaged through the pocket.

A syringe filled with the purple substance.

Breaths heaving, I stared at it in my hands and looked at him, unconscious and seizing.

I could've called emergency, but they might not have gotten there in time.

"Fuck!" I took hold of his trembling arm, studying the map of veins sticking up. "Fucking drug addicts do this shit, Lilia. Just give it to him!"

Using the sleeve of his coat, I tied the fabric around his arm like a pathetic tourniquet. An emergency kit lay scattered over the passenger seat, and I rifled through it for an alcohol swab. With trembling hands, I swallowed back the thought that I was too late. That he'd been seizing too long. That his heart may have long since clocked out.

Panic goaded me as I tore open the alcohol packet and scrubbed it over a vein in his forearm. Breathing hard through my nose, I popped the cap of the syringe and lined the needle to his pulsing vessel, the tip of it bouncing with both of our shaking. I closed my eyes and took a deep breath. *Please.*

Through a mist of tears, I pushed the needle, praying I hit the spot, and dispensed the fluid into his arm, as I'd watched him do that night in his office. Seconds ticked by, his body still wracked with tremors.

"C'mon, Devryck, please. Please!" I ran my hand over his damp hairline and choked back a sob. "You can't leave. I won't let you. You hear me? I won't let you fucking die. You are my most important thing, and I swear, if you don't come out of this, I will fucking hunt you down in the afterlife." More seconds. "Wake up, Devryck!" I scrambled for my phone, tucked inside my bag that I'd left in the car, but by the time I returned to his side, he'd stopped shaking.

A cold hollow expanded inside my chest as I stared down at him lying so still on the ground. *No.* "Devryck, wake up. Please."

He didn't move. His chest didn't move. Eyes didn't flutter. There was nothing but a sickening stillness that tore at my ribs.

Dread stirred in my gut. It slithered up into my chest and wrapped its cold fingers around my heart, squeezing until I couldn't breathe. I shook my head, falling beside him once more. "No. *No*!" I punched his chest.

His lips parted for a loud gasp of breath. Another gasp. And another. Eyes still closed, he rolled his head to the side, and on a terrified wheeze of relief, I zeroed in on his chest, clocking each rise and fall that told me he was breathing. It was then I noticed the sweat sticking to his face and neck.

With the inner part of my wrist, I felt his forehead and cheek. "Oh, God, you're burning up."

I needed to get him somewhere I could administer some water and something to bring down his fever. My dorm certainly wasn't an option, and I'd never been to his staff apartment on campus. The hospital maybe, but what if they did a blood test and found the toxin? Could he have gotten in trouble for that?

He let out a quiet grunt, but when I lifted his eyelid, his eyes remained staring, pupils constricted. Unconscious.

I shoved my arms under his armpits and lifted his upper half. The guy was so bulky and heavy, I could hardly manage, but after a few deep breaths, I strained my muscles and turned him just enough to pull him into the backseat of his car. Awkwardly fumbling to heft him onto the seat, I heaved out of breath with the toil, and shifted his legs over the seat to close him in.

It'd been a few years since I'd driven a car, and as I slid into the driver's seat, anxiety coiled itself around my nerves. I fired up the engine and drove back toward Emberwick, which we'd passed on the way. In the backseat, Devryck groaned and grunted, and when I peeked in the rearview, I caught the shine of sweat thick on his body. Minutes later, I finally reached the downtown area and pulled into a spot in front of the apothecary I'd visited weeks back. Leaving him in the car with the windows cracked, I jumped out and dashed into the shop, where the older woman who'd helped me before greeted me with a smile.

The smile faded as she seemed to catch on that something was wrong.

"I need help! My ... my ... professor. He's got a fever. He's burning up pretty bad."

"Oh, my!" She shuffled around the shop, grabbing various things from the shelves. My mind was so wired and wound around Devryck's condition, I didn't even notice what she'd grabbed. The two of us dashed out into the parking lot, and she opened the door, sliding into the narrow space between him and the front seats.

"Oh, he is very warm. Very warm."

I waited outside the car, pacing, biting my nails. I'd always put a lot of faith into holistic medicine, but what if it didn't work? What if the toxins screwed with the healing properties of the herbs?

She dragged a cool cloth over his brow and left it there, before crawling her way back out of the vehicle. "I'm going to make him some iced black rock tea. It sometimes helped bring my son's fever down. Just cool him with the cloth. I'll be right back."

With a tearful nod, I slid between the seats, as she had, noticing that she'd unbuttoned his shirt and rested his head on his crumpled coat. It took me back to the day in his office, when he'd yelled at me for using it. The thought somehow managed to break through my fear, and I chuckled.

"If you don't come out of this, I'm burning all of your expensive coats."

"You're not ... burning ... my coats," he mumbled, and a wheeze of elation shook my muscles.

"Devryck? Open your eyes. I need to see that you're okay."

He squinted and grimaced, as he shifted on the seat, but

he opened his lids to show those beautiful, fiery eyes. Though his pupils were blown, he seemed to have awareness. Lucidity.

I brushed the hair from his damp forehead and shuddered out a panicked breath. "You scared the shit out of me. What the hell happened back there?"

"The ... toxin ... stopped working."

Disappointment loomed like a dark cloud between us. "Why? I thought you figured out how to make it sustainable?"

"I ... was wrong."

"I administered the dose in your coat. Are you mad?"

"Mad ... that you ... saved my life?"

A frustrated chuckle escaped me. I didn't want to laugh, damn it. That whole scenario still had me shaking.

"Here," the woman said, as she passed me a tall glass of black liquid whose surface sparkled as if there were diamonds in it. "Have him drink some of this."

"What is it?" Devryck asked, his voice delirious.

"It doesn't matter. You're drinking it whether you like it, or not. I saved your life, therefore you have to listen to what I tell you."

"Fuck. You're going to ... hold this over me. Aren't you?"

"For as long as necessary. Now, drink." Steadying his arm, I helped him as much as I could, as he scooted himself to a sitting position.

He frowned, as if still in pain, and the sweat still clung to his chest and neck. With an unamused expression, he took the drink from me and sipped it. With a slight raise of his glass, he nodded at the woman. "Thank you."

"I'll be back to check on you in a minute, okay?"

"Oh! What's your name?" I asked, before she walked off.

"Francesca."

The sound of that name rippled across my heart, and I wondered if she'd been the one to inspire my mother's alias. "I'm Lilia. Thank you."

With a wink, she hustled into the store, and I turned back to Professor Bramwell.

"So, what ... you can't feel anymore? Is that why you've avoided touching me today?"

Brows lowered, he stared down at his drink. "Perhaps the most vindictive torment was having a brief moment of knowing what you felt like."

"So, what does this mean?"

"Back to the drawing board." On a sigh, he took another sip, longer than the last, and handed me the glass. "Not a fan of tea. Not even your disturbing gothic variety."

Through an uneasy smile, I accepted the glass and stared down at the sparkling fluids. "It's black rock. And it's apparently very hard to come by, so I'm not letting this go to waste." I chugged the rest of it, which wasn't a whole lot, and wiped my mouth on the back of my hand. Another failure meant that he was at risk again. That he might've died in my arms back at that cove. I didn't even want to think about what might've happened back there. "I think it's pretty good, actually." Pushing away those somber thoughts, because goddamn it, he'd be fine, I smiled. "How does it feel to know I just swallowed your spit?" I asked and forced a chuckle, desperate for distraction.

"You've swallowed worse." He groaned and pushed himself forward, toward the passenger door. "Let's get out of here before she brings more of that shit."

"Be nice. She's the reason you're not having a febrile seizure right now."

"The toxin is the reason. But I suspect this dose won't last more than a couple days. The seizures will get worse. So, I should get back to the lab."

I scrambled out of the backseat, allowing him to stand up alongside the car, and when he did, he tottered to the side a step. "Maybe I should drive?"

"Maybe not. I just need a minute."

"I'm going to thank Francesca again and let her know you're okay. You're sure you're okay to drive?"

"I'm fine."

"Okay, be right back." I jogged back into the shop, where Francesca greeted me with a smile, and as I handed off the empty glass, she held up a bag for me. "A bit more black rock tea."

"Oh, no. I can't. You've given me so much already."

"Please. In case his fever returns." As she handed it off to me, she clutched my hand in hers. "He's a Bramwell."

"Yes." I hesitated to admit it, though, already suspicious of her opinions.

"They've lived on this island a number of years. Just be careful, dear."

I offered a smile, in spite of the urge to tell her that what she'd heard about Devryck was nothing but gossip. "I will."

"Take care."

When I exited the store, Bramwell was already in the driver's seat, the car revving as he teased me to hurry up. I slid into the passenger side, and he took off back toward the university.

"I have to leave on business for a couple of days," he said, glancing over at me.

"Oh. Okay." Man, today turned out to be a roller coaster, what with Gilchrist's visit and what'd happened at the beach. Now the disappointment of him leaving.

"Have you registered for next semester?"

I'd gotten the email from Langmore, but hadn't taken the time to do that yet. "No, not yet. I will."

"Good. I'm going to pre-approve you for the second semester neuroparasitology. And my gross anatomy lab."

"I thought that was reserved for med students," I countered.

"It is. But I'm the professor. I can add whoever the hell I want, if I think they're smart enough to keep up. So, make sure to add that one."

A smile teased my lips. "What if I don't want to take it?"

"You'll take it whether you want it, or not." He gripped my thigh and quickly recoiled, jerking the car with his movement. Frowning, he held up his hand, twisting it around as if it were something foreign in front of him.

"What's wrong?"

"My sense of feeling's returned."

I glanced at his hand and back. "That's fantastic."

"That's impossible." He pulled the car over, off the main road, and down some obscure little side street. As the car skidded to a stop, he depressed the lighter. When it popped, he held the heated end of it near his skin, and his frown deepened. "It's reversed."

"The toxin is working, then?"

"I don't think so." He flexed his hand and curled it into a fist. "I was still numb after the injection."

Puzzled, I shook my head. "Then, how?"

"What did she give me back at the apothecary?"

"I didn't see everything, just kali phos, I think. And elderflower. And the tea, of course." I tugged the small satchel she'd gifted from my bag and handed it to him.

He snatched it out of my hands and held it up to the light, where the sparkling surface glinted through the bag. "Lilia ... this might be what's been missing. This might be what can sustain the toxin."

"I mean ... it would make sense, right? The birds that don't get infected. The ... the ... the ... natives who used the black stones as teeth." I gestured toward my own, noticing the tremble from excitement running through me.

"I have to test it. To make sure it doesn't degrade the toxin, at all. But you might've just figured out a brilliant complement."

"Well, technically, I didn't–" Before I could finish, he dragged my face to his, crushing my lips with a kiss.

"Get over here," he said, pushing the seat back to a lying position. "Get the fuck over here." The rough and needy tone of his voice mirrored the need pulsing through me. After the stress of earlier, I'd had a rush of pure adrenaline pumping through me. The prospect of burning it off enticed me enough to move without thinking too much about how the hell we were going to do so in his car.

I climbed over the console and straddled his knees in the cramped seat, the steering wheel pressed against my back, as he hustled to unbuckle his pants.

With hasty hands, he sprang himself free and hiked up my dress. "The condom," he said, staring up at me. The dangerous turbulence in his eyes sent my heart in a frenzy. He looked at me as though he were fantasizing his baby in me, then quickly blinked out of it.

Groaning, he lifted his hips just enough to nudge me upward. He stuffed his hands down into his shrugged pants pocket, and after tearing it out of the package, he smoothed the condom over his jutting shaft.

I only just pulled my panties aside, before he took hold of my hips and brought me down over his groin. Already wet, I sank onto him with ease, biting my lower lip as his cock filled and stretched me.

"Fuuuuck!" He tipped his head back, eyes lost to ecstasy.

Hand to my nape, he dragged me in for a kiss and pressed our foreheads together.

My hand shot out against the window, fingers scratching at the glass, desperate to clutch something. To tear and scratch and claw. My hands longed to destroy, the way he destroyed me from the inside, turning me ravenous and greedy for him.

"You're the fever in my veins," he said through clenched teeth, as he drove into me with furious determination. "An incurable madness I can't shake. Fucking you is the only thing that keeps me sane, Lilia." He fused our lips together, stealing my breath, and when he broke away, his hand moved to my throat, squeezing just enough to part my lips and trap the next breath. A dizzying euphoria swept over me, and my body jostled as he tore the bust of my dress down, exposing my breasts so they bounced and jiggled with every decimating thrust. "This pussy is all I think about. All I crave. You've infected every part of me, and I can't stop. I can't stop this obsession."

The lack of air, his words, and the feel of his cock filling me had my head in chaos, my body in a state of paralysis. He squeezed tighter and a mewling sound spilled from my lips.

"No. No quiet sounds from you. I want to hear you fucking scream. You're in the throes of fire now, Little Moth. Show me how much it burns." He loosened his hold just enough that I let out a hoarse and throaty moan.

I gripped the seat behind him and rode him hard, relishing the pained look of ecstasy on his face when he tipped his head back, jaw tight, veins popping from his neck.

"Ahhh, fuck!" His fingers dug into my hips, as I upped the pace, the wet sounds a testament to how hot the man made me.

"I want to feel you come all over my cock." he rasped.

The car jerked and bounced with his aggressive thrusts.

My moans escalated as a hot, coiling pleasure surged through me.

I clenched my eyes, but opened them at a grip of my nape.

"Eyes on me. I want to watch you come."

A bolt of lightning struck my muscles, pulling them to a wire of tension, and his name reverberated inside my skull as I screamed it over and over.

He crushed his lips against mine and bit my lower lip as he pulled away. "You are a merciless vision of perfection."

His hips shifted below, urging me up, and he lifted the hem of my dress as he pulled out of me and slid off the condom, tossing it into a trash receptacle beside him. While I settled back on his thighs, he continued to thrash his cock, and seconds later, hot jets painted my thighs, as he directed his release across my flesh.

With his lip caught between his teeth, brows pulled tight, neck shimmering with the sweat of his rough and overworked body, he grunted, watching himself come all over me. As if he was marking me. Making me as his.

The sight of it made my womb clench.

He pulled me on top of him, holding me there, and I rested my head against his marble chest, hearing his heart beat a wild cadence. Such a beautiful sound after what had happened earlier. "We probably shouldn't have done this here. Out in the open."

I smiled, my cheek still pressed to his warm skin. Although I hadn't seen another car, or house, in sight when he'd pulled off, he was probably right. We needed to be more careful, though admittedly, that had been part of the thrill for me. My hair lay plastered to my damp skin, the windows fogged with our intense fucking. "Devryck," I said breathlessly, every muscle spent and liquefied. "I'm scared."

"Of what?"

"This is beginning to feel like more than just sex for me."

"So, why does this scare you?"

"Because I can't see past the void, and it feels like this is when things fall apart." The sting in my eyes was an irritating nuisance. I didn't want to cry in front of him. Not after this. My emotions felt like livewires bouncing on hot sparks. "If you ditch me now, if you cast me aside–"

"Hey." Fingers tangled into a tight grip at my crown, and

he pulled my head back, staring down at me. "You don't have to be scared. I will never hurt you, Lilia. In fact, I'll rain hell on anyone who ever hurts you again."

I loved him. Every cell, every fiber of my being couldn't hide that truth. Even if I wasn't bold enough to say it or brave enough to risk the universe stealing it away from me, the words were as real as my fears.

The words I kept secret like all my other trinkets–safely tucked away.

Chapter 58

Lilia

"Access denied?" Frowning, I eased back in my desk chair, then clicked the button on my laptop to login for registration a third time.

The same error message returned. What the hell was going on?

"Trouble?" a voice said from the doorway, and I turned to find Mel leaning against the frame with her arms crossed. While Gilchrist had promised not to rat me out, I still felt a sense of guilt from having given up her name.

"Just trying to register for next semester."

"And there's a problem?"

I froze, staring back at her, studying the amused expression on her face. "Is there?"

"Perhaps Daddy didn't like getting called out."

"What do you mean?"

"Lilia Lippincott. Has a catchy ring to it."

A sickening realization crawled over me, and it was then I knew exactly what Gilchrist had done. She'd traded one scandal for another. Muscles strained for the poker face I held in place, I refused to confirm something that hadn't actually been confirmed for me, either. It was speculation. Rumor. I didn't have a blood test to prove anything.

"I don't know why I thought I could trust you. Covington trash."

"What did you do?"

"My blog has never been so popular as it is now. Over four thousand hits in a matter of two hours. And next week's scandal is going to be an absolutely delicious follow-up. *Provost's alleged daughter fucking Doctor Death.*"

"I don't know what you're talking about," I lied.

She rolled her eyes, and when she yanked her phone from her pocket, my knees nearly buckled. The photo showed Bramwell's car, windows steamed up and my hand pressed against the glass. No faces, though.

"I don't know what you're talking about," I said again without so much as a twitch.

Groaning, she zoomed in on my hand, and just below it, I could make out my *Momento Mori* tattoo on my forearm. "Nobody else on campus drives a black Maserati Ghibli."

The idea that she'd spied on us, that she'd gone so far as to take pictures for a fucking scandal, had my stomach twisted up in knots. I'd always joked that Covington was home to the worst souls, but here, they were a different breed. A scheming, manipulative genre of human beings. "Why?"

"Seriously? You rat me out, and you're asking why?"

"She was withholding information on everything. My father. My mother!"

"Oh, boo-fucking-hoo." The way she mocked me sent an itch to my palm–the longing to haul off and smack her tempting my restraint. "You tried to get me kicked out. Lucky for me, Lady Gilchrist was willing to strike a deal."

"Yeah. She struck a deal with me, too." I sneered. "Good luck with that."

"You're pathetic, you know that? You have no sense of self-preservation. It's fitting, though. You and Spencer as siblings. A whole pathetic family."

Except that Spencer had told me that Lippincott wasn't his father. Not that I planned to divulge that information to the gossip-mongering bitch. "Fuck you. Get out of my room."

"Seems it won't be your room for long," she said, and she slinked away like the snake she was, offering some reprieve from the smug grin plastered to her face.

Spencer.

For reasons I couldn't explain, I wanted to talk to him right then. I snatched up my phone and dialed his number. It rang and rang, and when it went to voicemail, I hung up and dialed again. Every nerve in my body quaked as I waited for the voicemail to kick in, Dean Langmore appeared at my door, flanked by two security guards in uniform.

Confused, I lowered the phone, trying to imagine why they'd be at my dorm.

Langmore adjusted his spectacles and crossed his arms in front of his body. "Miss Vespertine? I'll ask that you pack your things immediately."

The lingering stares of passing students had my cheeks burning, while my body jittered into a shocking tremble.

"I'm sorry?" I asked, my voice wobbling with his disorienting command.

"Please pack your things. You will be escorted to the ferry immediately."

Escorted out? Out of Dracadia? "I'm ... you're expelling me?"

"Yes, Miss Vespertine."

"Can I ask why?"

Langmore slid his glasses off and pinched the bridge of his nose. "Please don't make this difficult. Your ferry and train expenses will be paid, so no need to worry about that."

Worry about *that*? That was the least of my worries right then. I glanced around the room, not knowing where to start. I'd made this room my home. My safe place. Where did one begin with folding it up and packing it away? Tears wobbled in my eyes as I pulled my suitcase down from the shelf and began with my clothes, folding them neatly. I then packed my books, pictures, trinkets, and the shell Devryck had given me.

I wanted to call him so badly, and while I had his phone number, I feared contacting him, particularly while he was away on business. Who knew how this would all shake down, and the only thing that would've made me feel worse was the school finding out about us and bastardizing our relationship. Punishing him for it. We'd avoided all communications over the phone, absolutely no paper trail with email, but right then, I wished I could've texted him. If for no other reason than to say goodbye.

Once everything was fitted into my suitcase, I stood in the center of the room, tears blurring my vision.

Langmore's expression held remorse, at least. He didn't wear the same smug grin that Mel had. And at least he'd offered me a small bit of dignity when he called off the security guards.

As much as I wanted to, I couldn't call Jayda. I refused to put my problem on her with the new baby. I had no choice. Grim as it might've been, I'd be forced to return to the apartment.

Langmore led me down the corridor, which suddenly felt like a walk of shame, the way everyone stared at me. When we passed Mel's room, I didn't even bother to look at her. Could my expulsion have been a reaction to her blog? Had Lippincott gotten wind of it, somehow?

The sound of her snorted laugh as I passed grated on my nerves, and something inside of me snapped.

On a capricious twist, I dropped my bag and suitcase and slammed my fist into her cheek. A scream tore out of her, as she stumbled backward into the wall.

"Miss Vespertine!" Langmore wrangled my arm, as I drew back for another punch. "Let's not make a spectacle!"

Adrenaline pounded through my veins, as I breathed hard through my nose and took in the aftermath of what I'd done, where Mel lay slumped against the wall, blood already trickling out of her nose. Tears welled in my eyes, as I gathered my things, and we made our way to the elevator and down to the first floor.

In silence, he drove me to the ferry dock, and as we stood in the cold boathouse, waiting for my ride, he cleared his throat. "I didn't want this. Just so you know, Miss Vespertine. I am incredibly sorry."

Tears spilled down my cheeks.

I didn't want this, either.

But wasn't that the way of happiness? Perhaps the reason there was always a black void on the horizon. Because I was doomed for loneliness.

The train arrived at the abandoned station where I'd first set off for Dracadia, and as it chugged to a stop, I stared out the window to see the Uber driver I'd called. Thankfully, I still had cash left over from the money Devryck had given me. By the time I finally arrived back at the apartment, I was exhausted, both emotionally and physically. My phone had died halfway between the train station and the apartment, making the ride with the Uber driver a bit harrowing.

A sickly dread churned in my stomach as I climbed the staircase to the apartment. When I reached the door, Conner opened it, wearing a look of sympathy.

"Hey, kid," he said, grabbing my suitcase for me.

My eyes wandered cautiously for Angelo—the only thing that could make the unwanted homecoming worse.

A horrible smell assaulted my nose, and as we passed the kitchen, I noticed a pile of dishes in the sink, discarded food containers and beer cans littering the table and floor.

"Don't .... Don't worry about all that. I'm gonna clean up. I just got home from work not too long ago."

I didn't say anything, as he led me down the hallway toward my bedroom. My gaze shifted to the right of him, toward the darkened hallway, and he glanced over his shoulder and back.

"Still ain't found a roommate. Callaghan decided to keep her own place. I don't want you to worry about anything, though. I'll take care of shit until you find some work, okay? Just, uh ... get yourself settled again." He opened the door to the old bedroom, and for the most part, it looked to be the same, like nothing had been touched, thankfully. Just emptier, since most of my stuff was still packed in the suitcase, but clean.

I didn't even have the energy to unpack, as I zombie-walked toward the bed. *The* bed. Not mine. Nothing in the apartment felt like mine anymore. I felt like I'd slipped into a stranger's world, trying to find comfort in a place that had become foreign to me. Dracadia was my comfort. My home. Not this. Not here.

"Good to see you again, Lil," Conner said, and the click of the door signaled his exit.

With his retreating footsteps, I curled up on my bed and finally broke.

Chapter 59

Devryck

Two hours earlier…

Addicts stumbled about as I prowled slowly through the streets of downtown Thresher Bay, along a strip known as Meth Mile. Makeshift tents lined the sidewalk, where the homeless shot up drugs and prostitution was rampant. Eyes scanning, I searched for my next test subject.

Back at the lab, I'd administered the black tea to both Patroclus and Achilles, and watched as both moths, who'd previously returned to their paralyzed state, took flight again. Now that I had a method of sustaining the toxin's effects, it was time for a new test subject. To harvest fresh toxin with my most recent larvae, and attempt to produce a synthetic version, bypassing the need for human harvesting. I just needed a bit more of it.

A brunette stood at the corner of Gratis and Vine Road, wearing a short black mini dress with high heels and a coat. It wasn't her choice of attire that told me she was a prostitute, but the way she immediately sauntered over and leaned into the passenger window of my car, when I pulled up to the curb.

"Hello, handsome. Please tell me you're looking for some company."

I couldn't bring myself to look at her and kept my gaze locked forward, staring through the windshield at the hundreds of others I could've chosen. It wasn't personal. I'd only opted for her over a drug addict because I didn't care to drag around a half-conscious body. "I am," I lied.

"Well, all right, then." The door swung open, and she slid into the passenger seat smelling like rose perfume. Fuck, I hated that scent.

"Are you willing to go outside of the city?"

"Depends on how much cash you got, honey."

I lifted a folded stack of bills. Three thousand dollars that she'd never get the opportunity to spend if she said yes.

"I'm willing to go wherever you want, baby. For that much? You can *do* whatever the fuck you want."

Surely, that wouldn't have included infecting her with parasites.

As she buckled herself in, I stowed away the cash in my pocket and took off down the road. On a bold move, she reached over, brushing her fingers across my groin, and I lifted her arm to set it back in her lap.

"Not while I'm driving."

"You don't like road head?"

I did. But only when a certain redheaded pain in my ass was giving it to me. "Not particularly," I answered. I planned to get her on Dracadia Island, then once we reached the cadaver entrance, I'd anesthetize her and infect her with the larvae.

"Fine with me. You let me know what you want, handsome."

I wanted to laugh at that, but an uncharacteristic guilt tore at my conscience. To some extent, killing had become natural to me. Biological. Maybe even genetic and, dared I say, fascinating to observe. Except for the fact that, unlike the others, she hadn't done anything to deserve my cruelty. She was innocent, and because of that, I took no joy in the thought of killing her.

I didn't have time to shop around for my next subject, though. There was a small window of opportunity before the new batch of eggs would hatch, and with the information I'd received about Angelo DeLuca, I might've never tracked the asshole down.

When we reached the ferry launch, she sat up in the seat, looking around. It somehow reminded me of the day I'd taken Lilia to the old mansion. The innocence and curiosity.

"We goin' on a boat ride?"

"Yes. You said you're willing to go out of the city, correct?"

Her brows winged up, and she looked back toward the dark sea. "You talkin' about the island?"

"Yes. I'm a professor there."

"Are you now?" Whatever small bit of apprehension she might've had a moment ago faded for a wily grin. "Well, hot damn, tonight is my lucky night!"

Hardly.

In the distance, the ferry boat approached, and I ran my hand through my hair and down my face. I couldn't do it. I couldn't fucking do it, because all I could think about, all that mattered to me, was the girl. The beautiful girl with her autumn hair, and eyes that reminded me of both the sea and the sky. And she was everything. The earth, the sun, the moon. The air I breathed, and the tenacious beat that kept my eroded heart pumping.

What I felt for Lilia wasn't healthy. Beyond simple obsession, it was a sickening possession. Savage and rapacious, bordering on violence.

Just as I was about to order the woman out of my car, my phone buzzed in my pocket, and I pulled it out to see Langmore's number flashing across the screen. The only time I received personal calls was when the asshole was about to do something I didn't approve of.

"Excuse me," I said, stepping out of the vehicle. Once the door was closed, I answered, "Hello."

"Devryck, it's Lang–"

"Yeah. I know."

"I'm calling because .... Well, I tried to call you in your offices, but there was no answer."

The passing seconds chipped away at my patience. "I'm busy."

"Right. I suspect you're going to be quite angry, and ... I want you to know I had nothing to do with this." The shaky quality of his voice immediately put me on alert.

"Nothing to do with what?"

"Lilia Vespertine was expelled. I don't entirely know the reason behind it, but I received an order from Lippincott to have her leave the premises immediately. And seeing as you were quite adamant about her remaining enrolled in your class, I thought I should make you aware."

I gnashed my molars, doing my best to reel in the urge to pound my fist through something. To hell with trying to keep the thing I had with Lilia under wraps. I couldn't give a fuck at that point. "And she was sent where?"

"Back to her home in Covington."

"I want the address."

He let out a huff. "I find that highly inappropriate, Dev–"

The anger exploded out of me. "Address! Now!"

"Very well. I'll text you her address. Again, please know I had nothing to do with this."

Through deep breaths, I clutched a small bit of control and tempered my voice. "I appreciate your call. I'll consider this kindness when I return," I said through clenched teeth. "Tell no one that we spoke, or by God, I will make you regret it."

"You have my word."

I hung up the call, and as the rage tore through me, I pounded my fist into the hood of the car. Exhaling a breath, I slid back into the driver's seat. "Change of plans." I reached into my coat pocket and pulled the stack of bills, handing off five hundred. "For your trouble."

"You're canceling? Why?"

"Please just get out."

"I said I'm fine going–"

"Get the fuck out!" I barked, and snapped my attention away from her. "Please."

"Fine. I'll get the fuck out. Asshole." She tucked the hundreds away in her shirt. "You change your mind, you know where to find me."

The moment she exited the car, I fired up the engine. My phone buzzed with a text–Lilia's address. When I punched it into the car's GPS, it showed some theater on Prather Street. "If you gave me the wrong fucking address, you're a dead man," I muttered, and I threw the car in drive.

Hands shaking with rage, I dialed Lilia's phone number.

Straight to voicemail.

"Fuck!" I growled and dialed again.

Still, the call failed to connect.

I tried three more times, each unsuccessful attempt only raising my blood pressure. After tossing the phone onto the passenger seat beside me, I flexed my hand to a tight fist and breathed on counts of four, a half-assed attempt to calm the rage brewing in my gut. The last thing Lilia needed, after the shit day she'd undoubtedly had, was for me to show up ready to kill something.

Chapter 60

Lilia

At a soft knock on the door, I opened my eyes that were sticky with dried tears. Darkness blanketed the room, save for the soft glow of Christmas lights around my window.

"Lil?" Conner peeked his head inside the door. "I'm gonna go up to Callahan's. She's got–"

"Conner, I know you two have something going on, okay? It's fine."

His lips flattened, and he rubbed the back of his neck. "Was just .... I didn't know if it was too soon after your mom."

"It's been four years. It's fine."

"Okay. You need anything?"

"I don't think so. You're not ... planning to have Angelo over anytime soon, are you?"

"Nah. I ain't seen much of him, at all. The guy is so fucked in the head after he heard what happened to that rich prick."

"What happened to him?" Part of me didn't want to know. While I'd always been peripherally aware of Conner and Angelo's shady dealings, I'd never dipped too much of myself into their business.

It was a shadowy world I'd kept on the fringes. One that scared me.

Not that I had much choice, anyway, the way Conner was so secretive about it.

"Had his eyes gouged. Dick cut off. All of his guts were stretched out on the floor around him. Whoever did that was one sick bastard."

"You told me the guy he killed was some kind of sadist. Not a saint."

"Right. I'm sure he did worse. Anyway, I haven't talked to Angelo in about two weeks."

A small relief after the shitstorm I just went through. "I'm just gonna sleep. Tomorrow, I'll go out and see if I can find a job." The last thing I intended to do was stick around in the apartment all day, lamenting in my bedroom.

"Okay. But again, I got you for a couple weeks, okay? You don't have to rush into something. I still feel like shit for Bee's tuition." As he should have, but I kept that to myself. "How'd you get them to let her stay?"

"Just figured things out. She's good for a couple months."

"Cool. All right. You get some sleep."

With a nod, I rolled back over in bed, staring out at the night sky. I touched the screen of my cellphone, and when it remained black, I shot up in bed. Following the trail to the end of the cord showed that I hadn't bothered to plug it into the wall to charge earlier. "Damn it!" A low battery light lit up the screen when I shoved the cord into the socket. I fell back onto my pillow, sighing.

Devryck having left on business meant not even he would've been looking for me just yet. But when he returned, what would he think?

My mind drifted back to the day on the beach, when he'd taken me for my first dip in the ocean. The drive in his car along winding roads. The moments we stole away. The kisses. His touch. Would I ever see him again? Or would he one day fade into the perfect dream?

I reached over the edge of my bed, and from my suitcase, I pulled out my mother's painting of the swing and the ocean. Through a mist of tears, I stared at the view I'd hoped to one day make a reality for me and Bee. Even as brief as my visit at the house had been, it felt like home. My true home.

I held the painting to my chest, and as the tears slipped down my cheek, my finger dragged over a lifted corner of the canvas's backing, where I must've shoved it too hastily in my suitcase. I ran the frayed edge through my finger and caught sight of something behind it. Stuffing my pinky into the small gap, I felt something inside. I tugged at the backing's loose corner, popping it free from the staples, and once peeled back enough, I found a folded paper had been secured to the inner part of the canvas.

What the hell?

I unfolded the paper to find a letter.

Signed by my mother.

Two weeks before she'd died.

My Sweet Lilia,

If you're reading this, I either forgot about it, in which case, I suspect we'll be having a lengthy conversation afterward. Or my illness got worse and you're looking for answers. Either way, I suppose it was meant to be.

I've spent hours, days, deciding how to go about telling you things I've kept to myself for a number of years. Important things. As my illness seems to be progressing, I feel compelled to leave something behind, and it wouldn't be fair to carry all my secrets with me.

I'll preface this by saying that no one in this world is more important to me than you and your sister. Every decision I made, I did out of love for the two of you.

That said, I've lied to you, my love, and I hope you can find it in your heart to forgive me.

While you've always known me as Francesca Vespertine, my real name is Vanessa Corbin. I was born on a small island off the coast of Maine called Dracadia, where generations of our family have lived. In fact, we are descendants of the first colonists. Which would've probably been a cool conversation to have, if my past weren't so riddled with dysfunction.

A year before you were born, I met a charming doctor who convinced me to join a study at the university to help cure my diabetes. We fell in love, but he was married at the time, so things were a bit complicated. Particularly when I got pregnant with you, and he asked that I terminate the pregnancy. The mere suggestion of such a thing tore at my heart, and I refused—a decision that angered both him and my father.

Your father threatened that if I decided to go through with the pregnancy, he would ensure that I'd never get custody of you.

I was young and stupid and scared. So I fled with nothing more than the clothes on my back and cash in my purse. And the longer I stayed away, the easier it was to stay away, because having to explain nearly two decades of avoidance just seemed harder. The lies to protect you had snowballed out of control.

Then about two weeks ago, I went home for my mother's funeral. I know you thought I was looking into surgery for Bee, but telling you the truth at the time was complicated. Again, forgive me. I only wanted to see my mother one more time and perhaps find a way to secure the home that I grew up in, a place where you, me, and Bee could live freely. Unfortunately, the house had gone into foreclosure and it turned out the new owner was your father.

I should've walked away. I wish I had. I was foolish to

think the years had made him wiser. Had changed him in any way. I was wrong.

He doesn't know about you. I lied and told him that I'd suffered a miscarriage and lost the pregnancy. Not because I didn't want you to have a relationship with your father, but because he's a dangerous man who can't be trusted. I lied to protect you, Lilia.

Therefore, I won't give you his name. While I suspect you're smart enough to put pieces together based on what I have told you, I'm urging you to set aside your anger for me and stay away from him. Believe me, you're better off without him.

In the event that I do not get well, do not seek him out for anything. You'll get through things. You always do.

I love you and Bee very much. Infinitely. And I'm so proud of you, my sweet girl.

Love Forever,

Mom

Tears slipped down my cheeks, which I quickly wiped away as I frowned down at the letter. I suspected it was Lippincott she was referring to, even if she'd refused to say. She must've met with him about the house—the timing of it all precisely just before she'd gotten sick. Could he have been the one to infect her?

The sound of a hard thump somewhere in the apartment interrupted my thoughts. Muscles steeled, I glanced back toward the door, and after slipping the note and painting back into my suitcase, I tiptoed toward it, pressing my ear to the wooden panel.

Had Conner returned?

Cracking the door, I stepped out into the hallway for a better listen. "Conner? Is that you?"

No answer.

Another hard *thunk*, and I jerked.

I padded halfway down the dark hallway, ears perked, and scanned the kitchen and the small living room across from it.

No sign of anyone.

Cold tendrils of fear slithered across the back of my neck, and I dashed back to my room for my phone to call Conner. I swiped the phone still charging on my nightstand—only ten percent battery—and sprinted back toward the door. When I swung it open, Angelo stood in the dark hallway, his form illuminated by the small bit of light from the kitchen.

The air stalled in my chest, and my stomach dropped.

His hair stood at cocked angles of disarray, and the beard and mustache covering his face told me he hadn't shaved in a while. Red rimmed eyes spoke of little sleep, or drugs, and he appeared thinner than the last time I'd seen him.

On a frenzied beat of my heart, I pivoted toward the front door and dashed down the hallway, in the opposite direction. Body slamming into the door with the momentum, I fumbled with the lock.

Searing pain lashed my scalp, as Angelo wrenched my hair back. "'The fuck you think you're going, bitch!" A hard slam against my hand knocked my phone loose, and it bounced out of reach.

I opened my mouth to scream, and a dirty hand palmed my face, his fingers digging into my cheeks. Scream muffled, I clawed at his hands and bit down on his thumb. Hard.

"Ahhh, you fucking cunt!" He released me, and I spun out of his grasp, standing face to face with him.

He blocked the doorway, licking the blood from his thumb.

My phone lay to the right of him.

Adrenaline coursed through me in hot pulses, while my mind scrambled for a plan.

The knife. I'd tucked my pocketknife under my pillow

earlier. And the fire escape sat right outside my window. I darted back toward my bedroom, Angelo's heavy footfalls chasing after me. The moment I entered my room, I spun around and slammed the door shut, pressing hard against the wood, and reached for the lock.

He plowed into the other side of it, kicking me back a step, and a scream shot out of me.

I pushed hard, muscles straining to close it. *C'mon!*

Even in his weakened state, he was bigger. Stronger.

Abandoning the fight, I let go and scrambled toward my bed for the knife. The door flew open, and Angelo crashed through on a curse.

I held out the knife between us with a trembling hand. "Leave me the fuck alone," I said on a shaky voice.

"Lily Cat ... you always were a little fighter, weren't you?" Licking his lips, he stepped closer, and from his back, presumably his waistband, he pulled a gun. "Bring a knife to a gunfight ... well, it's just stupid."

"What are you doing here, Angelo? You're gonna hurt me?"

"Yeah. Yeah, I'm gonna hurt you. I'm gonna fuck you. Hard. And I'm gonna take that knife and slit your throat, 'cause ... you know, poetic justice, and shit. Then I'm gonna cut you up in pieces so I can carry your ass out of here without anyone gettin' wise."

"How're you gonna do all that with Conner here?"

"Conner isn't here. He's been fucking that Callahan bitch every night. Got her knocked-up, did you know that? Congrats. You're gonna be ... something." He snorted a laugh and scratched the back of his grown-out hair. "Guess it's Bee who's gonna be a big sis. But no matter. You were never really a part of things, anyway, right?"

"Why? What have I ever done to make you so hostile, Angelo?"

"It's not about what you've done to me. Seems somebody at that school has it in for you."

Faces flashed through my mind. Gilchrist. Lippincott. Even Mel.

"Someone from my school put you up to this?"

"Yep. Not gonna say who, though. It's a secret," he whispered, pressing a finger to his lips and grinning.

When he lurched again, I jerked the knife.

Sighing, he narrowed his eyes on me. "I'm bored of this shit. I got a long night ahead, so what do you say we get started?"

"Angelo, don't. I know people. People who can pay you."

"You don't know the *right* people. See, power is where it's at, Lily Cat, and you ain't got that kind of pull in your corner. Taking you out means protection for me. Means I don't have to sit rotting in a fucking room waiting for death." Meaning he struck some deal with someone to kill me. The question was who? He edged toward me. "Take your clothes off."

"No." My hand still trembled as I held out the knife.

"Take. Your fucking. Clothes. Off. Or I'll blow out your kneecaps." He raised the gun, pointing the barrel of it toward my legs.

A suffocating fear filled my lungs as I stared back at him. "Don't do this," I whispered.

"You know what a bullet feels like? It burns. And when it shatters a bone? There's nothing like that pain. So, I'll give you to the count of ten, and then I'm just going to empty this fucking gun into that body. If I gotta fuck you dead, so be it. Wouldn't be the worst thing I've done." Beady eyes sharpened on me, his lips peeled back for a snarl. "*One. Two.*"

Still holding the knife, I unfastened my pants and one-handedly pushed them to the floor.

"Shirt," he said.

I shook my head.

"*Three. Four. Five.*"

Uneven breaths shook out of me, as I hooked the hem of my shirt and quickly yanked it over my head so I wouldn't get trapped in it. I crossed my arm over the lace bra I still wore.

Eyes alight with a sickening fascination, he licked his lips, staring me up and down. "Panties, too."

A sob broke in my chest as I stood paralyzed, trying to wrap my head around what was happening right then.

On a whim of adrenaline, I spun around and scrambled across my bed for my window. I only just managed to open it a crack before his palm slammed into my throat, knocking the air out of me as he took me to the floor.

A scream tore from my chest, cut short by his hand pressing hard against my mouth.

"Shut the fuck up! Shut the fuck up!"

I swiped out at him, the blade connecting with his cheek. On a shocked jerk, he touched the wound I'd made there, wiping some of the blood, and eyes wide, he stared down at it, as if in disbelief.

With my hand raised for another strike, I swung toward his throat this time.

He caught my arm before the fatal blow could land.

A growl roared out of him, and he crushed my hand against the floor, the small shocks of pain zipping over my knuckles breaking my grip of the knife. Over and over, he hammered my hand, crushing my bones. A flash in my periphery was the only warning before knuckles plowed into my cheek, vibrating my teeth. The jarring hit blurred my vision and sent a shooting ache up into my ear. The same hand that hit me clamped back over my mouth, his fingers digging into the ache he'd planted there.

I screamed behind his palm, tears distorting his form.

"I wanted you to be a little more lucid for this, but I guess it doesn't fucking matter, does it?" From somewhere below, he pulled out a small baggie with pills inside.

I thrashed my arms and legs, screaming until my voice turned hoarse, and he pressed the full weight of his body over me, pinning me down.

His hand slid from my mouth, and I clamped my lips shut. Fingers dug into my jaw, prying at my chin so hard, I felt like he was trying to crack my bones. The gurgled sound in my throat snapped short when he deposited the pills into my mouth. He forced my lips shut and pressed both hands over my mouth and nose. The air waned. Dizziness wobbled my view. Lungs punching at my ribs for a sip of air.

"Swallow it, bitch!"

A sob cracked inside my chest, and the pills slipped down my throat. I choked and gagged behind his hand, and only then did he remove the palm blocking my nose. I gasped for air and coughed again, the godawful scent of metal clogging my sinuses.

"That's it. You're about to get nice and fucking pliant in a minute. Just lay still." A slimy tongue dragged across my cheek. "Relax," he whispered.

Something inside of me snapped like a fragile twig.

Relax.

The word echoed in my ear.

In the haze of chaos inside my head, a vision appeared.

Blood. The tub. I look up to see a dark form standing over me.

Lilia! Lilia!

The sound of my mother's voice reverberated off my skull, and I flinched.

The dark figure steps over me toward the tub, where my mother's slender legs dangle over the edge.

Her leg kicks.

She's alive. Alive! I thought she was dead, but she's alive!

"My ... my mother. She was alive," I whisper, narrating the vision as it played in my head.

Angelo paused somewhere in my periphery.

More memories filtered in.

"Stay away from me!" she screams.

Pain throbs in my skull on jagged flashes of light across my eyes. The air is too thick to move. "Mama," I rasp.

The shadowy figure grunts, with his arms outstretched. Drowning her. He's drowning her! My mother's leg stiffens, toes curled.

I scream.

Blackness.

The loud gurgling of water draining rouses me, and I blink awake.

I'm clawing at wet tiles, trying to get to her, but my muscles won't move.

"Relax," the shadow says to me, the smell of dirt and metal sticky in my sinuses.

My throat tightens as realization stabs my chest. "You were there that night."

Even more echoes of memory filter in.

Knock knock knock.

I glance back toward the front door of the apartment.

"I'm a friend of Conner's."

"It was you at the door. Then ... I saw you drown her. You drowned her!" The smirk on his face blurred behind more memories.

The figure runs a blade over my mother's wrists. Thick drops of red blood plink across the stark, white tiles.

"You killed her. She was alive, but you killed her!"

"I was sent to finish the bitch off. Imagine my surprise when you beat me to it."

I stilled. An icy mist of panic expanded inside my lungs, as

I fought to absorb his words. A flash of memory slipped behind my eyes.

Hands reaching out for me. Screams. Horrible screams.

Eyes screwed shut, I shook my head.

No. No. Don't look at it. It's not real. Not real.

"You don't remember much about that night, do you?" A wicked chuckle in my ear stirred demons from their slumber. Teeth and claws snapping at my conscience.

My stomach stirred with a horrible dread that scratched at my guts.

"Mama! Stop!"

A distant scream rattled through my skull, and I let out a whimper as it picked at my brain like nails on a scab.

"You're lucky," Angelo kept on. "I'd have loved to forget those fucking disgusting things wriggling around the tub, feeding on her blood before I sent them down the drain."

Blood on the tub. My mother's fingernails digging into my skin. Worms coming out of her like black smoke curling and shifting through the water.

The blackness in my gut crawled into my chest, squeezing its poisoned-dipped fingers over my lungs. I couldn't breathe. I couldn't breathe.

"Mama! Please!"

"I can't breathe!"

I screamed and thrashed beneath him, the monster inside of me desperate for escape. *Please!*

"Yes. You held her underwater."

"She was still alive," I growled back at him.

"Barely."

Liar. A fucking liar! "No. *You* slit her wrists. The coroner's report ..." My voice trailed off, watching his lips stretch to a grin. "Oh, God. You made it look ..."

Angelo's laughter only goaded the panic rising into my throat, pulsing like a living thing. A dark and wicked beast that gnawed at my ribs. "That coroner was pissing his pants, making sure her death looked like a suicide. That's power, Lilia." He let the tip of the blade scratch my cheek. "You passed out. Hit your head on the tub. Good thing, too. Made the whole scenario more believable." The stench of dirt and metal clogged my throat as he leaned in closer to me. "I saved your ass, Lily Cat. Between that and lying about your existence to Lippincott," he said, inadvertently spilling the name. "I saved your ass so many times, you owe me that ass. And I'm sure as hell gonna take it."

Lippincott. It *was* Lippincott.

"Best part of sticking around this shithole city was getting to watch you blossom into a woman. A woman I intend to break." He held up my pocketknife, twisting it in front of me. "Some couples? They get matching tattoos. You and me? We're gonna have matching scars. Only yours ain't gonna be so pretty."

My body shook with the effort of trying to break from his grip, but he pressed his full weight on my chest, crushing my lungs. White-hot pain streaked along my face, from the corner of my eye to my jaw. I let out a hoarse scream behind his palm, as tears slipped down my temples.

"It's a shame, really. You were so pretty. Now you're a monster. A used-up fucking whore. Although, I'm sure you were spreading your thighs for every college dick, weren't you? I bet you had a rotating door of dicks sticking it in that little pussy of yours, didn't you?"

Fuck you!

The drugs must've been kicking in, as vertigo shifted my vision. That, or I was passing out, I couldn't tell. In my periphery, the room widened and shrank and spun. A drowsy warmth settled over me, like I wanted to sleep, desperately needed to close my eyes.

Through the haze, I heard a distant pounding.

Angelo froze over me, attention turned toward the door.

"Lilia!" That voice. I recognized it. Deep. Authoritative.

A sob caught in my throat as more tears slipped down my temples.

Devryck! I wanted to call out. *Please!*

"You keep your fucking mouth shut," Angelo whispered, nearly crushing my jaw with his grip. "Keep your fucking mouth shut until he leaves."

No! No! Devryck! Help me!

Another pound against the door. "Lilia! It's Professor Bramwell. Are you there?"

Behind Angelo's palm, I sniveled, coughing and choking on the snot gathered at my nose.

"Professor, huh?" he said quietly. "You fucking a teacher, slut?" His hand snaked down to my panties, and he curled his fingers to a tight fist around my flesh, squeezing.

A wild cry rattled my throat, the pain unbearable as I kicked to get him to release me.

"Did he break you already? Huh?" Angelo said with a snarl.

That was it. I needed to get him angry. Mad enough to want to hurt me. To distract him from Devryck.

I nodded. "He fucked so good," I said behind his palm and laughed through tears.

"'The fuck did you say?"

I intentionally distorted my voice again and forced a laugh.

He removed his hand, squeezing my jaw instead. "Say it again, cunt."

"He fucked me so good."

A hard blow struck my cheek on a flash of light, vibrating the bones. "Whore!" he screamed over the ringing in my ears. Grip tight to my throat, he trapped the air in my lungs. "We'll see how good it feels when I fuck you with the business end of my blade."

A gurgling scream sputtered up my throat.

Pounding at the door grew distant beneath the blood pulsing in my ears.

My body jerked and jostled as he gathered his arms beneath me, my limbs heavy and numb. Whatever he'd given me had rendered me useless and nerveless. He dragged me toward the wall with ease, holding me against him, my back to his chest, and he held out his gun. "Ain't nobody coming through that fucking door without me filling them with lead."

No. The minute Devryck appeared, he'd be shot. I couldn't let that happen. Even if it killed me, I refused to let this ruthless bastard murder him in front of me.

Fight him.

Something caught my eye underneath my bed.

My old trophy for track and field that I'd haphazardly thrown there while cleaning my room. Closing my eyes, I took in a deep breath. Fucking this up meant he'd surely kill me, then Devryck. I had to be precise. And fast. An impossible thought, when my arms had begun to turn numb.

Mustering what little strength I had left, I reached behind and gripped Angelo's nuts so hard my hands shook with the effort.

A boisterous, gurgling scream hammered my ear, and the moment he released me, I fell awkwardly to the side, fighting the effect of the drug that had me feeling like I was swimming through quicksand. Ragged breaths razed my lungs, as I dragged myself toward the edge of the bed, clawing at the floor. As my body got yanked backward, I snagged the weighted metal base of the trophy.

"Fucking bitch!" Angelo bellowed, and as he twisted me around, I swung out with the momentum, knocking him in the skull with the heavy iron. He fell to the side on a thunk, groaning.

A prickling weakness shot through my arms, as I struck

him again, bashing him square in the forehead. Blood seeped from his crown and over his temples, as he rolled his head back and forth with heavily-hooded eyes that made him look drunk.

A curling black void seeped in from the fringes, crawling over me with determined fingers that slowly pulled me out of consciousness.

Screams breached the darkness. Horrible screams. Mine? I couldn't tell.

The noise fractured inside my head, as I was once again hurled toward an inescapable silence.

Blackness.

Incendiary eyes stared down at me. Furious eyes that glowed a hot molten copper. "Lilia," he said, his voice like a dark angel's. My avenging angel. Was I dead? I had to be.

Blackness.

Warmth engulfed me. A cozy heat. I curled into myself, falling deeper into sleep.

Deeper.

Deeper.

Silence pulled me under.

Chapter 61

Lilia

I turn to see my mother laughing, as she glances back at me from the swing that overlooks the sea.

I smile, as she stares back out over the endless blue beyond.

The swing slows to a stop, and she hops off.

"C'mon," she says, grabbing my hand. "Come with me."

She pulls me toward the cliff, and when we reach the lip of it, I stare down at my feet, toeing the edge. "Come, Lilia. Jump."

A ballooning tickle expands in my belly as I leap toward the water below. Wind blows through my hair. The sun heats my face. Down, down, down, I fall.

I open my eyes to the expanse of open sea. My mother is nowhere in sight.

Frowning, I look around, the waves bobbing me up and down. An ice cold fear settles over me, sucking the heat from my muscles. "Mama?"

Something tugs at my foot, and panic spirals through my bones. I peer down through the water, to below the surface, where my mother reaches for me.

"Come, Lilia. It's so peaceful," she whispers through the water. "Come stay with me."

I flap my arms, smacking them against the water to keep her from pulling me under. "No!"

"Lilia!"

She pulls harder.

An invisible force presses against my shoulder.

"Lilia! Lilia!"

I snapped my eyes open to a dark room and a hard clutching of my arm. On a gasp, I jerked away, but the grip tightened, and I turned to find Devryck reaching out for me. Fear panted out of me on shallow breaths, as I trailed my gaze over the unfamiliar room. The long dark drapes, furniture covered in white sheets, excessively ornate wall trim, and a fireplace mantle. Confusion lingered on my brain like a heavy fog, and I frowned, desperate to figure out where the hell I was and how I'd gotten there.

I'd gone home. Fell asleep in my room. Woke up to Conner.

An intense burn throbbed at my face. Memories snapped into place, and I gasped and touched my cheek, fingertips running over a rough, contractured surface. I shifted my jaw, flinching at the pain of having stretched it.

I turned away from him, hiding what must've been a hideous gash.

"You've been out for two days," he said in a calm and level voice, taking a seat beside me on the bed. "I did my best with the stitches."

Through a wobble of tears, I touched the scorching ache again, the puckered skin that extended from my eye down to my jaw.

"I wouldn't touch it too much."

The horrible memories that Angelo had dredged floated through my head, and on a sharp inhale, I remembered. I stared up at Devryck, silently pleading. As if he could take it all away. As if he could destroy and erase the monster that lived inside of me.

"What is it?" he asked, and as he reached to brush a stray hair from my face, I winced, kicking myself away. "Lilia?"

"My mom ..." Something inside of me begged not to say it aloud, because if I didn't say it aloud, maybe it would remain a lie. It would exist at the back of my head and return to the blackness where it'd come from. That was how I survived, after all. I'd practiced telling everyone she'd killed herself over and over in my head, until it became reality. Until I could say the words without the flinch, or a hint of guilt. While I now knew that Angelo had ultimately been the one to kill her, one horrifying fact remained.

I'd held her under water. I'd almost killed her first.

"I suspect I may already know." Lips forming a hard line, he lowered his gaze. "You talked in your sleep on the way back to Dracadia."

Silent in my thoughts, I stared down at my hands, trying to wrap my head around how I'd explain such a thing. What kind of child tried to kill her mother? It was a question I couldn't answer. I loved my mother. She'd always been my best friend. My home. She was my whole life.

But what kind of mother tried to drown her own child?

She was sick. So sick that she hadn't looked at Bee as the lovable teenager we'd known all her life. My mother had seen her as a threat, somehow. The look of terror in her eyes, when I'd caught her trying to drown my sister in the bathtub, was a vision that would haunt me in the afterlife.

And I'd desperately tried to stop her from hurting Bee that night. I'd done my best to hold her back, but she wouldn't stop. She'd bitten and pushed and fought like a wild animal, in her determination to eliminate what she'd considered the enemy in her head.

The monster.

Why she'd set her sights on Bee to begin was the tragic mystery of it all.

"She tried to drown your sister, yes?" Devryck's question broke through my thoughts.

I felt numb. Heartless. I nodded in response, a tear streaking down my cheek that I quickly wiped away.

"Then, it's not your fault, Lilia."

"This isn't the same as you and your brother. I fucking held my *mother* underwater." Even if I hadn't been the one to end her life, I'd tried. I would have. Even then, I could practically taste the adrenaline that'd coursed through me that night. The determination to make her stop.

"You're right. It's not. But the fact remains, it's not your fault. You were trying to save your sister's life, and believe me, your mother would've killed her. I've studied these patients enough to know the way their minds work. What this parasite does to their brains. You saved Bee. Don't doubt that." He reached for me, but I pushed his arm away.

Arms wrapped around my stomach, I bent forward, as the pain tore me apart inside. "I loved my mom," I said on a choked sob. "She wouldn't stop, though. I begged her to stop, and she wouldn't."

"She wasn't your mother. Something else had commandeered her mind that night, and your sister got in the way of it."

I shook my head, refusing to accept this unwanted exchange–his clemency for what I'd done to her.

"Listen to me. Was she the kind of mother who'd have willingly given her life to protect you from harm?"

"Yes, of course."

"Yes. You did the right thing protecting your sister. Your mother would've wanted that."

No matter what semblance of truth that might've held, I would never pardon myself for what I'd done. He was right on one point, though. My mother was the kind who'd have done whatever she had to do to protect us.

Even fleeing her home with nothing more than the clothes on her back.

The fact was, the world didn't always play fairly, and sometimes we were placed in shitty positions we didn't want to be in. Forced into decisions we didn't want to have to make.

I'd had the choice that night. To watch my mother drown my sister, or do what I had to do to save Bee.

As I compelled my head to relinquish some of the guilt, and push those thoughts back inside their compartment, a new anguish surfaced. I raised my hand, retouching the lower portion of the wound that ended at my jawline.

"Angelo ... he ... tried to ..." My words were broken by the shame and panic clogging my throat. Through tears, I stared back at him. "Can I see?"

"It's early yet, Lilia. It's going to heal."

"Please."

With a sigh, he pushed to his feet and opened the drapes a bit more, then plucked a sheet-covered object from what must've been a dresser across the room. He slipped the covering off to reveal a tabletop mirror and handed it to me. In the reflection, I took in the horrific line of tight stitches, perfectly spaced apart. The memory of Angelo holding me down as he'd carved it into my skin played back inside my head, and eyes closing over tears, I lowered the mirror and turned away.

"It will heal." Devryck reached out, and again, I flinched away. Why? He hadn't been the one to hurt me, after all. Sympathy and understanding flashed across his face, which only made me feel worse, as he lowered his hand. "It's going to take some time."

"I'm not .... I'm not afraid of you." In spite of myself, I reached for his hand, holding it in mine. "I was so scared. He told me that ..." Tears choked my words again. "He planned to–"

"It's okay, you don't have to say." It seemed he'd said that for his benefit, as his brows came together in a troubled frown.

"You were brave to fight him. My brave Little Moth." He brushed his thumb over my temple.

"Is he ... dead?"

A terrifying vacancy swirled in his expression, something feral and uncivilized—the way I imagined a shark might look upon its kill just before sinking its teeth into it. A cold and lethal glint that curled the hairs on my nape. "He won't hurt you again."

The words imprinted themselves in my head, as I tried to imagine what he'd done to ensure such a thing, and I dared myself to push forward and hug him.

Do it, Lilia.

An inexplicable wall of shame stood between us, though. For reasons I couldn't explain, I somehow felt at fault. Like I'd taunted Angelo into hurting me. It didn't make sense. Nothing made sense. I felt like an empty husk, absent of the emotion I should've felt right then. The problem was, there was too much at once, so much that I couldn't feel anything, at all.

Desperate for distraction, I trailed my gaze over the room again. "This is your old home? The mansion you showed me?"

"Yes. I couldn't take you to my campus apartment, or the lab. There really was nowhere else. You'll be safe here, though."

"I don't feel safe anywhere anymore."

"You're safe with me, Lilia."

Tears slipped down my cheeks, and on a bold breath, I pushed forward, wrapping my arms around him. He held me against him, shifting my body so my legs wrapped around him. Strong arms enveloped me in warmth. Safety.

We embraced for what seemed like an eternity, and with my head tucked into the crook of his neck, I lay staring, absorbing, processing everything.

"I need to know what Gilchrist told you about your

father. And please, be honest with me." The question spun within the mire of thoughts inside my head. The weight of all the emotions pressing down on me.

"She told me my father was Lippincott. I found a letter from my mother that somewhat confirmed it, and then Angelo told me someone at the school had it in for me. I think he might've been the one to hire him."

His brows came together in a mask of contemplation. "He hasn't trusted you from the beginning. Not since he first saw you and realized who you were."

"So, what do I do?" It wasn't like I had proof he'd tried to kill me.

"You don't do anything. At the moment, he likely thinks you're dead."

"How?"

"Before I excised his tongue, I had Angelo make a very convincing call to his contact."

The confusion must've been written all over my face. The Angelo I knew wouldn't have done anyone any favors.

"I had a blade propped at his balls."

That might've been motivation enough.

If it was true that Lippincott was, in fact, my father, his malice toward me made no sense. "I know this is going to sound incredibly naive. Maybe stupid, but ... I don't understand why. I wasn't going to ask him for anything. Not money. Certainly not any special favors. It doesn't make sense to me."

"Your existence is a threat to him and his position. Should his wife find out about you, I've no doubt she'd leave him destitute. He's desperate to keep his position in The Rooks."

"The Rooks ... they're a secret society, right?"

"Yes." His brows came together in a frown, and he unraveled my arms from his neck, urging me to sit beside him on the bed. "Lilia ... there's something I need–" A buzz interrupted him, and he pulled his phone from his pocket, his frown deepening.

"What is it?"

"A notification from the security system at the lab. Someone tried to punch in the wrong code." He kissed the top of my head, stroking his hand down my hair. "I need to find out what's going on."

"You're ... you're leaving?"

"Could be students fucking around, but I want to be sure. Besides, you need more antibiotic cream for the stitches, as well. I promise no one knows you're here."

Exhaling a breath, I glanced around the dark room, imagining how creepy it'd look if he didn't return until nightfall.

As if reading my mind, he said, "I'll try to be back in an hour. And I'll grab some food. I'm sure you're probably starving."

My stomach grumbled in response, as if it appreciated the acknowledgement. "Okay."

"I gave you a sponge bath earlier, but you're welcome to shower, if you'd like. Just don't get your stitches wet.

I caught a glimpse of my suitcase propped in the corner, which he must've grabbed from the apartment. "Oh, God. Conner's going to freak."

"I sent him a text from your phone, telling him you decided to stay with a friend."

"Where's Angelo?"

A look of vexation knitted his brows as he turned away. "When I entered that room and saw you practically naked on the floor and blood everywhere ..." A muscle ticced in his jaw. "Believe me when I say you don't want to know what happened to Angelo."

The blackness from before shifted inside of me. I somehow felt less alone, less heinous. He'd hurt Angelo for hurting me. Could Devryck have been considered a murderer for something like that? Who knew what Angelo would've done to me when he'd eventually come to?

At the same time, I knew damn well what my mother would've done to Bee, had I not found her. I'd seen that glint of madness in her eyes. Had Devryck seen the same thing in Angelo?

He'd told me he was going to rape me with a fucking blade–a fact I didn't bother to tell Devryck right then, given the way his jaw hardened to a harsh angle and those eyes blazed with a murderous gleam. Maybe it was best to count my blessings and understand there were certain justices in the world that went beyond what I considered fair and humane. Like animals. Lions who tore other predators apart for daring to threaten their prides. Was that what I was to Devryck? His pride? His untouchable thing?

For the first time since my mother's death, I saw through the eyes of the victim. The one grateful to walk away. To be alive because someone had given a fuck, had been bold enough, to do what needed to be done.

In my ruminating over it, I didn't notice Devryck had fallen into something of a trance, staring off at nothing. Quiet, at first. Until, at last, he cleared his throat. "There was ... the briefest moment ... when I was running toward that room. Your screams had silenced. And I thought—" Lips pressed to a hard line, he flashed me a sullen scowl that tore at my heart. He shook his head, refusing to say it. "That was the first time I truly felt that something could hurt me. That I could be brought to my knees. I don't ever want to feel that again, Lilia."

Through another shield of tears, I nodded. "I know that feeling well," I said, recalling the day at the cove when I thought I'd lost him.

I decided to leave it at that, with the understanding that Angelo had chosen his path, his fate. He was a predator who'd happened to be cut down by a bigger predator, and in the case of my mother, she had challenged my love for her, my loyalties, by harming my sister.

He pressed another careful kiss to my lips, urging me back onto the pillow beneath me. "Are you okay?"

"No. But I hope to be." As he stared down at me, the pain at my cheek flared with the memory of Angelo's words. *Now you're a monster. Nothing but a used-up whore.* Biting back another round of tears, I turned away from him.

His finger hooked beneath my chin, drawing me back to him. "Don't hide from me, Lilia. You are no less beautiful than that day you walked into my classroom and stole my fucking breath."

"It'll scar." I said, not only referring to the wound on my face.

"It might. But it'll also serve as a reminder that you fought a professional killer and survived. You're stronger than you realize."

His words tunneled through me, and I gave a small nod, letting them smother Angelo's relentless whispers that looped through my head.

He planted another kiss to my lips. "I'll return soon." With that, he strode across the room and closed the door behind him.

Chapter 62

Devryck

Tension burned in my muscles, as I drove back toward the university. Unbeknownst to Lilia, I'd stored Angelo in my father's old lab, down in the mansion's catacombs, and had given him the dose of larvae that I'd intended to give the sex worker back in Thresher Bay.

Every fiber of my being had compelled me to kill him for putting his hands on her, but I needed to keep him breathing in order for him to serve as my next test subject. I took comfort in knowing he'd suffer a much slower hell than that which a quick bullet or severed artery might've inflicted. Not even flaying him alive would be considered tortuous enough to quell the rage burning inside of me.

I also planned to administer a dose to Lippincott. Because there was no doubt in my mind that he'd put Angelo up to killing Lilia. And the connection between the two bastards had me believing he'd likely also been behind Caed's kidnapping. So blind in my pursuits and desperation to cure my illness, I'd failed to see what was in front of me the whole time.

He'd fucked with the only two people in the world who'd ever mattered to me, and for that, he would die a slow and painful death. As he was well known to stop into my office for a drink, I figured the means of inoculation would be relatively simple. I'd call him in to discuss the new variant, offer him a drink, then watch his world crumble.

I slowed my car to a stop in the small parking lot, just outside of the cadaver entrance, and made my way inside.

As far as he knew, Lilia was dead. I hadn't given him any reason to suspect that I was involved with her, so unless he'd come to his own suspicions, he wouldn't have made the connection that she was anything important to me. I'd sent him a text the day before, informing him that she hadn't shown up to classes. I was merely serving as the informant he'd requested of me. It was then he'd made the lame excuse that, due to budgeting issues, he hadn't been able to approve another semester for her. I hadn't squawked about it, hadn't given the slightest indication that I'd cared–a reaction further reinforced when I'd told him that I'd had success with the latest variant, to which he'd responded favorably.

As far as Lippincott was concerned, he'd dealt with Lilia quietly.

Thanks to Langmore, to whom I'd make a point to offer my gratitude, he'd had the rug pulled out from under him.

I hustled toward my office, peeking in on Achilles and Patroclus, who continued to respond well to the black stone concoction I'd administered. I could attest—I'd also sustained my sense of feeling for days without any decline.

In my office, I prepared the contaminated liquor that I intended to offer Lippincott, injecting the fresh eggs into the decanter. As I placed it back into the cupboard of my desk, I noticed a figure standing in the doorway.

Lippincott.

"Pardon the intrusion," he said, crossing the room toward the seat across from me. "Been a long day. Someone took it upon themselves to trash my office. I have a feeling it was Spencer."

I fell into my chair across from him. "Any reason why he'd do that?"

"He's a fuck-up. That's why." He let out a mirthless chuckle. "Can I tell you a secret, Devryck?" The slight lack of focus in his eyes hinted that he'd already gotten into the liquor. "He isn't even mine," he whispered and snorted a laugh.

Frowning, I stared back at him, wondering if he was telling the truth, or just drunk. I pulled the decanter of alcohol from the cupboard of my desk and held it up.

Nodding, he flicked his fingers, and I poured the liquor into a glass, pushing it across my desk.

"You're in deep shit, Devryck. That's why I'm here."

"For what?"

He screwed his eyes shut and snorted another laugh. "For what! For what? Are you fucking with me right now?"

I didn't respond, unsure if it was the alcohol talking, or not.

"Melisandre Winthrop has accused you of holding her at knife point and threatening to cut her fucking nipples off with a blade. That's what."

The accusation slapped me across the face like a wet towel. "*What*?"

"Yeah. She claims you attacked her for some files."

Files? I had no clue what the hell he was talking about. "When did she claim this happened?"

"The night before last. In her dorm."

Bullshit. I was cutting out Angelo's tongue and stitching Lilia's face the night before last.

"Are you trying to bring this crap back to the fore, Devryck?"

"I'm admittedly gobsmacked by this. I've no idea what you're talking about."

"C'mon, man. It's me. *Me*!" He lifted the glass of liquor

from the desk, as if he might drink it, but paused. "What the fuck are you thinking, Devryck? Melisandre Winthrop? The Chairman's daughter! Are you nuts?"

"I never threatened her."

Shaking his head, he pulled his phone from his pocket and clicked on a video. "As you know," Lippincott prattled on, "the chairman does not take kindly to any sort of threats."

A figure wearing a black hoodie entered the front door of what appeared to be Corbeau Hall. He glanced toward the camera just as Lippincott hit pause, and the breath exploded out of me.

Like staring at a fucking mirror.

An exact replica of me.

Caedmon?

It was a wonder Lippincott couldn't hear the frantic pounding of my heart, as I stared down at what I was certain was my twin.

My brain refused to accept it, though, even as I studied his features, unable to summon a goddamn word beyond *what the fuck*.

"A number of witnesses saw you enter the dorm, Devryck."

My mind scrambled for a reason. An explanation. Every fiber of me stood paralyzed in shock.

My brother. My twin.

For years, I'd thought he was dead. Mutilated.

Was I imagining it all? I couldn't be. Lippincott had said others had seen him, too.

I schooled my face to avoid showing any of the utter chaos swimming in my head right then.

Lippincott stared down at his drink, swirling it around. He tipped back a sip–a sight I should've relished, but I was too busy untangling myself from impossibility. "The Rooks are coming for you, Devryck. Winthrop is fucking pissed. Melisandre is his princess, as you know."

His voice remained a distant sound to the incessant pounding inside my head right then.

It was only when he drew a gun, pointing the barrel at me, that I broke from my trance. "You've always been like a son to me. Hell, more of a son than my own."

"What are you doing, Edward?" I asked, silently calculating how long it would take, how many days of suffering would have to pass, for him to realize that I'd already ended his life in that single sip.

As he took another, I held back the maddening desire to laugh.

"The way I see it, this ship is sinking. Fast. I'm just claiming my lifeboat, is all."

"I don't understand." No. Not so much that I didn't understand, as I didn't give a damn. Bigger fish to fry.

"I want everything you have on the toxin, Devryck. All of your research." He stuffed his hands inside his pocket and held up an external chip, tossing it onto my desk. "Copy everything onto the chip, and I promise you won't have to die. I want all the data. All the formulations. Everything."

"That's two generations of work you're asking me to hand over to you." In truth, I didn't care about any of it right then. I wanted to go find my brother. To disprove the impossibility clamoring inside my head. This shit with Lippincott was nothing but a distraction.

"Yes. You're about to crash. You realize, when Winthrop comes for you, he's not going to let you off, right? Not even your name will spare you."

My name had never offered much to spare me, anyway. It was only the promise of what I could offer to redeem it. I glanced down at the chip and back to him. "Did you hire

Angelo to kill Lilia?" At that point, I didn't give a shit if he knew about the two of us.

Knowing eyes narrowed on mine, and he tipped his head. "Now, what would you know about that, Devryck?"

"Answer the question. Or I'll destroy every shred of this study."

"And how would you accomplish that in a matter of seconds before the bullet hit you?"

Idiot. If he thought for one second that I ever trusted him entirely, that I ever trusted any Rook, for that matter, he was far more foolish than I'd originally estimated. "I've installed a failsafe. A virus, in the event something should happen to me. One click, Edward. And everything would disappear."

His jaw shifted, his eyes a psychotic shade of black. "You were always good at this game. Far more clever than your father." He rubbed the back of his neck and let out a groan. "Yes. I had her killed. I tried to be discreet about it, but that didn't work out, so I had to take more *aggressive* measures. She was a liability."

Discreet. "You were the one who drugged her with the noxberries at the gala."

"Well, technically no. The server did. For a rather excessive gratuity." The fact that Lilia hadn't gotten infected either proved that he was ignorant about the infectivity of noxberries, or posed a whole new mystery about my little moth that I'd have to unravel later. "Lilia was a liability to me," he babbled on. "I made a mistake years ago, fucking her mother, and it nearly cost me my career, my marriage, my fucking *life*."

"How are you so sure she's yours?" The last word arrived strangled, my head refusing to allow him any level of possession over her—even fatherly.

"She's mine. That bitch promised me. Four years ago, she came to me, soon after her own mother had died. She'd claimed she wanted to save their family home. She had *assured* me then that she'd lost the pregnancy. But when I saw Lilia that day in the dining hall, I just *knew* the bitch had lied to me."

"Four years ago. That was about the time when her mother got sick."

"I suppose it was." He shook his head on a dramatic sigh and clicked his tongue. "Tragic thing."

"You killed her mother."

"I eliminated a problem. She should've met a watery grave with the other six women. Why she didn't is a fucking mystery of the ages." Perhaps not so much of a mystery, if she'd been exposed to the black rock. If my hypothesis proved true, it would've protected her for a short time. "Unfortunately, she was too much of a threat to investigate the why of that. And then the bitch took off. I thought maybe she'd died, after all. Until she walked back into my life again like a goddamn herpes infection. Then that other lunatic showed up. Accusing me of putting worms in her."

"You had her report altered, just like you had me alter Andrea's."

Wearing a smug grin, he lifted his glass like a toast, and I wanted to laugh at the irony of it, but I was too busy imagining what he'd look like with a mouthful of busted teeth. "Blackmail is a beautiful thing. I had so much shit dug up on that coroner, he'd have fucked her corpse, if I'd asked him."

"Why Lilia? She wouldn't have even known, had you just left it alone."

"It was Gilchrist who couldn't leave it alone. That relentless cunt!" Rubbing his fingers together, he shifted in the seat, seething in his rage. "She's had it in for me for two decades now. The woman is desperate to sabotage my career and my marriage. She was the one who told your father about my little affair with that whore." On a long exhale, he rolled his shoulders back. "A whore who *swore* to me that she'd lost the baby.

Imagine my fucking surprise when a walking replica of her, about the right goddamn age, came strolling into the lunchroom that day. I should've never listened to you and kicked her out right then and there." Hands shaky, he frantically tipped back another sip. "It's a game for Gilchrist. A sick game to watch me fail, and I, for one, am tired of being pushed around by fucking women!" Breathing hard through his nose, he sat quiet for a moment, as if trying to collect himself. With his face lobster red, I wondered if he was about to keel from a stroke. "I'm going to let you in on a little secret, Devryck. One I haven't told anyone. I shouldn't be telling you, but you've been like a son to me. More of a son than my own."

"Why do you keep saying that?"

"Because it's true. Spencer isn't even mine. He was a product of my wife's affair with your father."

The man just couldn't help himself, dropping bomb after bomb in my lap. "Was there a paternity test to confirm this?"

"There was a paternity test to rule *me* out. Your father refused."

There was no point in asking if it could've been someone else's. I'd seen my father with her. Had watched the two of them together.

"So, you fucked Lilia's mom to get back at your wife."

"I'm not going to lie. Vanessa Corbin's cunt was worth the risk. In another life, I might've even loved her." A sickening thought, where Lilia was concerned. "But enough of this. Copy the files, Devryck. Please don't make me blow your brains out of your skull."

Teeth grinding in my head, I logged into the computer, thoughts spinning with how to outsmart the drunken fool while my head felt like it was about to explode. A notification popped up on the screen.

An email from Spencer.

Chapter 63

Lilia

In the bathroom mirror, I twisted my face to the side, eyeing the bottom of the wound, where I recalled the blade scraping against bone. Sickened by the thought, I turned away. Even if Devryck had meted out his own form of justice, I'd never rid myself of Angelo. He'd always be there, every time I had to look in the mirror. Every time I'd find myself desperate to forget that night, the vestiges left behind would take me right back to it.

I brushed my teeth with the toothbrush I'd rifled out of my suitcase, cringing each time the movement of my jaw stretched the stitches. I'd changed into a pair of jeans and a T-shirt, and after relieving myself and applying some deodorant I'd scrounged from my suitcase, I decided to leave my room and explore the expansive mansion.

The crack created by my ajar door showed a dark hallway. Spying an ornate light switch a few steps down from my room, I stepped out into the corridor and flicked it. Antique sconces on the wall lit up, glowing as if a flame burned inside of them. I padded down the hallway, passing enormous portraits, some of which were covered in white sheets. From the paisley print runner across thick wooden floors, the beautiful crystal chandelier that hung from the ceiling beyond the staircase, to the rich detail in all of the trim, the house carried a very regal appeal about it. A far cry from where I'd grown up. I found it strange that Devryck had let the house sit unused. Abandoned.

When I reached the staircase, I turned toward one particularly striking portrait on the wall. An austere man, with light hair and intense eyes, stood flanked by two identically handsome boys, perhaps no more than sixteen years old, by my estimates. I couldn't say that, with their serious expressions, I'd have been able to tell the two apart. Trouble, for sure. Both boys carried a deviant glint in their eyes, one a slight smirk to his lips that'd probably turned a lot of girls into a gooey mess.

Tired wood creaked beneath my feet, as I made my way down the stairs to the foyer of the house. Nothing there looked familiar to me. I couldn't recall one moment when I'd awakened to see anything, the night he'd carried me up to that room. I must've been out cold.

A den stood off to the right of the foyer, all the furniture covered in sheets, and as I made my way down the hallway, I passed a library, a small bathroom, a storage room under the staircase, and an empty utility closet.

A faint sound reached my ear as I stepped back from the closet, and closing the door, I frowned. I listened again, more intently. Closing my eyes brought the sound to the fore. An agonized scream. Crystals of fear skated down my neck, and my eyes shot open.

Go back to the bedroom, my head urged.

I knew in that instant what Devryck had done with Angelo. A wild fear shook my muscles, and I touched the wound at my face.

"He won't hurt you again." Devryck's words echoed in my mind.

For reasons I couldn't grasp, I needed to see for myself. I needed to know if there was even the remote possibility that he'd come for me again. I wanted to take something from him, so that if he ended up dying at Devryck's hands, he wouldn't haunt me in death.

While every muscle in my body warred with my head, my feet moved on their own toward the door through which the screams seemed to bleed. My hand brushed against my thigh, an instinct to grab my pocketknife. I lifted my gaze to the kitchen and dashed ahead, searching for a knife block. Instead, I opened a drawer to a collection of fancy steel blades. I opted for a thick cleaver, the edge of which looked sharp enough to cut bone.

Of course, I didn't want to imagine that, but in the event that Angelo may try to attack again, at least I was armed. I tiptoed back to the door and listened again. The cries seemed fainter than before, but still carried a pitch of agony.

As I placed my hand on the knob, I tried to imagine what state he might've been in. *Don't do it. Leave it alone.*

I couldn't, though. The bastard had threatened to fuck me with the sharp end of a blade. And I believed he would've carried through on that.

I opened the door to a staircase that descended into darkness below. A flip of the switch beside me brought the old-fashioned sconces flickering to life, lighting the path ahead. Cold air sent puffs of steam from my mouth, and shivers only added to the anxiety pulsing through me, as I made my way down the cold, stone staircase.

Down.

Down.

Until the bottom finally opened onto a dark corridor that extended in both directions. I flipped on lights, illuminating the long stretch to my left, and waited. Listening. Anxiety crushed my lungs, and I breathed hard through my nose. Cleaver still in hand, I held my arms to stave off the cold.

Quiet moans directed me to the left, and I padded in that

way. A door at the end of the corridor stood cracked. *God, please. Let him be restrained, or something.*

Swallowing past the lump in my throat, I peeked inside. The moans grew louder. Pulse pounding, I widened the crack of the door.

Across the room, Angelo lay on a steel examination table. His arms had been removed and cauterized, leaving only a dark, burned stump.

Air sawed in and out of me, as my feet brought me closer and my eyes swallowed up the gore laid out before me. I'd clocked some of it in my periphery, my head locked on the necklace covered in blood at his throat. With a trembling hand, I reached out for it, curling it into my palm, and he turned toward me on a scream. My breaths choked on a jolt of terror, as his body wriggled in panic, and a jerk of my hand tore the necklace away from him.

Blood streaked down his temples from eyes that had been maliciously gouged. I trailed my gaze lower, toward the slaughter I'd avoided looking at directly. His stomach had been cut open, his entrails spilling out. Blood everywhere I looked. Body writhing on the surface, he opened his mouth and released a moan, and I caught sight of the sawed tongue still oozing blood, which he spat as he turned to cough.

A slithering cold stirred in my gut. I dropped to my knees, the knife hitting the cement on a clatter. Acids shot up my throat, burning my nose, and poured out onto the floor, spattering over the surface. Angelo's moans heightened into a panicked howl. Beside me, a piece of his bowels lay on the floor, and I upchucked again, arms trembling as I fought to remain upright.

A clammy, cold sweat settled over me, my head dizzy as I turned away from him. Necklace clutched in my hand, I pushed to my feet, and a wave of vertigo struck, knocking me to my knees again.

It was too much. Too fucking much.

Hands pressed to my ears to keep from hearing him moan, I stumbled toward the door, and once out of the room, I fell against the wall, every muscle quaking with fear and repulsion. Not so much for the fact that Devryck had punished him. I didn't even want to imagine what the scene must've looked like to him, when he'd walked in on Angelo assaulting me, but I needed to. I needed to force myself to imagine what could've brought a man to inflict such brutality. My head pushed through the shock and summoned the horrible things Angelo had promised to do to me. Slicing my throat. Cutting me up so he could easily remove me from the apartment. Yes. All those things he'd promised to do. And he would've.

I didn't doubt that.

With renewed anger, I pushed off the wall and made my way back toward the staircase. Another high-pitched scream from the room brought me to a halt. Icy branches of fear skittered down the back of my neck as I turned toward the room where Angelo lay.

His screams fell to an eerie silence.

I waited to hear if they'd start back up again.

A figure stepped out into the corridor.

Ripples of terror coiled around my spine as I stared back at the obscure form of someone in a long cape and a plague mask. In his hand was the cleaver I'd dropped, its surface wet with what I had little doubt was blood.

Air stuttered in my chest, and I closed my eyes.

Not real. He's not real. He's not real.

Except, when I opened my eyes, he was still standing there. And when he prowled toward me, my muscles seized up. Lungs locked. I couldn't scream. I couldn't move. For what seemed like an eternity, I stood watching this apparition I'd made in my head trek toward me at a sickening pace.

The doorbell rang.

He ground to a halt.

I broke from the trance and glanced to the side, where a light shined at the top of the staircase. Adrenaline surged through my veins, and I pivoted and dashed up the stairs. A tearless sob broke from my chest. I glanced over my shoulder to see him chasing after me, and I let out a scream.

The moment I breached the staircase, I sprinted down the hallway to the foyer and swung the door open on Professor Gilchrist, who let out a wild screech of flying hands.

"Please! Please, he's after me! He's coming!" A light push knocked her sideways, as I bolted past her. I damned near leapt down the stone staircase toward the gravely, overgrown circular drive. It was there that I twisted around and waited for the masked man to come flying out at me. Wheezing and gasping, I stood bent over myself. Waiting.

He didn't appear.

Seconds ticked by, the air cold on my skin as an autumn breeze swept over me.

Frowning, Gilchrist tipped her head and peered into the house.

I imagined it to be the moment the killer cracked her in the skull with the blade, but instead she turned to me with a frown. "Lilia? Are you all right?"

"I was … he was … it was …" I couldn't catch my breath, the fear and sickness still twisting up my insides. "I swear there was someone."

God, maybe I'd imagined it again. Maybe the sight of Angelo had triggered the visual. With a trembling hand, I rubbed my forehead, and took long, easy breaths.

"Lilia, are you sure you're all right?" Her voice held a guarded edge of uncertainty.

Head lowered, I let out an exasperated exhale and nodded. "Yeah. I'm okay."

"What happened to your face?"

"I fell," I lied, watching the skepticism deepen her frown. I needed to get back inside, to shut her out before she got nosey. With quick strides, I hustled back up the stairs for the door, frowning when the strangeness of her visit finally struck me. Devryck had told me no one would know I was here. Had he sent her? "What are you doing here?" I asked, my voice as guarded as hers had been moments ago.

"Perhaps I should be asking you the same question. It's my understanding you left."

Devryck hadn't sent her, then.

"Devryck isn't here," I said, backing myself into the house, ready to slam the door in her face, if necessary.

"I'm here, Beautiful." At the sound of the deep, spine-tingling voice, I turned to see him casually strolling down the hallway, toward me, his hands tucked in the pockets of his dark jeans. A black, form-fitting T-shirt was a contrast to the white button-down he'd worn earlier.

Confused, I took a step back, as he approached. "Where ..." Gaze shifting toward the opened door of the cellar staircase and back, I shook my head. "When did you return?"

"Just a few minutes ago," he said, slowing to a stop. Eyes adoring, he cupped my face and gave a gentle stroke of my cheek just outside of the scar, the urge to turn away from him pulling at me.

In returning my attention to the driveaway, I noted his car wasn't there. Had he parked it in the garage? Or out back? Had he arrived with Gilchrist?

When I turned back to him, I caught sight of a red splotch at the corner of his eye, as if he'd broken a blood vessel there. My staring also drew attention to a scar just outside of the same eye that I hadn't noticed before.

The corner of his lips curved to a smirk, and he turned his attention to Gilchrist. "I trust you brought what I asked?"

She held up a black memory chip, and he stepped past me

to her side, grabbing her by the waist in a way that looked too intimate.

He pressed a kiss to her lips.

What the fuck.

Jaw unhinged, I stared back at the two of them, trying to discern whether, or not, I was caught up in a nightmare. Perhaps a hallucination. My heart withered, and it was only when my chest punched for air that I realized I'd held my breath.

"What is this?" I managed through choked breaths.

Devryck twisted toward me and smiled, swiping the chip from Gilchrist's hand. "Isn't this what you wanted from her, Lilia? All the files on the Crixson Project?"

I shifted my gaze from him, to her, and backed myself further away from the two of them, my head spinning in chaotic confusion. It must've been a dream. A horrible, fucked-up dream. "Devryck? W-w-why would you do this?"

He didn't answer. Didn't wear a single ounce of remorse in his apathetic expression, as he stepped toward me, reaching out a hand that I swatted away.

"Don't fucking touch me!"

"Don't be like that, baby," he said, while I mentally fought to make sense of the scenario.

Baby? He never called me baby. What the hell was this?

The smug grin on Gilchrist's face twisted to repulsion as she stared back at me. "Oh, God, your ... your wound is bleeding." An air of disgust clung to her words, and I lifted my hand to my wet cheek, drawing my hand back to show bright red blood painted across my fingertips. "That looks positively awful," she added, still grimacing.

Devryck's lips curved to a snarl, and he took a harsh grip on Gilchrist's hair, tugging her head back, the reaction so out of character, I jumped back on a sharp breath.

"Devryck!" she said, her voice affected by the angle of her head. "What are you doing?"

He turned back to me and, from a holster strapped at his hip that I hadn't noticed earlier, he tugged out a knife, pointing it at me.

Air exploded out of my lungs on a shocked exhale. He planned to hurt *me*?

"Go, have a seat in the den," he commanded in a gruff tone. "We need to talk."

I didn't want to talk. I silently begged my head to wake up. Wake up from this horrible nightmare that was tearing at my heart.

"Just let me go. Please. I won't say anything, just let me go." My gaze shifted toward the door, gauging if I could slip past him and Gilchrist.

As I lurched toward it, he released Gilchrist and stepped to the side, blocking my escape. "Sit."

Fuck this.

I spun around on my heel and headed in the opposite direction.

A sharp woosh rushed past my ear and thunked against the wall ahead of me.

I skidded to a halt.

The hilt of his blade stuck out from the wall, taunting me with the realization that it'd just missed my head.

"Don't make me hurt you."

Hurt me? I hadn't thought him capable of such a thing.

I turned around to find him unlatching a second holster at his hip, and before he could remove what I assumed was another blade there, I shuffled past the two of them into the den.

Arms crossed, I plopped down on the couch, my whole body trembling from a mix of adrenaline, anger, and fear. Something I never imagined I'd ever feel with Devryck. I studied the room in search of escape, while my head continued to spin in disbelief.

What had happened in the moments from when he'd left until now?

He directed Gilchrist toward a chair and removed the sheet covering it.

As she took her seat, he placed his hands on her shoulders, rubbing them, and again that smug grin found me. From the floor where he'd discarded it, he swiped up the sheet that'd covered the chair and held it in front of her. "Arms crossed," he commanded.

Frowning, she kicked her head to the side. "Excuse me?"

Instead of answering, he grabbed one of her arms and pressed it into her chest, then the other, roughly forcing her to cross them.

Wearing a mask of confusion that mirrored my own, she held them there without moving, and he trapped her inside of the sheet, gathering the ends of it behind her chair, back around to the front, and behind her again, securing her.

"We're gonna play a little game. Lilia. I'm going to ask her some questions, and she's going to answer. If she doesn't, you get to watch me soak this sheet in her blood."

Jesus.

Gilchrist gasped, her face twisting with new fear, and I watched her throat bob with a swallow.

I eyed the exit again, wondering if he had the balls to throw a knife in my skull.

Once she was secured, he stepped back and turned to me. "Are you ready?"

Still frowning, I stared back at him, searching for any sign that this was some crazy scheme he'd conjured, and I just hadn't caught on yet.

I looked back to her, and for once, I imagined we both

agreed on one thing: something was absolutely fucked about this.

"How did Lilia's mother become infected?"

I snapped my gaze to him, taken aback that he'd ask the very question that'd plagued me since I'd found out about the Crixson Project. The very one she'd offered to tell me, had I left Dracadia.

While I suspected, from my mother's note, that she had somehow gotten infected in her meeting with Lippincott, I wanted to see what Gilchrist knew. If there was something tangible that I could use against him.

She didn't answer at first, but with a hard nudge from Devryck, she glanced over her shoulder and shifted in her chair. "Her mother seemed to have natural resistance, as was documented in her chart. When that changed, I don't know. What I do know is, I saw Vanessa with Lippincott four years ago. About the time she got sick. And I firmly believe it was that encounter which sealed her fate."

"*How* do you know this?" he asked, as if he were inside my head right then.

"If you're asking for proof? All I can say for fact is that I distinctly remember her leaving his office. Beyond that, it's speculation. Who else would've wanted her dead?"

I didn't like this game with him, but I couldn't deny the relief in knowing that her timeline seemed to match the one from my mother's note.

"Did you kill Jenny Harrick?" Devryck circled her, coming to a stop in front of her.

At first, she didn't answer, but when he reached for his holster, she cleared her throat. "No. Of course not. She nosed around, but she wasn't a threat to me, by any means."

"In other words, I didn't want to fuck her, so you had no reason to be jealous."

She shot him a disgraced-looking glance and nodded.

"Tell her what you told me about Spencer."

"I learned from Spencer that Mel had made a drunken confession to him, the night he drugged her." She seemed to shift in her chair, as if uncomfortable in her restraints. "She claimed to have a sexual relationship with his father." Her eyes fell on me, the expression in them far less cavalier. "Your father, essentially."

"And? Why do I care about that?" I snipped, eyeing the door again.

"Don't be so quick to dismiss the small details, Lilia," Devryck warned. "They might be important."

"So we're clear, I had no part in getting you expelled. I may be a bitch, but I'm not *that* ruthless."

I begged to differ. "Spencer mentioned that someone had put him up to drugging Mel. Was it you?"

"I asked him to see what he could gather from her. Drugging her was not *my* idea."

"But you manipulated him. Took advantage of him. Why?"

"To live among the wealthy, you have to learn how to manipulate the game, or they will eat you alive. There's no better way to learn your enemy's secrets than befriending the son he can't stand. Spencer was merely a pawn and nothing more."

Eyes narrowed in disgust, I shook my head. "I was right. You are a horrible woman."

"It's time to play a different game now," Devryck interrupted, his eyes on me again. "The one where I fuck you in front of her."

Needles of panic numbed my throat, and I shook my head. "You touch me, and I'll–" I choked on the last word.

"You'll what?" He stared back at me with a cagey grin. "Fighting only makes it better for me."

"Fuck you."

His eye twitched. "That's a fantastic idea." He spun Gilchrist around to face the fireplace. As he strode toward me, he peeled off his shirt. Tattoos and scars colored his chest and abdomen–a skull jester, a dagger piercing a heart, another skull in barbed wire with gears and a clock's face, and two pissed-off looking dragons at each flank that disappeared behind his back.

My heart stuttered.

Not Devryck. Definitely not Devryck.

Oh, God.

I scrambled backward, as he lowered to his knees in front of me, tongue sweeping over his lips.

Rough hands gripped my ankles, jerking me toward him.

"You're ... you're ... Caedmon," I whispered. A part of me felt relieved, the other part of me still reeling from the shock.

"What is going on?" Gilchrist asked, neck craning over her shoulder.

Fists planted at either side of me, he pushed forward, caging me against the back of the couch, as if he might kiss me.

I kicked my head to the side in refusal, and he licked the edge of my wound that'd bled moments ago, twisting my stomach.

"So loyal to him, aren't you?" He nipped my earlobe with his teeth. "Pity. I love a good revenge fuck." Where Devryck smelled of cinnamon and cologne, Caedmon smelled of mint and leather with a hint of campfire. "Did you like my artwork? I made it for you."

"You did that to Angelo?" I spoke as low as I could to keep Gilchrist from making out what I'd said.

"Devryck had a head start with his tongue, and some severed body parts. Appendages, mostly. His hands are in a specimen jar. How fucking romantic." His dark chuckle spiraled around my nerves, squeezing them. *Oh, God*, Devryck had actually cut them off, as promised. "My brother's come a long way, hasn't he?" A gentle grip of my jaw turned my face back to his. He shared the same copper-colored eyes as Devryck, though his held more of a feral glint. "He isn't like us, though."

"How so?"

"This scar that Angelo put on your face?" He shifted his gaze to my wounded cheek and back. "He put one on me, too." He leaned back, offering a view of his torso, where a white scar marked a slash in his stomach, covered by his dragon tattoo there. "You and me? We're gonna go on a little ride together." He released me and jumped to his feet, swiping up the discarded shirt. "Now."

A glance to Gilchrist and back, and I frowned. "You can't just leave her like that." I had no good reason to help the woman, but it wasn't right to leave her tied up there. I scurried toward her, keeping my eyes on him, in the event he tried to stop me with one of his blades.

Once her binds were loosened, she scrambled out of the chair, letting the sheet fall to the floor as she pushed to her feet.

At the tight grip of my arm, I turned on a gasp to see Caedmon pulling me after him. I wrenched my arm to get loose, planting my heels as firmly as I could. "Where are you taking me? Just tell me, and I promise I won't fight."

His eyes shifted from Gilchrist to mine, and no doubt, he'd picked up on my intent to have her privy to the location in the hope she'd run into Devryck. "The university," he said, as if it didn't trouble him to reveal it.

"You won't get in. Not without an admin code," Gilchrist argued.

Caedmon swung back around. "I already have a code." Devryck's, no doubt. A rough jerk of my arm had me stumbling after him.

I had no reason to trust him. I had no reason *not* to trust him, either, even if he was a hell of a lot scarier than Devryck. He was still Devryck's brother, after all. The one he'd thought was dead all this time. The one who plagued him with guilt.

I followed Caedmon out of the house to Gilchrist's car in the driveway. At first, I thought he'd try taking her car, until he unsheathed his blade and slashed two of her tires.

"Why would you do that?"

He didn't answer, just tightened his grip, yanking me after him toward the gate.

"So, that was you. In the cellar. With the mask?" All the time I'd thought of it as nothing but a trick of my head, it turned out to be real. When he didn't bother to answer, I added, "Interesting choice of costume."

"It belongs to your boyfriend."

"What?" A divot in the lawn rolled my ankle, and I stumbled, bringing Caedmon to a stop. A mild ache throbbed in my foot, only a minor distraction to the turbulence pummeling my thoughts, as I grappled with his admission. No. Devryck had told me the costume I'd seen was all in my head. "You're lying."

"The liar is the one you've been fucking all this time." Grip tighter than before, he pulled me after him as he continued on his path.

"What is the costume for?"

"To hide their faces when they murder."

"Who's they?"

"The Rooks. Your little fuck-toy is one of them." It was clear, in that moment, that Caed harbored animosity toward Devryck. Did that extend to me, as well?

I twisted my wrist, testing the strength of his grip, only to find it was immovable.

"Was it you following me around on campus?" I asked, as we breached the iron gates that I recalled seeing with Devryck when we'd visited the mansion.

He didn't answer, but offered an insidious half-smile that reminded me of his twin. The similarity between them was unmistakable, but the more I stared, the more I noticed the differences, too. The small, subtle scars on his face. A wound at the back of his neck, as if it'd been cut open at some point. Scars on his hands, some discolored and stretched, like his skin had healed wrong. He was the broken version of Devryck.

He headed toward the woods with little concern over the sharp twigs that scratched at my feet, as I hopped over the brush after him.

"Why did you kill Angelo? I don't believe that was for me." It seemed far too passionate of a kill for him to have done that for me.

"Had I known Angelo was hiding out with you the whole time, I'd have spared you that scar."

The pieces suddenly snapped into place. Realization dawned on me. "It was you. You were after him. You were the one he was afraid of. You're the one who brutalized that rich guy, the CEO, or whatever he was."

He swung around, and before I could even so much as breathe, he gripped my throat. "Don't," he said through clenched teeth.

Fear shook me as I took in the deadly glint in his eyes. Whoever that man was, he'd done something to him, that much was clear.

I stared back at him, not saying a word, until he finally released me.

With another yank, he dragged me forward toward a small stone structure that reminded me of a petite cottage. Behind it stood a sleek black motorcycle–the sporty variety.

Shaking my head, I backed up a step. "I'm not getting on that thing. Not with you."

Ignoring me, he shoved a helmet toward me, which I pushed away.

"Don't fuck with me. Put it on."

"At least tell me this much. Do you plan to kill me?"

"Every minute that you stall putting that helmet on, I find less reason to keep you alive."

With trembling hands, I slid the helmet over my head, letting out a pained hiss as the cushioned interior of it slid across my stitches. Helmetless, Caed kicked his leg over the bike and jerked his head for me to get on.

I could've run, but I didn't trust that he wouldn't kill me.

So I did as he told me.

I got on the fucking bike.

Chapter 64

Devryck

As Lippincott downed his drink, I clicked on the email from Spencer–an attached video clip with a message that read: *To think the arrogant prick thought this was encrypted. Guess he shouldn't have roomed me with a computer genius. At midnight, this will go out to every student and faculty member on campus. Just thought you'd want an early viewing. Ask him about the file Jenny had that night.*

Lippincott prattled on, bitching about Gilchrist and how he planned to pay her back for all the trouble she'd caused.

As subtly as I could muster, I clicked on the video, which opened to a scene of the cadaver tunnel–obviously, from before I'd had the cameras removed. A figure strode toward the camera, a young blonde, clutching the strap of her bookbag as she hustled down the hallway while glancing over her shoulder. Jenny Harrick.

The screen flickered to the next clip, of her entering the incinerator room. As she made her way toward the exit at the opposite side of the room, she came to a halt and backed up. The video had no sound, so I couldn't make out what had her backing away from the exit.

Not until another figure moved into the frame.

Melisandre Winthrop.

The body language and throwing of arms told me the two

of them were arguing. I gave a quick glance toward Lippincott, who leaned forward, pushing his glass toward me.

I poured him more of the contaminated liquor, then turned my attention back to the video in time to see Mel grab hold of the shovel used to remove ash from the incinerators. She whacked Jenny over the head so hard, I flinched, noting that Lippincott had his face buried in his glass. The nauseating impact sent the girl tumbling to the floor, and as if stunned by what she'd done, Melisandre backed herself away, dropping the shovel.

Looking toward the door and back to Jenny, she seemed to be contemplating whether, or not, to help her, or flee. She pulled a cellphone from her back pocket and made a call.

Time lapsed on the video, then sped up, as if it'd been edited. T*wo minutes. Three. Four. Five.* Nearly ten minutes later, a third figure entered the room.

Lippincott.

Another glance showed the real version of him sinking into his chair, tapping his finger on the rim of his glass with impatience as he waited on me.

Back on the video, Mel threw herself at Lippincott, and I had to swallow back my repulsion when she kissed him. Strange, given the way he'd flocked to his son's side sometime after Jenny's disappearance, when Mel had accused Spencer of assaulting her. To save face, of course. It wasn't as if he gave a shit about Spencer.

She spun around for the door, and the moment she was out of the frame, Lippincott knelt to the floor and rifled through Jenny's bookbag. He pulled what appeared to be a manila envelope and flipped through the pages. Paused, seeming to read, he rubbed a hand down his face. After scrambling to his feet, he darted for one of the incinerators, pressing the button to fire it up, and continued to flip through the folder. Another brief perusal, and he tossed the entire file into the incinerator and ran a hand through his hair, looking back at Jenny.

"This is taking quite some time, Devryck. Let's hurry it along," he said in a bored tone across from me.

"You're asking for two decades of data, Edward. Relax."

In the video, Lippincott dragged Jenny's limp body toward the incinerator.

Teeth grinding, I watched as he opened the door of it.

He laid her out on the steel bed.

No. Fuck.

One hard shove sent her body into the awaiting flames. When he slammed the door shut on her, I had to bite my fucking cheek to keep from making a sound. Fire flickered through the window of the incinerator door.

A hand appeared on the other side.

In the video, Lippincott jumped back at the same time I did. I ran a hand through my hair to calm the alarm beating through me.

He killed her.

Burned her.

Alive.

All captured on a video he'd somehow suppressed. I didn't know how the hell Spencer had managed to get his hands on the footage, but he'd just cleared my name in a sixteen-minute-and-thirty-seven-second clip.

"What's the problem?" Lippincott asked, holding the gun loosely in his hand.

"Program crashed. I need to reboot. It's going to take a minute."

"I don't have a fucking minute."

"Then, I guess you should've approved the fucking request from finance to boost the internet."

"Fine." Groaning, he rubbed his gun-toting hand across

his brow. "But hurry. This gun is getting heavier by the minute."

As I pretended to wait for my computer to restart, I crossed my arms, staring back at him. "Do you remember that weird glitch we had a while back? Shut everything down for an hour?"

"How could I forget? Everyone blamed me for it. They blame me for everything. Lack of internet, lack of department supplies, tidal waves and full moons," he said in a mocking voice. "I hate this goddamn job. When President Whiting leaves, I will bulldoze my way to his position and be done with this menial shit."

Ignoring his comment, I asked, "That was the glitch that affected the Harrick feed, wasn't it?"

"Why are you asking this? Are we really going to revisit Jenny Harrick right now? Are you feeling so kicked down, you need me to shove your nose in shit all over again?"

I looked him square in the eye. "What was the file you threw into the incinerator?"

Sharp amusement carved his expression, and he ran his tongue over his teeth. "Careful, Devryck. You're walking the same fine thread that your father walked."

"What does it matter? If you don't kill me, Winthrop plans to do the job. You might as well tell me what it was that branded *me* a fucking monster."

"That file she stole held incriminating evidence against your father."

"Since when did you give a shit about *his* reputation? You've smeared his name through the dirt throughout all of my academic career."

He let out a mirthless laugh. "You're an ungrateful shit. I was protecting you! You, Devryck! It was your reputation on the line. Not his. And I cleaned up, didn't I? Did you spend so much as a fucking hour in prison?"

"On my father's death bed, he told me you sabotaged the experiment. You're the reason it was shut down. At the time, I just thought he was desperate and pathetic, looking to blame someone else. But now I'm wondering if maybe those files spoke a different truth."

His jaw shifted with obvious anger. "That study was supposed to have been *mine.* Mine! I should've been the primary investigator."

"You got Lilia's mother pregnant. My father kicked you out, so you got pissed off and swapped the injections. You infected those women. You sent them to their deaths, and our family took the blame!"

"Someone needed to knock him off his throne, didn't they? Imagine the power he would've amassed had that study been a success!" Snarling back at me, he sat forward in his chair. "Enough of this fucking history! Give me the files, Devryck. Now!" He shot up from his seat and rounded my desk. The barrel of his gun bit into my flank. "I want to see them copied onto the chip. And I want you to delete them from your computer afterwards." A pause followed, and I felt a slight nudge of the barrel at my ribs. "It just occurred to me ... you didn't bother to pour yourself a drink this time."

"It was the bottle you bought me for Christmas. I don't care for inferior quality."

"Pour yourself a drink."

"Do you want these files tonight, or ..."

"Pour. Yourself. A drink."

From the cabinet, I grabbed another glass and poured the liquor into it. At the press of his gun, I lifted the glass as if to drink it.

Before it got to my lips, I pivoted around and flung the liquor into his face.

"Fuck!" Squinting, he stumbled backward, and I cracked

the glass over his head. He fell against my desk, the flail of his arm knocking the decanter onto the floor, where it shattered.

The gun went off, and although a thudding pressure hit my shoulder, there was no immediate pain. Just a sickening numbness.

I knew I'd been hit, though.

"Motherfucker!" I barreled forward, taking him to the floor, and slammed his gun-toting hand into the sharp corner of my desk, until the weapon tumbled from his palm.

"Ah, fuck! Fuck!" he cried out, cradling what was undoubtedly two broken fingers, given the way they bent at an unnatural angle.

Swiping up the gun, I jumped to my feet and pointed at his skull with a steady hand, as I held my wounded arm limp against my body. A quick sideways glance showed a blossom of blood, confirming that I'd been hit. "You had my brother kidnapped. It was you. Say it."

"That research was mine. Your father stole it from me."

Bullshit. If that were true, he'd have found the funding for his own lab, the moment the grant had become null. He hadn't known where to begin with the research, which was why he'd recruited me to carry on my father's work.

Teeth clenched, I dared myself to pull the trigger. "You had my brother kidnapped. Fucking say it."

When he didn't answer, I knelt down and propped the gun beneath his chin.

A look of fear claimed him as he tipped his head back, staring up at me. "Yes. I took Caedmon. I didn't plan to kill him, though. Who knew your father was such a greedy prick?"

A numb chill slid through my veins, my muscles burning with the urge to pull the trigger and end him. "All these years, I believed your bullshit. Your *lies*. You handed him off to Angelo. And what happened then?"

"He was just going to keep him for a while. See if your old man had a change of heart."

I nudged the gun firmly beneath his skull, visualizing the beauty of watching his brains shoot out the top of his head. "And when he didn't?"

He hesitated, the gun bobbing with his harsh swallow. "I told Angelo to get rid of him."

I didn't bother to tell him that Caed was alive. Had I not seen the proof of that myself a few moments ago, I'd have happily dragged Lippincott into the autopsy room and dissected him alive.

"Do it," he taunted. "You don't have the balls to kill me."

I grinned at that. "What makes you think I'm so merciful as to offer you a quick death?" I pushed off him, biting back laughter when his eyes damn near bulged out of his sockets.

He looked toward his glass on my desk and back to me. "What have you done?" When he tried to lurch toward me, he let out a pained groan, cradling his hand again. "What the fuck have you done!"

At the sound of a distant thud, I snapped my attention to my computer, where an alert notified me that someone had opened the door to the lab from upstairs. I yanked the plug on my computer and hustled across the room, peering around the corner.

"Winthrop has had it in for you for a while," Lippincott said, pushing to his feet. "You're fucked, Devryck. The Rooks are coming for you."

Three men in black suits strode toward my office. All three of them I recognized as current members of The Rooks.

I knew damned well it wasn't me they'd punish, though. I was too important. Years, I'd gone with little liability. Nothing they could use against me.

Lilia. I needed to get to Lilia. If they imagined for one

moment that she was alive and had any connection to me, at all, they would use her against me.

I slipped out of my office, and at the first crack of gunfire, I ducked low and plowed through the laboratory doors.

Perhaps I was wrong about them not wanting to kill me.

Footfalls told me the men were in pursuit, but by the time they reached the lab, I was already crashing through the door to the autopsy room.

A searing hot pain flared in my shoulder as the adrenaline from before wore off, but I pushed the agony aside, making my way toward the cadaver entrance. Another shot fired. And another. As I rounded a corner, a bullet whizzed past me, exploding against the stone wall ahead.

With my gun-toting arm, I slammed through heavy steel door on a jarring ache that spiraled up my neck and found my car still parked in the lot where I'd left it. The cool nighttime air failed to extinguish the scorching burn of my muscles as I jogged across the lot and skidded around the back of the car to the driver's side. Once the men had breached the exit, I fired a shot. One of them let out a curse and fell to the ground, holding his leg.

The other two kept on toward me.

I scrambled into the driver's seat, fired up the car, and threw it into reverse before gunning it right toward them. The car plowed at them like a bowling ball, scattering the men as they dove out of the way. A quick shift to drive, and I hammered the gas on a squeal of tires, catching a glimpse of them clambering to their feet in the side mirror.

A bullet hit the back passenger window, shattering the glass. Another hit the back of the car somewhere. Given the shitty aim, it seemed they were only trying to slow me down. To apprehend me, rather than kill me. The plinking metal sound beneath the car confirmed that theory, as one of them shot toward my tires. Once outside of the lot, the surrounding trees swallowed me in darkness, and the gunshots faded.

As I sped along the mountain road, I dialed Lilia's cellphone number.

No answer.

I dialed again.

Again, no answer.

A searing ache throbbed in my shoulder, and using the hand of my shot arm to steer the car, I palpated the back of it for an exit wound. My nerves screamed a fiery hell and nausea gurgled in my throat, as I ran my fingers over ragged flesh that marked the bullet's passage. Meaning, I wouldn't have to dig the thing out of me, thank fuck.

I sped through town, toward the mansion, and caught sight of someone flagging me from the side of the road.

Gilchrist.

Part of me wanted to zip past her without bothering to stop, but her presence sent up red flags, particularly when she kept glancing over her shoulder, as if something followed her. I slowed the car and rolled down the passenger window.

"Devryck, thank God. If you're headed to the Bramwell Estate, know that Lilia isn't there."

"How do you know that?"

With a shake of her head, she gave a dismissive wave. "It's a long story. I apparently met your charming twin?" she asked the question as if expecting me to confirm, which I didn't. "Lilia is with him. Some men in suits arrived, looking around. I snuck away, as I noticed they were carrying guns."

The Rooks, if I had to guess. Probably waiting for me to return.

"Where was Lilia taken?"

"They're headed back to the university, as far as I know. You didn't pass them?"

I couldn't recall having passed a single car on the way

there. Teeth clenched, I let out a growl of frustration. "If you need a ride, get in."

As she hurried to open the door, my muscles bunched with annoyance for having to wait on her. Once she'd plopped into the seat, I turned the car around and headed back toward the university.

"Oh, my, your ... your shoulder is bleeding!"

"Brilliant observation."

"Are you hurt?"

I slid a frown toward her. For an expert, she certainly asked her fair share of stupid questions. "I'm fine." I jerked my head toward the glovebox. "Hand me the betadine, tape, and gauze from the first aid kit, will you?"

"Of course." She shot forward for the kit and pulled out the requested supplies from inside. "Would you like me to dress the wound for you?"

"No." I didn't want her hands anywhere near me. "Tear off a piece of tape and stick it to the dash. Then take the wheel."

She did as I asked, and as she gripped hold of the wheel, I pulled up on the gas a little and peeled my shirt back. Ignoring her gasp, I sprayed both the entrance and exit wounds thoroughly, allowing the excess fluids to drip at either side. One-handedly, I wrapped my shoulder in gauze and secured it with the piece of tape.

She lowered her hand from the wheel, as I took control of it again. "Are you in some trouble? Who were those men in the suits I saw back at the manor?"

"Evangelists. Looking to spread the word," I said in a humorless tone. I twisted my arm, checking the seal of the tape, when I heard her give a small chuckle that withered to a sigh. I wanted to ask what the hell she was doing back at my father's home, but wasn't interested in engaging her.

"Devryck, I .... You love her?"

I didn't answer her. I hadn't said those words to Lilia, so why she thought she deserved to know first was beyond my scope of giving a fuck.

"Silly question, I suppose," she prattled on. "I'm sorry. And I'm not saying that for her sake, or for the sake of whatever relationship you have with her. I'm saying it to you."

"Perhaps it's best we remain silent on this drive." I didn't have time for petty platitudes. Especially not when they arrived so late. Neither did I have time for conversation with a person I had no interest in talking to. With my foot to the floor, I ignored the woman who'd stirred so much trouble and gunned it toward where I hoped I'd find Lilia.

Chapter 65

Lilia

The helmet pressed into my wound as the wind whipped around me. I'd never been on a motorcycle in my life, but I could honestly say I found nothing appealing about the ride right then–particularly with how fast Caedmon was speeding down the road. The fact that I was forced so closely to his body troubled me. It felt too intimate and wrong. Even so, I held on for dear life, terrified that I would fly off the back of the bike, if I released him.

He slowed his speed and pulled off the main road, down a wooded path where a sign read Cascadin Falls, with an arrow pointing deeper into the woods. Panic swelled in my lungs, my panting breaths beating against my face inside the helmet, while he rolled the bike to a stop and cut the engine.

As he sat up, his back pressed to my breasts, I immediately pushed off him and climbed from the bike, shoving the helmet's face shield up. "Why are we stopped?

"We're not sticking around." He glanced down at his watch, which flashed with some kind of alert. "Get back on."

"Caed, please. I'm not an enemy here. Just ... tell me where you're taking me."

"I told you. To the university."

"This isn't the university."

Brow quirked, he didn't bother to look up at me. "I can see why he likes you. You're brilliant."

"You're angry at him. Why?"

Like every other time, no answer. He stared at his watch, as if counting down to something.

I looked around at the surrounding trees, which had begun to darken with the oncoming dusk.

"Don't even think of it. I'll put a blade in the back of your skull, the moment you step off the path."

His words somehow brought to mind the other night, with Angelo. The helplessness I'd felt then. The fear. It angered me that I had found myself in that position again. Imprisoned to some psychopath.

No. Anger wasn't the right word.

I was pissed. *Enraged*.

I ground my teeth as the fury took hold and climbed from my belly to my throat. "If you're planning to kill him, know that I'll kill you first," I blurted before I could stop myself.

Feral eyes lifted to mine, and he slowly lowered his arm. His lips twitched as if to smile. "Where I'm from, that's called foreplay."

"Where I'm from, it's a promise."

"Get on the bike."

"Tell me whether you plan to kill him," I challenged.

He stared at me for a moment, as if silently contemplating if I was worth the extra weight on his motorcycle. "Get on the fucking bike. Now," he said, resting his hand on the holster at his hip.

Instead, I remained fixed where I was, as if my body refused to comply. Yet, every cell quivered with the uncertainty of whether I'd pissed him off just enough for him to follow through on his threat.

"You want to save him? Get on. Or I'll leave your ass here."

It might've been a bluff. He could've very well been lying to my face.

But it was better than every other alternative swimming through my head right then, so I climbed back onto the bike, as he commanded.

"You try anything tricky when we arrive at the gate, and I'll gut you open in front of the guard." Admittedly, the *frequency* of his threats had begun to wear on me a bit. They no longer held the same punch as when we were back at the mansion. While Caed's intentions and motivations remained a blur to me, I had a sense he didn't want to kill me. It was hard to say what it was exactly that gave me that impression. Maybe just the simple fact that he *hadn't* put a blade in me yet.

He steered the bike back onto the main road, and within minutes, we arrived at the university's entrance, where the tyrannical guard stepped out of the gatehouse.

Caed slowed his bike, and as the wind died down around my head, I pushed up from him a bit.

"Evening, Professor Bramwell," the guard said.

"Evening," Caed responded in a clipped tone.

The guard tipped his head, eyeing me, clearly unable to see my face through the black shield, the way he so brazenly stared. "That a student with you?"

"Just company."

Another onceover, and the guard's gaze lingered on my bare feet, where I curled my icy toes around the knurled foot peg. Frowning, he shook his head and turned his attention back to Caed, his hand resting on the gun at his hip. "This must be your midlife crisis ride, eh?" He chuckled.

I could've probably screamed right then, let the guard know that I was in trouble, but doing so would've surely put me back on Lippincott's radar, and I didn't know which was the lesser of two evils right then. At the very least, I was closer to Devryck by being on campus.

"Yeah," was all Caed said in response.

The guard waved us on and strode back to the gatehouse. "Have a good night, Professor."

Not a minute later, the bike lurched into motion again, and I watched Caed punch the same code onto a keypad that I punched to get into Devryck's lab. The gate opened, and he drove through.

My heart pounded, waiting to see where he was going to go from there.

He turned the bike into a parking ramp just outside of the admin building and punched the code again. The gate opened, allowing us access to the ramp, and Caedmon parked on the ground level.

It occurred to me right then what he'd come to do. I climbed off the bike, and as I carefully pushed the helmet off, I winced at the burn streaking across my stitches. Blood coated the inside of the helmet when I handed it back to him. "You're going to kill Lippincott," I said boldly. It should've troubled me more that he planned to kill the provost, but it somehow felt like karma. For my mother. For me.

Lippincott deserved what was coming to him.

"Why bring me with you?"

The hardness in his eyes softened only a bit, and he reached out to thumb the blood from my jaw. "You're better off with me."

"Better off?" Scowling at the implication behind his words, I shook my head. "What the hell does that even mean?"

"Weeks, I've watched you. In class. While you sleep." His confession sent a shiver of distress up my spine, while the visual of him watching me sleep played inside my head. "He doesn't deserve you. None of them do."

"He loves you, you know. I have no idea what you've been through, but I know he still grieves for you."

His lip snarled. "He's a liar. Or have you forgotten

already?" he asked, undoubtedly referring to his involvement in The Rooks.

I didn't know what Devryck had done to him, how he'd lied to his brother, and I suspected Caed wouldn't tell me. "I haven't forgotten. He did lie to me. And for that, he's an asshole. But I'm allowed to forgive him. That's my choice, Caed. Not yours."

Jaw shifting, he studied me for a moment. "Then, I guess this is where we part ways."

As he climbed off the bike, I turned for the exit, but paused. "You don't have to do this, you know? Devryck would help you."

He sneered and unlocked a small storage compartment strapped to the back of his bike, from where he lifted out the plague mask. Moving to his pocket, he fished out a chip, presumably the one he'd swiped from Gilchrist, and handed it to me. "Get out of here. Don't make me regret letting you take off on your own."

I tucked the chip into my pocket. "I can handle myself."

"I'm sure you can, Covington."

Not sparing another minute, I sprinted out of the garage and across campus, barefoot. By the time I reached the incinerator room, my feet throbbed, cold and stiff as a day-old corpse. I nabbed one of the lab coats on the way into the lab to stave off some of the chill still wracking my body.

When I entered Devryck's office, I skidded to a stop on spying his upturned chair, and dashed around the desk to make sure he hadn't had another seizure. Something pricked the bottom of my foot, and I lifted it to find a tiny shard of glass sticking out of my heel. After plucking it out, I looked around to see a shattered decanter and a spattering of blood across the floor. The scene suggested a fight had broken out, and my thoughts spun back to the notification he'd received on his phone earlier, that someone had broken in. Oh, God.

Had he fought someone, or had someone ransacked his office?

What to do ...

I ran another search of the lab and offices, peeking into the doors and the cadaver fridge, in search of Devryck. Jogging out to the cadaver entrance showed that his car wasn't parked in the lot there.

Perhaps he really had fought an intruder, then headed back to the mansion.

Damn it.

I decided to return to his office and wait, in the event he called the phone there. Skirting the broken glass, I uprighted the chair and noticed that the computer cord lay unplugged from the wall. Frowning, I plugged it back in, and when the login screen popped up, I punched in the password I'd seen Devryck type at least a dozen times over the last week.

The screen populated all of the applications he'd had open before it'd gotten unplugged. One of which was a video. I clicked on it.

The scene played out a gruesome attack on what I was certain was Jenny Harrick, given the features I recognized from missing persons posters I'd seen around campus. When the hand appeared on the other side of the incinerator window, I tumbled backward into Devryck's seat, both hands covering my mouth.

Oh, my God.

Oh, my fucking God!

An eerie dread crept over me, raising the hairs on the back of my neck. I stared off for a moment, trying to absorb what I'd just seen, my pulse pounding in my ears. Lippincott had killed her. Murdered her by burning her alive, and had remained silent about the whole thing, letting the campus turn Devryck into a monster.

I hoped Caed gutted the sick bastard.

Rubbing a hand over the back of my neck, I mentally batted away the last ten seconds of the video clip that played on loop inside my head, and stuffed the chip from Gilchrist into the drive. Numerous files popped up, all of them dated and labeled in order.

I clicked on one of the files–a letter to the board that appeared to have been written by Bramwell, describing an adverse event: swapped inoculations. "*January fifteenth*," I read aloud. "*Dr. Darrows administered doses of toxins that he'd noted were discolored. Possibly contaminated.*"

Who'd swapped them?

A vision of Lippincott rifling through Jenny Harrick's bag just before he'd killed her slid into my thoughts. Was it possible those files contained the same information?

A notification flashed across the computer screen at the same time that I heard a loud *thunk* echo down the hallway. The only time the notification popped up on screen was when a code, other than Devryck's, had been punched into the keypad.

"Shit." I scrambled to remove the chip, which I stuffed into my pocket, and unplugged the computer, just as it had been before. Glancing around the office showed very few places to hide, and with the sound of approaching footsteps, my pulse roared through my veins.

I dashed across the office for the closet and shut myself inside.

Less than a minute later, I heard a crunching sound, like whoever it was had stepped on some of the glass–slow footfalls that seemed to trail off, as if they'd retreated.

I cracked the closet door enough to see a figure standing in the doorway, peering out into the hallway. When they turned back toward the office, I was greeted by the plague mask.

Caed?

I didn't dare utter a word as I watched him twist away again. He stepped out into the hallway, and I exhaled a sigh.

The closet door swung open.

A second figure wearing the plague mask loomed over me.

A scream ripped from my throat.

Chapter 66

Devryck

About a mile from campus, my phone buzzed in my pocket, and I answered immediately on seeing a call from Langmore.

"What is it?"

"It's Winthrop. He's asked you to return to The Roost. They have Lilia."

Dread twisted up my insides, and I pulled the car over to the side of the road as I clicked out of the call. "You need to get out," I said without looking at Gilchrist. "I'm sorry."

"Good grief. I am just about tired–"

"Get out!"

"Okay. Fine. I'll get out." She slid from the passenger seat, and the moment she closed the door, I hit the gas toward The Roost.

The main building was an old Catholic church, built long before the monastery, but like parts of the monastery, it'd survived the great fire. What had made it such an inviting piece of real estate for The Rooks, was that it happened to be connected to tunnels that ran beneath the entire island, built into the rock. The Rooks had it remodeled and updated with all the latest technology, turning the old church into something of a fortress.

I pulled up to the gate, which was manned by a brute more tyrannical than Sam at Dracadia's entrance. He didn't even bother to check my credentials as he allowed passage.

They'd been expecting me.

I drove into the underground parking garage, my head spinning with how the hell I'd get out of this one. Caedmon had fucked me by threatening the chairman's daughter. Intentionally, I imagined. My brother had always despised The Rooks, and my father's affiliation with them. Knowing that I'd followed in our father's footsteps would've undoubtedly seemed like an act of betrayal to Caed.

Nabbing my suit coat from the backseat, I carefully slid my arm inside, flinching at the sting. The last thing I wanted was to give them the satisfaction of thinking one of their goons had actually nailed a shot.

A fellow Rook met me at the elevator and escorted me up one floor, to the room where trials were held.

I kept my breathing steady as I entered the room that was packed with Rook members wearing the usual ceremonial garb.

Seemed a bit much for a threat. No doubt, Mel was Winthrop's princess, and he certainly seemed protective of her in that respect, but calling on members for a meeting like this just seemed to be overkill. As far as I knew, Caedmon hadn't actually cut her. The garb, often worn for a death sentence, was the first sign something was amiss.

I'd stepped just inside the room, when the Rook who'd escorted me there threw out his hand to stop me. The center floor shifted to allow an enormous golden cage to rise up from below.

Inside the cage stood Lilia.

It seemed death was precisely what they had in mind.

Relief claimed her face as she rushed toward the bars, her

hands shaking as she curled her fingers around them. "Devryck!"

My muscles lurched, my body keening with the urge to kill every bastard in the room. The escort lowered his arm, and I strode up alongside the cage, wearing a mask of indifference. Showing any emotion would've been foolish.

The associate chair, sitting next to what I knew was Winthrop, stood to address me. "Dr. Devryck Bramwell, you've been brought forth on accusations of having threatened the chairman's daughter, and for the brutal slaying of fellow Rook and provost, Edward Lippincott, who was found moments ago in his office."

Fuck.

Fuck!

Caedmon again. However, they'd have likely obtained video evidence that, in their eyes, showed *my* face, not my brother's. Threatening the chairman's daughter was bad enough, but killing a fellow Rook was the most grievous crime one could commit. A death sentence.

"Why is Miss Vespertine here?" I dared to ask, already knowing the answer. "She's innocent. She had nothing to do with any of this."

"Due the importance of your role in the Noctisoma study, Miss Lilia Vespertine will stand in your place as The Accused. It has come to our attention that the two of you have had relations together. There lies the possibility that she might be complicit in your crimes. While the nature of your relationship is of no consequence, the significance of it is, in this case." Mel had obviously reported the news to her father, alongside the accusation of my having attacked her. "Do you have anything to say to your fellow Rooks?"

"I do." I stepped closer, refusing to look at what I imagined was fear and confusion plastered to Lilia's face right then.

"I'll ask my brethren to pardon Miss Vespertine, on the basis that the chairman's daughter conspired with Dr. Lippincott to murder a student believed to have gone missing."

Chairman Winthrop sat forward, his fingers curled in tight fists. "Lies!"

I lifted my phone and twisted to show the members standing at my back. "I have proof. Security footage that captured the crime."

The associate chair flicked his fingers for my phone, and once I'd handed it over, he stared down at it for a number of lingering minutes. He slowly lowered the phone, passing it to the man seated next to him.

Chairman Winthrop viewed the video next.

Seconds ticked by, and he lowered the phone beside him, clearing his throat. If I had to guess, the man was fuming with humiliation right then, probably ready to strangle his daughter–particularly after the sickening embrace with Lippincott.

"Ms. Harrick possessed data recorded during the Crixson Project, which implicated Lippincott in the crime of having swapped inoculations." A bold accusation, but one I was willing back with my name and rank. "In essence, he murdered the six women involved in the study and passed the blame onto my father."

"You've no proof of that," the Chairman volleyed. "We've no idea what was burned in that fire."

"I have the files. All of them," Lilia said beside me, her fingers curled around the bars of the cage. "On the computer chip that you confiscated. They were given to me by Professor Gilchrist. She served as a secretary and data entry person for the study. January fifteenth is the date Darrows noted a change in the inoculations. You should find his notes there."

My brazen little moth. I bit back a smile watching her address these powerful men like she was prepared to fly right into the flame. Of course, she'd have to get past me first.

One of the nearby Rooks handed off what I presumed to be the confiscated chip to the associate chair. In turn, he handed it off to another man sitting two seats down from him, whom I guessed to be Dr. Fausten, and said, "If you'd be so kind as to confirm the notes on January fifteenth."

Another Rook placed a laptop down in front of Dr. Fausten. Minutes passed in agonizing quiet, as he seemed to scroll through the notes.

I prayed they were in some kind of order. Knowing Gilchrist's meticulous nature, I suspected they were.

"I'm sorry," Lilia whispered beside me.

How badly I wanted to hold her hand, to assure her that everything would be okay. Perhaps in any other courtroom, the evidence would've held up, but I was up against more than suspicion and doubt. I was up against corruption, politics, and favoritism, and there was no guarantee that they'd find the facts compelling enough to spare Lilia.

My mind scrambled for another solution, another means of saving her life, because there was no fucking way she was going to be killed on my watch. I'd burn the whole damned project down and walk away with a smile. Fuck the consequences.

Another minute passed, and Dr. Fausten eased back in his chair. "The Accused is correct–the notes on January fifteenth demonstrate that the samples had been noted as discolored and possibly contaminated. Darrows did, in fact, administer the inoculations. It seems Dr. Warren Bramwell attempted to file a report, which was rejected by former Chairman Lowenstein." Winthrop's predecessor, who'd been exceptionally tight with Lippincott. He was the one who'd petitioned for Lippincott's position as provost. "Lippincott was noted as suspect in Bramwell's report."

"We will investigate this further, in an effort to restore the Bramwell name," the associate chair said. "As for Miss Vespertine, we find ourselves in a rather precarious position. Her awareness of our organization poses a threat to the security and anonymity we've upheld for centuries. As you know, in the past, this has resulted in swift execution."

"I propose to make her a member," I said without hesitation. "In the time that she has worked in my lab, Miss Vespertine has made a rather significant contribution in the stability of the Noctisoma toxin."

"And what is this contribution?" Chairman Winthrop asked with an edge of dubiety.

"I'm not at liberty to say." I glanced over at Lilia and back. "The research belongs to her."

Chairman Winthrop tapped his finger on the polished wood of the bench. "One does not become a Rook without proper *assessment*."

I was all too aware of their assessments. The initiation. The missions I was tasked with carrying out to prove my loyalty. Every member in the room had suffered at the hand of the elders. "I offer my personal endorsement."

Doing so ensured that, if she messed up, both of us would ultimately pay the price. Not even fathers personally endorsed their sons, for fear of the consequences. They needed to know just how much I was willing to place on the line for her.

"You are aware of the repercussions." An air of satisfaction hung on the Chairman's words.

"I am," I answered assuredly.

"Miss Vespertine." The associate chair crossed his hands in front of his body. "Is it your interest to become a fellow Rook? To be indoctrinated into our society, bound by our rules, and branded with our emblem?"

She lowered her gaze, as if contemplating the question. As if *contemplating* the fucking question?

What the fuck?

The alternative was a cozy eternal nap.

When she lifted her gaze again, every muscle in my body tensed, not knowing what the hell the wild card would say.

"I want my scholarship reinstated. All four years and a master's degree. And I want my childhood home. Paid for in full."

Bold little shit.

Again, I had to hide the smile itching to escape, the pride that was damned near beaming out of me.

"A-a-and I feel emboldened to make such requests based on the significance of my contribution. It's proven to sustain the effect of the toxin, ensuring its success." She was nervous, hands shaking, but beautifully dauntless at the same time.

"Do you agree with this claim, Dr. Bramwell?" Chairman Winthrop asked, dragging my attention back to The Seven.

"I do. I'll provide a report by the end of the week with the early *in vivo* results. You'll find them most favorable, I assure you."

"Then, we'll vote on the matter to enlist Miss Lilia Vespertine as a member of The Seven Rook Society, with the accommodations that she has *so brazenly* requested."

It could've gone either way. There'd only ever been one female member prior to her–a ruthless woman who'd had far more money than Lilia. They could've easily told her to fuck off, killed her, and attempted to force me to reveal the black rock discovery. Of course, they'd have had to torture me at that point. No fucking way I'd give them what they wanted if they dared to lay a finger on her. I'd carry that information to the grave on the promise that Lilia and I would reunite in the afterlife.

Each of The Seven removed their pins from their gowns.

My heart rampaged inside my chest, slamming against my bones. I knew every face behind every mask, and I would hunt every one of them down, starting with Winthrop. I'd start a collection of flayed skin and severed tongues, if they dared to issue a death sentence right then.

One by one, each of The Seven laid their gavels out.

All of them gold.

Chapter 67

Lilia

My stomach gurgled as the brand pressed into my skin on a sickening sizzle. What felt like white-hot knives sank deep into my flesh, and my arm shook as a Devryck held my hand in his, watching me with intensity.

Nails digging into his palm, I let out a quiet cry of pain as the searing heat beat down into my bones.

He sent the man branding me a murderous glance, and the hot metal released its hold, leaving behind an unbearable agony that rendered me dizzy.

"Look at me, Lilia. It's over. It's all over." Devryck brushed the hair from my face, which must've been as white as snow right then.

I swallowed back the urge to throw up, as the man standing before me yanked my shirt back in place, covering up the mark he'd just scorched below my collarbone.

"It's done," one of the masked men said, his voice flat. "Having taken our vows and branded your flesh, you are now a member of The Seven Rook Society. Welcome, Miss Vespertine."

The surrounding Rooks clapped in a clamor, as I breathed hard through my nose, willing myself not to pass out. I had no idea what any of it meant, what I had agreed to, but I had a pretty good idea that not agreeing to their membership would've resulted in death. Not that I could see their faces behind the masks, but I got a sense these men didn't fuck around.

A particularly wild glint lit Devryck's eyes as he pulled me to my feet, which felt unsteady, at first. My knees wobbled, and at a rush of acids up my throat, I swallowed hard, desperate not to puke all over the tiles below. One of the masked men approached me, handing off my own neatly folded mask and robe.

"Miss Vespertine, you will be given access to a password protected website," the one I'd come to learn was Chairman Winthrop said. "There, you'll find the handbook and resources at your disposal. This meeting is adjourned."

All seven men at the front of the room filed out.

The surrounding masked faces exited, as well.

Resources at my disposal?

Devryck took hold of my hand and led me out of the room. Instead of following the rest of the crowd toward what I assumed was the exit, he guided me down the hall in the opposite direction. The two of us slipped into a dark room, similar to the one we'd just left, and he backed me against the wall.

"Are you all right?"

"Well, I mean, it burns a little, but I'm sure it'll heal okay."

"No. I mean, did anyone ... *hurt* you?"

"Are you asking if Caedmon hurt me? No. He didn't. No one hurt me." I gave a hard shove to his chest. "Except you. You lied to me, Devryck. You told me that it was all in my head!"

"Shhh. I did it to protect you, and it was wrong, but goddamn it, Lilia. You don't know these bastards. You don't know what they're capable of." His brows came together in a tight frown. "If they would've hurt you, I'd have found myself in a very dangerous place."

From what little I'd already seen, and the way they seemed to protect their identity, I understood his concern. Even having reported the birdman costume I'd seen the night of the gala to Dean Langmore as a means of steering them away from Devryck, I was probably walking a thin wire. "Is Langmore a member?"

"He is. Perhaps one of the more diplomatic ones."

"What do they mean by resources at my disposal?"

"As a member, you will have access to whatever you want. There is a lot of money and a lot of power in this organization, Lilia. I suspect they made you a member based on the potential of what the research will bring."

It seemed like they were offering the world for a lie. "But you were wrong. It's not my research. I'm just an undergrad here."

"Who has a very significant role in my lab."

I dropped my gaze to his shirt, just noticing a speck of red at his collar. "What happened to you?" I peeled back his coat and took in a much bigger splotch of what definitely looked like blood, and he let out a groan.

"I was shot. Seems your father didn't much care for the worm cocktail I made him."

"Shot?" Panic goaded me to tear away at the buttons on his shirt, trying to see for myself.

He grabbed my wrists and kissed my knuckles. "It's all right. I'm fine. Hurts like fuck, but I'll live."

I relented my mission to check him over, but couldn't peel my eyes from the blood that bloomed over his shoulder. Blood the others in the room hadn't taken notice of. "You were going to make Lippincott one of your test subjects?"

"Seemed a waste to kill him outright."

"You're a sick man, Doctor Death." I wrapped my arms

around his neck, careful to avoid his shoulder, and pulled him in for a kiss. "Positively crazy, I think."

"I am. Crazy enough to admit that I would've killed every person in that room a moment ago. I'd have killed Lippincott, Gilchrist—my own brother, if he'd laid a hand on you."

My brows came together in disbelief. While I suspected I ranked higher than Lippincott, or Gilchrist, I couldn't have imagined the man would've offed his own twin.

"I've staked my claim on you, Lilia. God help you."

"I've done just fine without God's help," I said, pressing my lips to his. "I just have one request. Can we not sleep where Angelo is tonight?"

"We'll stay the night in my lab office. I'll deal with Angelo tomorrow. If you'd like, I can grab your personal things from the house."

It was the pictures of Mom, Bee and me, and my mother's paintings that concerned me most. And clean underwear, of course. "Thanks, but only if you're okay to drive with that arm. Otherwise, maybe you want to give me the keys?"

"I'm fine."

We headed back to his car, and as I approached, I took in the backseat passenger door, riddled with holes, and the blown-out window. Glancing back at his shoulder and to the holes again had my stomach gurgling. "How the hell did you only end up with a shoulder wound?"

"I don't think they intended to kill me," he said, opening the undamaged front passenger door, and I sank into the seat, ignoring the lingering sting where I'd been branded. He exited the underground parking garage and back onto the seaside road toward the Bramwell Estate.

When we arrived, a heavy exhaustion tugged at my eyelids. The mansion stood dark and ominous, as he rolled to a stop in the circular drive.

"Wait here," he said, throwing the car in park. "I'll be right back."

"Are you sure? I can go with you."

"It's all right. I'll only be a minute."

Nodding, I curled up in the seat, ready to fall asleep, and he planted a kiss on my forehead.

Chapter 68

Devryck

I made my way inside the miserable, old mansion, and up the staircase, to the room where Lilia had slept the last two nights. Once I'd gathered her cellphone and suitcase, I headed back toward the foyer, and stopped alongside the portrait hanging on the wall, of me, my father and Caed. I remembered the day it was painted. Caedmon and I had gotten into a silly argument over a girl at school that I'd kissed. One he was particularly fond of. In the portrait, my face held a smug expression, while his undoubtedly held back the anger burning inside of him. Ten days later, a week after our seventeenth birthday, my brother was dragged from that closet, and I never saw him again.

And yet, he was alive.

First thing in the morning, I'd begin my search for him.

I carried Lilia's suitcase down the winding staircase to the foyer, and as I reached the door, a prickling cold danced across the back of my neck. Turning around showed a figure mostly hidden in the shadows behind me.

"Caed?" I asked, squinting past the darkness that concealed him.

The obscure form stepped forward, illuminated by what little moonlight shined through the windows, and my suspicions were confirmed.

An ache stabbed my chest, crushing my lungs. Muscles locked and stiff, I dropped Lilia's suitcase on a hard thud.

Fuck.

It was him.

Standing in the hallway like he'd never disappeared from the house.

As if I'd been transported sixteen years into my past, he looked no different to me. Perhaps slightly aged, but beneath all of that was the twin I remembered. Half my soul staring back at me like a dark reflection in the mirror.

The brother I'd prayed for every night, for years.

"Hello, Devryck," he said in a voice as stoic as his expression.

Crystals of shock spun around my muscles, leaving me frozen in place.

Alive. My brother was alive.

Fucking alive.

My pulse thundered a deafening beat in my ears, as I stood stupefied, staring back at him, silently calculating the statistical improbability of the moment. "You haven't changed," was all I could manage, as if even my vocal cords were paralyzed.

With a sneer, he lowered his gaze, picking at his palm. "Oh, I've changed quite a bit." Eyes that mirrored mine trailed over me. "But so have you, it seems. Gone is the boy who wouldn't dare touch a corpse."

"I've since found peace in death."

"As have I." As simple as his words might've been, they swelled with the weight of pain. Suffering. Whatever torment I couldn't possibly imagine that he'd endured.

"I thought you were dead. I saw a video of them torch–" The word choked in my mouth, and I shook my head, refusing to slip into that memory again. "They sent what I thought were your ashes."

"Angelo had a flair for the dramatic."

"You're telling me all of that was fake?"

"Oh, it was real." He lifted his pant leg, where every inch of his shin was marred in grotesque scars. "As I said, a flair for drama."

"Where've you been?" The stream of questions swirling inside my head was endless. I felt like Lilia, bombarding him with one after the next.

The repulsed curl of his lip told me I didn't want to know the answer, which only amped the rage burning in my blood. "I see you've done well for yourself," he said, ignoring my question. The hard edge in his voice gave breath to the animosity that must've ground him every day, thinking how different our lives must've been. A stark contrast of pain and contentment. Death and life.

"Why didn't you come to me?" I asked, ignoring his comment also. "Why stay hidden?"

"I want nothing to do with a *Rook*." He spat the word like a bad taste on his tongue, his eyes blazing with bitter resentment. "You're one of them. One of *him*."

Whether he was talking about our father, or Lippincott, I couldn't tell.

His jaw shifted, his hand balled into a fist. "You whored yourself out for power."

"Is that what you think?" The accusation in his words stirred my own anger. This was hardly the reunion I'd dreamed of for so many years. "I was fucking dying! Have you forgotten?"

He twitched and rolled his head on his shoulders, rubbing the back of his neck. The reaction had me frowning. "You would've never survived the shit they did to me." A haunting darkness clung to his words, and he twitched again, as if he was short-circuiting before my eyes. As simple as the comment was, it felt like a blow to my chest. "You're nothing. A rich, prick asshole, and nothing more." He rested his hand against the holster at his hip.

Frustration escaped me on a mirthless chuckle. "You let me believe all these years that you were dead. And *I'm* the asshole? That's rich. Who the fuck do you think took the brunt of our father's rage? Who do you think he blamed every minute of every year that followed, huh?"

While he may have looked the same, a replica of me, the man standing before me was not the brother I remembered and loved. Whatever hell he'd suffered had turned him colder, detached.

"So you got cozy with Lippincott. Even went so far as to fuck his only daughter. Is that how you learned how to forgive him?" A malicious smirk lifted the corner of his lips. "Maybe I should've fucked her, too."

The fury exploded inside of me, and I curled my hands into tight fists, the will to keep my temper in check gnawing at my spine.

As if sensing my anger, he tipped his head and smiled. "Oh, it seems I've found a weakness, Brother." His anger made no sense to me. His desire to taunt left me baffled, as I fought the urge to smash his teeth. "She tell you I watched her sleep? How easily I could've fucked her, pretending to be you."

"I'd have fucking killed you myself for touching her."

Something flashed over his face, and he twitched again. "What'd you say?" The tone of his voice dared me to say it again.

I wanted to, just to see what the hell he'd do, but something told me he was waiting for that. Much as his words goaded my violence, I didn't want to fight him. "What the hell did they do to you, Caed?"

His spine snapped. Like a bull seeing red, he barreled straight into me, the shock of pain from where I'd been shot spiraling up my arm into my neck. The impact knocked me to the floor on a jarring zap that struck my spine. He scrambled over top of me, his pupils blown, crazed like a rabid animal. In a haze of blinding rage, he hammered his fist into my face, kicking my head to the side. As he drew back for another hit, I slammed my stronger fist into his flank with a sickening thud, and the moment he curled himself into the hit, I twisted to the side, knocking him just enough to plow another punch to his jaw.

We rollicked across the floor, all fists and growls, until I got the upper hand and pinned him beneath me. I pounded two quick punches to his temple. Another spurred blood from his nose. A hint of a smile played on his lips like he enjoyed the hits.

I railed another to the other side his face, and he let out a sound of pleasure.

"What the fuck is wrong with you?" I drew my fist back again, but a sharp blow struck my ribs, knocking the wind out of me.

He drilled another powerful blow to my wounded shoulder, and I shook away the jagged flashes of pain that flickered behind my eyes. The moment of distraction cost me, as Caed plowed me over again, knocking me onto my back, and in two quick moves, he propped his blade at my throat, bringing my movements to a halt.

The razor thin edge of the knife scraped against my stubble, casting a slight burn where he must've cut me. Body shaking with adrenaline, I stared up at him, into eyes that held so much enmity and hate, I was certain he'd slice me open. "Impervious," I gritted, the rims of my eyes stinging as I lifted my chin, giving him full access to my throat.

His brows came together in a tight frown, and his cheeks twitched as if the emotions inside his head cross-wired.

"Impervious," I said again, and eyes screwed shut, he shook his head.

"No." A rage-filled growl vibrated out of him.

"Do it. Kill me." I kept on with my taunting that seemed to be breaching the haze clouding his head. "The day they dragged you from that closet, my whole fucking world caved in, and I've been living in death ever since."

"Shut the fuck up! Shut the fuck up!" He pushed off me and clutched his temples, as if something rattled inside his head. A war between his thoughts and my words. "Shut the fuck up!"

He was coming undone.

I fought the emotions brimming to the surface as I watched it happen before my eyes. Decades of pain, confusion, and anger. Anger that I had to stuff into the quiet recesses of my head, hardening my heart. "You were my protector. My whole fucking world." Voice faltering, I cleared my throat.

He scrambled away and backed himself into the wall beside us, where he struck the butt of his knife against his temple and whispered something in a string of incoherent words that I couldn't make out.

"You remember, don't you?"

Another angry growl broke from his chest, and he punched his temples harder. "Shut up!"

I reached for his arm, and he recoiled, scrambling away.

"Don't fucking touch me!" As he held the blade out toward me, I caught the high shine of tears in his eyes. "IamashadowIamaghostIamnothingIamashadowIamaghostI-amnothing," he whispered over and over.

"You're no ghost, nor shadow. You are my brother." I edged closer, careful to keep some distance between me and the business end of that blade. "It's me, Caed."

The blade trembled in his hands as he held it outstretched. His eyes shifted with unseen images, as if memories came flooding in too fast to keep up. The hard edge of his jaw loosened, at the same time his brows turned up. Jaw trembling, he lowered his weapon and let out a pained growl that echoed over the clang of his fallen blade.

Palms clamped over his ears, he whispered the string of words again.

I lurched forward and wrangled him into a tight embrace. A harsh blow struck my chest as he tried to push me off, and fuck, my shoulder felt like it was on fire, but I didn't let go of him. I held firm, while he snarled and growled like a cornered dog, pushing and clawing for escape. A searing burn licked my flesh where he dug his fingers into me, both of our muscles locked and trembling in paralysis–a balance of two opposing forces.

Until, at last, he relented.

He let out a pained sound and gripped my arms. "Fuck! Fuck!"

"I'm sorry," I whispered.

He finally broke.

I fought tears as I held him, listening to the sounds of agony that broke from his chest. Whatever he'd been through had ravaged his mind, no differently than the parasites that infected my victims. It was clear to me that he'd somehow been brainwashed into thinking I was his enemy. That I was somehow responsible for what he'd suffered. Whoever had taken my brother had broken him into an animal. A cold and callous machine.

He quieted again, and when he lowered his hands from my arms on a shaky exhale, I released him.

I fell to the side, against the wall.

We stayed that way, in silence, for a minute or two, while I wrapped my head around what the fuck could've happened to him to make him this way.

He daubed the blood from his nose with the back of his hand, smearing it over his upper lip.

I yanked the sheet covering the console table next to me

and slid it across to him, using the other end of it to daub some of the blood from my shoulder.

"D'you get shot?" he asked, wiping the blood from his lip with the corner of the sheet.

"Lippincott."

"His trigger finger is pinned to the wall of his office, next to his ears." He drew his knee up, resting his elbow there. "He held a gun to my head once. Told me he'd put a bullet between my ears."

"Tell me what happened to you."

Twitching again, he rubbed the top of his skull. "So much of that day, with you, is gone now. Things I remember come to me in flashes. Like flickering scenes of a movie."

"Someone kept you imprisoned. Who was it?"

"Angelo had me chained up in some abandoned building somewhere." His voice carried an aimless drawl, as if his mind were lost to memories. "Lippincott showed up. Told him our father refused to make the deal. So, Lippincott told him to get rid of me."

Frowning, I tried to imagine the level of betrayal Caed must've felt. The hopelessness. "You should've let the parasites kill him slowly."

He shook his head. "Couldn't take a chance he'd live. I vowed to kill them all." He swiped up his blade and pressed the tip of it into his palm, toying with it, which drew my attention to scars even there. His entire hand was riddled with them.

"No way Angelo let you walk. What happened?"

"I was sold to some rich prick out of Massachusetts." He stared off, as if his mind had taken him back to that day. "He was part of a sadistic group. A society of rich and powerful men, like The Rooks. Only they weren't academics. They made sport of torturing people."

I rubbed the back of my neck, hesitating to ask more. But I

needed to know. I needed to understand what he'd suffered. Even if I had to live it myself. "They tortured you."

"It was him, mostly. But I didn't break as easily. I had this crazy fucking notion that I was going to get out of it. That I'd escape." He snorted and drew a bead of blood on his palm, where he continued to toy with the knife. "He saw that as a challenge."

"He brainwashed you."

He pressed his forehead against his bicep and breathed deeply, as though he needed a moment to collect himself before answering. Something told me this was the part that'd messed him up. The stretch of his history where everything had changed for him. "He found out I had a twin," he said, lifting his head again. "At first, he told me he was going to find you and sell you to those sadist pricks. When that didn't seem to work on my psyche, he began to feed me lies. Not outright. It was a slow-drip feed." Frantically rubbing the back of his neck, he inhaled hard through his nose. He twitched and grunted, fighting some invisible force inside of him. "He'd go for days without feeding me anything else. I'd get delirious, seeing shit. He started invading my dreams with images of you siding with Lippincott. Worse things than that, too." His voice cracked, and he shook his head. "I can't even think about that shit."

Part of me wanted to know what could've been worse than betrayal, but the other part of me thought it better left alone. Fuck. No wonder he wanted to kill me. He must've thought I'd conspired against him all these years.

"When I finally gave up the idea of trying to escape, he began to *reward* me." His voice held a tight clip of disgust. "Like a fucking dog. Little by little, he fed my loyalty to him. To *them*. It wasn't long before I forgot who the hell I was. That's when he made me kill for him. I became his protector. His guard dog."

I thought back to the report I'd been given, about him having murdered the businessman back in Massachusetts. "You killed him?"

The repulsion on his face faded for a gratified smile. "Killing sounds merciful for what I did to him."

"Why now? After all these years?"

"A few weeks back, I attended a meeting with him. Some bigwig pharmaceutical CEO. Another member of Schadenfreude."

Schadenfreude. I knew the word to mean something about pleasure from another's suffering. Must've been the name of the society he'd mentioned earlier.

"He'd met with Lippincott about buying some research for a breakthrough treatment." Goddamn. The shady deal The Rooks had gotten wind of a while back. The conniving bastard was behind that the whole time, and he'd let Darrows take the fall for it. Eyes still spacey, Caed shook his head. "Soon as I heard that name, something snapped inside my head." He rubbed his skull back and forth. "It hooked my fucking guts, and I couldn't let it go. It brought to mind Angelo and the pricks who'd swiped me up. I couldn't fucking see past this blinding rage. For the first time since I was seventeen, I wanted to kill them all."

"You pretended to be me to get close to Lippincott."

"Imagine my surprise when I found Barletta in that cell, too. Then you delivered Angelo, and it was like Christmas fucking morning."

"You planned to kill me, too," I dared to say aloud.

Lips snarled and trembling, he lowered his gaze. "I don't know what I would've done. That's what scares me."

"And now?"

"I'm trying to flush it down the mental fucking toilet over here, so let's just move on, okay?"

I snorted at that. Then chuckled. My chuckle became

laughter, and when I looked over at Caed, he was laughing, too. The laughing became hysterical, a release of something I couldn't even pinpoint exactly, but it felt good. Purgative. I laughed until I was wiping tears across my arm, and it died down to quiet again.

Both of us stared off.

"Remember when we were kids, and dad would lock you in that closet? You'd hear voices talking to you?" he asked, his tone calmer than before, sounding more and more like my brother.

"Yeah."

"What'd they tell you?"

I pulled my knee up, resting my elbow atop it. "They told me to run. To get as far away from our father as I could."

"But you didn't. You stayed, and you endured every punch he threw at you." Sniffing, he thumbed at his nose. "When they threw me in that dank, cold fucking cell, I heard a voice, too."

"What did it say to you?"

"It told me to stay alive and to kill them all. But it wasn't the voice of dead people. It was your voice I heard."

Brows pulled tight, I swallowed down the emotions constricting my throat.

"I wouldn't have killed you. I wouldn't have killed my own blood." His throat bobbed, and he pushed to his feet, holstering his knife again, as I stood up from the floor.

"So, what happens now?" I asked, rubbing the muscles around the bullet wound that ached like a bitch. "You plan to stay here on Dracadia?"

Weary eyes held the vacancy of a man who'd fulfilled his vengeance and hadn't thought what would come after. "This place, this life, isn't for me. I never wanted it." Those bleak words wrapped around my lungs and squeezed the breath out of me.

"You're leaving, then."

"Yes."

I lowered my gaze to stave off the agony threatening to rip me apart all over again. "Where will you go?"

"Don't know. Away."

I shook my head, my jaw tightening with stubborn protest. "You can't leave. Now that I know you're alive ..."

"I need to figure shit out, Dev. My head isn't right."

"There's money. Plenty of it. I can set up an account."

"I don't need your money. I need to find a reason to live again."

Gaze lowered, I rubbed my hands together and released an uneasy breath. It troubled me that he needed to get away from me to set himself straight. I didn't want to think about what he might do at the end of that journey. What he might find there. I hoped there'd be enough to keep him from deciding he was better off dead, but I knew that pain. I'd clung to that rope once myself, feeling my grip loosen. "If it's time you need, then go. But for fucks sake, Caed, promise me you'll come back if it gets too heavy for you. Because ..." Scowling, I blinked back tears. "I won't lose you again."

After a moment of stillness, he scratched the back of his head and strode toward the door, but came to a stop beside me. With what seemed like reluctance, he held out his hand.

I reached for him, and the moment his palm hit mine, I pulled him in for a tight hug, holding him against me. An image flashed through my mind: *lying on the floor, bleeding out of my skull after my father had struck me too hard, and Caedmon's arms wrapped tight around me, telling me I'll be okay.*

Impervious.

"I'm sorry," I whispered. "If you stay, I swear to Christ I'll protect you this time."

He gave one hard squeeze. "You let him convince you of his lies, Brother. You were never weak. Not to me."

I gripped the back of his neck, not willing to let go.

At the sound of the door, I lifted my gaze to see Lilia standing there, her eyes wide as she took in the two of us. "Oh. God. I'm sorry. I didn't mean .... You were taking a while, and I got worried–"

"I was just leaving." Caed released me and, with determined strides, kept on toward her, grinding to a halt beside her. "You're about the feistiest little fox I've ever met," he said and leaned into her, whispering something in her ear that I couldn't make out.

With a smile, she lowered her gaze and nodded.

A quick kiss to her cheek, and he glanced back at me. While his comment earlier was likely nothing more than an attempt to piss me off, I still felt a wire of tension in my muscles having seen his lips on her. "Give my best to Chairman Winthrop." The tone of his voice carried a threat. "If he even thinks to retaliate, I'll have reason to return."

"I suspect he's reeling from humiliation right now," I said, as Lilia padded across the room to my side and slipped her arm in mine. "Take care of yourself. Maybe send some proof of life every now and then. And Caed ... if you ever need me. I'm here."

His brow flickered, but he said nothing in response.

And with the click of the door, he was gone.

"Are you okay?" Lilia asked, giving a squeeze of my hand.

"I will be." I lifted her hand to my lips and kissed her knuckles. "What did he say to you?"

"He just said that I was too beautiful to fret over this scar. And that I should look out for you because you're all he has left."

Brows pinched, I pressed a kiss to her forehead. "He's right. You're far too beautiful."

"Do you think you'll ever see him again?"

"I don't know."

Chapter 69

Lilia

Seven weeks later …

I held up the test tube, marveling at the perfect homogenous mixture of purple fluid and black sparkles. With the stability of the toxin, Devryck was able to have some lighting installed throughout the lab, seeing as it didn't particularly bother the uninfected moths we'd begun to study–the ones injected with a synthetic version of the purified toxin he'd taken from Andrea Kepling's frozen sample. Turned out, the toxin he'd saved from her autopsy was still viable, which meant no more killing. Devryck had been able to replicate it, modify it *in vitro*, to produce a small supply that he planned to test on mice in the upcoming weeks.

"So pretty," I whispered, before turning to him. "What do you plan to call it?"

"I was thinking Lilia's Elixir would be appropriate." Professor Bramwell stood off to the side, injecting the substance into the moth I'd named Hybris, for the annoying way it constantly flitted its wings against the glass for attention.

Multiple domes stood about the lab, housing a number of different test groups–all of whom I'd named. Moths we'd spent weeks observing, who'd once been paralyzed and were probably itching to break free from their cage to fly.

"I don't know." I carefully slid the tube back into its tray alongside the others. "Doesn't feel right naming it after just me. How about BramLil?"

"No."

"Okay, then, how about LiliBram? Oooh! DevLil? Sounds like Devil."

"Definitely not." Bramwell said, placing the fluttering moth back into its cage.

I playfully groaned. "Fine. If you want to name it after me, I'll let you, I suppose." I lifted another of the test tubes, studying the fluid inside that one, searching for any sign that it hadn't combined properly after centrifuging. "You think this black rock is the reason my mother didn't get sick with the swapped inoculations?"

"Considering the timeline you gave me, and Francesca having confirmed that she enjoyed the black rock tea from the apothecary, yes. I think it gave her enough resistance to avoid infection."

"Not enough to keep Lippincott from reinfecting her, though."

His expression turned somber. "I'm afraid not. I've since learned the effects of the tea wear off, if not consistently replenished."

A shadow of despair hung in the pause that followed, and I quickly switched subjects. Conversations about my mother needed to remain surface. Anything deeper, and I'd slip into the dark space that terrified me. The shadows of my past that would forever dwell in the corner of my mind. I still suffered the occasional nightmare and hallucination of her, but her form ultimately morphed into something else—the root of my fears that took the shape, scent and sound of Angelo. "I can't believe you move to clinical trials soon," I said, switching the topic.

"Still a few months away, thankfully." He tossed the needle into the sharps container and removed his gloves to wash his hands in the adjacent sink. "We've got a whole team to assemble and some details to work out before then."

"Details shmetails. It's going to be great. You're going to be known as the doctor who reversed Voneric's Disease. And who knows what else. There's so much potential."

"Let's not get ahead of ourselves."

Perhaps it was his prior failures that weighed heavy on him, but the man refused to get excited. He'd taken one of the synthetic injections himself, a few weeks back, and in spite of his loathing toward the black rock tea, he drank it every night. Since then, he hadn't suffered a single seizure. Not so much as a cramp.

I was practically bursting out of my seams with how incredibly well the black rock casteyon had stabilized the toxin. It made sense, though, the way nature offered a sense of balance. The only issue was sourcing the casteyon from the treacherous underwater caves. The Rooks had agreed to fund a team to collect samples of the element, but the deep ocean currents at Devil's Perch still made it dangerous.

As a Rook myself, I'd since been given access to more of the sensitive information in the library, and I learned that the black rock had long been observed in the Cu'unotchke tribe–in their teeth, in the water they drank. It was where the black tea had originated, passed down to later generations. Unfortunately, they'd been branded evil by Dr. Stirling–wild animals that he'd taken to kidnapping and using to test his Stirlic acid, to banish the evil from their souls.

Ultimately, it wasn't the Cu'unotchke tribe who'd attacked Stirling and Adderly, but the patients that'd been kept locked up and tortured. Those who'd become infected with the black worms–the devil's serpents as they were called then. They went mad. Plundered and raped. When Adderly tried to stop them, they burned him and his men, the whole island, and then drowned themselves in the sea–hundreds of bodies washing ashore at what had become Bone Bay.

"So, I enrolled in Advanced Biochemistry next semester." A quick study of another test tube showed the same perfect mix as all the others. "I understand Professor Golding is a prick."

"He is. Stay on top of your reading and you'll be fine."

"A bigger prick than you?"

"I wouldn't know." He shot me an unamused glance. "And I suggest you stay away from any other pricks, unless you'd like one gift wrapped under your tree this Christmas."

I chuckled at that. "What if I need help?"

"You know I'm always available to you."

I placed the test tubes back under the hood and turned to Devryck, who peered into his microscope. With quiet footsteps, I snuck up behind and slid my arms around him.

Never breaking his study, he grabbed one of my hands, holding it to his chest, fingers gently stroking mine. "You make it impossible to concentrate," he said.

My other hand reached down to his groin, and I felt him jerk against me.

"Lilia," he warned, but his cock hardened beneath my palm.

The teasing was fun, but no more than a game. A distraction from myself. Something dreadful still lived inside of me since the night I'd been attacked, and if I wasn't engaged in something else, I'd see it sometimes in the shadows on the wall–beady eyes staring back at me, silently threatening to cut me into small pieces. The playful banter with Devryck kept it hidden and tucked away. Safe in its burrow.

Another minute, and he twisted around on his stool.

"So, this team you're assembling, do I get to be on it, Professor?" I wrapped my arms around his neck and pressed my lips to his, smiling against them when I added, "I'm extremely flexible and work well with others."

At the tight grip of my ass, I gasped. "There might be an opening that needs to be filled."

"Oh, it definitely does."

"This particular position isn't a team effort, though. More one-on-one."

"I can handle that."

"You certainly can." His teeth grazed my earlobe, and he pushed to his feet, backing me up a step. "Meet me in my office, Miss Vespertine," he said, and turned toward the adjacent sink, where he washed his hands a second time. As he rinsed, he sent me a *what-are-you-still-doing-there* cock of his brow, and wearing a grin, I quickly padded toward his office.

Once there, I crossed the room to his desk and caught sight of something on one of the bookcase shelves behind it. Two small black frames each held a moth, and frowning, I rounded his desk, coming to a stop before them. *Patroclus* and *Achilles* had been etched into small gold plaques below each preserved moth. They'd passed two weeks prior, having completed their lifecycle. What had compelled him to keep them? The gesture was so wildly out of character for Devryck, yet adorable at the same time, that it brought a smile to my face.

A slight turn and I caught sight of something on one of the lab coats hanging on the nearby coat rack. Tipping my head, I squinted my eyes, catching the purple stitching just outside of the lapel. I tugged the arm of it, to find my name above the title, *Associate Researcher*. Smiling again, I ran my thumb over the stitched lettering that, as simple as it was, felt so official.

At the sound of approaching footsteps, I abandoned my examination and turned to face the door.

The moment he strode into the room, my heart kicked up like windswept leaves. The man looked like a walking thunderstorm ready to strike, as he rolled up the sleeves of his black shirt and glanced at his watch, the sight of him casting a burn in my thighs. "I have a board meeting in two hours. I need to kill some of this tension." Having rounded the desk, he scooped me up into his arms, and our lips practically sizzled when he seized my mouth in a fiery kiss. A growling impatience rumbled in his throat as he set me down on the desktop.

"You kept Patroclus and Achilles?" I asked.

He planted his palms on either side of me and kissed me again. "Had to keep my first successful specimens. Naming them was brilliant, on your part."

"I told you."

"And I'm telling *you* to turn over and spread your knees," he whispered.

As commanded, I twisted around on the immaculate desk, knees and palms pressed against its surface, as I stood on all fours.

Hands reached up under my skirt, all the way up to the waistband, and he pulled down the thick tights I'd begun to wear since the temps had dropped. When he peeled them over my naked ass and halfway down my thighs, he paused. "No panties?"

"Panties are for the modest," I said with a smile, lifting my leg to allow him to slide them down over my knees.

A devilish grin slanted his lips as he removed my boots and slipped the tights off entirely.

At the first brush of his tongue against my overly sensitive flesh, I arched like a cat, moaning with the welcomed intrusion. My ass twitched, fingers curled against the unforgiving surface of the wood, as he licked and sucked and drove his fingers up into me. Arousal leaked down my thighs, and he groaned, pausing to suck his fingers before plunging them back inside me.

"Why does the forbidden have to be so fucking sweet?" He dragged his tongue over the back of my thighs, lapping up every drop.

A ravenous greed throbbed in my belly, and I backed myself to his knuckles and circled my hips, desperate for more.

A tight grip of my throat lifted my chin, sealing off the air to my lungs as he held me steady. In and out, he pumped his fingers while squeezing my throat just enough that I could feel my pulse hammering against his palm. He withdrew his fingers on a wet sound and ran the pad of his thumb in small circles over my swollen and aching hole. "Do you need a proper fucking, Miss Vespertine?"

"Yes, Professor," I breathed, my pussy clenching with his relentless teasing.

For the two weeks after Angelo's attack, he hadn't attempted to touch me that way. Part of it was my own insecurity over the scar on my face and the yellowing bruises across my body. I'd struggled to look at myself in the mirror without seeing those hateful black eyes and hearing Angelo's promise to mutilate me. Devryck had told me that he'd wait until I was ready, and while he'd remained affectionate, even more so than before, he'd never gotten sexual–not even as I'd slept beside him. Not even the one time I'd broken down while showering, and he'd held my naked body against him. I hadn't realized how much I'd yearned for that, how much I'd needed that level of closeness without actual sex.

In the weeks that'd followed, my wound healed, the bruises faded, and I no longer heard Angelo's whispers. My desire for Devryck intensified, a hungry beast that twisted and curled with its appetence, until he'd finally caved. What followed was a craving for the man like I'd never felt before.

It'd peaked that first night, from sundown to sunrise, when he'd taken me against his desk, the chair, and every wall of his office. We'd eaten, showered, and fucked away every horrible thought still lingering in my head.

I'd come alive, resurrected.

I'd felt beautiful, desired, whole again.

Yet, there seemed to be something looming between us. Something unresolved.

A sting smarted the cheek of my ass, and with a nudge of my hip, he urged me to step down to the floor. "Lower your face to the desk," he commanded, and I did, feeling the hem of my skirt lift higher up the cheeks of my ass, giving him a full-on view of my needy flesh. It seemed to be his thing, staring at me before he took me. Part of me felt like he enjoyed the torment of having something he considered forbidden on display.

Palms flat to the desk, I stared toward the bookcase to the right of us, waiting as he visually devoured me in silence. I sucked my bottom lip between my teeth, the anticipation of his touch like sex itself.

Peering over my shoulder, I watched him unbutton his shirt, peeling it away from his shoulders, where a scar marked the bullet that'd plowed through him. He unfastened his belt buckle and sprang himself free, giving a few languorous pumps of that deliciously thick cock.

Still bent over his desk, I waited for his ruthless plundering. The rapacious desire we had for ruining each other. The tearing of clothes and scratching of skin. The biting and smacking, and filthy words that sank themselves in my head, erasing every hateful thought about myself that I stored there.

Instead, I felt him notch the tip of his cock at my already soaked entrance, drawing soft circles over my flesh. The maddening lust for his lechery had me feeling like I might combust from the tension, and I turned to rest my forehead against the desk, balling my hands to fists. Slow and lazily, he gave small thrusts–just enough to stir the desperation coiling in my stomach, until, at last, he pushed to the hilt, and a sound of utter relief spilled out of me.

A guttural groan rumbled in his throat as his hips drove into me on a rough thrust.

Yes. This was what I wanted. What I *needed.*

Pain zapped my scalp, as he gripped a fistful of hair and lifted my head from the desk. "Look how well you take my cock, Little Moth. You were made for me," he said on a ragged breath, and he released my hair, gripping my hips in a way that felt possessive and dominating. A few hard thrusts had the shiny veneer burning my breasts as my body jerked across the desktop, and he pulled out on a wet glide. The absence of him had every cell in my body screaming with a voracious hunger.

I craned my neck to see him flicking his fingers, urging me off his desk, and he fell into his chair, his cock standing proud and threatening as he stroked the thick shaft.

I impaled myself over the monstrous fiend that'd tormented me so many times with his teasing, biting my lip while he filled me completely. As I pushed to draw myself back up his length, he held my shoulders, keeping me in place. Finger hooking my chin, he guided my face to his, those implacable copper eyes searching mine.

"Do you feel that, Lilia?" He ground my hips against him, rooting himself so deeply it sprang tears to my eyes. We'd had sex countless times before, had fucked in nearly every position, but why, in that precise moment, didn't it feel the same? Why, the second the question tumbled from his lips, did my heart pound in my chest, as if I'd anticipated his inquiry? As if I'd thought it at the same time.

As we sat wrapped around each other, breaths hastening with need and desperation, something clawed inside of me. It begged me to turn away from him. To push off and curse him.

Twisting and writhing in my gut with a furious determination to break away. An unfamiliar intruder that hooked itself into my belly and climbed its way to my ribs.

"Yes," I whispered. "Why does it feel different?"

He ran his thumb over my scar and pressed his lips to the jagged surface. "Tell me what feels different?"

I focused on the foreign pressure blooming in my chest. The way he held me. The freedom and security, and our heated bodies entwined together like two flames.

Soulmates.

It was his eyes. The way he was looking at me. The feelings he stirred inside of me with that obnoxious gleam of reverence.

No.

I pushed against his chest, but he held me closer, digging his fingers into my hips, refusing to let me go. His hands climbed beneath my shirt, to the column of my spine, where he pressed me against him.

The monster scratched at my ribs, punching at my bones for escape.

"Say it."

"Just fuck me already," I snapped, frustrated for reasons I couldn't tell him.

"Is that all you want? A quick fuck? You know I can give you that, but I think there's something inside of you that craves more."

How could he have known that? How could he have possibly known the hungry shadow, the vacuous hole that longed to eat my heart?

"I feel it, too," he said, as if reading my mind. "It's inside of me. Burning like a fever I can't shake. It's a spiteful, prideful anger that refuses to admit the truth."

"What truth?" I asked, my voice shaky. Nervous.

"That I would kill for you without a beat of hesitation, or remorse. And yet, at the same time, I could be reduced to nothing more than a pile of ash without you. I'm weak for you, Lilia."

Through an irritating blur of tears, I chewed on his words, savoring them. How strange that I felt so different. Stronger. More confident because of him.

As many times as I'd had to look at the scar Angelo had left, Devryck made me forget it was there. He somehow infused courage into my most discomposed moments, when the world felt more foe than friend. "Why do you have to make me cry?"

"Because I know there's a truth inside you, too. One you refuse to admit, but I want you to say it. Say it to my face."

"I can't."

"What are you afraid of?"

I shook my head, a swell of panic rising up into my throat and yearning to break free on an angry bellow.

Teeth clenched, he gripped my jaw. "What are you afraid of?"

"That the universe will hear it, too! And it'll steal you away." The wobble of tears broke, skating down my cheek. "I wanted to say it to you so badly that day at the ocean, when you were slipping away from me. I was screaming inside my head. *Tell him! Tell him before it's too late.* But I couldn't, because I knew if I did, you'd be gone forever. And now? Now it feels cursed. Like I'm carrying a cursed secret inside of me that I can never say aloud."

His brows came together as he pushed a strand of hair behind my ear. "I'm not going anywhere. You and I? This? There's no escaping it. Doesn't matter how fast you run, or how far you get, I will always be inside you just like this. In your bones and in your blood and in your head. It doesn't matter what you tell the universe–what secrets you spill. Nothing can change what we are, what we've become."

It was there, on the tip of my tongue, begging to be said, as

I imbibed his confession like an addict. "I want to tell you. I've wanted to tell you for a while, but my heart feels too hard. Too guarded. And in some ways, I'm glad, because the harder I am, the less I feel, and the less I feel, the less everything hurts."

"I know that feeling well." He brushed his thumb across my cheek. "You and I are the same, Lilia." A gentle kiss to my scar and then to my lips. "I know the demons of your past still plague you. I know you see Angelo sometimes when you wake in the middle of the night." His brows came together in a tight frown. "But he will never hurt you again, Little Moth. I will bleed out every one of your demons until you feel safe."

God, was it possible to desire the man any more than I already did? "I don't see them when I'm with you. I think they're afraid of you."

"As they should be." A darkness shadowed his eyes with the threat.

"It's when I'm not with you that scares me, though." The forbidden words tickled my tongue, begging to be cut loose. I dared myself to say it. To put the curse out into the universe and risk everything that had brought me happiness these last few weeks. "I love you. And I don't think I can stop loving you." I leaned forward to kiss him, but hesitated, uncertain if I'd confessed too much.

A firm hand gripped my nape, preventing my retreat. "I will never reject you, or turn you away." Lips pressed to mine, he held my face so delicately in his hands, as if I were something too precious to grasp tightly. "I have lived a lifetime in death–a cold existence in an endless void. Never feeling. Never knowing the warmth of touch. Every unfulfilling breath a suffocating reminder of how hollow I'd become. It wasn't until you came along and cast the first ray of light that I felt a pulse of life. A pull that I couldn't resist." He thumbed the seam of my pressed lips. "Don't ever hesitate to touch me, Lilia. You're the only one who can. It was you who dragged my heart from this insensate slumber. And it's you for whom it beats now." Sighing, he stroked his hand down my hair, brows pulled tight. "It's a fucking wreckage, though. Scarred and caged by ravaged bones. But it belongs only to you."

Passion burned across my lips with his kiss, and he unbuttoned my shirt, slowly peeling it down my arms to my elbows, where he gathered the fabric around my wrists at my back, holding me captive.

"You're mine, Lilia." Eyes on mine, he bent toward me, flicking his tongue over my stiffened nipples. "And I am yours."

When he finally released his hold, I threaded my fingers through his hair, drawing a tight grip in my palm. "Mine," I whispered.

Strong arms wrapped around me, pulling me against him. What began as a lazy thrust quickly heightened with fervor. Powerful hips drove into me as he fucked me hard. Mercilessly. I dug my fingers into the deep grooves of his muscles, letting him plow into me like he was searching for God in every moan that escaped me. He fucked me so deeply, fresh tears sprang to my eyes.

The intensity of the man lashed out at me like a bolt of hot lightning, electrifying the air around us. I was breathless and panting. Deliciously defiled.

My body tautened, and what sounded like a cross between a sob and relief shook from my throat. Both of us slick with sweat, he held me tighter, those deep, guttural sounds in his throat telling me he was desperate to climax.

I threw my head back on a flash of light and cried out, shattering in his arms.

His climax followed, sending jets of warm fluids up inside of me, and boneless, I rested my scarred cheek against his scarred shoulder, the malicious marks where both of us had been branded monsters.

He shuddered around me, his arms shaking at my back.

When I dared to lift my head, his eyes held the glint of promise beyond that euphoric exhaustion, as he stared up at me with heaving breaths.

I stroked a hand across his dampened forehead, studying the adoration I refused to see before. The veneration of a powerful man. One the monsters in my head feared the most. It was in that moment, I believed him when he said he belonged to me. Like a vast ocean claimed by a single grain of sand.

My dark sea. The mystifying depths that both captivated and terrified me.

For so long, I struggled to accept and give love. I'd become jaded. Stingy. Untrusting. And because I so rarely relinquished a piece of myself to others, it hurt worse when it was stolen away–the times when the world reached its greedy hand into my life and tore away the pieces of what I loved most. I'd come to learn that at the heart of life was suffering, and pain was an inevitable consequence of love. A slow gnawing ache that began the moment we dared to admit what it was. The shadow behind every adoring glance. The anguish that punctuated those fleeting moments of peace.

Love was also a sickness. An incurable disease. The kind that crawled inside the muscles and bones, and persisted long after death. As much as I wanted to bury the love of my mother, to harden myself so I wouldn't have to face the crippling truth, I couldn't. Burrowed deep into the roots, it blossomed from the wounds of my broken heart, tearing through the stitches that burned with memories of those who'd tried to hurt me. Sometimes, the pain was too much to bear. But sometimes it felt good, because it meant that I was capable of feeling *something*.

I glanced up at the plaque on the wall–the one I'd noticed my first day working in the lab.

Mortui vivos docent.

The dead teach the living.

I hadn't come to Dracadia with any notion of falling in love with my professor, or Death, as some had referred to him. Perhaps that was the nature of the world, to take so cruelly, then swoop in and blindside us when we least expected it. There was an implicit truth in the dead teaching the living, though. It was my mother, my refusal to accept her death, to accept what the world had taken from me, that had brought me to Dracadia in the first place. And it was there that I'd faced death head-on. So smitten, I fell in love with him–his abrasive heart and blood-stained hands. The dangerous and erudite professor, with fiery eyes and cold steel flesh. We hid away in shadows, stealing kisses under midnight stars. He taught me passion and courage, and to seize what I wanted by the teeth.

And in return, I taught him to feel again.

Epilogue

Lilia

Camped out in my dorm room, I printed off the syllabus for Bramwell's gross anatomy class next semester, when a text from Bee popped up on my phone. Smiling, I clicked on it.

Five more days!

She was due to spend Christmas with me on the island. I'd sent her a train ticket, and itinerary of activities. Such as skating in Canterbury park, perusing the book shops in Emberwick, and of course, coffee at Dragon's Lair. I also planned to introduce her to Devryck. Professionally, seeing as I hadn't uttered a word of our relationship to her.

Mom's old house was still being renovated and wouldn't be ready for another couple of weeks, but come summer, the house would be fully updated with all the modern amenities. A home for me and Bee. A place we could come back to whenever we wanted, because it was ours.

After Devryck had submitted the results of the last variant, The Rooks were all too eager to offer me whatever I wanted to remain involved in the study.

Devryck, of course, was a huge part of that.

Inspired by my efforts, he decided to update the Bramwell

Estate, as well, and rent it out as a summer getaway–obviously once he'd disposed of Angelo. I supposed he'd hoped that Caedmon would've returned at some point, but he hadn't.

I suspected he wouldn't.

Devryck had also agreed to a DNA test, confirming Spencer was, in fact, his half-brother. Once the shock of that had worn off, Spencer seemed to embrace the news. And eventually, the awkward exchanges between us fizzled back to friendship.

I'm so excited! You're going to love Dracadia.

Can I tell you a secret?

Always

Promise you won't judge or get mad.

I promise?

In truth, she worried me a little. Bee had a reckless side to her that'd always put me on edge.

I have a huge crush on the new English Lit teacher here. I caught him staring at me today.

Jesus. I rubbed my brow, trying to decide how to respond, without sounding like our mom. Really, though, who the hell was I to judge?

Just be careful okay? No doing anything crazy that'll get you kicked out.

I felt like a hypocrite typing those words.

No, I know. I won't. But Lil, he's so hot. I mean, smokin' hot. All the girls in my dorm are going nuts over him. Wanna see a pic?

I groaned, shaking my head.

Sure. But Bee, seriously, just be careful, okay?

Yeah, I know. Okay, sending a pic now. It's not the best–had to snap it quick during class.

I waited for what seemed like an eternity.

A picture popped up, of a guy standing in front of the class in a pair of dark jeans and a black shirt.

The air stalled in my chest.

I clicked to enlarge it and zoomed in on his face.

An exact replica of Devryck.

This is Mr. Caed. Isn't he yummy?! He drives a fucking motorcycle to school, Lil. Think I'm going to ask him out for coffee tomorrow!

I breathed hard through my nose to calm the frantic thrumming of my heart.

Shit.

Shit.

Shit.

Acknowledgments

First, to my readers, booktokkers, and bookstagrammers—this story took a number of months to write and in that time, you remained enthusiastic, showing your support and excitement. I'm so incredibly grateful for all of you. Thank you for trusting me with these stories. For sharing your love for the characters and their worlds. For your kind messages, reviews, edits and videos that mean the world to me. No matter how many books I write, it never gets old. I'll always feel a sense of gratitude and appreciation.

For my husband and daughters who give me space when I need it and who accept that as much as I'm a part of their world, I'll always be divided by other worlds. Thank you for being understanding when an idea pops into my head in the middle of conversation or the middle of the night and I have to jot it down. I could not pursue this dream if you didn't support it the way you do. I love you.

My long-time editor and friend, Julie Belfield. Thank you for your honesty. I truly feel the level of investment you have in making these stories shine, and I'm so grateful for it. As painful as the story edits can be to work through, the fact is, I'm ALWAYS happy with the changes in the end and you're right, they always seem worse than they really are. One of these days, I'm going to hug you and thank you in person, but in the meantime, just know that I appreciate you so much.

To my incredible alpha reader, assistant and friend, Diane Dykes—this book would not be what it is without the care and attention you have gifted me. I cannot thank you enough for the many times you've read through this, have pep talked me out of my doubts, have lent an ear when I had a different idea about a particular scene or needed to bounce an idea. Your friendship, advice and support has meant so much to me. Thank you for sticking with me.

Many many thanks to the incredibly talented Sarah Hansen of Okay Creations. You took a few ideas and turned them into a stunning work of art. This cover perfectly matches the tone of this story and is one of my absolute favorites. 🖤🤍🖤

To Debbie, Kelly, Courtney and Lana—my fearless beta readers who jumped into an unedited copy of this story, thank you for your bravery and invaluable feedback. This book is better because of you!

To my wonderful ARC Team readers who read an early copy of the book, thank you for leaving honest reviews so that others might discover this story. I appreciate each and every one of you. Big hugs for all of the love and support!

To the Vigilante Vixens who cheer me on and lift me up, thank you so much for sticking with me and giving me a safe little corner of the internet. Your support and positivity means so much to me!

To all of the hardworking bloggers who read, review and promote, while asking for nothing in exchange, I see you and I appreciate you. Thank you for all you do.

And finally, to the incredible authors who have been so kind and supportive, and inspire me to be a better writer, I can't thank you enough.

THE GOTHIC COLLECTION

LOOKING FOR ATMOSPHERIC BOOKS LIKE NOCTICADIA WITH A TOUCH OF EERIE AND TWISTED?

"This is the dangerous combination I truly adore: a gothic mansion made of bones, dark, intense, erotic, horrific, psychological, soul crushing story ..." ***-Nilufer, Goodreads Reviewer***

"I'm saying it now. This is hands down my favorite book of 2021. I'm going as far as placing it in my top 10 of all time. It was magical and so emotional my heart aches. I kept laughing because this book just felt epic. I disappeared within the pages and lived this story." ***-Coffee and the Bibliophile Blog***

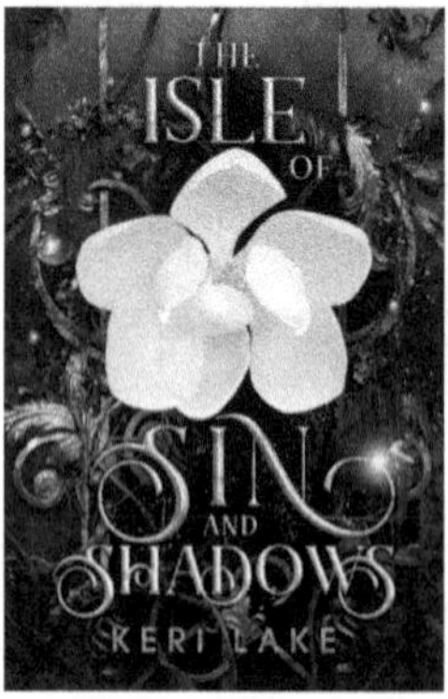

"A spine chillingly, majestically dark, engrossing read. Utter brilliance." ***-Zoe, Goodreads Reader***

Other Books By Keri Lake

<u>THE NIGHTSHADE DUOLOGY</u>

NIGHTSHADE

INFERNIUM

<u>STANDALONES</u>

MASTER OF SALT & BONES

THE ISLE OF SIN & SHADOWS

RIPPLE EFFECT

<u>VIGILANTES SERIES</u>

RICOCHET

BACKFIRE

INTREPID

BALLISTIC

<u>JUNIPER UNRAVELING SERIES</u>

JUNIPER UNRAVELING

CALICO DESCENDING

KINGS OF CARRION

GOD OF MONSTERS

<u>THE SANDMAN DUET</u>

NOCTURNES & NIGHTMARES

REQUIEM & REVERIE

About the Author

Keri Lake is a dark romance writer who specializes in demon wrangling, vengeance dealing and wicked twists. Her stories are gritty, with antiheroes that walk the line of good and bad, and feisty heroines who bring them to their knees. When not penning books, she enjoys spending time with her husband, daughters, and their rebellious Labrador (who doesn't retrieve a damn thing). She runs on strong coffee and alternative music, loves a good red wine, and has a slight addiction to dark chocolate.

Keep up with Keri Lake's new releases, exclusive extras and more by signing up to her VIP Email List:
VIP EMAIL SIGN UP

Join her reading group for giveaways and fun chats:
VIGILANTE VIXENS

She loves hearing from readers ...
www.KeriLake.com

Milton Keynes UK
Ingram Content Group UK Ltd.
UKHW050626210624
444358UK00005B/85